## Love for *Expectation*

'A brilliant exploration of friendship, feminism
and thwarted ambition.'
PANDORA SYKES

'Profoundly intelligent and humane. Deserves to
feature on many a prize shortlist.'
*GUARDIAN*

'Thoughtful, beautifully written, honest. A sensual
book. I URGE YOU TO READ IT.'
MARIAN KEYES

'One of the most intensely readable novels this year.'
*METRO*

'A generation-defining book on motherhood,
ambition and sex. Like *Normal People* with female
friendship under the microscope.'
ERIN KELLY

'The most buzzed-about, addictive read.'
*STYLIST*

'Sublime.'
*GOOD HOUSEKEEPING*

'A grown-up, honest take on female camaraderie.
Packed with talking points.'
*MAIL ON SUNDAY*

# Expectation

Anna Hope

doubleday

TRANSWORLD PUBLISHERS
61–63 Uxbridge Road, London W5 5SA
www.penguin.co.uk

Transworld is part of the Penguin Random House group of companies
whose addresses can be found at global.penguinrandomhouse.com

First published in Great Britain in 2019 by Doubleday
an imprint of Transworld Publishers

A CIP catalogue record for this book
is available from the British Library.

ISBNs 9780857524904 (hb)
9780857524911 (tpb)

Typeset in 11.5/16pt Minion Pro by Jouve (UK), Milton Keynes
Printed and bound in Great Britain by Clays Ltd, Elcograf S.p.A.

Penguin Random House is committed to a sustainable
future for our business, our readers and our planet. This book
is made from Forest Stewardship Council® certified paper.

57 9 10 8 6 4

For Bridie, when she's older,
and for Nimmi, who wove me back into the tale

*You do not solve the problem or question of motherhood.*
*You enter, at whatever risk, into its space.*

Jacqueline Rose, *Mothers:*
*An Essay on Love and Cruelty*

# London Fields

## 2004

*It is Saturday, which is market day. It is late spring, or early
summer. It is mid-May, and the dog roses are in bloom in the
tangled garden at the front of the house. It is still early, or early
for the weekend – not yet nine o'clock, but Hannah and Cate
are up already. They do not speak much to each other as they
take turns at the kettle, making toast and tea. The sun slants
into the room, lighting the shelves with the haphazard pans, the
recipe books, the badly painted walls. When they moved in here
two years ago they vowed to repaint the dreadful salmon colour
of the kitchen, but they never got around to it. Now they like it.
Like everything in this shabby, friendly house, it feels warm.*

*Upstairs, Lissa sleeps. She rarely rises before noon on the
weekends. She has a job in a local pub and often goes out after
work – a party at a flat in Dalston, one of the dives off Kingsland
Road, or further afield, in the artists' studios of Hackney Wick.*

*They finish their toast and leave Lissa to sleep on, taking
their faded canvas shopping bags from the rack on the back of
the door and going out into the bright morning. They turn left
and then right into Broadway Market, where the stalls are just
getting set up. This is their favourite time – before the crowds
arrive. They buy almond croissants from the baker at the top
of the road. They buy strong Cheddar and a goat's cheese
covered with ash. They buy good tomatoes and bread. They*

1

buy a newspaper from the huge pile outside the Turkish off-licence. They buy two bottles of wine for later. (Rioja. Always Rioja. They know nothing about wine but they know they like Rioja.) They amble further down the road to the other stalls, looking at knick-knacks and second-hand clothes. Outside the pubs there are people, in the manner of London markets, already clutching pints at nine o'clock.

Back in the house they lay out the food on the table in the kitchen, make a heroic pot of coffee, put on some music and open the window out on to the park, where the grass is filling with small clusters of people. Every so often one of those people will look up towards the house. They know what the person is thinking – how do you get to live in a house like that? How do you get to live in a three-storey Victorian townhouse on the edge of the best park in London? Luck is how. A friend of a friend of Lissa's offered her a room, and then, during the same year, two more rooms came up, and now they live in it together; the three of them. In all but deed the house is theirs. There is an agent somewhere in the far reaches of Stamford Hill, but they have a strong suspicion he does not know what is happening to the area, as their rent has remained stable for the last two years. They have a pact not to ask for anything, not to complain about the peeling lino or the stained carpets. These things do not matter, not when a house is so loved.

Sometime around eleven Lissa wakes and wanders downstairs. She drinks a pint of water and holds her head, then takes her coffee to the steps outside and rolls a cigarette and enjoys the morning sun, which is just starting to warm the lowest of the stone steps.

When coffee has been drunk and cigarettes smoked and

morning has become afternoon, they take plates and food and blankets out into the park, where they lie in the dappled shade of their favourite tree. They eat their picnic slowly. Hannah and Cate take turns to read the paper. Lissa shades her eyes with the arts pages and groans. A little later on they open the wine and drink it, and it is easy to drink. The afternoon deepens. The light grows viscous. The chatter in the park increases.

This is their life in 2004, in London Fields. They work hard. They go to the theatre. They go to galleries. They go to the gigs of friends' bands. They eat Vietnamese food in the restaurants on Mare Street and on Kingsland Road. They go to openings on Vyner Street on Thursdays, and they visit all the galleries and they drink the free beer and wine. They remember not to use plastic bags when they go to the corner shop, although sometimes they forget. They cycle everywhere, everywhere, all the time. They rarely wear helmets. They watch films at the Rio in Dalston, and then go to Turkish restaurants and eat pide and drink Turkish beer and eat those pickles that make your saliva flow. They go to Columbia Road flower market and buy flowers in the very early morning on Sundays. (Sometimes, if Lissa is coming home early from a party, she buys cheap flowers for the whole house – armfuls of gladioli and irises. Sometimes, because she is beautiful, she is given them for free.)

They go to the city farm on Hackney Road with hangovers, and they eat fried breakfasts in amongst the families and the screaming children, and they swear never to go there again on a Sunday morning until they have children of their own.

Sometimes on Sundays they walk; out along the Regent's Canal to Victoria Park, and beyond to the old Greenway, to

Three Mills Island, savouring the sideways slice of London that the canal offers up.

They are interested in the history of the East End. They buy books on psycho-geography from the bookshop at the bottom of the road. They try to read Iain Sinclair and fail at the first chapter but read other, more accessible books instead, about the successive waves of immigration that have characterized this part of the city: the Huguenots, the Jews, the Bengalis. They are aware that they too are part of a tide of immigration. If they are honest, they would like to halt this particular tide – they fear encroachment by those who resemble themselves.

They worry. They worry about climate change – about the rate of the melt of the permafrost in Siberia. They worry about the kids who live in the high-rises, right behind the deli where they buy their coffee and their tabbouleh. They worry about the life chances of these kids. They worry about their own relative privilege. They worry about knife crime and gun crime, then they read pieces which suggest the violence is only ever gang on gang and they feel relieved, then they feel guilty that they feel relieved. They worry about the tide of gentrification that is creeping up from the City of London and lapping at the edges of their park. Sometimes they feel they should worry more about these things, but at this moment in their lives they are happy, and so they do not.

They do not worry about nuclear war, or interest rates, or their fertility, or the welfare state, or ageing parents, or student debt.

They are twenty-nine years old. None of them has children. In any other generation in the history of humankind this fact would be remarkable. It is hardly remarked upon at all.

*They are aware that this park – London Fields – this grass on which they lie, has always been common land, a place for people to pasture their cows and sheep. This fact pleases them; they believe it goes some way to explaining the pull of this small, patchy patch of green they like to feel they own. They feel like they own it because they do; it belongs to everyone.*

*They would like to pause time – just here, just now, in this park, this gorgeous afternoon light. They would like the house prices to remain affordable. They would like to smoke cigarettes and drink wine as though they are still young and they don't make any difference. They would like to burrow down, here, in the beauty of this warm May afternoon. They live in the best house on the best park in the best part of the best city on the planet. Much of their lives is still before them. They have made mistakes, but they are not fatal. They are no longer young, but they do not feel old. Life is still malleable and full of potential. The openings to the roads not taken have not yet sealed up.*

*They still have time to become who they are going to be.*

## Hannah

Hannah sits on the edge of the bed, holding the vials in their plastic case. She runs her thumbnail along the thin wrapper and brings out one of the tubes. It weighs almost nothing. A quick fit of the needle, one flick of her fingertip to release the bubbles – she knows what she's doing, she has done this before. Still. Perhaps she should mark the moment somehow.

The first time, two years ago, Nathan bent over her with the needle, kissing her belly each day as the injections went in.

He kissed her differently this morning.

*Promise me, Hannah, after this, no more.*

And she promised, because she knew after this there wouldn't need to be more.

She lifts her shirt and pinches her skin. A brief scratch and it is over. When she has finished she stands, straightens her clothes and heads out into the morning to work.

Lissa is not there when she arrives at the Rio, so Hannah gets a tea from the little bar and moves outside. It is September but still warm, and the small square beside the cinema is busy with people. Hannah spots Lissa's tall frame threading its way up the street from the station and lifts her hand to wave. Lissa is wearing a coat Hannah has not seen before; narrow at the shoulders, fuller below the waist. Her hair, as ever, is long and loose.

'I love this,' Hannah murmurs, as Lissa leans in to kiss hello, catching the rough linen lapel between finger and thumb.

'This?' Lissa looks down as though surprised to discover she's wearing it. 'I got it years ago. That charity shop on Mare Street. Remember?'

Never anywhere you might be able to go and get one for yourself, always a charity shop, or *that little stall in the market, you know, the man in Portobello?*

'Wine?' says Lissa.

Hannah wrinkles her nose. 'Can't.'

Lissa touches her arm. 'You've started again then?'

'This morning.'

'How are you feeling?'

'Fine. I'm feeling fine.'

Lissa takes her hand and squeezes it lightly. 'Won't be a sec.'

Hannah watches her friend weave over to the bar, watches the young man serving light up at her attention. A bright, shared laugh and Lissa is back outside in the sun, her red wine in a plastic cup. 'All right if I have a quick cig?'

Hannah holds the wine while Lissa rolls. 'When are you going to give that up?'

'Soon.' Lissa lights up and blows smoke over her shoulder.

'You've been saying that for fifteen years.'

'Have I? Oh well.' Lissa's bangles clink as she reaches back to take her wine. 'I had the recall,' she says.

'Oh?' It's terrible, but Hannah never remembers. There have been so many auditions. So many parts almost got.

7

'A fringe thing – but a good thing. A good director. The Polish woman.'

'Ah.' She remembers now. 'Chekhov?'

'Yeah. *Vanya*. Yelena.'

'So how did it go?'

Lissa shrugs. 'Good. In parts.' She takes a sip of wine. 'Who knows? She worked with me quite a bit on the speech.' And then she launches into an impression of the Polish director, replete with accents and mannerisms.

*'Here, do it again. Make it real. None of this – how do you say it? Microwave emotion – put it on high. Two minutes. Ping! Tastes like shit.'*

'Jesus,' says Hannah, laughing. It always astonishes her, the crap Lissa puts up with. 'Well, if you don't get the part, you could always do a one-woman show, *Directors I Have Known and Been Rejected By.*'

'Yeah, well, that'd be funny if it weren't true. No. It is funny. Just . . .' Lissa frowns, and throws her cigarette into the gutter. 'Don't say it again.'


'Not bad,' says Lissa, as they emerge from the cinema into the darkness of the street outside. 'Bit Chekhovy, actually.' She threads her arm through Hannah's. 'Not much happens for ever and then the big emotional punch. The Polish director would probably have loved it. Long though,' she continues, as they head down towards the market, 'and no decent parts for women.'

'No?' It hadn't occurred to Hannah, but now she thinks of it, it's true.

'Wouldn't pass the Bechdel test.'

8

'The Bechdel test?'

'Jesus, Han, call yourself a feminist?' Lissa steers her towards the crossing. 'You know – does a film have two women in it? Do they both have names? Do they have a conversation about something other than a man? This American writer came up with it. Loads of films fail it. Most of them.'

Hannah thinks. 'They did have that conversation,' she says. 'In the middle of the film. About the fish.'

They both snort with laughter, as arm in arm they cross the street.

'Speaking of fish,' says Lissa, 'you want to eat something? We could head down and get some noodles.'

Hannah pulls out her phone. 'I should get back. I've got a report due tomorrow.'

'Through the market then?'

'Sure.' This is their favoured route home. They weave their way past the shuttered-up fronts of the African hairdressers, past sliding piles of cardboard boxes, crates of too-ripe mangoes buzzing with flies. The blood-metal stink of the butchers' shops.

Halfway down the street a bar is open and a knot of young people stand outside, drinking lurid cocktails with retro umbrellas. There is a rackety, demob air to the throng; some of them still wearing sunglasses in the dusky light. At the sight of them Lissa hangs back, tugging on Hannah's arm. 'Come on – we could just have a little drink?'

But Hannah is suddenly tired – irritated by these young people laughing into the weekday night, by Lissa's spaciousness. What does she have to get up for in the morning? By her constant capacity for forgetting that, lately, Hannah does not drink.

'You go. I've got to be in early. I've got to do that report. I think I'll get the bus.'

'Oh, OK.' Lissa turns back. 'I guess I'll walk. It's such a lovely evening. Hey' – she brings her hands either side of Hannah's face – 'good luck.'


## Cate

Someone is calling her. She follows the voice but it twists and echoes and will not be caught. She struggles upwards, breaks the surface, understands – it is her son crying, lying beside her in the bed. She brings him to her breast and gropes for her phone. The screen reads 3.13 – less than an hour since his last waking.

She had been dreaming again: the nightmare; broken streets, rubble and her with Tom in her arms, wandering, searching the burnt-out carcasses of buildings for something, for someone – but she did not recognize the streets, or the city, did not know where she was, and everything was over, everything destroyed.

Tom feeds, his grip slowly slackening, and she listens for the change in his breathing that signals the beginning of sleep. Then, with the barest of movements, she slides her nipple from his mouth, her arm from above him, turns on to her side and pulls the covers up over her ear. And she is falling, falling down into the pit of sleep and the sleep is water – but he is crying again, escalating now, announcing his distress, his indignation that she should fall like this away from him, and she hauls herself back awake.

Her tiny son is writhing beneath her in the gritty light. She lifts him and rubs his back. He gives a small belch and she puts him back on the breast, closing her eyes as he suckles and then bites. She cries out in pain and rolls away.

'*What?* What is it?' She pushes her fists into her eyes as Tom wails, hands and legs flailing, fists closing on nothing. 'Stop it, Tom. Please, please.'

On the other side of the thin wall there are low voices, the creak of a bed. She needs to pee. She moves her crying son into the middle of the bed and goes out towards the landing, where she hovers. To her right is the other bedroom, where Sam sleeps. Nothing wakes him. Downstairs is the narrow hallway, filled with piles of boxes, the lumped, heaped things she has not attended to since the move.

She could leave, leave this house, pull on her jeans and boots and walk away from here, away from this wailing creature that she cannot satisfy, from this husband wrapped in the interstellar blankness of his sleep. From herself. She would not be the first woman to do so. In the bedroom her son's cries grow louder – a small animal, afraid.

She hurries to the toilet and pisses quickly, then stumbles back to the bedroom, where Tom is howling. She lies beside him, pulls him back on to her breast. Of course she will not leave – it is the last – the very last – thing she would do – but her heart is beating strangely and her breath is ragged and perhaps she will have no choice, perhaps she will die – die like her mother before her, and leave her son to be brought up by his father and his family in this sterile house in the far reaches of Kent.

Tom flutters finally on her breast, slackens and sleeps. But she is wide awake now. She sits up in bed and pulls back the

11

curtains. Through the window she can see the car park, where the cars sit in their neat, obedient rows, then the dark shape of the river, and beyond that the orange lights from the ring-road, where the traffic is already thickening; lorries moving out to the coast, or returning from the Channel ports, cars on their way to London, the great greased machine of it lumbering towards the light. She feels her heart, the adrenaline swill of her blood. The moon comes out from behind clouds, illuminating the room, the rucked duvet, her tiny son beside her, abandoned now to sleep, his arms flung wide. She wants to protect him. How can she protect him from all the things that might fall upon his unguarded head? She reaches out and touches his hair, and as she does so sees the picture tattooed on her wrist, silver in the moonlight. She brings back her hand, traces the image slowly with her opposite fingertip – a filigree spider, a filigree web – a relic, now, from a different life.

She wants to see someone. To speak to someone. Someone from another lifetime. Someone who made her feel safe.

She is sitting on her bench, facing the river, where a low mist is rising from the water and a tangle of nettles clogs the bank. There is movement on the towpath now, a thin stream of humanity; joggers, early-morning workers, heads down, heading towards town. Tom is calm at least, a warm weight on her chest, face framed by a little bear hat. He woke again at five or so this morning and would not be placated, so they came out here. Her phone tells her it is almost seven o'clock, which means the supermarket will be open soon, which means there is somewhere warm to go, at least, and so she stands and follows the banks of the little tributary, over the humped bridge, under the underpass and out by the car park. By the time she joins the small crowd outside the supermarket doors, it has begun to drizzle.

Tom grinches in the sling and Cate shushes him as a uniformed woman comes out and casts a look to the sky, then goes back inside, and the doors slide open. The people bestir themselves and follow, funnelled through the bakery aisle, where the heated air circulates the smell of sugar and yeast and dough. She makes for the baby section, filling her basket with several little foil packets. She bought these packets in ones or twos at first – always sure the next meal would be the one she prepared properly – now she buys them in bulk. Nappies too; at first she was sure she would use washables, but after the trauma of the birth she started on disposables and then came the move, and now here she is lifting huge packets of nappies into her basket, the sort guaranteed to take half a millennium to decompose.

It is a two-minute walk back home, past the trees encased in concrete and wire cages, the bin store with its padlocks, the car park with its barriers, the signs alerting you to the anti-climb paint on the walls. She reaches her front door and lets herself into the narrow kitchen, puts down the bag and lifts Tom from the sling and into his high chair. She selects one of the little foil packages – banana and blueberry – and Tom holds out his hands for it as she untwists the seal and holds the plastic teat to his lips. He sucks away happily, like a little astronaut with space food.

'Morning.' Sam wanders in, hair mussed from sleep. He looks as though he slept in the clothes he was wearing last night – a faded band T-shirt and boxers. Straight to the kettle he goes, without looking up; hand out to test the temperature, switch flicked, used grounds dumped into the sink, the cafetière barely rinsed before the fresh grounds are shaken in. The swaddled luxury of the morning trance – no point in speaking till the caffeine has entered the blood.

'Morning,' she says.

Sam looks to her, eyes with an underwater glaze. 'Hey.' He raises a hand.

'What time did you get in?'

'Late,' he says with a shrug. 'Two-ish. We had some beers after the shift.'

'Sleep well?'

'Oh. OK.' He sighs, cricking his neck. 'Not great, but OK.'

How many hours straight through? Even a late night gives him, what? Six, maybe seven hours of uninterrupted sleep – the thought of it, of seven straight hours, of how it would feel. Despite this, he still looks tired, with heavy shadows beneath his eyes – the indoor pallor of the professional chef. He sleeps in the spare room, which is no longer, it seems, spare: it is his room now, just as the room that should be theirs is hers – hers and their son's, Tom's cot unused, a dumping ground for clothes, while Tom sleeps with Cate. Easier that way, for the many, many times Tom wakes.

He turns back to the coffee, plunges, pours. 'You want one?'

'Sure.'

He makes his way over to the fridge for milk. 'On an early one today,' he says. 'Doing lunch.'

He works as a sous in a restaurant in the centre of town. *Ten years behind London*, was what she heard him say on the phone to a friend back in Hackney the other night, *but OK, you know, OK. Getting some input already.*

He was on the verge of opening a place in Hackney Wick, before the rents went crazy. Before she got pregnant. Before they moved out here.

He hands her her coffee, takes a sip of his own. 'Did you wash my whites?'

She looks around, sees the pile in the corner, three days' worth. 'Sorry, no.'

'Really? I left them in your way, so you wouldn't forget.' Sam goes over to the pile, lifts the least stained overall to the light, starts scrubbing it viciously with the scourer at the sink. Outside the drizzle is thickening into rain.

'What are you two up to today?' he says.

'Washing, I suppose. Unpacking.'

'What about that playgroup? The one Mum mentioned?' He nods to the brightly coloured flyer stuck up on the fridge, the flyer Alice brought around the other day. Alice, Sam's mother, with her concerned face, mouth pursed somewhere between a grimace and a smile. *It's a lovely little group, it really is. You might make some friends.* Alice, the mastermind of the plan to *buy a little house for you all. In Canterbury.* Alice, their saviour. Alice, who has a key to the lovely little house and likes to pop round unannounced.

'Yeah,' Cate says. 'Maybe.'

'And we've got that thing tonight,' Sam says, giving up on the scouring, hanging his overall on a chair to dry, 'don't forget. At Mark and Tamsin's.'

'I haven't forgotten.'

'I'll pick you up, shall I?'

15

'Sure.'

'But Cate?'

'Yes?'

'Try and get out today, won't you? Take Tom out?'

'I was out while you were still asleep. Buying nappies and food.'

'I mean out-out.'

'Define out,' she says under her breath.

Sam looks at the kitchen. 'You know,' he says, taking a tea towel and wiping down the counter. 'It's really easy to clean at the end of the day. You just do what chefs do and put the day's tea towel into the wash. Along with my whites.' He holds up the damp dirty cloth. 'Where's the washing basket?'

She looks up at him. 'I'm not sure.'

'You just need a system,' he says, shaking his head. 'A system is all you need.' He puts the cloth on the side, then leans in and scoops Tom out of the high chair, lifting him up above his head, and their baby squeals with delight, kicking his heels. The moment plays out, passes, and then Sam gives him back, dropping a hand on Cate's shoulder. 'Knackered,' he says, to no one in particular.

'Yeah,' she says. 'Me too.'


*Lissa*


It's at the Green Room, Wardour Street. Scene of too many castings to count. The receptionist is young and glossy and hardly looks up as Lissa gives her name.

'Lissa Dane. Sorry, I'm a bit—'

16

'It's fine. They're running late anyway.' Her name is ticked off a long list, and a clipboard and biro are handed over the counter. 'Take a seat. Fill in your details.'

Lissa nods, she knows the drill. A quick glance at the room: four men, two women, the women both in their thirties, one dark, one red-haired. The redhead is speaking on her phone, low and stressed and apologetic: 'No, no, I know I said half past, but they're running late. Not sure. Half an hour maybe. Maybe more. Do you mind? I can come round and fetch him from yours. Oh God, thank God, thanks, I owe you one, thanks, thanks.' The woman flicks off the phone and catches Lissa's eye. *'Forty fucking minutes,'* she whispers furiously.

Lissa pulls a sympathetic face. Not great, but not so bad. She's had worse – has waited for almost two hours to be seen. But then, she doesn't have kids at the school gate. She glances at the casting brief in her hands.

*A PTA meeting, a teacher and two parents, both concerned about their son.*

At the top of the page she recognizes the name of a well-known brand of chocolate cookie. Across from her a man is diligently marking and highlighting his piece of paper. She flicks to the second sheet and begins filling out her details.

Height. 5'7.

Weight. She pauses, can't remember the last time she was weighed. Sixty? She usually puts sixty. She scribbles it down.

Waist. 30.

Hips. 38.

She tries to tell the truth nowadays; it's not worth stretching it on these things. For a long time she put any old thing down, not lying, just being . . . inexact. But then she was caught out at that shoot in Berlin; that old flat with the hundreds of Japanese paper lanterns, the assistant bringing out outfit after outfit, none of which fitted the measurements she had scribbled down in the London casting a month before, as the little designer fussed around her, tutting his disapproval.

*But you look so fet. So fet in these.*

In the end, she had to borrow the costume assistant's trousers. In the end, she was cut out of the ad.

As she scrawls across the pages, Hannah's comment from last night comes back to her: *a one-woman show. Directors I Have Known and Been Rejected By.* It was funny, of course it was, but it had stung. She wouldn't make a comment like that about Hannah.

Hey! Han! What about *All the Times I've Tried IVF and It's Failed.* What about that? Wouldn't that be hil*arious*?

But of course the comparison doesn't stand. Because nothing beats Hannah's pain.

The casting director puts in an appearance, and the atmosphere lifts and sharpens. 'All right, folks. Running a bit late.'

He is tanned, meaty, running to fat. His face the face of a self-satisfied baby. But he gets her seen for these things often, and so Lissa smiles and laughs and flirts with him despite herself.

The red-haired woman is up. Lissa watches her seal away her fury and paint on a smile.

She gives a quick, reflexive glance to her phone. Still no news on the recall. The Chekhov. That in itself doesn't mean anything – you can wait weeks for these things and then be surprised, but she can feel hope begin its long, tidal ebb. By tomorrow, if she has still not heard anything, she will be twitchy; by the weekend, fractured and emotional; by the beginning of next week, defensive, patched up. She has become more, not less, thin-skinned as time has gone on.

She ignores the hat and glove measurements – sometimes it seems as though these forms haven't changed since the 1950s – puts down her shoe size, then stands and hands the paper back to the young woman behind the desk.

The young woman rises. She is tall and skinny and wearing black. She picks up the Polaroid camera before her and waves it languidly towards the blank wall.

Lissa sees the other women look up as she takes her place against the exposed brick, their quick assessment of her figure, her clothes. Looking for the shadows, the wrinkles, the greys.

She arranges her face.

She used not to go up for these things at all.

When she left drama school, her new agent, who met her sitting on a yoga block and ran briskly through her impressive client list, said she wouldn't put her up for commercials unless she really wanted her to.

*And if you do*, said her new agent, *then they'll only be for Europe. We wouldn't want you to be seen over here.*

They both laughed at that. *Hahaha.* That was when she used to go up for three movies a week. When the casting directors made sure you never crossed paths with anyone else up for the same part. When you waited in hushed anterooms clutching your script, a racehorse, primed and ready. When the director leaped up as you entered the room, holding out his hand (always his, never hers). *Thanks so much for coming in.*

The Polaroid clicks and whirrs.

'Thanks,' the young woman says, wafting the photograph dry. 'Take a seat.'

Lissa does not sit. Instead she makes her way down the line to the small bathroom to check her face. In the mirror she sees that her mascara has run and little black dots mark her under-eye. *Fuck.* She rubs at them with her thumb. No matter how good you feel. No matter how well you think you have pulled together an outfit, put your game face on, something always occurs to prick it.

*You've just got to play the game, Lissa,* her first agent's assistant had sighed down the phone to her once, when she had refused to buy a Wonderbra for an audition. *You know that. They said they wanted someone with bigger boobs.* The Wonderbra had been cited in the phone call in which the agent dropped her.

She makes her way back out to the waiting room, threads past the legs of the waiting actors, takes a seat and closes her eyes.

She has tried.

As time has passed, as her twenties have given way to her thirties with little to show for them, she has really tried to play the game. Has bumped down through three agents, each further down the food chain than the last. Has gone from never having commercial castings to having nothing else. From being protected from the scent of desperation to being sure that she gives it off, sweating from her pores, at castings, at parties, in the street.

*Please. Give me a job. Any job. Please, please, please.*

Like that programme her mother used to watch in the eighties. *Gis a job. Gis a job.*

'Lissa. Rod. Daniel.'

She snaps open her eyes. The casting director is back. It is her turn. She makes her way into the darkened box where two men sit on a sofa, scrolling idly through their phones. The air is stale, the table before them littered with coffee cups and half-eaten sushi and e-cigarettes. Neither of the men looks up from their screens.

She takes her spot on the X on the floor. The camera pans up and down her body. She says her name, says the name of her agent. Turns to the left. Turns to the right. Shows her hands to the camera.

When the men have done the same, the casting director claps his hands.

'OK, so, Lissa, you're the mum, Rod, you're the father. Dan, you're playing the teacher.'

Dan nods wildly. Lissa can see he read the brief last night, since he has come dressed for the part in a jacket with patches on the elbows, and a tie.

'So, Lissa, Rod, you sit here.' The casting director gestures to a couple of chairs behind a table. 'And Dan, you here on the other side. And here's the cookies.'

Lissa looks at where a plate of cookies sits on a stool, anaemic-looking in the fetid air.

'So yeah, why not just do a bit of improvising then?'

One of the men on the sofa glances briefly up at the monitor, then back down at his phone, as Dan leans forward, eager to begin.

'So – erm, Mrs . . . Lacey. Mr . . . Lacey, I'm a little, um, worried about . . . Josh.' He sits back, obviously pleased with this first sally.

'Oh?' The actor beside Lissa leans forward now. He is handsome in a bland sort of way. She can see his muscles tensed beneath the cotton of his shirt. 'That's very ... concerning.'

'*Look at me.*'

Lissa looks up, startled, to where the casting director is reading from a script in a gruff baritone.

'The cookies,' the casting director says to her, waving her gaze away, 'I'm the voice of the cookies. Look at the cookies, not at me.'

'Oh,' she says. 'Right.'

'*Look at me,*' he says again.

She looks down at the cookies.

'*You know you want to. Yeah. That's right. Come a little closer.*'

Lissa leans tentatively towards the plate.

'*Yeah.*' His voice drops another half an octave. Is he moving into an American accent? He sounds like Barry White.

The men on the sofa have both looked up now. She can see the monitor – a tight close-up of her face, her cheeks red, her expression confused.

'*Yeah,*' the casting director murmurs. He too is looking up at the monitor now, waiting.

Silence.

'Go on,' he says, in his normal voice.

'Sorry?' She can feel sweat spreading over her back. 'I'm a bit lost here.'

Dan leans forward, eager as ever. 'You're supposed to pick them up,' he says. 'It said in the brief. To *shove them in your mouth.*' He points to the paper. 'It says you can't concentrate on the teacher. On what the teacher's saying. Because of the cookies. You just can't help yourself.'

'Ah. I see.'

The men look at her: the two actors, the casting director, the cameraman, the men on the sofa. One of the sofa men marks something on a piece of paper. The other reads it, nods, looks back down at his phone.

The casting director sighs. 'Did you read the brief, Lissa?'

'Obviously not quite closely enough.'

'No.' He flicks the sofa men an apologetic look. 'Shall we go again? And Lissa, could you flirt a little more with the cookies this time?'


Oxford Street is a scrum of lunchtime shoppers. The entrance to the Tube gapes, but she walks past it. She doesn't want to go down, not home, not yet.

Fuck the cookies.

Fuck the fat casting director with his three holidays a year. Fuck those two directors sitting behind their monitors like bored teenagers. Fuck the camera that pans up and down your body more slowly than it does the men's. Fuck the scriptwriters for these fucking commercials. *You just can't help yourself.* Fuck the men that run this fucking show.

Without thinking, she heads north and east, picking up Goodge Street, emerging on to Tottenham Court Road and then Chenies Street, past the red door of her old drama school. Now Bloomsbury, past the gates of the British Museum, the lung of Russell Square; the relief of it, the green. She walks on, further north, through Gordon Square to the clamour of Euston Road, where she ducks into the courtyard of the British Library, opens her bag for the man on duty, stands in the hush and bustle.

How long since she has been in a library? She takes the escalator up to the first floor, where banks of people sit at chairs with small armrests as though they themselves are some sort of exhibition, some sort of display. But here – ah – here are the Reading Rooms. Rare Books. Humanities One. She pushes the heavy door open; perhaps she can sit here for a while, in Rare Books, and let the rare books calm her, bring her back to herself.

'May I see your card, madam?' A pleasant-faced guard has his hand out to stop her walking further. 'Your reader's card?'

'I don't . . . I'm sorry.'

There is someone behind her, tutting, his belongings in a see-through plastic bag, card held out already in one bristling fist.

'You need a card, madam, to enter the Reading Rooms,' says the guard, waving the man along.

'Oh, I see.' The world is full of spikes today. She turns, pushes back out towards the main concourse, where she sinks on to a nearby bench.

'Lissa? Liss?'

For a moment she doesn't recognize him, here, out of context, but then – of course – 'Nath!' She stands and they hug hello.

'What are you doing here?'

'I . . .' What is she doing here? 'I thought I'd do some reading for something,' she says.

'Oh?'

'Yeah – a . . . course I'm thinking of taking. But they won't let me in.'

'Oh? Well. They're funny like that in here.' He smiles, and she is glad of him. She needs someone familiar today. 'Listen' – he gestures behind him to the crowded restaurant – 'I'm just on a break. You fancy a coffee?'

As they queue she scans the crowd: people of all ages, clutching laptops beneath their arms, tapping away on phones, all with those same see-through bags. She orders her coffee and as Nathan orders himself a cappuccino, double shot, she thinks of Hannah – no coffee, no booze, not for years now. She used to wave the wine bottle in her face – *Go on, Han, surely a little won't hurt* – but by now she has learned not to. How many years have they been trying? Four? Five? She has lost count.

In the early days, when Hannah and Nathan first started trying and nothing was happening, she remembers Hannah weeping one evening. *But I've worked hard. I've worked so hard all my life.* And her saying something back, like, *Of course it'll happen. It has to. It's you two, isn't it?* as though the universe gave two shits whether or not you'd worked your arse off and paid your taxes and your TV licence fee, whether you were the deputy director of a large global charity and married to a lovely man who was a senior lecturer at a leading London university and put your hand up first in class. What she had wanted to say was, *Bad things happen to good people all the time. Every day. Do you watch the news?*

'So,' Nathan says, letting Lissa go first as they thread their way towards an empty table. 'What sort of course?' He sits down before her and she sees his eyes are tired. But he looks well, still has something of the boy in him, still wearing the same flannel shirts he wore twenty years ago, the sleeves rolled up to the elbows. Even his hair has hardly changed, thick and dark, cropped close to his head.

'Ah . . . well.' She takes a sip of her coffee. 'Um . . . film.'

'Film?'

'Yes – it's a . . . PhD.'

'A PhD? Blimey. Careful. You can cut yourself on those things.'

'Yeah. So I hear.'

Now she has lied she should feel worse, but she feels marginally better. Why not? Why not do something different? Why not change her life?

'Hannah didn't mention it,' says Nathan.

'No, well, it's quite a new idea.'

'So, tell me,' he says, his gaze levelling with hers.

'Um.' Lissa stirs sugar into her coffee. 'It's a sort of . . . feminist appraisal. Using the – you know, the Bechdel test . . . looking at films now and in the seventies, and . . . the forties. Comparing parts for women. How they've shrunk. Changed. *All About Eve, Network . . .*'

'*Network.* Isn't that the one where he dies on screen?'

'Yes. Yes! But Faye Dunaway in that – she's incredible, totally fierce, totally unlikeable. And all those pictures of the forties, the "women's pictures"' – she makes quote marks in the air with her fingers – 'they were actually pretty great. Bette Davis, Katharine Hepburn . . .'

'*Autumn Sonata,*' Nathan says, leaning forward.

'What's that?'

'You don't know it? Seriously? Liv Ullmann. Ingrid Bergman.

26

Two incredible parts for women. Fierce doesn't even cover it. I needed therapy after that film.'

'I'll watch it,' she says, laughing. 'Thanks.' She leans over and takes his pen, scribbles the title on to the back of her hand.

'Hey,' he says, 'maybe you should invest in a notebook, for this new academic career.'

'Yeah.' She hands him back his pen. 'Maybe I should.'

'How's the acting then?'

'Oh. You know.' She shrugs. 'Appalling. Humiliating. Ask me tomorrow.'

'Really? But I thought it was going OK. There was that thing . . . the Shakespeare. You were great.'

'That thing was three years ago, Nath.'

A fringe *King Lear* at the back of a pub in Peckham. Playing Regan for two hundred a week plus expenses. Raising her voice even louder when the racing was on in the bar.

'So how do you live? You don't still work in pubs?'

She pushes her cup away. 'I do shifts in a call centre. Raising money for charities. And I do the life modelling.'

'Still? Jesus, really?'

'Yeah. Well.' The look on his face pricks her. 'It's not so bad. They're good charities. And the life modelling's fine. I work at the Slade. It could be worse.'

'Yes, but surely there's something else. You're so bright.'

'Thanks, but it's not so easy to find a world-beating part-time job that lets me go to auditions at short notice.'

He nods, chastened.

'What about you, Nath?'

'What do you mean?'

'How are you doing?'

'Oh, OK. Overworked. Underpaid. Drowning in admin.'

*I didn't mean that. I meant the baby stuff. The no-baby stuff. How are you doing with that?*

'But, you know, we academics love to moan.'

As they stand to say their goodbyes her phone buzzes – her agent. She gestures to Nathan, who waves his hand for her to take the call.

'Lissa?'

She can tell by the tone it's good news. 'Yes?' She tries to keep the eagerness from her voice.

'They want you. The Chekhov. You're in.'

## Cate

Sam is at the wheel as they drive westwards, through the terraces and pound shops of Wincheap, out to where the city thins and frays into the ribbons of A-roads that lead to London, to the coast. They are late. She and Tom were asleep when Sam came back from work, both of them sprawled together on the bed. Now Tom nods again in the car seat as they take the Ashford Road, passing garden centres, small industrial estates housing soft-play zones, motor-home dealers, stands of scrappy-looking trees.

She's wearing the first decent blouse she could find and her maternity jeans, the ones with the huge black waistband. An old cardigan on top. She could have done better. Should have done better. 'So is anyone else going to be there?'

'I don't think so. Just Tamsin and Mark.'

'What is it he does again?'

'He's got a company. Agricultural machinery. He's doing really well.' Sam turns to her. 'He might invest in a restaurant. He's got the cash. We've talked about it for years.'

She tries to remember Mark's face but cannot quite picture it. She's only met him once since the wedding, the time they came down to see the house. But everything then was a blur. 'How long have they been married?'

'Forever. They got together at school.' He turns to her, a small tightness at the edge of his mouth. 'They're lovely people. Really. Just stay away from politics and you'll be fine.'

She nods, smiles, circling the spider at her wrist with her finger and thumb.

They turn up a country lane with large houses on either side, past a huge fruit wholesaler where even at this time of the day forklifts roam around the forecourt. Pulling up at a wooden gate, Sam presses the button on an intercom. There is a buzz and the gate slides open. A black Land Rover Defender stands on the driveway. Sam parks beside it and lifts a sleeping Tom out of the car. In answer to the bell there is the tinny yap of dogs, the scuttle of claws on a wooden floor, footsteps.

'Sorry we're late,' says Sam, as his sister opens the door. 'We had to get Tom dressed. Then traffic.'

Tamsin is dressed in jeans, heels and a grey jumper. Sequins crust like icicles at her shoulders. She hugs them – brief, angular, fragrant – then shoos them through to the kitchen, where a vastness of shining floor is punctuated by a large granite island. Cate pulls her cardigan tighter around her while Sam hoists Tom and the car seat on to the dining table. Three large black pendant lights hang suspended above it. On the wall, a sign reads 'EAT' in large wooden letters, as though without it Mark and Tamsin and their two children might forget what this side of the room is for.

'They're here!' Tamsin calls to her husband, who emerges from a different room. Mark is tall, broad. His shirt hugs his frame. He looks like an advert for a certain sort of manhood, a certain sort of success. He kisses Cate, fist-pumps Sam. A watch the size of a small mammal grips his wrist.

'Would you like a drink?' Tamsin ushers Cate towards an armchair. 'Fizzy water?'

'Actually,' says Cate, 'I'd love some wine. A red wine. If that's OK?' Her voice sounds odd. She has hardly used it today. 'I'd love a small red wine,' she says again, giving each syllable equal weight, as though speaking a language that is new to her.

'Mark!' barks Tamsin. 'Glass of red for Cate.'

'Coming up.' Mark moves towards the kitchen counter, behind which cabinets are lit from within, and pours wine from an open bottle into a goblet. He looks like a mortician, standing behind his slab, dealing in blood.

'There,' Mark says, bringing it over and setting it on the glass table before her. 'Put some colour in your cheeks.' And he laughs. And Tamsin laughs. And Sam laughs. And Cate laughs too, though at what she is not quite sure. Both Tamsin and Mark are deeply tanned. Their teeth are extraordinarily white against their skin. She remembers now Sam telling her – they have recently been on holiday. She can bring it up later, when she is at a loss for something to say.

'Antipasti,' says Tamsin, lifting a plate where meats and cheese and olives glisten in the bluish light.

30

Cate takes an olive and rolls its saltiness on her tongue.

Outside is a large garden, laid to lawn; beyond it, a fold in the hills where the river runs. The Great Stour, the same river that runs behind their house – she knows this because they walked there together, she and Sam and Tamsin and Mark, when they came down the first time to *get a sense of the area.*

*Let's walk through the orchard!* Tamsin had said. And so they did, the route taking them over the lane, past the whole-saler, past the cabins with the numbers spray-painted on the sides housing the fruit pickers, the dartboards, the mothers on camping chairs with their babies in their laps, watching them warily, the radios, the sound of Russian being spoken, then the orchard, which was simply lines and lines of trees. It was summer and the trees stood penned, grafted on to wire, their arms stretched in supplication, or defeat. *It's not an orchard,* she wanted to say, *it's a factory farm.*

'So how was your holiday?' she asks, turning back to the room.

'Oh, amazing,' says Tamsin. 'We were in Turkey. All-inclusive. The kids loved it. They were gone from breakfast till dinner. Had the run of the place.'

'Where are they?' Cate has the sudden terrible thought that they have been left somewhere, forgotten.

'In the snug.' Tamsin gestures to a door half open, and she sees them, their son Jack, their daughter Milly, faces stunned and immobile in the blue TV light. 'Hey! You should come, next year. We should all go together. We could bring Alice too, a big family holiday – she's amazing with the kids. Wait – or Dubai. Christmas!' She claps her hands together. 'Mark! Tell them. Tell them they should come to Dubai.'

'You should come to Dubai,' says Mark, with an indulgent smile to his wife. 'We go every year. I do a bit of work, then we have a week at Atlantis. You seen it?'

Mark brings up pictures on his phone and they all crowd round. Cate sees a huge pink stone edifice, a strip of sand, the ocean beyond. 'It's a man-made island,' he says. 'They've got everything – Gordon Ramsay restaurants. An aqua park. The kids go mental for it.'

It looks terribly fragile, its hugeness, its hubris. 'Atlantis?' says Cate.

'Yeah.' Mark nods. 'Check it out.'

'Didn't Atlantis disappear in the flood?'

'Which flood?' Tamsin looks bewildered.

'The Bible.'

'Thanks,' says Sam hastily. 'But I don't think we can get away this year – maybe next time.'

Cate looks over to where Tom lies. He looks tiny there, vulnerable, a small craft floating on a sea of polished oak. He is so still.

'Excuse me.' She rises quickly, goes to him, puts her hand to his nose, feels the soft relief of his breath. Outside, beyond the glass doors, the hillside is turning russet in the last of the light. The lawn is mown to within a millimetre of its life.

Tamsin comes over and joins her. 'Gorgeous, aren't they, when they're asleep?' Her face, dusted with a light pink powder, shimmers in the overhead lights. 'So how's the house?' she says.

'Oh.' Cate shifts a little. 'It's good – it's great. We're so grateful.'

'When are you going to invite us round?'

'Soon. When we've unpacked.'

'You're kidding?' Tamsin laughs. 'You haven't unpacked yet?'

'Still a few boxes left to go.'

Tamsin's hand lands on her sleeve. 'You look tired,' she says. 'Sam says you're sleeping together?' Her voice drops to a whisper. 'You and Tom? In the same bed?'

'Yeah.'

'Are you sure that's a good idea?'

'It's just easier like that. For the night feeds. You know.'

'You should stop.' Tamsin is gripping her now. 'Get that baby off the boob. You know what? You should have some time off. One day a week. What do you say?'

'I—'

'Say yes! Alice will do it. She's desperate to spend some time with Tom. Hang on – Sam!' Tamsin turns to the men, clapping her hands. 'Sam! Cate's going to have a day off! We'll arrange it. Me and mum. Alice is *dying* to help.'


It is almost dark when they return. Tom stays asleep as she lifts him from the car seat and into her bed. She goes down to the living room, where Sam is lying on the sofa, plugged into his computer. He pulls his headphones off as she comes into the room and raises his beer. 'You want one?'

She shakes her head. He makes room for her to sit. 'That wasn't so bad, was it?'

'Why did you tell your sister I share a bed with Tom?'

'Because you do.'

'Don't you like it?'

'Well, I'd rather share a bed with you.'

She laughs. She cannot help it. The thought is too absurd.

'I'm worried about you, Cate.'

He looks genuinely concerned. Or perhaps it is not concern, perhaps it is disappointment – the disappointment of one who has bought something online and then, just when the warranty has run out, realizes that it is faulty in all sorts of hidden ways.

'Did you ask Tamsin to arrange a Tuesday with your mum?'

His face tells her.

'Did you not think of asking me first?'

'I thought it would be good for you. I thought you would be relieved.'

'I thought you might have the courtesy to check with me before you rearrange my life.'

'Wow. OK. I'm just trying to help. I thought that's what mothers needed.'

'This isn't help. It's an ambush.'

'Jesus Christ, Cate.' He holds up his hands.

She gets up and goes into the kitchen. She is shaking. She looks through to the living room, where Sam's back is to her. He has already clicked on to some computer game or other, put his headphones back over his ears.

This is the pattern of their evenings. A little passive-aggressive banter and then separate computers on separate chairs. If she is lucky, she gets the sofa. Then they go to bed. In separate beds. Repeat.

Her phone buzzes. A message from Hannah – a missed call. Her heart leaps. She can navigate by Hannah. Hannah is true north. She lifts the phone and calls her back.

'Cate?'

'Hey.'

'How are you? I've been trying to get in touch with you.'

'Sorry. I've been . . .' What has she been? She has no idea.

'How's Canterbury?'

'Funny,' she says.

'Funny how?'

'I don't know.' She thinks of how it's funny. Tries to frame a joke. 'We went to see Sam's sister. They want to take us to Dubai.'

'That sounds nice.'

'Seriously?'

A small sigh. 'I'm sure you'll get used to it. These things take time.'

Cate is silent.

'How's my godson?'

'He's good. Asleep.'

There is a pause, the sound of Hannah's computer keys in the background, of Hannah doing two things at once – the great world swirling around her, summoning her back.

'Han?' says Cate.

'Sorry, just catching up on work emails. Had to send that one.'

'Do you fancy meeting up? Next weekend? Saturday, maybe? I could bring Tom into town. We could go to the Heath? I haven't come in since we've been out here. He's growing so fast . . .'

Cate braces herself for the no, but then, 'Hang on,' says Hannah, 'let me check . . . Saturday? Yeah. Why not?'

They speak a little more, then Cate ends the call, and goes

over to the window. It has been six weeks since she moved to Kent. Gulls sleep on the pointed roofs of the flats opposite. A man is out there, climbing out of his car. Perhaps he is the one who lives on the other side of the wall, whose sleep is broken nightly by Tom.

The man looks up. Cate lifts her hand. He stares at her – a dark shape in the window – with a baffled look of incomprehension on his face, then looks away.

# Abjections

## 1995

*The seminar is called Feminisms. It is not full. There is a general feeling, in the popular culture, that feminism has done its work. It is the era of the Spice Girls. Of the ladette. Lissa, the daughter of a feminist, has taken it for granted that she is a feminist too. A wholly unexamined position. She chooses Feminisms because the other option is Science Fiction.*

*The reading list is daunting and mostly foreign. Lissa reads none of it in preparation for the course. No one really does the preparatory reading for courses in the English department. You just skim the books in the week you have to write about them. This, to Lissa, seems to be the main thing that university teaches you – how to bullshit convincingly. The better the university, the better the bullshit. She has expounded this theory regularly in the bed of her new boyfriend, a Mancunian drug dealer with a terraced house in Rusholme who walks like Liam Gallagher and has a way with a parka. He is dark and funny and clever and the sexiest thing she has ever seen.*

*The girl is sitting close to the front of the room, long hair almost hiding her face, small frame drowned by a baggy jumper, the cuffs pulled down over her thumbs. One of those long patchwork skirts, DM boots, a heavy hand with the eyeliner. She is of a type – suburban rebels, indie kids, packs of them roaming Manchester on a Saturday night. Flailing around the dance floor of the student union. Sitting Down to James. Lissa and the girl (who is called Hannah) are assigned to present together – Kristeva and the abject. Having not done the reading, Lissa has no idea what any of this means. Why don't you come to my room? Lissa asks Hannah. Tomorrow? Three o'clock?*

*Hannah turns up at Lissa's room on the dot of three. She carries several weighty books in her arms. She knocks on the door and pulls her cuffs over her bitten fingernails. So far, for Hannah, university is not what she had hoped. She has only come to Manchester because she did not get into Oxford and her second choice – Edinburgh – was full. And so, after a year out – which she spent, not 'travelling' like the majority of students she seems to meet, but working to save the money for clothes and books and anything extra she might need – here she is at university number three, still living at home in Burnage. Cheaper this way, so she doesn't have to pay for her accommodation in halls. And her parents are happy about it. And she pretends she is too, but really she is seething. Seething because she fudged a question about Keats in the Oxford interview. Seething because her best friend, Cate, got in. Seething because she didn't put somewhere far from home for her third choice. And, mostly, seething with the discovery that the city she has lived in all her life is infected by privileged students. For the last few months she has had a bar job in the student union, and she, who is naturally a watcher, has learned much. Forget Feminisms – she could already write a dissertation on class. There are the boarding-school kids, who wear their shirts with the collars up and play sports and roam in unadventurous, braying packs. The state-school kids, who occupy different tables but eye the rugby boys and match them pint for pint in the bar. The misfits, who wear their misfit status like a badge, thus signalling to the other misfits and forming misfit cliques. And then those like this blonde girl whose door she stands at now. These are the ones who trouble her: they are slippery, hard to categorize. And Hannah is fond of categorization. This girl sounds posh, but does not necessarily act it. Hannah has never seen her in the student union. She is beautiful, but careless with her beauty – at the eleven o'clock seminars, for instance, she often has last night's make-up crusted around her eyes. The tip of her index finger is stained orange from smoking. She barely seems to brush her hair. But this girl possesses something indefinable, something that, although she cannot name it, Hannah knows she wants desperately for herself.*

*The other girl opens the door and Hannah steps inside. The room is a mess. It smells of fags, and ashtrays overflow on every surface. There are half-full glasses of water in various places. An empty bottle of wine. The single bed is covered with an Indian throw. There is a collage on the wall – photographs of young people on a far-flung beach, Lissa sitting on a scooter, no helmet in sight, Lissa and a dark-haired young man in a nightclub, both with large pupils, faces crowded into the frame. So far, standard fare. But Hannah's eye is caught by a different picture, this one propped carelessly against the wall – an oil painting of a fair-haired girl curled into a chair, reading a book.*

*Is that you? she asks, kneeling before it.*

*Yeah, says Lissa carelessly. My mum did it. Years ago.*

*It's really good.*

*Lissa sits on her bed, watching, a little amused, as the dark-haired girl takes her hungry inventory of her possessions, then*

39

sits at the desk and opens the first of her books. The girl moves precisely. Her pencils are sharp.

These are the things that Lissa thinks she knows about university and Manchester and class: she is the daughter of a socialist. She went to a North London comprehensive. She would rather hang out with a drug dealer than a public schoolboy. There are far too many public schoolboys and girls in Manchester, but scratch its grimy post-industrial surface and the city waits. That Manchester is, at this point in its history – if, like Lissa, you are a fan of dance music and of ecstasy – possibly the greatest city on earth.

She is interested in this long-haired girl because she has a Mancunian accent – a rarity at the university. She likes Mancunians. And she likes her serious, slightly cross face. She enjoys hearing her spar with the other kids in the seminar group. Hannah is chippy and Lissa likes it. And she is also interested in her, this spring afternoon, because she thinks she might help her to get a good mark.

OK, says Hannah. The abject.

Hit me, says Lissa.

Hannah bends her head and reads, twisting the ends of her hair in her fingertips.

Abjection preserves what existed in the archaism of pre-objectal relationship, in the immemorial violence with which a body becomes separated from another body in order to be.

Immemorial violence, says Lissa. What does that mean?

Well, says Hannah, it's birth, isn't it? And infancy – before we enter the symbolic order. Language. All of that.

If you say so, says Lissa. Tell you what. She leans over and pulls a small bag of weed from a drawer in her cabinet. She has been given it this morning by her boyfriend.

*But . . . Hannah feels a mild panic as she casts her hand over the ranged books. It's three o'clock. I mean – we've got to give a presentation tomorrow, haven't we?*

*I know, but this might help.*

*Lissa feels Hannah's eyes on her as she rolls the joint. She takes her time, enjoying her skill, finishing with a flourish before she opens the window and leans out of it, four floors up above Owens Park. Go on then, she says, lighting up.*

*Hannah sighs and reads on.*

*On the level of our individual psychosexual development, the abject marks the moment when we separated ourselves from the mother, when we began to recognize a boundary between me and other, between me and (m)other.*

*Lissa thinks of Sarah driving her up here last September, her mother's old Renault 5 packed high with her stuff. She took her out to lunch at a restaurant in town. Now, darling, she said over the pudding, you are on the Pill, aren't you? Then she gave her twenty pounds, a rather beautiful portrait of Lissa aged eight sitting in the flowered attic chair, a large packet of Drum tobacco, a brisk kiss on the cheek, and drove off back down the motorway to London. A separation which hardly seemed to bother Sarah at all.*

*. . . as in true theatre, Hannah reads on, without make-up or masks, refuse and corpses show me what I permanently thrust aside in order to live. These bodily fluids, this defilement, this shit are what life withstands . . .*

*Wait – does it really say that?*

*Yeah. Hannah looks up and smiles. It is the first time Lissa has seen her smile. She has a lovely smile. Interesting. All the better for not being easily won.*

41

*This shit . . . this shit are what life withstands, hardly and with difficulty, on the point of death. There, I am at the border of my condition as a living being.*

*Wow, says Lissa.*

*Yeah, says Hannah.*

*Lissa blows out smoke on the evening air. There is the sound of traffic on Wilmslow Road below, the hazy, blurred sounds of the tower block; Portishead, 'Glory Box', drifting out of some-one's nearby room.*

*So . . . says Hannah. The presentation?*

*Oh. Yeah. OK. How about, Lissa says, how about, for start-ers, we name all the sorts of abject we can come up with?*

*Why? says Hannah. She is not a fan of thinking around things. She has a linear mind.*

*Well, why not? Go on – Lissa waves the joint at Hannah – how many can you name?*

*Hannah scrunches her nose. Well, there's piss, obviously – urine. Shit. There's blood; two types of blood. Vein blood. Menstrual blood.*

*I'll bet there must be more types of blood than that.*

*There probably are.*

*That'll do for starters. Vomit. Snot. Earwax.*

*We need to write these down. Hannah snatches up her pen-cil and starts scribbling.*

*How many is that? says Lissa.*

*Seven so far.*

*What about eye gunk?*

*Definitely eye gunk. What's the right term for eye gunk?*

*I don't know. Here, don't you want some of this?*

*Hannah has only smoked a joint once before. It was at the*

Ritz with Cate last summer, and it made her feel dizzy and ill. She is self-conscious as she makes her way over to the window. She takes the joint from Lissa – a short, exploratory drag. Lissa watches, amused, from the corner of her eye, then takes up the pad and pen.

Spit, says Hannah, taking a longer drag this time. Speaking of which, I might have made this a bit wet.

It's fine, says Lissa, keep going.

Phlegm, says Hannah.

OK. Don't say phlegm again.

Phlegm.

They both snort.

Dandruff?

Dandruff will do. Lissa stops scribbling and comes back to the window. They are close to each other. She catches Hannah's smell of incense and shampoo.

What about babies? says Lissa, taking back the spliff.

What about them?

Well, aren't they a form of abject in themselves?

Maybe. Hannah scrunches her nose. Or at least what's around them. What's it called? Some sort of fluid. Amniotic.

Yeah. That's it. We should form a band, says Lissa, giggling. The Amniotics. No – wait – the Abjections.

They are laughing properly now.

Oh God. We should. The Abjections. I love it.


They print out band T-shirts: black with hot-pink writing across the chest. The hot pink is allowed, they decide, as it is ironic. They name their Abjections, giving examples of each *from their own life. They discuss whether a man's sperm leaving your body – leaving its trace on your knickers after sex – can be seen as an abjection in itself. (Having not yet had sex, Hannah lets Lissa do the talking here.) They declare there are many different types of vaginal discharge: the one that leaves a white crust, the one that leaves a yellow crust, the one that floods you when you're turned on. They discuss whether discharge – with its pejorative connotations – is itself a patriarchal term. They decide that there are as many different types of vaginal abject as Inuits have words for snow.*

*They watch with satisfaction as the boys cringe. They feel a new power. They become electric. They become friends.*

## Hannah

She waits in the queue for the fishmonger, hovering over the threshold, the sun strong in the window, the shouts and calls of the market behind her. It has been a warm day; the ice is melting and the remains of the day's catch are blood- and scale-streaked. Two young men in waders pass between the front and a chopping block at the back, where the fish are gutted and bagged.

Eight years ago, when she moved to the area, a Jamaican guy owned this place. It was painted the colours of the Jamaican flag. He sold fresh and salt fish and vegetables, and other bits and bobs in the back; incense, reggae on bootleg cassettes. He had the most beautiful face. There was a campaign to help when his shop was sold from underneath him to a property developer: articles in the *Guardian* by local writers, a sit-in in the premises of a cafe on the street – a place owned by the same developer. An angry meeting was called in the church hall, to which they all went along – Hannah remembers a guy in his fifties, face livid with anger, standing and shouting, *I remember when it was shit round here. It was much better then.*

But now the ripples have been smoothed over, now marble tiles and line-caught fish have replaced pineapples and salt cod and plantains. This fishmonger is no longer new. And, despite an occasional, residual queasiness, Hannah likes it, with its day boats and its flirty young men and its sense that the sea is still full of abundance – that all might yet be well with the world.

It is her turn at last, and she duly flirts a little as she buys medallions of monkfish, asks advice on what else she might add to the pot, buys saffron and samphire and stows them in her bag. She is sweating as she leaves the shop – the first sign of the hormonal dip. Her scalp is laced in it. This is the hard part, the part they don't tell you about, the *down-regulation*, the menopause brought about in three weeks, your hormones suppressed to ground zero: the day sweats, the night sweats, the constant urge to cry.

But she is good at not crying – has it down to a fine art. She does not cry when woman after woman at work announces her pregnancy. As day after day she takes her temperature and marks it on a graph. As month after month she bleeds. And when her oldest friend told her she was pregnant, Hannah held her very close, so Cate would not see the expression on her face.

Outside she weaves past the coffee shop with its inevitable buggies clogging the pavement, her gaze grazing the babies, the parents with their fists clutching cappuccinos and flat whites. (She is good, too, at not looking closely at the children, it is not wise to stare at a baby's plump arms, at a toddler hand in hand with its mother, a newborn slung across a father's chest.) But as she passes the flower stand, she stops, her eye caught by the display. The woman with the stall turns to her. 'What do you need?' she asks. She is in her late fifties or early sixties, her eyes are blue.

'I—' For a moment Hannah is taken aback. What does she need? 'What are these?' She gestures towards a tall spiked flower.

'Teasel. They came from my own garden, we had a bumper crop this year. And here,' – the woman bends to her buckets – 'these are Michaelmas daisies.'

'I'll take some of both.'

The woman ties the flowers loosely with twine, and as she hands them over, her rough knuckles brush Hannah's own. Hannah heads to the bottom of the market, where the crowd thins out, crosses the canal and turns right, through the estate, towards her flat, jostling her bags as she opens the unprepossessing metal street door, then climbs the external stairs to the third floor of a three-storey building, an old pub, converted and sold before it was even finished. They had to elbow their way round with twenty other couples, then send their offer in a sealed bid the following day. Before the decision to move to Canterbury, Cate would visit, stroking her bump, staring out at the view, wondering aloud at Hannah's luck.

*It's not luck*, Hannah wanted to say. *It's how life works. You work hard, you save throughout your twenties, and by the time you're in your thirties you have enough for a deposit. It's not magic, it's simple maths.*

And now here is Cate, living in the house that has been bought for her by her husband's parents, for which, it seems, she has to pay no money at all, with her healthy, beautiful son, conceived with the utmost of ease – here is Cate, unhappy again. Or at least so she sounded on the phone last night.

Hannah slides her purchases from her bag, places the fish and samphire and wine in the fridge, cuts the stems from the

47

flowers and arranges them in a vase, which she places in a long slant of afternoon light. The teasels are unexpected, their beauty severe, precise. Her laptop is open on the table, and as she goes to close it, she sees the report she was working on this morning, before the sun called her outside. She saves the document and shuts the lid.

She is sweating still, so goes to the sink to splash her face with water. It is the strangest feeling, as though her skull is being scraped out. The urge to cry is on her again. She wants Nathan here, beside her, wants to feel his arm steady on her back. But he is only at the library, only a cycle ride away, along the canal. He will be home soon. They will eat together. He will tell her about his day. She looks up, her gaze resting on the flowers, the table, the light.

This is the house that Hannah built.

Here is the table she found in a junk shop in an old railway arch and spent a weekend sanding herself.

Here is the framed photograph of the garden of the house in Cornwall where Nathan proposed, each blade of grass frosted, whole.

Here is the bookshelf along one wall, filled with poetry, with novels, with Nathan's journals. (She, who grew up in a house with no books, can spend minutes standing in front of it, letting it speak back to her, the spines arranged by author, alphabetical: Adiche, Eliot, Forster, Woolf.)

Here is the rug they bought on a weekend in Marrakesh. The night shopping in the souks, the haggling and then the final capitulation and the exorbitant price to take it back on the plane. But it is beautiful, Beni Ouarain – from the Atlas mountains. A thick cream wool. *It will bring you fortune*, said the seller, tracing the diamond patterns with his fingers, and was it her imagination or did his glance flicker to her womb as she took out her credit card and paid?

Here is the sofa they bought from a warehouse in Chelsea, and chose for its low mid-century lines, its dark slate-blue linen. The sofa on which she sat, two weeks after the first round of IVF, holding her test – the jubilation of those two clear pink lines. The sofa on which she sat cocooned in blankets while Nathan cooked – soups and risottos for his pregnant wife.

Here, a little way down the hall, is the bathroom. The white bevelled tiles. The lotions in their plain brown glass jars. Here is the place where, three weeks after that test, she writhed in pain, where after a day of bleeding she passed a clot. The fibrous sac which held the baby that did not live. That she and Nathan did not know how to dispose of. That, in the end, they took to the park late at night, where they dug a hole and buried it deep in the ground.

But wait, here – come, walk this way, down the hall to a little room – open the door and stand within, watch how the light falls, softer here, more diffuse. This room waits, nothing in it but a quiet sense of expectation.

This is the house that Hannah built, three floors above London, floating in light.


The stew is cooked and bubbling on the stove. There is crusty bread and a bowl of aioli. A bottle of white stands glistening on the counter and two glasses wait beside it. Hannah takes parsley and chops it, adding lemon and salt. She hears the front door and then Nathan is behind her, his hand on her back. 'Hey.' She turns to him – a brief kiss on the mouth. 'How's the chapter going?' When he has writing to finish, her husband takes himself off to the British Library. He says he likes it there on weekends, when the Reading Rooms are quieter; says he finds it easier to work there than at home.

'Oh, you know. Getting there, slowly.'

She hands him a glass of wine which he takes gratefully, then ladles out stew, sprinkles parsley over the top, and hands Nathan his bowl. She takes her place at the table before her husband, aware of a slight sense of ceremony. It is Saturday; she is allowed to eat and drink what she likes. She sips the wine. It is clean and hard and bright and she could down it in one gulp, but she puts it back on the table beside her plate. Discipline. This is what she has always had, and this is what she has brought to bear on this situation. No caffeine. No alcohol. Apart from Saturday nights.

Nathan looks up at her, catches her watching, reaches his hand across the table and takes hers. 'This is delicious.'

'Thanks.'

'How about you? Did you work today?'

'A bit, this morning. And then it was too lovely, so I walked to the park.'

'Hey,' he says, 'I meant to tell you, I saw Lissa.'

'Lissa? Where?'

'At the library. Yesterday.'

'The library? What was she doing there?'

'She said she wants to do some reading, for a PhD.'

'That's funny. I'd never have imagined that.'

'Well. You know Lissa. She seemed a bit haphazard about it all.'

He reaches for the bottle. She watches as he pours himself another glass.

'Nath?' she says softly.

'What?'

'I thought . . . it's daft really, but I had this thought, earlier in the week, when I started the injections. When I was there with the syringes . . . I wondered about doing some sort of . . . ritual.' The word tastes strange. As she speaks, a fresh wave of sweat breaks on her forehead. She lifts her sleeve to dab it.

'What sort of ritual?' Nathan puts down his spoon, folds his hands in front of his chin. Rituals are what he teaches – they are his butter and his bread.

'I don't know.' She can feel herself begin to flush, the heat rising again. 'Something to mark it. I mean, if we did . . . If we did do something, how would we go about it, do you think? What could we do?'

'Well,' he smiles, 'you know, a ritual can be anything. It doesn't have to be serious, even. We can do something simple.' He reaches over and catches her hand. 'We could light a candle or . . .' Then, when she doesn't respond: 'Or we could just do nothing. We could just wait and see.'

'Yes,' she says, embarrassed now, releasing her hand from his. 'Yes. Let's just wait and see.'

## Lissa

'Sweetheart.' Sarah opens the door, and immediately begins walking back into the darkness of the hall. 'Come in. Got something on the stove.'

Lissa follows her mother through the hall into the kitchen.

'I'm making soup, though God knows why. It's still so bloody hot. Want some?' Sarah goes over to the range and lifts the lid off a pan, giving it a stir. Her mother's long grey hair is twisted on top of her head, held in place by two Japanese combs. She is wearing her work apron, ancient and brown and covered in paint.

'Love some,' says Lissa. She never refuses a meal at Sarah's – her mother is a fantastic cook.

'Ten minutes,' says Sarah, putting the lid back on the pan. 'And I'll do a bit of salad to go with it.'

Lissa lifts the cat from one of the dining chairs and sits. The mess is, if anything, messier than usual: drifts of letters on the table, some opened, some not. Her mother's periodicals: the *New Statesman*, old editions of the *Guardian Review*; missives from charities: Greenpeace, Freedom from Torture. One official-looking envelope is unopened and being used to make a list, Sarah's elegant hand spidering across the paper.

*Judy??*
*Cortisol? Ask Dr L.*
*Ruby – pills.*

'What's wrong with Ruby?' Lissa looks up.

'Something with her tummy. Poor thing's been puking and shitting for days. That vet. You wait years for an appointment, you really do.'

'How's your hand?'

'Oh. You know.' Sarah flexes her fingers. 'OK.'

'This one looks important.' Lissa lifts a letter and waves it at her mother.

Sarah turns back to the stove, dismissing her daughter with an airy hand. 'Not really. You can tell by the envelope.'

'Really?'

'It's a charity asking for more money. Or someone wanting me to take out a credit card.' Sarah plucks tobacco from the pocket of her apron and rolls herself a cigarette. 'Cig?'

'Sure.'

Lissa takes the proffered packet, enjoying the sweetness of the sugared paper on her tongue as she rolls – always the same brand, always the same liquorice Rizla papers, her mother's fingertips, for as long as she can remember, orange-stained, her breath murky and low. Her mother is making work again, that much is clear; the apron, the mess, and a distant edge of manic energy to her, as though there is a gathering somewhere nearby, a better conversation happening in an adjacent room. Lissa knows enough not to ask, though, not this early in the game. Whatever Sarah is working on, it is new.

'Cumin.' Her mother is rattling in the cupboards. 'Needs cumin. Course it does. Bugger.'

Lissa tosses the envelope back on to the pile where it triggers a minor landslide across the table, only stopped in its tracks by the fruit bowl. If her mother isn't going to worry about unpaid bills, she isn't going to do it for her.

'Sweet paprika?' Sarah turns, herbs in hand.

'Whatever you think, Ma.'

'I think it'll have to do. It's just – cumin seeds. I'm never without them. It's odd.'

'Can I do anything?'

'I'm going to do something salady. You can chop if you like. Wait a bit, though. Here.' Her mother chucks a greasy box of Cook's Matches over to her, Lissa catches them and wanders over to the door, which is propped open to the late summer air.

The garden is the nicest thing about this place. Her mother is a fine gardener, and what feels like chaos inside the house makes sense when you step outside – her mother's sensibilities; everything poised just on the edge of wild. Lissa strikes a match and smokes. 'I got the part,' she says softly, to the lavender and the honeysuckle.

'Sorry, darling?' her mother calls from inside. 'What did you say?'

'That part.' She blows out smoke in a thin line, turns back to the kitchen. 'The one I told you about?'

'Tell me again.' Her mother's face is in shadow.

'Chekhov. Yelena.'

'Oh, wonderful. That's wonderful.' Her mother comes to embrace her and Lissa inhales her smell of paint and herbs, the dry crackle of her hair.

Lissa laughs, feeling again the bubble of excitement she has been carrying in her stomach since she heard the news. 'Thanks. It is. The director – she's a woman. She's good, I think. Tricky, they say, but good.'

'But how wonderful. We must celebrate!'

Before she can object, her mother is rooting in the cupboard where she keeps the booze. 'Hmm. White wine. Lidl Pouilly-Fuissé. Supposed to be OK. Not cold, though. Or there's a bit of Gordon's – what about a G and T? Hang on. Not sure I've got any ice. I can chip a bit off the roof of the freezer. Shall we start with that? See how we go?'

'Sure.'

'Chuck me a lemon then.'

Her mother hums as she pours out large measures of gin and splashes a bit of tonic on the top. 'Bit flat but it'll have to do. Here.' Sarah hands her the glass with a flourish. 'Come and sit in the garden. The salad can wait.'

Sarah leads the way down a crooked stone path, through lavender bushes, past tomatoes and squash and herbs to where a small weather-aged table and chairs stand beneath a wooden trellis.

'You've gone out, darling.' Her mother leans forward and re-lights Lissa's cigarette. 'Cheers. Goodness. Here's to you.' She raises her glass. 'Here's to Chekhov. So Yelena – that's . . .'

'*Vanya.*'

'*Vanya.* Marvellous. Hang on, remind me, is that the one with the gun?' Her mother picks a stray strand of tobacco from her lip.

Sarah taught English before she retired. English and Art at the local comp; a good North London school, the sort that middle-class parents fought with their elbows out to get their kids into.

'That's *The Seagull.*'

'Ah yes. *The Seagull.* The one with the failing young actress. So – *Vanya?*'

'He's the failed . . . well, he's just failed. Failed at life. They're all failing, aren't they? It's Chekhov.'

'And you're the wife of the . . .'

55

'Failed academic. Serebryakov.'

'That's right. Oh gosh, yes – I think I saw Glenda do it, back in the day.'

Glenda Jackson is her mother's touchstone for all things good and wholesome about the acting profession.

'Or no – wait, it was that gorgeous one – Greta something or other.'

'Scacchi?'

'That's it. She was wonderful. So will you be.' Sarah leans forward and grips Lissa's wrist. 'Goodness, well done, darling. A proper part. About time too. You should tell Laurie. She'll be thrilled.'

Laurie, her mother's oldest friend, who taught drama at Sarah's school, who gave up her time to coach Lissa to get her into drama school all those years ago.

'You tell her,' says Lissa.

'I will.' Her mother sits back and regards her through the smoke. Sarah's gaze. Nothing escapes it. How many hours has she suffered it? She used to model for her mother as a child – hours and hours for years and years of sitting in that battered old chair in the attic. Until one day she refused to do it any more.

'I must say,' says Sarah, 'it's wonderful you can pass for . . . whatever it is she's supposed to be. I mean, they're never more than thirty, are they, these women in these plays? Unless they're fifty. Or the maids. They shuffle on and off a bit, don't they, the maids?' She waves her cigarette in the air. 'Light a samovar or two.'

'Yes,' Lissa says, though to what she is saying yes she isn't quite sure. All of it, she supposes. Yes, it's wonderful she can pass for thirty. Yes, there's bugger all between thirty and fifty, not just in Chekhov, but in everything else. Perhaps in life. Perhaps this is it – Womanhood. The Wasteland Years.

'Gosh.' Her mother takes a healthy swig. 'This is fun, isn't it? Haven't drunk in the day for aeons. So who's the director then?'

'She's Polish. Klara.'

'I can't believe you didn't say anything.'

'I've stopped. I mean, it's hardly worth it, is it, any more?' She picks at a stray piece of skin on her thumb with her opposite nail.

'Oh no, don't say that. You must let me know, when things come up. I can wear my lucky earrings.'

'Yeah, well. I'm not sure they've been that helpful. In the grand scheme of things.'

'They helped when you got that telly part. And when you were ill.' Her mother points the cigarette reprovingly in Lissa's direction.

The sun rounds the corner of the wall and falls on to the grass beside them. Lissa angles her face towards it. The cat winds itself, mewling, against her mother's calves.

'So when do you start?'

'Week on Monday.'

'So soon? And how long do you have?'

'Four weeks.'

'That's decent then. And are they paying you well?'

'Not really. Enough.'

'Good,' says Sarah, putting her cigarette out in the nearest plant pot. 'Good.' She claps her hands together. 'Right. Hungry?'

'I'll help.' Lissa goes to stand, but her mother waves her away.

'You sit. Enjoy the sun. It's just coming round the house. Lovely this time of day.'

So she sits while her mother clatters in the kitchen. Sarah is singing snatches of opera. In the sky above, contrails purl and lace against the blue. It is hot. Lissa looks up at the house; three storeys of Victorian brick. She can see the window of the room that used to be her bedroom. The attic skylight. Her mother bought the house with the settlement from Lissa's father, thirty years ago now. She has never spent any money on it, never had any money to spend, only a teacher's salary, enough for good food, for paints and materials, a holiday now and then. If she sold this house, her mother would be rich.

'Salad's coming.' Sarah brings two steaming bowls to the table, heads back up the path and returns with a large wooden bowl. Bitter red leaves mixed in amongst the green, walnuts and goat's cheese crumbled on the top. There is olive oil in a separate bowl, with a pool of balsamic at the bottom. Good, chewy bread with salty butter. They eat for a while in silence, the sounds of the neighbourhood around them: kids in paddling pools, barbecues, people laughing, the dusty, easy end of the holidays; summer in the body, sun on the skin.

'And how's everything else?' says her mother when she has finished, pushing away her bowl, rolling and lighting up again. 'How's Hannah? How's Cate?'

'Cate's in Kent. I'm not sure, really. I haven't spoken to her for a while.'

'Why?'

'Oh, you know. It happens like that sometimes.'

'Like what?' Sarah's gaze is hawk-like.

Lissa shrugs. 'We've sort of lost touch.'

'You must keep hold of your friendships, Lissa. The women. They're the only thing that will save you in the end.'

'I'll remember that.'

'Do,' says Sarah. She regards Lissa through the smoke. 'I always admired Cate.'

'I know.'

'She has principles.'

'Really?' says Lissa. 'I suppose she does.'

'And Hannah?' Sarah says.

'Hannah's OK. I saw her the other night.'

'Is she still . . . ?'

'She's doing another round of IVF, yes.' Lissa presses a hunk of bread into the bottom of her bowl.

Her mother tuts. 'Poor Hannah.'

'Yes,' says Lissa.

'That poor woman,' Sarah says again.

'Hannah's not poor.'

'It's a figure of speech.'

'I know,' says Lissa, 'but it's an inaccurate one. She's pretty successful. She and Nathan. They've done pretty well.'

Her mother puts down her spoon. 'Goodness. You're testy suddenly, Melissa.'

'I'm not testy, I'm just – you might as well be accurate, if you're going to pass comment.'

'I say *poor Hannah*, because I know she's been trying to have a baby for years. Trying and failing to have a baby. And I can't think of anything worse.'

59

'Really? What about trying and failing to have a career?'

'What do you mean?'

'Nothing.'

'No, really.' Her mother's eyes are sharp now; she has caught the scent of something. 'What do you mean? Do you mean yourself? Is that how you feel, darling?'

'Yes. No. Actually, no. Forget it. Let's just forget it. Please. This is nice. Let's not spoil it.'

'All right.' Sarah reaches down, scoops Ruby on to her lap, strokes her skull with an absent hand. There is quiet, the sound of Ruby's motorboat purring. Lissa finishes the last of her food.

'Your generation,' her mother says quietly. 'Honestly. You baffle me, you really do.'

'And why is that?' Lissa pushes away her bowl.

'Well. You've had everything. The fruits of our labour. The fruits of our activism. Good God, we got out there and we changed the world for you. For our daughters. And what have you done with it?'

The question hangs heavy in the summer air. Sarah closes her eyes, as though summoning something from the depths.

'When I was at Greenham. Standing there with thousands of other women. Hand in hand around the base. You were there, beside me. Do you remember?'

'I remember.'

A dusty campsite. A fence, covered with children's toys. Other children who knew all the words to all the songs. Ruddy-faced women huddled beneath tarpaulins drinking endless cups of tea. Her mother's friends: Laurie and Ina and

Caro and Rose. No men. The only men the soldiers who patrolled on the other side of the wall, their guns held against their chests.

She remembers a terrible blue dawn when the police came and dragged her mother out of the tent by her hair. She remembers the fear that her mother would be shot.

She remembers crying, asking to go home. Sarah taking her to a phone box and calling Lissa's father, who came to get her in his black Volvo. She remembers the look on Sarah's face as her father drove away. The disappointment. As though she had expected more.

'We fought for you. We fought for you to be extraordinary. We changed the world for you and what have you done with it?'

Lissa stares at the wall where the wisteria fights for space with the ivy.

'I'm sorry,' she says, a tight, familiar feeling rising in her chest. 'If I let you down.'

'Oh God,' says Sarah, grinding out her cigarette in the remains of her lunch. 'Don't be so bloody dramatic. That's not what I meant at all.'


She takes the overground from Gospel Oak to Camden Road. It is full, this Saturday afternoon, packed with families heading home from the Heath. Children yowl and carp, their faces pink and smeared with the remains of sun cream and ice cream and crumbly bits of picnic, their parents harassed and rosy, a couple of bottles down. Women her age, fresh from the Ladies' Pond, the ends of their hair damp. At Camden she manages to find a seat. The heat is terrible, the day overdone. Beside her, a teenager, the whites of his eyes red, blasts music from his headphones.

The train empties out at Hackney Central and Lissa makes her way across the park. Here – the province of the young – things are just getting going, the barbecues cranking up, people in groups of five or ten or twenty, the drift of cigarette smoke and charcoal and weed and the undertow of booze and coke and the night to come. She passes two young women, skirts hitched to their waists, holding on to each other and cackling as they piss behind a tree.

Her flat is just adjacent to the park, in the basement of the old house. She moved down here when she was still with Declan, who gave her the money for the deposit and helped her with rent. Since the break-up she has managed to hang on to it through a precarious combination of her life modelling, the call-centre work, the occasional acting job and some tax credits to top it up. She has stumbled through, has survived. Just.

Inside it is mercifully cool, and she drops her bag in the tiny hall, goes into the kitchen, fills a glass, and drinks down water from the tap. On the other side of the garden wall someone is being sung to – *Happy Birthday*, sing the half-cut voices, *to youuuuuuuuu!!!*

She lies down in the bedroom and shuts her eyes. Her head hurts – from the alcohol, from her mother, from the sun. *We changed the world for you and what have you done with it?*

She knows what Sarah thinks. That she has wasted time – fumbled the baton in the intergenerational feminist relay.

What she should have said – *Our best. We're just doing our fucking best.*

The tinny blare of music from the park is irritating her and she goes next door to the living room, closing the blinds against the low sun.

She slides a DVD from her bag – *Autumn Sonata*. Sarah had a copy in the dusty TV room, a Bergman box set. The cover is an intense close-up of the two actresses. She weighs it for a moment in her hand, then takes it and her computer over to the couch and slides it in.

At first she is bored, put off by the simplistic, static camera work, the clunky monologues to camera, and considers turning it off, but then Ingrid Bergman sweeps in and the film ignites. It is like watching a boxing match between two heavyweights, evenly matched, round after round of brutal pummelling, as a mother and a daughter go head to head, raking over the bones of their relationship. Half an hour in and Lissa is aware she is holding her breath. By the end of the film she is a small tense ball, arms locked around her knees.

When it is finished, she gets up and walks around the living room, feeling the blood come painfully back into her limbs. She rolls herself a cigarette and pulls up the window, sitting on the sill as she smokes. It has grown dark outside, and the night air lifts her skin in her vest top. The smell of petrol mingles with the smell of fried food, the charcoal of the barbecues drifting from the park.

She thinks of Nathan, of his face in the library. *I needed therapy after that film.* The sort of thing that most men don't say. But then, Nathan has never been most men.

It was down to Sarah that she met him. The first time was just after she turned twelve, when she refused to sit for her mother any more, and since Saturdays were Sarah's painting day, Sarah found herself a different model and Lissa was left to herself.

After a few weeks of watching crappy Saturday-morning telly, she began leaving the house and walking down the hill to Camden without telling Sarah where she was going. Kids not much older than her were hanging out in groups on the canal. She took to buying a Coke from a newsagent's and then sitting on the bridge to watch them. Nathan was one of those kids. No particular tribe, just a North London teenager who hung out and smoked weed on a Saturday afternoon on the canal.

Once, on a chill afternoon, he came over to her. *Are you all right? You look cold.* She admitted she was and he lent her his jumper. It was big and warm and he had done that teenage thing of making holes for his thumbs, and they shared a can of cider. He gave her her first cigarette.

A few years later they would see each other at Camden Palace. They would hug each other – the way you did then, with your whole wide self – you could tell each other you loved each other and mean it, high and platonic in your tracksuit on a Friday night. Then he went off to university and she never had his number and she didn't see him for years, until that night at Sarah's opening, bumping into him just after graduation, introducing him to Hannah. When she was already with Declan.

He must be nearly forty now.

She takes out her phone and composes a text.

*Bergman slayed me. Thank you, I think.*

She puts a kiss. Takes it away. Adds it again. Deletes the text. Writes another.

*How did you know?*

Deletes it. Puts down her phone.
*How did you know? Did you know? Did you know it would make me feel like this? Can I call you? I need to speak.*
She picks up her phone again and writes:

*Thanks for the Bergman. Loved it. Liss. X*

# Soulmates

## 2008–9

*The night of Hannah's wedding Cate has sex with the only other single person on her table, one of Nathan's cousins, a thirty-eight-year-old banker in the City. They get slaughtered on cava during the reception and fuck in the toilets at the Pub on the Park. After that she meets him quite often. He calls her sometimes at eleven o'clock at night and she goes over to his house. He owns a whole house to himself, which he lives in alone, on the far reaches of London Fields, over towards Queensbridge Road. He has already flipped a house in Dalston. He has a kitchen with a huge range on which he never seems to cook, as there are always takeaway packets filling up the bin.*

*Mostly they have sex there, in his house, but sometimes, if he is away on business, which he often is, they meet in hotels in Manchester or Birmingham or Newcastle, rooms of featureless luxury. They watch porn together. Having rarely watched porn before, she is surprised by how much she enjoys it. Once, they have sex in front of his computer in front of another couple who are having sex in their room in front of their computer somewhere in the southern states of the USA. It definitely turns her on.*

*This arrangement continues for several months. They never meet in the daytime. He never asks her to a gallery, or out for dinner. He is her secret. She feels shame when she thinks of him. Sometimes he goes quiet for a few weeks and she knows* he is having sex with someone else. Sometimes she wants to hate him for not being someone else. But he is not a bad man. He is not a wanker. He has many good qualities. He just does not want her to be his girlfriend and, in truth, she does not want him to be her boyfriend either.

One day he stops calling. She tries him a couple of times, then waits for the text that will signal he is ready to resume intimacy. Instead she receives a short, polite message that tells her he has met someone and is getting engaged.

She is thirty-three years old. She understands that this man has taken up a space in her life, space that could have been filled by a proper partner. She has not had a proper partner since she left Lucy, in a forest in Oregon, almost ten years ago. But then, in the intervening years, she has come to suspect that Lucy was never really hers.

She is seized by a sense of desperation. She will do Guardian Soulmates. It is the only sensible option. She chooses a photograph of herself from Hannah's hen do in Greece. It is taken from a distance and she is sitting on a wall and she doesn't look too fat. The drop-down option gives her pause:

Women seeking Men.

Men seeking Women.

Women seeking Women.

Men seeking Men.

For simplicity's sake, she chooses number one. She calls herself LitChick, talks about her love of books, of politics, of Modernist writers, of the history of the East End.

She goes on a date with a guy who is in a band. He is skinny and short and Scottish and wearing black jeans. He has no bottom. His eyes scope the room behind her while he speaks.

After one beer he gets a text and stands up. *Gotta go*, he says, and leans over to kiss her on the cheek.

She travels to Covent Garden, to a huge outdoor pub in the plaza that is full of tourists. She meets a man in a suit who looks shifty and depressed. He is recently divorced, he tells her. His wife wants custody of the kids. When she is with him she feels as though she can't breathe. She excuses herself to go to the toilet and walks quickly out of the pub towards the Tube.

She carries on, more dates, more men, aware that this is not good for her – that it hurts her – but like gambling, like an addiction, she is compelled to carry on.

In despair, one afternoon, she goes downstairs to Lissa's flat. She is nervous as she knocks. *I wouldn't have come*, she wants to say, *unless I was desperate. I know you don't want to see me. I know you're still angry.*

But Lissa, when she opens her door, is pleasant enough.

She shows Lissa her profile. *Jesus*, says Lissa. *Do yourself a favour.* With Lissa's help she chooses another picture – one closer up, of her laughing.

*And boobs*, says Lissa.

*Really?*

*Definitely a bit of boob.*

They craft a different profile, one that sounds less serious. *You want to sound as though you're OK without a partner*, says Lissa. *Nothing scares them off like need.*

She wonders when and where Lissa learned these rules.

This time she is more successful. Lots of men seem to want to date her. She meets a man – good-looking in an unobtrusive way. He has ginger hair and glasses. Her heart rises when she meets him. They have a drink and then they go to a restaurant.

They argue about Philip Roth. He writes freelance book reviews while temping. He takes his glasses off and wipes them quite often. It is a tic she decides is endearing. He is small, but she doesn't mind. They finish dinner and pay half each. They kiss lightly on the lips – the tiniest bit of tongue – and say how great it was and go their separate ways. She hears nothing from him. She checks her computer constantly. She sends him a message. Another one. She starts to feel she might be going mad. After a while she sees he is active on there. He has changed his profile. Changed his picture. He says he would like to meet someone who likes books.

In these moods everything is black. In these moods all men are damaged monsters. As is she. Everyone tells her that everyone meets online nowadays, cheering her on from the sidelines, but in these moods she knows it is just the leftovers. The leavings. She cannot imagine Lissa, for instance, ever going on there to find a man.

She shows Lissa the pictures of the men. These leavings. These leftovers. Listen, says Lissa. You're going for the wrong ones. They're all too skinny. Too cerebral. What you want is a bear. What about him? She points to a man with a beard and bags underneath his eyes. He looks kind. Or him? She leans forward and clicks the profile of a tattooed man with a baseball cap. There you go, she says. Try him.

They meet in the Dove on Broadway Market. They drink ale and talk about music and food. He is a chef. He knows nothing about politics or books. He has no A levels. He left school to go to catering college and he has lived in Paris and Marseilles and speaks fluent French. She feels she has been waiting her whole life to meet a man with no A levels who speaks fluent, backstreet Marseilles slang. He does not flirt. When he takes off his cap she sees that he is starting to go bald. She sees his small reflexive flinch as he monitors her reaction. But now, two hours into their date and several pints down, she has no reaction to monitor because by now she has decided that he could have lost all of his hair and she would not mind. He tells her that one day he would like to own a restaurant. No pretensions, simple cooking, local food. He asks her about herself. She tells him about her job, working for a small company, pairing community projects with big banks. The office on the edge of Canary Wharf. Queuing on her lunch break with all the suits. She makes it sound funny. She tells him about a five-a-side football match between local kids and a German bank. How the kids thrashed them. How pleased she was. He likes this story, as she hoped he would. About the Bengali women's group she took to a meeting this morning at the Bank of America, nervously fluttering in their saris like beautiful birds.

That's good, he says. That's good work. Those bankers. You should take that lot of bastards for whatever you can.

Yeah, she smiles, I'll drink to that.

When he goes up to get more drinks she sees that he is trying to hold his stomach in. By the end of the third pint he has stopped trying. They kiss on the street outside, their hands in each other's hair.

They go back to his. It is a large studio in a run-down block overlooking the canal. He has a futon and a wall of records. He plays her vintage reggae and opens a bottle of wine. The bed is messy and he hastily covers it with a throw.

I wasn't expecting anyone back here, he says. She believes him, and she likes him even more. They are hungry and he says

71

he will cook. She watches him chop vegetables with startling efficiency. He must be drunk but his knife does not slip. His tattoos. His wide forearms. Lissa was right. What she needed was a bear.

He cooks pasta with capers and chilli and fresh tomatoes. It is unbelievably delicious. When they have eaten they have sex on the unmade bed. She is astonished by how lovely he is to fuck.

In the morning the sun rises over the gas tower, over the canal. She counts his tattoos; he tells her the story of each one.

And what's this? he says, catching her wrist, tracing her spider with his fingertip.

Oh, that? she says, pulling her hand away. Just a nineties thing.

Three months later she is pregnant. Nine months later they are married. Seventeen months later she is living in Canterbury.

It is as though life has decided for her. Has picked her up and turned her round and deposited her a long, long way from home.

## Cate

'Come on,' she says brightly to Tom in his high chair, where he sits solemnly eating a banana. 'We're going on a trip today. To see Hannah!'

Sam looks up from his phone. 'It's Saturday,' he says.

'I know.'

'Saturday is my day.'

'I know,' she says. 'But I want to see Hannah and she works in the week. I thought you'd be pleased. You can go back to bed.'

'I mean . . .' He pushes his baseball cap back on his head. 'I was going to go to Mum's, but if you're sure. Where are you meeting her?'

'In Hampstead. On the Heath.'

'*London?*' He stares at her, uncomprehending. 'Why?'

'Because I miss her. I miss London. And Tom's growing so much, and she misses him and . . .'

'Really?'

'What?'

'Well, I mean, with everything . . . I just – can't imagine that's true.'

'What do you mean?'

'Well – if you were Hannah, would you miss Tom?'

She looks down at her hands, takes a breath. 'He's her god-son. And yes, I think I might. They say being around babies is good for women trying to conceive.'

Tom giggles and she looks up. He is grinning at them both, clapping his hands together, his latest trick.

She sources those little Tupperware cartons she bought, back when she thought she was going to mash and purée and blend his food herself, finds them at the back of the cupboard, stacks two with apple slices, rice cakes, fills his sippy cup with water, the changing bag with nappies, gathers the sling, a change of clothes, bundles Tom into his coat, grabs her wallet and makes for the door. Sam rises to open it, staring sceptically at the world outside. 'What shall I tell my mum?' he says, scratching his beard.

'Tell her I had to see Hannah. Tell her we'll see her next week. Tuesday. Tamsin's arranging it. Remember?'

'Oh. Yeah. Cool.' He leans in, high-fives Tom, gives her a brief kiss on the cheek. 'Look after yourselves. You sure you're going to be all right?'

'We'll be fine!' The brightness in her voice makes her wince.

She pounds down the road, past the scrubby patch of grass with its one tree, past the supermarket, down the underpass and out at the crumbled edges of the city walls. If she keeps going like this, she might outpace her tiredness. Sun strikes off flint, but it is chilly. The season is turning; the air here has a bracing twist that she doesn't remember feeling for years. The sea – it must be something to do with proximity to the sea. She is wearing only a thin jacket. She thinks about returning to the house, but to do so would be to risk defeat – if she does so, she might pluck Tom from the buggy and give up. And he is happy enough, kicking his legs, looking from left to right, practising his wave on the dogs and the passers-by.

He is good on the train too, standing on her thigh and bouncing, trying his legs out for size as the flat estuary lands of England pass by. Her phone buzzes. Hannah.

*You still OK for this morning?*
*Yes!*

She adds a smiley face, something she would have avoided in the past, but today, for the sake of speed and this new primary-coloured brightness she feels, it seems appropriate.

But by the time the train is slowing for London, Tom is tired and fractious and has missed the window for his nap. He protests when she tries to get him into the buggy on the platform, bucking and twisting away from the straps. She bends down and rummages through her bag for the Tupperware, but the bag, large and voluminous and many-pocketed, is reluctant to give it up. She locates it eventually, takes out a rice cake and brandishes it towards Tom. 'Here! Here, darling.'

He is crying properly now, real tears on his cheeks. He doesn't want a rice cake. He probably wants a feed. She kneels before the buggy. 'Just – hold on. Please. You can sleep soon.'

She pushes the buggy a little way down the platform, but Tom is beside himself and so she stops and takes out the thinner of the two slings, the one she has used since he was tiny, the one Sam would put him in and sing to him. Sam. She would put up with any number of his comments and sideswipes to have him here beside her. But he's not here. There is no cavalry, no *deus ex machina*. She is the grown-up now.

'Hang on,' she says, her voice getting tighter, as people cast quick, worried looks towards her. 'Hang on, darling.' She slots the sling in place, ties its origami folds tightly and manages to get Tom into it. It is like wrestling an octopus. He twists against her chest, but finally the crying eases and soothes and they both breathe together.

'OK?' she says, stroking his back through the sling. 'OK. OK?'

He is drifting into sleep. Now. She can either pace up and down the platform until he sleeps more deeply, or walk on, to the Tube, and risk him waking up. After a look at her watch she decides on the latter.

The Tube is loud, louder than she can ever remember it being, but Tom, mercifully, stays sleeping, his head on her chest. People look and smile, and she smiles back, but her heart is clanging. What if something were to happen – an attack of some sort? It just feels entirely wrong to have this tiny, sleeping infant in this carriage, this metal carriage in which it feels as if death could come in so many guises – which is tunnelling past the heaped bones of the dead, past the hungry ghosts of the city, and under the river – *the river* – which in and of itself must be dangerous, must it not? How has she not considered these things before?

She should never have left the house.

Tom sleeps on but she is a tight knot of worry now, her hand rigid against his back. *Please. Please don't wake. Not now. Not yet. Not till we're there.*

And he doesn't, the movement of the train keeping him

rocked and unconscious – he sleeps still as she wrangles the buggy on to the escalator, leaving the Underground at Camden, as she walks to the overground, as she takes the train to Gospel Oak, and it is only as she is rounding the gates of the Heath that he lifts his lovely sleepy head and looks around.

'Oh, hello! Hello, darling!' She is jubilant, on the verge of tears, she is so relieved. 'Look! Look at all the trees. The leaves! Can you see? Can you see?'

It is a beautiful morning. The broad swathe of Highgate Hill in the distance is alight with reds and golds and browns. There are runners, dog walkers; elegant couples in matching down jackets gesticulate as they talk in French, Italian, Arabic. It is the Great World and she is a part of it. 'Isn't it lovely?' she says, taking him out of the sling and strapping him into the buggy, then making her way to the cafe at the bottom of Parliament Hill, the cheap one, their favourite, the old Italian where you can still get ice-cream sandwiches and scrambled eggs on toast. She sees Hannah before she has been seen herself, sitting alone at a table outside.

'Hey! Hey, Hannah!'

She is shouting, sweaty and shouting, but she doesn't seem able to lose this terrible jaunty tone. Hannah looks up.

Hannah stands, a hug – the scent on her neck of something expensive and restrained – and then she bends to Tom. 'Hey, little one.'

Hannah is dressed in a sleek woollen winter coat; her hair looks as though it has recently been attended to by a very good hairdresser.

'You look nice,' says Cate, gathering her breath.

'Thanks.'

77

Cate searches Hannah's face for signs of stress, but can see none, finds rather that her gaze falls off it, as though Hannah is coated in something smooth and impenetrable, a rock face with no hand- or footholds, while she feels porous. More than. It is as though there are great gaping holes in her that anyone might be able to see into, poke around in and pass judgement upon the mess within. She is sweating, and Tom, when she lifts him out, is sweating too.

'Oh,' says Hannah, staring at Tom. 'He's wet.'

'It's just sweat.'

Hannah nods. 'But his chest, it's soaked. It's quite chilly, isn't it?'

Hannah is right. He has drooled all over himself. He is teething and she should have brought a dribble bib. Why didn't she bring a bib? His chest is covered with sweat and drool and he is tiny and he is teething and Hannah is right, it is not warm – the season has changed while she was hiding inside the house. 'Here, just a sec.' She thrusts him at Hannah, who takes him and puts him on her knee.

'Hey, Mister.' Tom twists round and stares at Hannah doubtfully, and Cate can see the momentary flash of panic on Hannah's face.

'He's fine. He's just woken—'

'Don't worry.' Hannah lifts her hand. 'We're cool.'

Cate bends to the buggy, rummages for his change of clothes. The bag again. The fucking bag is terrorizing her. 'Here!' She has a clean jumper in her hands. She holds it up to Hannah, who nods and smiles. It is impossible to convey the sense of achievement inherent in this find, so Cate says nothing. Instead she begins to wrest the jumper over Tom's head, then thrusts him a rice cake, which he takes happily as she shoves a hat on his head.

*Breathe. Breathe. Breathe.*

'Will you be OK with him if I go and get a coffee?'

'Sure. We'll be great, won't we, Tom?'

Tom kicks his feet and grins.

'You want anything?'

'No. Really, I'm fine.'

Cate stands, makes her way into the cafe and joins the queue at the counter, casting frequent looks back towards where Hannah and Tom sit, Hannah with her hand raised, pointing to something just out of sight. She scans the herbal teas, decides against them, orders a cappuccino and a pastry, dumps two sugars into the coffee and carries them back out into the morning.

*Breathe.*

'Tell me what's happening then.' Cate puts down her coffee and sits.

'There's really nothing much to tell. I'm having a menopause right now. I'm sweating. I'm irritable. It's pretty horrible, but it won't last long.'

'But you look great!' cries Cate, and she reaches out and touches Hannah's sleeve. A strange, reflexive action – she wants something of that sleekness for herself. Hannah's hand comes down on her own.

'And you?'

'I'm fine,' says Cate.

*I think I might be losing my mind.*

There is a pause. Cate blows on her coffee while Tom chirrups on Hannah's lap, and she stares at her lovely child in the arms of her oldest friend and feels sudden, stupid tears in her eyes. She bends to wipe them before Hannah sees. But she has seen, of course she has.

'Hey, you're crying.'

Cate nods. The tears are streaming now. 'I'm OK. I promise. It's just—'

There is snot; there is nothing to deal with the snot, only a small, thin napkin on the side of her coffee, beneath the plastic-wrapped biscuit. She blows her nose and the napkin dissolves in her hands.

'Here.' Hannah reaches into her bag for tissues and Cate takes a tissue from the packet and blows her nose. 'You look tired.'

'I am tired. Tom wakes so often to feed in the night.'

'That's tough.' Hannah nods. She leans in to Tom and whispers in his ear. 'Hey. Listen, you. You give your mum a break. She needs to sleep.'

'You watch,' Cate says. 'When you have this baby, you'll have a sleeper. You'll have it on a routine from day one.'

Hannah laughs. 'Yeah, well, let's see. How's Sam?'

'He's OK. Well, maybe he's OK. I'm not sure. They offered to take Tom for me, one day a week. Tamsin, Sam's sister, and Sam's mum.'

'But that's great!' says Hannah. 'Free childcare. Isn't that part of why you moved out there?'

'I suppose it is.' Cate looks at Tom, who is flapping his arms with great enthusiasm at a nearby dog. 'But what if he turns out like them?'

'What do you mean?'

She shakes her head. 'I'm sorry. I don't really mean that. I just—'

'What?'

'Sometimes I feel I failed.'

'At what?'

'Everything.' She lifts the balled-up tissue in her fist. 'I didn't even have tissues today. My mum always had tissues. That's just what mums do. And I'm scared.'

'What of?'

'Everything. The future. Climate change. War. I keep thinking what sort of world it will be, when he's our age.' She circles her hand with her opposite wrist, her thumb touching the spider, just hidden from sight. 'And I keep thinking about Lucy. About where she is.'

'Lucy? Really?' Hannah's expression darkens. 'I'm sure wherever she is she's fine. Come on, Cate, you've got Tom. You've got Sam. You've got your life.'

'But what if it's not my life?'

'What on earth does that mean?'

'I just feel—'

'What? What do you feel?'

*Lonelylonelylonelyallthefuckingtime.*

'Sometimes I feel . . .'

'What?'

'That maybe it was irresponsible. Having a child at all.'

And just like that she feels Hannah detach – arms folded, head turned. Feels the morning, with all its promise, drain away from her, drain from them all.

'Cate,' says Hannah, her voice tight, 'listen to me. Take the offer of childcare. Have a day a week to yourself. Sleep. And I think you should see someone. A doctor.'

'A doctor?'

'If you're depressed,' says Hannah slowly, 'there are things you can do. You've been here before. Go and see the doctor. Take some pills. Get better. Please.' She lifts Tom, places him back on Cate's lap. 'Come on, Cate, nip it in the bud. For Tom, if not yourself. And he's cold,' she says. 'Tom's cold. Let's go inside.'

## Lissa

The first day of rehearsal is a crisp, early autumn day and Lissa rises early. In the shower she hums, sounding out her voice, running her tongue round her jaw. She chooses her outfit with care: a loose cotton shirt open at the neck, jeans and a necklace of red beads. No make-up other than a touch of mascara. She pins up her hair, shrugs on a man's oversized jacket and winds a light scarf around her neck. She is nervous, but it is a manageable feeling, a sharpening, a slight fizz at the edge of things as she walks across the park, enjoying the pull of the morning tide, the fast pace of the walkers, the bikes. The air is clean, the leaves of the plane trees catch the early sun.

As she walks she speaks to herself in a low voice, running over the speeches she has half memorised; they are using the Michael Frayn version, and she is coming to know it well already, to internalise its cadences, imagining herself into the part: Yelena, the young wife of an old man, buried in her marriage and thirsty for life.

*Yelena: You know what that means, having talent? It means being a free spirit, it means having boldness and wide horizons . . . he plants a sapling, and he has some notion of*

*what will become of it in a thousand years' time; he already*
*has some glimpse of the millennium. Such people are rare.*
*They must be loved . . .*

She is interested to see who is playing Astrov, the doctor
with whom her Yelena will fall in love. Interested to see who
is playing all of the parts she has been reading to herself over
and over for the last three weeks.


She arrives fifteen minutes early at the address written on the
front of her script, a basement studio in Dalston tucked away
on a side street between two Turkish restaurants, their fronts
shuttered up against the morning. The director, Klara, is there
already, in a corner of the room, speaking to someone who
can only be the designer, their heads bent to a scale model of
the set. She is shorter than Lissa remembered, dumpy even,
grey hair in a dandelion frizz around her head. Ten or so
chairs are set out in a circle for the actors, another row behind
them for the technical staff. On a small side table a kettle
steams into the bright air. A clear-faced young woman comes
up, pumps Lissa's hand and introduces herself as Poppy,
the ASM. 'Great to meet you! There's coffee, pastries, help
yourself.'

Lissa drops her bag by a chair and wanders over to the
table.

'Might as well take advantage of the hospitality.'

She turns to the voice and sees a man about her height
standing beside her.

'God knows when we'll see its like again.' There's a faint
northern accent to the bass growl. Scouse? He is clean-shaven,

fifty or so, with grey in amongst the brown of his hair, which is longish, falling past his ears. His eyes are the most extraordinary blue. She knows him from somewhere. She must have seen him on stage but she cannot remember when. She goes to say something back, but he has turned and gone already, croissant in hand, over to his seat.

'Lissa?'

She turns to see a much younger man this time, thin-faced with wide-set eyes and thick lips. She meets his proffered hand. Does she know him?

'Lissa Dane, isn't it?'

'Yes. I'm sorry, I—'

The young man laughs. 'I just recognize your face. From pictures.'

'Really?'

'Didn't you use to go out with Declan Randall?'

'Oh. Yes, I did.'

'I love his work.'

She nods. 'Well, he's a talented man.'

'That last film – the one in the prison. The French director? Awesome.'

'I haven't seen it,' she says.

'You're kidding.' He shakes his head. 'If I could have anyone's career, it would be his.'

She nods, finds her gaze sliding out to where the older actor is sitting. It is bugging her. His face. Where does she know it from?

'So you're not together any more?'

'No,' she says. 'Not for a couple of years. He dumped me. For a make-up girl.'

'Jesus,' he says, shaking his head. 'That's harsh.'

'Yeah, well. He was an egotistical monster. So, you know.' She picks up her coffee. 'Silver linings and all that.'

The room is filling up now, the hubbub around the coffee table increasing, the knot of actors spilling out into the room. The assistant stage manager is clapping her hands and gathering everyone together. Lissa and the young man, who tells her his name is Michael, wander over to the circle, where she takes her seat beside the older actor, who acknowledges her with a slight nod of the head.

All of the chairs are taken. Klara makes her way to her place but stays standing, her gaze sweeping the circle as one by one her actors fall silent. She lets the silence swell until it fills the room, then touches her hand to her heart. 'Here you are,' she says. 'Here you all are. And who are you? Tell us. Johnny.' She nods to the man beside Lissa. 'You begin.'

'Johnny, Vanya.'

A young, intense-looking woman in black jeans and a polo neck speaks next. 'Helen, Sonya.'

One by one they speak – *Richard, Serebryakov*; *Greg, Astrov* – and as they do so, the play populates itself: the elegant older woman playing Maria, Yelena's mother-in-law; the woman who looks to be in her seventies playing Marina the nurse. Lissa watches Klara watch her actors – they all watch each other with wariness, with excitement, until the circle is complete and it is Lissa's turn. 'Lissa,' she says, 'Yelena.'

'So,' Klara says, 'let us read this brilliant play.'

As Johnny bends to the black leather bag at his feet and fishes out his script, it comes to Lissa where she knows him from – the call centre. She can picture him there now, sitting in the grotty break room with the same faintly disdainful look on his face. Something regal about him. Something tragic. Dressed all in black, with the same black leather briefcase at his feet.

## Hannah

They have been told to report to the hospital early, and she and Nathan sit silently, side by side on hard plastic chairs nailed to the floor, as dawn breaks over London.

Nathan scrolls through work emails on his phone as Hannah counts the couples. Seven of them. She knows the statistics: 24 per cent of those in her age bracket will conceive, 15 per cent of those older than her, slightly higher for those under thirty-five. She watches faces, guesses ages, tries to do the maths. How many of those sitting here will be lucky? One couple? Two?

The women's names are called and they rise, their small bags in their hands, saying goodbye to their partners. Nathan stands before Hannah and presses his forehead against hers.

Then the women are taken away through swinging double doors, to a waiting room where a television is playing – the gaudy blare of morning TV. It scratches at Hannah's nerves and she does not want to watch it or listen to it, so she pulls out her book and tries to read, wishing she had brought headphones. Her name is halfway down the list that is pinned to the wall.

They are given hospital gowns to wear – strange garments, open at the back. They sit so their knickers are not on show.

The morning passes like this. There is weak squash to drink. One by one the women leave and Hannah watches them go – each with their precious cargo, full of hope. She tries to read their faces, their bodies, as though she might see their destiny written there – which one of them will have the longed-for child. As though if they win, then she loses. As though fertility were a zero-sum game.

She thinks of Cate. *Sometimes I feel I was irresponsible, having a child at all.*

The carelessness of her comment. The luxury of a gift that came so easily.

In truth, her words had made Hannah furious, but she'd said nothing, packing away the anger she has no spare energy to feel.

The woman beside her is nervous. She keeps getting up to go to the toilet. It is making Hannah nervous too.

'Is it your first time?' asks Hannah, when she returns.

The woman nods. 'You?'

'Third.'

'Really?' The woman looks unhappy to hear this, and Hannah wishes she had kept quiet.

'I don't like anaesthetic,' the woman says. 'Don't like being knocked out.' Her face is ashy in the hospital light.

By the time Hannah's turn comes, she too has grown nervous. How many eggs will there be? The more she has, the higher her chances. It looked like eleven on the monitor, when she had the last scan, but sometimes they are just empty sacs.

'Hannah Grey? Follow me.'

She pads after the nurse into the small cupboard-like anaesthetic room, where she climbs on to the table.

'OK there?' The anaesthetist shoots her a quick look.

Her hand is taken, the anaesthetist asks her to count back-wards, and Hannah does and . . .


'Thirteen,' she says to Nathan, in the recovery room. 'I got thirteen.' She is dizzy, jubilant.

'Blimey.' He reaches over to kiss her. 'Aren't you clever?'

'How was yours?'

'Fine.' He grins. 'It was funny, though, they had the same magazines in the drawer they had last time.'

'You're kidding.'

'I'm not!'

'Do you think they disinfect them? Do you think that's someone's job?'

'I've no idea.'

They are laughing and she is light, sitting here, high on hospital tea in the wipe-clean recovery chair. Other women sit opposite her. Some look happy, some less so. And she knows. She knows this is their time.

It is still early afternoon. They walk home, through the back streets, over the park, where leaves spin and fall in golden light. The flat has the calm, clandestine feeling of a midweek afternoon and they are playing truant, together. They open the windows and let in the day, and then, for the first time in weeks, they lie on their bed and make love.


She wakes early. She has been dreaming but she is not sure of what.

Beside her, Nathan sleeps on. She stands softly, pulls a blanket from the bed and goes into the kitchen, where she makes herself camomile tea and then takes out her laptop, wondering if she should distract herself with a movie, but there is nothing she wants to watch, so she clicks through some other pages, the IVF message boards – the thousands of women posting their queries, and the thousands who answer them – the pastel-hued sorority of anxiety and reassurance. She cannot bear these message boards and yet they call her, again and again, with their siren, sister song.

After a while she casts the computer aside, takes the blanket and goes over to the window, looking out over the park to the city beyond. She thinks of those embryos, tinier than sight. How many of them have fertilized? How many of them pulse now with the smallest possible pulse of life? She wants to be near them. To walk back to the hospital and find the room where they lie and sit beside them. To watch over them in these long, small hours before the dawn. She is their mother, after all.

They call her the next morning while she is at work. As soon as she sees the unknown number on her phone she jumps up and takes the call in the corridor. 'Eleven have fertilized,' the nurse tells her, and she feels her heart leap.

She tries to call Nathan, but his phone rings and rings and she gets his voicemail. A text comes through. *In a meeting. All OK?*

*Eleven*, she writes, and he sends back one word. *Great!*

Now she must wait.

*

There is no news the next day. Nathan is working late, and the flat feels large. She opens the door of the little room. This small room faces west, towards the hospital. She slides down to the carpet and sits there in silence. After a while she lifts her phone and calls her parents' house. Her father answers.

'Hi, Dad.'

'Hannah. How're you doing, love?'

'I'm good.'

'Glad to hear it.'

'How're you?'

'Grand.'

Have they ever said more than this to each other on the phone?

'Hang on a sec, love. I'll just get your mum.'

'Thanks, Dad.'

His soft call. She sits in the dusk of her empty room and imagines her mother getting up from whatever she is doing, watching telly most probably, feet up on the low table in front of her. Wearing the slippers Hannah bought for her from the catalogue last Christmas. Here she comes, padding into the hall. Shooing the dog away from the little armchair by the telephone table.

'Hannah, love.'

The soft vowels.

'Hiya, Mum. Did I disturb you?'

'No, love. Not at all. Just catching up with a bit of *Strictly*. Hang on a sec, I'll just get comfy.' She can hear her mother settle further into the chair. 'How're you? Have you had the thingy?'

'Yes.'

'And how did it go?'

'Well, I think.'

She doesn't go into details. Her mother's concept of IVF is hazy at best.

'Oh, that's good, love. You know, I saw Dot the other day. Her daughter's little one is one now.' The talismanic properties of Dot and her daughter's daughter – conceived by IVF and born last year – are strong. They were wheeled out last Christmas, all three generations, invited over for an awkward cup of tea.

'One?' says Hannah into the darkness. 'That went quickly.'

'Such a poppet.'

'How's Jim?' she asks.

'Good. They've exchanged on the house. They're moving in a week or so. Just in time for the birth.'

'Hayley must be getting close now.'

'She is. She's big all right. You'll be an aunty soon.'

'That's good,' says Hannah.

'How's work?'

'Quiet.'

'Well, that's a blessing. And Nathan?'

'He's . . . good.'

'Well, that's grand, love.'

She closes her eyes. She wants to be up in Manchester in her parents' little living room, watching *Strictly* with her mum with the gas fire turned up too high.

'I'll pray for you, love,' her mum says.

'Thanks,' says Hannah. She never knows what to say in response to this.

*Thanks, Mum, but there's no such thing as God.*

'I'd better go. Leave you to your telly.'

'All right. If you're sure?'

'Nathan's got something on the stove,' she lies.

'Oh good, well, you give him our love, won't you?'

'I will. Bye, Mum. Love you.'

'Love you too, Han.'


The next day, early, there is a call from the hospital.

'The embryologist would like to do the transfer today.'

She thanks them, and goes into the bathroom, where Nathan is brushing his teeth.

'They want to do it today.'

He spits, rinses his mouth. 'Did they say anything else?'

'It was just a receptionist. They must not look good, the embryos.' The smallest flickering pulse.

'I'm sure it's fine, Han. It's just – science.'

She fiddles with a bit of toilet roll.

'Hey. Hey, Han.' His hand on hers.


They are shown into a tiny, dimly lit anteroom. She is told to take off her clothes from the waist down and given a gown to wear.

The room is dark but for small lowlights set in the wall. There is a nurse. A doctor. Her on the gurney. Her feet in stirrups. The monitor beside her. Her heart. Her heart. Nathan's hand, steady on her arm. The embryologist appears. 'Ms Grey? Mr Blake?'

She nods.

'Well, the thirteen eggs that were taken three days ago have been watched closely. There were seven still developing last night.'

She nods.

'There are three that look viable. One is excellent. A 3.5. The others are a 2.5 and a 2.'

'And the others?' asks Nathan.

'Less viable. Our recommendation is to transfer the top two.'

'Yes,' says Nathan. 'Of course.'

The ceiling has small pinpricks of light, like stars.

'Han?'

'Shall we proceed?' says the voice of the doctor.

'Yes.'

She lies back, gasps at the chill of metal as a speculum is inserted. There is a deep, strange almost-pain as her cervix is stretched wide.

'Now, just watch the screen.'

Nathan grasps her hand.

'There we are,' the doctor says. 'There they go.'

Two points of light appear in the darkness of her womb.

She looks at them.

'Here,' the doctor says kindly, reaching down and tearing off a printout. 'Would you like this to take with you?'

'Thank you.' Hannah stares down at the photograph, at those two smeared points of light. She looks. She looks and looks and looks.

# Resistance

## 1998

Cate puts her full stop on her final finals paper (Greek Myth in Spenser's Epithalamium) and steps out into the mild May sun, where she is duly pelted with flour and rice by a small cluster of waiting friends, with whom she drinks a bottle of champagne in the cobbled street. Then she goes to the pub and drinks pints of lager in the beer garden until the ground is tipping, when she goes to the toilets and is sick.

The next morning she wakes late and sits and stares at the wall, which is peppered with Post-it notes, quotes by Spenser, Rochester, Congreve, Donne. She takes them down one by one and puts them in the bin. She has to be out of this room on Monday. It is over. She has limped to the finish line, patched up on Prozac, pills she has been taking since the end of her second year, when, quite suddenly, standing in the college quad, her mind began to fracture. Grief, was what the college counsellor said to her. Delayed grief, agreed the doctor, writing out his prescription. And of course, he went on, Oxford can be very stressful in itself.

She took a year out. Went back to Manchester. Stayed in her father's house.

She knows she will not finish first or last, but somewhere in between. From her mullioned window she can see hungover students stumbling to the shop for soft drinks and cigarettes.

To her right, just visible, the ghoul masks of the Sheldonian Theatre. The Bodleian beyond. She will never set foot in the library again. She has packing to do. She wonders what it was all for.

There is nowhere to go home to. Her mother is dead and her father is in Spain. Her sister is in Canada. So she goes to stay with Hannah, who is living in a small flat on the edge of Kentish Town, walking distance up a long hill from where Lissa lives with her mother. Cate sleeps on the sofa in the living room of Hannah's flat. Hannah has a new boyfriend, a man called Nathan. She met him through Lissa (of course.) He is tall and handsome and gentle, and walks with a slight stoop, as though apologizing for his height. In all other respects, though, he seems like a winner in life. Nathan spends nights there, in the small Camden flat. Sometimes, waking in the darkness, Cate hears them through the walls.

They talk, just once, she and Hannah, about Hannah's new job – entry level in a management training firm.

Why would you want to do that? Cate asks her.

It's not for ever, says Hannah. But I need money. I want it. I'm sick of not having it. I'll do it for a bit and then I'll do something worthwhile.

But what about Patti Smith? Cate wants to say. And Emma Bovary? And the Pixies? But she says nothing, only nods.

So, what are you going to do? asks Hannah of Cate. And Cate has no answer to that at all.

She doesn't like London. The transport system alone makes her head hurt. Hannah leaves copies of Loot on the kitchen table, drops hints about people who might have a spare room going, but Cate follows up no leads. She is ill at ease with

96

*Hannah and Lissa, a friendship that has grown and eclipsed her own. Ill at ease when they go out to dinner together with Nathan and Declan, Lissa's boyfriend, a laughably good-looking Irish actor, to a restaurant Lissa knows, an Ethiopian place where food is served without cutlery on sour flatbread, which they all tear into with their fingers and dip in sauces with equal alacrity, and drink coffee which is brought to the table and roasted on the spot. They talk emphatically at these meals, using their hands as they speak, they seem certain about all sorts of things, like which films to see, and which books to read, and who they are and what they are going to be.*

*Cate herself is certain of nothing. Life seems at once becalmed and full of danger, as though a wave could come at any moment, rising out of the still waters, a great towering wave, and take her down.*

*She receives her finals results. She has scraped a first. She tells Hannah, who looks shocked. It was an accident, says Cate hurriedly. And then hates herself for saying it. Still, she thinks, it was an accident. She never expected that.*

*Her tutor calls to congratulate her. So what are you going to do? he says.*

*She can only think that she would like to tell her mum. To give her the good news.*


*She gets an email from Hesther, a friend from Oxford who is living in Brighton, inviting her down for the day. There is a room going in her house.*

*As she steps off the London train, Cate can smell the sea. She walks down to the seafront and stands on the pebbled beach and stares out at the pale horizon. She walks through the city to Hesther's house. Brighton seems appealingly ramshackle, human-sized. The room is cheap and small with a window that lets in good light. She takes it. She buys herself some furniture from the charity shops on the Lewes Road.*

*The other room is occupied by a woman called Lucy. Lucy wears combat trousers and vests and boots with strong soles, as though she is a foot soldier in an unnamed war. She has thick dreadlocks that hang down her back, and her face is small and fine. She is studying for a Master's in International Development at the University of Sussex. She is half American – grew up between Devon and Massachusetts, and her accent is deliciously confused. Two summers ago Lucy lived up a tree in Newbury, sleeping on a wooden platform a hundred feet above the earth, protesting the destruction of ancient woodland for the building of a bypass road.*

*Lucy teaches Cate how to use a drill, how to put up shelves in her room. She has a light cloud of armpit hair and does not use deodorant. When they stand close, Cate catches her musky scent. Walking around the city with Lucy is an education – she has a scavenger's eye: wood for the wood burner, wine crates for shelves, just-out-of-date food from supermarket skips. Lucy carries herself lightly, as though she still walks in the forest. As though at any moment she might be predator or prey.*

*A rhythm establishes itself. Once a fortnight Cate signs on at the job centre, and once a month money lands in her account. It is not much, but enough to cover the small bedroom, and to buy cheap food – enough to allow her to breathe. She is pleased to find her needs are few. Hesther tells her there is a job going in the cafe in which she works, a cycle ride away, on the other* side of town. Cate takes the job. At the end of her first shift she is paid money from the till in cash. The first time is hard – she feels like a cheat. She tells Hesther this, and Hesther tuts. You know how much the British government spends on weapons? Besides, it's just till you get sorted, till you get on your feet.

It is easier after that.

At the weekend they go down to the seafront and drink cider and watch the sunset, watch the starlings stream in to roost on the skeleton of the West Pier, watch them cast themselves in great clouds of murmuration against the evening sky.

Lucy and Hesther are part of a group of young people who like to gather together at the house and talk – about capitalism, about hierarchies, about horizontal power and the potential for change. They plan actions. Cate has no idea what an action is until, one dawn in late summer, Lucy knocks on the door of her room and tells her to get out of bed. Cate pulls on her sweater and tracksuit bottoms and they drive out along the High Street, where Lucy stops the van and instructs Cate to sit in the driver's seat. Which she does, nerves jangling, as Lucy covers her face with a bandana and neatly spray-paints the word SLAVERY – the V made by the swoosh of Nike – on the front of a trainer shop. Lucy jumps back in the van and shouts at Cate to drive. Which she does – giddy and fast. She feels like Bonnie, or Clyde.

She begins to read again, different books: Chomsky and Klein and E. P. Thompson. She starts to join the discussions. At first it is odd to hear her voice in a group – it has been so long since she felt she had anything to say. She begins to think that Oxford, that place of power – that place she hoped would confer power on to her – robbed her of her voice, or rather, that she gave it away. Or perhaps, she thinks, it was only hidden. Perhaps she had only to follow the trail of breadcrumbs to find it again.

She and Lucy and Hesther go up to London and they march in the streets. They dress up in costumes which they run up on sewing machines; they don fat suits with pinstripes to protest at the fat cats in the City. There are bicycles everywhere. There are solar-powered sound systems blowing bubbles into the crowd. Passers-by stop and shake their hips.

She goes to dance classes on a Monday morning, where the teacher plays loud music and people of all ages throw themselves around the room and sweat and shout as though possessed. Sometimes in these classes, when the music is at its height, she screams. No one takes any notice, for this is what you are supposed to do. She realizes that she is angry. Very, very angry indeed.

On the other side of her anger is something else.

One morning, in Cate's room, Lucy finds her anti-depressants.

What do you want these for?

I had a breakdown, says Cate. At uni. I've been taking them since then.

You don't need anti-depressants, says Lucy, looking up at her with a smile. You just need better friends.

She throws away her pills, waits for the crash that she fears will come – but feels only relief at the ebbing of the fog.

She is aware, somewhere at the back of her mind, what Hannah would say if she could see her, how easy all of this would be to parody, this benefit fraud and cider drinking and dancing and horizon watching. But she is starting not to care.

She writes Hannah a postcard, an old-fashioned picture of an old woman with her skirts hitched up and her ankles in the sea – *Come on in*, it says, *the water's lovely.*

Lucy and Hesther both have vans and with her small savings Cate buys one too – a decommissioned ambulance which she parks at a cement works outside the city and, over the winter, with a little help from Lucy and a small Makita drill, converts herself. Tongue-and-groove cladding inside, a bed made from sawn plywood, shelves above and drawers beneath. It is ready by spring, and when it is finished she thinks she has never been prouder of anything in her life.

There is an album they all listen to, all autumn, winter, spring. Clandestino, *by Manu Chao. There is a song, 'Minha Galera', that Cate loves above all.*

*Oh my waterfall.*

*Oh my girl.*

*My Romany girl.*

*She plays it over and over, and when she listens to it she thinks of Lucy.*

Summer comes. They stock up on muesli and coffee and rice from the local wholesaler and take to the road. They drive west. They swim naked in rivers, emerging jubilant, silver-backed. They go to small festivals tucked into folds in the green hills.

Cate comes to recognize some of the faces around the evening fires: young people like themselves, and older people; people whose faces tell stories, of weather and work and lives lived outside. At night, with tea and whisky, these older people loosen their tongues – they speak of Enclosure, of the Commons, of an older, wilder Britain, of gentle and of not so gentle defiance of the status quo. Cate thinks she can touch it, this life-giving current, ribboning out into the clear western night.

And then they dance.

One black night, at one small gathering, in high summer, when the air is still warm at midnight, where there are no lights, when there is no moon, Cate loses Lucy. She wanders around for hours, searching, feeling panic bite at the edges of her. She finds her again as dawn begins to break, sitting in the middle of a pile of people, naked from the waist up, her nipples painted gold.

Lucy holds out her arms for Cate and Cate steps into them and then, filled with love and relief and a desire to claim, she bends her head to Lucy's golden nipple and takes it into her mouth. It tastes of salt and metal and earth.

Soon after, as the sun presses itself against the windows of her van, Cate slides her fingers into the slick warmth of Lucy and encounters no resistance. She watches Lucy buck and arch beneath her, her eyes half closed. She sees a tattoo on Lucy's inner thigh, a filigree spider, a filigree web, and she puts her mouth on it, kisses it. She herself is shivering with desire – she doesn't even need to be touched to come.

## Cate

Mid-morning and Tom is sleeping. Cate sits at the kitchen table, the bag of pills beside her.

*Come on, Cate, nip it in the bud.*

As though it were that easy.

This morning she went to the doctor, as Hannah suggested. The doctor was nice, was kind; she asked about Cate's eating, sleeping, libido. She asked about the manner of the birth and Cate told her.

*Caesarean section.*

*And was that hard?*

She thought about the fear – for her child, for herself. The confusion. The knives and numbness, the smell of burning flesh.

*Yes. I suppose it was.*

The doctor asked about whether she thought of hurting herself, hurting her son. *No*, said Cate. *Not that.*

The doctor said that yes, she thought Cate was depressed. She said there was CBT, but a long waiting list, or antidepressants. But if she took anti-depressants, she would have to wean her son. She asked if Cate had ever been on antidepressants before.

*Yes, Prozac. At university.*

*Good*, said the doctor. *Well, perhaps we'll start with that.*

Cate reaches for the packet of pills, pops one from its packaging and holds it in her palm. The innocuous white and hospital green. They used to make her head fizz. If she drank while she was on them she would black out.

She puts the pill down on the table and brings her computer towards her, searches 'breastfeeding anti-depressants' and reads that the amount of medication that gets to the breastfed baby is usually less than 10 per cent of the amount found in the mother's blood. Which still sounds like an awful lot.

*You don't need anti-depressants. You just need better friends.*

Her fingers hover over the keys, then she types 'Lucy Skein' into Google, feels her heartbeat increase. Several pictures appear, but none that resembles Lucy, although she would be older now of course, much older. She was four years older than Cate, so forty now, or nearly so. Perhaps Lucy Skein was never even her real name.

They parted in the States. They had gone there to Seattle, to take part in the protests against the WTO. Had locked themselves into Perspex pipes and shut down the city. Had watched the police on their horses, their black uniforms, their masked faces, like a scene from a fairy tale, good against evil, light against dark. Had sat and chanted with thousands of other protestors as they were sprayed with CS gas till they were burning and almost blind. She remembers the pain, the inrush of feeling – the ecstatic logic of the binary. Of black and of white. Of being right.

After Seattle they went down to Eugene, Oregon, and lived

in a squatted warehouse for a couple of months with ten other activists, and that was where Lucy heard about the protest camps by Mount Hood – loggers cutting down ancient trees. They caught a ride out there together, walked out into the forest on a crisp November morning, the mountain rearing before them, the tang of earth and resin and snow in the air. They reached the camp, and there were the trees, and the people in those trees, their shouts and whistles as they moved about in nets high above their heads. And Cate saw the look on Lucy's face, and watched, helpless, as Lucy pulled out her ropes and strapped herself on, and then she was climbing away from her, and Cate stood earthbound, leaden-hearted, as Lucy climbed up into green and light.

They rode back to Eugene. Cate's visa was running out. Lucy didn't need one. They went to a tattoo parlour downtown, where Cate sat while Lucy held her hand, as an unsmiling man leaned over her arm and drew a filigree spider in a silver web. She flew home, determined to fly back again as soon as she could. She went down to the internet cafe every day to check her email, but there was never a word. Those first weeks, as the tattoo scabbed and healed, when missing Lucy grew too much she would press her fingernail into it, would lift the scab to feel that pain again.

She went back to her job in the cafe, signed on, trying to save for another flight, waiting for word, but no word came. Spring came and went, and brought nothing from Lucy. Then in the early summer, an email – a few words.

*Some of us in the camp have been arrested. They say we're terrorists. I won't use this account any more.*

*Spin always.*
*Weave always.*
*Love always.*
L. X

And then nothing. Severance. Free fall.

Years. Years in which Cate thought she saw her constantly, on the beach in Brighton, or cycling through the city, her long hair down her back. Years in which Cate stayed working at the cafe, still watching the door, waiting for Lucy to walk back in.

It was Hannah who finally walked through the door. Hannah who came down to Brighton one day, who stood in her smart work clothes and looked around the cafe – at the cakes on their cake stands and the menu chalked up on to the board, the pitta and hummus and the bean burgers and soya lattes, and said, *You have a first-class degree from Oxford University. What the hell are you still doing working here?*

It was Hannah who told her about the room in the house Lissa had found in London Fields. Cheap rent. On the park. A chance to start again. And because she knew she was rotting behind that counter, corroded with waiting, Cate took it.

She stares back at the pictures on her computer screen, feels the old twist of loss.

She could have searched harder. Could have gone back to the States, could have found her. Could have claimed her, claimed that part of herself.

And then a thought comes to her – Hesther. Perhaps there are pictures of Lucy in Hesther's feed – perhaps they have stayed in touch. She searches for Hesther, finds her profile, the pictures of her family, her Georgian house in Bristol, her high ceilings and her lovely kitchen. Clicks back and back and back. There are a few photographs from the Brighton days but none of Lucy.

She clicks on Hesther's name.

*Hey Hesther, long time. Hope all is well.*
   *Just thinking about some old friends today. Wondered if you had Lucy Skein's contact details?*
      *Much love*
      *Cate.*

She presses send.
*Fuck.*

There is a knock at the door. Cate stays where she is, but the knock comes again, imperious this time, and then the sound of a key turning in the lock. Horrified, she goes out into the hall where she sees Alice coming through the door.

'I thought you might need a hand.' Sam's mother is brisk, dressed in a scarf and padded gilet, her cheeks rosy. A bulging bag stands at her feet. 'So I brought some help.' She lifts the bag, which is bristling with lurid plastic bottles. 'Shall I come in?'

Cate steps back as Alice passes her into the kitchen. The pills are still on the table, next to the computer, open to a series of photographs of women's faces. Cate moves, putting herself between the table and Alice, her heart beating wildly.

'Still haven't unpacked those?' Alice takes off her gilet and hangs it on the back of a chair, then points to the tower of boxes behind the door.

'Not yet. I mean – I've been waiting to borrow a car, for a charity-shop run.'

'You can borrow Terry's,' says Alice, taking a crisp, ironed apron from the bag and tying it around her waist. She lifts bottles from the bag. 'I thought we could tackle the kitchen and bathrooms then go for a bit of tea and cake. Get you both out of the house.'

Cate eyes the bottles. Alice's cleaning cupboard is a temple to carcinogens in all their many varieties. 'Oh, well, that's so lovely of you, Alice.' She turns around, gathers her computer and the pills and brings them all into the safety of her cardigan. 'The thing is . . .'

'Yes?'

'I'm actually just heading out.'

'Out?' Alice's head is cocked; she appears to be sniffing the air for untruths.

'Yes. To playgroup.'

'Playgroup?'

'The one you recommended.' Cate nods at the flyer on the fridge. 'I've just been waiting for Tom to wake up. I'm just going to check on him now. Excuse me a sec.'

She races upstairs to the bedroom, where Tom is fast asleep, his arms flung out at right angles on the duvet. She shoves the pill back in the packet, puts the packet in the paper bag and the bag at the very back of the bathroom cupboard, covered with a towel, scrubs her face with a flannel, returns to the bedroom, pulls a jumper over Tom's Babygro, pulls on the sling and manoeuvres him swiftly into it, then makes her way downstairs as he begins to properly stir.

'There we are,' she says, snatching the playgroup flyer from the fridge and one of the space-food packets from the cupboard. 'I'm really sorry to miss you, Alice. And I'm so grateful for your help.'

Alice stands in the middle of the room. 'Well, all right then. But don't forget Tuesday.'

'Tuesday?'

'Tuesday, my grandson and I have a *date*!'


The address on the flyer is a low, unprepossessing municipal building. She walks quickly past, further up the hill, then curves back around the block, in sight of the hall once more.

She need not actually go to playgroup at all. She could take Tom and go somewhere else, perhaps to a cafe, one with wifi, drink coffee and jitter through the morning, spending her finite energies on more fruitless internet searches, but it is starting to rain, and Tom is grizzling and here she is. She crosses the street, over the threshold, coming into a hallway which is a chaos of buggies and shoes and coats. She lifts Tom from the sling and gives her name to the woman at reception. A tidal roar comes from behind double glass doors.

'It's five pounds for the session,' says the woman, 'but you can pay three. It started an hour ago.'

Cate pulls some coins from her wallet and tosses them down. Inside she is greeted by a thrashing sea of children and plastic toys. She grips on to Tom, who grips back, his head turning this way and that. There seems to be no safe harbour anywhere. Her heart is thumping, sweat breaking on her back.

'It's circle time now.'

Cate turns to see a brisk, grey-haired woman standing beside her.

'There's a baby mat over there for when we're done.' The woman points into the far corner and claps her hands. 'Circle time!' she calls in a sing-song voice, and Cate watches as the hordes form themselves into a ragged approximation of a circle. 'Come on,' says the grey-haired woman to Cate, in a tone that brooks no opposition. 'Come and join in.'

The woman launches into a joyless version of 'The Wheels on the Bus'. Larger children practise commando crawling across the space, and Cate shields Tom between her legs. Here, amongst the older children, he seems terribly small.

*When do we get off the bus?* Cate wants to ask, as the grey-haired woman grinds on. *When does the bus actually stop?* The last time she sat on a mat like this was when she was a child herself. *Miss? Miss? Are we nearly there yet? Please, Miss, I want to get down.*

Eventually the bus judders to a halt, and after a few rounds of 'Twinkle, Twinkle' and 'Wind the Bobbin Up' the woman claps her hands. 'All right, children. It's free play!'

There's general screaming as the larger children dive towards racks of dressing-up clothes. A girl emerges from the melee in a fireman's suit; her hijab-wearing mother grins back at her and gives the thumbs-up. Superheroes twist and flail across the room. Cate retreats to the corner, to the baby mat, where a scattering of toys have been put out.

'Jesus Christ, it's like World War Three in here.'

She looks up to see a woman standing close to her, a baby around the same age as Tom in her arms. 'I was told it was OK for little ones.'

'I know. I think perhaps you have to keep to the corner.' Cate gestures to the mat beneath her.

'Really?' The woman looks cross. 'Well, what's the bloody point in that?'

The woman's baby has seen Tom and is reaching out for him. The mother notices, amused. 'You want to get down?' She kneels and puts her child on the mat. The baby is dressed in a hand-knitted, haphazard style. She wears a home-spun bonnet which gives her the look of a small mushroom, or a Bruegel peasant. The woman plucks her daughter's hat from her head and black curls spring forth, then throws off her own cardigan. She is small, with a gentle intensity to her features, short brown hair, an angular fringe.

On the mat, their children are groping for each other. Their hands touch and they both scream in delight. The woman laughs. 'Who's this then?'

'This is Tom,' says Cate.

'This is Nora,' says the woman.

'That's a good name.'

'You think? My partner decided on it. All the ones I wanted had some sort of tragedy attached to them. Antigone. Iphigenia.'

Is she joking? Cate can't tell, but the woman catches her eye and smiles. She sits back and blows her fringe from her forehead. 'Where's the Tom from then?'

'Oh, well, we just liked it, I suppose.'

'Fair enough.' The woman reaches out and places a toy in front of Nora. It has lots of buttons which Nora presses in turn, blaring out Americanized versions of nursery rhymes.

'Oh, nononononono.' The woman leans in and turns the

111

sound off. 'We've had quite enough of that for one morning.' Nora presses the buttons a few more times, but when they yield nothing, loses interest and crawls over to where Tom is bashing a block against the side of a table. 'I like the Babygro,' says the woman, gesturing to him.

'Oh.' Cate can feel herself colour. 'We were late, and he was sleeping, so—'

'I'd wear one myself if I could. Can you imagine, someone putting you in a Babygro and tucking you in? Letting you sleep? Heaven.' The woman closes her eyes, and for a moment exhaustion takes over her features, until there is a cry and she snaps them open again. Nora is reaching for the wisps of hair on Tom's head. 'Oh, no no, we don't grab, darling,' says the woman, lifting her child away and on to her lap as Nora's fingers clutch on air.

'Nora Barnacle!' says Cate. 'Joyce.' She has spoken before she has thought.

The woman looks up. 'Yeah.' She grins. 'That's right. She's certainly growing into the Barnacle bit. Crusty and clinging. Here, poppet.' She reaches down with her sleeve and swipes at her daughter's nose. 'My partner's writing about Joyce,' she says. 'I'm Dea.' The woman looks up, smiling. 'So, what happens next?'


## Lissa

Her head hurts and her tongue feels swollen. The pint glass beside her bed is empty – she must have woken and drunk it all at some point during the night. She didn't eat after rehearsals, going straight to the pub with the other actors, and

112

was three glasses of wine down before realizing how hungry she was. By then the pub kitchen was closed, so she had two packets of crisps for her dinner.

From her bed she can see through the window, out to where rain falls dully on to the sodden garden. There must have been a strong wind as the trees have lost many of their leaves. At least the park on the other side of the wall is quiet – you can usually hear the chatter from early on a Saturday, but today the weather has obviously kept the crowds at bay.

She hauls herself out of bed, pulls on her old dressing gown and pads through to the kitchen, filling the glass from the tap and drinking it straight down. She rummages in the cupboard for ibuprofen but finds only an empty packet. A further search turns up a couple of paracetamol, which she swallows gratefully. The fridge yields a lump of Cheddar, badly wrapped and hard, and a bit of butter, knife-gouged and jam-stained. She takes the cheese and nibbles on it, staring out at the rain.

When Declan used to visit, it would send him mad, this habit of hers, of not replacing things, not using things up properly, or putting lids back on empty jars. Once, during the last stint of his living here, she came home from work to find five almost-empty Marmite jars piled up on the little kitchen table with a note beside them: *See what I mean?*

It was a strange thing about Declan – how he came across as so easy when you met him, loose-limbed and wolf-grinned, happy to sink several Guinnesses in the pub with you, to sit up polishing off a wrap of cocaine, but it was always she somehow that was the messy one – always she that drank more than him and didn't remember the night before. He would be up and out and running around the park, even on a few hours' sleep. He liked discipline, did Declan. He liked a clean kitchen. He liked a hairless vagina. He had a streak of cruelty which cut through the craic and kept you in your place. She thinks of Michael, that conversation on the first day of rehearsal – *If I could have anyone's career, it would be his.*

She'd lied. Of course she'd seen the film. She's watched them all. Several times. Declan's a brilliant actor. He makes clever choices. He works with who he wants. He's such a good actor she can watch his films and forget who it is and forget that she hates him for a while.

She pulls up the hood on her dressing gown and rolls herself a cigarette, lights it at the table, takes two puffs and puts it out in disgust.

She wants to be touched. When was the last time anyone touched her? When was the last time she had sex? She doesn't even want sex. She just wants to be touched. She might wither if she isn't touched soon. She's no good at being single. Good single people plan for the weekend – they know the wretchedness of this ambush and head it off at the pass with yoga and brunch dates and exhibitions and dinners – but she has nothing planned, only a hangover and her own company and the long day ahead.

She considers going back to bed and attempting sleep again, but that feels even more depressing, so she makes herself some tea and brings it into the living room. The blinds are drawn and she leaves them that way.

Her eye falls on the Bergman DVD and she remembers Nathan's face in the library cafe, laughing at her as she scrawled on her hand with his pen.

Do they discuss her together – he and Hannah?

114

*Lissa's thinking of doing a PhD. Oh hahahahahahahaaa.*

She takes out her phone and scrolls back to the brief text exchange.

*Thanks for the Bergman. Loved it. Liss. X*
*I'm glad. Hope you got yourself a notebook. See you in the library sometime. Nx*

Since then she has been back to the library a couple of times, got herself a reader's card, ordered up some books on Russian history. She likes it there, likes putting her possessions in the locker, likes drinking good coffee in the cafe. She looks for him, often, but has not seen him there again.

Her bag is on the sofa beside her, contents spilling out: script, scarf, tobacco, phone. She pulls the script towards her. It is folded open at the scene they were working on yesterday, she and Johnny, the scene where Yelena berates Vanya on behalf of all men: *You recklessly destroy forests, all of you, and soon there won't be anything left standing on the face of the earth.*

It is only the end of the first week and yet there is already an atmosphere in the rehearsal room. Klara is prone to outbursts, flying off the handle at the slightest provocation. Greg, the actor playing Astrov, was half an hour late on Thursday, a doctor's appointment for his son having overrun. He was screamed at and told he would be sacked if it happened again.

Usually, by this stage, at the end of the first week, there is a sense of how things are going, but this time she cannot tell – yesterday, for instance, when she was working through Yelena's monologue, the director's expression was one of barely contained disdain, ultimately erupting in her banging the table. 'Stop this microwaved emotion!'

*Microwaved emotion*, it is rapidly becoming clear, is Klara's favourite phrase. They went on to try the monologue several different ways but each time Klara shook her head, muttering under her breath. Yet when it came to Johnny's turn, Vanya's speech to Yelena – *You're my happiness, my life, you're my youth . . . let me look at you, let me listen to your voice* – Klara sat back, nodding, murmuring her assent. If she were a cat, she would have purred.

There is no denying that Johnny is a superb actor. Last night she heard Greg raving to Michael in the pub about a performance he'd seen Johnny give twenty years ago in Liverpool – *Best Hamlet of his generation. Made me want to be an actor. Total fucking tragedy he's not a star.*

Despite the fact that most of the men and most of the women in the cast seem to seek his approval in some unspoken way, Johnny keeps himself to himself. He didn't stay long at the pub last night, just the one pint, which he drank at the bar in the company of Richard, the older actor playing Sereb-ryakov. He is careful with his energies, unlike the others, who spill over already into easy intimacies, into kisses and hugs and the swapping of tales. As he left she overheard him telling Richard that he had his kids this weekend. *They always want to go to soft play – it's hell on earth with a hangover.*

She has no idea what Johnny thinks of her. His expression is unreadable. Yesterday, when she was rehearsing alone with Klara, she saw Johnny slip quietly into the room. He stayed at the back silently watching her – those blue eyes, the calm intensity of his gaze.

A thought comes to her, and as it does she slides down further on the sofa, opens her dressing gown, reaches into her knickers and puts her hand to her crotch. She closes her eyes and thinks of herself standing there, alone on the stage, and of Johnny watching her, of taking off her clothes for him, one slow layer at a time. And his face, his blue eyes, the way he watches, the way he wants her – and then it is not Johnny, it is Nathan, Nathan sitting in Johnny's place, at the back of the room, watching her, wanting her, and her standing naked now, and she is coming, coming into her hand.

She lies there, gathering her breath, staring up at the ceiling.

Then she curls over herself, groans and pushes her head into the cushion with shame.


## Hannah

'Shall we do something this weekend?'

Nathan is standing in the shower. It is the second day after the transfer. The door to the terrace is open, and autumn sunshine streams into the flat.

'Like what?' he calls over the water.

'Like – I don't know – get out of London? Go to the countryside. The sea.'

'Yeah, why not? Oh, wait . . .' He turns off the shower and reaches for a towel. 'I've got that paper to turn around for publication.'

She watches him towel himself dry, stretch in a shaft of sun. He comes towards her. 'You look well,' he says.

'I feel it.'

He tastes of coffee and toothpaste and soap.

'But you should,' he calls behind him, as he goes into the bedroom and pulls out a pair of boxers and jeans from the chest of drawers. 'Get out, I mean. Why don't you go and see someone? See Cate? Go to Canterbury? Or – what's that place by the sea? Nearby? The one with the oysters?'

'Whitstable.'

'Yeah, that's it.' He comes back over towards her, buttoning up his jeans. 'Why not go there?'

'Maybe.'

'Wait. Can you eat oysters? If you're—?'

'Oh. No,' she says, closing her eyes, warmth inside, warmth without. 'No, I don't think you can.'

In the end she does nothing – finding that she does not want to stray far from home after all. But as she goes about her weekend, she thinks of the embryos inside her. Often, she takes out the photograph and stares at it, tracing them with her finger, those two points of light, surrounded by an immensity of dark.

On Monday, the fourth day, they call. She is in a meeting, and feels her phone buzz in her bag. She excuses herself, goes out into the corridor and answers.

'I'm sorry,' the nurse says. 'Nothing has been frozen. The other embryos were not doing well.'

'Oh,' says Hannah. 'Thank you.'

The pulse, the flicker of life. Gone out.

'What happens?' she says softly. 'To the other embryos? Can you tell me?'

'I . . .' The nurse falters. She sounds very young. 'They're . . . disposed of, I imagine. I'm sorry, no one's ever—'

'It's OK,' says Hannah. 'Thanks.'


On the sixth day, a Wednesday, she goes to meet Lissa at the theatre. She gets out of the Tube at Embankment and walks slowly over Hungerford Bridge, where dusk is falling and the lights are jaunty in the river.

The clear days have continued and the nights are crisp. She pulls her coat tighter around her, weaving around the buskers, finding a pound for a young girl who sits at the top of the stairs. She tries to remember what play they are going to see. A family drama. Lissa's choice. Theatre rather than cinema this time. In truth, she does not want to go inside. She would like to keep walking, this clear autumn evening, carefully, carefully along the river – a pilgrim, carrying her lights inside her. How long would it take to reach the sea?

The Long Bar is thronged. A jazz band plays in the corner. Hannah scans the space for Lissa, and finds her eventually, tucked away on a leather bench by the picture window, the remains of an espresso on the table in front of her. Her head is bent over a script, her pencil poised, her mouth moving soundlessly. Hannah touches her shoulder and she jumps. 'Oh, hey.' Lissa rises and kisses her cheek. She is wearing a little more make-up than usual; her long hair is pinned on top of her head with Japanese combs. She looks extraordinarily like her mother. Hannah perches beside her on the bench.

'Did you have the thingy?' says Lissa.

'The transfer. Yes.'

'And how did it go?'

'Good, I think. I hope. Is this your script? How's it going?'

'Oh, OK,' says Lissa, frowning, folding the script in half and putting it in her bag. 'She's tough. The director. I mean, I knew she was going to be, but she really is. I'm not sure she thinks I'm any good.'

Hannah looks past Lissa, to the wide river outside, the winking lights.

'It's just so ... gladiatorial,' Lissa is saying. 'Having to prove yourself every minute, every day. There's nowhere to hide. And the guy playing Vanya. He's brilliant – but I just don't know where I am with him.'

*Oh Lissa,* she wants to say. *You chose this. Are actors never happy?*

What she says is, 'Sure, I understand.'

The bell rings for the performance. Lissa lifts the tickets from her bag and Hannah follows her into the dark mouth of the theatre.


The play is long, the cast large, the tickets cheap and the seats far from the stage. Hannah can't keep track of who is who, and the action seems to be happening in a little box very far away.

In the interval they go outside and wander without speaking over to the river wall.

Lissa takes out her pouch of tobacco. 'Do you mind?'

Hannah shakes her head. Lissa rolls and lights up and blows the smoke away from them both. They fall silent, watching the water. Beneath them the small beach has appeared, its sand and rocks glistening in the half-light. Hannah breathes in the tang of mud and salt and dirt.

'I'm thinking of studying,' Lissa says, 'thinking of making some changes in my life.'

'Oh?' Hannah brings herself back. She remembers then. 'Didn't you see Nath at the library? A few weeks ago? I'm sure he mentioned something about it.'

Lissa nods as a thin stream of smoke leaves her mouth.

'Something about a PhD?'

'Yeah. Maybe.'

'What would you want to do with it?'

Lissa shrugs. 'I'm not sure. I've been doing some reading.'

'Really, Liss?' Hannah pulls her coat close around her. 'If I had a fiver for every overqualified person with a PhD who applies for an internship . . .'

Lissa gives a brief laugh. 'You'd be rich. I know.' She turns to where the interval crowds are making their way back inside. 'We should go back.'

'Would you mind . . . ?' says Hannah. 'I'm really tired. Do you mind if I don't?' She wants to go home, to keep herself close, she doesn't want to spill a drop.

Lissa takes a quick last drag, then chucks her cigarette over the wall. 'Sure,' she says. She leans in, a quick hug. 'You look after yourself, Han.'

Hannah walks towards the steps, up to Waterloo Bridge. She waits for her bus. Thinks of the river beneath her, fast-flowing, thinks of its course – out through Wapping, out beyond the Thames Barrier, out, out, salt and sweet water swirling as its wide mouth meets the sea.


As the days go on she can feel it, she is sure of it. Traction. A catching. The points of light have buried themselves inside her and taken root. Her breasts are heavier. There is a fullness inside her that was not there before.

'It's happening,' she says to Nathan over breakfast, on the morning of the eighth day.

He reaches over and takes her hand. He is smiling, but it does not reach his eyes.

'What?' says Hannah. 'What's wrong?'

'Nothing's wrong, I just – don't want to get my hopes up.'

'Really? Why?'

'Hannah, please.'

'I'm telling you.' She grips his hand. 'I can feel it. It's happening. I *know*.'


On the afternoon of the eleventh day, when she goes to the toilet at work, there is a trace of blood in her knickers, tiny, but there.

She looks away. Looks back again. She wants to scream but she tries to breathe.

It is nothing. It is normal. She goes back to her desk and googles 'blood post IVF'. Her search leads her to the message boards, where she reads the blood could be a good thing – *implantation bleeding*. Meaning she is right, and they are burying themselves inside her, those twin points of light.

She does not visit the toilet again. She holds on for the rest of the day. She works on a report. She takes a conference call with the States during which she smiles and nods and takes diligent, copious notes. There will be no more blood. It is nothing, it is normal, it has worked. Everything is fine. *Itisnothingitisnormalithasworkedeverythingisfine.*

On the Tube journey home every bump of the carriage makes her wince, and there is pain now, deep in her abdomen, a claw tracing its way along her womb. By the time she reaches home she can hold off no longer. Her knickers are soaked with blood. It is over. It is done.

She is curled up on their bed when Nathan returns from work.

'Hey.' He kisses her.

'I'm bleeding,' she says to him.

'What? Oh God. Oh Han, I'm sorry.' He does not sound surprised.

'You're sorry?' Her voice is dull. 'Who for? For me? For you? For our child? Who doesn't exist?'

'All of it. You, mostly, Han.' He lies on the bed behind her, fits himself to her back, laces his arm around her waist. 'Are you OK? How long have you been here?'

'An hour. Or two.'

'You're cold,' he says, holding her closer.

And she is aware of her body suddenly, of how he is right – how cold she is, how it has grown cold.

'Oh, Hannah.' He puts his cheek on her shoulder. 'Oh Han, my love.'


The next morning she is hunched at her computer before Nathan wakes.

'What's going on?' he says, coming into the room, dropping a kiss on her head.

'I've found a clinic. Harley Street.'

She feels his fingers grip her shoulders. 'Hannah—'

'Please,' she says. 'Just look.' She gestures to the pictures of babies on the screen.

'No.' He moves away, over to the window.

'Nathan—'

'*No*, Hannah. You promised. You promised this would be the last time.'

'This man is the best. He's—'

'Hannah. I'm not listening to this.'

'Why?' She is standing, fists clenched. 'Why?'

'Hannah? Can't you just . . . Just let me . . . Can I hug you? Please?'

'Why? Why do you want to hug me?'

'Hannah. God, Han. Why do you think?'

'I'm going,' she says. 'I've made an appointment. I'll pay for it. Come with me. Please. Just – come.'

# True North

## 1987–92

*They are suspicious of each other. They know of each other's existence because they got the first and second highest marks in English last year, and these things are talked about. But they have not shared any classes together, until now. And here they are in the same classroom. Top set English, Miss Riley. They are twelve years old.*

*Miss Riley has long curly hair and glasses like Su Pollard from* Hi-de-Hi! *She passes round a poem by Thomas Hardy. Who would like to read first? She looks over the faces. They are in one of those prefab classrooms, the mouldy ones built after the war.*

*Hannah and Cate do not, this first day, put up their hands. They watch each other like snipers, each waiting for the other to make the first move. When the poem has been (badly, haltingly) read out loud by someone else Miss Riley lifts her face to her class.*

*Right then. Cate? Can you tell me what this poem is about?*

*She is not particularly pretty, Hannah thinks, this girl who got a full 5 per cent more than her or anyone in the English exam – 97 per cent. She has a round face. In an era in which girls wear their socks ruched around their ankles and hoist their skirts above the regulation height, Cate wears her skirt at the ordinary length. Her hair is cut to just above her shoulders*

*and she is a little bit overweight. But she has something about
her that Hannah doesn't have the words for, something going
on under the surface, some force.*

*It's about love, says Cate. And losing that love. He loves his
wife and she's gone.*

*Good. Anyone else?*

*Hannah raises her hand. Her hand feels hot.*

*Yes, Hannah?*

*She's dead, she says.*

*How can you tell?*

*She's* dissolved to wan wistlessness. Heard no more again
far or near. *She's a ghost.*

*Yes.*

*But he's feeling bad. He's feeling guilty about something. You
can tell by the metre, by the way it stumbles, changes in the last
stanza. It doesn't end well.*

*Excellent! Miss Riley beams.*

*And Cate, from the other side of the room, stares at this tri-
umphant girl, her long dark hair, her eyes intent, like a bird's.*

*The game is on: from that day forth they are locked in
vicious, ecstatic rivalry.*

*After a certain time has elapsed – half a year or so – they go
on a school trip together and end up sitting side by side in the
coach on the way to Styal Mill. They get along surprisingly
well. The next weekend Hannah stuns Cate with an invitation
to tea, and Cate surprises Hannah by accepting.*

*Hannah's house is small, a semi on a council estate off the
Parrs Wood Road. It has a long garden out the back. It still has
a hatch between the tiny kitchen and the dining room, through
which Hannah's mum passes oven chips and Angel Delight.*

Hannah's room is tiny – smaller than her brother James's, even though he is younger. The injustice of this makes Hannah fulminate.

Her parents go to church and Hannah is expected to go too, every Sunday morning. She often takes books to read in the sermon. After she tells Cate this, Cate lends her a copy of Forever by Judy Blume, backed in William Morris wallpaper and made to look like an innocuous book of poems. I've turned down the corners of the good bits, she says.

Next Sunday, while the vicar drones on, Hannah opens it and reads:

He rolled over on top of me and we moved together again and again and it felt so good I didn't ever want to stop until I came.

Hannah grins, and begins to understand that the force she saw running beneath Cate's mild exterior, although she does not have the words for it yet, is subversion. She is a girl with a rebel heart.

Cate's house is an Edwardian semi in Didsbury, on the other side of the Parrs Wood Road, with four big bedrooms and a garden. She has a mum and dad and an older sister, Vicky, who is seventeen and stalks the landing like a wrathful deity.

Cate's mum is a nurse, pretty and round. She has long red hair which falls around her face and freckles scattered over her nose. She laughs a lot. She makes her own bread. Hannah has never eaten homemade bread before. Cate's dad is tall and has a beard, and when he is around he plays music in the living room; he has a collection of old vinyl and plays Bob Dylan and Paul Simon and Cat Stevens. Sometimes, after tea, they put on music and dance in the kitchen. Cate's mum is a really good

*dancer. So is her dad. Sometimes they dance close to each
other, sometimes they laugh and kiss. Hannah has never seen
parents touch each other before. Cate's sister, if she ever witnesses this display, rolls her eyes. For fuck's sake, she says.
Leave it out.*

*Compared to her own parents, Cate's mum and dad seem
young.*

*Cate's family vote Labour. Hannah's vote Conservative.*

*Cate's family have Zola and Updike. Hannah's have* Reader's
Digest *and the* Encyclopaedia Britannica.

*Cate's dad does something to do with engineering. Hannah's
dad works at Christie Hospital as a porter.*

*Cate's family have olive oil. Hannah's have salad cream.*

*When they are thirteen Cate's mum becomes ill. She loses weight
and loses her hair and experiments with scarves. Sometimes she
comes to pick Cate up at the school gate but Cate wishes she
wouldn't. She wishes she could walk straight past the strange
thin woman with the headscarf and the earrings and the lip-
stick, who is trying too hard, whose teeth are too big in her face.*

*After a while, though, her mother gets better. Her hair grows
back, though a little differently, a little more thinly than before.
Cate's dad still plays music, but they don't dance in the kitchen
any more.*

*When they are sixteen Cate puts a picture of Patti Smith on
her wall, a life-sized poster of the cover of* Horses. *She got it at
the Corn Exchange in town. They go to Affleck's Palace and
search the musty rails for jackets like Patti's. Hannah actually
suits the look better, as she has no breasts to speak of yet. All
that summer, on Monday nights they tell Hannah's mum she*

is having a sleepover at Cate's and they take the bus into town to the Ritz, where they jump up and down on the bouncy dance floor to the Pixies and Nirvana and R.E.M. Cate wears tutus and DM boots and stripy tops with frayed edges. Hannah wears long patchwork skirts and DMs. If she pushed it any further, her mum would have a heart attack. As it is, when she applies kohl pencil her mum nearly has a fit.

They go to a small town to the west of Paris on their French exchange and come back speaking halfway decent French. They walk on Saturdays, arm in arm in Fletcher Moss Park, where they practise speaking French in loud voices. They test each other on past exam questions.

How is Emma Bovary responsible for her own downfall? Or do the nature of provincial society and the people around her make her unhappiness inevitable?

Their English teacher that year is a dedicated, energetic woman who believes in social mobility, in empowering girls. She suggests that they both apply for Oxford and she puts in extra time in the evenings, tutoring them both for the exam. They enter a new era of competition, spurring each other on.

One Saturday morning Cate's mother falls, crumpled over herself in the cereal aisle in Asda. She goes back into hospital and Cate stays at Hannah's, on a camp bed in Hannah's room. At night, when Hannah is asleep, Cate lies beneath the duvet and looks at Hannah, cocooned in her sleep, in her security, and feels horror waiting for her in the dark.

She goes to see her mum in the hospice the week before she dies. Her mum's eyes are enormous. She seems to take up so little room on the bed. The room smells sharp and thick at the same time. Oh, her mother says, when Cate comes into the room. It sounds as if someone is pressing her stomach, letting out all the air. Cate walks slowly towards her. She thinks this is probably the last time she will see her mother. Part of her wants to laugh; she puts her hand to her mouth and presses it to stop the laugh from coming out.

Here you are, says her mother as she gathers Cate to her. Here you are.

After the funeral Cate's sister Vicky moves into her boyfriend's house. And now it is just Cate and her father, rattling around at home. Her father gives up cooking, and Cate often forgets to eat. She stops writing essays for the extra Oxford classes. Hannah is simultaneously horrified, appalled for her friend and, in a small uncharitable place, relieved.

They apply for their colleges. Since neither they nor their teacher know anything about the university, they choose them randomly – Hannah hers because it looks the most beautiful, Cate hers because it says it takes the largest number of state-school pupils each year. They take the exam. They are both invited up for interview, one dank weekend in November. Hannah is given a room looking over a quadrangle, which is misted in the morning and makes her heart rise with the beautiful future that seems to breathe from its walls. Cate is in modern accommodation round the back of the dining hall. Her window backs on to a ventilation shaft and the smell of cooking infuses her room.

They get their letters a month later, just at the start of the Christmas holidays. They call each other, as they have arranged they will. They open the letters. Hannah looks down at hers in disbelief.

Cate looks at hers. Shit, she says. Oh shit.

## Cate

'Morning, my little soldier!'

Despite the early hour, Alice is her usual immaculate self: gilet, hair, ironed jeans. 'How's my little soldier doing today? Are you ready for our date?!'

Tom grins and flaps his hands and makes eyes. 'Good,' Cate says. 'He's good. We're good.'

'Have you got a kiss?' Alice swoops on Tom. 'Have you got a kiss for Grandma?'

Tom lunges delightedly for his grandmother. 'Terry's in the garden.' Alice takes Tom into her arms. 'Terrible wind last night.' She nods through the window to where Sam's father is wrestling gamely with a leaf blower. The three of them regard him for a moment in silence. Terry seems to be creating as much mess as he is managing to contain.

'I never know quite what they do,' Cate ventures. 'Those things.'

'They clean up the leaves,' says Alice.

'Ah. Yes.'

Terry looks up, sees them and manages a wild wave, while Tom kicks and bucks in Alice's arms. 'He wants to be with the big boys,' says Alice. 'I'll take him out for a bit. And we'll see you later.'

Cate swallows down her horror; her tiny son, that stupid machine. 'Whatever you think.'

'I think,' says Alice crisply, 'that it will do him good.'


Cate waits at the bus stop but no bus comes, and so she walks down the hill into town, the cathedral ahead of her. She has five hours to fill – five hours in which she can do anything, within reason. She could take the train to Charing Cross, go to the National Portrait Gallery. Look at the Sickerts. The Vanessa Bells. Walk up St Martin's Lane, through Covent Garden, go to the Oxfam bookshop at the bottom of Gower Street, buy a cheap paperback and sit in one of the squares with it, begin to feel the old contours of herself.

She knows what she should do – go home, wash tea towels and Babygros and chef's whites. Fold clothes. Unpack boxes. Finish moving into her house. But she does none of these things – instead she walks, her feet finding the old Pilgrims' Way, in through the city walls, down Northgate, Palace Street.

At the cathedral entrance the inevitable line of foreign students and international Christians wait to go inside. Cate ducks into Pret, where she buys a coffee and a pastry and sits in the window looking out at the half-timbered heart of the city. There are stalls selling tourist tat, baseball caps with LONDON emblazoned on them. Sweet shops selling gobstoppers and rhubarb and custards with 1950s lettering over their fronts. Red-jacketed young men cruise the crowd, selling punting trips, touting for business. All the ersatz thrills of Merrie twenty-first-century England.

Her eyes are caught by a small stall amidst the throng, a banner along the front reading: PROTEST TUITION FEE HIKES. VOTE 10TH DECEMBER.

A young woman stands in front of it, handing out leaflets, her hair long and dyed pink. Cate watches the way she talks to passers-by. Her small frame wrapped in a large jumper. The animation on her face. She reminds her of Lucy.

Despite checking her emails almost hourly, Cate has heard nothing back from Hesther yet.

When she has finished her coffee, Cate goes outside, approaching the stall shyly.

'May I have one?' she says to the young woman with the pink hair, pointing to the leaflets.

'Of course,' smiles the young woman, taking one and pressing it into Cate's hand. 'Do you want to sign the petition too?'

'Sure.' Cate leans in and does so, and then, suddenly self-conscious, and with no real idea of what to do next, mumbles a goodbye and moves away, joining the queue for the cathedral. It is ten pounds to go inside. She baulks, but pulls out her wallet and pays with her card. A cobbled road leads to the cathedral entrance and the building itself rears ahead. She goes inside, to the nave, where the roof soars above her and sweet-faced tabard-wearing guides stand selling guidebooks. She moves away, past the racks of candles, over to the far wall, reading the inscriptions on tombs set into the stone. They are a maudlin scrapbook of colonial misadventure: young men dead at Waterloo, in India, in West and South Africa, all the way up to the greatest hits of the First and Second World Wars. Tattered black flags hang from the walls. Somewhere in the distance is the sound of an organ. She stops before an oval-shaped monument, tomb of a certain Robert Macpherson Cairnes, Major of Royal Horse Artillery, 'taken from this sublunary scene June the 18th 1815 aged 30'.

*This humble monument*
*erected by the hand of friendship*
*is a faithful, but very inadequate, testimony*
*of affection, and grief which no language can express,*
*of affection which lives beyond the tomb,*
*of grief which will never terminate*
*till those who now deplore his loss*
*shall rejoin him*
*in the blest realms*
*of*
*everlasting peace.*

All these boys. All these mothers. All that grief. And here, no apology for any of it. It would be nice if somewhere, even on a tiny little plaque, it read: *Sorry. We got it wrong. All that colonialism and empire and slaying our children. All that God. Lands grabbed. Resources plundered. Patriarchy upheld. Church and military hand in hand.*

*Who's a little soldier then?*

She wants her son back. Wants to run up the hill to Harbledown and snatch him from his grandmother's arms. It is suddenly difficult to breathe. She hurries out through the side door into the cloisters, where the wind bites and the grass of the quadrangle is a deep green. She sinks to a stone bench carved into the wall and takes great gulps of air. And it comes to her, why she doesn't like this city: it reminds her of Oxford – the churches, the tourists, the grass on which you cannot walk. Even down to the punts, generations of students taking to the river, grasping for the *Brideshead* dream.

*Evelyn Waugh was a fascist and a sentimentalist. Discuss.*
She hated that fucking book.

There are footsteps on the flagstones. Cate looks up, sees a figure moving towards her, walking quickly. She is wearing a large man's coat, a beanie hat pushed down on her head, but Cate recognizes her from the playgroup and pulls back against the stone wall – she does not want to be seen today, but it is too late.

'Oh,' says Dea. 'Hey, hi! Cate, isn't it?' She smiles, stretches out a gloved hand. Her face is tired, wind-blown. 'I didn't recognize you at first. Without the baby. Where is he today?'

'With my mother-in-law. In Harbledown.'

'That's good.' Dea puts her head on one side. 'You don't look sure. Is that good?'

'Oh, no – it is. It's just the first time that I've left him. It's all a bit strange.'

'I know what you mean,' says Dea, nodding. 'I have the day to myself on Tuesdays. I look forward to it all week, and I'm supposed to be working, but I just . . .' She pulls a face.

'What's your work?'

'Church art. I'm writing a book. But it's taking me forever.'

'What sort of church art?'

'Some of it right here.' Dea points to the roof and Cate

looks up. At first she doesn't know what she is looking at but then, 'Here' – Dea takes her by the elbow – 'see that Green Man? And the mermaid?'

It is hard to see at first, but as Cate looks closer the details emerge – not just Green Men, but coiled dragons, lizards, shepherds with pipes. 'Oh,' she says. 'Yes. You'd never know they were there.'

'Exactly! I like to think of them as little nodes of subversion. Pagan deities holding up the buttresses of the established church.' Dea looks back. 'Did I actually just say that? Sorry.' She gives a rueful smile.

A chill wind is funnelling around the cloisters. 'It's cold,' says Dea. 'Shall we go back to mine? It's just around the corner. We can have some tea.'

'Sure.'

They walk out of the cathedral, past the stall manned by the students, where Dea stops for a second to speak to the pink-haired girl. Cate hangs back, watching as the girl proudly shows Dea the list of signatures.

'She's one of my students, or she was before I took maternity leave,' says Dea as she rejoins Cate. 'We're asking our Vice Chancellor to speak out about the tuition fees, but I don't think she will. It's interesting, though – all these kids. They're really taking a stand. I'm proud.'

Dea's house is close, just off the high street – tucked in a terrace of similar small houses. The front door is painted a muted grey-green; beside it, a window box blooms with late crimson flowers. The narrow hall is a tangle of coats and scarves. Dea leads her through into a kitchen at the back, where the house opens up and becomes light-filled and welcoming. A tall black woman with a loose Afro stands at the stove.

'Hey, Zo.' Dea unwinds her scarf. 'This is Cate. I met her at Playmaggedon. That terrible group I told you about. And I just bumped into her in the cathedral.'

The woman turns. Everything about her is long: long limbs, long neck, long fingers laced around a mug. She is surpassingly beautiful. 'Nice to meet you, Cate, I'm Zoe.' Her accent is American; Cate thinks she hears the sounds of the south. Dea wanders over to the stove and kisses Zoe. Cate watches Zoe's hand briefly linger on Dea's back.

'Take a seat, Cate,' says Zoe. 'Excuse the mess.'

Cate perches on the seat of a battered sofa, which is covered with throws and cushions. Sunlight slants in from the window behind, warming her back. Kilner jars compete for shelf space with books and toys and bottles, glinting in the sunlight. More books lie in piles on every other surface. A biography of Louise Bourgeois is being used as a plant stand. There is dust on the dado rails and the floorboards are scuffed. Washing-up is piled in the sink. The sight of the dirty plates invokes in Cate a mild but profound sense of relief. 'Have you lived here long?' she asks.

'Five years.' Dea shakes herbs into a pot. 'We were in the States before that. I was teaching at a university out there, which is where we met. But I'm a Kent girl. I grew up just outside the city. What about you? Have you been in Canterbury a while?'

'Almost two months. We moved when Tom was five months old.'

'That can't have been easy.'

'It was OK,' Cate lies.

'Where are you living?'

'Over the other side of town. Wincheap way.'

'I know it over there,' says Dea. 'We have an allotment, round the back of Toddler's Cove.'

'Well, lovely to meet you, Cate,' says Zoe. 'I'm just off to do a little work while Nora naps.'

'Oh, the spacious joys of a funded PhD.'

'Oh, the joys of fully paid maternity leave,' says Zoe, blowing Dea a kiss. 'Hey,' she says, turning at the door. 'You should set something up, you two. Something chilled. Something where mothers get together.'

'We're doing it.' Dea walks over with a cup of tea and hands it to Cate. 'Aren't we, Cate? This is it. This is our group. Right here. Right now.'

'Er . . . yeah, I guess so,' says Cate. She lifts her tea – it is pale yellow and gently fragrant. Small flowers float on the surface.

Dea slides herself on to the sofa beside Cate. 'Mum Club. The only rule of Mum Club is that we don't talk about Mum Club. Right?'

Zoe laughs and rolls her eyes. 'I'll leave you two to it,' she says with a wave.

When Zoe has gone, Dea turns to Cate. 'Chocolate biscuit? I've got a stash.'

'Um. Sure.'

Dea reaches into the cupboard behind her and takes out a tin. 'Amazing the stuff you find yourself buying when you become a mum. I'd forgotten how delicious chocolate fingers are.' Cate leans in and takes one.

'So . . .' says Dea. 'How are you doing, Cate?'

'I'm . . .' Cate falters, taken aback, her mouth full of biscuit. 'I'm OK,' she says.

'We tell the truth in Mum Club,' says Dea reprovingly. 'I'll go first. Ask me. Ask me how I'm doing.'

'Um . . . how are you doing, Dea?'

'Hmm. Let's see.' Dea closes her eyes for a moment. 'Well, I sleep on average five hours a night. I used to be a person that slept for eight or more. If I didn't get my sleep I would freak out. I'm still that person, somewhere inside, but I don't think I've completed a full sleep cycle since my daughter was born. My knee has flared up. It's an old injury, exacerbated by lugging my daughter in a sling, which seemed like the best and most wonderful thing to do when she was three weeks old and now is feeling like a less good idea. But it's the only place that she'll sleep. So. My boobs are enormous. I was told they would go down. They haven't gone down. My left shoulder has seized up. I'm assailed night and day by visions of horrors: my daughter falling, my daughter hurting herself, someone hurting her. I can't listen to the news without crying or switching it off. I haven't had sex since my daughter was born.'

Cate smiles.

'You think it's funny?'

Dea sips her tea. The chocolate fills Cate's mouth with sweetness.

'There's more, but – you know. I can keep it till next time. Now,' Dea says, turning to Cate. 'Tell me. How are you?'

She has made pasta and tomatoes; olive oil, a little bit of chilli. A knuckle of Parmesan she forgot she had at the back of the fridge is grated over the top. A portion for Tom in his little green bowl is ready to go, and a bottle of red is open on the table.

The door goes and she hears Sam hang up his coat in the hall. 'Hey.' He sniffs the air. 'Something smells good.'

'I thought I'd make some food.' She scoops Tom up from where he has been playing on the floor. 'C'mon, poppet. Come and try some pasta.'

The pasta is rather successful. Tom proves surprisingly adept at fingering farfalle and sucking off the sauce. When the meal is finished, when she and Sam have both had a glass and a half of wine each, Sam offers to give Tom his bath and Cate sits at the table, listening to them giggling and singing together. When the bath is done Sam brings him back down, his hair curly and wet, and she kisses his forehead. 'Who's my boy?' she says. 'Who's my lovely boy?'

'Shall I get him in his PJs?' says Sam.

'Yes, please.'

When she collected Tom from Alice's he was happy and calm.

She rises and does the washing-up, wipes down the table, and pours herself another half glass of wine.

*The truth?*

*Yeah. We tell the truth.*

The way Dea had said it, as though she wanted to hear the answer. As though anything other than the truth would not be good enough.

*The truth is I'm scared too.*

*Go on. What of?*

*Of everything. All the time. I'm lonely. I'm in pain. I still can't*

140

*deal with the fact that they sliced me open. I feel like a failure. As a woman. As a mother. I get everything wrong. My mother isn't here. I miss her. I realize I've always missed her. She didn't prepare me at all. I'm angry that she left me on my own. I'm not coping. Not coping. No one told me it would be like this.*

*I think I married the wrong person.*

She didn't say the last bit, but she said all the rest. Once it started, it didn't stop. And Dea sat there, listening – the simple, heady oxygen of being listened to.

*So. Same time next week? Mum Club?*

*Yeah. Same time next week.*

'Hey.' Sam comes into the room. 'Tom seems on good form. Did it go well with Mum then?'

'Oh,' says Cate. 'Yeah.' She drains her glass. 'I think it's going to work.'


## Lissa

They are going to play a game, Klara says. Although it is a serious game, a *technique*, a technique for getting *out of the skin*. They need this technique because they are stiff. They are stiff in an English way. Not like the Russians. The Russians are not stiff, not at all. They have vodka and grief and the blood of the land in their veins, and the English have weak tea and the damp.

So.

The director stares around the room – her cast is assembled before her, a full roll call. It is first thing Monday morning, the beginning of the third week.

'Leesa.' She narrows her eyes. 'You are stiff. Always you are stiff. See how you sit? What does Vanya say about Yelena?' She turns to Johnny. 'About the way she is?'

'*If you could see the way you look*,' says Johnny, fixing Lissa with his eyes. '*The way you move. The indolence of your life. The sheer indolence of it.*'

'Thank you, Johnny. So, Leesa – does Yelena sit like this?' She crosses her hands over her lap in imitation of Lissa's posture. 'No. You are English. You are all wrong. Why did I choose English people to interpret this Russian play? I am crazy. Never again. Leesa – do you know the Meisner technique?'

Lissa nods; she does. 'We did it at drama school. Although it's years since—'

'Good. Sit here, please.'

A chair is produced and Lissa dutifully makes her way into the middle of the space and sits upon it. 'And you' – Klara turns on her heel and points to Michael – 'you are also stiff. You are only on stage for five minutes but you are stiff. It is horrible. Come here.'

Michael stands, runs his hand through his hair. He is grinning. 'Great,' he says. 'Nice one.'

'Michael, do you know this technique?'

Michael shakes his head.

'Leesa. Describe it to Michael, please.'

Lissa crosses her legs at the ankle, then uncrosses them. 'So . . . as far as I can remember . . . it starts by one or other of us noticing something about the other person. I will notice something about you, something on the surface at first. It may be what you are wearing. I might say, *You are wearing a*

142

*blue top*. And you repeat it back to me. *I am wearing a blue top*. We do that for a bit, and then we go deeper—'

'Stop!' Klara slaps the desk. 'Enough explanation. Begin.'

Michael gives a quick barking laugh. Lissa takes a breath.

'Your hair,' she says, 'is . . . shaped like a quiff.'

Michael smiles. 'My hair is shaped like a quiff?' he says, giving the word a little upward tick.

'STOP.'

Michael turns towards the director.

'No *acting*.' Klara bangs the table and Poppy the ASM jumps. 'You are acting. If this is your acting, I am glad you have no lines in this play. The point is *not to act*.'

Chastened, Michael turns back to Lissa, who shoots him a compassionate look, and they begin again.

'You look pale,' says Lissa.

'I look pale.'

'You look pale.'

'I look pale.'

She can see he is frozen now, too frightened to make a move.

She remembers her teacher at drama school, a small intense man who believed passionately in this way of working. *Call what you see*, was what he always said when they used the Meisner technique. *Put your attention on the other person, look closely, and call what you see*. 'You look scared,' she says to Michael.

'I look scared,' Michael agrees.

'You look scared.'

The game stumbles on limply as Klara hisses and tuts and shakes her head.

143

'STOP. This is terrible. Terrible.' She waves Michael off the stage with a vicious hand.

'*Je–sus*,' he says under his breath, as he stands and hitches his jeans. 'Good luck.'

'You.' Klara twitches her head towards where Johnny sits. 'Johnny. Your turn.'

Johnny rises silently and comes to take Michael's place.

He is still, very still, for a long while, watching her. His gaze is soft. She feels it brush her shoulders, her stomach, her feet, her breasts. She is aware of her legs, tightly crossed again – when did that happen? – the position of her hands. Aware of the heat in her palms, under her armpits. She is aware of the balance of power, of how it belongs to him. Then, 'You look sad,' he says.

'I look sad,' repeats Lissa, surprised.

'You look sad.'

'I look sad.'

'You look sad.'

'I look sad.'

'You're turning red.'

'I'm turning red.'

'You're turning red.'

'I'm turning red.'

'You're upset.'

'I'm upset.'

'I've upset you.'

'I've upset you, no' – she stumbles – 'you've upset me.'

'I've upset you.'

She can feel her cheeks flaming. 'You – have a black shirt,' she says.

144

Johnny raises an eyebrow. 'I have a black shirt,' he repeats.

'STOP.' They turn to Klara, who is out of her chair now, incandescent.

'Why did you do this? Why did you talk about his *shirt*? Something was *happening*. Something was starting to happen for the first time in this stinking fucking room and you talk about his *shirt*? No. Now. Go again.'

Johnny turns back slowly, smiles at her. It is the smile of an assassin. His blue eyes barely blink. 'You're uncomfortable,' he says.

'I'm uncomfortable.'

'You're uncomfortable.'

'I'm uncomfortable.'

'I make you uncomfortable.'

'You make me uncomfortable.'

'I make you uncomfortable.'

'You make me uncomfortable.'

'You look sad.'

'I look sad.'

'You look sad.'

'I look sad.'

'You have a sad face.'

'I have a sad face.'

Her throat is tightening. There is no time to recover from the last blow before he is on to the next.

'You've lost something.'

'I've lost something.'

She can feel it – the other members of the cast, sitting forward in their seats. As the ranged faces become an audience,

145

the invisible filaments between her and them tightening, something is happening.

'You're crying.'

'I'm crying.'

'You're crying.'

'I'm crying.'

'Good!' Klara is hopping. 'Now. *Now*. Begin your scene.'

She needs fresh air. She pushes her way outside and stands in the grotty stairwell, staring up at the sky.

Michael is out there already. 'Fuck,' he says. 'That was harsh. But electric.'

Lissa says nothing.

Behind her, Johnny appears.

'Fucking electric, mate,' says Michael. Johnny ignores him. Michael nods to himself. 'Electric,' he says, into the void.

'That was rather good,' says Johnny to Lissa. 'You could be a much better actor, you know, than you allow yourself to be. If you just let go.'

She has the afternoon to herself. She does not wish to go home. Nor does she wish to stay any longer in the room and watch the rest of the day's rehearsal, and so she climbs on the bus into town, the rackety old 73: Kingsland Road, Shoreditch, Old Street, Angel, King's Cross. The sky is low and yellow, and it is starting to rain as she descends at the library. She stows her coat and bag in the lockers, flashes her reader's card at the guard on the door of Rare Books, finds a seat and sits down. In the hush she closes her eyes.

She is hollow; there is nothing inside her, nothing tethering her, not talent, not success. Johnny is right – she has lost something. Or many things. Or she never had them. She is the sum total only of her failures. She is so hollow she could float up over these people, their heads bent in industry, up and out over this city, this city that she has loved but which does not love her back, which does not give her what she needs to live, only to survive.

She is going to go downstairs and get her stuff and call her agent and tell her she is pulling out of the play, that she is giving up this excuse of a career.

She goes down to the cloakroom and collects her coat and bag, walks out across the echoing foyer towards the doors, and then she sees him. She knows it is him even though he is facing away from her. He is hunched and he is not speaking but it is clear that whoever is on the other end of the phone is speaking a great deal. Lissa hangs back, hands in the pockets of her coat. After a short time he turns off his phone and she sees him stand, perfectly still for a couple of seconds, and then look up. She goes to him and touches him on the arm. Nathan jumps.

'Lissa. Hey.'

'You OK?'

He pushes his hands through his hair. His eyes look wild. 'I just need to . . . Cigarette. Have you got one?'

'Sure.'

They make their way past the security guards, out to the

small overhang that offers a little shelter from the rain, which is falling in earnest now. She hands him the tobacco, stands back while he rolls.

'Sorry,' he says, as he puts the cigarette to his mouth.

'For what?'

He looks up at her and his eyes are startled. 'I don't know. I'm just – used to saying sorry, I suppose. Sorry for smoking. I shouldn't be smoking.'

She hands him a lighter and he flicks it gratefully, leaning his head back with the release of smoke. She takes the leather pouch from him and rolls one of her own, and their smoke mingles in the damp air. On the concourse, people hurry over concrete, which is rain-slicked now, carrying their bags and their books. 'Have you eaten?' he says.

'No.'

'There's a pub somewhere around here. Does . . . tapas or something.'

Something about the way he says 'tapas' makes her smile.

He looks disoriented as they cross the road, and she has to fight the urge to put a hand on to his arm and steer him through the traffic to safety.

'It's round here somewhere,' he says, leading her through the redbrick flats that lie to the south of the Euston Road, along a wide Georgian terrace to a dark-looking corner pub. 'I think this is it. It'll do, anyway.' He holds the door open for her. 'Drink? I'm going to have a pint. And a whisky. You want a whisky?'

There is no further mention of food. She looks at the clock above the bar – two forty-five.

'Sure,' she says. 'Why not?'

She finds them a table in the corner of the bar, tucked away from the window. He comes back with two pints of Guinness and two glasses of whisky. 'Your health.' He gulps the whisky down, chases it with a healthy swig of Guinness. Then, as though he notices her presence properly for the first time, 'How was your day?' he says.

'Awful.'

He nods grimly.

'You?' she says.

'You don't want to know.' He lifts his head to her and she sees his despair. 'It didn't work. The IVF. The last go.'

She is not surprised. She wishes she were but she is not.

'I'm lost,' he says. 'We're lost. In all of it.' He looks away to where rain has begun to dapple the window, and downs the rest of his Guinness in three open-throated gulps. 'I'm going to get another drink. You want one? Another whisky?'

'Sure.'

She fiddles with her phone when he has gone. Turns it on. Turns it off again. It is strange, she thinks, that Hannah has said nothing to her of this news. She finishes her whisky. Sips her pint.

There are two more Guinnesses when he returns, and two whiskies. 'I'll drink it, if you can't.' He gives a small smile as he slides them over the table towards her. 'So go on then, why was your day so bad? Hannah says you're in a play?'

She wants to tell him that it doesn't matter. That she doesn't want to talk about herself. 'Yes,' she says. 'I am.'

'Something Russian?'

She nods. '*Uncle Vanya*. Chekhov.'

'How's it going?'

'It's OK.'

He leans forward. 'OK? That doesn't sound too good.'

'It is. It's just . . .' She gives a small laugh. 'I don't know. I'm doubting everything today.'

'I could have said that.'

'Really?' She is silent, waiting for him to go on, watching his hands around the pint glass. His eyes – the thin skin beneath them, the curled edge of his mouth. *Call what you see.*

*You're sad.*

*You're angry.*

'I don't know.' His fingers drum the stained wood of the table. 'I just – I can't even remember why we are doing this, this thing that our lives have become. Hannah. This *constraint*. Every. Single. Fucking. Thing. Regimented. Policed. Whatever I put in my body. I see her, hovering. Watching the coffee I drink. Asking me how many drinks I've had if I go out after work. Counting. Always counting. She's become a policewoman.'

He falls silent.

'She's just trying to have a child,' says Lissa softly.

'Don't you think I know that?' He is furious now. 'But that's all she's become. She has become a creature that is trying to have a child. And it's not fucking *working*. Shouldn't a child be conceived from love? And abandon? And good sex? Not a timetable. A spreadsheet. *A graph*.'

He has said too much. She sees him step back from his words.

He looks up at her. 'Did you never want kids?' he says, in a low voice.

'I – no. Once. I mean, I was pregnant once.'

'Really?'

150

'Yeah.' A blurred shape on a scan photograph at the Marie Stopes clinic in Fitzrovia. The end of the first year of drama school.

'What happened?'

'I had a termination.'

'I'm sorry.'

'Don't be. Here.' She lifts her whisky to his. '*Sláinte.*' It burns her throat. 'Cigarette?' she says.

'You read my mind.'

They step outside, huddling in the doorway, taking it in turns to roll.

'Go on then,' he says again, when they are both lit. 'You still haven't told me why your day was so shit.'

'Someone . . . criticized my acting. I took it badly, I suppose.' She tries to find an anchor – the rain, the cars with their lights on. The people manoeuvring their umbrellas. She is veering rapidly towards being drunk.

'Sometimes . . . I don't feel real.' She turns to him. He is watching her. He is close. He shakes his head.

'What?' she says.

'It's just so strange to me, to hear you speak that way.'

'Why?'

'Because I always saw you as so vivid. More than real.'

She gives a small laugh.

'I remember the first time I saw you. You just – you shone. And then those parties. When we were older. That gorgeous thrift-shop raver.'

'Yeah. What was I thinking?'

'They were good, weren't they, those days? We didn't care, did we? We were free.'

He leans forward, catching her wrist in his hand. She looks down, sees his fingers, the nails trimmed haphazardly, feels a pulse in her heart, her wrist, her crotch.

'I miss that,' he says.

*Call what you see.*

*You want me.*

'Who?' she says to him, looking back up into his face. 'Who am I? To you?'

'You're beautiful, you're bright, you're wild, Lissa. You're real.' And he lifts his hands to her face, her face towards his, brings his lips to hers.

The surprise.

The lack of surprise.

Her lips parting for him. The taste of his tongue.

'Sorry,' he says, pulling away.

'No,' she says.

'I shouldn't have done that.'

'It's OK. It didn't happen.'

He shakes his head. 'Hannah,' he says, and his voice is strangled.

'It didn't happen, Nath.'

He passes his hand over his face. 'Not that. It's just – she wants to do it again. The IVF. Wants to go to another clinic. On Harley Street.'

'That must be thousands.'

'And the rest.'

'So what are you going to do?'

'I don't know.' And the despair is back, cloaking him. He looks up at her. 'What would you do?'

'Oh God.' She laughs softly. 'Don't ask me.'

'But I am,' he says. 'I am asking you. You're the first person I've managed to talk to about this. You don't know how good it is to talk. Liss. Tell me,' he pleads. 'Please. What would you do?'

'I wouldn't do it,' she says, pulling her cardigan around her, staring out at the rain-washed street. 'I'd say no.'


## Hannah

They come out of the Tube at Regent's Park, walk past the cream colonnaded buildings, then along the Marylebone Road before turning into Harley Street. She walks quickly, as if by hurrying – by ushering Nathan past these mini mansions, past the huge cars disgorging skinny, headscarfed women, past the elderly ladies carrying their tiny dogs in their arms – he might not register where they are.

She rings the bell of a three-storey house, mercifully slightly less grand than those that surround it. The buzzer admits them and they step into a black-and-white flagged entrance hall, where pictures of smiling babies decorate the walls and the slim curve of a Regency staircase stretches upwards towards the light. They give their names and are shown into a waiting room the size of their flat. Squashy sofas face each other over angular tables and magazines are arranged in tight-cornered piles. A couple sit on a sofa, twenty feet away. They eye Hannah and Nathan across the room.

Nathan sits, his ankle crossed over his knee. His trainers are scuffed. His leg jiggles on the deep pile carpet. In the corner, a coffee machine gurgles. 'I'm going to get a drink,' he says, jumping up again. 'You want one?'

'No, thanks.' Hannah leans down to the table: *Tatler*, *Harper's Bazaar*, *Country Living*, *Elle*. She slides out *Elle* and flicks through it, aware her breath is shallow and short.

Nathan comes over with a small white plastic cup.

'This coffee's terrible,' he says accusingly. 'How much do they charge?'

'Seven thousand.' She speaks quietly, but precisely. He knows this. She knows he knows this.

'Wonder what the rent is on this place?' His voice is a little too loud. The couple on the other side of the room lift their heads. The receptionist puts her head round the door.

'Dr Gilani will see you now.'

Hannah stands, smoothing down her skirt. 'Thank you.'

Nathan follows her up the stairs. 'Nice paintings,' he says, as they pass a series of lurid abstracts.

Dr Gilani sits behind a broad desk in a huge room. He is a large, smiling bear of a man. He leans forward to greet them, grasping their hands in his paws. 'Good to meet you,' he says, and looks as though he means it. 'Please, sit down.'

'So,' he says, as they sit. 'I've been reading through your notes. As you know, Hannah, there are a large proportion of women like yourself for whom there is no known cause of infertility.'

Hannah nods.

'And the fact that you have been pregnant once already, despite the miscarriage, is a good thing. The good news is that you might still conceive at any time. The bad news is that there is nothing, other than the usual, that we can tell you to do to help. But' – he smiles – 'we are very well equipped here.'

Nathan looks around the room, as though scanning it for equipment, but the room, despite its vast size, looks empty.

Dr Gilani runs through the treatments he can offer that the NHS cannot: the time-lapse cameras, the frequent scans, the womb scraping, the egg transfers at the weekend. All of it adding up to success rates in the 30 per cent range, for patients of Hannah's age.

'What's womb scraping?' says Nathan. 'It sounds barbaric.'

'It's a technique,' says Dr Gilani, 'that has been shown to help with implantation. Here.' He passes a piece of paper over the desk. He has underlined the numbers: 32 per cent pregnancy, ages 35–38. The live birth rates that follow are lower. The fee is in small figures at the bottom of the page.

'Can you give me an idea,' says Nathan. 'A breakdown of the costs?'

Dr Gilani's smile is immovable. 'Of course, I can have my secretary prepare it.'

'It's just – it's an awful lot of money,' says Nathan. 'Isn't it? For something that is seventy per cent likely to fail.'

Hannah presses the nail of her thumb into the palm of her opposite hand.

'I understand.' Dr Gilani gives the smallest of glances to the clock on the wall. 'Many of our patients use their insurance to cover—'

'We don't have insurance,' says Nathan. 'We believe in the National Health Service.'

Hannah leans over Nathan, sweeps the paper into her bag. 'Thank you,' she says.

'So – if you decide to go ahead, please make an appointment with my secretary and we can get you started straight away.'

'Wait,' says Nathan. 'Han – don't you need time? To recover? Hannah's just had a round of IVF. She's exhausted.'

'I'm fine,' says Hannah. 'And I can speak for myself.'

'Of course' – Dr Gilani spreads his large hands – 'if you'd rather wait. But every month that you wait, of course, is a month that—'

'No,' says Hannah. 'I'd rather not wait.'

Nathan is looking out of the window, his jaw clenched. 'Thank you, Dr Gilani. You've been very helpful.'

Dr Gilani presses their hands in his.

Nathan walks in front of her down the staircase, but does not stop at the receptionist's desk. Instead he pushes his way out on to the street. By the time Hannah catches up with him he is round the corner, halfway through rolling a cigarette.

'When did you start smoking?'

'Recently. And I haven't started smoking.'

'What's this then?'

'A cigarette.'

'Were you smoking? Last cycle?'

'No, Hannah. I wasn't. But now I'd quite like a cigarette.' He lights up. She stares at him. The traffic roars. It is a grey, polluted day.

'I can't believe you,' she says.

'What can't you *believe*, Hannah?'

She casts her hand towards him.

'Oh. I disgust you, do I? Well, this' – he waves his cigarette at their surroundings – 'disgusts me. All these doctors making thousands, *millions*, out of people's desperation. This is a street of quacks. You might as well go and chuck seven thousand pounds down a wishing well for all the good it will do.'

'Really?'

'Really. They're fucking faith healers, Han.'

'What about the children on that wall? They exist. Because of this doctor.'

'They might have existed anyway.'

'You don't know that.'

'No, I don't. I don't know anything. Neither do you. Neither does Doctor fucking Gilani. No one does. Because the human body is a mystery. Because fertility is a fucking *mystery*, Han.'

'There are things you can do . . .'

'We've been doing them. We've been doing every single one of those things, Hannah. For months. For years. We still don't have a baby.'

'I've been doing them. *I've* been doing those things. What have you done, Nath? Tell me. What?'

He looks at her, takes a deep drag of his cigarette. 'I'm sorry, Hannah, I really am. I want you to know that I love you, but I can't do this any more.'

'What? What can't you do?'

'This,' says Nathan.

'What does *this* mean?'

He throws the cigarette out into the street, where cars growl at the traffic lights, and shakes his head.

\*

157

Her father meets her on the platform at Stockport. She sees him through the window before he sees her – always the momentary shock at his hesitancy, the white of his hair. As she gets down she sees his head twisting this way and that, searching for her.

'Dad,' she calls, and he turns towards her, holding out his arms.

He smells of soap and the sharpness of her mum's washing powder.

'Let me take that.' He moves for her suitcase.

'It's fine. It's not heavy.'

'Shush. Give it here. Got your ticket? There's barriers at the back now.'

The car is parked where it always is. 'Now,' he lifts her case into the boot, 'your mother's made shepherd's pie. She's worried about you, love.'

It is raining, a light drizzle. The leaves are brown; autumn is already making itself felt up here. Her mother is in the kitchen when they arrive, the windows steamed up, the dog jumping up to say hello.

'Come here.' Her mum presses her to her chest. 'You've lost weight,' she says, tutting as she hugs her.

They eat the shepherd's pie and broccoli, then fruit and cream for pudding, and after they eat they go into the living room and sit in front of the telly.

'What would you like to watch?' Her father turns on the TV, hands her the three remote controls with a small flourish. 'You decide.'

'I don't mind, really. What would you normally watch now?'

She sits beside her mother. They watch an episode of a costume drama.

When the adverts come on, her father goes into the kitchen and comes back with tea and chocolate.

He hands her hers with a wink. 'Aldi,' he says. 'They do these lovely little bars.'

She goes to bed when her parents do, at half past nine, and lies down in her childhood room, in her old single bed. There's a photo on the wall of her and her dad on her wedding day, standing outside in the park – the afternoon light. That green dress.

Her mother pops her head around the door on her way from the bathroom.

'Anything you need?'

'Thanks, Mum, I'm fine.'

'Hot-water bottle?'

'I'm OK.'

'I know, but it's nippy tonight. And I just thought, for your tummy . . . after everything.'

'I'm fine. Thanks, Mum.'

'All right, love. Night-night.'

'Night, Mum.'

Her mum closes the door softly, and it strikes Hannah, not for the first time, that her parents, whose sphere of life has always seemed so small, so constrained, have mastered the art of kindness. She used to lambast them – the newspaper they read (the *Daily Mail*), the telly they watched (soaps and nature programmes). Their politics. Their religion

(C of E). Their horizons, always so narrow. Their naivety. Their class.

And yet they are kind.

They love their children, and they love one another still. How do they do it? Did they learn it, over time? The slow accretion of habit, of days built from these small, simple acts?


On Sunday morning her parents get ready for church. Hannah watches her mother pull on her winter coat, then tut and fuss at her dad's thin anorak; trying to get him to wear an extra jumper, cajoling him into his scarf.

'Would you like to come?'

'No, I'll go for a walk. Get some bits from the shop. Maybe I'll make some lunch.'

She walks out along the cul de sac: pebble-dash and tiny windows and Union Jacks. It always used to amaze her, how quickly the houses changed, how on the other side of Fog Lane Park you were in Didsbury, where the streets had trees and the houses were huge. Not these little 1930s semis, huddled together as though apologizing for themselves.

She does a couple of laps of the local park, then goes to the Co-op and buys a chicken and some veg. Her parents are back by twelve, and she sees their faces light up at the smell of roasting meat.

Later, when lunch is over and she and her mum are washing up, Hannah turns to her mother. 'How do you pray, Mum?' she asks.

'What do you mean?' her mother says.

'I mean in church, when you pray. How do you do it?'

Her mother takes off her gloves and places them on the side of the counter. She rinses the bowl, placing it back in the cupboard under the sink, then turns to Hannah.

'I'm not sure, really,' she says. 'I close my eyes. I listen. I sort of . . . collect myself, I suppose. And then, if I'm praying for someone in particular, I bring them to my mind. If it's for you, I think of you. Sometimes you're like you are now, sometimes you're a little girl.' Her mother's hand takes hers. 'And then I ask. I pray.'

'Do you pray for a baby?'

'Yes, love. I did.'

'You did?' she says. 'And now?'

Her mother steps forward, takes Hannah's cheeks in her palms. 'Now, I pray for your happiness, love. For you to be happy. That's all. Oh, Hannah,' her mother says, as Hannah begins to cry. 'Oh, my lovely girl.'

# London

## 1997

*It is August 1997, the summer of graduation, when Hannah arrives in the city.*

*Tony Blair has been Prime Minister for three months. For eighteen years of Hannah's life there has been a Tory government. They watched the election together, she and Lissa, just before their exams, in an Irish club in Chorlton. They drank Black Velvets until they were reeling. Even her father voted for Tony Blair.*

*The invitation from Lissa was issued casually, on a postcard from Rome showing the Trevi Fountain.*

*I have been doing my best Anita Ekberg. It's too beautiful here. I will undoubtedly be bored and lonely on my return. Please come to London soon.*

*Lissa meets her at Euston, wearing jeans and scuffed plimsolls. She is tanned and her hair is loose. Hannah herself is scratchy with self-consciousness. She has recently had her hair cut in a close bob; her hand moves often to the place where the hair tapers to a sharp point at her neck.*

*Wow. Lissa greets her on the concourse with a hug. Louise Brooks. I love it.*

*Really? says Hannah, touching her hand to the nape of her neck.*

*They wait outside King's Cross station for the bus, and when*

163

*it arrives Hannah follows Lissa as she runs up the back stairs. The seat at the front is free and Lissa grabs it, swinging her plimsolled feet up on to the rail, chattering away, as the bus takes them through the wastelands behind King's Cross, where Lissa points out warehouses where she has gone to parties, a club that she goes to most weekends. She tells Hannah about her new boyfriend – Declan – an Irishman ten years older than her. Of how he took her to Rome, where he is filming a series, and they wandered the sound stages of Cinecittà, and stayed in an apartment in Trastevere and saw medieval paintings and religious shrines.*

*Declan says he's going to get me an agent, says Lissa. So I can go up for things in the holidays.*

*She says this with no particular surprise, just a happy acceptance of her lot.*

*And Hannah watches Lissa as she speaks and thinks she is more beautiful, if possible, than before. Lissa will be a successful actress. This is clear. She might even be a star. She has talent and looks and insouciance and golden things fall into her lap. And there is no point envying her, for this is simply how it is.*

*Outside the bus window the industrial land gives way to council estates as the bus climbs a long hill. They get down opposite a Tube station, and Lissa leads the way through streets where tall houses are set back from the road and Hannah can hear music practice through open windows. These streets are quiet, the city softened. They stop at a house with hollyhocks in the front garden and a battered green front door.*

*Your room's at the top of the stairs at the back, says Lissa, letting them in. You can put your bag up there, if you like.*

*The stairs are covered with an old Moroccan carpet. There*

are things piled on almost every step, either on their way up or down – it is not quite clear. A collection of pictures line the wall: framed cartoons, postcards, and other larger paintings – a big canvas at the top of the stairs of Lissa as a girl. Hannah stares at it; she recognizes the style – there was one in Lissa's room in halls. She puts her bag down in a narrow room with a single bed, which looks out on to a long garden with a green-house at the bottom. The sound of a radio comes from somewhere up above.

She sits on the bed for a while then goes to use the bathroom, which is large and grubby and painted a dark grey-green. Magazines are strewn in haphazard piles on the floor. She picks up a wrinkled copy of the New Yorker, which is open at the fiction page. It is over four years old.

Downstairs, the living room has been knocked through and one whole wall is taken up with bookshelves. The window on to the street is covered in vegetation and lets in a greenish light; the effect is a little like being underwater. Ashtrays in various states of overflow are set on side tables. There seems to be no order to the books on the shelves: Tolstoy, Eliot, Atwood, Balzac. Hannah takes down one of them, Eliot, Four Quartets. Its margins are filled with writing, a looping scrawl. There is a movement behind her and she jumps.

A woman is standing at the bottom of the stairs. She is tall and wears a long brown apron which is covered in paint, and her long greying hair is caught up on top of her head in two combs. She is arrestingly beautiful.

Who are you? the woman asks.

Hannah, says Hannah. Sorry.

Why are you sorry? says the woman, her head on one side.

*She looks both curious and dangerous, like a bird of prey. She comes closer, peers at the book in Hannah's hand.*

*Ah. Eliot. Are you a fan?*

*Hannah looks down at the text, with its spidery marginalia. What is the right answer?*

*I think so. I mean – I did* The Waste Land. *I liked that. But . . . wasn't he horrible to his wife?*

*He was, unfortunately. He was an absolute shit. But he could write.*

*I'm Sarah, by the way, she says, holding out her hand. Borrow it. But don't worry if you don't enjoy it. Eliot is wasted on the young.*

*They go into the large, messy kitchen, where Sarah takes over lunch from Lissa, insisting that she is starving and a sandwich isn't nearly good enough. When the food is ready, Hannah watches Lissa and Sarah as they eat, alert to the ease with which they attack their food. The salt is not in a cellar but in a mortar bowl, into which the women reach with their fingers. They pour oil liberally over their salad, then dunk with their bread to mop it up. When the salad is finished they suck their fingers dry. They eat like animals, but in doing so they are more elegant than anything she has ever seen. She thinks of her parents; of her mother in her M&S cardigans, the salad cream poured on to pallid lettuce: their politeness, their serviettes, their insistence on manners.*

*Afterwards they smoke. Sarah has a similar leather pouch to Lissa's, uses the same dark tobacco papers. Sarah and Lissa speak about films they have seen, plays. There is an edge to these conversations, a competition. When Lissa talks about the art in Rome, Sarah grows silent, listening with her head to* one side. Before she went to Rome, Sarah says to Hannah, Lissa thought a Bellini was a cocktail.

It is, says Lissa, reaching over and putting out her cigarette in the remains of the olive oil. Art and life aren't mutually exclusive. You taught me that.

Touché, says Sarah, raising her glass.

Hannah feels herself like a plant, tendrils reaching out, hooking on to this house, these women, this life.

You should stay a few more days, says Lissa, when Hannah's time is almost up. My mum likes you. She thinks you're good for me. She's got an exhibition opening next week. Declan will be back. You can meet him too.

Hannah calls her mum, who sounds small and tentative on the other end of the phone. If you're sure, love? Are you sure they're happy to have you? You won't be in the way?

The house is huge, Mum.

Oh, in that case. Well, you thank her mum from me, won't you?


It is hot the night of the opening. Hannah wears a slim vest, some wide trousers. She touches her hand to the newly shorn place at the back of her neck. The gallery is tiny, on a cobbled street in East London. Sarah's canvases are displayed in a stark white room. There is wine and barrels of beer. The crowd stands on the street outside, mingling with the crowds from the other galleries.

Hannah looks at the people and thinks, Here – here is life. It is as though all along a part of her has been hard at work making a skin for herself in the dark and the silence, and now she is ready to wear it, to step into the light.

*She loses Lissa for a while, and when the crowd thins she sees her again, further down the street, speaking to a tall young man in a flannel shirt rolled up to the elbows. Lissa is telling a story, gesticulating, and the man is laughing, leaning in to hear. She watches as they pass a cigarette between them. So this is Declan, Lissa's boyfriend. Hannah feels a strange shifting at the sight of him. A recognition, almost, and a disappointment that threatens to prick the evening's magic and let in something darker. Lissa sees her and waves, and Hannah makes her way slowly towards them.*

*The tall young man turns towards her and takes her hand in greeting.*

*Somehow, he does not seem like an actor.*

*Hey, says Lissa. Hannah, this is Nath.*

## Lissa

She does not contact Nathan and he does not contact her. Often, though, she replays the kiss in her mind – taking it out when she is alone in bed at night, or in the morning, as she comes to consciousness. She has not heard from Hannah for days. She trusts Nathan has said nothing – still, she hears it, a faint yet shrill alarm, ringing somewhere at the edge of thought.

She throws herself into the life of the play. Klara's approach is starting to work – they are indeed becoming less English, their acting is raw, there is blood in it and sinew and bone. And as Klara grows happier with her cast, the cast, in the way that happy casts do, is becoming a living, breathing entity of its own. The actors arrive earlier and stay later, taking pleasure in watching each other's scenes. They begin to run the play from start to finish, feeling its rhythm, the places where it needs pace, the moments when it needs to slow down and feel itself breathe. When a scene becomes sticky, or does not feel alive, the actors step out of the play text and use the Meisner technique to observe each other, keeping in character, repeating what they see, before moving back into the scene again.

Michael suggests they sing together – an idea taken up enthusiastically by the rest of the cast – and so they learn a

Russian folk song and rehearse it in the morning before they start work, Michael strumming a few chords on the guitar while they sing.

As they move towards opening night, Lissa can feel her own performance improving; her body feels different, there is indolence in it: heat and sadness and sway. Even Johnny is softening. Since the day he made her cry, something has shifted between them, and Lissa finds with surprise that she looks forward to their scenes above all.

The evening before her technical rehearsal, her phone rings – Hannah.

Lissa stares at the name and waits. After a moment there is the buzz of a message. She picks it up, calls voicemail, brings it to her ear.

'*Liss?*' Hannah's voice is soft. '*Can you call me? I need to speak.*'

The alarm in her head sounds louder, more shrill. She rolls herself a cigarette, goes to the kitchen door, and calls Hannah back.

'Hey.' Hannah answers after the first ring. 'What are you doing?'

'Just getting ready. It's my tech tomorrow.'

'Oh shit. Of course.' There's a catch in Hannah's voice. 'Can you come over? There's something I need to ask you.'

*Fuck.*

'Sure.' Lissa tries to keep her voice steady. 'Now?'

'Please. And Lissa? Maybe – will you bring a bottle of wine?'

She pulls on her parka and makes her way towards Broadway Market, stopping to buy wine and chocolate at the Turkish off-licence on the way.

Hannah buzzes her in through the metal door and Lissa

climbs the old external staircase, to where her friend is waiting at the top. Hannah looks pale, slight in the dusk, infused with a restless, spiky energy. 'Did you bring wine?'

Lissa holds it up. 'Rioja.' She tries a smile. 'Old times' sake.'

Hannah takes it from her, goes inside, to the kitchen counter, opens the wine, pours two glasses and hands one to Lissa. 'Cheers,' she says grimly.

'Cheers,' says Lissa, taking her wine, keeping her coat on.

'Are you cold?' says Hannah.

'No – I can't really stay. I've got to get up early. We've got tech.'

'Lissa. Please. I need to talk.'

She takes off her coat, which Hannah hangs behind the door. Outside, dusk is settling over the park, over the lights of the city beyond. A vase of flowers stands on the table. Small lamps are lit. It is the flat of an adult, and yet sitting before her, on the blue sofa, with her legs folded beneath her, her hair tucked behind her ears, Hannah looks like a lost child.

'What's happening, Han? Where's Nath?'

'Working, I guess. I don't know. We had a row.'

'What about?'

'He doesn't want to do another cycle. The IVF. He said no. I thought he would change his mind. But he didn't. And now he says he wants a break.'

'From what?'

She can feel the way her breath moves, in and out, shallow and high.

'From everything.'

'What does he mean by that?'

'I don't know. I went back to Manchester for a few days. I

171

thought things would be different, but we've hardly spoken since I've been back.'

'Maybe he's right. Maybe you need a break from it all for a bit. Don't they say that? That it's often when you give up that it actually works?'

'Do you know how many *fucking* times people have said that to me?' Hannah throws her cushion to the other side of the room, where it bounces and falls still. 'Too many.' And then, quite suddenly, Hannah folds in on herself. 'Why?' she says. 'Why is this happening to me? Am I cursed? I feel like I'm cursed.'

Lissa moves towards her, sits beside her on the sofa. 'Hey. Han. You're not cursed.'

Hannah lifts her face from her hands. 'Will you speak to him?'

'I can't—'

'Please.' Hannah grips her arm. 'Get him to change his mind. He'll listen to you, Lissa. Talk to him. Please.'


She takes the bus down to Bloomsbury, gets off at Southampton Row and walks up towards Russell Square, where the trees flare orange and red, the sky an iron grey.

When she contacted him she said she needed to speak to him, but was only free in the morning on Thursday. He texted back immediately: *Sounds intriguing. I'm in uni on Thursday. Come and see me there?*

It took her five changes of outfit to get out of the door. In the end she put on an old faded sweatshirt, jeans and her parka. Trainers. No make-up, hair scraped on top of her head.

At the reception they direct her to the third floor – she climbs the stairs, pushes her way through double doors into his corridor. His door is closed, but as she approaches it opens and a young woman emerges. She is tall, her hair loose. Long limbs in tight jeans. She walks past Lissa without a second look.

There are posters on his door, in the manner of academic offices: one advertises a talk, another a union meeting about the tuition fees. She raises her hand and knocks.

'Come in.'

He is sitting at the desk with his back to her. 'Hey,' he turns. 'Liss.' He looks pleased to see her.

'Hey.' She steps inside, closes the door behind her. The room is pleasant, a high window through which the trees of Russell Square are just visible, a wall lined with books, a small sofa, his desk. Him. He is wearing a soft-blue T-shirt with a wide neckline. 'So this is where the magic happens,' she says.

He smiles and she realizes she can't really look at him, so she goes over to his bookshelves and looks at them instead. They are neat, arranged alphabetically.

'*Coming of Age in Samoa*?'

'Classic. You should read it.'

'What's it about?'

'Sex.'

'Oh.' She can feel herself turning red.

He is grinning. Is he teasing her?

'How's the play?' he says.

'Better. We open tomorrow.'

'That came round quickly. Can I come?'

'Of course. But you need to book.'

'Then I'll do that.'

'Good.'

'Why don't you sit down?'

She sits on his sofa. It is still warm. She thinks of the young woman who was in here before her.

'You look like a student,' he says.

'Thanks, I think.'

'You want a drink? Tea?' He gestures to a small tray, a kettle, cups. 'I have whisky in the drawer.'

'Seriously?'

'Only for emergencies.'

'Student emergencies?'

'Academic emergencies.'

There is a pause, a stillness in the room. She realizes it is her turn to speak. 'I'm here for Hannah,' she says.

'Ah,' he says, 'right. And why is that?'

'I promised her I'd come.'

'Why?'

'Because she seems to think I can influence you.' Lissa looks away, down at her hands. 'And I feel bad. I should never have said that thing, that day in the pub. About not doing IVF. I was wrong.'

'Really? But you seemed quite clear. You told me not to do it.'

'But I didn't mean that.'

'Then what did you mean?'

'I meant *I* wouldn't do it. I only spoke for myself. Not you and Hannah – I didn't think—'

'What? You didn't think what? That you influence me?'

His gaze is steady. He does not flinch. 'Please,' she says.

174

'Please don't say that. It's not fair. I didn't realize what I was saying. I didn't think of Hannah.'

'You know,' Nathan says softly. 'I have spent most of my adult life thinking of Hannah. Of what she wants. Of how to make her happy. And for most of my adult life, that was what I wanted to do.'

The curve of his cheek, the swell of his Adam's apple as he swallows.

'Why did you really come, Lissa?' he says.

'For Hannah. I told you.'

He nods, then, 'Can I tell you something?' he says.

'Yes.'

'Can I lock the door before I do?'

She nods, watches him stand. Feels her heart, the thrum of her blood. His hands on the key. The sound of the lock. He comes and kneels in front of her. 'Liss,' he says. 'The thing is that lately I keep thinking of what you want. Of what might please you.' He reaches out and takes her hand. 'Your hand's cold,' he says.

'Yes,' she says, although now it is hard to speak.

He takes one of her fingers and puts it in his mouth. His mouth is warm. She can feel pleasure radiating from her fingertip, into her breasts, her crotch, the backs of her eyes. She closes her eyes, leans her head against the sofa.

'Can I do this?' he says.

'Yes,' she says, although it is hard to speak.

She keeps her eyes closed, and now his mouth is on her stomach, very light, and now he is unbuttoning her jeans and easing them down and she is lifting herself, helping him. And now his finger is inside her, and she hears a sound, quite low in the room, and then she realizes the sound is coming from her. And his thumb is rubbing her, and his finger is inside her, and the sound carries on.

'Can I do this?' he says.

'Yes,' says the sound of the voice that is hers. 'Yes, please, yes.'


## Cate

'So the second rule of Mum Club is . . .'

'What?'

'We have to do something that scares us.'

They are sitting on a bench in the cathedral gardens, or rather, a flint-walled secret garden in the grounds of the cathedral. Dea had asked Cate to meet her at a small car park on Broad Street, where a small booth was cut into a thick wall, behind which a man waited, and Dea had flashed her university card and the guard waved them through. And it is quiet here, the walls crenellated and fortress-thick, as though the city outside with its traffic and its buses and its shopping and car parks and tourists has momentarily ceased to exist. It is cold, but the sun is out and the sky is blue and clear.

'OK,' says Cate. 'So, what scares you, Dea?'

'Having sex with my wife.'

Cate laughs out loud, and an elderly couple on the adjacent bench turn their heads towards them.

'Don't mock. I'm talking scared on all levels. I'm talking X-rated horror. I'm practically incontinent.' Dea grins. 'What about you?'

'What about me?'

'Any incontinence?'

Cate laughs. 'Caesarean, so no, not really.'

'Aha, yes, of course. So, bits intact?'

'Something like that.'

'So, sex then?'

'Not much, no. I haven't been up for it lately.'

'And how's that going down? With your husband?'

'Um. I think Sam might be finding it hard.'

'Tell me about him,' says Dea.

Cate turns to her. 'Who, Sam?'

'Yeah. How long have you been together?'

'Not long. A year and a half.'

'Where did you meet?'

A small hesitation and then, 'Online,' says Cate.

'Go on,' says Dea. 'I love a good origin myth. What was it you fell for?'

'He's funny. Or he can be. He's talented. He's a chef. For our second date he invited me to his flat. He cooked for me there.'

'Nice. What did he cook?'

'Chicken,' she says, 'roasted in cinnamon. He made his own flatbreads.' She smiles. 'That was pretty much the clincher. No one had made me a flatbread before.'

Dea gives a low whistle. 'Me neither. I might have turned, for a homemade flatbread.'

'Yeah, well, they were pretty good. And then he took me to Marseille – he'd lived there for years – and I sort of loved that, the way he knew his way around the city . . . the way he spoke French. And not long after that I was pregnant.' The look on his face when she told him. The unsullied joy. How disarmingly cellular her own response. 'He asked me to marry him, and I said yes.'

'Blimey, quick work. How was it?'

'Which bit?'

'The wedding?'

'Oh.' Cate wrinkles her nose. 'You know – pretty weird. I was huge. It was just a few of us – a registry office, a meal at a restaurant. All I wanted was to have a few drinks, but I couldn't, obviously. My dad flew in from Spain and made a terrible speech. My stepmother got out of it on champagne. It was the first time they met Sam. I just kept thinking that it was all a bit shotgun and entirely unnecessary and wishing I could get drunk. I couldn't work out who we were doing it for.'

'And now you don't want to have sex with him.'

'Yeah. No. Yeah.'

'Well,' Dea grins, 'you know, I think that's entirely normal. I think having sex with a man is extraordinary. All that *penetration.*'

'It's not all bad. Sometimes it's actually quite good.'

'If you say so.'

Cate hesitates and then, 'I was with a woman once,' she says.

'Really? Well I never.'

'Yeah.'

'And?'

'And . . . I think I was in love with her. I miss her.'

'Who was she?'

'Lucy? She was an activist, I suppose. She liked to climb trees.'

'Sexy.'

'It was.'

'Where is she now?'

'I have no idea. The States, probably. That's where I left her. If she's still alive. She was going to be arrested, so she went to ground. I've been looking a bit, lately. Trying to find her again.'

'Okaaay.'

'What?'

'So you don't want to have sex with your husband but you're looking for old lovers online? Sexy, *illegal* lovers online.'

'It's not like that.'

'Really? What's it like then?'

'She was important to me. For all sorts of reasons. Not just sex. Anyway, it's probably good I haven't found her.'

'Why?'

'I'm not sure she'd approve of what I've become.'

'What have you become?'

'Less.'

Dea is quiet, regarding her. That expression she has – curious, amused, alive. It is strange, thinks Cate, but she does not mind being seen by her, being stretched gently on the rack of her attention.

'So, come on,' says Dea. 'Just one woman? Or more?'

'One more. After Lucy. But it was a disaster. It ended very quickly. And I realized I wasn't gay. I just loved a woman. One woman. Once.'

'Aha, the old Gertrude Stein line.'

'Do I have to define it?' Cate says, defensive now.

'No,' says Dea. 'Sorry. Of course you don't.'

Cate watches her face, but there is no judgement, just that same amused look.

'Does he know?' says Dea.

'Who, Sam? A bit, not all.'

'Don't you think you should tell him?'

'I think it might be confusing.'

'Confusing for who?'

Cate falls silent. 'That's a lot of questions,' she says quietly. 'What about you?'

'Me?' Dea rolls her eyes. 'Jesus. Are we going to go into my sexual history now? Now that *is* an X-rated horror. I'll tell you one day. I'll give you the director's cut.'

Cate laughs. 'I'll look forward to it.'

Are they flirting? She can't tell.

'But not now. It's freezing. Come on,' says Dea. 'Let's go somewhere and get warm.'

They stand and Dea threads her arm through Cate's. 'Hey,' she says, as they near the edge of the garden. 'You never said what scared you. If I have sex with my wife, then what are you going to do?'

Cate thinks. 'Honestly? It's my house. Sorting it out. Unpacking the boxes from the move. I still haven't done it. It terrifies me.'

'Well, first of all, let me say that I think the pressure for women to have a perfect home is one of the greatest heists of capitalism. Which I am resisting daily on principle, as I'm sure you've seen from the state of my own house. But, you know, since it scares you so much, I think you should face it. Unpack the boxes. Sort it out. Have a gathering. Invite me round. And Zoe. Get Sam to cook. You never know' – Dea winks – 'maybe we'll all get pregnant again.'

*

Later that evening, when she hears Sam come home from work, Cate gets out of bed and goes down to the living room, where he is already installed on the sofa, beer in hand, computer propped on his chest.

'Hey,' she says, and goes to sit on the opposite chair.

'Hey.' He pulls off his headphones.

'What are you watching?'

'Just some crap.'

'How was work?'

'Tiring. Boring. I'm over it. Really. Plating up someone else's food.'

'I wanted to ask you . . .' she says.

'Yeah?'

'I met someone.'

'What?' He raises an eyebrow. 'Who?'

'Another mum. At that playgroup, the one Alice told me to go to. The one you told me to go to – so I could make friends. And I was wondering if I could invite her over, for a gathering. I was wondering if you would cook.'

'A *gathering*? What's a gathering?'

'Sam. Please.'

'When?'

'I don't know. A few weeks' time. I thought I might invite Hannah down, Nathan. Make an evening of it.'

He frowns. 'I don't know, I have to check my shifts.'

'Sam,' she says. 'You said I should meet people. I've done it. I've met people. Dea, and Zoe.'

'Wait, they're gay?'

'Yes.'

'Canterbury has lesbians?'

'Very funny.'

He takes a swig of beer.

'So can I tell them we'll do it? Will you cook?'

He thinks. 'OK,' he says. 'But let's invite Mark and Tamsin too.'

'Really?'

'Why not? We owe them a dinner. It's been ages since Mark has eaten my food. It might get the ball rolling. Encourage him to invest.'

'Great!' she says.

*Fuck.*


## Lissa

He does not call. She does not call him. He does not text. She does not text him. She looks at her phone. Keeps it in her pocket. Waits for the buzz of a message, but a message does not come.

She has forgotten how this goes. How you cede your power to the man after sex. How this appears to be a fundamental universal law. How you can move from sane to crazy in a few swift moves. Even if they are the husband of your best friend.

The. Husband. Of. Your. Best. Friend.

Think about that for a moment. Examine it. Let it sink in.


Press night goes well. The cast may be a little pushed, a little forced, but the play has its own engine, its own life force, and as they take their curtain Lissa can sense the excitement, see it reflected in the eyes of her fellow actors – it is working, the play is alive, they are part of something good.

The whispers go round the bar after the show that there were plenty of press watching, that they should expect a decent handful of reviews, and this news evokes in Lissa a familiar sense of relief and dread.

By Saturday morning there are four reviews online. The *Telegraph*, the *Independent* and *The Times* are all four stars. The *Evening Standard* carries a five-star review: *Where has Johnny Stone been? With a talent this rare he should be a household name. It's taken an out-of-the-way theatre and a little-known director to give him the opportunity to shine.*

Helen is *a young actress on the cusp of something huge.*

And of Lissa, the reviewer writes that she is *as languid, lost and dangerous a Yelena as I have ever seen.*

She gets a message from Cate.

*Saw the reviews! Wish I could come. Having a thing in Canterbury – December 10th. But I think you're performing?*

*Thanks*, Lissa writes back. *But you're right. I'm performing. Hope all's well.*

She leaves her phone in the house and goes for a walk around the park. It is market day, but the weather is cold and the crowds are thin. She feels conspicuous, there is every chance she might bump into either Hannah or Nathan or both of them together – buying bread or bacon or croissants or fish. Are they still having sex? Hannah and Nathan? What are they doing now? She could go round there. Just knock on the door and stay for a coffee. *Hey, Han! Nathan seduced me. Yeah, on Thursday, in his office! Have you ever fucked there? On the sofa? And that thing with his thumb. Is that what he does to you?*

Perhaps he is fucking all of them, she and Hannah and the long-limbed, succulent girls who rise from his sofa and leave it warm. Perhaps none of them knows him at all.

Or perhaps it is she who does not know herself.

She wonders if there is a word for a woman like her, perhaps a Greek word – a special sort of word for a special sort of woman, one who betrays her friend.

*Oh, Hannah. Oh, Jesus.*

She buys herself a croissant and takes it home and eats it alone, standing up at the sink.

Ticket sales rise in response to the reviews; they are 80 per cent full on the weekdays and then sold out on Friday and Saturday evenings. Their group warm-ups take on a celebratory air. When they have all completed their vocal exercises, their stretches, their articulation exercises and their pacing out of the stage, they gather in a circle and throw a ball to each other to tune up their reflexes. Ten minutes before the first half they sing their Russian folk song. Occasionally the younger men try out Cossack moves, before they high-five each other and whoop as they disperse to their dressing rooms to listen for the call for Beginners on the tannoy.

Only Johnny does not warm up. Instead he sits on the stage on the lounge chair that Vanya favours, wearing his crumpled linen costume, hat pushed down on his head, and does the crossword, looking up occasionally at the antics of the other actors with one eyebrow raised. When they sing he gets to his feet and wanders out for a cigarette.

Lissa is grateful to have something to do, somewhere to go

in the evenings; grateful to have the ritual of performance to hold her, to know where to stand, how to speak, where to put her hands.

She gets a text from Hannah. *Bought tickets! Me and Nath coming a week next Thursday.*

*Great!* she writes back, as her stomach swills with queasy fear.

The end of the first week, her mother comes with Laurie. After the performance they are waiting for her in the bar. Sarah holds Lissa's face in her hands. 'Wonderful, darling, wonderful – properly good. No review in the *Guardian*, though?'

*If a play goes on stage and the* Guardian *doesn't review it, does the play really exist?*

'Nothing in the *Guardian*, Ma, no.'

Laurie steps up and hugs her close. 'Best you've been, Liss, best you've been.'

On the Monday of the second week her father comes with his wife in tow.

'Well done, sweetie. You looked beautiful,' he says. 'Reminded me of your mother when she was young.'

Beside him her stepmother nods away like a nervous bird, gripping her handbag beneath her arm. 'I enjoyed it,' she says. 'Not a lot happens though, does it?'

No, Lissa agrees, not a lot happens. When she suggests a drink her father looks willing, but she sees her stepmother touch his arm and he turns to Lissa with a small, helpless shrug.

People's agents come, those with pulling power bringing casting directors with them: The Globe, the National, a TV company. The inevitable whispers pass around the dressing room before the show – *so-and-so is in tonight, so-and-so is in* – and the knowledge of these people watching, people who have the power to change the course of your life, spikes the blood. Now the pecking order shifts and changes, no longer the simple calculation of talent, the meritocracy of the stage. Michael's agent seems to bring half of London's TV and theatre people with him, and Helen's agent comes three times, each night with a different casting director in tow. Lissa sees them in the bar after the show, huddled in a corner as though engaged in vital affairs of state, the industry people leaning in, faces attentive, serious, as they listen to what the young actors have to say.

Her own agent comes finally – unaccompanied by casting directors, in the middle of the third week, when the show is a little flat. She sees her sitting in the back row, a small woman with unruly red hair, and as she is changing out of her costume Lissa gets a text.

*Wonderful. Had to get away, speak tomorrow?*

The next day she checks her phone often, waiting for a phone call that doesn't come.

Thursday arrives and she spends the day feral with anticipation. She writes Nathan a message. *You coming with Hannah tonight?* She hears nothing back. But as soon as she steps out on stage she sees Hannah, sitting alone, an empty seat beside her, and she is flooded with disappointment and relief.

Afterwards in the bar, Hannah hugs her. 'Amazing, Liss. Loved it. So she was worth it in the end?'

'Who?' She feels strangely disoriented. Her friend here before her, the knowledge of her transgression blazing within her.

'The Polish director.'

'Oh, yeah,' says Lissa, 'I guess she was.' Her eyes rove over Hannah's face. 'Nath didn't feel like coming then?'

'He got held up at work. He sends his love.'

'His love? Really?'

'Hey, did you get a message from Cate?' Hannah says. 'Inviting you to Canterbury?'

'I can't. I'm performing. Are you going to go?'

'I think so. We need to get out of London. Me and Nath. Do something spontaneous for a change.'

Lissa laughs. 'Spontaneity's not your forte, Hannah,' she says. 'If you want to do something spontaneous, go somewhere else. Go to Berlin. Go to New York. Go to Belize.'

Hannah looks at her – a quick, hurt look. 'Well,' she says quietly, 'maybe I'll start with Canterbury and see how I go.'

Lissa smiles, and a strange, bitter taste fills her mouth.


Her birthday comes around – she is thirty-six now, playing twenty-seven. She tells no one in the cast. It is freezing, as she leaves the house to visit Sarah, with a fierce, bitter wind. Sarah gives her the usual handmade card, but there is no present this year.

'I'm just rather busy,' Sarah says in the kitchen. 'The new work's consuming me somewhat. Did I tell you? I've got an exhibition in the summer. The gallery in Cork Street came through.'

'Can I see?' asks Lissa. 'What you're working on?'

'I'm not sure.' Sarah tilts her head, pondering, then: 'No . . . I rather think not.'

When their coffee is finished, Lissa lingers as her mother rises. Outside, the wind has died down, and sunlight strikes the winter garden. 'Do you fancy a walk?' she says. 'It's brightened up. We could go up on the Heath.'

'Work,' Sarah says, already heading for the door. 'You're welcome to stay but I have to work.'

Lissa stays where she is, listening to her mother's footsteps mount the stairs.

On the wall of the living room is one of Sarah's portraits, a picture of Lissa at the age of eight, or nine. She remembers sitting for it so clearly still: it was summer, and hot in the attic, but she didn't mind being up there, Saturday morning after Saturday morning in that old flowered chair. She would sit there with her book – her legs flung over the arms of the chair, the sunlight slanting in from the skylight – as Sarah prepared her paints, set up her easel. Then finally, when everything was ready, she would turn on the radio and start to paint, and Lissa would sense it, the concentration, the way she had all of her mother's attention at last. How safe it made her feel.

Then, one morning, on the pavement outside the school gates, a different sort of painting appeared. Simple white lines, the silhouettes of children drawn in chalk. Everyone standing around, disturbed, as at a crime scene, wondering what they were.

At home that evening, Lissa told her mother about it and Sarah turned to her with a strange smile.

*I painted them. Caro and I. We went out, in the early morning, while you were still asleep. They were all that was left. Of the children. In Hiroshima. We painted them so that people would understand.*

She remembers the way Sarah spoke, the pride, the particular smile she had, as though she had done something good. When really, Lissa knew, she had done something terrible. She had no words to tell her mother how those pictures made her feel. The hollowness of those children who had disappeared.

The day stretches ahead of her, with nothing in it till she must be at the theatre at six o'clock. She heads down to the South Bank, to the BFI, where they are showing a Bergman season. She gets tickets for the longest of the films, then buys coffee and a slice of cake and sits in the window to wait for the cinema to open, watching the faces of the people as they pass. Perhaps he will appear. It is not, surely, beyond the realm of possibility that Nathan might treat himself to an afternoon film. Perhaps that will be how it happens – to bump into him, to let coincidence take care of the plot. Or she could text him again. Tell him where she is. Invite him down.

But of course he doesn't come. He is a busy man. It is only people like her who can sit in a cinema on a weekday afternoon, tasting the equivocal pleasures of time on their hands. She should make a joke of it, she thinks, of Bergman on a birthday. But there is no one to make the joke to.

She is the first into the cinema when it opens, handing her ticket to the usher, sitting in the darkness before the thin safety curtain rises, before the adverts come on.

## Hannah

She searches for a hotel in Whitstable for the Friday and the Saturday night, finds one that has only recently opened but has good reviews on TripAdvisor. There is the requisite mention of Egyptian cotton. There are driftwood mirrors in the bedrooms. A neutral palette of white and grey. She calls them up and a pleasant-voiced woman tells her she is in luck, they have had a last-minute cancellation, a room is free but there is a shared bathroom. It is either that or the Travelodge so Hannah takes it. As she hands over her credit-card details she pictures wide skies – walking on the beach on Saturday morning. She books lunch at a restaurant she has heard of further along the coast, an unprepossessing pub with a reputation for spectacular food. She looks at the menu: oysters, salt-baked celeriac, Aylesbury lamb. They will eat oysters. They will walk on the beach. It will all fall into place. She has been wrong. It is the controlled, clinical side of things that has brought them to this. Nathan is right, Lissa is right: they should take a break – let things happen naturally. Maybe everyone is right. The message boards are full of people's stories of conceiving after IVF has failed. It is not the end. It is only the end of the beginning. She has been holding too tight. There is still time, there is still a chance – she just needs to relax. To be spontaneous. It will do them good to get away.

# Bras

## 2008

Hannah is getting married. Nathan has proposed in a cottage in Cornwall. They have been a couple for ten and a half years. She is having a little gathering at the new flat to toast the announcement, with her best women, Lissa and Cate.

It is February, but sunny and mild as Cate and Lissa walk the small distance from the big house, down Broadway Market towards Hannah's flat. They stop at the off-licence on the way. Cava? says Cate, lifting a bottle. Champagne, says Lissa. Let's get a bit of Veuve.

At the bottom of the canal they turn right, where they announce their arrival at a plain metal door and Hannah buzzes them inside. The flat smells both earthy and clean – the interior staircase has been newly covered with sisal. Hannah appears, smiling at the top of the stairs, dressed in simple trousers, a silk shirt. Cate and Lissa take off their shoes and walk slowly up the stairs, the sisal pleasantly rough beneath their feet. The stairs give on to a large, open kitchen and living room, where a long blue sofa lies along one wall.

Cate has seen this flat before – visited often since Hannah and Nathan moved here last year – but tonight it looks different; it is as though the definition has been turned up. Her eyes graze the details of the room: the elegant sofa, a table of lightest wood, a brown jug placed just so upon it, knives arranged by *size on a magnetized strip on the wall. They seem to look back at her, these objects, with a cool judging gaze. They seem to ask her how she measures up.*

*They take their drinks and go through sliding doors on to a large terrace with a view over Haggerston Park where they drink their Veuve and toast their friend.*

*Hannah carries a particular radiance, this springlike evening, as though she herself is the chief exhibit in this backdrop of her own curating, as though all of this – the terrace and the park and her home glowing gently on the other side of the glass doors, were simply there to reflect her radiance, her status as a bride-to-be.*

*After a little while Cate excuses herself – she has to go to the toilet. In Hannah's bathroom there is no clutter, there are no bottles on the bath or in the shower. Instead, in the cabinet, there are matching jars of brown glass.*

*In the hall, on the way back out, Cate hesitates, for Hannah's bedroom door is ajar. Outside there is laughter, the red tip of Lissa's cigarette carving the air as she talks. Cate steps inside. She fingers the linen throw that lies on the large bed, then goes over to the wardrobe, where she takes out one of Hannah's simple silk shirts, feels its supple weight between her fingers, then puts it back. She goes to the chest and opens the top drawer, and here she stops, breath caught – Hannah's bras and knickers are laid out in matching sets. She fingers one of the bras – it is the sort of bra only a woman with very small breasts can wear: two thin triangles of lace with a bright flash of silk on the edge. One is red. One petrol. One is the colour of lightest pink. Cate can feel her heart racing. She did not know Hannah owned bras like this; Hannah, whose exterior is so spartan, whose edges have always been so clear. There is something about the sight of these* bras – something insolent and secret and potent – that hits her like a punch to her stomach.

Quickly, furtively, she takes off her jumper and her own bra (large, nondescript), managing to fasten Hannah's on its widest clasp. She turns it round to the front, pulls up the straps, and stares at herself in these two triangles of nothing, edged in petrol-coloured silk. She knows then – she has lost. More than the house and the sofa and the engagement and the knives on metal strips and the jug just so, and the successful ten-year relationship, it is the sight of these bras that tells her that in the fierce, unspoken race she and Hannah have been running since they were children, she has lost.

Over the next days she feels herself slipping, as though happiness were a dance whose steps she has forgotten. She counts her breaths. She counts her blessings, she tries to rationalize – why should it matter what her friends are doing? Why should her happiness be indexed to theirs? But it is. Somehow, it is – she cannot help but take inventory of her life; her lack, at thirty-three years old, of any of the markers that constitute real adulthood. She is beginning to loathe her job, taking the Tube every day to Canary Wharf, going cap in hand to meetings with bankers who believe that in giving you a minute of your time they are changing the world. This job which will never give her enough to buy a home, to buy good clothes.

And Hannah – Hannah who always said she would do something worthwhile and did – who moved from her management training job at the age of twenty-nine and is now senior advisor in a large global charity on a salary twice that of Cate's own. She didn't sell out. She sold in. And it turned out her stock was high.

Cate, who has prided herself on living simply, finds she wants things. She wants a home of her own, a functioning relationship, a child, or at least the possibility of one, money for decent clothes, a knicker drawer that is not a frantic tangle of odd socks and old M&S briefs. Her wants proliferate, metastasize in the darkness inside her.

The other two rooms in the shared house are occupied by people she does not really know. The house, always shabby, feels grotty – the salmon colour of the kitchen, the terrible cheap carpet on the floor. The kitchen is no longer a place to gather. She makes her food and scuttles out again, eats it in her room, at her desk.

Cate tries to speak to Lissa about it, to spin it into humour somehow, but Lissa is preoccupied, on an upward swing. For Lissa there is hope on the horizon. Last week her agent called her with news of an audition. A feature film. A young indie director. A lead role. The director had seen her in a short film she made for no money last summer as a favour to a friend and called about her availability.

Lissa has read the script and it is extraordinary.

Somewhere, she knows, this one is for her.

Declan is away, and so Lissa practises her speech for Cate, while Cate sits on the battered old sofa in the living room, listening, prompting her when she stumbles, which she rarely does. She is good, thinks Cate, she deserves this. Her career will finally ignite and she too will move up and away.

Lissa gives up drinking for the week before the audition, makes sure she drinks plenty of water, sleeps as much as she can. She takes herself off to yoga classes and returns radiant.

*The day of the meeting arrives. The director seems as excited to meet her as she is to meet him. He tells her he loved her in the short. She already knows one of the speeches by heart, and she delivers it on camera without looking at her script.*

*Wow, he says. That was awesome.*

*She does another speech, equally well. When she gets up to leave the director envelops her in a hug. See you soon, he says.*

*A day passes. Another. And another. Lissa checks her phone constantly. She checks that it is on. She turns it on and off. Cate watches her face cloud and darken, elation turn to doubt. By the Wednesday she is quiet, by Thursday belligerent.*

*It's gone to someone else, she says.*

*Cate watches her take a call from Declan, who is filming somewhere in Scotland.*

*I'm going to go and see him, says Lissa. I need a break.*

*Lissa leaves on Friday afternoon. She takes the plane from City Airport to Edinburgh, where Declan has sent a car to pick her up. She sits in the back of the car and watches the city slide by. It is grey and raining. They drive out, up into the country-side, until they reach a castle in large grounds. Behind it there is a large loch. There is no mobile reception. She is relieved.*

*Cate comes home from work at half past five, locks up her bike, climbs the stone steps and lets herself into the house. There is no one else there. She feels the harsh, grainy texture of her loneliness.*

*The landline rings. A rare event. It rings and rings and rings and rings off. Then it rings again and perhaps it is an emergency, so Cate goes to answer it; a woman's voice, hectoring, asking for Lissa, who Cate informs her isn't there. Where is she? says the woman, who speaks to Cate like she is shit on her shoe. I don't know, says Cate truthfully. Somewhere in Scotland, I think.*

*Well, her mobile's not working, says the woman. Tell her, she says, tell her she needs to come back to London. He wants to see her. Again. Monday morning. First thing. Tell her to come back as soon as she can.*

*Cate puts down the phone. She honestly does not know where Lissa is. She could find out. She could make it an emergency. She could call Sarah, Lissa's mother, who would probably know. She could go into Lissa's room and search the chaos of her desk for a piece of paper which may or may not contain the name of a hotel. Her diary. Her computer. Cate knows the password. It may be in there. She could do any or all of these things, but she does nothing.*

*On Sunday night she is sleeping when Lissa arrives in the house. It is gone midnight. She barely wakes, she goes back to sleep.*

*On Monday morning Cate rises and showers and dresses and leaves for work.*

*When Cate comes home that afternoon Lissa is sitting at the kitchen table, a ball of damp tissues in her hand. Did you get a call from my agent?*

*Who?*

*My agent. She said she called here, on Friday. That he wanted to see me for the audition. It was this morning, first thing. She begins to cry. I was asleep. I missed it. It's gone.*

*Can't you get in touch? Get him to see you again?*

*Don't you get it? Lissa hisses. It's gone to someone else. It's fucking gone.*

*Lissa spends the next day in bed with the curtains closed. Cate knocks on her door, but she does not answer.*

*She does not speak to Cate for weeks.*

*And Cate is queasy with guilt. She has done something, or not done something – she is not sure which. She should have done more.*

*But if Lissa had been made to get the part, she would have done so, wouldn't she? It was Lissa's decision to go away to a place in the middle of nowhere. It was Lissa's destiny, wasn't it – to lose out?*

2010

## Cate

*Dinner. Friends for dinner. A dinner party. Supper. Friends for supper. A gathering.* However Cate frames it to herself, the thought is excruciating – she is no good at such things. But Sam seems happy about the arrangement. On Sunday, his day off, he brings out his knives and pans. He hands Tom a milk pan and a wooden spoon and Tom sits on the floor, happily playing with them both as Sam flicks through cookbooks.

'I want to do something Kentish,' he says. 'You ever eaten whelks? I could do a ceviche with shallots and tomatoes and lime. And then something with dabs. I could get fish from that place on the coast. They supply the restaurant.'

Cate looks at him in the narrow kitchen, in the grey light of the winter afternoon, sleeves rolled up, and realizes she hasn't seen him so happy for months.

The day of the dinner she spends the morning cleaning. She moves Tom with her from room to room, putting him on the floor with his toys while she scrubs toilets and sinks and vacuums floors. She has the radio on in the background.

*Parliament has voted by a tiny majority to increase student fees to nine thousand pounds a year. Large protests in central London yesterday.*

When the cleaning is done she turns on the TV and watches footage of protestors on the roof of the Conservative Party headquarters. Placards on fire. Charles and Camilla, their horrified faces as a window of their car is smashed. A close-up of one of the protestors, a young man with his mouth open wide. She knows the look. The war cry. Feels it land in her gut.

Sam is home after his afternoon shift, carrying a bulging bag of fish and vegetables, which he puts in the fridge, along with four bottles of wine. 'I got a good Burgundy,' he says, 'it was on offer in Aldi.'

She can hear him singing as he takes a shower. He comes down in a T-shirt and jeans. 'Come on, little guy.' Sam straps Tom in the high chair, gives him some carrot to play with, then ties on an apron, pulls out his knives and sets to work on an onion. She lingers, watching him, his wide forearms, his skill with the blade, the flash of the knife. When the onion is chopped he looks up. 'What are you looking at?'

'Just – I remember the first time I saw you do that. The first night we met.'

'Yeah.' He smiles, and holds her eyes. 'I remember that night too.' Then, 'Hey,' he says, after a moment. 'I went to check out a premises the other day. It's an old warehouse. Victorian. Backs on to the Stour. It was a grain store. I think it would be affordable.' She can see the excitement in him. 'But let's make this meal great first and then see what Mark says.'

She can hear him chatting away as she moves next door, telling Tom what he's doing – *so you take your onion, and then you sweat it in the oil* – and Tom's burbling responses.

She flicks on the TV again, but it is only the same rolling

pictures as earlier, Charles and Camilla. That same protestor, open-mouthed. She turns it off and texts Hannah: *You still OK for tonight?* Part of her, she is aware, a large part of her, would like Hannah to cancel – would like everyone to cancel – but she gets a text back immediately: *Can't wait!*

## Hannah

She decides to work from home, so she can pack and get everything ready in time. 'We have to pick up the rental car,' she says to Nathan as he leaves for work. 'But if we leave at three or so we can get to Whitstable and have some time together before we go to Cate's.'

The weather has eased a little. It is not so cold as it was. She works all morning, then takes herself for a run along the canal, and showers and dresses in her best underwear and a dress that she knows he loves, knee-length, supple black silk – bought for their anniversary last year. She takes time over her make-up. She has bought a good bottle of champagne, which she packs in her bag, then goes online, looking again at the pictures of the hotel, of the restaurant, of the beach at Whitstable. Perhaps this is the beginning of something new. Perhaps they can move to Kent. Walk under wide skies. Get a dog.

At five she receives a text: *Just leaving.* Which means they are going to be late. To calm herself, she goes into their bedroom and begins packing a bag for him, but as she does so she feels a sense of dread – as though their intimacy is suddenly contingent, fraught with a vague peril. She should have gone to get the car herself – she has had the whole afternoon – but the car-rental place is close to the road that leads to the A12, which leads to the A2, which leads to the M2, which leads to Kent. So it made sense, in that way at least. She finishes packing and goes to sit on the sofa, so she will be ready as soon as he arrives.

She is still sitting in the same spot when his key turns in the lock at six fifteen.

'We're late,' she says.

'I'm sorry. There was an emergency meeting. Industrial action. The tuition fees.'

He looks tired, irritable.

'Do you need anything?' she says. 'A shower? A drink?'

'If we're late, let's just go.'

At the car-rental office there are forms to be filled out, driving licences to be photocopied, excesses to decide upon. It is seven before they leave with an ugly Ford Fiesta, and Nathan drives out of London on the A2.

'I think we're too late to go to Whitstable first,' she says.

He nods. She studies his face in the dark. Something she thought she knew by heart has become inscrutable, opaque.

'So shall we go straight to the dinner, then?'

'Whatever you think.'

'Or maybe we should cancel the dinner? Just go to the hotel?'

'Won't Cate be disappointed? Isn't that the whole point?'

'Yes, I suppose it is.' She turns to look out of the window at the 1930s edges of London sliding past. 'I've never been to Canterbury,' she says. 'I only know it from Chaucer. The Wife of Bath. A level.'

He changes lanes. 'I went there once,' he says, 'for a conference.'

'Did you like it?'

She winces. It is as though they do not know one another. Or as though they are following a badly written script.

'Yes,' he says. 'From what I saw. It was nice.'

They fall silent. The script has run out. She feels panic rising in her. 'The hotel looks sweet,' she says. 'There are bikes we can borrow. We can cycle to Margate tomorrow. If the weather's OK.' She lifts her phone and checks the weather, but there is only one bar of reception. 'Apparently it's really up and coming. Margate. There's the Turner. Opening next year. Turner Contemporary. Someone at work went there last summer. Loved it. Sold up and moved.' His face. His shuttered face. 'Or, you know, we could just stay in bed. Sleep. They bring breakfast up to your room.'

What is she? A fucking tour guide? Shut up shut up *shut up*.

She switches the radio on; the news is full of the tuition-fees story. She leans forward and turns it up. 'Do we have to?' he says, leaning in and turning it off. 'It's depressing. I've heard enough of it today.'

They follow the instructions that Cate sent, but they lead only to a large roundabout, which they go around twice as Hannah tries calling to check, but the phone rings and rings and is not answered. 'She's probably busy,' says Hannah. 'With her guests.'

'Right,' says Nathan. 'Well, in the absence of any clear directions, shall we stop the car?' He swings off the roundabout and turns left at a set of traffic lights. There is nowhere to park. She watches the muscle tense in his jaw. 'There,' he says, pointing to the sign for a car park.

They go down into the depths of a multi-storey. What if it closes while they are at Cate's? How will they get to Whitstable? They go up in the lift and do not speak. He looks pale beneath the overhead light. Hannah's phone buzzes in her pocket – she fishes it out. Finally: Cate with the directions.

'She sounds happy,' she says, as she puts her phone back into her pocket.

It is cold on the street in Canterbury, colder than in London. She has dressed too flimsily. She wants to ask Nathan to hold her, but he is hunkered down into his coat. Has she ever had to ask him to hold her before?

He rolls a cigarette and lights it. She bites her tongue. They walk past a small supermarket, and then into a small estate, find number eleven.

She wants to go back to the car. To drive back to safety, to her home, which feels such a long way away. She wants to stop and hold her husband. To shake him until his water runs clear again, until his secrets fall out.

Nathan reaches up and presses the doorbell.

'Hannah!!' As Cate opens the door she stumbles forward. Nathan steps up to grab her elbow. 'Hannah! Nate! Come in, come in!'

Cate is flushed, talking loudly as she pulls them through a narrow hallway, a cramped sitting room, to where expectant faces crowd around a small round table. 'Everyone!' says Cate. 'This is Hannah! And Nate. The best couple in the world!'

## Cate

It is going well – surprisingly well – except for the fact that she cannot find her wine glass. She had it a moment ago – did she take it when she went to the bathroom? There it is, on the other side of the table. She reaches for it, but Nathan gets there first and passes it safely back towards her. Mark is talking, something about sailing.

'The coast is so close. Got a friend with a boat, takes me out sea fishing – you should come, Sam. Next summer. We take some decent wine, cook up on deck. He's got cash. If you cook like this, I reckon he might be interested in your food too.'

And Sam is nodding, looking pleased. And the food – they are all eating their food, and it is delicious, really delicious, they are all saying so – and here is Dea, her face intent, listening to something Hannah is saying. And Cate is filled with warmth for Dea – whose idea this was – who turned up bearing cordial, wine-dark elderberry cordial made from her allotment, which Cate stowed in the kitchen for Hannah to drink. But tonight Hannah is drinking – and Cate laughs to herself because it is so good to see Hannah here in her house, drinking wine.

And she looks so beautiful – has obviously made an effort – in that dress, the way her hair frames her face, her face which is flushed from the outside air and the alcohol. And she is so touched that Hannah cares enough to come, to make the journey, that she feels sudden tears in her eyes. She stands up and goes around the table to Hannah, puts her cheek against hers. 'Thank you,' she says.

'What for?'

'For coming here. You look gorgeous, Han.'

And Hannah laughs. 'Thanks. You too.'

And as she circles back to her seat, she catches Nathan and Dea talking together now: 'They've occupied the Senate building. Fifty of them in the War Room. Our VC signed a letter supporting the fees hike.'

And Nathan is nodding. 'It's a shit show.'

Cate puts her hand on Dea's shoulder. 'I saw them,' she says, 'this morning – they were handing out leaflets by the cathedral again. I was looking for that girl. The one with the pink hair, do you remember?'

Dea smiles. 'I do. She's inside. She's in the Senate.'

Zoe leans forward. 'It feels like the spirit of '68 or something. Like these young people are being radicalized overnight.'

'I agree,' says Nathan. 'But don't people always say that? Wheel out the *soixante-huitards*?'

'Well,' says Zoe. 'If my daughter was old enough, I'd want her to be in there.'

'Yeah,' says Nathan. 'I reckon I'd want that too.'

Cate looks around at her table, at her guests, and she feels happy – suddenly and completely happy. There is no future to fear, no past to regret, only this, only a series of moments, strung along, like lit globes on a string – there is warmth, there is food, there is comfort. Upstairs, Tom sleeps. She is grateful. And she sees that the bottles on the table are empty so she goes back into the kitchen and fetches another from the fridge – it is hard to open – and here is Sam, coming in behind her. 'Here,' he says. 'Let me do that.'

She turns around and there he is, her husband – and she leans in and kisses him – not a chaste kiss, and he laughs, pulls her closer, and she traces the rough line of his beard with her tongue.

'Wow,' he says. 'You must be drunk.'

She laughs. She has forgotten this, the fizz of his proximity, this man, this bear of a man. Dea was right. This was what she needed to do.

She helps Sam carry the food and the wine back in. They are configured slightly differently now – Dea and Tamsin are speaking together; Hannah, who is not talking to anyone, is looking over at Nathan and Zoe, whose heads are bent, looking at pictures on Zoe's phone.

'She's with a babysitter,' Zoe is saying. 'I'm pretty nervous but they seem to be going OK.'

'She's gorgeous,' Cate hears Nathan say.

Cate watches Hannah watch them and feels a sudden spasm of protectiveness towards her friend. 'Hey,' she says, nudging Zoe. 'Hey, you two.' Nathan and Zoe look up, startled. Now she has said it she doesn't know what else to say. She claps her hands as Sam puts the fish down on the table.

## Hannah

Cate is drunk. She is swaying, holding the plates; Hannah reaches up and takes them from her.

'Here, have some water.' Hannah holds out her glass.

'I'm fine,' says Cate. 'Really, I am.'

Hannah drinks the water herself. She has had two glasses

of wine and her head feels fuzzy. She already has a headache beginning at her temples. She is finding it hard to concentrate on the conversation that is swirling around her; she keeps thinking about the car, about how it will be stuck in the car park and they won't be able to get it out. She needs to call the hotel – she needs to let them know that they will be late, to ask whether that's OK, whether they need to have a special key. She can't remember how far it is to Whitstable. Twenty minutes? Maybe more? It is ten o'clock and they are just eating their main course – at this rate, they will be here till one.

The conversation is getting heated now: Dea, Cate's new friend, and that guy Mark with the big diver's watch, the one who's fond of the sound of his own voice. She recognizes him from the wedding – he was Sam's best man, wasn't he?

'It was needed,' Mark is saying, 'if the markets aren't going to turn their backs on us. You want to be like Greece? Didn't you see the note they left in the Treasury? *There's no money left*. Idiots. Fucktards.'

'Sure,' says Dea, 'and austerity is going to hit the poor the hardest. What about a tax on the banks?'

'They'll just take their business elsewhere.'

'So they are in charge?' says Zoe, leaning in. 'So they dictate policy now?'

Mark turns to Zoe. 'I'm not sure you quite know what you're talking about, love.'

'And why is that?'

'I mean, you're American, for a start.'

'For a start?' says Zoe. 'And what comes after that?'

The temperature has dropped a couple of degrees in the

room. Hannah stands and quickly makes her way to where Sam is sitting. She leans in and thanks him for the food and asks him if he has a landline. 'Sure,' he says, 'it's in the bedroom, first on the left.'

She kicks off her shoes and goes upstairs. In the bedroom she sits on the bed in the dark. She is breathing quickly. There is a tightening in her skull. Something is troubling her. Nathan – the way he was with that woman Zoe. Their heads bent together looking at her phone, his low exclamation at the sight of her child.

There is a noise beside her and she jumps. At first she does not know what it is, then she understands – it is Tom, he is here, sleeping in the big bed. She can see him properly now, in the small light from the landing, his arm flung out to the side. She lies down beside him. He stirs but does not wake. His breath smells sweet. It is so even. He is so deeply asleep.

She curls up beside him and puts her finger in his grip, tracing the small bumps of his knuckles beneath her thumb, her cells fizzing with a longing that might split her in two.

And she understands something, lying here – an understanding that arrives in her cells fully formed. She has lost her husband – or her husband is lost to her. Something fundamental, some deep river that fed them, has dried up.

For the moment – this small moment, with this small hand in hers – this knowledge does not hurt, but she knows there is pain waiting for her, on the other side of this. She knows it will come.

It is quiet, for now, up here, while downstairs there is music, louder now, and Cate's voice raised above it, exhorting everyone to dance.

208

'I used to love dancing!' she yells. 'Dea, Zoe, come on!' She pulls them to their feet. Someone needs to change the energy in here – rescue the evening, which is in danger of escaping, of slipping away. 'Where's the rest of the wine?'

There is a bottle by Mark, half full. She goes over towards him, lifts it and pours it into a nearby glass.

'Are you sure you need any more of that?' he says.

'I'm sorry?' Cate turns back to him. 'What did you just say?'

Something in the way he stands – an ancient violence, simmering just beneath the surface. As though on an unspoken cue, Tamsin moves towards her husband. Behind her, Cate can sense Dea and Zoe. Nathan is sitting watching to her side. Sam to her left. Hannah, where is Hannah? Cate lifts the glass to her mouth. The wine is no longer cold. It tastes tacky, overly sweet.

'I think your wife might have had enough. Don't you think?' Mark turns to Sam.

Cate splutters. 'Oh my God, you're not really saying that? *I think you've had enough, love.*' She is laughing hard now. 'Oh, wait – you are?!' She shakes her head. 'You're a joke.'

'Excuse me?'

'You're a fucking joke. Look at you, with that stupid watch. You're not a diver, are you? Wait a minute – shall we see if it works?'

She moves towards him, grabs his hand and turns it over, unclasps his watch, and drops it into her full glass of wine. 'Oops,' she says, as the wine sloshes out over her wrist.

The fury on his face. Tamsin, white with shock.

'You people. Do you have any idea how ridiculous you are? You people,' she says again, waving her glass at Tamsin and Mark. 'You're the problem, do you know that?'

'Cate.' Sam steps forward. 'Mark's right, you've had enough. You're a breastfeeding mother, for God's sake.'

'Oh. Oh, I'm a breastfeeding *mother*, am I?'

'You're tired.'

'Oh!' She bangs the glass down on to the table. 'Oh, that's *priceless*. Of course I'm tired. I haven't had a full night's sleep in almost a year. You know. I'm sorry I haven't got a system, Sam. I'm sorry I haven't got a functioning fucking *system*. It's a form of torture, you know. Sleep deprivation. Did you know that? They break soldiers with it. I mean – you may not be that bright, but at least you can grasp that.'

'I really don't think we need to have this conversation here.'

'Yeah, go on. Shut me down. Shut me up. I shouldn't even be here. I shouldn't even be in this fucking marriage. In this fucking town.'

She looks around at them all, the way they are staring, slack-jawed.

She watches as Mark moves towards Tamsin, as though to protect her, his arm around her, the way she shelters in her husband's bulk. And she understands, in a pure, clear moment that cuts through the wine, that she hates this man. Hates everything he is and everything he represents. She lifts her sleeve. 'Shall I show you what I wear on *my* wrist?' she says to Mark. 'It's a spider. To remind me to keep fighting. Not to capitulate. Not to forget to fight men like you.'

## Hannah

She hears Cate shouting from where she lies on the bed. The door banging. Concerned voices. She knows she should go to check, because whatever has happened sounds serious, but she is filled with a great exhaustion, all of her cells heavy with it, as though she has been walking, walking for such a long time, with such a heavy load on her back, and her body is so tired. She just wants to lie here curled beside this child, to feel the warmth of him, and maybe sleep beside him for a while. There are footsteps on the stairs, the door opening a crack.

'Hannah?' Nathan's voice.

'Yes?'

She does not want this crack of light, this light which is sharpening, filling the room, which carries the future within it, cold and hard and unforgiving. She wants to pull Nathan in here, close the door behind them. Lie down in the darkness together with this baby on this bed.

'It's Cate. She's gone. She's pretty drunk. I think she might need finding.'

Hannah rouses herself and comes to stand, then follows him slowly back down the stairs, and out blinking into the living room, where people are scattered in small groups.

'I'll go and look for her,' she says.

'Let her cool off,' says the man called Mark. 'She's pissed. She could do with the air.'

Hannah takes her coat.

'You want me to come?' Nathan says.

'No, you stay.'

Outside it is freezing, and she has no idea where to go. She calls Cate's name and her voice is thin and high. She traces their steps back out to the road, heels percussive on the hard ground, comes to a deserted supermarket car park. She feels vulnerable out here, in these heels, in this dress. 'Cate?' she calls. The road is busy, even at this time of night. She has a sudden terrible thought and she starts to run. 'Cate?' she calls. 'Cate?'

And then she sees her. She is standing on a small hump-backed bridge, leaning out over the river. 'Cate?' she calls.

Hannah is breathless when she reaches her.

Cate's eyes, when she lifts her gaze, are hard and bright. 'I'm leaving,' she says.

Beneath the bridge the cold black water moves.

'Cate,' says Hannah, taking her arm. 'You're drunk. It'll seem different in the morning. I promise.'

'Don't fucking *silence* me. Do you know what you're like, Hannah? You're just like all the rest of them. *Never mind that you feel like shit. Never mind that they cut you open and didn't tell you why. You have a healthy baby. Take some fucking pills and shut up.* You don't want to hear the truth.'

And Hannah feels her own cold fury rising now. 'What truth? What truth, Cate? Come on. Tell me.'

Cate shakes her head, mutinous.

'Well, I'll tell you my truth, shall I?' Hannah speaks quickly, clearly now. 'My husband is leaving me. Because we can't have a child. I lost a child. I had a miscarriage. Have you ever had one of those?'

Cate's eyes in the darkness, all pupil now.

'Shall I tell you the truth of that, Cate? It's like this.' She

212

takes Cate's hand, lifts her sleeve. 'It was about this big. About seven weeks old. A sac to hold a baby. It's fairly monstrous, actually. It's not the sort of thing that's supposed to be seen. It's supposed to stay inside you – to grow and grow and grow until it can't grow any more. You know what that feels like, don't you? A baby, growing inside you?'

Their breath plumes together in the freezing air.

'You didn't tell me.'

'I didn't tell anyone.'

'*Why?*'

'Because you were pregnant at the time. Because I didn't want to upset you. Because I felt ashamed.'

There is a slackening. Cate's hand drops to her side, her shoulders slump.

'I'm sorry,' says Cate. 'You should have told me.' Her voice is thick.

'No,' says Hannah. 'You should have asked.'


It is late when they arrive at the hotel. The room is smaller than she imagined. 'Where's the bathroom?' asks Nathan.

'I was too late to book the en suite,' she says wearily. 'I think it's down the hall.' She is cold. She got cold out there on the bridge.

He nods, goes to his bag. 'Can you tell me where you packed my toothbrush then?'

'It's here.' She takes out her wash bag, hands him his toothbrush.

When he has gone she sits down in the armchair. She sees herself reflected in the driftwood mirror. This stupid black dress. Her make-up, smudged now. All of it broken. All of it over. It is all so absurd.

In the morning two trays are left outside their door. She brings them in and puts them on the table. Nathan sits up in bed, pulls on his jeans. 'I'm going outside,' he says. When he comes back he smells of cigarettes.

She calls the restaurant and cancels the lunch reservation.

There will be no lunch. There will be no oysters or artisan bread or Aylesbury lamb. There will be no children. She kills things before they are even born. He does not touch her. In a way she is grateful. It is as though she has broken into tiny pieces inside, with only her thin skin holding it all together, and if she is touched she might shatter – might never find the pieces to put herself back together again.

They walk along the beach without speaking. They look out at the roiling sea, then they climb back into the car. They drive back up the M2 to London. She pretends to sleep. They drop off the rental car. They take the bus back to Hackney.

They walk up the three flights of stairs into their flat. Nathan packs a bag.

*Lissa*

It is the final Thursday night, and the play flies. It is the freest she has ever felt on a stage – the lines rise in her as though they are her own.

*You have mermaid's blood in your veins,* Vanya tells her, *so be a mermaid. Run wild for once in your life.*

As she comes off stage after her final exit, she realizes she has been unaware of the audience; entirely focused on the other actors, out of her skin. She has not thought about Nathan for an hour and a half. As they take their curtain, Johnny turns his face towards her, saluting her with a small nod. Then in the wings, in a gesture of old-fashioned courtesy, he takes her hand. 'Magnificent,' he says.

'You, too.'

He inclines his head. 'We should drink to it,' he says. 'You and I.' He still has her hand in his.

She hurries to the dressing room, aware she is happy, that something has been completed tonight, that a question she asked herself as a young woman has been answered. That she can do this, that it is worth doing. That she has not been deluded or stupid or wrong.

As she is unbuttoning her costume, her phone vibrates and she sees a message from Nathan.

*I'm here.*

She stares at it, then up at herself in the mirror. She sees her outline there – Yelena's dress for the final act: a long dark coat, the buttons fastening all the way to the neck, her hair pinned up. She sees the way her lips are swollen, the slant of her eyes, her chest moving up and down with her breath. She does not reply to the message; she knows he will wait.

She finishes unbuttoning her costume and slips out of it, hanging it up on the rail, then goes to the sink and splashes water on her neck. She pulls on her jeans and her top. Her make-up she leaves as it is – slightly smudged around her eyes. When she takes her hair out of its clips it falls in waves down her back.

*Mermaid's blood in your veins.*

She picks up her bag and makes her way out into the bar. Nathan is alone at a table in the corner. She approaches him slowly. He stands before she can speak. His face is a mixture of nervousness and awe.

He is wearing a blue shirt with the sleeves rolled up. She notices this. She notices his forearms. The way his hand moves to his chest as he speaks, referencing his heart. The way his shirt is open at the neck.

She bends her head – she is a queen tonight, and she accepts his tribute. As she sits before him she can feel herself, the parts where her skin touches her clothes, the hardness of her nipples, the tingling of her skull. There is an open bottle of wine on the table and he lifts it, pours her a large glass, and she nods her thanks. Behind the curve of his shoulder she sees Johnny standing alone at the bar, two drinks before him. He looks towards her; she sees his eyes slide over her and Nathan, then back to her, snagging on her with a question. She does not answer it – instead she turns away, to her drink, which is thick and red and looks like blood.

She sees the pulse at Nathan's neck. His mouth, stained a little with the wine. The span of his hands on the table before her.

She drinks her wine and he drinks his and they speak but she is not sure, exactly, of what. When her glass is empty he asks if she wants more. At a certain point the bottle is finished. She looks up and sees that Johnny has left the bar without saying goodbye. She registers this, but distantly. 'We could go back,' she says, turning to Nathan. 'We could go back to mine.'

And like everything else this night, it is surprisingly easy to say.

On the way he makes conversation, but as the train nears her stop the words dwindle and he falls silent. She catches him staring at his face in the window. They walk quickly, without speaking, across the park. In her living room, she paces around, switching on lights, while Nathan stands in the middle of the floor. 'Do you want another drink?' she asks.

'OK.' His voice is low and a little cracked.

She goes into the kitchen, where she leaves the lights off. There is a bottle of whisky at the back of her cupboard and she takes it out, pours a measure into two glasses.

There is a sound behind her and she sees that Nathan has followed, is standing behind her. He lifts her hair from her neck and holds it in his fist. He leans towards her and she feels his mouth at the place where her neck meets her shoulder. Then he presses her gently against the wall. 'Please,' he says, 'don't speak.'

She does not speak. Instead she turns to him and opens her mouth to his.


The next morning, when he has gone to work, she lies in bed and thinks of him. She can feel him still: his weight on her, the look on his face when she was above him, the feeling of him inside her. At the memory she is queasy with desire again, and when she puts her hand to herself she is flooded, swollen, slick with sex.

She goes out for coffee and sits in the weak sunshine, cradling her cup. She knows it is not wise to be out here, feeling this way, only streets from Hannah's flat. She knows the scent of him is still on her, knows she is drenched in it. Men stare at her. She is a battery that has been charged again. It is simple electricity – it is outside of morality. There is a dangerous, shimmering elation to the way she feels.

## Hannah

She begins to sleep in the little room. The sounds here are different from those she has been used to – she can hear the wind in the trees, the sounds of the canal: bikes clunking over loose paving stones, the mangled yowl of foxes, the shouts and laughter of drunken kids. She lies awake, staring at the play of light on the ceiling, and if she sleeps, she sleeps lightly and her dreams are full of strange, unknowable things.

In the mornings, for a few moments she is disoriented, lying here in this bed alone, and then she remembers – Nathan has gone, her husband has gone, and for the first time in over thirteen years she does not know where he is.

Outside, the winter city presses on her and she feels flimsy beneath its weight. She forgets to shop and eats little, small mouthfuls of food she has in the cupboards: crackers and butter, a slice of apple. There is no joy in cooking for herself. She is getting thinner. She knows this but does not care; there is nothing to take care of herself for, no future to safeguard, no limits to keep within.

She gets a text from her brother. *She's here! Rosie Eleanor*

*Grey.* A picture of a small wrinkled bundle of humanity held in her brother's arms. Her niece.

She writes back. *Congratulations!! Can't wait to meet her.*

*You're still coming for Christmas?* her brother replies.

*Yes! Can't wait!* she lies.

The next morning she writes to work and says she is ill – a virus, that she needs to rest. The weather has changed again, grown bitter and cold. She puts on the radio, but does not really listen to it. She moves slowly through this place that has all the hallmarks of her previous life – the same rooms, the same furniture, the same books on the same shelves – but is utterly foreign. She has arrived at a destination, but it is an unknown place. She is aware that she hurts, but that the hurt is so large it is beyond her. There is no solace outside, in the sky, the grass, the animals and the trees. She is not like them. She cannot multiply herself – she is aberrant, outside of nature, and she knows it is better for her to be up here, alone.

Sometimes there are children in the park below. From this distance they are small packets of energy, jerky and joyous and untrained. They ride scooters along the paths. They trail after their parents and stop and pick up stones and look at them. She watches the children look at the stones and their parents, more often than not hurrying back to them, grasping them by the wrist and hauling them to their feet. If she had a child, she thinks, she would not rush and pull, she would get down on the earth, she would get down beside them and look at the stones.


Outside the world marches on, and Christmas looms with all its gaudy inevitability. She has said she will go up north, to

Jim and Hayley's, but now she would like to refuse the invitation to her brother's house. But she has given her word, and there are presents to be bought: her parents, Jim, Hayley, Rosie. After work she walks towards Covent Garden, weaving past the tourists, the carol singers, everyone buttoned up against the cold, but she does not buy presents. Instead, she wanders into clothes shops, trying on things she would usually never wear: an ankle-length dress covered with a print of crawling vines, earrings that graze her shoulders, high-heeled boots the colour of blood. Her reflection surprises her – her fringe falling into her eyes the way it does. It is months since she has had it trimmed. Perhaps, she thinks, she will grow her hair long. Perhaps she will shave it all off.

One freezing afternoon, on Long Acre, her eye is caught by a child in a pushchair – a little girl. The child is grinning and giggling, clapping her hands. The buggy stops and Hannah looks up. The woman pushing the child is staring at her, her head on one side.

'I'm sorry,' says Hannah.

'What for?' says the woman. There is something crow-like about her, something unsettling about her gaze.

Hannah pushes her hands into her pockets. 'I just—' The child is chattering to herself, absorbed by her reflection in the shop window beside her. She has cheeks like a child in a picture book. Her hands are large and dimpled and strong.

'Do you need healing?' says the woman.

'Sorry?' Hannah's eyes switch back.

'Do you need healing?' the woman says again. 'Perhaps I can help?'

The woman reaches into the back of her buggy and pulls a printed piece of paper from a small stack. 'Here,' she says, holding the leaflet out. 'Take it.' Her tone is surprisingly brusque.

Hannah obeys, reaching out and taking it, folding it in half.

The woman nods and then, as though it is absolutely in her power, this holding and releasing of the gaze, she looks ahead and walks on.

At the entrance to the Tube Hannah finds she is breathless, as though she has been running. She pulls the paper from her pocket, sees an ordinary-looking flyer – something mocked up on a PC at home. It advertises the healing powers of Lindsay McCormack. There is a photo of Lindsay's sallow face in troubling close-up, and an address, somewhere in the outer reaches of West London. She pushes it to the bottom of her bag. Later, though, back at home, she pulls it out again and gazes upon it in the light of the lamp in the small room – blurred pictures of female forms and trees, text in coloured lettering that is difficult to read. A testimonial from a man who was in chronic pain who feels much better now. All of it badly done, nothing in the least bit compelling about any of it.

And yet.

She picks up her phone, calls the landline number. It is answered quickly. 'Hello?'

'Oh – hello. I saw you. Today. In Covent Garden. You gave me a flyer.'

'Yes?' The woman sounds harassed, and there is the noise of a crying child in the background. 'Yes, I remember.'

'I wondered if you had any space.'

'Space?'

'To see me, I mean.'

'Ah,' the woman says. 'Yes. How about tomorrow morning?'

She tells work she has a dentist appointment – an emergency filling – and then, just after rush hour, takes the Tube out west to the end of the line.

The address is deep in a warren of houses, an ungainly semi with a muddy patch of front garden. A trike rusts on the step, its trailing purple decorations soaked with rain. Hannah rings the doorbell and peers through the frosted glass. At first there is no sound, no movement, and she thinks she may have the wrong house – then the woman comes to the door. She is bundled in a cardigan the colour of porridge, her hair pulled back into a scruffy bun.

'Come in.' She leads Hannah through a dark hallway to a small back room with a table and two blankets. 'Hop up.' The woman pats the table.

The room is chilly, uninviting. 'Would you mind,' says Hannah, standing in the doorway, 'if I visited the loo?'

A flicker of irritation crosses the woman's face. 'It's just out the door on the right.'

Hannah locks herself in the toilet and stares at her reflection in the mirror. Her cheeks are flushed, but her lips are pale and set in a tight line. What is she doing here? She has a strange, uneasy sense that she has been summoned here, or that she has summoned the woman from the depths of her subconscious mind – that this woman holds some unearthly power, that if she goes back into that cold room, she might never come out again, might never leave this cheerless place. She uses the toilet, flushes, and washes her hands with the small hard sliver of soap. In the hallway she hesitates – there is still time to run.

But the woman is waiting. She holds out her hands for Hannah's coat, which she hangs on the back of the door. 'Hop up then,' she says again, gesturing to the table.

Hannah slips off her shoes and complies. It is cold. Should she tell her how cold it is in here? The woman is wrapped up in her cardigan, but Hannah is only wearing her work dress. She pulls the blanket around her knees. It crackles and sticks to her tights.

'So,' says the woman, her head on one side. 'What brings you here?'

Hannah's lips are dry. She licks them. 'It was strange. For you to approach me – and – and – this is unlike me, very unlike me, but I just felt compelled to call.'

The woman nods. 'I sensed it,' she says.

'Sensed what?' says Hannah.

'Your need.'

'Need for what?'

The woman pauses, shifts in her seat. 'A child.'

'Ah,' says Hannah, and then falls silent, her skin prickling with anticipation, with fear.

'Tell me,' the woman says.

'I – we've been trying. For a long time. For three years, and nothing. And then we started IVF. And I got pregnant. And lost the baby. And then we tried again. The IVF. And now my husband has left.'

The woman nods, as though none of this surprises her.

'Sometimes,' says Hannah, 'I feel cursed. I don't know why I should be cursed.' She is babbling now, gibberish. 'I try and be good.' The woman is staring. Hannah is silent a moment, then, 'It's cold,' she says.

The woman gets up and turns the radiator dial a notch. 'I have the heating off in the day.'

'Don't you heat it up? When you have clients? Patients?'

'They usually like the blankets,' the woman says.

'Oh.'

'Would you like another?'

She looks down at the shiny, unpleasant blanket over her knees. 'No. Thanks.'

The woman rolls up her sleeve. She takes Hannah's calves in her hands. Her palms are not warm. 'All right,' she says. 'I'm going to work on you now.'

'Work on me?'

'Just lean back and relax.'

The woman's eyes begin to roll back in her head. She nods to herself, as though her suspicions are confirmed by the feel of Hannah's feet, her calves. The woman's eyes are closed now; she seems to be listening.

'Mmmmm. Mmmmm.' The woman is making a low humming sound. 'Mmmmm. Mmmm. Mmmm.'

Hannah looks out of the window at the dreary little garden.

'Am I cursed?' she says to the woman. 'Can you tell me if I'm cursed?'

But she is not sure if she has spoken or not, if she has uttered or only thought the words.

## Lissa

On the last night the cast club together and buy salmon and dill and cream cheese and crackers and vodka, and one by one, when their final scenes have finished, they go into the men's dressing room and down shots – *Nostrovia!* By the time of the curtain call they are all tipsy, and when the final curtain has been taken they pile back into the dressing room, all of them in their costumes still, making Johnny and Helen – the last of them left on stage – drink three shots each to catch up.

Klara comes and finds them, hugging them all in turn. The technical staff drink beer and cider while the actors sink more vodka, singing their Russian song over and over again – until even the technical staff join in. Someone puts on dance music, and the dressing room becomes a shebeen as the noise level increases to a roar.

Lissa checks her phone. She has had only one message from Nathan since Thursday.

*No regrets.*

At first she read it as a question, but then realized it was a statement, and replied: *None.*

The music has changed – Greg has got hold of the stereo and is playing old dance tunes from the 1930s – and the actors have coupled up to turn each other around the floor.

'Lissa.' Johnny is before her, hand outstretched. 'Would you like to dance?'

She takes his hand and he pulls her to her feet. She is drunk, she realizes, and she leans on him for balance as he moves her around the room. She closes her eyes briefly, enjoying his proximity, his warmth, his smell of tobacco and soap.

'I'm sorry,' she says into his chest.

'What for?'

'The other night. Standing you up at the bar.'

'S'all right.' Johnny's voice rumbles against her ear. 'He your boyfriend then?'

She gives a gesture, part shrug, part shake of the head. 'It's complicated.'

'Ain't that always the truth.'

They stop moving and he steps back a moment, holding her at arm's length, regarding her. He reaches out and tucks a piece of her hair behind her ear. 'It's been a pleasure, love. Here.' He takes out a piece of paper, scribbles a number on it. 'Just so you've got it,' he says, handing it to her. 'Look after yourself, won't you?'

'I'll try.'

'None of my business,' he says quietly. 'I know.'

Then he lifts her hand in that same courtly gesture, his lips to her knuckles, and turns away. She watches as he slings his black leather bag over his shoulder and slips out of the door without any elaborate goodbyes.

On the other side of the room, Michael and Helen are kissing, their hands in each other's hair. Lissa checks her phone again. The sand is running out – soon the magic will dissipate and the play will truly be over. Soon the night will end and there will be nothing but the flat and the call centre, and she will no longer be a queen.

*Mermaid's blood.*

She lets herself out of the dressing room, walks down the darkened corridor. After a few steps she stops and calls Nathan. He picks up on the second ring. 'Liss?' Wherever he is, it sounds quiet.

'I want you,' she says. 'Can you come here? Now?'

There is a pause and then: 'Where are you?'

'At the theatre.'

'How long will you be there for?'

'An hour. Maybe more.'

'I'll come.'

She clicks off the phone, holds it lightly in her palm. Hears her breath in the corridor. It is as though she has taken half a step outside her skin, to a place where things are weightless, where there is only the logic of desire. She feels no guilt, only interest. She wonders if it would be this easy to murder.

At half past eleven, her phone buzzes in her pocket and she slips out of the room without being seen, making her way through the bar, where the bar staff are clearing up, to where Nathan is standing waiting outside on the street, hunched into his winter coat, smoking a cigarette, smoke pluming in the cold air. It has started to snow, and flakes tumble from the sky. Already an inch or two has gathered on the pavement.

She steps towards him, reaching and taking his cigarette from him, bringing it to her mouth. The smoke hits her bloodstream, mingling with the alcohol, meeting the cold, making her reel.

'You're her still,' he says.

She looks down at herself – her velvet coat, her boots. She had forgotten she was wearing her costume. 'Yes,' she says, and she can see how this pleases him – how it excites him. 'Yes, I'm still her.'

He takes her wrist and pulls her to him. His mouth tastes of smoke. She can feel him against her, already hard. 'Where can we go?' he says.

'Here,' she says. 'You can come in here.'

She leads him back through the bar to the dark corridor to the women's dressing room, which is empty, the lights turned off. Soon the women will be back, changing from their costumes, moving out into the night, but for now they are occupied – she can hear the party continuing, the men Cossack dancing; she can hear the thump, thump of their heels on the floor.

She sits on the table and lifts her long, heavy skirts, feels the cool air on her thighs. Nathan bends towards her, and puts his mouth on her flesh. There is the cold shock of his cheek, the warmth of his mouth, his tongue. When he stands before her, she opens herself for him, and he spreads her wide.

# Hens

## 2008

*Hannah is getting married. She does not want a hen do. Instead, she wants to go on holiday with Lissa and Cate. Since she is getting married in May, she decides Greece would be perfect in late April. She clears the dates with the others and spends hours searching for a place to stay – finally booking them a villa for a week on one of the islands, close to the beach with its own pool. It is expensive, but not hideously so. She has recently had a promotion at work – since she knows neither of her friends is earning much, she does not ask them for any money towards the cost. And she gets a thrill from this, from treating her friends, her best friends, her best women, Lissa and Cate.*

*They have fun in the airport. They try different perfumes and sunglasses. They drink champagne at the champagne bar. They make jokes about the gaudy horror show of late capitalism but they enjoy it really. They are so busy enjoying it that they almost miss their flight.*

*The villa is beautiful. They each have their own room, their own bathroom. The towels are thick and the thread count is high. Hannah takes pleasure from watching her friends squeal like young girls as they run around the tiled floors, opening cupboards, finding chocolates and wine and fruit. They are all implausibly touched that the owners have left them a bottle of cheap wine. They drink the cheap wine from the bottle and they put on their swimming gear and jump into the pool.*

*They sleep late. They eat long breakfasts of yoghurt and honey and nuts and toasted white bread and strong coffee. They angle their chairs towards the sun. It is twenty-two degrees at ten o'clock. By noon it is twenty-five. There are wild flowers everywhere. They agree this is the perfect time of year to visit Greece.*

*In the afternoons they go to the beach, a short walk along a rocky path that is fragrant with thyme. They take books and rent loungers and swim in the blue sea.*

*They put cream on each other's backs, exclaiming gently over the softness of each other's skin. They eat lunch at beach tavernas which are knocked together with driftwood and serve inevitable but delicious Greek salad peppered with oregano. They drink sharp retsina served in small glass jugs, misted with condensation in the heat.*

*In the evenings they go out to restaurants. They try several and then settle on one they like and go there every night – a small pretty place with tables overlooking the harbour. They dress carefully for these outings, even though the restaurants are only village tavernas – they wear dresses and put on make-up, they thread earrings in their ears.*

*They grow peaceful on this holiday. They go to bed early. They soak up the sun. They remember how well they live together. It does them all good to get away.*

*But as the week comes to a close, happiness grows gritty and begins to chafe. Lissa thinks of the call centre, realizes she has forgotten to book shifts for the week of her return. Which means she will not have enough for her rent. Which means she* will have to ask Declan again. And Declan is growing tired of these requests, she knows. Just as he is growing tired of her.

On the final morning, Lissa regards herself in the mirror in the early-morning sun. She knows she is beautiful, has always known this, but now, in her thirties, this beauty that once was something abundant, something she threw away on cigarettes and alcohol and late nights and coffee and no real exercise to speak of, lately this beauty has come to seem a finite resource, one she must attend to, take better care of. And this care, it would appear, takes money, money she does not have. More than once, lately, she has come to find herself standing at the counter in Boots or Selfridges or Liberty's holding an expensive face cream in her hand. More than once she has considered slipping the expensive face cream into her bag.

Last week, her agent dropped her.

These chances, Lissa, her agent told her on the phone, they come along once in a blue moon for people your age. I'm sorry. I just don't think I can represent you any more.

In the mirror, Lissa's mouth is set in a straight, tight line. She is angry. Angry with Cate. Cannot help but blame her for what occurred. And angry too – though she knows this is unfair – with Hannah, all this generosity, this villa, this holiday. She wishes it were her, able to be generous, able to treat her friends. But Hannah is good. Hannah is dutiful. Hannah works hard, and so is justly rewarded. Whereas she is broke. Perhaps it is her beauty that is to blame. Her beauty, this unasked-for gift. Perhaps it has warped her – made her lazy. Made her expect too much.

Last week, before coming out here, she bought a dress in Liberty's, on her credit card, a wrap in silk crêpe de Chine. It has a print of Japanese flowers. She has brought it out here but she knows she won't wear it. It stays at the bottom of her suitcase. It is the outfit of someone who has achieved things she has not. Who is living a life she is beginning to expect is not destined for her.

On the last evening of the holiday, Lissa insists they go for cocktails. There is a little bar she has seen tucked down an alleyway. They all go out to the bar and drink Kir Royales and champagne cocktails in its dark interior. They have three cocktails each but they do not feel drunk, just merry, as they make their way down the cobbled streets to the harbour and to their restaurant. It is their restaurant now. They order wine and drink it quickly, and then have more. They eat bread dipped in olive oil and salt, and drink more wine. They start to feel drunk.

So, says Lissa, lighting a cigarette. What happens next? She is speaking to Hannah.

What do you mean?

Well, after you get married. You going to have kids?

I suppose so, says Hannah. Yes.

Does Nathan want them?

Yes. I think so.

You think so?

Yes, says Hannah. He does.

Right. Lissa nods.

What? says Hannah.

Nothing, says Lissa.

What? Why are you making that face?

I just, it's quite a big deal, isn't it? Having kids. Don't you think you ought to think about it a bit more than that?

*I have thought about it, actually. I've thought about it a lot. And I want children. What about you? Do you want kids?*

*No.*

*No? Just no?*

*Yeah.*

*Don't you think you ought to examine that a bit more? What if you regret it?*

*Sure, says Lissa, blowing the smoke of her cigarette out into the evening air. I'll examine it. I don't want kids because I think you should really, really want kids to have them. And if you want to do anything else in your life, then maybe you should do that instead. I saw enough of that with my mother.*

*What do you mean? says Hannah.*

*I was in the way. Of all of it: her art, her life. Her fucking* activism. *She should never have had me. Everyone would have been a lot better off.*

*Oh, for God's sake, says Hannah. Don't be ridiculous. Your mother is amazing.*

*Is she? says Lissa. Of course. Of course she is, Hannah, and you would know. Since you know my mother so well.*

*Hannah stares at her friend. She has rarely seen this side of Lissa before. This drunken curdling. This bitterness.*

*Leave it, Lissa. Cate leans in. Give Hannah a break.*

*Oh? Give Hannah a break? Lissa turns to Cate, her teeth bloody with wine. What about me? What about giving me a break, Cate? Cate the moral compass. Showing us all the way. You think you're so fucking squeaky clean? Whose fault is it that I didn't get that part?*

*Not mine, says Cate.*

*Fuck you, Lissa spits.*

*Hannah watches Cate reel back as though she has been hit.*

*Then – I'll tell you why you don't want children, Lissa, says Cate, leaning back into the fray. Because you're fundamentally selfish. Because you're never going to want to put another person before yourself.*

*They have never argued before, Cate and Lissa. Not like this. It is exhilarating. With the wine and the cigarettes and the balmy spring night, it is like a drug. They want more. They could imagine brawling in the street. Tearing each other's hair out. Taking bites out of each other's skin.*

*Hannah watches them. There is something erotic, she thinks, in their arguing. She feels strangely bereft.*

*People look towards their table. These three English women with their quirky clothes and their loud voices and their empty bottles of wine. How rude they are. How incontinent they all seem.*

## Cate

Since the dinner Sam has refused to meet her eye. He is asleep in the mornings, waking late and hurrying out of the house to work, then stays out later and later after his shifts. Still, she is often awake herself when he comes in at one, two, three o'clock. She does not go to him.

She has called Hannah but Hannah has not picked up. She has sent her messages – *Can we talk? Call me when you're ready. Han, we need to talk, call me. Please.* Hannah has not replied.

She remembers Hannah's face on the bridge. The cold, clipped way she spoke. The razor-sharp edges of her hurt.

She wants to say sorry, but she wants to say, too, that it is not fair. That Hannah did not tell her – did not give her the chance to do the right thing.

The only person she has heard from is Dea.

*Emergency Mum Club? Whenever you're ready. Just say the word.*

She has not written back.

The days are short and bitter and she stays inside, the heating on too high. Tom is fractious, picking up on her lack of ease, and her patience with him is thin and frayed. She shouts at him often and often he cries. And then she shouts some more. When she does go out, the pavements are icy and treacherous. There are carol singers raising their reedy voices to the spires in the centre of town. They are selling Christmas trees in the garages of Wincheap – trussed in plastic. The students are still in the Senate building. The wet black branches of the trees.

At the weekend Sam rises early and dresses Tom himself. They come in to where she lies in bed, Tom dressed haphazardly in an ill-fitting jumper which barely covers his belly. 'We're going out,' he says.

'Where?'

'Mark and Tamsin's. Mum'll be there.'

'Right,' she says. 'I don't suppose I'm welcome then.'

'No, I don't suppose you are.'

When they have gone she takes out her computer. Checks her emails. Searches again for Lucy Skein. Nothing.

She leaves the curtains drawn and burrows back into bed.

The sound of the front door wakes her in the late afternoon. She pulls on tracksuit bottoms and a sweater, makes her way downstairs, sees Tom asleep in his buggy in the hallway, finds Sam in the kitchen, sitting at the table, a small zippered bag in front of him.

'Are you leaving?'

'You should be so lucky. They're from Tamsin. For Tom. Jack outgrew them.'

Cate unzips the bag. A pile of clothes, neatly folded. They smell aggressively clean. 'That was nice of her.'

'Yeah, well. She's pretty nice. But you could always give them back. I mean, we wouldn't want too much of my family. Contaminating the air.'

'Sam—'

He holds up his hand. 'Wait,' he says. He leaves her, goes upstairs. She hears his footsteps above her head. When he comes back down he has the prescription bag in his hands. 'What are these?'

'They're pills,' she says flatly. 'Anti-depressants.'

'And are you taking them?'

'No.'

'Don't you think you might need to?'

'No. Yes. I don't know.' She shakes her head. 'I'm sorry,' she says.

'For what? For marrying me? For saying I'm not that bright?' His face is twisted.

'I just – I think I've been confused.'

'About what?'

'Me. You. Everything.' She looks at the floor. 'There's someone—'

'Someone else?'

'Not like that.'

'Like what then? Like what?' He bangs the table in front of him. 'Come on, Cate. You might as well tell me now.'

Behind her in the hall, Tom stirs, grizzles, then is quiet again.

'Someone I used to know,' she says. 'A long time ago. I've been thinking about her. A lot. That's all.'

Sam nods. 'OK. A woman?'

'Yes.'

'So, what, you're gay now?'

'No. I mean . . . I was. I wasn't. It was just her. Just Lucy. I just loved her.'

He looks at her for a long time. 'OK,' he says. 'When was this?'

'Eleven years ago.'

'And where is she now?'

'I don't know.'

'But you want to?'

'I don't know.'

He looks at her for a long time, then nods, as though something has been decided. Then he stands, takes a can of Red Bull from the fridge. 'I'm late for work,' he says. 'I'll see you later tonight.'

The next afternoon, when Sam comes home she is screaming at their son. Tom is wailing, some half-eaten food on his high chair, the rest on the floor. 'I'm calling Mum,' he says, going to pick up Tom. 'She can take him for the day tomorrow.'

Alice arrives with Terry the next morning, and Cate hands Tom over. It is a cold clear day, the sun low in the sky. They exchange few words. She thinks she can see the relief on her son's face. When they have gone, she closes the door and cries. When the crying has stopped she goes upstairs to the bathroom, pulls out the bag of pills, and sits on the floor of the bathroom with them between her legs. In her pocket her phone rings. Dea. It rings and rings, then stops. The buzz of a message is loud in the silence of the house. She lifts the phone and listens.

*I've got a bonfire needs tending. What are you doing right now?*

238

Cate lifts her head to the window, sees the thin sun, calls back.

The allotment is surprisingly close, just on the other side of the river. There are a couple of other figures dotted there, bent to the cold earth, but she sees Dea immediately, standing alone on a plot halfway down. A small fire going, a pile of bracken and leaves beside it.

'Wow,' says Dea as Cate approaches. 'You look terrible.'

Dea is dressed in faded canvas dungarees, a parka, her beanie on her head, and a large mug in her hands.

'Thanks.'

'Is this still the aftermath of the other night?'

Cate shrugs. A couple of old camp chairs sit around the fire. At the back of the plot stands a rickety-looking shed with potted marigolds in front of the door.

'This is nice.'

'Yeah, well, I like to keep my end up.' Dea looks down at herself. 'Lesbian allotment-holder. Dungarees. I'm ticking a lot of boxes right now.'

Cate raises the ghost of a smile. 'Where's Nora?'

'With Zoe. Her family are over already for Christmas. They're great, but they're loud. And the house is small. Where's Tom?'

'With Alice.'

'Well,' says Dea, raising her mug. 'It was a great dinner party. Thanks.'

'Please.'

'No, really, it's the most excitement I've had for a while. I particularly liked the line about the breaking soldiers.' Dea raises her mug. 'And that guy Mark. I liked seeing you stick it to him.'

'I'm glad you had a good time.'

'You want a tea?'

'Sure.'

'Chuck some brambles on the fire,' Dea calls as she heads to the shed. 'They're extremely satisfying to burn.'

Cate eyes the pile, then goes and lifts a prickly armful, throws them on the flames, watching them twist and buckle in the heat. Dea comes back out with a mug of tea. 'Lemon balm,' she says, handing it over.

'Thanks.'

'The food was great, though. He's a talented man, your husband. You were right.'

'Can we stop talking about it now?'

'Sure.'

Cate sips her tea, which is green and gently fragrant, and stares into the flames. There is the sweet smell of woodsmoke. Gulls calling in the high thin sky.

'I went up to the Senate building today,' says Dea. 'To check in on the students. They've turned off the heating in there. The university authorities.' She shakes her head. 'It's barbaric. I took them a couple of blankets. They're asking for more.'

'They should come out,' says Cate sullenly.

'Oh?' says Dea. 'Why's that?'

'What are they going to change? What does anyone ever change?'

Dea looks at her.

'You know how it is.' Cate shrugs. 'Young people become older people. They'll compromise. That's what we do. We stop fighting. We capitulate. We become part of the problem.'

'Right.'

'The vote's over. The Tories have won. If the students are cold, they should go home. See their parents. Have Christmas. Get warm. Don't you think?'

'No,' says Dea. 'I'm not sure I do. I'm not sure you do either.'

She goes over to the pile of bracken, taking an armful of brambles and feeding them to the fire, regarding Cate through the flames.

'Have you compromised then?' she says. 'Is that what's going on?'

When Cate does not reply, Dea crouches to poke the fire with a stick, rearranging it, raking the burning embers. 'I meant to tell you,' she says, after a while. 'There's a job going. At the university. It's just maternity cover, but I thought of you.'

'What sort of job?'

'Outreach – all over Kent. Going into schools, helping kids get into higher education. We've got some of the poorest areas in Britain on our doorstep – Sheppey, Medway. I'm sure it would suit you. It could be quite creative, if you gave it some thought.'

'Right. So poor kids can go to university and be thousands of pounds in debt when they finish?'

'What would you rather? That they didn't go at all?'

Cate is silent.

'Anyway, they're interviewing early in the New Year – they want someone to start in the spring.'

Cate turns back to the fire. 'Who are you? My careers advisor?'

'No,' says Dea, throwing a stick into the flames. 'Just a friend.'

## Hannah

In the car on the way to Jim and Hayley's, she sits in the back seat, behind her mother, her head leaning against the window as the edges of the city give way to villages and then the villages to moorland, to dry-stone walls, all of it with a thick covering of snow. Every so often, her father brakes for a grouse or a sheep in the road.

Her dad sings tunelessly, happily, to the radio, banging the steering wheel to the beat, while her mother chuckles and tuts and shakes her head. They are excited, on their way to visit their son, their granddaughter: grandparents at last.

She always used to sit on this side, on family holidays – Jim to the right of her, this exact view of the back of her father's head. Often they would bicker. Once, she remembers, on the way to a campsite in Wales, her dad finally lost his temper and stopped the car, ordering them both out on to the grass verge. He pulled away and left them, and they were silent, horrified, for a full five minutes until he drove back around. Now her little brother is a father. Soon he will be driving on family holidays of his own.

They pull up outside a stone cottage on the edge of a village; it has thick walls and small windows. As they climb from the car Jim appears in the driveway to meet them. He is bigger than Hannah remembers – has put on weight – but it looks well on him. Somehow he manages to be everywhere at once – opening the door for their mum, carrying on a conversation with their father about Christmas traffic and the weather and enveloping Hannah in a hug. 'How are you doing, sis?'

His vowels. She always forgets how northern he is. She would like to shelter here, in his arms, in his vowels for a while. 'OK,' she says into his shoulder. 'I'm OK.'

He leads the way inside, carrying their luggage into a narrow hall, a Christmas tree in the corner. 'The bedrooms are all up there. You and Mum are first on the right,' he says to their father, 'and you're at the end, Han. But Hayley's up there napping with the baby.' He claps his hands together. 'Right then. Who's for a drink before they wake up?'

He serves them all – gin and tonic for their mum, a glass of wine for Hannah, and ale for their dad, and she sees how proud he is, her brother, how proud to be witnessed by them: householder, father, host.

Later, when they have been through the tour of the house, they sit in the living room, where peanuts and crackers wait in small bowls on the tables and a picture of Jim and Hayley's wedding hangs above the fireplace. Hannah and her parents sit, slightly stilted, slightly hushed, perched on the edge of sofas – an audience waiting for the main actor to take to the stage. There is the creak of the stairs and there she is, Hayley, standing in the doorway, plump with sleep, creamy-cheeked, a tiny parcel of humanity held in her arms. For a moment, no one moves; the tableau is too perfect: the soft-faced Madonna and child. Then: 'Oh.' Hannah's mother gets to her feet. Hannah watches as she sweeps the baby up from Hayley's arms, her face beatific, transformed. 'Rosie,' she breathes. 'My lovely little Rosie!'

Hannah stands, makes her way over to the group, and sees James's features on a tiny old woman's face peering out from beneath layers of blanket. 'Oh.' She stretches the tip of her finger to touch the baby's cheek. 'She's so lovely, Jim. She looks just like you.'

Soon the baby starts to cry, and Jim gets to his feet. 'You sit down, love,' he says to Hayley. 'I'll do the feed.'

He comes back from the kitchen with a tiny bottle for his tiny daughter. Hannah watches him take her, the care with which he lifts her, the love and absorption on his face as Rosie takes the bottle and feeds. They are all silent, watching, listening to the sounds of suckling.

'Never did that in my day,' says Hannah's father.

'Don't know what you're missing.' Jim looks up with a grin. 'The oxytocin. It's incredible.'

'Oxy what-what?' Their father beams.


She goes to bed when her parents do, at ten o'clock. On Christmas morning she wakes early, stands at the window and looks out at the snow-covered fields. The rise of the moor beyond. The baby is lovely. The house is lovely. Jim and Hayley are lovely. It is exhausting, how lovely they all are. She can feel their compassion, their concern whether this is all right for her: Hayley's gentle, almost apologetic movements with her daughter. Their eyes on her when she takes the baby for a cuddle. Their collective in-breath, hoping Rosie won't cry in her aunty's arms. No one has asked her about Nathan. Have they decided amongst themselves that they will not?

This house, with its thick stone walls, its low lintels, its view of the fields and the moor and the steel-grey sky, its family sleeping in the room next door, oppresses her. She does not want to be here. She imagines walking out, through the garden, on to the high, snow-flecked moor. The air would be pure and clean and scouring. She wants to be scoured.

But she would need boots and waterproofs – she has not packed the right clothes.

She wonders how quickly she can get away – whether she can take the train back to London on Boxing Day. She checks the services, but they are scant and expensive, and she already has a ticket for the twenty-seventh. Two more days then, two more days to bear.

She thinks of the books she read as a child – all those maiden aunts, the illustrations showing the glasses and whiskers and good humour and cheer. Always in chairs. Always in the corner. She used to be in the centre of things. She is an edge dweller now.

She is aware that there are different, competing Hannahs within her: the polite Hannah, the good Hannah, Aunty Hannah! who is happy with the invitations to stay, who smiles and sits quietly, and parcels up her pain. And the bad Hannah, who is capable of poison, of madness – the one who wants to stand up, to upend the table, to take the baby and run away with her, to claim what should have been hers. To scream, *It should have been me.*

*It should have been me!*

*It should have fucking been me.*


## Lissa

The front door is hung with a homemade wreath; woven willow studded with mistletoe and holly, taken from the bush in the garden. Lissa lifts the knocker and lets it fall. Sarah answers the door in her apron and takes Lissa's face in hands that smell of turpentine and spices. 'Happy Christmas, darling.'

'And to you.'

Lissa has brought gifts: a mug, speckled with a brown glaze like freckles, two beautiful new pencils and a vase to keep them in. Sarah coos and smiles and is pleased. Lissa opens her gift from her mother: a scarf, hand-knitted in fine green wool. 'It's beautiful, Mum,' she says. And it is.

Sarah has made food – seasonal but not traditional, something she excels at, that she invests with an almost moral purpose. When Lissa was small, she used to feel hard done by for the lack of tree – *a Victorian invention* – the absence of chocolate, of all the *tinselly baubley nonsense* her friends' homes were filled with. But now the times have caught up with Sarah, and each corner of the house contains something beautiful: leaves salvaged from walks on the Heath, a table decoration made from raffia and twine. Small glass bulbs are suspended over the table. Candles stand ready to be lit.

Lissa sits in the low armchair; Ruby pads over towards her and she lifts her on to her lap. They drink wine mulled with cloves and cinnamon and star anise. 'So tell me, any more meetings?' says Sarah from the stove.

'One. For Salisbury.'

'Oh darling, that's great. Any joy?'

'No.' Her agent had called her, apologetic. *You're just not quite what they were looking for.*

In truth, she had known the part was not hers as soon as she read the script: a blowsy blonde in an Ayckbourn comedy.

'I don't mind,' she says, stroking the cat. 'After *Vanya* it's hard to imagine doing something like that.'

Sarah brings over the soup, which is a vibrant orangey yellow – there are toasted cumin seeds and yoghurt to spoon on top. 'Squashes from the garden,' says Sarah.

They eat in companionable silence, until Sarah puts down her spoon. 'I wanted to say, darling. You were really wonderful in *Vanya*. I haven't seen you be better. There's a quality you have. A radiance. It's rare.' Her mother sounds surprised, as though it has occurred to her for the first time.

'Really?' Lissa looks up. 'Why do you say that?'

'What do you mean?'

'Why now?'

Sarah's brow creases. 'Because it occurred to me. Because it's true.'

'Oh.'

'Darling, I'm trying to be nice.'

'Trying?'

'Oh God, Lissa.' Sarah puts down her spoon. 'Don't.'

'Don't what?'

'Don't turn a compliment into its opposite.'

'I just think it's strange you choose to be complimentary about my choice of career now.'

'What do you mean? What's different about now?'

Lissa looks at the clock – she has been here for an hour. There is no one else: no brother, no sister, no father, no child. Only she and her mother, grinding away together like an unoiled axle.

'I'm seeing someone,' she says quietly, curling her spoon around the last of her soup.

'Oh?'

'Yes,' she says. 'Someone lovely.'

'Oh, darling. Oh. But that's *wonderful*.' Sarah leans forward. 'Who is he?'

'He's a . . . friend.'

'Anyone I know?'

'I don't think so.' Already she regrets speaking. Already she is somewhere dangerous. She did not mean to say this – she is a fool. 'He's someone I met . . . online.'

'Oh. Well, everyone meets there now, don't they? The internet.' Sarah waves her hand. She makes it sound like the village green. 'It would be stranger if you hadn't, in a way. So.' Sarah's face is hawk-like, hungry. 'Can't you tell me anything? Does he have a job? A name?'

'He's called – Daniel.'

'And what does he do?'

'He's an academic.'

Sarah's hands come together in an involuntary clap. 'Well. Well. You must bring him around,' she says, reaching over and gripping Lissa's hand. 'Bring him over for supper soon.'

'Yes,' says Lissa, as her mother stands and clears the plates. It has grown dark outside, and when Sarah comes back with plum pudding, she lights the candles on the table. They reflect the room through the dark, gleaming surface of the window, and Lissa sits there, in her borrowed robes, and she shines.

He comes to her flat on Boxing Day. It is sunny, and the snow has started to thaw. They undress quickly and do not speak.

248

She pulls herself on top of him and makes him stay still, watching him, moving very slowly. When she comes she cries out. And when he comes she leans down and takes his lip in hers and sucks it, feeling him judder and fall still.

'Melissa,' he says to her afterwards, his hand tracing the curve of her hip, 'of the Melissae. The guardians of the honey.'

She leans in and kisses him and it is true – with him her core is molten and sweet.

When the evening comes she finds she is ravenous, and he stays in the flat while she goes out to the Turkish shop and buys food: noodles and vegetables and beer.

She cooks for him – she is hungry: for food, for sex, for life, and this hunger is beautiful, voluptuous. They eat noodles and drink the cold beer and she watches him eat, loving to watch this man eating this food she has prepared for him, listening to the low, resonant hum of his voice. She reaches across for his wrist, catches it, kisses him there.

'Are you happy?' he asks her.

'Do you mean now? Or generally?'

'Both. Now.'

'Now, yes.'

'And generally?'

She shrugs. 'Is anyone? Are you?'

He looks at her. 'How come you don't have a lover?' he says.

'I do,' she says, watching the complexity of the emotions on his face.

'I mean – you know what I mean.'

'I don't know.' She pushes her plate away. Outside it is dark already. 'It's harder than it looks, finding a good man. So many are so disappointing.'

'That's sad.'

'It's true.'

'I always hated Declan,' he says.

'Yeah,' she sighs. 'He was a bastard. You were right.'

'I've boycotted his films on principle.'

She laughs.

'I'm loyal,' he says. And the way he says it makes her stomach contract.

'Thank you,' she says, although she knows he is not. For if he were, he wouldn't be here at all.

'You never wanted kids?' he says softly.

She looks up at the ceiling. 'Not with him.' She levels her gaze with his and she feels it – loosened, filling the room, leaving space for nothing else. If they were to go back to bed now, she knows, if they did not use protection, she knows in her body that she would conceive – that this is how children are made, this desire, this drenched desire.

'You could stay the night,' she says. 'No one would know.' She watches his face, sees the struggle there.

'It's worse,' he says.

'What do you mean?'

'For Hannah. Me staying. It feels – worse somehow.'

'Really?' she says. 'Worse than us fucking?'

He flinches.

'Hannah doesn't know,' she says softly. 'Hannah doesn't have to know.'

He looks down at his hands, then back up at her. 'Sure.' He leans to her, a clumsy kiss that lands on the side of her mouth. 'I'd love that.'

Outside, it is cold. Inside, the room glows, golden. Time is somewhere else. She could live here, she thinks, and – in this moment – she could love this man.

## Hannah

She is grateful to get home, back to the flat – grateful for these in-between days – between Christmas and New Year. The pendulum has stopped swinging, time has stalled and pooled, and she is here, held in the lees of the year. Still, she feels restless. There is something rising in her, some itch, some need.

She takes to buying wine. She drinks most evenings, one glass, then another. The sales are on and she goes back to the clothes shops in Covent Garden, where she buys the boots the colour of blood and the dress that is covered with creeping vines.

On New Year's Eve, she dresses for herself in the dress and the red boots, and puts on music and dances, turning slow circles in the room. She drinks red wine, one glass and then another, and then her eye falls on to a pouch of tobacco Nathan left. One cigarette. What would be the harm? She slides out the papers – black liquorice papers – and rolls herself a cigarette. She lights it from the stove, then steps outside on to the terrace, where the air is crisp and a handful of stars are visible in the high black sky. She brings the cigarette to her lips, and immediately the taste of sugar paper makes her think of Lissa.

And then, suddenly, the knowledge arrives – hitting her body before her mind. It spikes her blood, makes her heart race, her palms damp.

*Lissa.*

Nathan and Lissa.

She holds on to the terrace rail, then she throws the cigarette into the park below. She goes back into the flat, picks up her phone and calls Nathan.

'Lissa,' she says when he picks up.

'What?'

'What happened?' she says.

'What do you mean?'

'With you and Lissa?'

He hesitates a moment too long. She holds the phone away from her ear. Feels her stomach heave into her mouth. Hears his voice, speaking to the cold empty air.

## Cate

At New Year she gets an invitation from Dea for dinner, and accepts, since Sam will be working.

*We're going up to the Senate building first if you'd like to come?* Dea writes. *There are five students still holding on inside. I think they're freezing. There's a vigil for them at sunset. Bring a candle and something for them to eat.*

Cate brings some mince pies and wine, and takes Tom up the hill to the university, where Dea and Zoe and a small group of others are clustered round the Senate building, candles in their hands. They talk in low voices and pass food parcels in via the security guards. Afterwards they walk back down the hill to Dea and Zoe's for food.

'I downloaded the application form,' Cate tells Dea, as she helps her tidy up after the meal.

'Really?' says Dea. 'Glad to hear it. Are you going to fill it in?'

'Yeah,' says Cate. 'I suppose I am.'

At nine o'clock she straps Tom into the car seat and drives him home. She knows Sam is due to finish work at eleven. She goes over to her computer, prints out the form, and begins to fill it in. The time goes quickly, but half past eleven comes and she is tired, and Sam is not home so she puts on the television and wraps herself in a blanket with a cup of tea.

She is dozing when her phone rings, and she jumps awake to see Hannah's name on the screen.

'Han?' She snatches the phone to her ear. 'Hey! Happy New Year!'

It is a while before she can make out any words, because at first there is only weeping, weeping that sounds as though it has been happening for a long while already – thick, clotted, exhausted sobs. 'Hannah?' she says softly, waiting for her friend to find her voice.

'Lissa,' says Hannah eventually.

'What about her?'

'Lissa and Nathan.'

'What?'

'Together.'

'No,' says Cate, sitting up on the sofa, wide awake now. 'No, Han, that's impossible.'

'Don't tell me what's possible,' hisses Hannah. 'I know it's true.'

On the television people are singing together, 'Auld Lang Syne'. There are Scottish pipers in bearskins and serious faces. She mutes the sound. The room is dark, only the light of the screen. She is silent. A strange taste fills her mouth.

'Hannah,' she says. 'Is there anything I can do? Do you want to come here? Can I come to you? Are you in the flat? I can drive – I'll put Tom in the back and leave now.'

'No. No.'

'Is there anyone near by that can come and be with you?'

She almost says *Lissa* – Lissa who lives moments away – and stops herself in time.

'No,' says Hannah. 'Are you there? Will you stay there? I might – I might call again.'

'Of course, Han. I'm here.'

When the call is finished Cate stares, stunned, at the television screen, where people are holding hands and dancing. She is aware of several conflicting and equally powerful emotions – of shock and disbelief, and a strange sense of inevitability, the last of which makes no sense at all.

She is sitting in the same spot when Sam returns home two hours later. She has stayed awake, but Hannah has not called again. She watches him come in, take off his jacket and hang it on the peg with careful deliberation. He takes two beers out of the pockets of his coat. 'I got these, they were giving them out at work – you want one?'

'Sure.'

He opens them with his lighter and passes her one, coming to slump on the sofa beside her. He looks tired, she thinks, tired and drunk.

'I just spoke to Hannah.'

'Oh?' His eyes are unfocused.

'Nathan cheated on her.'

'What?' He looks at her, mouth agape, beer bottle halfway to his mouth. 'Who with?'

'Lissa.'

He sits forward. 'You're joking?'

'No. At least, Hannah's convinced of it.'

'Fucking hell.' He takes off his cap, runs his hands through his hair. For a moment he looks horrified, and then he starts to laugh. She stares at him, appalled, and then she starts laughing too. They put their hands over their mouths as though they might be overheard, as they shake and shake with strange twisted exhilaration, until, abruptly, they stop. Cate feels the guilt swilling around her body.

'Shit,' says Sam, shaking his head. 'Poor Hannah. Shit,' he says again.

Cate puts down her beer. 'Sam,' she says.

'What?'

'I'm sorry. I'm sorry about Mark.'

'Yeah, well. He probably deserved it. He's always been like that. Even when he was at school.'

'Will they forgive me?'

'It's not them you need to worry about,' he says. 'It's me.'

She goes over to him. 'Will you forgive me?' she says.

'That depends.'

She slides her hands into his palms. 'Can I kiss you?' she says.

He says nothing. She lifts her lips to his. He lets her, but does not respond. Then he turns his face away.

'I need to tell you something,' he says. 'I asked you to marry me because I fell for you. And I thought you felt the same. I'm not here to be your consolation prize, Cate. I want to be chosen. Not settled for.'

And he slides himself out of her hands, stands, and leaves her where she sits on the floor.

## Lissa

She lies in bed late on New Year's morning. She wears only a T-shirt and knickers. He is coming to see her – there is no need to get dressed.

She jumps up at his knock, but as soon as she opens the door she sees that something is wrong.

'She knows,' he says.

She puts her hand to her mouth.

'Come in.' She sees his hesitation. 'Come in,' she insists, taking him by the wrist.

He steps over the threshold into the kitchen, where he stands, his coat still on. She turns on the light, the ugly old electric ceiling light, and his face is pale beneath it. 'I said nothing,' she says.

'No. I didn't imagine you had.'

They fall silent, and the silence is painful and inert. She wants to fill it, with desire, with violence. She crosses towards him and takes his hand in hers. He looks down at her hand, then back up at her face. 'I'm sorry,' he says.

'What for?' She puts her hand over his eyes, tenderly, as though shielding them from the sun. She feels him close them – the eyelids flickering beneath her palm. She reaches behind her and turns off the light again. She moves her hand away gently, running her fingertips down his cheek, his neck. His eyes remain closed as she gets to her knees before him and begins to unbuckle his belt.

'What are you doing?' he says.

He is hard already when she takes him into her mouth,

and she holds him there for a moment. She moves her mouth against him and he pulls her up to standing, then he turns her around and pulls down her knickers and pushes himself into her, roughly, and she gasps in pain. He pulls out of her. He cups himself, pulls up his jeans, turns away from her. 'Sorry,' he says. 'I'm sorry.'

She turns around to him. He is still wearing his coat. It is a strange sight, him in his coat, cupping himself like that – she could almost laugh.

'It's OK,' she says, pulling her knickers back up. But it is not OK. Not really. Not at all. 'It's OK,' she says again.

He pulls up his jeans, buckles his belt. 'I'm going away,' he says. 'I'm going to go away for a couple of weeks. I need some space.'

'You need some space,' she repeats. Her voice sounds strange. She wants to cry, but she knows she has no right. She can feel it coming towards her, like a wave, a wave that will flatten her. And how afterwards there will be nothing left, nothing left to say what this was, how this felt. How no one will be interested in her version of events.

'I won't contact you,' she says.

He nods. 'I think it would be best.' He reaches out and his hand lands briefly, gently, on her cuff. He touches her as he might a child.

And she is furious now. And she sees that he wants it to be easy. He wants the water to cover this over, for the bubbles to rise to the surface and disappear, for the smooth surface to give no sign of what was underneath. 'It wasn't worth it,' she says.

'What?'

'The sex.'

She sees the shock on his face. He steps back into the room. And his expression has changed. It is needy now. Now she has hurt his ego. He wants something from her – she sees that, despite it all, he wants her to tell him it was good. That he was good. How pathetic, his need. How desperate the pair of them are.

'Lissa,' he says, holding out his hands in supplication.

'It wasn't worth it,' she says again. 'None of it.' And she gestures as she speaks, at herself, at him, at the sudden painful squalor of it all.


## Hannah

She dreams of violence, of Lissa's face lacerated with a thousand tiny cuts. Of holding Nathan's severed head, his blood soaking her lap. Sometimes the violence is chasing her and she is running from it across a wide open space. It is gaining on her and there is nowhere to hide – a dark presence, its long fingertips touch her neck.

At night, sleepless, she travels over the roofs to Lissa's house, to where she lies in her guilty bed. How does she sleep? Does she sleep?

Finally, she sleeps herself, and when she wakes, when the world assembles itself in the dawn light, she understands it is a new world – the old one blasted to shards – and that this new world is a place that operates by different physics, different laws. She imagines them together, her husband and her friend – their hands, their lips, their naked flesh, the parts where their flesh has met. The secret, beloved places on his body that she had come to think she owned. How did he touch her? Was it animal and nothing more? Or was it, is it, more?

She may not ever know. And this fact – the knowledge of his subjectivity, these experiences of his to which she will never have access – feels more violent, somehow, than the betrayal itself. What she feels when she thinks of this is beyond pain; it is close to delirium – colours seem brighter, sounds louder. Many, many times she lifts her phone, or goes to her computer – to curse him, to accuse her – but each time she turns away, puts down the phone; for what words could she find that would encompass this?

She avoids the park, no longer walks down the market. She walks to the bus stop and then back, that is all. She makes sure there is little chance of seeing Lissa in the street. Still, she thinks she sees her often – a tall fair frame ghosting at the edge of sight.


Winter turns, becomes spring. It stays cold. She has annual leave to spend. Two weeks of it. She has no real idea of where to go.

She clicks through pictures of cottages, of white-sand Scottish beaches, of lochs that look deep enough to drown a city in. Of places where she knows no one, and people are few. She is hungry for something that she cannot quite name – some elemental nourishment, something wild. She wants to taste salt water. Be scoured. Feel wind and weather on her skin.

One day, riding the Tube home from work, she sees a poster for Orkney. Sea and wide skies and wildlife. She goes home, and within minutes has booked planes, and a hotel and a car. She will go in March.

At night she dreams of running fast across open country. She wakes breathing quickly, the room altered, the silhouette of the tree's branches thrown starkly on to the wall.

# Epithalamium

## 2008

*It is Saturday, which is market day. It is late spring, or early summer. It is May, and the dog roses are in bloom in the tangled garden at the front of the house.*

*They take turns in the shower, Lissa and Cate, then dress quietly in their rooms. It is cool and overcast, but the forecast for later in the day is good.*

*As Lissa dresses she thinks of Nathan. Her friend. She knew him first. And she has always suspected that all those years ago, when they met again after university, had she been more available, he might have wanted to be with her. Would he have been hers now? Somehow, today of all days, she wants him to notice her, notice her beauty. She would not admit it to herself, but she wants to outshine Hannah, she wants to be seen. So she cuts the tags off the silk dress from Liberty's which she definitely cannot afford, and slips it on. She outlines her eyes in green kohl. She wears heels that make her over six feet tall.*

*Over in her morning flat, Hannah dresses. Her mother and father are with her. Nathan has spent the night away, at his brother's house. Her mother knocks on the door to come in.*

*Oh, Hannah, she says, when she sees her daughter in her dress. Oh, Han.*

\*

They stand waiting in the largest of the municipal rooms in the registry office. It is, they all agree, for a couple like Hannah and Nathan, the best possible place to get married – its very utilitarian nature invests it with a sort of magic.

Nathan waits at the head of the room. Lissa watches him, his face, his blue suit, asking his brother for the third time to check his pocket for the rings, and as she watches he looks up, catches her eye and smiles.

The music starts, they stand, and Hannah appears on the arm of her father. She is wearing a simple green dress, her eyes shining, and at the sight of her, Lissa is chastened – how could she have thought she would ever outshine her? This woman that she loves. Here, in her green column of a dress, walking slowly towards Nathan, Hannah is mythic, archetypal. And Nathan here, standing at the front, has eyes for no one else, his face eager, lit, waiting for his bride.

As Hannah and her father pass her, Cate is thinking of her own father, and trying to remember when the last time was that she touched him – years ago now. And how she wants him here, in this moment, wants nothing more than for her own father to hold her like this – wants her own father to look at her like this, transfigured with pride and with love. Perhaps it is only for this that weddings are made.

And Cate thinks of Lucy, and where she is – and whether she ever thinks of her. And whether she is alive or dead, and whether she will ever love anyone like that again, and how time is passing and they are all getting older, and she is crying, standing here, thinking of Lucy and of Hannah and Nathan, of her mother and how she misses her, of her father and love and of time, and how it is all so beautiful and so impossible, really.

*And Hannah looks at Nathan and thinks of how she loves him. And how she is happy. And when the serious-faced woman who is holding the ceremony turns to her and asks her if she will take this man – Yes, she says, yes. I will.*

*Afterwards, when the wine has been drunk and cake has been eaten and speeches have been made, Hannah finds her friends. She takes Lissa by the hand and threads through the crowd in the pub to find Cate, and takes Cate by the other hand, and leads them outside, into the May sunshine, through the gate, into the park, into London Fields. The cherry tree by the gate is heavy with blossom.*

*The forecast was right: it is a beautiful day. They walk out on to the grass, and as they walk, in this golden, tipsy light, the world feels full of love, of possibility. Hannah brings her friends towards her, presses her forehead against theirs. I love you, she says. And, their heads bent to hers, Cate and Lissa murmur their love back, for this is what marriage does – it flows out beyond the couple, engendering love, engendering life, making us believe, even for an afternoon, in a happy ending, or at least, at the very least, in the expectation that a story will continue as it should.*

## Lissa

'You can change behind the screen,' says the teacher. 'Or go to the toilets.'

He is young, younger than her anyway, short and wiry, dressed in a striped woollen jumper and jeans. Expensive-looking glasses. Mild grey eyes.

Lissa nods. She knows the drill. She doesn't bother to tell him she has done this many, many times before. They don't want to hear you speak.

She takes her bag and walks down the corridor to the women's toilets. There are high shelves on either side, the smell of paint and clay and turps. She locks herself in one of the stalls and takes off her coat and T-shirt and bra, her jeans and her knickers. She folds her clothes and puts them back in her bag, then puts on her kimono, keeping on her socks, as the floor is chilly. She pees quickly. The last thing she wants is to need a pee before the first break. The first break is not for forty-five minutes.

She makes her way back down the corridor, and pushes open the heavy door of the studio. The students are here already, busy preparing their easels. A thin, clear light falls from high windows. She makes her way over to a raised platform in the middle of the room.

'OK, Lisa,' says the teacher.

'Lissa,' says Lissa.

'Right, Lissa. So – when you're ready, just take whatever pose you like. We'll do some short ten-minute sketches, and then move on to the longer poses later in the morning.'

Her toes are already cold, but there are a couple of heaters, which are on. She slips out of her kimono and sits down.

The teacher looks at her for a moment, then: 'Actually – what about we begin standing?'

She stands, finds a pose, one foot in front of the other, arms behind her back.

'Right,' says the teacher to his students. 'Charcoal or pencil. Ten minutes. Let's go.'

There is the scribble of charcoal and pencil on paper.

So, thinks Lissa, here she is again.

She has managed to eke out her savings from *Uncle Vanya* by living on soup mix and porridge, rarely going out, spending her days watching old films on her computer, feeding her melancholy, and now she is down to the last two hundred pounds in her account.

She always thinks that somehow she won't be back here. She's always wrong.

For a long time she waited, bracing herself for Hannah's fury, but when weeks had passed and she heard nothing she wrote her a single message – *I'm sorry. I'm here if you ever want to talk*. It was weak at best, craven at worst.

Nothing from Nathan. Not since New Year's Day. Not since the scene in her flat. She wrote him a letter, then burned it. Wrote him another, then burned that too.

In the break she goes out to use the loo, and on the way

back she casts a look at some of the students' sketches. Her haunches. The rise of her breasts. The shortness of her hair.

In the early spring, she took herself to the hairdresser and told him to cut her hair. He approached her warily – an inch? he asked. More, she said. He cut off two. More, she said. And then he capitulated, sliced it, sheared it, and they both watched the locks fall silently to the floor. And she cried when she saw herself in the mirror, for she did not know herself any more, and he looked at her in horror. I'm sorry, he said. I thought it was what you wanted. It is, she said. It was.

'OK, Lissa.' The teacher comes over to her. 'So, now we're going to do a longer pose.'

'I know.'

'So, just make sure it's something simple – something you can hold for forty-five minutes.'

She sits down on the raised platform, still in her kimono, and finds a pose, one knee up, the other leg bent beside her. She clasps her knee in her arms to brace against. She has a small repertoire of longer poses. There are some people who can sit for hours in the most contorted of positions – dancers usually, acrobats. She is not one of their number.

After a few minutes the room settles down. They are painting now – there is the sound of brush on canvas, the teacher's footsteps as he moves quietly from easel to easel. Sometimes he says nothing, sometimes he leans in – *Good*, he murmurs, or *See this – the line here?* He traces his hand on the paper, lifts it, moves it through the air.

She looks down at herself – her lower legs, the stubbled hair which she forgot to shave this morning. The heat in here

266

is patchy – part of her lower calf is turning mottled and red. She can smell the scent of herself.

She is aware that she has lost much, so much that she cannot quite comprehend its scale: she has lost Nathan, she has lost Hannah. She has lost Cate, who will not return her calls.

But she has lost much more than that, as though loss were a black hole, pulling all the potential futures, all the things you might have been, all the successes, the loves, the children, the self-respect you might have had, down into it.

'We want to capture something,' the teacher is saying. 'Some essence. It is not our job to interpret. We want to *transmit*.'

Her left buttock is already growing numb. There are pins and needles starting in her foot. She shifts slightly, hears a tut from the teacher.

'Lissa,' he says. 'Please try to keep still.'

There is a cough and she looks up into the eyes of a young woman. She is twenty or so. Beautiful in a precise way. She looks like a serious little doll.

She imagines the young woman's body beneath her clothes, smooth like alabaster. What does she think when she looks at her?

Does she think of why she is doing this job still, at her age?

Does she look at the curve of her belly? Does she wonder if she has had children?

She looks back at the young woman, who is staring now at her thighs, making larger strokes with her charcoal. Her doll-like, impassive face.

All I am, thinks Lissa, is a collection of lines. There is nothing real inside. Like those bodies her mother drew, all those years ago on the pavements of Tufnell Park. As though it were prophecy – this hollowness. There is only the outline left. She feels dizzy suddenly, and she moves again. There is an audible groan from the other side of the room.

'Excuse me,' she says. 'I don't feel well.'

She stands up, wraps herself in her robe, goes out into the corridor and lays her cheek against the cool, hard surface of the wall.


## Hannah

Gatwick, early morning, and she is an oyster, newly shucked. The wide world presses upon her; the women in their heels and coats, the people who walk quickly because they have somewhere better to be. She feels at once invisible and far too visible in her waterproof jacket and walking boots.

Thirty-six. She is almost middle-aged. Is it worse if men look at her, or not? The tip of her thumb nudges the space left by her wedding ring, a small groove, a ridge of callused skin, and then an absence. The callus has almost disappeared now, although her thumb still returns to it, like a tongue to the gap where a tooth used to be.

At Aberdeen, she has a wait of an hour before the connecting flight. The airport is full of men. Men with the look of squaddies – although less fit, many of them are huge, red-faced, balding, tucking into breakfast and pints at the bar. She avoids them, browsing the stands at Smiths, thinking to buy a magazine, but they all seem faintly ridiculous, so she moves to the book stands. She has read nothing for months.

What used to be an innocuous activity is now trip-wired; she wants nothing about love, nothing about children, nothing about infidelity. She lifts guidebooks and puts them back again. She does not need a guidebook. She is capable of navigating by instinct. She is capable of spontaneity. In the end she buys a copy of *Emma* and a bottle of water. She has read it before. She is pretty sure there are no babies in the book.

The Orkney plane is tiny. Rain laces the window panes. She stows her bag beneath the seat. People greet each other as old friends. Just as the door is about to close, one of the men from the bar climbs aboard, breathing quickly, as though he has been running. He says hello to an older lady on the other side of the aisle from Hannah, before taking his seat a couple of rows in front. His hair is short and neat. He moves with the exaggerated precision of someone who knows it is still morning, and that he is drunk. The first glimpse of the islands is through a break in the cloud – choppy sea and then the low-lying grey-brown of the land. As the plane banks she sees rain, and almost-empty roads.

It is not yet midday – too early to check into the hotel – and so she collects her hire car and decides to drive up the island. The sky has lifted a little. She knows the main concentration of sites is forty minutes or so away; burial chambers, standing stones. She might as well see them while the rain holds off.

She passes through the town: a large red-bricked cathedral, stone-fronted houses, a huge Tesco on the route out to the north. The landscape is sodden, unpromising. The radio in the car is tuned to Radio 2 – some inane chatter, some cheesy songs. She tries for something else but gets only static, and so turns it off. This was not what she expected, when she booked this holiday, in the quiet of her flat. She expected something craggy, magnificent, some sort of scale to dwarf her interior landscape, but there is barely a hill or a tree to be seen, only tussocky grass and pebble-dashed bungalows. It is, if she is honest, all quite bleak.

She parks at a set of three huge standing stones and climbs out of the car. A large sheep with a broad face stands in the middle of them, cropping the grass. The sheep is remarkably ugly. So are the stones. They look like a piece of Brutalist civic architecture – something an overeager county council might have thought was a good idea some time in the 1970s. She walks around them dutifully. She stands in the middle. The sheep eyes her suspiciously. She waits to feel something but feels nothing other than mildly self-conscious.

At the far north of the island is a Neolithic village. Her internet searches have told her it is five thousand years old. As she climbs out of the car, the clouds are feathered overhead. She can smell the sea. The track towards the village is studded with stones, each one marking an event: a man on the moon, the French Revolution, the fall of Rome, leading all the way back to when the village was built, at the same time as the pyramids of Egypt. The gift shop is stocked with Viking hats, the sort made from hard plastic with two plaits of synthetic hair hanging down on either side, with Fair Isle sweaters and stuffed puffin toys.

A pleasant man behind the desk in the gift shop sells Hannah a ticket, and tells her she must watch a short film first before visiting the site, which she duly does, sitting behind an older couple in matching waterproofs. She is then funnelled through a small exhibition, each one of whose cases she reads diligently, learning about the food the villagers would have eaten (fish and deer and berries), the pots they made, the strange, lovely balls they carved; and it is not without interest, this exhibition, if you are a schoolchild, or a historian. Or someone with nothing better to do. Outside the museum is a replica house – she ducks inside, sees two beds, a dresser made from stones, a stone-bordered hearth.

When she comes out and goes to explore the village proper, it starts to rain again. She walks around the houses, peering down into their interiors, and they are impressive, moving even, and yes, it is easy to imagine these people going about their lives, inhabiting their houses, with their beds for children and their beds for adults and their stone dressers, as though from an episode of *The Flintstones*, carving their jewellery, eating their trout and deer and berries, and loving and fighting and fucking around the hearth. She turns away from the houses and looks out at the sea, a wide, gently shelving bay along which the rain is coming in hard now. She feels a fresh wave of anger and pain. What is she doing here? What was she thinking, coming to the edge of things, to stare at hearths and homes and places where families lived and loved, and only feel more of what she does not, will not, have?

She wanted something wild, something that exists only unto itself – nature without audience. Must everything be made human-size? She does not want the domestic. The domestic is what she came here to escape.

Tesco is the size of a large aircraft hangar and she is grateful it exists.

She wanders the aisles, letting the supermarket's white noise wash over her.

She buys a bottle of Rioja and some cheese crackers and crisps.

The hotel has been billed as one of Orkney's finest. It is tired, and has not been decorated for years. There are queasy swirls of colour on the carpet, and a smell of fried food and burnt coffee seeps from the restaurant. Her room is pleasant enough, despite the pictures of lurid purple flowers on the walls. The bed is huge but uncomfortable – two beds pushed together. The pillows are unspeakable. She twists off the top of her wine and pours a third of a bottle into her tooth mug.

By six o'clock she is hungry and has almost finished the wine. There is no answer at room service and so she goes downstairs to the restaurant. 'Can I order food here?'

'Aye,' says the young woman behind the bar. She has a small, heart-shaped face, make-up, a pretty mouth.

'Can you deliver it to my room?'

'I'm the only one on right now. Do you mind waiting? You can take it up yourself?'

Hannah looks around her at the near-empty restaurant. She is alone apart from an older couple who look as though they are on a business trip, their heads bent over a computer screen. 'OK.'

'You can have a drink on the house,' says the young woman with a wink, 'seeing as I'm in charge.'

'OK,' says Hannah. She looks over the menu. 'I'll have fish and chips,' she says.

'Perfect,' says the young woman.

'And a glass of wine. What wines do you have by the glass?'

'Just the Merlot.'

'A glass of that then.'

'Perfect,' the young woman says again, taking a large glass and filling it almost to the rim. 'There you go.'

*Perfect?*

She takes it to a seat in the window. A vase of plastic flowers stands on the table before her. Outside, the harbour is rain-washed. Shafts of fading sunlight pierce the drizzle, then disappear again, leaving steely grey light in their wake.

'Tomorrow's better. Weather-wise.'

She turns and sees a man beside her. It is a moment before she recognizes him from the airport, from the plane. She nods in response. He looks as though he has sobered up, whereas she is on her way to being drunk. He takes a seat at the next table, diagonally opposite her, and she feels a vague sense of annoyance. Now she will either have to make conversation or ignore him. She looks in her bag, finds the paperback she bought at the airport, slides it out on to the table. She takes a sip of her wine, opens the book. *Emma Woodhouse, handsome, clever, and rich—*

The young woman comes over, puts a pint down in front of the man. 'There you go.'

'Thanks.'

The murmur of the couple in the corner – something about a meeting. Something about figures. The world of work. The man lifts his pint and drinks. 'That good then?'

She looks up. The man is large, but not overweight; her age, or a little older. He looks ruddy, as though he has recently showered. The hair at the back of his neck is damp.

'Your book?' He gestures towards it. 'Is it good?'

She holds it up to him. 'I'm on page one.'

'Ah,' he says.

'But I've read it before.'

'Right.'

'They all learn lessons. And live happily ever after.'

'Ah,' he says. 'Right enough.'

She looks back down at the page, but the words are dancing now.

'You up here on holidays then?'

'I suppose.'

'You suppose?' He gestures to the chair in front of her. 'Do you mind if I join you?'

'I'm just waiting for my food. I'll be gone soon.'

'Then you won't get bored of me.' He lifts his pint and takes the seat opposite her, his back to the woman behind the bar.

'Cheers.' The man lifts his pint and drinks. His fingers are thick, the skin chapped and red. There is a wedding ring on his hand. His phone is beside him on the table. She sees a picture of a woman and a child on the screen. 'So what is it then? If it's not holidays? You here on work?'

'No,' she says. 'Not work.'

'Mystery,' he says.

'Something like that.'

'I'm from here,' he says, as though in answer to a question she has not asked. 'Grew up here. I work on the rigs. Off Aberdeen. Two weeks on, three weeks off. I stay up on Papa Westray when I come off. Work a farm up there.'

She has a vision of a cottage. A view of wind farms and the

sea. A wife and child. The woman on his phone. Managing alone while he is gone.

'You?' he says to her. 'Where are you from?'

'London. Manchester. London.'

'That's a lot of places.'

'Manchester.'

He nods. 'There's some lads from Manchester on the rig.'

'Oh?'

'They don't sound like you.'

'Well. I've lived in London for years.'

He leans towards her. 'What's that like then?' he says. 'London?' There is something about him, his energy, something untethered. Something hungry in his eyes.

She leans back. 'Oh,' she says. 'You know.'

'I don't get on with cities,' he says.

'No.'

They fall silent. He turns his phone over on the table, so the blank back faces upwards and the picture of the woman and the child has gone. 'What have you seen then, today?'

She shrugs. 'I saw the main sights. Apart from that burial chamber. Maeshowe. I suppose I'll go there tomorrow.'

'Did you like the main sights then?'

'Not really. I thought Orkney was . . . something else. I thought it would be wilder. It's all a bit . . . polite.'

'Polite!' He throws back his head and laughs.

The diners at the next table look up, then down again at their food.

'You should go south,' he says.

For a moment she thinks he means the South: the hot South. Sun and sea and warmth on the skin.

'Go down to Ronaldsay,' he says, 'see the tomb there. The Tomb of the Eagles. On the cliffs there. That's wild. That's a good one to see before you go.'

She looks down at her hand, fiddles with her ring, but her ring is not there. The man looks at her finger, then back up at Hannah's face.

She is aware, in the moment, that an invitation has been extended. Aware of a conflicting set of emotions, the answering leap of desire.

Is this how it was? With Lissa and Nathan? Was it spoken or unspoken? Did they think of her, before they crossed the line?

'Is that your wife?' she says.

'Where?' He looks startled.

'There.' She reaches in, takes his phone, turns it over and presses the button on the side. There she is, a young woman, squinting into the light, a child of four or so before her.

The man looks down at his phone, back up at Hannah. 'That's her,' he says.

'So what are you doing here?' She is furious now, hissing her words. 'Talking to me?'

He takes the phone from her, looks at the photograph briefly.

'She's dead,' he says. 'She died a year ago.'

'Oh.' It is as though he has kicked her in the stomach. 'God.'

'It's all right,' he says. 'It's not your fault.'

He looks away, to the rain-washed harbour, then back again.

'Anyway,' he says, 'I didn't come here to talk about my wife.'

She is silent. And then, without anything more being said, something is agreed.

They ride up in the lift. She watches his hand press the button for the second floor. His thick fingers. His wide palms. He leads the way down the corridor and she follows, half a step behind. He opens the door, then steps back to let her enter, and for a moment she feels a sharp slice of fear – he could be anyone – but then the fear dissolves. He goes to put the key in the socket but she puts her hand on his wrist. 'No,' she says. 'Keep it dark.'

The visitors' centre at the Tomb of the Eagles is staffed by a soft-voiced woman. The woman speaks about the tomb, about how it was found on her father's land, a mile or so from where she and her family live today. About the human remains that were found there – no skeletons, only jumbled bones, thousands upon thousands of them. About the eagle talons found in amongst them. About the theory that the bodies were left out to be eaten by the birds. Like the sky burials of Tibet. How only the clean bones were saved.

'Excarnation,' the woman says in her soft voice.

'Excarnation,' says Hannah, tasting it. A new word.

When the small tour has finished, the woman tuts at Hannah's jacket and boots, and kits her out in proper waterproofs. When she is ready, Hannah laughs.

They go to the window and the woman points the way to a hunkered mound in the distance. 'Come back along the cliffs,' she says, 'that's the best way. You might see the seals then.'

The track is muddy and rutted with puddles; Hannah walks through them, not around them. When was the last time she wore wellington boots? A scrap of song comes to her and she sings out loud. A dog bounds out of one of the farm buildings, weaving through the fence ahead of her, trotting back to make sure she is keeping up, then running ahead again, chasing the swallows, who skirl and dive, loving the wind. Primroses stud the path and she bends and picks them, and then is unsure what to do with the picked flowers, stowing them in the pocket of her coat.

The chamber looks like nothing so much as a heap of rocks, almost indistinguishable from the shelved rocks around it. The entrance is covered with a trolley. She feels a tremor of fear, but moves the trolley away and gets down on her hands and knees, crawling along the tunnel before emerging into a small, chambered space. It is not dark – small skylights have been built into the ceiling – nor is it cold, or eerie, even; it is simply rock and earth and a deep insulated quiet. Outside, back through the tunnel, she can see the wind in the grass, the white spray on the sea.

She sits there for a moment, uncertain what to do. There is a scrabbling in the tunnel and the dog appears, coming close to her, panting. She holds him to her, feels his heart, the warmth of his flank. 'Hey,' she says. 'Hey there.'

Ahead of her, leading off from the chamber in which she sits, is a smaller, darker space. From here it is impossible to see just how far it extends. A torch lies on the ground and she reaches for it and switches it on, flashing it into the chamber, which is revealed to be small, but big enough for a person to lie within.

She turns off the torch, crawls under the stone lintel and lies on her belly, her cheek on the cold ground. It is strangely comforting – lying like this, she can feel her heart beating in her belly, her chest, the rush of her blood. The distant thump of the sea on rocks. The soft sound of the dog, breathing close by.

She thinks of the bones that were piled in here for so long, thousands upon thousands of them.

Soon enough her flesh will be no more.

She thinks of the night before. The shock of his body: the difference of it, the shape of it. His smell. The places where she put her mouth. And she was different. Her body different. The way they moved together. The strange animal noises they made. Afterwards, lying in the dark with this familiar, unfamiliar man, she thought of Nathan. Of how she had forgotten to see him as separate. Forgotten to feel his unfamiliarity. Forgotten to acknowledge the animal inside him. Lissa would have kindled the animal in him. And with this thought comes something else: a sort of grief, for her own animal nature, for its own wild desires.

She turns on to her back, switches off the torch, and there is only the darkness – the low, intimate sound of her breath.

After a long while she crawls back out to the main chamber, and then pushes herself out into the brightness of the day. The dog follows her, and they walk along the rocks back to the car. The clouds have lifted, the wind has stilled, the day is clear.

She drives back up the island, past a strip of white sand, the sea gentle beside it, and she is seized with a desire so strong and immediate that she stops the car. She climbs down and walks back along the sand until she is no longer in sight of the road, takes off her clothes and runs into the sea. She lets out a sound, a shout – of cold, of joy, of exhilaration – as the water lifts her off her feet and slaps her skin.


## Cate

Spring arrives early, and the city turns green. She takes her bike out of storage and cleans and oils it, and then she cycles up the hill to work – watching the trees come into bud and then leaf, the candles of the horse chestnuts that stand by the side of the wide road.

At first it makes her breathless, the climb – she has to stop and wheel her bike several times to make it up the hill. But soon she is feeling fitter, feeling her muscles respond, the air flood into her lungs.

The ride is lovely, but it is when she is driving that she sees it most – out on the B roads, between Canterbury and the coast, the radiant springtime sweep of the land.

Dea was right; the job fits her – two days a week in the office and then a day a week visiting schools. Sam has dropped a day at work, and so they manage the childcare between them, she and Alice and Sam. She likes the teenagers she meets – their attitude, their sass. They give nothing for free. She is working on a scheme to get kids from a school in Sheppey to visit the campus, working with the Creative Writing department to publish an anthology of the teenagers' work.

Tom is almost walking now. He likes to pull himself up to standing, cruising around the living room in his tights, delighted at his new-found mobility. Cate watches him, fascinated. It is extraordinary, she thinks, this urge to stand, to walk; extraordinary to watch the human animal evolve before her eyes. Everything he comes across he puts in his mouth: pencils, elastic bands, scraps of food from the floor. He becomes enamoured with putting pencils in holes. She buys plastic guards for the power sockets. It becomes imperative to get out of the house.

On a sunny Sunday in March, a week before his birthday, he takes his first steps across the living room; one, two, three and then he sits on his bottom. She applauds, calling to Sam, where he sleeps upstairs, and he rushes down, rubbing his eyes and blinking. They coax and wheedle and Tom manages another few steps. Sam brings out his phone and manages to catch it, sending it immediately to Alice. Cate sends it to her dad.

Often, at the weekend, she straps Tom in the buggy and walks over to the allotment, where he and Nora toddle on the ground, amateur naturalists investigating stones and eating earth, while she and Dea dig over the beds for the new season's planting. She likes the work, likes the way it makes her sweaty, likes the sweet smell of the soil.

She goes for walks. Sometimes she goes with Dea; sometimes, if she is alone, while Tom naps in the buggy, if the weather is fine she simply sits on a bench in the sun. When he wakes there is often a short gap of time in which he comes to himself, in which he looks out at the world from his seat, not looking for her, not looking for anyone. She sits behind him, letting him have this moment, a minute when she is not immediately there hovering over him. It occurs to her that it begins so early, this process of letting go – of not inserting yourself between your child and the sun.

They are tentative with each other, she and Sam, but they have grown easier, grown closer. Still, they give each other plenty of space, as though whatever small fire has been rekindled will be smothered with too little air. But Tom sleeps in his own bed now, and sometimes, in the quiet of the night, it is easy to turn towards Sam, curling into his frame, waking with her arm over his chest.

She texts Hannah every day, just a single line to check in.

One morning in early April, she cycles up the hill to the

university, arrives in the office and opens her email. She sees it immediately. A message from Hesther – subject line *Lucy Skein.*

Cate begins to shake. She looks up and out at the room, but no one is watching her – the sun slants in through the window. It is still the same morning that it was.

She opens the email.

Hesther is sorry to have taken so long to reply; she has been away – travelling for work. It is lovely to hear from Cate after so long. Cate's eyes travel hungrily over the words, down to the bottom two lines.

*I haven't seen Lucy for years, but funnily enough I bumped into her when I was in Seattle for work last year. She seemed really well. Seems she changed her name. I have her contact if you'd like it.*

And below, an email address. A name.

She types it immediately into her search engine. And she is there before her. Dr Lucy Sloan. Dept of Int. Development. University of Oregon.

Her face. The way the lip curls up when she smiles.

A relic from a different life.


*Lissa*

*You must bring Daniel*, Sarah says to Lissa on the phone and, in the subject heading of the email that contained the exhibition invitation, she put in bold letters – *Bring Daniel! Excited to meet him.*

In the end, in desperation, Lissa texts Johnny: *Got a plus one to an art opening. Don't suppose you'd like to come?*

*I'd be delighted*, he replies, almost at once.

They meet at the Tube. He is dressed as always in black with his black leather bag, but his shirt looks new, and he is wearing a smart jacket. He is freshly shaven and looks well. She is surprised by how happy she is to see him, to have him lift her hand in that courtly, gentle way he has. 'Hiya, sweetheart,' he says. She has forgotten the soft Scouse rumble of his voice.

'You look good,' she says. 'Very natty.'

'I'm working. Got a bit on *Doctors*.'

'Ah ha.'

'And,' he says, half apologetically, 'I seem to have scored a season at the RSC.'

'Whaaat? That's great!'

'Don't get too excited.' He holds up a hand. 'It's small parts mostly, but then Enobarbus in *Antony and Cleopatra*. It's set in Liverpool in the sixties. Don't ask. They'll probably mangle the fuck out of it, but hey ho.'

'Johnny, but that's proper!' She finds she is unconditionally happy on his behalf.

'You'd be a good Cleopatra.'

'In another life.'

'What about you? Any meetings?'

'Not really. Actually,' she says, 'I'm thinking of giving up.'

'Hush, child,' he says.

'No, really.'

'Come, come,' he says, taking her by the arm. 'Less of that.'

'When do you start?'

'May,' he says. 'Apparently they're all quite civilized, the Stratford lot. Voice classes together every morning – that sort of thing. A year's worth of the mortgage too.'

'Well,' says Lissa. 'You deserve it.'

'So whose exhibition is this then?' he says.

'Oh,' says Lissa. 'It's just my mum's.'

'Blimey,' he says with a wink. 'Then I'd better behave.'


The gallery is busy, thronged with faces she has not seen for years. Her mother is surrounded by people. It is a month or so since she has seen her and Sarah has lost weight, but she looks extraordinary – regal in a long red dress. It is she who should be Cleopatra, thinks Lissa, not herself.

The pictures are few; there are no more than seven. In each one the painted area takes up only a third of the canvas, then there is an expanse of white space around it. They are hung without frames, so the effect is of the image being suspended in space. As the eyes adjust to the canvas, objects emerge. In one there is a young girl wearing a cotton dress, half turned away, her face in profile; she is stooping to look at something on the ground, but the ground is not there, has disappeared into blankness beneath her feet. The face is smudged, but Lissa knows it is her.

In the largest of the canvases, which takes up most of one wall, a smudged line suggests a figure, or a creature, walking on the horizon, thinning to nothingness; it could be the Bolivian salt flats, it could be the surface of the moon. There are few distinguishing features, but Lissa knows the figure is Sarah – her mother with her back turned – walking away.

The canvases are not cheap – between two and five thousand each – but there are already three red dots on the cards tacked to the wall.

'She'll sell the lot at this rate.'

Lissa turns to see Laurie beside her. The older woman threads her arm through Lissa's. 'I think she knew when she started these, don't you?'

'Knew what?'

'How ill she is.' Laurie gestures at the paintings. 'It's as though everything inessential has fallen away.'

And Lissa feels something falling away from her – the ground, her stomach. She looks down at her hands, which Laurie is squeezing.

'And you, Liss?' Laurie is saying. 'How are you? How are you coping with it all?'

'Fine,' Lissa hears herself say softly. 'I'm doing fine.'

By the time the gallery owner climbs on to a crate to stand above the crowd and speak, the place is packed. Lissa has walked around the block, decided she will leave – decided she will come back again. She has smoked four cigarettes, drunk four glasses of wine. She has lost Johnny, found him and lost him again. She hangs back as the crowd makes a tight circle around Sarah and the gallery owner, silent while Sarah says a few brief words, but Lissa hardly hears above the hard thrum of her anger, and when the crowd parts, she pushes her way towards her mother and takes her by the arm.

'Why didn't you tell me?'

'Tell you what?'

'Laurie told me. She thought I knew.'

'Oh,' says Sarah. 'That.'

'*That?*'

'I didn't want to concern you.'

'You didn't want to *concern* me? How ill are you?'

'Fairly ill.' Sarah wipes a hand over her forehead. 'I have stage four cancer.'

It is hot – hot everywhere, inside and out. 'And how long have you known?'

'Since Christmas.'

'*Christmas?*'

'I refused the chemo.'

'Of course you did. And you didn't think I might have something to say about that?'

'It's my body, Lissa. My life.' Her mother looks weary, cornered, and Lissa senses the people behind her – knows they are being observed.

Sarah's face changes. 'Is Daniel here?' she says quietly. 'Did you bring Daniel?'

'No,' says Lissa, her voice rising. 'No, he's not. Do you know why? Because he doesn't exist. Or he does – but he's Nathan. Hannah's Nathan. I fucked Hannah's Nathan and I told you he was someone he wasn't and now he doesn't speak to me. And nor does Hannah. Because my life is a mess. Because you never taught me how to love.'

Sarah reels as though she has been hit. Lissa steps in for more, grabbing her mother's arm. 'You're so selfish,' she says to her mother. 'So fucking selfish. You know that? You always have been and you always will be.'

Sarah steps away, a small, elegant parry.

'Goodness me,' says Sarah. 'And you say *I'm* selfish? Dear

me, Lissa, I know you wish you were more often on stage, but for once, please can you spare me the drama?'

'Hey.' There is a steady hand on her arm. 'Hey, love.'

Lissa turns to see Johnny beside her. She sees Sarah surrounded, Laurie between them. 'Time to go home, Liss.'

'Come on,' says Johnny, as he beckons her into his arms.


## Hannah

It is, apparently, the warmest spring in years. The cherry trees on her walk to the bus stop are in full blossom. The Georgian cafe on the corner has its tables and chairs on the street.

She gets up with the dawn and crosses the park to the lido. It is fairly quiet at this time of the day. Only the serious swimmers in their lanes. She goes into one of the small changing rooms, puts on her costume. Takes her cap and goggles. The morning air has a chill but the water is warm. She swims, long fifty-metre lengths. She takes pleasure in her strokes. She watches the light ripple and refract on the water. She remembers Orkney, the horizon, the light. As she swims, her thoughts change. They become less jagged. In the water there is no past and no future. By the time she comes out of the pool her body is tingling and her mind is clean.

She takes to walking everywhere. She walks to work. She walks back along the canal in the afternoons, savouring the light – the changing sky. She sits outside on the terrace, feeling warmth on her skin. She buys herself flowers, each Sunday at the market. One Sunday morning her eye is caught by some plants, which she buys and puts in terracotta pots and arranges on the windowsill in the little room, where it is sunny and they will receive the light. The evenings are lengthening; it is light now at seven o'clock.

The heat increases as April passes; by the end of the month it is as hot as July. Each morning, before work, she rises early and goes to the lido and swims – further and further every day. Work is fine, but she knows she is ready for a change. She thinks she might apply for a different job – swapping Farringdon for Lisbon perhaps, or New York. All those jobs she didn't apply for, all those opportunities she didn't take, back when she was waiting, treading water. She has no ties – can do anything, go anywhere she likes.

After work, in the still of the flat, Hannah pours herself water and stands at the sink and drinks it, then goes into the little room, takes off her clothes and lies naked in the evening sun. She closes her eyes and lets the light play in purple and red and green across her lids. She feels full, although of what exactly she cannot say.

One evening, lying like this, her phone buzzes with a message.

She lifts it, sees the name – Nathan.

*Need to collect some stuff. Is that OK?*

She stares at it while long seconds pass. She does not reply. Half an hour later the phone buzzes again.

*Would it be OK to come round later?*

She puts the phone down, picks it up again.

*What time?*
*Soon? I'm close by.*

Her heart beats faster.

*OK. Come. I'll be out.*

She stands and pulls on knickers and an old black summer dress; one that has been worn so often it cleaves to her. She leaves her phone behind, in case she is tempted to change her mind and call him, then takes her keys and walks towards the canal. It is still warm. The bars on Broadway Market are full, but she walks away from them, following the canal towards Victoria Park. She takes her time, doing a lap of the evening grass, moving between the lengthening shadows of the trees, and then makes her way back home in the gathering dusk.

She knows he is still inside as soon as she turns her key in the lock – a difference in the quality of the silence, a slight disturbance in the air. She does not see him immediately, as she kicks off her sandals, standing at the doorway in her bare feet. A small sound comes from the little room. She walks over the wooden boards, down the hall, where she pushes open the door. He is standing staring out of the window at the tree.

He turns to her. 'I couldn't bring myself to leave.' His voice is hoarse. There is a small bag at his feet.

She should feel angry, she thinks, but anger is far away.

'You changed things in here,' he says. 'You painted.'

'Yes.'

'It's nice.' He gestures to the plants on the sill, the print on the wall. 'It's funny we never touched it, isn't it? This room. All that time.'

'I suppose it is.'

Outside there are the sounds of running footsteps, the percussive slap of trainers on pavement, of children playing in the street.

'How have you been?' says Nathan.

'All right,' she says, and she leans against the wall behind her, sliding slowly down to the floor. She brings her knees towards her, clasps her arms around them. She can feel her breath coming shallowly, in and out. The evening sun is an oblong slice on the carpet between them. 'Bad, for a long time. Better now.'

Nathan nods.

'What about you?' she says.

'Han,' he says softly. He takes a small step towards her, but she puts her hand up to stop him.

'No,' she says. 'Don't come any closer.'

And so he stands there, unmoored, in the middle of the floor.

There are many things she wants to say:

*How could you do this to me?*

*How could you ever show your face here again?*

But what she finally says is,

'How was it?'

'How was what?' he says.

'With Lissa.'

'Han.' His face contracts. 'Don't.'

She puts her head back on the wall and looks at him. The

sadness on his face. How is it, after all of it, that she feels so strong, but sitting here, like this, he looks as though he will break? 'Tell me,' she says. 'I want to know.'

She has been in the fire, all this time – this is how – she has been tempered by the fire.

He turns away. Puts his hand on his bag, lifts it, puts it down, takes his hand away. 'It was . . . It felt dangerous,' he says. 'And it felt wrong.'

'And that was good?' she asks.

'Yes,' he says. 'In a way.'

'Did she come?'

'What?' He looks wretched.

'You heard me. Did she come?'

'Please,' he says. 'Don't do this.'

'It's my right,' she says. 'Isn't it?'

'I don't know.'

'Did she come?'

'Yes.'

'Was she loud? What noise does she make when she comes?'

'She wasn't loud,' says Nathan. 'No.'

It is as though she is drilling down into something hard and deeply satisfying. 'How does she fuck? Did she turn you on?'

She slides the straps of her dress off her shoulders; slowly the fabric falls to her waist. Her nipples are hard.

For a long time she does not move, until she slides out of her dress, and now she is just in her knickers. 'Do you want me?' she says.

He nods, and his face is slack with desire.

'Do you want me as much as you wanted her?'

'More.'

She stays where she is, in the sun, on the floor. The animal in him. The animal in her. 'Say it again,' she says.

'More,' he says, then slowly crosses the floor towards her. When he reaches her he kneels before her, his head on the ground. Then he lifts his head, pushes her knickers to the side, slides his fingers inside her, and she arches to his touch.


## Lissa

They speak little on the train as it makes its way through the western edges of London. They are in an uneasy truce – this trip a peace offering of Lissa's, accepted by Sarah, the first day they have spent together in weeks. Once they leave Reading the land opens up and there are wider skies, smaller villages. The summer is in full, glorious bloom.

Sarah dozes, her hat beside her on the seat, a novel open on her lap. Lissa studies her mother's face. She does not look ill – she looks, if anything, more beautiful than ever. The weight she has lost serves only to display more clearly the fine architecture of her face – which in sleep has none of the slackness of age. Her hair is as long and thick as it ever was.

Her mother opens one eye, latches it on to Lissa, and Lissa turns away.

They get down at a country station and cross a river. Sarah walks slowly, leaning on her stick, a red scarf trailing jauntily from her wide-brimmed hat. There are swans in the river – two cygnets that have not yet turned white. They swim closely to each other's side, their parents close behind. Cows meander in the opposite field. It is lovely, but in the way of certain country roads there is no pavement, only a thin grass verge, and the traffic is fast and loud and harries their backs.

'Hang on, Mum, wait a sec.' Lissa puts a hand on her mother's arm to halt her, then turns back to the road and reaches out her thumb. A man in a Range Rover stops almost immediately. He is pleasant and hearty, and Lissa senses her mother's silent relief as he drives them up a hill towards the Common, dropping them in a car park, where Lissa helps her mother down. Sarah walks to the fence, where an old control tower still stands. Lissa wanders over to a board, which tells a little of the history of the Common, of the airbase, of the flora and fauna to be found. *Greenham Common, it says, restored to lowland heath.*

*Past grazing by commoners' livestock has enabled a rare heath plant-life to develop, consisting of heather, gorse and other acid-loving plants.*

*The removal of the runways and the erection of fencing allows commoners to once again exercise their grazing rights.*

She squints. In the middle distance is a concrete pathway – the old runway – where two girls, young teenagers, stand playing aeroplanes, their arms out to catch the breeze, their laughter high on the air.

'This way,' Sarah says. The sandy gravel crunches beneath their feet; heather blooms in all directions, star-like white flowers studding the grasses by the path. They walk parallel to the old runway, past a pond, a fire hydrant. Sarah's head turns this way and that, occasionally nodding to herself, as though things are falling into place. 'That was the Blue Gate,' she says, pointing with her stick, 'over there.'

Cyclists pass them, families lumbering along together, older men in packs of three or five, wearing their wrap-around sunglasses, their helmets. Sarah tuts at them as they shoulder their way over the path. It is warm, getting hotter. Lissa takes water from her bag, offers it to Sarah, who takes it and drinks deeply.

'There,' Sarah says suddenly, her eyes fixed on something behind Lissa. 'There they are. The silos. Where the missiles were held.'

Lissa turns. They are huge, grass-covered. They look, she thinks, like nothing so much as burial mounds, the sort where Bronze Age kings would be interred with all their loot. They make their way slowly over the Common towards them. Triple barbed-wire fences still stand in front of them; someone has painted over them in red paint.

*Pussy*
*Cunt*
*Fuck*
*You*

A sign still stands amidst overgrown vegetation – *Ministry of Defence*.

Sarah rattles the fence with her stick. 'Bolt cutters,' she says proudly, 'made short work of this.' She smiles. 'We always had our bolt cutters on us.' Then she throws her head back and begins to make the most extraordinary noise – a ululation – at once utterly earthed and utterly unearthly. Lissa sees some walkers look up, wondering. When Sarah stops there is silence; she smiles a wicked smile. 'It frightened the daylights out of the soldiers,' she says. 'They didn't know what to make of us.'

'I'm not surprised. I'd have run for my life.'

'Did I tell you we danced?'

'Where?'

'Over there.' Sarah gestures with her stick to the silos. 'We cut the fence, put ladders up, climbed over and danced in the moonlight. It was New Year's Eve. We made our own music. We danced beneath the moon.'

*She is a witch*, thinks Lissa, as Sarah begins to sing again, softly this time. *My mother is a witch.*

She wanders a little away, to where brambles crowd the path. The blackberries are ripe, and she plucks a handful and brings them back to Sarah; an offering held in her palm. 'Delicious,' says Sarah, 'thank you.' She has found a feather from somewhere, and put it in the band of her hat. 'We should pick more. Take them home and make a crumble.'

They do so, Lissa lifting the brambles so Sarah can reach in and pick the darkest, ripest berries from the middle of the bush, taking the sandwiches she has packed for later out of their box and filling it instead with the glistening fruit. When the box is full they walk on, through a small, thick copse, where birches and sycamores dapple the light and bracken is chest-high and the silos are invisible. 'Ah, yes, this way,' Sarah says, 'I know this path.'

They reach a tree with many trunks, and Sarah steps off the path towards it, reaching her hands up to it. 'Hello, old lady, I remember you. This is where I camped,' she says, 'just beside this tree.'

'I remember,' says Lissa. 'I was there.'

'Yes,' Sarah turns to her. 'Of course you were. For a short time. I always forget.'

They walk on slowly and emerge again into the sun by a gate. A section of perimeter fence still stands, a concrete panel set behind a newer fence. It is painted with serpents, with a simple green butterfly – they are crudely done, little more than daubs, but they have an eerie power to them. It is like coming across forgotten cave paintings. Beneath the rusted metal, green paint is still visible, flaking with sun and with age. The air feels close, the vegetation pressing at their backs.

'I remember this,' Lissa says, threading her fingers through the gate. Tarps slung up in the rain. Women's ruddy faces. The smell of wool and fire and bodies.

'Thirty thousand people,' says Sarah, 'hand in hand around the base. They came and dragged us from our tents. Told us we were unnatural' – she laughs – 'as though it were natural to keep missiles of death on common land.'

'I remember them coming.' Lissa's hands close on the wire of the fence. 'Taking you from the tent. It frightened me. I hated it. You being here.'

'Why?'

'I thought I would lose you. That you would be shot.'

Sarah turns to her. 'The world is a fearful place,' she says evenly. 'It was not my job to lie about that. It was my job to try to make it safer. If you had your own child, you'd know.'

The comment lands. Twists. Does its work.

'I was pregnant once,' says Lissa quietly. 'With Declan.' She turns back to the fence, where a tiny insect crawls across the flaking green paint. 'It wasn't easy. The decision. I thought it would be, but it wasn't. But I couldn't have done it. Not with Declan. Not on my own.'

'My God. Why didn't you tell me?'

'I felt stupid for letting it happen, I suppose.'

'And why didn't you keep it?'

Lissa exhales. 'I was young and selfish and I wanted to have my life. I wanted to work. I didn't want a child who felt in the way.'

Her mother is silent, then she says quietly, 'Is that how you felt? Is that how I made you feel?'

'Sometimes. Often. Yes.'

Sarah shakes her head. 'That was never how I felt about you.'

'Really?'

'Truly.' Sarah regards her, steadily. 'But I had to live my life. All my life. Otherwise I would have been no mother at all.'

Lissa nods. 'I understand,' she says. And standing here, her hands threaded through this fence, she finds she does.

After a moment she speaks again. 'I'm sorry,' she says, turning towards her mother.

'What for?'

'That you're not a grandmother. You would have been a wonderful grandmother.'

And she would – she would have been magical. That would have been the right distance to love her from. To have been loved.

'Thirteen,' says Lissa. 'My child would have been thirteen.' And she finds she is crying, properly crying, her shoulders heaving, the sobs coming in shudders. Her mother steps towards her and folds her into her arms.

After a long moment, Lissa pushes the heels of her palms into her eyes and Sarah takes her arms away. Then they turn and walk back through the copse on to the Common and Lissa is glad of the space, the fresh air. In the distance a herd of cows is visible on the flat land. As they grow closer it is clear that they are in the middle of the runway, some standing, some lying. 'Look at that.' Sarah chuckles. 'You wouldn't get many warplanes past those ladies.'

The wind is high now. Sarah's hat is whipped off her head; Lissa runs to fetch it from where it has landed in a nearby bush.

As she walks back slowly towards her mother, she thinks, *It is here – the catastrophe. My mother is dying. I am losing my mother. Soon my mother will be gone.*

'Hold it a moment, would you?' says Sarah.

And Sarah steps on to the runway and turns to face the wind, eyes closed, her arms outstretched as though she is flying, and Lissa comes beside her, and does the same, feels the wind beneath her as she lifts her arms.


## Hannah

She is tired. The spring has given way to early summer and the heat. Then the weather changes; it grows cooler and begins to rain. She feels tired still.

One day, when she is at work, she puts her head on her desk and falls asleep. When she gets home she climbs into bed and pulls the covers over her head and sleeps deeply. She wakes in the middle of the night thirsty, and goes to get water.

*I'm pregnant*, she thinks, standing by the sink. The thought seems to come from above her, beyond her.

She goes to the bathroom; in the back of the cupboard there is a box of old tests. She pees on one and sits in the darkness. She does not have to wait long; almost immediately a strong line appears in the second box.

She looks at it. She looks and looks and looks.


It is a fizzing in her blood.

It is anxiety.

It is great piercing shafts of joy, joy so pure she has to stand and hold on to something and wait for it to pass.

It is fear.

She has lost before. She knows how losing looks and feels, and what it leaves you with.

She tells no one. Not Nathan. Not her mother. Not Cate. She knows it may not last.

At the weekend she sleeps late, and wakes full of dreams. She lies in the bath and looks at her toes.


## Cate

She takes the train to Charing Cross, the Underground to Bethnal Green, and then the old bus route up Cambridge Heath Road, gets down on Mare Street and walks along the canal, past the gas tower, past the gate to Sam's old studio, right down Broadway Market. It is a Thursday, and the road is fairly quiet, although the tables outside the deli are full. At the top of the road she turns left, following the terrace of Victorian houses to the end, where she stops, looking up at the tall house, the high windows, then walks on, through the park, where the London planes are in full splendid leaf.

The cafe was Lissa's choice – a bakery in one of the arches by the train station – and Lissa is waiting for her already, sitting outside. She stands hurriedly when she sees Cate approach.

'I got you a coffee.' She gestures to the table before her.

'Thanks,' Cate says, sitting down.

Lissa is dressed soberly, jeans and a plain T-shirt, no make-up, her hair caught on top of her head. She looks different. Her face, for so long seemingly immune to time, has begun to be claimed by it. There are greys in amongst the blonde of her hair.

'I wasn't sure you'd see me,' Lissa says.

'I wasn't sure I'd come.'

'Do you mind if I smoke?'

Cate shakes her head, and Lissa takes out her pouch and rolls.

'I went past the old house,' says Cate. 'On the way here.'

'Oh?'

'It was funny. Looking at it and not going in. Are you still in the basement?'

'Barely. I can't really afford it. I think I'll have to move.'

'Then it really is the end of an era.'

'Yes, I suppose it is.' Lissa lights her cigarette, blows the smoke away from them. 'How's Tom?' she says. 'And Sam?'

'He's good. Tom's walking now.'

'Do you have pictures?'

Cate takes out her phone, bringing up a couple of recent photos as Lissa leans in. 'He looks like a sweetheart.'

'He is. Sometimes.'

'How's Hannah?' asks Lissa softly.

'She's OK, I think. As far as I know they're still apart. I'm seeing her later. I guess I'll know more then.'

Lissa nods, turns to look out into the street. 'I won't bother to defend myself,' she says.

'OK.'

Above their heads, the rumble of a train, the squeal of its brakes. The hiss as it opens its doors.

'It's funny,' says Lissa, turning back. 'I've been thinking, lately, about that audition. That film. Do you remember? Before we went to Greece?'

Cate's stomach tightens. 'Yes.'

'And how I couldn't forgive you for it. I've sort of hated you, I think. Ever since. For not telling me about it in time.'

'Lissa—'

'No.' She holds up her hand. 'Let me finish. I know you have your own version of events. I just wanted to say that, lately, I've come to understand that I'm capable of things I didn't ever imagine. And I wanted to say that, whatever happened, I forgive you. That I wish you well.'

Cate opens her mouth to defend herself, then closes it again. 'Thank you,' she says. 'That means a lot.'

There is the rattle of the train leaving the station above, bound for Liverpool Street, or for the north, for far reaches of the city.

'Sarah's ill,' says Lissa. 'She has cancer.'

'Oh God,' says Cate. 'How far?'

'Stage four.'

Cate puts down her cup. 'I'm very sorry to hear that, Liss.'

Lissa's hands move to her hair and back down again. 'Yeah,' she says, 'it's all a bit shit.'

'Is she having treatment?'

'She refused it.'

Cate waits for Lissa to speak.

'I sort of admire her for it,' Lissa says, 'but I'm angry too – I mean, I'm fucking furious actually.'

Cate nods.

'And . . .' Lissa looks up. 'I know you went through it with your mum, and I wanted to ask you what to expect?'


She has the afternoon to herself, until she needs to be at Hannah's at six, so she wanders down to the bookshop, where she finds a picture book for Tom. The tables outside the deli are still full. Everyone sitting at them seems terribly young. As she queues inside for salad she watches them, these young people in their summer clothes, the self-consciousness of the way they sit, as though ready to have their photos taken, with their lemon water and their flat whites, starring in the movie of their lives. The way you do, when you are twenty-four or twenty-five, and you only see yourself from the outside in. She buys her salad and takes it into the park, where she sits beneath the old tree at the back of the old house and eats it, and then lies in the dappled sun.

At quarter to six she takes the back route to Hannah's flat. Hannah buzzes her in and she climbs the three flights of metal stairs to where her friend is waiting at the top.

Hannah looks well – she is tanned, wearing a short-sleeved

dress, her hair a little longer. Cate doesn't know what she expected, some lingering sadness perhaps, but the flat feels lovely, homely, the way the light catches the flowers on the table. Hannah makes tea, which they take out on to the terrace and drink in the last of the evening sun.

'You look good,' says Cate. 'How are you, really?'

'I've been swimming,' says Hannah. 'Every morning. It helps. And you? How're you and Sam?'

'OK, I think. Good.'

'That's good.'

'I heard from Hesther,' says Cate.

'Who?'

'Hesther. From Oxford. I wrote to her to ask for Lucy's address. A while ago. In the winter. She wrote back. Sent me her contact.'

'Oh Jesus, Cate. Really?'

Cate looks out, at the sun, setting now in the trees. She thinks of the days after the email – the letters composed, scrapped, written again. And then waking one morning in early summer, dressing Tom, dropping him off at Alice's, cycling through the morning to work, and knowing, or understanding what she had known, really, all along. There was nothing to be gained from writing. There was much to be lost.

'I didn't get in touch,' she says lightly, 'in the end.'

She hears Hannah exhale. 'That's good.'

She turns to Hannah. 'I did see Lissa, though.'

'Lissa?'

Cate sees the momentary shock on her friend's face. 'We met up this afternoon.'

'To talk about me?'

'Actually, no. Not really. Although she asked about you. She seemed different. Sad. We talked about Sarah.'

'Sarah. Why Sarah?'

'She's dying. She has cancer. Lissa asked to see me, to ask me about it. About how it might be.'

'Oh,' says Hannah. 'Sarah? Oh no.' For a long while she is silent, then she leans forward and puts her face in her hands.

'Han . . .' Cate puts her hand on Hannah's arm, worried she has punctured her frail bubble of happiness, but when Hannah looks back up her face is unexpected, shining.

'I'm pregnant,' she says, quite quietly.

'What?'

Hannah laughs, puts her hands to her face.

'Oh my God,' Cate says. 'Who—?'

'Nathan. He came to the flat. To collect some things. It was quick. So quick.' She shakes her head. 'All that time, and then . . .' She makes a gesture, her palms upturned, and Cate sees the surprise still, on her face.

'Does he know?'

'No.'

'Are you going to tell him?'

'Yes. No. I don't know. Not yet.'

'You have to tell him, Han.'

'I want to wait. Wait to see if I'll manage to keep hold of it. If it will stay.'

'How many weeks are you?'

'Eight, or nine. I'm not sure. I've got a scan booked at the end of the month.'

Cate watches her hands move to her abdomen, rest there. 'Can I come?'

'To the scan?'

'Yes. Can I come with you?' Cate reaches across, takes hold of her friend's hand.

## Lissa

It was suggested that Sarah might want to move downstairs, to the old study at the back of the house, but she has refused. *I'll die in my own bed, thank you very much.*

Laurie has moved in, taking the bedroom beside Sarah's, the one that faces out on to the street. They have established an easy rhythm, Lissa and Laurie; they are solicitous with each other, taking turns to sit with Sarah while the other cooks or cleans, or sleeps.

Sarah is a surprisingly easy patient – whatever pain she is in, and Lissa knows it must be great, she rarely complains.

Sarah's friends visit. Some of them Lissa hasn't seen for almost thirty years: June and Caro and Ina and Ruth. They congregate round Sarah's bed. Lissa leaves them to it. Sometimes the laughter is raucous and wild. Sometimes they sing.

While Sarah sleeps they gather around the kitchen table. They take over. They make Lissa sit and drink wine, or tea. They take Lissa's face in their hands and cry and kiss her cheeks and tell her how much she looks like her mother, and when they hug Lissa to their chests in their embrace, she knows that they have lived through illnesses and lived through children and lived through no children and that they are a tribe, these women, with their battered bodies and their scars.

She is awed by them, these women of her mother's generation; they appear to her shining, like a constellation that is
setting in the west. These women, these caretakers. What
will happen to the world when they have gone?

When they are gone the house is quiet.

She cycles back along the canal to Hackney in the summer
sunshine, and packs up the flat into boxes, which she loads
into a rental van and drives to a storage facility on the North
Circular. She goes back to the flat and cleans the oven, washes
the windows. Has a last cigarette on the wide stone steps. She
posts the key through the letterbox of the house of the estate
agent in Stamford Hill then she takes a taxi to Tufnell Park
with three small bags of her stuff.

She moves into the attic, where she sleeps on a futon on the
floor. She likes it up here, though it is hot at this time of year,
at the top of the house. The old chair is still here, and she sits
in it and reads, while Sarah sleeps downstairs. She roams her
mother's bookshelves, reading at random – Carson McCullers,
Zola, Katherine Mansfield. Many of the books have her
mother's notes in them; some from her time as a teacher,
some from earlier, from her university degree. There is something moving about reading like this, alongside her mother,
feeling the youthful energy in her mother's scrawl, keeping
her company while she sleeps downstairs.

One afternoon, as she sits there reading, an idea comes to
her, a surprising one, and she lets it settle in her body, feeling
its contours, trying it out for size.

In the early mornings she takes the battered old hose and
douses the garden – *It must be early when it's hot like this,* Sarah
tells her, *so their leaves don't burn.* Lissa stands in the greenhouse

at the bottom of the garden inhaling the musky tang of the tomatoes and green growing things, and looks up at the house, at Sarah's bedroom, where the curtains are still drawn and her mother sleeps. She is starting to have her favourites: the lady's mantle, which cups the water like mercury; the sweet peas, racing up their trellis. Sometimes she bends and takes the tendrils in her fingers and strokes the ends of them, watching them reach out for life. She attempts to cut the lawn with the ancient mower, whose teeth are rusted and saw at the grass.

In the long, light evenings, they sit in Sarah's room and read to her. She loves to be read to; poetry mostly – *more bang for the buck,* she says, *no time for* The Brothers Karamazov *now.* She sends Lissa and Laurie to the bookshelves over and over again – knows where each book stands on the crowded shelves, knows its neighbours, can direct you to a volume in the dark. She treats poems like medicine and knows what she needs.

She asks for Shakespeare, and Lissa and Laurie take it in turns to read the sonnets. One sunny Sunday, Lissa calls Johnny, who comes to join them, arriving freshly shaved, bringing flowers and pastries and good coffee and wine. They read *Antony and Cleopatra* all the way through, taking it in turn to read the parts. It takes all day, and is one of the nicest days she can remember. Sarah has her eyes closed for most of it. Sometimes Lissa sits beside her, takes her hands, which Sarah squeezes now and again.

Later, Johnny helps to carry Sarah down to the garden. It is the first time in a week since Sarah has left her bed. When Lissa and Johnny make a hammock with their hands and lift her, she is noticeably lighter. Laurie disappears into the kitchen to roast a chicken, waving them all outside.

'Fetch my sketch book, would you?' says Sarah, when she is sitting in the chair. Lissa does so, bringing it, and her tin of charcoals. Then she retreats to the bench behind her, watching her mother's charcoal move over the paper, the garden spring to life beneath her hand: Johnny dozing in a deck-chair, Ruby stretched belly up in the sun.

Later that evening, when the chicken has been eaten and Sarah is asleep in bed and Johnny has departed, Lissa and Laurie stand by the sink, clearing the last of the plates.

'Is he your lover?' says Laurie.

'Who?' Lissa looks up, startled.

'Johnny?'

'No.'

'He'd like to be. He's a lovely man.'

'I don't need a lover,' says Lissa. 'Not now.'

Laurie nods.

'And he's complicated.'

'We're all complicated,' says Laurie. She stows plates in cupboards, wipes down surfaces. It is the tidiest the kitchen has ever been.

'I'm giving up acting,' says Lissa. 'I realized that earlier, when we were reading. I don't want to do it any more.'

'That's a shame, Liss,' says Laurie softly.

'No,' says Lissa. 'It's not. I never want to go to another audition again.'

She feels this land, the certainty of it. The relief.

'Do you know what you're going to do?'

'Sort of.' Outside, the light lands in the pear tree. 'I've been thinking. I'd like to train to be a teacher.'

'Really?'

She nods. 'An English teacher.'

'Like your mother.'

'Like Sarah, yes.' She turns to Laurie. 'But I'm not sure. I'm going to go away first. To make up my mind.'

'Where?'

'I don't know.'

It is hard, hard to think of a destination that does not seem contrived – she does not want to find herself. Or perhaps she does. Perhaps that is exactly what she wants.


A few days later, when Sarah is dozing and Laurie has gone for an evening walk on the Heath, Lissa goes downstairs to feed Ruby. While the cat is busy at her bowl, she fills the old watering can in the dim kitchen, goes outside and drenches the beds with water. The garden is full of the smells of evening – the jasmine, the honeysuckle and the lavender – and the low humming of the bees. As she makes her rounds, she feels how her mother loved her garden – easily, simply, without rancour or friction or pain. She feels her mother's choices, her mother's care, her mother's subjectivity, like a veil hovering over this small patch of earth, merging with the night. Perhaps, she thinks, this is what remains.

She thinks of smoking a cigarette but does not. Instead she goes back into the house, puts the kettle on the stove and makes herself a cup of tea. She takes it back up the stairs, her eyes adjusting to the lack of light. As soon as she enters the room she senses it. She puts down her tea and walks slowly over to where her mother lies in her bed. She lifts Sarah's hand, which is cool, and she rubs her mother's thumb with her own.

At first she wants to rub and rub, to rub the life back into her mother, the way you would rub warmth back into someone who is cold, but then she understands that she cannot – that the time for that is passed – and so she stops, and holds her mother's hand instead. She reaches over and brushes her hair gently from her forehead. Someone has shut the window – it must have been Laurie – and Lissa stands and opens it. Then she comes back to sit beside her mother, to hold her hand.

The morning after Sarah's death, Ina arrives. She is a hospice nurse and knows what to do. Lissa watches as Ina unpacks her bag beside Sarah's body: small brown bottles with stoppers, scissors, string, muslin squares. Ina is small and steady and purposeful. 'Can I watch?' she asks her.

'You can help,' says Ina. 'If you like.'

First Ina straightens Sarah's limbs, then takes her head in her hands and moves it gently from side to side, placing it down on the pillow, placing another pillow beneath her jaw. 'We'll clean her now,' says Ina.

Lissa fetches boiled water from the kitchen, and Ina adds lavender oil and sage, and soaks swabs of muslin in the fragrant water. The women clean Sarah's armpits, her chest, her legs. Ina swabs in between her legs. She takes a fresh square of muslin and folds it, placing it in a pair of clean knickers.

'She might leak,' she says matter-of-factly. 'We all leak.'

*These bodily fluids, this defilement, this shit are what life withstands, hardly and with difficulty, on the point of death.*

She misses Hannah. She wants to talk to Hannah.

'Here,' says Ina, moving around Sarah's body. 'We need to

wrap the fingers, to take off her rings. The fingers will swell and then we can't.'

Lissa watches as Ina wraps Sarah's fingers with cotton thread, massaging in oil, moving the fluid gently down towards her mother's wrist so the rings might ease off. She does the same for the rings on her mother's left hand. 'That's it,' says Ina approvingly. Then, under Ina's instruction, they place Sarah's hands gently on her chest. 'It's better that way, so the blood doesn't pool.' She is like a midwife, thinks Lissa, in her gentle, certain ministrations; a midwife for death.

'Can I have a moment?' she asks Ina.

When Ina steps outside, Lissa takes her mother's hands. She lifts her fingers to her face, as though her mother might read her – read the Braille of her daughter's features, even now, even beyond death. Then she slowly places the hands back down on the sheet.


## Hannah

Cate is waiting for her outside the hospital. Hannah sees her scanning the car park, watching for her.

'They'll think we're together,' says Cate as Hannah approaches, and she laughs. Her hands move like birds, unsure where to land.

'Well,' says Hannah, threading her arm through hers. 'That's all right.'

They are the first couple there and they do not have to wait to be seen. A sonographer in jeans and a T-shirt calls them into a small dark room.

She gets up on to the table. The monitor faces away from her. Her heart. Her breath coming quickly.

The sonographer glances at Hannah's file, then turns to Cate. 'And you're the partner?'

'No,' says Cate. 'I'm just a friend.'

'Well,' says the woman gently, 'why don't you go and sit down there.' She gestures to a chair at the head of the table.

The woman puts cold gel on to Hannah's stomach. Hannah catches her breath as the sensor rolls over the tautness of her skin. She looks at the woman's face. The woman is silent, staring at the screen, at the dark places inside her – her face impassive. She is a seer, a diviner of meaning, a reader of the runes. But why is she so silent?

A wave of fear and nausea breaks over Hannah. 'Is everything all right?'

The woman looks up. 'So far,' she says.

Hannah clenches her thumbs into her hands.

'Just taking measurements,' the woman says.

The woman rolls a ball, the keyboard clicks, and then, 'Here,' she says, turning the monitor around to face them, 'here's your baby. Everything looks fine.'

A creature is projected there, waving its limbs. A heart flickering, flickering, beating faster than Hannah's own.

*Lissa*

All week Sarah's friends, her colleagues, her ex-pupils, all those who knew and loved her, are encouraged to come to the house and write their messages on scraps of cloth. Lissa and Laurie make coffee and tea, they give out glasses of wine and of water, put crisps and toast and soup on the table, and listen.

She imagines this is a little like it must feel after the birth of a child: this liminal space where time behaves differently, is gentled and held.

There are middle-aged men whom Sarah taught as teenagers, who tell of her classes, of her importance in their life. Younger women with their children in tow, who stare at the house – at the books and the paintings in it – and nod, as though it is exactly what they had expected, or hoped. Sarah's dealer comes, bearing a spectacular bouquet, leaving a trail of expensive scents in his wake.

Johnny brings his oldest daughter, a tall girl of seven, with straight brown hair that hangs past her shoulder. 'This is Iris,' says Johnny. Iris is dressed in high-tops and a hoodie. She stands hand in hand with her dad. 'We're going for ice cream,' says Iris. 'Do you want to come?'

'Sure,' says Lissa.

They walk the streets and the streets are strange – it is the first time she has been out properly in days. 'Is your mum dead?' asks Iris.

'Yes,' says Lissa, 'she is.'

Johnny reaches out and puts his arm around Lissa, and she lets him, and his daughter watches them and she does not seem to mind.

She sleeps in her mother's bed – the bed she died in – and it is not eerie, but comforting. Her mother had the death she wanted, she thinks. She understands now what a gift that was. How many people can say the same?

\*

The morning of the funeral Lissa puts on a yellow sundress. It is October, but unseasonably warm. Johnny and Laurie arrive to help – they wind the fresh flowers through the weave of the wicker basket.

*Don't call it a coffin, darling. It's a basket, that's what I want, a basket filled with flowers.*

The basket is indeed filled with flowers, dried ones and fresh ones, and posies of herbs and the ribbons of cloth covered with messages to send Sarah on her way. As she and Laurie and Johnny lift Sarah into the back of her old van, which still smells of turps and canvas and coffee, the ribbons lift and flutter in the breeze.

Sarah joked that she wanted to be buried under the pear tree in the garden, but they take her to Islington and St Pancras Crematorium instead.

*Which is actually in Finchley*, Sarah had said with mild disappointment, when she looked at the map.

The room is packed; there are hundreds of people there. When the ceremony is over, one by one the mourners come to speak to Lissa to say goodbye. Her dad is there, with her stepmother, and he holds her for a long moment before releasing her again. It is then that she sees them – Hannah and Cate. They must have been here all along.

'Oh,' says Lissa, looking at her friends. 'Oh,' she says again.

Hannah reaches her hand to Lissa and Lissa takes it.

'You're pregnant,' she says, and it is only now that she begins to cry.

'Yes,' says Hannah.

And now she is nodding, grinning stupidly in this sun.

'Look at you,' she says. 'You look wonderful.' And it is true, Hannah does; she is a fine ripe fruit.

'I came for Sarah,' says Hannah. 'I came to say goodbye.'

'Yes.' Lissa nods. 'Thank you.' And then, 'I'm sorry,' she says. 'I'm so sorry. Please, forgive me.' And then, for she cannot truly believe it, 'You're pregnant,' she says again. 'Can I? May I?' She holds out her hand.

Hannah nods, lets her place her hand there.

And now Lissa is laughing, standing in the sunshine with her hand like this, on the taut skin with the life beneath, laughing and crying and shaking her head.


The house is quiet. Laurie had offered to come back with her, as had Johnny, but Lissa refused. *I'll be fine*, she said.

There are books left open on the tables, and she lifts them gently and closes them, placing them back on the shelves. The kitchen has their breakfast things still sitting in the sink. She rinses the bowls and puts them on the side, then props open the door to her mother's garden. Sunlight pools on the floor. She pours herself a gin and tonic and rolls a cigarette.

She lifts the drink to the urn, which rests on the kitchen table. On Monday, as promised, she will go to Greenham with Laurie and Ina and Caro and Rose, and leave some of her mother's ashes by the tree. The rest Sarah has asked her to scatter in the garden, *wherever you like*. She'll do it tomorrow, alone.

In her inbox is a ticket to Mexico. Her flight is next week. She has no plans, only a vague destination – a town on the

Pacific coast. It is not an ending or a new beginning. Or perhaps it is. But if it is an ending, it is not clean, or neat – it is simply the part where one pattern joins another. It is made of blood and sinew and bone.

When she has finished her cigarette, Lissa shuts and locks the door. She comes over to the table. How many hours spent here? How many breakfasts and lunches and dinners? How many times was she put here, with drawing materials or crafts, and told to look after herself?

Once, she remembers not being able to sleep, hearing voices in the kitchen, coming down to find her mother and her friends here, sitting around the table. 'What are you making?' she had asked.

'They're cranes,' her mother replied. 'Here, look.' Sarah lifted her into her lap and showed her how to fold the paper to make the origami birds, and explained they were making them to mark an anniversary, of a bomb dropping in Japan, that they were a sign of peace, a sign that nothing like that should ever happen again. They sat around the table, the women, speaking in low voices, as Lissa followed her mother's instructions and a bird emerged, like magic, like something beautiful being born.

The women murmured to each other, and there was the soft, susurrating sound of their voices, the ripple of their occasional laughter, the warmth of her mother, the smell of her, of turps and of spices, the feeling of being allowed to stay up, of being held, the whiteness of the paper and the pleasure in folding and in making something fine.

She remembers all this, standing here in the evening kitchen – the peace there was in this room. She remembers the sense of peace.

## Hannah

It has not been easy to sleep, these last nights. Even with all the pillows she cannot find a comfortable place to lie.

The baby wakes her often. She lies there, feeling the baby move her limbs in the small space left to her. Hannah thinks she feels a heel bone, an elbow. She touches the baby through the skin of her stomach. The baby is a selkie. An underwater swimmer. An habitué of the dark.

The baby is a girl. At first, this knowledge troubled Hannah. A boy felt simpler somehow. How to be a mother to a girl?

But now the thought of a girl is wondrous.

Now she is impatient to meet her.

There is a line to be crossed first. A birthing. She is not scared, she thinks, of pain. It is only the surrender, perhaps, that frightens her.

She speaks to Nathan sometimes. He has a room in a flat close by. He visits and when he visits he is quiet, solicitous. He cooks for her, soups and risottos. He makes a large pan and he leaves it for her on the stove. Sometimes they walk together, along the canal. Sometimes, when she is tired, she takes his arm. Sometimes, before he leaves her where she sits, huge on the sofa, she catches him looking, catches the look on his face.

He asks for little, but he has asked to be present at the birth. She has not said yes to this. She does not know if having him there will make things easier or harder. There are many things that she does not know. And this not knowing, in these cold January days lit from a warmth within, feels OK somehow.

Cate stays one night a week. Hannah looks forward to her visits, when they will sit and talk and laugh. She has asked Cate to be her birth partner, and Cate has said yes. It will take her an hour and a half to drive from Canterbury, two hours at the most.

Hannah wakes in the night.

It is very late, or very early. It is four o'clock. It is the time at which people are born and the time at which people die. It is dark and she is wet – the bottoms of her pyjamas are soaking. She reaches for her phone and calls Cate.

'She's coming,' she says.

She feels the leap of her heart, the beat of her blood in her ears.

She is coming. Here, in the darkness, a new story is beginning.

Her girl is on her way.

# London Fields

*It is Saturday, which is market day. It is late spring, or early summer. It is mid-May, and the dog roses are in bloom in the tangled garden at the front of the house. Lissa sees them as she passes, on her way to the park.*

*It is warm. She is dressed simply, in faded jeans, an embroidered peasant blouse. Her feet are in thin sandals and she carries a canvas bag on her shoulder – inside it: good tomatoes, bread, Rioja, a goat's cheese covered with ash.*

*As she enters the park, she pauses on the path, looking over towards the back of the big old house with its crumbling garden wall, the old tree beneath which they used to love to sit. Today, the grass beneath the tree is packed with bodies, the air filled with the scent of barbecues and cigarette smoke, the blare of competing sound systems. It looks like a festival for the young. She looks up once more at the house, at the open windows, at the distant, shadowy figures that move around inside, then turns and walks on. They have arranged to meet on the other side of the park – close to the lido – the side where the families go. Here the grass is quieter and still green. She finds a spot and puts down an old rug and kicks off her shoes. The grass is lovely beneath her feet. She is nervous. This meeting was her idea – she wrote to them both, on a whim, one morning from the balcony of her small flat in Mexico City, telling* them she was coming – a rare visit to England, to London, for Laurie's funeral, asking if they might want to see her again, after all this time. She was surprised, and pleased, when they both replied and said they would.

Presently she hears a shout and looks up to see Cate, dressed in a light summer dress, and a young girl of five or so coming over the grass towards her. Lissa sees Cate pause, bend to the girl and point, reminding her, no doubt, who this tall woman with the short fair hair is, for Lissa has never met Cate's daughter, born the year after she left for good.

This is Poppy, says Cate, when they have hugged hello. She's been excited to meet you. I told her you used to be an actress. She loves to perform.

Ah, says Lissa, yes, a long time ago. And she kneels beside Poppy, a round-faced, smiling child, and asks the right questions, listening as the girl chatters about her ballet classes, about the play she did last Christmas at school.

Another call, and they turn, and here is Hannah, come from the lido, with her own daughter walking beside her – a tall six-year-old, another child that Lissa has never met, a girl with the look of her mother – the same sleekness, the same dark hair, the same graveness of expression. Clara, says Hannah, this is Lissa. Hannah and her daughter take their places on the rug and the food is brought out and smiled over and tucked into.

The talk, though, is only small talk, and Lissa, who has been imagining this moment for weeks, for years – feels a creeping sense of disappointment. Somehow she had hoped for more. But what, truly, can there be to say to each other, after all this time? Small talk is small, but the inroads to intimacy were savaged years ago. And who is to blame for that?

320

But then, as the afternoon deepens, as the wine is drunk and the light thickens, the women start to relax. They talk about the old days. They raise a toast to the old house. Hannah asks Lissa about her life in Mexico and Lissa tells her about her job, teaching English in a language school, about the city she has grown to love, the mornings when she takes herself to a cafe with her laptop and sits and writes. Small moments, really, but they make her feel alive. And as Lissa talks, carving the air with her hands, Hannah feels a part of herself unfurl, just as she did that first time she met her – Lissa carries colour in her, she always did, and Hannah feels herself draw a little closer, warming herself at the small fire of her old friend.

When Cate and Hannah talk, they talk about their children mostly – talk through them, even, reaching for them, touching them often, smoothing their hair. And their children talk, too – they know each other well, it is clear; they tell Lissa about a holiday they all took last summer to France. As Lissa watches, she feels a familiar ache. She will be forty-four next birthday. As the years in which she might conceivably conceive have diminished, she has felt a corresponding, surprising sadness rise. It is not that she wants a child, not really, she is happy with her life, with her apartment in a cool-tiled building in Coyoacan, with her partner, who is a kind and gentle man. She and he sleep late on the weekends. They have their lives to themselves. It is just that sometimes, lately, on the way to work, or walking through the weekend markets, she will stop, made suddenly breathless at the sight of a baby. And Mexico is full of babies. But mostly, most days, she is fine. Her partner has a son, a boy of fifteen, who lives with his mother nearby. He spends every other weekend with them. Lissa likes him. He is kind and studious and funny, like his father. He likes to sleep late, too.

Hannah's daughter talks about her dad – who is coming to pick her up later, as she is staying at his house tonight – and the mention of Nathan hovers dangerously in the air between the women, but as the girl chatters on, oblivious, the moment loses its charge, is lost in the next moment, and the next.

They look at each other, these women, as the girls talk, noticing the ways in which they have aged. They are not the same women they were.

They worry. They worry about their parents – their fathers mostly. Hannah's father, who forgets things – more and more, it seems – who no longer meets her on the platform at Stockport station when she travels north. Cate's father, in Spain, who drinks too much, and is lonely. Lissa's father, who seems to have no joy in his life at all.

They worry about summer, which is coming earlier and lasting longer each year – a worry that taints their enjoyment of this beautiful May afternoon like a dark drop of ink swirled in clear water. Most of all they worry about the future, about their children, about the world they will inherit, a world that seems so fractured and fast and ever more splintered. They worry about how their generation will be judged by those who come after, and if that judgement will be hard, about whether there is still time to rectify this, because, more and more these days, they would like those who come after them to look back and be proud.

Sometimes it seems that the list of their worries is endless, that they are corroded by worry, hollow with it – they and everybody else they talk to, these days.

*But long, too (although sometimes harder to name), is the list of things for which they are grateful: for small mercies, which no longer seem so small. For moments. Like this morning, for Cate, saying goodbye to her husband and her son, knowing they will be there to meet her again this evening, when she returns, knowing there will be food to eat, a table to sit around, the talk of her children. Her husband's continued steady presence in her life. And for Hannah, the pride she still takes in her work, the fact that she is still friends with the father of her child, the ongoing, unceasing miracle of her daughter's presence – a love so strong and fierce she feels no loneliness and no need for another, for she has found the love of her life. For Lissa, the quietness of her flat in the morning, when she rises early, and feels the warmth of the day to come in the air, and sits in the cool dawn and writes and feels sufficient unto herself.*

*They are grateful for these things because they know that old age and illness are not, perhaps, so very far away, and are not kind. They have seen this already, understood this, been humbled by it. They are humbled often, these days.*

*At a certain point in the afternoon, when the two girls have picked at the picnic and eaten their cake and are full of sugar and spiky energy and impatience, they jump up and move away from their mothers and from the other, blonde woman they do not know and whose name they will soon forget, on to the grass – called by the sun and the sky and by something else, something within that tells them they must move, right now. The same impulse, perhaps, that calls the seed to push up from the earth and reach for the light.*

*And Hannah's daughter takes Cate's daughter by the hand*

*and they spin round and round, round and round, and the women watch them, caught by their clumsy grace, the assertiveness of their small bodies in space, filled with a joy that is close to – that might, in fact, also be – pain. And the girls whirl on, laughing – glad to be free of the blanket, of the weight of their mothers' attention, of their mothers' need for them, of the looping, dipping, hard-to-follow thread of the women's conversation – giddy with movement, their hands clasped tightly together, round and round, round and round, in this spun-gold moment, dizzy with, drunk with life.*

# Acknowledgements

If it takes a village to raise a child, then it takes a very special village to raise a child *and* support the mother while she writes a novel. While writing this book I was fortunate enough to move to such a place – thanks to all my family in the Shire, but especially to Judith Way for deck therapy, to Cherry Buckwell for the walking cure, to Kate Christie for goddess-mother love, to Fionnagh Winston for wit and wisdom, to Rebecca Palmer for a home from home for my daughter, to Kelly Tica for boundless love, support and chicken soup, and to Rachael Stevens for sorting my life out, on so many levels, more times than I care to count.

Thanks to Ben and Toby for great chats about Seattle and LA – even if they didn't make it into the finished book.

To Olya Knezevic, who told me to watch *Autumn Sonata*.

To Judith, for taking me to Canterbury, lending me her library card and sharing her love of the city.

To the lady who opened the Tomb of the Eagles on a wild and wet day in November and gave her time so gently and generously.

To Philip Makatrewicz, Thea Bennett and Cherry Buckwell, who read the book in early drafts and whose clarity and enthusiasm were incredibly helpful.

To Josh Raymond and his legendary skinny black pen, whose edits are worth an ISBN number in themselves.

To the Unwriteables, still going strong after a decade of love and support.

To Naomi Wirthner, who called me in to her *Seagull*, and wove the magic round us all.

To my mum, Pamela Hope, whose activism inspired and shaped me, and who came with me on a memorable walk to Greenham Common.

To Dave, for making it work somehow.

To Bridie, for hearing the call, and answering with your wild bright wondrous self.

To my wonderful editor, Jane Lawson – she who understands what an ending must be.

To the inimitable Alison Barrow. I feel so lucky to have you on my team.

To my agent Caroline Wood, whose dedication to this book and desire to see it be all it could be were unwavering. Caroline, you have helped more than anyone else to bring this book into being – thank you so much for your rigour, enthusiasm and support.

And finally to the beautiful women who have shaped my life, the horizon watchers, the fierce dancers, the van converters, the river swimmers, the caretakers, the ones who know the old ways. Thanks for all you've taught me and all we've shared. More, please, more.

# About the Author

ANNA HOPE studied at Oxford University and RADA. She is the acclaimed author of *Wake* and *The Ballroom*. Her contemporary fiction debut, *Expectation*, explores themes of love, lust, motherhood and feminism, while asking the greater question of what defines a generation. She lives in Sussex with her husband and young daughter.

# Challenging Silence

## Other titles in the Studies in Society series

# Challenging Silence

Innovative responses to
sexual and domestic violence

Edited by Jan Breckenridge and Lesley Laing

ALLEN & UNWIN

First published in 1999 by
Allen & Unwin
9 Atchison Street, St Leonards NSW 1590, Australia
Phone: (61 2) 8425 0100
Fax:    (61 2) 9906 2218
E-mail: frontdesk@allen-unwin.com.au
Web:   http://www.allen-unwin.com.au

National Library of Australia
Cataloguing-in-Publication entry:

Challenging silence: innovative responses to sexual and
  domestic violence.

  Bibliography.
  Includes index.
  ISBN 1 86448 725 9.

  1. Sex crimes—Australia. 2. Child sexual abuse—
  Australia. 3. Family violence—Australia. 4. Sexual
  abuse victims—Services for—Australia. I. Breckenridge,
  Jan. II. Laing, Lesley.

364.1530994

Set in 10.5/12 pt Bembo by DOCUPRO, Sydney
Printed by SRM Production Services Sdn Bhd, Malaysia

10 9 8 7 6 5 4 3 2 1

*For Dominic,*
*with love*

# Contents

# Preface

MANY FRIENDS, FAMILY members and colleagues would tell you that this book was a very creative way of avoiding the completion of our doctoral theses. However, this would be only partly true. The impetus for this book comes from two separate but interrelated concerns and interests. The first of these is reflected in Part I where we explore the apparent 'backlash' against the public acknowledgment of sexual and domestic violence. The second, reflected in Part II, is a firm commitment to sharing innovative and creative responses to sexual and domestic violence with a wide audience of health, welfare and legal professionals. We believe that the contributions comprise a rich and representative collection from both New South Wales and interstate.

Many people who have been associated with this project deserve thanks. The research project described by Frank Astill, Joan Bratel and Christine Johnston was carried out with the assistance of a National Staff Development Fund grant. They gratefully thank Louise Cahill, Cherie Saunders, Sarah Pritchard, Robin Hunt and the Speech Department of the Spastic Centre of NSW and, most of all, the children and their families for agreeing to participate in the project.

The chapter by Shelagh Doyle and Claire Barbato is based on a detailed report published by the NSW Department for Women: *Heroines of Fortitude: the Experiences of Women in Court as Victims of*

*Sexual Assault* (1996). The authors thank their fellow *Heroines* team members, Pia Van de Zandt, Gina Leotta and Jenny Bargen, who, with the assistance of the authors, co-wrote the original report. Their chapter is written in a personal capacity and does not necessarily represent the views of the NSW Department for Women.

Elisabeth Shaw, Akivra Bouris and Sheena Pye acknowledge the assistance of Kerrie James, Clinical Director, Relationships Australia, in preparing their chapter and in her development of the Family Safety Program. The Ackerman Institute's Center for Family Safety, New York, inspired both their service model and name.

We would both like to thank Elizabeth Weiss from Allen & Unwin for her patience and support during this project. Thanks also to Tony Vinson for his support and ideas in the conception of the structure of the project. We both thank many colleagues and friends who have had to listen to the trials and tribulations of producing this book within the time frame and word length.

Jan Breckenridge would like to thank Jane Waddy for her creative ideas, love and support and more than her fair share of childcare, and Dominic Breckenridge who was born into this project and is possibly heartily sick of it distracting from playtime. Lesley Laing would like to thank Chris Burke for her support throughout the project, and for generously sharing an office where the book often took up most of the available space!

'Walking on Eggshells: Child Sexual Abuse Allegations in the Context of Divorce' was originally published in the *British Journal of Social Work* 1997, vol. 27, pp. 529–544, and is reprinted by permission of Oxford University Press.

'Recovered Memories of Child Sexual Abuse: The Science and the Ideology' was originally published in *The Judicial Review* 1977, vol. 3, no. 3, p. 163, and is reprinted with the permission of the Judicial Commission of New South Wales.

'Truth or Fiction: Men as Victims of Domestic Violence?' was originally published in *The Australian and New Zealand Journal of Family Therapy* 1996, vol. 17, no. 3, pp. 121–125, and is reprinted with permission.

'A Comprehensive Approach: the Family Safety Model with Domestic Violence' was originally published in an extended version in *The Australian and New Zealand Journal of Family Therapy* 1996, vol. 17, no. 3, pp. 126–136, and is reprinted with permission.

# Contributors

FRANK ASTILL is Director of the University of Sydney Law Extension Committee. He has practised law and taught in both Law and Education faculties. His particular interests are legal education and dispute resolution strategies.

EILEEN BALDRY BA, DipEd (Syd), MWP, PhD (UNSW) has participated in and researched social and community action, has published in the areas of prisons and child abuse and is presently a Lecturer, School of Social Work, University of New South Wales.

CLAIRE BARBATO completed a Bachelor of Arts (Honours–Women's Studies) in 1991. Between April 1994 and July 1996 Claire worked at the New South Wales Department for Women as a Research/ Policy Officer where she was part of the research team that conducted the *Heroines of Fortitude* project. She is now working in the community housing sector.

AKIVRA BOURIS BSocStud (MSW) is a Social Worker and Family Therapist. She is currently in private practice, teaches in the Social Work Faculty and Couple and Family Therapy training programs at the University of New South Wales and is an educator/group leader in the Family Safety Program at Relationships Australia. Akivra has a background in child and adolescent psychiatry, sexual assault, medical social work and child and family health.

JOAN BRATEL is a psychologist with over 16 years' experience in the fields of child development and disability. Her particular areas of interest are children with disabilities, child protection and family support. She currently manages an early childhood intervention program and an intensive family support program for the North Eastern Sydney Region of the Spastic Centre of New South Wales. She is also involved in various research projects which examine child protection issues for children living with a disability.

JAN BRECKENRIDGE is Senior Lecturer in the School of Social Work at the University of New South Wales, teaching in the areas of contemporary social theory and social work practice and offering specialist electives in the areas of sexual and domestic violence. She is attached to the Centre for Gender-Related Violence Studies and is the co-editor of *Crimes of Violence—Australian Responses to Rape and Child Sexual Assault* (1992). Currently Jan is involved in a three-year research study funded by the Australian Research Council, undertaking a comparative analysis of counselling strategies used to address child sexual assault.

CHRIS BURKE is Director of Jannawi Family Centre, a child protection service in Sydney. She has worked for over 20 years in the areas of domestic violence, child sexual assault and child protection service delivery, community education and training. She co-wrote and produced *Change Could Come*, a community education and training package using lifelike puppets for adults about overcoming the effects of domestic violence on children.

ANNE COSSINS is a senior lecturer in Law in the Faculty of Law, University of New South Wales. She has published in a wide variety of fields, such as administrative law, freedom of information law, environmental law, feminist legal theory, evidence law and sexual assault law reform. She has recently completed her PhD thesis entitled *Masculinities, Sexualities and Child Sexual Abuse.*

JANE DAVIDSON has worked in women's health and sexual assault for the last 20 years, including several years as a sexual assault counsellor and coordinator of the Sydney Rape Crisis Centre. Her research into the sexual abuse of women in psychiatric institutions, *Every Boundary Broken*, was completed in 1997. She is currently working at the University of New South Wales on research into counselling interventions for children who have been sexually assaulted and also works as a sessional trainer educating mental health workers on adult and child sexual assault.

SHELAGH DOYLE has a BA (Hons) in Women's Studies and History from Macquarie University and a Bachelor of Laws (LLB) from the University of New South Wales. She has worked for four years as a policy adviser in the Law and Violence Unit at the New South Wales Department for Women. During that time she has served as Executive Officer of the New South Wales Sexual Assault Committee and was a member of the research team for the project *Heroines of Fortitude: the Experience of Women in Court as Victims of Sexual Assault.*

ANN-MARIE HAYES currently works as a Manager of a Youth Accommodation Service in the western suburbs of Adelaide. Prior to this she worked at a Women's Health Centre as a social worker. This work involved counselling, group work and broader activist work around the areas of sexual/ritual abuse, violence against women generally and women's mental health issues.

CATHERINE HUMPHREYS is currently employed at the University of Warwick in the Department of Social Policy and Social Work. She worked for 15 years as a social work practitioner in the child protection and mental health fields in Australia. In 1994 she moved to England to take up the University of Warwick post. She has a longstanding interest in work in the areas of domestic violence and child protection, focusing particularly on issues of child sexual abuse. Her recent research and writing has been in the areas of domestic violence and child protection, attending to the crossover in the child abuse area.

ROSEMARY HUNTER is an Associate Professor of Law at the University of Melbourne and, during 1998/99, principal researcher at the Justice Research Centre, Sydney. Her general research interests are in the areas of anti-discrimination law, women's employment and feminist legal theories, her doctoral research investigating ways in which women's experiences of violence are heard and (re)constructed in various court settings. She is the author of *Indirect Discrimination in the Workplace* (1992) and the co-editor of *Thinking About Law: Perspectives on the History, Philosophy and Sociology of Law* (1995).

JANE HUTTON is a therapist and educator in private practice in Montville, Queensland. She has a particular interest in narrative therapy, group work and therapy with adolescents and survivors of abuse. She has provided specialist training in these areas for organisations across Australia.

KERRIE JAMES MSW, MLitt (Women's Studies) is the Clinical Director of Relationships Australia (NSW). Her background is in family therapy and she currently teaches in the *Masters in Couple Family Therapy* course at the University of New South Wales, School of Social Work. Kerrie has published widely in family therapy about feminism, child abuse, domestic violence and couple work and is currently involved in a qualitative study of men's violence in relationships.

CHRISTINE JOHNSTON is a lecturer in Developmental Disability in the Faculty of Nursing, University of Sydney. Her particular interests are in early childhood intervention and the development of self-concept in children with disabilities.

MELVA KENNEDY has worked in child sexual assault counselling, community education and training with Aboriginal communities. She was the first Aboriginal person to become accredited to conduct the Protective Behaviours Program. She has conducted training workshops on child sexual assault throughout New South Wales, and in Canberra and the Northern Territory. She has been awarded a Churchill fellowship to travel to Canada in 1999 to study indigenous approaches to dealing with child abuse, sexual assault and domestic violence.

LESLEY LAING is Director of the Education Centre Against Violence, a specialist organisation providing training in the areas of sexual assault, domestic violence and child abuse. Her background is in work with children and families in community health, child and family psychiatry and sexual assault services. Her doctoral research evaluated Australia's first incest treatment program. With Jan Breckenridge, she is currently undertaking a three-year study, funded by the Australian Research Council, of outcomes for children and families attending specialist sexual assault services.

LORNA MCNAMARA RMRN, RPN, BachHlthSc (Nur) has been employed as an educator at the Education Centre Against Violence since 1994, training mental health professionals on the issues of sexual assault and domestic violence. She has worked in the mental health sector and in community organisations for the past 20 years and is Chair of Women & Mental Health Inc., a non-government organisation committed to the improvement of services for women experiencing a mental illness. Lorna has been actively involved with the research report, *Every Boundary Broken*, which examined the sexual abuse of women in psychiatric facilities.

SHEENA PYE AAMFC has been involved throughout the development of the Family Safety Program at Relationships Australia (NSW) as a Clinical Supervisor and Group Leader/Educator. She established and facilitated the women's support groups, and coordinates and supervises all the family safety services in South West Sydney.

ELISABETH SHAW BA (Hons), DipFamTher, MMgt (Comm) is a psychologist currently working as a Regional Manager at Relationships Australia (NSW) and in private practice at Drummoyne, Sydney. She has worked extensively with perpetrators and survivors of domestic violence in the Family Safety Program at Relationships Australia, and teaches and supervises working with domestic violence as well as other specialist clinical issues for the professional community.

MAILIN SUCHTING has a longstanding interest in issues of race, culture and identity and the ways in which these intersect with feminist practice. She is currently employed by the Education Centre Against Violence and is working towards the completion of a Master of Arts (Communications and Cultural Studies) at the University of Western Sydney, New South Wales.

JANE TIGGEMAN is a former Co-director of the Dulwich Centre (1988–98) and has been practising psychology in the clinical area for 20 years. She has worked with survivors of emotional, physical, sexual and ritual abuse for many years. Upon the birth of her son Saxon in 1997 she began part-time work and is currently based at NADA, a counselling centre in Adelaide that encourages respectful intervention in domestic abuse and workplace harassment.

TONY VINSON BA, DipSocStudy (Syd), MA, PhD, DipSoc (UNSW), now Emeritus Professor, was previously foundation Professor of Behavioural Science in Medicine at the University of Newcastle, New South Wales, and Professor of Social Work at the University of New South Wales. He has undertaken research on behalf of the Child Protection Council of New South Wales and is currently Director of the Centre for Gender-related Violence Studies.

# Introduction

THE 1970S WERE marked by the breaking of silence about the prevalence and impact of sexual and domestic violence. This period can be characterised as one in which the community was confronted by a new, feminist analysis of violence against women and children, and in which demands were made for services to address these issues. The 1980s saw governments respond by funding programs in the public and community sectors to provide services for victims. In Australia, service development was predominantly underpinned by a feminist analysis. However, the 1990s have seen challenges to established views of violence, and have been marked by attempts to silence victims and survivors again, and also to discredit those who believe their stories and advocate on their behalf. A notable example is the rapidity with which the view that adults reporting sexual victimisation in childhood are suffering from 'false memory syndrome' has gained currency in the popular press, legal system and therapeutic discourse. These challenges have demonstrated the need for research-based intervention and service development, and for innovative practices designed to meet the emergent challenges.

This book provides a compilation of contemporary Australian research and practice and reflects an interdisciplinary approach to sexual and domestic violence and the physical abuse and neglect of children. Each of the contributions in Part I explores an aspect

**1**

of the process of silencing the victims of violence, while the contributions in Part II include examples of innovative practice and research which provide a foundation for new responses. Chapter 1 examines the context for the two parts of this collection. Jan Breckenridge explores the ways in which professional discourses about sexual and domestic violence have confined the voices of the victims to the margins of what was accepted as knowledge. Silencing practices, such as speaking about domestic and sexual violence in mythologised ways, are also explored and their role in silencing the victim exposed. She then traces the impact of the second wave of the women's movement in the 1970s and 1980s in publicly challenging the unhelpful dominance of professional discourses, before discussing the backlash that these same activists and victims are now facing. She concludes by looking at strategies that offer a basis for withstanding the ravages of backlash and moving beyond its influence.

In Chapter 2, Catherine Humphreys explores the paradox by which women who attempt to protect their children from sexual assault by taking action in the Family Court are themselves victimised and accused of either overreacting or exacting vengeance through false allegations of abuse. Through an examination of empirical studies, Humphreys exposes the myth of the 'falsely accusing mother' and explores possible explanations for the lack of congruity between practice and research in this field.

An important theme of Part I is the failure of attempted modifications to the legal system adequately to address the needs or protect the interests of victims. In Chapter 3, Shelagh Doyle and Claire Barbato illustrate the failure of sexual assault law reform to overturn entrenched prejudices about victim/complainants in the criminal justice system, through a discussion of some of the findings of the *Heroines of Fortitude* study. In the area of civil law, Rosemary Hunter argues, from her research on the experience of women who attempt redress against violence and harassment by family members or work colleagues, that the emphasis on 'consent'—mutually agreed settlements—results in a lack of institutional affirmation of women's stories of abuse. Thus the existence of violence against women, and the scale of that violence, fails to enter the realm of public knowledge: men's denial and minimisation of violence is echoed by the state.

In Chapter 5, Mailin Suchting explores why improving access to sexual assault services for people from non English speaking backgrounds might seem so hard and for whom. She examines the ways in which cultural, ethnic and racialised differences have been, and are currently, addressed in the provision of sexual assault services and proposes ways in which we can think about access in practice by using a politics of difference.

In Chapter 6, Jane Davidson and Lorna McNamara present the findings of a research study on the sexual abuse of women in psychiatric facilities, and make evident the failure of the system to respond to that abuse. This chapter also presents an interesting first-hand account of the barriers faced by the researchers in their attempts to conduct the study—constituting an attempt at another level to 'silence' victims of sexual abuse within the psychiatric system.

In Chapter 7, Anne Cossins cuts to the heart of 'backlash politics'. In a rigorous analysis of research and literature, she exposes the lack of evidence for the so-called 'false memory syndrome' and contrasts this with the empirical evidence confirming the existence of delayed recall of traumatic events. Since this phenomenon only became controversial in relation to the trauma of child sexual assault, she argues that the recovered memory debate is more an ideological debate than a legitimate scientific enterprise. She poses a question that underpins each of the chapters in Part I—namely, why some professions, and society generally, so quickly accept and promulgate attitudes, beliefs and theories that effectively silence the voices of victims of violence.

Part II begins with two chapters that interrogate the issue of offenders. Lesley Laing's research on a treatment program for incest offenders exposes the ways in which offenders continue to abuse power after disclosure and in treatment, and the challenges that this poses to treatment aimed at changing the power balance within the family. In Chapter 9, Kerrie James reviews the research about men's and women's violence within relationships, and concludes that, while it is true that women can be violent, female violence is qualitatively different from male violence, making it a fiction that women's violence is equivalent to men's in intent, severity and outcome.

Chapters 10 and 11 provide examples of creative therapeutic responses to survivors of child sexual assault. Jane Hutton conveys insight into the unique challenges and importance of working with adolescents—often a group that falls through the gaps in therapeutic services. In Chapter 11, Ann-Marie Hayes and Jane Tiggeman present therapeutic suggestions for ways of working with people who experience dissociative identity disorder. They contend that the therapist's courage to hear clients telling the story of their abuse is a fundamental requirement of therapy, and involves the therapist in the process of being a witness to healing and supporting clients' choice of overcoming habits of dissociation.

The vulnerability to abuse of children living with a disability such as cerebral palsy is exacerbated both by the nature of their disability (which affects speech production) and by ill-informed perceptions of decreased abilities, both in the community generally, and within the criminal justice system. In Chapter 12, Frank Astill, Joan Bratel and Christine Johnston describe ground-breaking research that shows a way forward in giving a voice, including a voice within the criminal justice system, to this group of children.

In Chapter 13, Melva Kennedy describes the process of raising the issue of child sexual assault with Aboriginal communities in ways that promote the development of culturally appropriate solutions. She also discusses issues that non-Aboriginal service providers need to understand when working with Aboriginal clients and communities, particularly the ongoing impact of colonisation and racism.

In Chapter 14, Eileen Baldry and Tony Vinson explore the question of whether community matters when considering prevention strategies for child protection. The discussion is based on their research study of the neighbourhood or local community as a potential source of support for families living in two socio-economically depressed localities in Western Sydney. The authors present ideas about possible strategies and existing programs that aim to make community matter in the promotion of the well-being of children and the prevention of child maltreatment.

Chapters 15 and 16 describe innovative responses to domestic violence. Elisabeth Shaw, Akivra Bouris and Sheena Pye outline the development of a comprehensive and integrated approach to addressing domestic violence in response to the needs of clients. Issues, dilemmas and practice frameworks are outlined in service provision to women, men, children and couples affected by violence.

In the final chapter, Chris Burke highlights the dilemmas and practice pitfalls for workers intervening in families in which there are both domestic violence and child protection concerns. She illustrates how gender-biased interventions have commonly encouraged a focus on the mother and her perceived deficiencies while failing to address the responsibility of the perpetrator. She goes on to provide a framework for intervention that aims to protect children, empower women and hold the perpetrators of violence accountable. This provides a fitting conclusion to this book. When perpetrators are held accountable and the voices of victims/ survivors are no longer silenced, then injustice and suffering can no longer continue unchecked.

# 1 Subjugation and silences: the role of the professions in silencing victims of sexual and domestic violence

## Jan Breckenridge

> Many people who wish to impose their definition of reality would deny that they are involved in gaining power. They would say that because of *their greater knowledge, wisdom, training and experience* they know what is best. The most dangerous people in the world are those who believe that they know what is best for others. [emphasis added] Masson (1988, pp. 16–17)

INDIVIDUALS WHO EXPERIENCE domestic and sexual violence as adults and children are likely to struggle to speak of the 'truth' of these events in ways that make sense of their own experience. The choice of the term 'struggle' may at first seem puzzling but it is only so until we give serious consideration to why it has been, and even in the 1990s is still, so difficult for both adults and children to voice their experiences of sexual and domestic violence in a public arena where they will be heard and believed.

Judith Herman (1992, p. 1) suggests that this struggle is inevitable because certain violations are too terrible to utter aloud; they are unspeakable. While this proposition may explain the difficulty that 'victims'[1] have in speaking publicly of their pain, it is only one part of a complex story of subjugation and silences. To understand fully the reasons why, in many western countries prior to the 1980s, the voice of the victim of sexual and domestic violence was not heard, it is crucial to look beyond the horror of violence to the ways in which victims were, and still are, silenced. This chapter addresses this issue in detail by exploring the role that various professions[2] have played in shaping social and cultural understandings of sexual and domestic violence—understandings that often bear little resemblance to victims' own experiences.

To unravel the operations of the dual concepts of subjugation and silences, examples of professional practices are drawn from aspects of sexual and domestic violence. This discussion is then followed with the case study of Sigmund Freud's psychoanalysis, 'the talking cure', and the very particular impact this professional intervention has had in the area of child sexual assault.

It would be depressing and perhaps a little unbalanced to concentrate only on the unhelpful dominance of professional discourses up until the public challenges of the second wave of the women's movement in the 1970s and 1980s. Consequently this chapter concludes by looking briefly at those challenges and the ways in which the strategies used by activists and survivors to 'break the silence' surrounding sexual and domestic violence have been incorporated into contemporary professional practice and research, and could be further incorporated.

## SUBJUGATION AND SILENCES . . .

The dual concepts of 'subjugation' and 'silences' provide a useful conceptual framework within which it is possible to understand the operations of what are known as the 'psy' professions (such as medicine, psychiatry, psychology, and the social sciences) and the law in relation to sexual and domestic violence. These concepts are drawn from the work of the French philosopher and historian Michel Foucault but are at the same time consistent with contemporary feminist accounts of sexual and domestic violence.[3] The following discussion focuses mainly on professional discourses prior to the public challenges of the second wave of the women's movement in the 1970s and 1980s. However, there is still evidence today of the operations of subjugation and silences in professional practice, which is taken up in greater detail at the end of this chapter.

### Subjugation

Subjugation refers to processes that subordinate or discount certain types of experiences or sources of information, by either ignoring or reinterpreting the content (Foucault 1980, pp. 81–82). In relation to domestic and sexual violence, subjugation occurs when various professional 'knowledges', and their ways of talking about violence (discourses), are privileged over the knowledge that victims hold about their own experiences. Prior to the 1970s, members of the 'psy' and legal professions had all put forward theoretical perspectives that hid or obscured the actual incidence, prevalence and dynamics of sexual and domestic violence. Despite contradictions within and between professional discourses, victims' experiences were not heard in any public arena but were instead buried or disguised in historical accounts, formal theoretical frameworks and government policies.

For example, sociological surveys in the nineteenth century[4] unearthed substantial information about the prevalence of incest in the colonies. In these accounts incest was understood to be, and was portrayed as, the product of environmental conditions such as poverty and overcrowding due to inadequate housing. Like child physical abuse and neglect, incest was seen as an inevitable part of working class life and little or no attention was paid in these reports to the effects sexual violence may have had on individual members of that class. Typically, lack of housing and poverty were the issues that were publicly spoken about and which became the public's concern. Consequently the protection of children was awarded little value and the victim's own knowledge and experience of abuse effectively remained invisible.

With the emergence of essentialism in the early part of the twentieth century, incest and child physical abuse became the subject of psychology and like professions. These professions sought to 'treat' and therefore control 'mad' or 'bad' behaviours that were understood to be the manifestations of genetic or biological problems. Consequently the tenor of social surveys changed. Incest and child physical abuse and neglect were no longer mentioned at all as there was now a strong reluctance to discuss publicly such 'unnatural' and, by implication, unpleasant practices (Finch 1993, p. 68). A parallel, culturally induced shame of admitting to being a victim of violence in the home privatised and subjugated the issues of sexual and domestic violence. This allowed the professions to assert the sanctity of family life and the associated civil liberty of privacy. Importantly, where incest and child physical abuse were not ignored, they were 'treated' within the confines of the therapeutic relationship.

Professional and cultural values around the sanctity of the

family were clearly reflected in government policies and in legal redress for victims of domestic violence. Despite the tacit legal recognition of domestic abuse, there was a strong reluctance to enforce any penalty on the part of the police. Other policy barriers were also evident in accessing protection. In Sydney, at the turn of the century, a summons cost six shillings and sixpence—half the weekly wages of a domestic servant (Allen 1982, p. 4). For non-working women the difficulties were profound. They would have had to request money from their husbands (unless their family of origin agreed to help) to ensure their own protection—a paradox to say the least. It is clear to see, in these particular examples, that the knowledges of social science, psychology and the law worked together to subjugate the experiences of those who suffered domestic violence, child sexual assault and physical abuse in the home. Their stories remained unspeakable.

So the concept of subjugation is critical, as in the first instance it identifies and names the process by which a whole set of knowledge, that of the victims of domestic and sexual assault, has been disqualified as inadequate or insufficiently developed. Within this framework, victims' experiences are assumed to be naive and subjective knowledges, and are consequently located further down the hierarchy of belief (and status), beneath the required level of objectivity and 'scientificity' claimed by professional knowledges. An excellent example of this can be found in an examination of the ways in which the 'truth' of events is defined in the legal system. Frequently, other knowledge is heard only to the extent that it can be recast as pertinent to legal issues and is therefore admissible in a court of law (Bell 1993, p. 10). For example, in cases of adult and child sexual assault, or for an adult incest survivor, any knowledge the victims may possess of events is heard only when it touches upon what the law sees as relevant. Conversely, the legal method may highlight aspects of the situation that the victim may not see as relevant, such as whether they were able to say 'no', their truthfulness in other situations, or whether they told anyone the assaults were occurring. The 'truth' that is propounded in any given case is not necessarily based on the experience of the victim. Their stories are confined to the margins of knowledge and are only admissible to the extent that they conform to the legal method of establishing 'the facts'.

The concept of subjugation provides an equally important means of understanding how the documentation of sexual and domestic violence has been disguised or masked through the scholarship of professional discourses. Halberg and Rigne (1994, p. 155) express a concern that is raised throughout much of the contemporary literature by asserting that there has always been evidence that professionals knew that sexual and domestic violence occurred. However, these same professionals often knowingly recorded information in ways that obscured the actuality of such violence by simply calling it something else. Allen (1990, p. 14) provides abundant evidence of this occurring in the Australian context. A telling example from this text is the legal declaration of teenage girls as 'uncontrollable' when removed from their family of origin, with their experiences of incest to be found only in confidential case files, and not in any other official statistical record of their circumstances.

Subjugation, when understood in relation to the regulation of Aboriginal children, has had a very particular and dramatic impact. In New South Wales, the amendment of the *Aboriginal Protection Act* 1909 led to the establishment of the Aboriginal Protection Board in 1915. The Board gained total control ('loco-parentis') over Aboriginal children in New South Wales, and proceeded to remove them from their families under an apprenticeship scheme. Aboriginal children were not removed because they had been abused—rather, they were randomly 'rounded up' and removed because of the belief that Aboriginal families could not, by virtue of their Aboriginality, ever provide a suitable environment for their children. Physical abuse and mistreatment after their removal was commonplace, one specific consequence being that many Aboriginal girls were sexually abused when in care or servitude, although the only official indication of this was the recording of Aboriginal teenage pregnancies.

It has really been only in the last decade that the historical rationale for the removal of Aboriginal children and the consequent sexual and physical abuse many suffered has been publicly questioned and discussed. Importantly, this occurred in no small part after Aboriginal people themselves spoke out about the devastation they experienced as a result of this particular government policy. Showing little regard for the damage caused by past decisions, the Howard government appears not to want to hear or acknowledge the pain and suffering that indigenous people wish to speak of. Instead, there is a preference to stick doggedly with the simplistic and hollow explanation that past governments and philanthropists were simply doing what they thought was best at that time.

The strategy of subjugation, then, provides an understanding of how professionals asserted that 'they knew what was best for others', and how the marginalisation of the voice of the victim of sexual and domestic violence necessarily complemented the privileging of professional knowledge in Western cultures.

## Silences . . .

Subjugation is only one part of a dual system that facilitates a context in which victims struggle to speak of their experiences in the public domain. Victims' experiences of sexual and domestic violence are subjugated alongside the operation of 'silences' within professional discourses. Foucault is not suggesting a blanket imposition of silence about an area as a whole, or even a mere reduction in what is said. Rather, silences refer to 'the things one declines to say, or is forbidden to name, that function alongside the things that are said with them, and in relation to them' (Foucault 1981, p. 27). Silences, then, have been an equally effective technique operating to omit or mask different aspects of a narrative, thereby changing its meaning and significance.

Silences have had a very particular and dramatic effect on the victim of sexual and domestic violence and are evidenced in professional discourses in two ways. First, silences are apparent in ways of speaking about sexual or domestic violence that fail to distinguish particular instances and events within a generic discussion of issues. In such a strategy, child sexual assault may be omitted from explicit mention. For example, the generic child abuse category, used by critical social theorists and some members of the medical profession, does not distinguish between child physical abuse and neglect and the differing features that characterise child sexual abuse. The effect of such generalised discussion is that it hides the different gendered dynamics and any specific effects it may have on its victims, thereby making the different features of child sexual assault invisible. Similarly, in New South Wales, the change of name from Apprehended Domestic Violence Order to Apprehended Violence Order, is another way of avoiding naming and speaking about violence in the home as a specific and prevalent problem.

The second way in which silences may be incorporated in professional discourses encompasses speaking about domestic and sexual assault, but in mythologised ways that effectively silence a particular voice, that of the victim. The concept of 'mythology' is intended to portray the process by which explanations of events are interpretations imposed from above, rather than constructions that reflect the experiences of the victims from the bottom up. Bell (1993, pp. 79–88) provides an excellent account of the operations of myths in relation to child sexual assault, arguing that they are obvious within a number of professional discourses, successfully obscuring the victims' experiences of childhood sexual violence, despite asserting contradictory and unsubstantiated propositions.

The inconsistent nature and content of mythology is clearly seen when comparing the core assumptions of a select number of professional discourses. For example, the psychoanalytic theory developed by Freud denies that child sexual assault occurs. However, in family dysfunction literature there is a clear acknowledgment that it does occur, perhaps even frequently, although its impact is minimised by the suggestion that it should be considered a symptom of a more significant problem for the family (Goldthorpe 1987). Even when abuse is considered a problem, it is argued by a selection of psychological 'trait'/deviance theorists such as Weinberg (1955) that, once again, it is only a rare occurrence, perpetrated by a small number of psychopathic or 'feeble-minded' men. Alternatively, offenders are often portrayed as 'normal' men who may be seduced by a precocious child or forced into the situation by an inadequate mother and/or wife (e.g. Justice & Justice 1979). It would seem that the only consistent feature of these myths is the patently telling silence regarding the actual experiences of abuse by the victims, and the accompanying silence in relation to the offenders and any responsibility they should assume for their actions.

Importantly, the operations of mythology in legal discourse can function to shift the location of domestic and sexual violence sideways, creating an ambiguity about the necessity and appropriateness of the application of legal prohibition in other than a few highly sensationalised cases. There is a tendency for disclosures of child sexual assault to be seen as better addressed by therapeutic means rather than pursuing criminal charges. For example, the judgement of the 'Mr Bubbles' case in New South Wales, made subsequent to the allegation that a pre-school proprietor had sexually assaulted a number of pre-school children, is a telling example of the difficulties faced in prosecuting cases of child sexual assault. The presiding magistrate claimed that 'I am satisfied that the children, due to their stage of cognitive development, and other factors, are not of sufficient intelligence to justify the reception of evidence from them . . .' (cited in Hatty 1991, p. 262). In this situation, children were disqualified from speaking of their experiences so their stories remained unheard. Very obviously, the legacy of Piaget's work in the area of developmental psychology has, from the early 1930s onwards, at best cast doubts on children's competence and ability to tell the truth, and at worst has allowed children to be constructed as malevolent creatures, liars, or both. Either way, the thought of pursuing legal redress after an allegation of child sexual assault is automatically problematised.

The theme of blaming the victim and obscuring the responsibility of the perpetrator was, and frequently still is, evident in professional discussions of sexual and domestic violence and, in particular, affects those victims who have experienced sexual assault. For example, after the perpetrator of a rape had pleaded guilty, Judge Bland stated in his judgement that '. . . often, despite criticism that has been directed towards judges lately about violence and women, [and] men acting violently to women during sexual intercourse, it does happen, in the common experience of those who have been in the law as long as I have anyway, that no subsequently means yes' (*The Age*, 6 May 1993, p. 11). In another case where three young men were raped at knifepoint on the Sydney University Campus, the security guard alleged that if the men 'had been doing the right thing' they would not have been raped (*The Sydney Morning Herald*, 21 January 1993, p. 9). The most insidious aspect of such mythology is that very often victims internalise these beliefs and therefore struggle to make sense of their experiences, let alone speak of them publicly or in a therapeutic relationship.

Generally, the mythology surrounding domestic and sexual violence both informs and is informed by professional and cultural values and beliefs. This is particularly evident in relation to adult sexual assault where the myths of rape incorporate and mirror cultural attitudes towards women and towards male sexuality. Excuses such as 'she provoked me', 'women often fantasise about rape', 'she really wanted it' and 'she changed her mind and then cried rape' have functioned to cast doubt on the genuineness of allegations and the good character of the victim. Moreover, the perpetrator effectively remains invisible while these same myths justify and excuse violent behaviour. Schultz (in Armstrong 1996, p. 20) typifies the insidious nature of this mythology, suggesting that 'so great can the role of the victim be in sex offences that many should be considered offenders themselves'. It is in this way that the victim is positioned as being responsible for the assault occurring in the first place. It would seem that even when women and children do attempt to speak of their experiences of violence in a public forum, there is no guarantee that they will be believed, particularly where a differing professional opinion is available.

## The inherent power of professional discourse

Within professional discourses, the strategies of subjugation and silences have selectively constructed what is to be counted as 'real' and 'true', as well as what is and isn't spoken about in relation to domestic and sexual violence. This situation remained largely unchallenged until the activism of second-wave feminism in the 1970s and 1980s. It is important to consider, however, the ways in which the professions maintained their stranglehold over the knowledges pertaining to these issues up until this time.

Foucault provides an interesting insight into the relationship between power and knowledge that allows an understanding of how this situation may develop. In his earlier work, Foucault stressed the importance of the relationship and interaction between power and knowledge, suggesting that '[P]ower produces knowledge' (1980, p. 27). He argues that, through the operations of power, knowledges are formed. This allows for the possibility of knowledge claims, which often allege a corresponding technical and conceptual expertise. The exclusive nature of this expertise is precisely what professionals claim when they seek to put forward their 'professional judgement' claim. It is in this fashion that the professions attempt to shape the 'truth' of a particular discourse by controlling who has the expertise to speak about an issue, in what context and in which particular time frame. There is an accompanying set of conditions and rules, which most often relate to obtaining the necessary academic qualifications before being awarded any credibility, but may also relate to professional regulation and accreditation.

The ensuing exclusivity of the holder of this professional knowledge automatically amounts to a limitation on who may be allowed to speak appropriately and legitimately of certain issues unless they have satisfied certain conditions or have been qualified to do so from the outset. Thus professional knowledge becomes the sole possession of 'experts' who are seen to have *greater knowledge, wisdom, training and experience*. The ensuing status and credibility awarded to the professions produces the power to create reality by controlling all discussion of the issues and appropriating meaning. Thus, 'truth' becomes a function of who controls a particular discourse or professional opinion. Therefore, it is crucial to acknowledge that any resistance offered by a victim necessitates having the capacity to 'speak' and be 'heard'.

It is important to remember, however, that professionals and practitioners have a vested interest in maintaining 'expert' ways of speaking in order to control access to the production of knowledge. More precisely, the professions attempt to control who has the authority to speak, for the control of knowledge ultimately depends on controlling the subjects who 'know' (Larson 1990, p. 32). Therefore, what has counted as the 'truth' about sexual and domestic violence in various situations has relied on the suppression of the voice of the victim and a privileging of professional knowledge that mostly supports the cultural status quo and pro-fessional self-interest. The critical point is that the professions' base in 'respected' knowledges and institutional settings provides the credibility that makes professional discourses so tenacious and so very effective in silencing the voice of the victim who is, after all, the 'object' of their knowledge.

This chapter now examines 'the heroic age of hysteria' with a particular focus on a case study—that of Sigmund Freud and his development of psychoanalysis, which he colloquially dubbed the 'talking cure'. Following the earlier discussions of the operations of subjugation and silences, a number of questions are addressed through this case study. First, how and in what ways has psycho-analytic discourse contributed to the struggle of the victims of sexual violence to speak of their experiences? And, crucially, how have aspects of psychoanalysis functioned so that the experiences of victims are not accepted or believed to be true?

## THE HEROIC AGE OF HYSTERIA

By the end of the nineteenth century the study of sexuality generally, but particularly incest, occupied a central place in the discourse of medical science (Foucault 1981). Incest featured in two distinct but clearly related disciplines. Medico-legal practition-ers (from forensic medicine) debated the alleged 'innocence' of the child in reported cases of child sexual assault. Alternatively, the psychiatric fraternity concentrated on adult 'hysterics', who were considered to be suffering from a strange disease with incoherent and incomprehensible symptoms that manifested in women and originated in the uterus, and which had been named 'hysteria'. This discussion concentrates on the study of hysteria and the work of Sigmund Freud who originally claimed to be interested in hysterics who he believed were 'suffering mainly from reminiscences' of childhood sexual assault (Freud & Breuer 1986, p. 58).

Initially, Freud's development of the aptly named 'talking cure' was a turning point in the treatment of women who had experienced childhood sexual assault. Freud had provided the opportunity for women to speak of their experiences of childhood sexual trauma, he had listened to them and, most importantly, he had believed them. Why then did Freud retract this particular theoretical premise for his work? This question is addressed by examining the process by which Freud came totally to repudiate his early work, arguably ensuring the perpetuation of psychoanalysis as an influential professional practice.

## Psychoanalysis—the 'talking cure'

Following the thread of memory, Freud and his patients uncovered major traumatic events of childhood that had been concealed beneath the more recent, often relatively trivial experiences that had actually triggered the onset of hysteria. In their writings on hysteria, Freud and Breuer (1986, p. 57) excitedly claimed that 'every individual hysterical symptom immediately and permanently disappeared when we had succeeded in bringing clearly to light the memory of the event by which it was provoked'. Hence the claim to the success of the 'talking cure' that would come to be known as psychoanalysis.

On the basis of his clinical work, Freud extended his findings to address the aetiology of hysteria, which was the title of his key paper presented to the Society for Psychiatry and Neurology in Vienna, in 1896. In this paper he put forward the thesis that 'at the bottom of every case of hysteria there are *one or more occurrences of premature sexual experiences*, occurrences which belong to the earliest years of childhood but which can be reproduced through the work of psychoanalysis in spite of the intervening decades' [emphasis in original] (Freud in Masson 1984, p. 271).[5] Freud believed he was showing his professional colleagues 'the solution to a more than thousand year old problem—a caput Nili' (Freud in Masson 1984, p. 272). However, he was also aware that

'The Aetiology of Hysteria' would make him 'one of those who disturbed the sleep of the world' (Freud in Masson 1984, p. 275).

Freud was so sure that he would be met with strong disbelief that he included in his text the type of 'myths' that would be used against his argument. Interestingly, Freud himself resorted to using those same myths when he recanted his thesis, and those myths have steadily prevailed and can be found in many a contemporary text. Even Krafft-Ebing, who had previously acknowledged increasing incidents of incest in criminal statistics at that time, commented that Freud's research sounded like 'a scientific fairy tale' (cited in Masson 1984, p. 9). In speaking publicly of women's and children's experiences of childhood sexual assault, Freud's work had led into the realms of the unthinkable.

There was little or no public response to Freud's paper (Masson 1984, p. 9). Contrary to all other papers given at the same conference, there was no summary of Freud's paper, nor was the discussion included in the proceedings. It was as if a complete silence had enveloped his work. Academics and professionals have only recently become truly aware of the professional censure that followed the personal victimisation he experienced and the consequent self-doubt he suffered. Had Jeffrey Masson, the Director of the Freud Archives (1978–81), not released previously suppressed information concerning Freud's personal correspondence with colleagues such as Wilhelm Fliess, the importance of Freud's theory of childhood seduction and certainly his reasons for recanting this work would have been lost. Immediately after he had given his paper, Freud wrote to Fliess claiming 'I am as isolated as you could wish me to be: the word has been given out to abandon me, and a void is forming around me' (cited in Masson 1984, p. 10).

Freud published his paper in defiance of his colleagues, but very quickly regretted his courage in publishing his findings. He privately recanted in his letters to Fliess in 1897, saying that 'I was at last obliged to recognise that these scenes of seduction had never taken place, and that they were only fantasies that they had made up' (cited in Masson 1984, p. 11). Freud was later to build on the work of Abraham, suggesting that the sexual constitution that is peculiar to children is precisely calculated to provoke sexual experiences of a particular kind—namely traumas (cited in Masson 1984, p. 131). In an astonishing turnaround, the child was no longer a victim, but was now to blame for childhood sexual traumas. In 1905 Freud publicly retracted his seduction theory. Giving up his 'erroneous' view allowed Freud to participate again in a medical society that had earlier ostracised him. By 1908, respected physicians had joined Freud and the psychoanalytic movement was born. But it is important to point out that an important 'truth' had been left behind—that of the victim of child sexual assault.

## An astonishing retraction

For Freud to successfully recant his theory of seduction, he had to completely reverse the professional context that he himself had created. This context had affirmed and protected the victims of childhood sexual assault. Freud now had to stop listening to women's experiences of child sexual assault, and to do this he had to construct another explanation for the repeated number of accusations that he had already heard. The implications of this were profound. Freud quickly insisted that women's experiences were no longer a source of 'truth' about child sexual assault, as they were not to be believed. Instead, they were now to be understood as fantasies, something that women wanted to have happened.

The shift in Freud's professional practice has consequently been labelled as misogynist by many subsequent researchers. For example, Young-Bruehl (1990, p. 41) aptly presents the concern, particularly of feminist researchers, that 'behind every specific criticism looms one large objection. Freud, so this objection goes, viewed femininity as failed masculinity'. There is also persuasive evidence of Freud's changed attitude towards women in his private correspondence and in his professional practice. His colleague Ferenczi reports that Freud wrote to him suggesting patients were only 'riff raff'. The 'only thing patients [read here women] were good for, was to help the analyst make money and provide material for theory' (Masson 1988, p. 19). The vindictive and cynical tone of this suggestion generalised to all Freud's ensuing work in relation to this area.

Within this newly constructed framework, Freud began to speak openly of childhood sexual assault in mythologised ways. The child that he had earlier claimed was the victim of sexual assault was now blamed for having a sexual constitution that provoked the sexual experiences he once termed traumatic. Freud's concern regarding the consequences for men of his earlier thesis was expressed privately to Fliess when he wrote in 1897, imagine 'the surprise that in all cases, *the father* [emphasis in original], not excluding my own, had to be accused of being perverse' (cited in

Masson 1984, p. 93). In his later work he concentrated on absolving fathers (including his own) from any possible responsibility by explaining his female patients' reported experiences of incest as fantasies that were typical of normal psychosexual development, which he called the Oedipus complex.[6]

However, Freud's last word on the theory of seduction is as astonishing as his original retraction of it. In his later work he was to make yet another allegation of childhood sexual assault, but this time, remarkably, he claims that 'the seducer is regularly the mother', and in these cases 'phantasy touches the ground of reality' (cited in Masson 1984, p. 200). The professional knowledge that Freud has managed almost to set in stone goes something like this. Any allegation of child sexual assault is the result of a child's fantasy. Where incest does occur, the child actively provoked the contact by being very 'seductive'. Furthermore, fathers are regularly falsely blamed, because the actual, as opposed to the fantasised, occurrence of incest is extremely rare. However, if there is someone to blame, it should be the mother who must accept the responsibility that, in physically caring for her child, she awakened sexual feelings.

The pervasiveness and enduring appeal of psychoanalytic practice cannot be overestimated. It no longer leads professionals into the realms of the unthinkable, nor does it accuse the male medical establishment of wrongdoing, and so it no longer necessarily 'disturbs the sleep of the world'. Undoubtedly, there are contemporary theoretical and practice reformulations of psychoanalysis that have moved beyond the tenets of Freudian interpretations only.[7] However, the legacy of Freud's mythological ways of speaking about child sexual assault is common parlance in most Western cultures. These ways of speaking about child sexual assault prevail to the exclusion of the voice of the victim, who, in any event, can be dismissed as a hysteric, a liar or both. The voice of the victim therefore has been successfully subjugated within the realms of professional and theoretical formulations and the ensuing silence remains deafening.

## THE (RE)DISCOVERY OF VIOLENCE AGAINST WOMEN AND CHILDREN

Judith Herman (1992, p. 9) argues that there is a curious history of episodic amnesia characterising the area of sexual violence generally. She claims that the study of sexual trauma does not languish for lack of interest. Rather, the subject provokes such intense controversy that it periodically becomes anathema. Indeed, the case study of Freud presents compelling evidence of how periods of active investigation have alternated with periods of oblivion. Herman maintains that to hold the traumatic reality of child sexual assault in either individual or collective consciousness requires a social context that affirms and protects the victims. More precisely, the victims must be positioned so they can speak and be heard, and their experiences must be acknowledged as credible before they can be believed. While the core of Herman's argument is concerned with instances of childhood sexual assault and adult survivors, it is of critical interest to this chapter when generalised to domestic and adult sexual violence.

Herman (1992, p. 9)[8] is not alone in suggesting that there have been times when victims have spoken, in an attempt to 'break the silence' enveloping their experiences of violence. Following Herman, Breckenridge (1996) similarly argues that women and children have only successfully resisted the total imposition of professional knowledge in relation to sexual and domestic violence, that their voices have only been heard, when they are in affiliation with a political movement. The following discussion outlines briefly the claimed 'successes' of second-wave feminism in relation to adult and child sexual and domestic violence in the State of New South Wales, although features of these collective actions are well evidenced in other States and Territories in Australia. This chapter concludes by considering the effects of the 'backlash' against these earlier achievements, and, most importantly, whether this backlash has reinforced old and reimposed new practices of subjugation and silences in relation to sexual and domestic violence.

## Breaking the silence

> How, then, did we get here? How, in just fifteen years, did we go from total silence—from what was said to be a 'dread taboo' . . . How did we get away from enforced secrecy, the suppression of children's experiences, women's experiences, such that they were not ever heard? (Armstrong 1996, p. 8)

The answers to these questions can be found, in large part, in a brief examination of the collective actions of second-wave feminism in the 1970s and 1980s that occurred in every State and Territory in Australia. This is not meant to suggest that child advocates and individual professionals were not helpful in lobbying for change—many were. However, the reforms that were achieved in the areas of sexual and domestic violence unmistakably reflect a feminist analysis of these issues, as did the ensuing strategies for policy reform and service provision. While it is fraught with difficulties to suggest that there was, or is, one feminist analysis, it is arguably true that self-proclaimed feminists at that particular time identified and accepted power and gender as the central features of sexual and domestic violence. Indeed, in New South Wales, the promotion of such an explicit feminist framework, and the accompanying decision to align child sexual assault with adult domestic and sexual violence has been described as 'astonishing' by more than one researcher (Sawer 1990).

By declaring the existence of violence against women and children as a fundamental arena of challenge to the structural and personal oppression of women, the women's movement raised the 'problem' of domestic and sexual violence to public prominence.[9] Importantly, these collective actions involved questioning the artificial division between private and public interests and highlighted feminist objections to stereotypic gender roles and the culturally condoned 'sanctity' of the family unit. The key strategy of 'breaking the silence' is perhaps best known in relation to the collective action targeting child sexual assault. However, this sentiment very much underpinned the movement's fight more generally to expose publicly the extent and nature of sexual and domestic violence.

The public nature of these collective actions certainly established violence against women and children as a significant and previously under-reported issue. In this sense, the 'personal' truly became the subject of political struggles. The strategies used by the movement to document the prevalence and dynamics of child sexual assault included research initiatives such as phone-ins and surveys, as well as responses to the issues involving government task forces, extensive legislative and policy reform and the funding and provision of specialist services and community education. In pursuing these strategies the women's movement combined grass roots activism and the work of 'femocrats' in the bureaucracy within sympathetic political contexts. This in turn resulted in considerable changes to the definition of, understanding of, and responses to, sexual and domestic violence.

However, an equally critical component of the movement's collective actions was the comprehensive challenge to the existing professional definitions of sexual and domestic violence and their (non)responses to 'victims'. Encouraging women and children to *speak* of their experiences enabled them to name what had happened. This in turn facilitated the public discussion of the nature and dynamics of gendered violence from the perspective of the victim. In so doing, Walby (1985, p. 12) claims that women's and children's experiences were 'elevated to the level of theory'. This process necessarily challenged the dominance of professional discourses, as it demanded that another 'truth', that of the victim, become central to cultural and professional responses to sexual and domestic violence.

Crucially, this newly developed theoretical base did allow for alternative theoretical frameworks and practices that responded better to the expressed needs of victims, and gave voice to their experiences. Women and children were now able to speak of their experiences of childhood sexual assault in a context where they were both heard and believed. By challenging the ways in which professional discourses had subjugated victims' experiences and the mythologised ways in which they had spoken of sexual and domestic violence, the women's movement had confronted the unhelpful legacy of professional discourses. Importantly, this very challenge influenced and reshaped professional discourse, thereby providing therapeutic alternatives and comprehensive policy and legislative reforms. The question is: Have these 'successes' been sustained?

## THE POLITICS OF BACKLASH

Just as the *Age of Hysteria* had been followed by Freud's vehement denial of the sexual assault of children, there were signs even as many of the initiatives were being implemented that second-wave feminism, too, had 'disturbed the sleep of the world'. The public knowledge of the reality of sexual and domestic violence was once again becoming unpalatable. As a consequence, a process that has come to be known as 'backlash' began to undermine hard fought gains, gradually growing in momentum from undercurrents of discontent to direct attacks. Initially, backlash framed the issues of sexual and domestic violence, particularly in relation to its incidence and prevalence, as possibly overblown and exaggerated. Now, self-proclaimed 'experts' openly dispute the veracity of feminist research while at the same time resorting to ideological accusations such as 'revenge feminism' to bolster their claims (Biddulph in *The Sydney Morning Herald*, 15 April 1996, p. 11).

Other critics emphasise and focus on the lack of 'neutrality' of alternative therapeutic responses to sexual and domestic violence, directly questioning the competence and motives of the therapist. This is most obviously evidenced in the debate about recovered memories of child sexual assault. Those involved in the backlash have renamed this issue 'false memory syndrome' and have even gone as far as setting up the False Memory Syndrome Foundation (FMSF) in the United States. The aim of this Foundation is to fight any accusations that are likely be heard in a court of law and to support those who, they claim, have been falsely accused by the work of therapists and 'bad' daughters who seek to disrupt family life with their stories.

Those therapists who choose to listen and to believe the recovered memories of adult survivors within the context of therapy are both personally and professionally attacked. They may be called 'hysterical' or be accused of having 'lost contact with rationality' (Guilliatt 1996c, p. 4). Even the Final Report of the Royal Commission into the NSW Police Service (1997, vol. V, p. 1189) talks of professional 'charlatans, who are obsessed or unbalanced and likely to occasion much distress and harm to persons who have *never truly* been victims of sexual assault' [emphasis added]. Yet again, it is as if listening to victims and believing their stories of violence automatically positions the therapist as being 'suspect' of some amorphous unprofessional practice. Ironically, the contemporary discourse of backlash appears to be remarkably similar in both process and content to the professional and personal censure Freud suffered after publishing 'The Aetiology of Hysteria' at the turn of the century.

Very obviously, backlash has attempted to reinforce old, and reimpose new, practices of subjugation and silences in relation to sexual and domestic violence. However, it is important to be aware that while backlash can be overt and vindictive there is also a subtlety to backlash tactics, which is well described by Susan Faludi. She claims that backlash:

> adopts disguises: a mask of mild derision or the painted face of deep 'concern'. . . It manipulates a system of rewards and punishments, elevating women who follow its rules, isolating those who don't. The backlash remarkets old myths about women as new facts and ignores all appeals to reason. (1991, p. xvii)

Print media provide excellent examples of the overt and covert workings of the backlash process. Editorials and feature articles can be found that question whether there is a rigorous enough system for determining the truth of sexual abuse claims (although not other kinds of claims) involving a wildly overinflated accusation that 'millions of dollars in compensation' may be at stake (Arndt in *The Weekend Australian Review*, 24 April 1994, p. 1). In 1993 there was an outcry about a 75-year-old man receiving a good behaviour bond after admitting to digital penetration of a nine-year-old girl. One commentator who was obviously irritated by the public concern expressed for such a minimal sentence, proposed 'a toast to all those we didn't hear from' (Murphy in *The Sun-Herald*, 7 March 1993, p. 11). A last, but pertinent example involves an accusation that the NSW domestic violence policy 'based their approach on a narrow ideological radical-feminist perspective' because the policy sought to enforce legal sanctions rather than offer therapeutic intervention as the alternative 'solution' (Arndt in *The Weekend Australian*, 11 March 1995, p. 27). When these tactics are ultimately exposed and their proponents cornered, backlash 'denies its own existence, points an accusatory finger at feminism, and burrows deeper' (Faludi 1991, p. xvii).

Regrettably, even though (or perhaps because) the women's movement achieved substantial progress in legislative and policy reform and in the development and provision of alternative professional services, the backlash has now eroded the integrity of many of the original reforms. Two significant issues have contributed to this. First, both before and after the collective actions of the 1970s and 1980s, many feminists were concerned about what they felt was too close an alignment with the state. And yet what other choice did second-wave feminism have? Franzway, Connell and Court (1989, p. 11) persuasively point out that this contradiction will remain in relation to sexual and domestic violence. Because the state holds the legal monopoly over both the regulation of violence among its citizens and the funding of services for victims, it was, and still is, inevitable that the women's movement must engage with the state in some way.

Arguably, the relationship between political activists and the state is a growing paradox for many contemporary social movements. On one hand, the state can provide much needed reform and funding for services. In relation to sexual and domestic violence, the state's acceptance and adoption of feminist principles in the areas of service provision, legal reform and policy reform made such instances of violence more visible and allowed for a different understanding of its dynamics and nature. On the other hand, what the state gives it can take away or water down just as easily. A telling example of this can be found in the words and actions of Virginia Chadwick, the (then) NSW Minister for Community Services, who immediately stalled the implementation of one of the most fundamental legal and policy reforms achieved through collective action, that of mandatory notification of child sexual assault. Mrs Chadwick was recorded in *Hansard* as stating 'Anyone who thinks there is a budgetary allocation to cope with such cases is wrong' (*Hansard*, 20 November 1988). This was a notable reversal of support but other commentators at that time argued that, in relation to many of the reforms, 'what feminism demanded, the state responded to, in turn, by incorporating and containing those demands' (Game 1985, p. 107).

The other factor making it difficult to maintain the political gains of the 1970s and 1980s has been the concurrent fragmentation of the women's movement. Even during the initial collective actions, criticisms were made of a feminist analysis that acknowledged only the oppression of gender and saw all women as equally oppressed. The influence of post-structuralism and the appeal of a politics of difference seemingly denies the movement its symbolic appeal as a specific and universal actor for all women. By giving everyone the chance to be different, it has cancelled its own separateness as a political force. Put simply, diversity has diminished the movement's capacity to emerge with a cohesive and collective voice in public forums because of unresolvable issues around diversity within and between different 'groups' of women. The fragmentation of the women's movement, combined with too close an alignment with the state, has made it difficult for feminism to locate its antagonistic nucleus. Together these difficulties have allowed the greater intensity of 'backlash' politics that so often follows substantial cultural change. Without any collective outcry, in the 1990s, when issues of sexual and domestic violence are spoken about in the public domain, notably the voice of the victim is ever more faint.

## FUTURE CHALLENGES

It is vital not to underestimate the force the backlash aimed at the alternative professional interventions developed by practitioners following the movement's feminist/power analysis of the 1980s. The operations of subjugation and silences are once again functioning to silence the voice of the victims. Moreover, activists and professionals are faced with the prospect of being worn down by the constant assault of backlash politics, largely because they face such attacks as individuals rather than as colleagues in collective action. These attacks are not only verbal. Many therapists were shaken when the administrator of Canberra Rape Crisis was jailed for 'refusing to produce her notes of sessions with a victim for the alleged rapist to use at his trial' (*The Sydney Morning Herald*, 15 December 1995, p. 1). Without the collective strength of a political movement, the proponents of backlash are often successful in their attempts to discredit individual professionals and re-pathologise victims, diminishing the capacity and credibility of both to speak publicly of sexual and domestic violence. How, then, do we maintain and build on the innovative alternative responses achieved by feminism in the 1970s and 1980s?

Put simply, the answer to this question is that it is imperative to revisit the earlier commitment to providing a context where victims are positioned so that they can speak, are able to be heard, and are believed. However, this can be achieved only if we are fully aware of the hazards facing professionals in the 1990s and as we head towards the next century. In the first instance it is imperative that we carefully consider and discuss the danger of 'professionalising' alternative responses as a strategy to gain legitimacy and credibility. There is no intention of suggesting here that there isn't a need and role for competent and skilled intervention. These are qualities that should underpin all professional practice. Rather, the use of 'professional' in this context refers to building an exclusive and excluding knowledge that assumes a specialised training, expertise or scientific basis that is imposed without dialogue with victims, thereby losing touch with their self-defined experiences and needs.

Presumably, attempts to talk about the issues of sexual and domestic violence in ways that are consistent with the more traditional professional responses hope to achieve credibility within that paradigm as well as in the broader context. For example, the use of medical metaphors such as 'syndrome', and psychiatric diagnoses, including dissociative identity disorder and post-traumatic stress disorder, now feature prominently in contemporary feminist literature. Arguably, the inclusion of these disorders in the DSM IV has achieved a tacit recognition of the possible effects of sexual abuse, albeit symbolic. But again, once the language used to describe and define sexual and domestic violence is medicalised, there is the danger of an associated shift sideways away from an analysis that incorporates power and gender as key concepts to one that focuses on diagnosis, illness and pathologies. This in effect can lead to a retreat to the professional status quo existing prior to the collective actions of the 1970s and 1980s.

In a similar vein, the Final Report of the Royal Commission into the NSW Police Service (1997, vol. V) chose to use the terms 'paedophilia' and 'pederasty' to replace child sexual assault as the preferred description of sexual violence against children and young people. While it is true that a particular type of child sexual assault was spoken about in this public forum, part of the discussion was devoted to criticising professionals—not all professionals, however, only those who were seen as independent of a recognised professional group. Particular references were made to the need to provide counselling 'by therapists who are trained to remain impartial, and who have a clear idea of the problems of contaminated evidence' (1997, vol. V, p. 1187). To address this issue the Report suggested greater controls over who can and should be able to provide therapy/counselling, calling for stricter accreditation or registration of professionals and claiming that 'many are well meaning but because of their absence of expert training they may be potentially dangerous' (1997, vol. V, p. 1188). These comments appear to ignore the structural and resource constraints that have existed in relation to the training and support of workers. Moreover, the Report does not define what 'expert' training would mean in real terms. A concerning implication remains, however, that if such guidelines were to be implemented many of the activists who pioneered alternative therapeutic responses would be excluded from the therapeutic arena.

Another associated danger emerging from the push to 'professionalise' the issues is that the needs of victims may once again be exclusively addressed (or perhaps not) in the privacy of the therapeutic relationship, or in therapeutic, rather than consciousness-raising, inter-agency or community education groups. Armstrong (1996, p. 213), speaking as a survivor of child sexual assault, suggests that a plethora of professional responses now use the words of 'second-wave' feminism to claim an expertise that effectively functions to re-silence the voice of the victim. She claims that a re-privatisation of the issues occurs because the discussion is contained solely within the therapeutic relationship. Armstrong is clearly distressed by this turn of events as she argues that 'instead of survivors being drawn to feminist designed solutions, feminists are now drawn to solutions designed for the defined pathologies of survivors'. Strong words indeed, but perhaps useful in pointing to the dangers to be faced when dealing with the issues of sexual and domestic violence on an individual basis, primarily by therapeutic means. Armstrong's fear is that the issues of sexual and domestic violence are only publicly spoken about as part of a battle of therapeutic discourses and, as such, professional voices are those most often heard. When this occurs, the voice of the victim is once again lost and, as a result, sexual and domestic violence is 'dis-located from its social, powered, context' (Radford, Kelly & Hester 1996, p. 11).

'Professionalising' responses to gain credibility and legitimacy is at best a gamble in that it can add to the privileging of the professions. This in turn can lead back to the situation described at the beginning of this chapter where the professions believe 'that because of *their greater knowledge, wisdom, training and experience* they know what is best for others' [emphasis added] (Masson 1988, pp. 16–17). Also, there is no compelling evidence at this time that shows this strategy even works. Despite all efforts made to 'professionalise' intervention there is still the likelihood that workers will face vehement criticisms, attacking the very heart of alternative practices and the professionals who seek to implement them. The aim of such attacks is to suppress the 'truth' of sexual and domestic violence as told by the victim and witnessed by the activist/ professional. The tenor of the following accusation by Guilliatt is typical of a genre of backlash politics where sweeping criticisms are made of alternative 'professionalised' responses. He states:

> . . . no knowledge of any substance can be derived from dubious research, inflated statistics, faulty medical techniques or shoddy so-called therapy. Ultimately, those who employ such practices undermine the very cause they hope to promote. (1996, p. 4)

Ironically, criticisms such as this are often poorly researched, providing little or no substantiation, the very thing backlash proponents claim to object to themselves. Nonetheless, it is difficult to disagree with these sentiments, testifying to the everyday general appeal of the language of backlash, particularly when couched in scientific or legal terms. The questions that are never addressed when making these criticisms are as follows. In whose vested interests are the judgements made that research is dubious, that statistics are inflated or that therapy is shoddy? And, importantly, who should make those kinds of judgements about whom?

Recognising the stressful influence of backlash and considering the dangers involved in 'professionalising' responses are the first steps towards regaining and maintaining earlier achievements. But how do we once more move forward and away from the 'level of cacophony such that children's voices, women's voices, are once more not, in any purposeful sense, being heard?' (Armstrong 1996, p. 8). Very often future challenges are best met by revisiting past successes and modifying them to suit the current situation. Looking back at the collective actions of the 1970s and 1980s, there were a number of key strategies that would assist those committed to providing a space where once again the issues of sexual and domestic violence are appropriately addressed.

For this to occur we need to re-open and intensify the public discussion of sexual and domestic violence. Professionals need to re-establish a more comprehensive dialogue with one another and, most importantly, with victims. This can be achieved in a number of ways—peer support and review within and between agencies, developing ways in which consumers can be involved in providing feedback about service provision and political debates, and by encouraging forums for discussion such as workshops and conferences. Such comprehensive dialogue would allow us to develop further creative therapeutic and political responses and would provide a crucial sense of collective action that has been diminished by the attacks of backlash over recent years. Notably, on the occasions when activists have established a dialogue about a certain issue, change has occurred. After the administrator of Canberra Rape Crisis was jailed for not providing counselling notes for the alleged rapist to use at his trial, the outcry that followed as a result of the collective response from victims, workers and activists succeeded in achieving legal protection for victim confidentiality. Such instances testify to the necessity of publicly airing such issues through collective dialogue and provide the incentive for future collective action.

Opening a space for dialogue is a crucial step from which other strategies build. The creation of innovative alternative responses to the self-expressed needs of victims must be evaluated by competent and credible research efforts. Activists in earlier campaigns excelled in gathering data about the incidence, nature and dynamics of sexual and domestic violence. These earlier efforts need to be replicated and extended to include marginalised issues and those 'identity groups' (people with disabilities or from culturally diverse backgrounds, for example) whose voices are very often absent from mainstream research. Without extending our understanding to incorporate possible differences experienced by individuals we will be unable to tease out the complexity of the issues and our analyses will lack sophistication. The privileging of qualitative research methodologies, alongside quantitative work, will necessarily assist victims to speak of their experiences publicly and ensure that the development of knowledge occurs from the ground up, rather than being imposed from above by the 'experts'.

The evaluation of our professional work situated within a broader research agenda should inform our responses to contemporary political issues. Yet again, well-informed collective action must demand policy and legislative change (where appropriate) and monitor its implementation. The pursuit of these goals best supports the development of creative professional responses, including a consideration of possibilities that complement or may in some cases replace therapy as the only intervention offered. Faludi (1991, p. xxi) observes that 'in times when feminism is at a low ebb, women assume the reactive role—privately and most often covertly struggling to assert themselves against the dominant cultural tide'. As activists and professionals, we must continue to aspire to provide a space where victims are positioned so they can speak, are able to be heard, and are believed. Only then will the 'truth' of the victim become central to our responses to sexual and domestic violence and the operation of subjugation and silences be unmasked. Ultimately, if we achieve these goals, we will be able to provide a solid basis for withstanding the ravages of backlash and will move beyond its influence.

# PART I

## STRUCTURES THAT SILENCE

# 2 | 'Walking on eggshells': child sexual abuse allegations in the context of divorce

## Catherine Humphreys

As the court cases go on I can see the hopelessness of the whole thing. It's getting stronger in me to want to take the law into my own hands. I wouldn't say it's revenge, its not . . . I mean a mother protects its young. You wouldn't see a lioness letting something attack its young. (A mother expressing her desperation that the Family Court of Australia has ordered her to send her child on visits to her ex-husband who she believes sexually abused their child.)

ON HEARING THIS woman's story, I was struck by the fact that, in another setting, outside the processes of divorce, unless this woman acted *with* an aggressive protection of her child she would be labelled as inadequate and as 'failing to protect' her child. It seemed as though the 'norms' established in one context were reversed in another. This woman argued that the significant medical evidence (which was backed up by reports from the statutory child protection agency) in any other situation would have been taken without question as evidence of sexual abuse. Similar cases occur in the United Kingdom. Hester and Radford (1996, p. 25), for example, report *Olive's Story* which shows clear parallels with the example mentioned above, as well as the experiences of other women in their qualitative research study of contact orders.

Undoubtedly, ambiguity, allegations and counter-allegations are persistent themes within the child sexual assault area more generally. Further complexity is added to the assessment of child sexual allegations by the persistent suspicion and blame cast upon mothers whose children have been sexually abused (Hooper 1992). Practices such as 'shooting the child's messenger'—whereby those who seek to protect the child are assumed to be either misguided or malicious—continue, and appear to be exacerbated by the already negative association with women in the divorce courts (Chesler 1986). The assessment of these allegations by child protection social workers and other professionals operating in the courts occurs against this contentious background.

This chapter explores the way in which knowledge in this area has been constructed and legitimated by social scientists, such that the ability of non-offending mothers to protect their children in this context is negated.[1] The 'common knowledge' that has developed often implies that a significant number of allegations are fabricated, or that indicators of child sexual abuse are misinterpreted by mothers during the intense emotions of divorce proceedings. Such 'knowledge' and theorising frequently form the basis of assessments and judgements, which have far-reaching consequences for the protection of children.

Initially, this discussion traces the development of the ways in which the mother of the sexually abused child has been portrayed in the literature. This chapter then goes on to make comparisons with contemporary ideas, practices and beliefs about mothers who raise the issue of the sexual abuse of their children during divorce proceedings.

## THE COLLUSIVE MOTHER

When social scientists first began writing about incest, the mother of the sexually abused child was ignored (Bender & Blau 1937). With the advent of family therapy, however, new constructions of sexual abuse developed which shifted the focus from the provocative child victim or the deviant abuser to dysfunctional family interaction (Lustig et al. 1966). In this process, the mother's behaviour and position increasingly became the centre of attention and the role of the offender in the abuse was marginalised. Hersko et al. epitomise this shift: 'The mothers remain in the background as outwardly the least important, but actually through their manipulations, essential persons in precipitating the overt incestual behaviour' (1961, p. 30). The mother steadily became the focus both of responsibility and of condemnation for the abuse, and clinicians and researchers framed their practice and discussion around this analysis.

The history of this development provides an interesting insight into the construction of social knowledge. Wattenberg (1985), who traces the evolution of the 'collusive' mother, cites the pivotal role of male doctors quoting each other on the basis of small, selected samples. Within a relatively short period, the notion of the 'collusive' mother became entrenched as fact. Successive authors merely quote previous papers, leaving out the criticisms and qualifications that may have been noted in the original article.

The rapidity with which notions such as the 'collusive' mother become accepted as 'common knowledge' is frequently a function of the already fertile ground established by particular socio-cultural values and the practices that stem from these values. In this instance, a culture adept at mother-blaming (Caplan 1989), and at passing emotional and sexual responsibility to women (Jenkins 1990), quickly grasped the social scientist's legitimation of these practices. Women who did not fit the scenario of the 'collusive' mother in the incest triangle were never discussed. Intra-familial child sexual abuse that remained within the domain of the family therapist, but in which the abuser was not the mother's partner, was rarely mentioned even though it is more common (Russell 1986). Similarly, the actions of the protective mother were rarely examined.

Feminist writers of the 1980s mounted a challenge to the construction of the 'collusive' mother (Ward 1984). They criticised the terms, assumptions and evidence used by clinicians. They highlighted, instead, the powerless position of the mother, her economic vulnerability, her poor health, and the frequently reported violence and alcohol misuse of her partner. They also focused attention on the majority of mothers who believed and supported their sexually abused children (Sirles & Franke 1989).

## THE FALSELY ACCUSING MOTHER

Interestingly, as an alternative knowledge developed which challenged the notion of the 'collusive' mother, literature on the 'falsely accusing' mother in divorce cases became a new focus. Thus began a new way of speaking, which again undermined the mother of the sexually abused child. Given the intensity of the earlier attack on mothers for their *lack* of protection of their sexually abused children, the undermining of women in the divorce context who attempted to protect their children seems somewhat paradoxical. Although there are also relevant issues in this area pertaining to the way in which children's evidence is treated or mistreated by the courts, this chapter concentrates on the particular themes that emerge in the attitude towards mothers and their representation in the literature.

First, as with the development of the 'collusive' mother, 'knowledge' became constructed by doctors and psychologists writing up their 'findings' on the basis of a small number of clinical cases and then continuing to reference each other's work. The notion that there was a high number of false allegations in the family court rapidly became accepted as fact, and mental health professionals were warned to be suspicious of these allegations (Green 1986).

One can speculate whether these studies say more about the sample group that has been seen, the mothers in the sample, or about the interviewing doctors. For example, Benedek and Schetky (1985) found that 10 out of 18 cases where sexual abuse was alleged were not confirmed. Does this suggest their sample was based at the extreme end of the spectrum? The number of contested custody cases is small relative to the total number of divorcing couples (Thoennes & Tjaden 1990), and the number of these families who are further referred for psychiatric evaluation is still smaller. Or does the finding say more about their techniques as assessors? For example, Schuman (1986) found that mothers were usually suffering from paranoia or hysteria. Again, does this suggest that these mothers are the extreme end of the continuum of psychiatrically disturbed clients? Or, is there something about the prospect for women, not only believing that their child has been sexually abused but then finding that they are unable to protect them, that creates hysteria and paranoia? Furthermore, discrediting the mother with psychiatric labels does not invalidate an allegation of abuse. Women who are psychotic can still have children who are being sexually abused. In fact, the statistics indicate that mothers who are disabled emotionally or physically have children who are significantly *more* vulnerable to sexual abuse (Finkelhor 1984). This is further confirmed by offender self-reports on their targeting of child victims (Conte, Wolf & Smith 1989). Moreover, Corwin et al. (1987) point out that the mis-categorisation of one case, shown by a re-analysis of the data in one study, can significantly skew the percentage of false allegations in these small studies. This example highlights the methodological problems with much of the research in the area—namely, that, with a few exceptions (such as Jones & McGraw 1987; Faller 1988), the basis on which cases are categorised as true or false is rarely made clear, and is not subject to checking by independent researchers or measures.

Whereas the clinicians mentioned above have argued that the rate of false allegations in divorce cases is significantly higher than in non-divorcing couples, there was also a group of mental health professionals who, in the 1980s, argued emotively that false allegations are not only more frequent in divorce situations, but are common. Thus, Coleman (1986) speaks of 'a wave of false allegations' sweeping the United States, while Blush and Ross (1987) felt the extent of the problem was worthy of the status of a new, 'medicalised' syndrome, 'the SAID syndrome' (sexual allegations in divorce). Wakefield and Underwager (1988) argued that false accusations were on the increase and highly prevalent in custody cases. Their papers have been widely criticised by clinicians and researchers (e.g. Berliner 1988; Conte 1995). In spite of the lack of any statistical basis for these generalisations and the discrediting of 'experts' such as Coleman and Underwager in major trials (Hollingsworth 1986), their ideas met a receptive popular press who gave them widespread publicity. This coverage contributed to the dissemination of their ideas within the broader socio-cultural context.

A second theme in the literature is the emphasis on false allegations. Papers often start or finish with a rider that the empirical evidence shows that false allegations in the context of divorce are rare, but then enlarge at length on these false allegations (Byrne 1991; Yuille et al. 1995). Other papers focus almost entirely on false allegations (Blush & Ross 1987; Wakefield & Underwager 1992) or, as mentioned above, highlight false allegations occurring in small selected samples (Benedek & Schetky 1985). The reader is left with the impression that the field is fraught with such allegations, feeding into the stereotype that disclosures in this context need to start from an initial point of disbelief.

A further thread running through many of the articles on the assessment of allegations of child sexual abuse within the context of divorce is a focus on the mother's behaviour. This primarily involves questioning whether she fits within the norms of expected behaviour for these circumstances (Benedek & Schetky 1985; Bresee et al. 1986; Green 1986; Gardener 1987; Wakefield &

Underwager 1988). Bresee et al. (1986) paint a picture of the 'normal', passive mother of the incest victim in contrast to the combative mother in the divorce scenario. Mothers who respond with early belief in their child's disclosure are viewed with suspicion (Jones & Sieg 1988; Schaefer & Guyer 1988). Mothers' reports, as against those directly from children, are viewed with even greater suspicion. Clinicians such as Green (1986) have developed tables that establish what they believe to be the differences mental health professionals should look for in true and false allegations. Similarly, Gardener (1987) has developed a scale for assessing true and false allegations. There has been biting criticism of much of this work. For example, Conte says of Gardener's scale, 'Probably the most unscientific piece of garbage I've seen in the field in all my life' (1988, p. 26).

Nevertheless, recent overview articles on the assessment of sexual abuse allegation in child custody disputes (Elterman & Ehrenberg 1991, 1995; Yuille et al. 1995) still cite Gardener, Green, Benedek and Schetky as providing the evidence that there is an elevated occurrence of false allegations in the context of divorce. Moreover, 'norms' for determining true and false allegations continue to be quoted (Byrne 1991).

The specification of a norm against which false and true allegations are measured is dangerous territory for mothers attempting to protect their children. Using the previously mentioned criteria spelt out by the 'experts', allegations of sexual abuse need to satisfy the following criteria. First, they must be made prior to the custody case; mothers must show initial disbelief; mothers must not show anxiety about their children (even toddlers) being seen alone by the psychiatrist/psychologist; mothers must not be angry or combative (hysterical), nor overly suspicious of the ex-partner's motives (paranoid). Then, mothers must happily accept the ruling of the court and believe that they were misguided in their suspicions, not 'destructively' fight on to protect their 'at risk' children; they must accept that out-of-court disclosures to them are only hearsay and could be a product of their overly suspicious minds. Importantly, mothers must not question their children about their suspicions as this will be construed as placing pressure on the child and coaching them to make false allegations against their fathers.

Mothers are often aware that the 'rules' are endless and report 'walking on eggshells' as they negotiate the court process, hoping that they will not unwittingly destroy their child's case for protection (Humphreys 1990). Unfortunately, not all disclosures of child sexual abuse fit the 'experts'' norm. Faller (1988) shows that in the 6.5 per cent of cases in her sample where the offender gave a full confession, the child's statements lacked any of the characteristics thought to make a statement true. Similar points can be made about child sexual abuse allegations in divorce cases, as not all cases follow a typical pattern (Berliner et al. 1988). It should be kept in mind, for instance, that non-abusing parents (usually mothers) and other relatives are the most frequent referers of child sexual abuse to the authorities outside the divorce courts (Sharland et al. 1995; Packman et al. 1986). Moreover, the uncomfortable notion that women can be angry, malicious or mentally ill *and*, at the same time, making true allegations of child sexual abuse is an issue that may need to be taken into account.

A third theme in the literature is that, until recently, issues of domestic violence have been treated separately from those of child abuse. Research over the last ten years shows that the group at greatest risk of child abuse are those children whose mothers are also being abused by a violent man. Such work is increasingly reported (Mullender & Morley 1994). Although the clearest links have been drawn between men who are violent towards their female partners and the physical abuse of children, there are also elevated rates of child sexual abuse in the context of domestic violence (Truesdale et al. 1986). This link has implications for the assessment of allegations of child sexual abuse in the context of divorce.

There are further themes from research on domestic violence which parallel themes in the child sexual abuse field. Hester and Radford (1996) exemplify the issues in their research on child contact, which was based in both Denmark and the United Kingdom. Among a range of concerns they found that mothers who raised the issue of past violence and the potential for continuing violence both against themselves and their children were often construed as avenging mothers unconcerned about the needs of their children for contact with their fathers. Women's claims that the contact experience for the child may be disturbing, particularly if 'hand over' occurs in the context of abuse towards themselves, and/or that the children are expressing fear and anxiety about contact, are minimised and treated with suspicion. These authors suggest that, in the context of divorce, unlike any other context, the rules for mothers are different. Protectiveness is construed as paranoia, and reporting abuse is treated as vindictiveness.

The extent to which this is a theme for women before the

Australian Family Court is less clear. The *Family Law Reform Act* 1995 certainly acknowledges the need for the Court to regard domestic violence as an issue for consideration in contact and residence decisions arrangements, and for decisions to be consistent with family violence orders in ways that United Kingdom legislators have entirely failed to grasp. Initially, the Family Court of Australia refused to acknowledge the significance of domestic violence as a legitimate issue for consideration in custody and access cases unless the child had been directly physically abused (*Heidt & Heidt* (1976) FLC 90–077; *Chandler & Chandler* (1981) FLC 91–008). However, from 1994 a number of cases have made it clear that domestic violence is directly relevant to the deliberations of the Court (*Jaeger & Jaeger* (1994) FLC 92–492; *Irvine & Irvine* (1995) FLC 92–624) and this has been reflected in the *Family Law Reform Act* 1995. Parkinson (1995) nevertheless sounds a note of caution. He points out that the Court still has some distance to go before recognising not just that 'the mother's parenting may be impaired' (*Grant & Grant* (1994) FLC 92–505), but that there are risks to women in their own right when contact continues with the child's violent father.

A further theme is that the link between domestic violence and child abuse, including child sexual abuse, has often been ignored. The ensuing artificial separation of the issues of violence experienced by children and those experienced by their mothers fails to account for the context in which abuse occurs or the ways in which this may influence disclosure and assessment. Ironically, when domestic violence *is* raised as an issue, it is not infrequently used as a reason for invalidating an allegation of child sexual abuse, since the allegation is construed as an attempt by women to overcome for themselves problems with 'hand over' and contact arrangements with violent men. The fact that many women are highly concerned to promote contact arrangements, even at the expense of their own safety (Hester & Radford 1996), and that child sexual assault often occurs in the context of domestic violence, may be ignored.

A final issue concerning the construction of 'knowledge' in this area is the fact that there have been substantial criticisms of much of the literature on false allegations by well-respected researchers and practitioners (Corwin et al. 1987; Berliner et al. 1988; Faller 1991; Conte 1995). These writers suggest that assessments of child sexual abuse in the context of divorce, although often difficult, should not be unexpected. They cite a number of reasons for children disclosing sexual abuse when their parents separate—disclosure of child sexual abuse can be the precursor to the parents' separation; the child may no longer feel the pressure to 'keep the family together'; children may feel they will now be believed given that the abuser loses the opportunity continually to enforce secrecy; equally, the child may be increasingly worried by lengthy access periods alone with the abusing parent; the abuse may escalate with increased time and opportunity; or sexual abuse may occur for the first time on contact visits. Such circumstances suggest that disclosure of child sexual abuse will not be uncommon during the divorce period, or even following the initial settlement of contact arrangements.

Many articles ignore this literature (Byrne 1991; Wakefield & Underwager 1991), or fail to account for it in overview articles citing the literature, which they criticise without evaluation (Elterman & Ehrenberg 1995). Furthermore, the literature appears to have little impact on practice. For example, Judge Schudson (1995) points out that, although the evidence of false allegations in the context of divorce is scant and the literature critical, there is a tendency for judges to be overly suspicious of allegations of sexual abuse in this context. Similarly, my experiences as a trainer with child protection workers between 1992 and 1994 indicated that many social workers came with a profound cynicism about sexual abuse disclosures that occurred in the context of divorce. Focus groups on this issue showed clearly that practitioners understood the 'common knowledge' and practice wisdom in the area to be that mothers (and sometimes other family members), whether maliciously or misguidedly, brought false allegations of child sexual abuse into the context of divorce proceedings.

## CLARITY AMONG THE MYTHS

The empirical studies of child sexual abuse allegations in custody disputes belie the popular conceptions of the 'falsely accusing' mother. Thoennes and Tjaden (1990), in a comprehensive six-month survey of eight domestic relations courts in the United States, found that there were over 9000 cases of custody/visitation disputes. Of these, 169 (2 per cent) involved allegations of child sexual abuse. These cases were substantiated by child welfare investigators at the same rate as other notifications to their agencies. Moreover, mothers accusing the child's father of sexual abuse occurred in only 48 per cent of these cases. The figures, if anything, suggest an under-reporting by mothers of child abuse in divorce proceedings.

Two studies examining the Australian Family Court Counselling Services (Bordow 1987; Hume 1996) found only a comparatively small number of cases in which allegations of child sexual abuse were made. Bordow (1987) discovered that only 1.6 per cent (n = 97) of new cases in a three-month period involved allegations of child sexual abuse. Again, mothers were the source of the allegation in only 42.3 per cent of these cases. Hume (1996) tracked 50 South Australian Family Court files in which allegations of child sexual abuse had been made between 1990 and 1992, though this did not completely represent the numbers of sexual abuse allegations for that period. She found that child sexual abuse was confirmed in these cases by the statutory agency at a slightly higher rate (42 per cent) than for the general population (37 per cent). Confirmation rates increased when the allegation directly involved sexual abuse by fathers (19 of 27 such cases confirmed), rather than allegations that the child was at risk of abuse, or allegations of inappropriate behaviour indicating possible sexual abuse.

Another Australian study drawn from child protection cases (Humphreys 1993) tracked every case of child sexual abuse confirmed by the statutory agency in four different regional centres over a six-month period (n = 155). In 12 cases, action was being taken or was pending in the Australian Family Court for changed contact or residence orders. This small study illustrates the worrying trend in decision-making within this court. Two cases were still pending, while in 50 per cent or half of the sample (five out of ten) fathers who were alleged sexual abuse perpetrators were granted access or supervised access to their children. In two of these cases, supervised access was in the presence of family members who did not believe the sexual abuse had occurred. These decisions occurred in spite of legislation and case precedents that should have precluded such a situation (*M v M* [1988], FLR 606).

The empirical evidence on the subject of false allegations is low. Jones and McGraw (1987) examined the frequency and nature of false reports. They took all the referrals of child sexual abuse (576) to the Denver Social Services Department over a one-year period and found their research team considered only 6 per cent of cases to be fictitious accounts by adults. Their research suggests that false allegations are rare, and in this study, such allegations occurred in the context of mental illness and complex divorce proceedings. A more recent study by Hlady and Gunter (1990) found no difference between children involved in custody disputes and children who were not in dispute in the patterns of sexual abuse and the behaviour indicators reported to the child protection agency. Other large, though clinically based samples (Horowitz et al. 1984) showed a 6 per cent rate of false reporting and, again, an association of this very low rate of false reporting with divorce proceedings. An interesting study by Everson and Boat (1989), drawn from a statutory child welfare agency, identified 1249 cases of reported sexual abuse. From the sub-group of 29 allegations designated as false by child protection workers, five occurred in contested divorce cases. This study showed that the designation of false reports had as much to do with worker attitudes to the evidence of children as it did to the details of the case. Ducote and Harrison (1988) make a similar point to Everson and Boat, arguing that child sexual abuse cases brought during divorce proceedings seemed to require a higher threshold of evidence. They illustrated cases in which substantial medical evidence and full disclosures by children, accepted in other arenas as confirming child sexual abuse, may be regarded as false because the disclosure occurred in the context of a contact dispute.

In summary, the empirical studies suggest a need for caution and careful assessment. However, the majority of reports of child sexual abuse arising in the context of the divorce courts are neither misconstrued nor fictitious. The lack of impact of this message in countering the construction of the 'falsely accusing mother' for many social workers, court welfare workers and the legal profession requires further explanation.

## CONTEXTS FOR DEVELOPMENT OF THE DISCOURSE ON THE 'FALSELY ACCUSING MOTHER'

The persistent undermining of the mother of the sexually abused child has taken different forms, which have been consistently legitimated by patriarchal discourses in the social sciences. The theme mirrors other practices in the child sexual abuse field which protect the offender and subjugate the knowledge of child sexual abuse. Interestingly, the micro-practices of predominantly male offenders, which frequently involve the undermining and blaming of the child's mother (Laing & Kamsler 1990), are reflected in parallel practices at an institutional level. This indicates the wider circulation of powerful beliefs and practices that perpetuate oppressive behaviour towards women and children more generally. An analysis of three particular practices may contribute to a feminist understanding of the ways in which mothers of sexually abused children are portrayed in the divorce court.

First, a consistent theme within the discursive field of child sexual assault has been to 'shoot the child's messenger'. This practice seeks to discredit those who act for the victim, rather than directly attacking the credibility of the child. Mothers and child protection workers who support/believe the child's disclosure of sexual abuse are targets. Defence lawyers and professionals from the social sciences acting as expert witnesses for the defence have epitomised this method of attack (O'Gorman 1991). In front of a judge or jury, there has been little to be gained by demolishing a child. A much more effective strategy has been to impute that those around the child have been misguided or malicious in their belief that child sexual abuse has occurred. Hollingsworth (1986) has carefully documented this process in her analysis of a case in which two day-care operators were charged with child sexual assault in Miami, Florida. Similarly, Franklin (1989) has traced the process in Britain, documenting the vehement attack by the press, the public and members of parliament on child protection workers. Like the mother of the sexually abused child, child protection workers are attacked when they are unable to protect the child and just as roundly attacked when they do. They are either 'wimps or bullies', 'passive or combative'. The end result, however, is the same. Those who advocate for the child are discredited, offenders are protected or not held responsible, and the child remains vulnerable to child sexual abuse.

A second important element in the portrayal of a woman seeking a divorce is that she is now tarred with the attitudes and beliefs that surround these court procedures. In a significant minority of cases these are very adversarial proceedings. The women's motives in this context are construed as suspect, which reinforces the portrayal of mothers as misguided or vindictive, a point brought out clearly in Hester and Radford's research on child contact. Mothers constantly reported being on the defensive and accepting agreements that put their own safety in jeopardy in an attempt to avoid being attacked as obstructive and revengeful.

Popular myth has it that men are disadvantaged when applying for a residence order for children in divorce proceedings. However, when *contested* custody cases are analysed separately, it is clear that men have an equal chance of gaining custody and a greater chance if they have already taken a new wife and established a new family (Scutt 1990a). In these contested proceedings, Chesler (1986) notes the powerful role of expert witnesses such as psychiatrists, psychologists and social workers in 'diagnosing' the unfit mother. Moreover, both by statute (Family Law Bill 1996, ss. 11(4)(c)) and through dominant professional values and practice, the notion is perpetuated that all contact with fathers in the wake of divorce is beneficial to the child (Hooper 1994). The mother bringing allegations of child sexual assault before the courts in divorce proceedings must contend with these judicial preconceptions and practices which disadvantage both her position and her advocacy on behalf of her child.

Third, the judiciary has a tradition of treating allegations of sexual assault with suspicion. The warning laid down by Judge Hale in the seventeenth century remains as the judicial system's maxim: ' . . . it must be remembered that it [rape] is an accusation easily to be made and hard to be proved and harder to be defended by the party accused though never so innocent' (Hales, quoted in Scutt 1990b, p. 317). He goes on to warn against the possibility of false allegations. Wigmore (1961), in the United States, continued the tradition. Jocelyn Scutt, the feminist criminologist, makes the following comment:

> Wigmore was so in awe of women's power to conceal, deceive and lie, and in fear of men being 'unjustly' treated by the courts, that he firmly concluded that no judge should ever let a sex offence charge go to the jury unless the female complainant's social history and mental make-up has been examined and testified to by a qualified physician. (1990b, p. 318)

The parameters have changed, in this case to include another woman, the mother of a child who alleges sexual assault. The theme and practices remain the same: the woman is regarded with suspicion and her social context and psychological make-up is the subject of intense scrutiny by lawyers, judges, psychiatrists and psychologists.

## CONCLUSION

It is probably predictable that allegations of child sexual abuse in the context of divorce would be treated with great suspicion and that mothers would bear the brunt of much of that suspicion. In any situation, disclosure of child sexual abuse is a source of huge controversy. It challenges the power of adults and particularly men, fragments a cherished notion of social cohesion based around a protective family, and highlights the abusiveness that occurs in sexual relations more generally.

Focusing on the mother and her inadequacies, rather than on the offender, has a long tradition within the literature on child sexual abuse. Divorce is similarly an arena in which powerful emotions are unleashed and where women are frequently construed as self-seeking and vitriolic, and as disadvantaging men by their claims for custody and financial settlements. The meeting point between the two arenas provides a volatile conjunction which goes some way towards explaining why, in the face of cogent and rational critiques, practices persist that lead some children to remain unprotected from sexual abuse when disclosure occurs in the context of divorce. This holds particular challenges for both welfare and court personnel.

Given this situation it is imperative that appropriate networks and supervision be established for workers. For workers, the emotionally charged nature of the area is compounded by the far-reaching implications of their recommendations and decisions in the lives of children and their mothers and fathers. Moreover, there is currently a sustained 'backlash' against women and children who disclose sexual abuse that increases the need for professionals not to be isolated when making decisions that challenge these formidable forces in the courts. Disrupting these entrenched attitudes and beliefs is not an easy task. It will be assisted by the pooling of research, practice and activism focused on women, and equivalent endeavours focused on children, to create new understandings that foster protective practice.

# 3 | Justice delayed is justice denied: the experiences of women in court as victims of sexual assault

*Shelagh Doyle and Claire Barbato*

. . . Delayed stories, stories growing out of silence that has gone before are disbelieved precisely because they are delayed. In the time that elapses between the event and the story, all sorts of new motivations can emerge to shape the story that is told, or so the informal rules of evidence would have it . . . (Scheppele 1994, pp. 1005–1006)

EVERY DECISION-MAKER who walks into a courtroom to hear a case is armed not only with the relevant texts setting out well-established legal doctrines but with a set of values, experiences and assumptions. The logic of law claims to be neutral, objective and impartial, claims incarnate in the concept of justice. However, in law, as in society more broadly, male views of what constitutes objectivity or experience are privileged. *Heroines of Fortitude: the experiences of women in court as victims of sexual assault* (NSW Department for Women 1996) is an example of rigorous and innovative feminist research which unmasks the purported ungendered nature of the law.

The broad objective of *Heroines of Fortitude* (henceforth *Heroines*) was to determine how victims of sexual assault are treated in their role as primary witnesses in the criminal justice process. The project examined the effectiveness of legislative provisions designed to protect the rights of a complainant/witness in sexual assault proceedings. Those provisions include the regulation of questions regarding a victim's sexual history (s. 409B *Crimes Act* 1900 (NSW)), corroboration warnings (s. 405C *Crimes Act* 1900 (NSW)), delay in complaint warning (s. 405B *Crimes Act* 1900 (NSW)) and provisions for the proceedings to be held in camera where the court so directs (s. 77A, *Crimes (Personal and Family Violence) Amendment Act* 1987 (NSW)). The research examined all sound-recorded sexual assault trials in the District Court of New South Wales over a one-year period (between 1 May 1994 and 30 April 1995) where the accused had been charged with one or more serious sexual offences and where the victim was an adult female. In this chapter we discuss the research findings surrounding judicial warnings and directions about evidence of complaint. 'Complaint' refers to the oral or written statement made by the victim of a sexual assault to another person and/or to the police about the incident.

## THE LAW OF COMPLAINT

In a criminal trial it is an established rule that previous statements of a witness that are consistent with the evidence given by them in court are not admissible as evidence. However, the testimony of sexual assault complainants at trial has always been treated with the greatest suspicion and a specific exception to this rule was developed, the 'recent complaint' rule. Evidence that a sexual assault complainant reported to a third party at the earliest reasonable opportunity was made admissible. The impetus for this rule was the belief that sexual assault complainants were inherently unbelievable and that legal exceptions were necessary to raise their credibility to a level attained by other victims of crime. Complaint evidence could not be used to prove the offence occurred but only to prove that the complainant acted 'consistently' with the actions of a person who has been sexually assaulted (Aronson & Hunter 1995).

The history of the 'recent complaint exception' extends from the Middle Ages, when it was a defence to an allegation of rape that the victim had not raised an 'immediate 'hue and cry'. As Henry Bracton wrote in the thirteenth century:

> When therefore a virgin has been deflowered and overpowered against the peace of the lord the king forthwith and while the act is so fresh she ought repair with hue and cry to the neighbouring vills and there dipole to honest men the injury done to her . . .

The recent complaint rule operated not only to admit evidence of a sexual assault complainant's 'recent' complaint; it also permitted the defence to infer that, where an alleged victim had failed to complain swiftly, the credibility of her testimony was undermined.[1] Thus sexual assault victims who did not complain to a third party at the earliest opportunity or who did not complain to the police could expect to be cross-examined about this by the defence. That the judge too could comment adversely upon the late complaint in his/her summing-up to the jury (a common law warning) was confirmed by the High Court of Australia in *Kilby v R* ((1973) 129 CLR 460).

To counter the negative effect of the recent complaint rule, the NSW Parliament in 1981 introduced s. 405B into the NSW *Crimes Act*. This provision made it mandatory for the judge in sexual assault proceedings to give a warning in relation to delay in complaint in certain defined circumstances. It was designed to offset the potential inferences often drawn from the failure to make an immediate complaint. The section provides that where evidence is given or a question is asked of a sexual assault witness which tends to suggest an absence of or delay in complaint in respect of the commission of the alleged offence the judge shall:

> give a warning to the jury to the effect that absence of complaint or delay in complaining does not necessarily indicate that the allegation that the offence was committed is false (s. 405B(2)(a));

and

> inform the jury that there may be good reasons why a victim of a sexual assault may hesitate in making, or may refrain from making, a complaint about the assault (s. 405B(2)(b)).[2]

The section serves to alert the court to the important point that failure to complain at the earliest reasonable opportunity is not evidence of fabrication or consent to intercourse. It was an appreciation that the traumatic and humiliating effect of a sexual assault often disabled a woman from disclosing the offence for some time, if at all (Woods 1981).

## MYTHS AND STATISTICS

Despite the major and significant legal reforms in the area of sexual assault over the last 15 years, such as s. 405B, many obstacles to the successful prosecution of sexual assault remain. Possibly the most powerful obstacle of all is the law's acceptance and perpetuation of the ubiquitous myths that prevail in the community about sexual assault. These false beliefs and images of sexual assault are well known—women precipitate sexual assault by their provocative appearance and behaviour; only women with 'bad' reputations are sexually assaulted; women are prone to sexual fantasies; women mean 'yes' when they say 'no'; men are not at fault for losing control in a confusion of sexual signals; the rapist is usually a stranger—and many more.

But perhaps no myth is more powerful in the law surrounding sexual assault than the myth of the lying woman; the spurned lover who seeks revenge; the pregnant woman who cries rape to cover up illegitimacy; the inexperienced woman who consented to sex but later regretted her actions; the woman who fraudulently seeks financial compensation—the vicious, vengeful, spiteful women who would lie about sexual assault. The *Heroines* research confirmed that these myths are regularly and mercilessly peddled and perpetuated in the courtroom, revealing yet again that the complainant is often unrelentingly cross-examined about every aspect of her lifestyle and relationships and routinely accused of lying. In fact, 84 per cent of complainants in the *Heroines* research were questioned about lying. A typical exchange goes as follows:

*Defence counsel:*     You weren't in shock, you were having consenting sexual intercourse on the lounge room floor, weren't you?

*Complainant:*     I was not.

*Defence counsel:*     You see this is a tissue of lies by you, isn't it?

*Complainant (crying):* It is not a lie—why would I go to the police station and make a 20 page statement and be here for 8 hours and go through hell for this! (Case 43)

By the end of this exchange the complainant was screaming, which gives some indication of her frustration. One complainant was asked a total of 98 questions about lying during cross-examination. The research findings support Adler's (1987, p. 15) contention that the rape victim 'occupies a unique position in the legal system which treats her with unequalled suspicion'.

It is not just the inherently untrustworthy woman we encounter in the eyes of the law—it is also the lying woman who is using the court for her own vengeful and/or fraudulent ends. One-third of complainants in the trials studied for *Heroines* were cross-examined about whether their motive for complaining was victim's compensation. One woman was asked a total of 43 questions on the topic and another commented herself on the relevance of this line of questioning:

*Defence counsel:*    Do you intend to claim compensation?
*Prosecution:*    I object to that, your Honour.
*Complainant:*    No that's all right, I'll answer it. That's got nothing to do with this. I am just seeking a bit of justice.
(Case 97)

Closely linked with the notion of the dishonest and unreliable woman is the belief—the myth—that if she delays in complaining about the offence then she has probably fabricated the allegation. The other side of this reasoning is that a woman's 'natural' reaction to sexual assault is to make an immediate outcry about the offence. This myth is embodied and enunciated in the law related to complaint in sexual assault trials and has been appropriately termed the 'timing myth' (Stanchi 1996). Belief in such myths about sexual assault creates biased jurors, judges and criminal justice personnel and a prejudiced community (Torrey 1991). Hence the urgent need to continue to confront and dislodge such myths with sound empirical evidence.

While there is no empirical evidence that supports the presumption underlying the 'timing myth', there is much evidence to repudiate it. Empirical research conducted over the past 20 years in fact reveals that most victims never report the crime of sexual assault. The Australian Bureau of Statistics Women's Safety Survey (1996) revealed that across Australia 1.9 per cent of women over the age of 18 had experienced sexual violence (a sexual assault or threat of sexual assault) over the preceding 12 months. A total of 1.5 per cent were sexually assaulted and 0.7 per cent were threatened with sexual violence. Of the women who had experienced sexual violence in the preceding 12 months, only 14.9 per cent had reported the incident to police (ABS 1996). Sexual assault, according to the annual Crime and Safety Survey, is the *least* likely personal criminal offence to be reported to the police (ABS 1994b).

The 1993 Australian Crime and Safety Survey found that the two most common reasons for not reporting sexual assault were that the offence was a private matter and that the victim was afraid of reprisal (ABS 1994a). The third most commonly stated reason for not reporting a sexual assault incident was the belief that the police would not take action. In their Bureau of Crime Statistics and Research (BCSR) study (Salmelainen & Coumarelos 1993) summarised the common reasons for lack or delay in complaint from a number of victim surveys as follows:

- victims believe that the police can't or won't do anything about it
- the incident is 'too trivial' to report
- victims' feelings of guilt and shame over the incident
- fear of repercussions from the offender
- fear the police will not believe them
- fear of the scrutiny and interrogation that they may have to face in the courtroom.

Salmelainen and Coumarelos also commented that it has been suggested that many of the reasons for not reporting arise from a set of false cultural beliefs or 'myths' about sexual assault. Among these myths, for example, is the misconception that sexual assault requires some sort of physical force on the part of the rapist. A 1995 Office of the Status of Women study confirmed that perceptions that women lie about being sexually assaulted continue to be held by some members of the community (OSW 1995). While almost 60 per cent of their respondents agreed with the statement 'women rarely make false claims of being raped', 34 per cent disagreed and 11 per cent strongly disagreed. However, there is no empirical evidence to prove that there are more false allegations of sexual assault than of any other violent crime. It is estimated that false reports for sexual assault are similar to those for other crimes, calculated at approximately 2 per cent of all reports.

The 1993 Sexual Assault Phone-in revealed that women were reluctant to report for a range of reasons that had nothing to do with their credibility (NSW Sexual Assault Committee 1993). The Phone-in found that women were more likely to report a sexual assault that conformed to the stereotype of a 'real rape'—a sudden, violent attack by a stranger which results in serious physical injury. Sexual assault victims hesitate to report non-stranger sexual assault because they are more likely to feel responsible for it. The authors of the report commented that this highlighted the fact that victims of sexual assault often internalise prevalent assumptions about their own blameworthiness. The Phone-in also revealed that distrust of police and the legal system, fear of retaliation and a desire to protect family and friends from the truth also combine to create situations where the majority of sexual assault victims suffer in silence. Stuart (1993, p. 97) despaired that: 'rape is a relatively safe crime for perpetrators to commit'—the best available estimates suggest that only a small proportion of the sexual assaults committed against adult women in New South Wales are reported to police. Even fewer cases end up in court.

## 'COMPLAINT' IN *HEROINES*

The *Heroines* study revealed that more than half (55 per cent) of the complainants told someone that they had been sexually assaulted within one hour of the offence occurring. Another 28 per cent of complainants told someone of the sexual assault within 12 hours. The vast majority (93 per cent) of complainants made their first disclosure within seven days of the assault. The study also found that over half the complainants reported the offence to the police within five hours; indeed, 31 per cent had reported to the police within one hour. The majority (81 per cent) of complainants reported the matter to the police within seven days.

If we compare these statistics with the empirical evidence available (detailed above) about what sexual assault victims generally do—never report the assault—then the NSW study reveals that the complainants in the research sample, on the whole, made exceptionally speedy complaints. Despite this being the case, the research revealed that defence raised delay in complaint as an issue in cross-examination of the complainant in over *half* the trials. In particular, delay was raised as an issue by the defence in 38.5 per cent of cases where the complainant had complained in less than one hour. In 75 per cent of cases where the complainant had delayed in advising someone of the assault for one to two days, the defence raised the issue at trial. Thus the research reveals that, despite speedy disclosures by complainants, they are still cross-examined in court about 'delaying' their complaint.

Hence the study shows that those women who do complain, complain at what might be regarded as the earliest opportunity and that the notion of 'reasonable complaint' is not value free but in fact has a gender basis. A 'delay' of half an hour can be interpreted and exploited by the defence as a late complaint in a sexual assault trial. This occurs because stereotypic, false beliefs about sexual assault complainants prevail in the criminal justice system and the general community.

It is interesting to note that, in 89 per cent of cases studied by the *Heroines* research, the police were not notified of the alleged assault until the complainant had told someone else such as a friend, family member or stranger. Of the 10 per cent of complainants in the study who were assaulted by strangers, 87 per cent of them reported to the police within one hour of the offence occurring. Complainants generally took longer to complain if the accused was someone described as a friend or partner. In fact, a quarter of complainants who described the accused as a partner took a week or longer to report to the police. A similar pattern was noted for the time taken when the accused was an ex-partner (husband, de facto or boyfriend).

Complainants gave varied reasons for the 'delays' in complaint when questioned during cross-examination. The most common single reason given by complainants for delay in complaint was that they feared reprisals (30 per cent). Other reasons included—the complainant was scared and ashamed (17 per cent), the complainant was fearful of not being believed (2 per cent), fearful of the police/court process (3 per cent) and there were no communications paths available (3 per cent). Complainants gave the following reasons in court when questioned about delay:

> I was frightened and didn't know what to do. (Case 9)

> When something like this first happens to you don't really know what to do 'cause . . . you don't want anyone to really know about it—you don't want your mother to find out . . . and so you're gonna hide, so you're gonna cover it up . . . I didn't know if I was going to have strength enough to speak out about it so it was better for me to try to cover it up and then I tried to sort of live with it and for a week I couldn't sleep and thought I'm gonna have to speak out about it. (Case 97)

> Initially I was too scared to do anything—but it was my own self respect that got me to the police station after a week. I went to the police station for my own self respect and pride because no man is entitled to do that to anybody. (Case 65)

The findings show that women who do not complain immediately and spontaneously are viewed as having fabricated the charge. Possible motives for such fabrication were canvassed in court with one of the most common being the fraudulent pursuit of compensation. Other reasons for making a false allegation that were alleged by the defence included:

- to gain revenge on the accused
- because the complainant felt guilty after having consensual sex with the accused
- to legitimate separation from a partner
- to avoid paying money to the accused
- to cover up for adulterous behaviour
- because of property settlements or child custody proceedings in the Family Court.

In one case studied, the complainant claimed to have been sexually assaulted by a tradesman who came to the house (Case 56). It was a 'typical' stranger rape with no previous contact with the accused, and an immediate report to the police showing significant signs of distress. During cross-examination the complainant was asked 19 questions about her possible motives for fabricating the report. The defence line was that she had fabricated the story to anger her de facto husband.

## JUDICIAL INTERPRETATIONS

At the end of a trial, and after closing submissions from the prosecution and the defence, the Judge summarises the entire proceedings for the jury. Part of the summing-up includes giving directions on the law that the jury must apply to the facts as they find them. In the *Heroines* study it was found that judges gave the mandatory warning to the jury that absence of complaint or delay in complaint does not necessarily mean the complainant's allegation of sexual assault is false (s. 405B(2)(a)) in *only 44 per cent* of trials where delay in complaint was raised by the defence in cross-examination. Further, where delay in complaint was raised by the defence in cross-examination, judges gave the mandatory warning that there may be good reasons why the complainant hesitated, delayed or refrained from making a complaint (s. 405B(2)(b)) in *just 51 per cent* of trials. We are left to speculate that these warnings were not given because the Judges were not committed to the spirit of the legislation.

Judges told the jury that evidence that the complainant did not report the offence swiftly could be used to undermine the woman's credibility in 39 per cent of trials where the delay in complaint was raised.[3] Such common law delay in complaint warnings delivered from the bench in the trials observed include the following examples:

> Your common sense tells you, from your experience of the world and the way people behave, that if something dramatic, something seriously life threatening happened to a person, one would normally expect that person to say something about it pretty quickly after it happened, rather than mention it weeks or months later. But of course if somebody doesn't mention a matter, at the earliest reasonable opportunity, then you may think that it's not consistent behaviour with what is said to have occurred. So it's in that limited background that you consider the evidence of the complainant . . . (Case 71)

> If events such as these occur one expects some complaint to be made and that such a complaint is made within a reasonably early stage of the events themselves. Take for example an allegation that someone was raped and the complaint is made a year later. That in the eyes of everybody, would cast some suspicion on the acceptability of the allegation. (Case 7)

> A complaint is admissible if made at the earliest opportunity—if a man runs out of a house and doesn't tell anyone the house is burning until the night following it is not consistent with him believing that the house was on fire when he ran out of it. (Case 21)

These statements are examples of assertions deeply embedded with political and masculine viewpoints. The judges do not claim to have encountered or studied the behaviour of sexual assault victims and thereby to have discovered that such victims tend to complain immediately. Instead they derive their instructions about how to distinguish 'true' sexual assault victims from 'false' ones exclusively by resort to their logic, to their common sense and untested beliefs about human behaviour. They assume that their assessment of 'ordinary human experience' is universal and the only experience on which to base justice.

They allege that we are all principally alike, disregarding the real experiential differences between men and women: white male experience imposes the norm and informs what may be termed an acceptable response to sexual assault. Thus it is a masculine morality and view of the world and objectivity that ultimately determines the way a specific case is to be considered. The empirical evidence about patterns of complaint is disregarded.

These legal perspectives and use of 'common sense' assumptions on complaint illustrate the law's involvement in and perpetuation of cultural myths surrounding society's conception of woman and the nature of her response, her experience (Graycar 1995). It illustrates the continued construction by legal discourse of sexual assault from the masculine viewpoint and a failure to acknowledge the diversity of responses and experience that can result from such an intimate crime.

Scheppele (1989) employs the notion of outsider/insider to arrive at an understanding of how these discriminatory patterns result. She explains that, in the courtroom, outsiders' interests are often discredited and disbelieved, while insiders' interests are legally sanctioned and received as creditable. Scheppele discusses this in the context of the 'perceptual fault lines' to be discovered in fact-finding in legal accounts. Scheppele explains that most of the 'perceptual fault lines occur at the boundaries between social groups . . . the "we" constructed in legal accounts has a distinctive selectivity'. That is, they support the perspectives of those who are white and privileged and male. Women are the outsiders in this script, Scheppele explains, who are often excluded by the daily operation of apparently harmless legal habits.

## CONCLUSION

It is almost a truism that many sexual assault complainants describe their experience of the trial process as like being raped again; a 'secondary victimisation' in the sense that it is not only the accused who is on trial but the character and identity of the primary witness—a 'status degradation ceremony' (Adler 1987). One victim described the experience as follows:

> I left the court with the same feeling of powerlessness as the
> night he raped me. I now know why the majority of women are
> too scared to put their trust in the system.

While attempts to reform legislation represent a step in the right direction, it is doubtful that legislation alone can abate the re-victimisation that sexual assault complainants routinely experience as they proceed through the criminal justice system. Evidence that legislative reforms engender insufficient change form the basis of this chapter and can also be found in other revelations uncovered by the *Heroines* research. For example, judges refused to consider the needs of the complainant in requests to close the court whilst the complainant gave evidence, despite express legislative direction to do so. Further, in 35 per cent of cases, sexual experience material was admitted without challenge or justification from the judge, despite legislative requirements to vet the admittance of such material.

Clearly, judges who wish to circumvent the legislation are able to do so. Thus, eliminating judicial discretion in procedural decisions should be viewed as only one method of attack. Misguided, erroneous, discriminatory and biased beliefs would be more effectively dealt with as a matter of education of the judiciary, the legal profession and the general public. The failure to recognise systemic discrimination is often a function of lack of information. It is important for people in positions of authority in the justice system to understand the daily experience of others unlike themselves. Once an understanding is gained of other experiences and the concomitant inequalities associated with those experiences, those in authority must in turn understand how these inequalities might be continued and compounded by the law.

In the meantime, however, women are still reluctant to report sexual assaults to the police or in many instances even to disclose to family and friends because they think they will not be believed or that the matter would never be effectively or sensitively dealt with in court. Hence proponents, agents and reformers of the criminal justice system must employ every strategy possible to convince women that, in defining their experience within the criminal justice framework, they will be treated with the dignity and respect commensurate with the status of the victim of a serious crime.

This means that feminist research must persist in challenging the law's claim to authority and continue to expose its alienation from women's lives—it must continue to agitate for a broad notion of justice that encapsulates the diversity of women's experience, and continue to strive to transcend the law's limited assumptions, its pretended neutrality and impartiality and its blind adherence to discriminatory conventions—as only then will women's right to sexual autonomy and freedom of movement in the community be affirmed.

# 4 | Having her day in court? Violence, legal remedies and consent

*Rosemary Hunter*

THIS CHAPTER IS based on a research project conducted in Melbourne on women's experiences of civil legal processes designed to address violence and harassment perpetrated by family members or work colleagues. The research involved court observations and interviews with lawyers, support workers and women litigants. One of the aims of the project was to evaluate the success of various avenues of redress for women who have been targets of violence and harassment—avenues that were created in response to feminist activism. Has the availability of these legal processes made the law more responsive to the particular experiences and needs of women?

Violence against women in Australia is the concern of both the criminal law (when perpetrators are prosecuted) and of various civil law proceedings. Civil cases have several advantages over criminal proceedings for women seeking an end to and/or a remedy for violence and harassment. The civil law, for example, enables women to take action directly against their abusers rather than relying on the state to take action, as is necessary in a criminal prosecution. In a civil case, the woman is the subject of her own proceeding, rather than merely a witness for the state. In civil law proceedings, too, the standard for establishing the legal truth of the woman's story is lower (on the balance of probabilities, rather than beyond reasonable doubt), and the perpetrator does not enjoy several other evidentiary and procedural advantages available to a criminal accused. A successful civil case also results in a direct remedy for the woman who has been the target of violence or harassment, rather than simply a criminal penalty for the perpetrator.

The traditional form of civil action that might be used to seek a remedy for violence is the ability to sue an abuser for damages for assault. This legal avenue remains a largely theoretical option for most women, since it is very rare for an abuser to have the resources to pay damages (although there is now some scope to overcome this problem in Family Court proceedings, as explained below). Other reasons for the inaccessibility of this kind of civil suit include the cost of initiating action (and the unlikelihood of obtaining legal aid), and the shadow still cast by the old doctrine of interspousal tort immunity, whereby one spouse could not legally sue another. Although the doctrine of interspousal tort immunity has been formally abolished in Australia (*Family Law Act 1975* (Cth), s. 119), it continues to influence women's sense of entitlement to sue, and courts' views of justice in family relations (Okin 1989; Graycar & Morgan 1990, pp. 285–286).

While the ordinary civil law has therefore offered little assistance to women seeking remedies for violence and harassment, feminist campaigns for improved legal protection for women have resulted in the establishment of a number of specialised avenues for this purpose. These avenues are intended to provide (although do not always do so in practice) low cost, reasonably efficient access to justice for abused women. They include intervention orders designed to prevent further abuse under threat of criminal sanctions,[1] and specific legislation outlawing sexual harassment and enabling action to be taken against harassers.[2]

The Family Court is another civil forum where violence may be raised and taken into account in determining arrangements for the long-term care, welfare and development, residence of, and contact with children[3] and in distributing marital property according to past contributions and future needs.[4] It has also recently become possible for women to combine a traditional civil action for assault with a family law property dispute, so that in effect the woman is suing her former husband for injuries caused to her during the marriage and claiming damages out of his share of the property.[5]

The availability of such remedies seems to indicate that women's harms are taken seriously. Australian state and federal governments have given legal recognition to family and workplace violence, and provided specifically tailored forms of redress. Women's experiences have been made the basis for legal claims (e.g. MacKinnon 1987, p. 103), rather than women being expected to work with legal tools designed by and for men. The results of this research project, however, suggest that the Australian legal system still takes little account of the particularity of violence and harassment. Women have been offered merely formal legal equality with men rather than substantive equality.

A major structural barrier to the civil law taking women's experiences of violence and harassment seriously is the role played by consent in civil proceedings. A mutually agreed settlement is the systemically preferred outcome in civil cases. This preference has both ideological and pragmatic dimensions. Liberal societies believe that individuals are in the best position to determine their own solutions and should be given maximum freedom to do so. Private agreements are thought both to enhance individual autonomy and freedom of choice, and to maximise social welfare, since parties will only agree to arrangements that make them both better off (Neave 1994, p. 111). This concern dovetails with and is reinforced by the fact that our legal system is endowed with insufficient resources to adjudicate all disputes (Galanter 1974, p. 95).

Thus, parties to civil cases will be actively encouraged by legal institutions to settle their differences between themselves, resulting either in the withdrawal of the formal grievance or the making of consent orders. This emphasis on consent applies equally (if not more so) to civil cases involving violence and harassment as to other kinds of civil cases involving personal injuries, property damage, debts or commercial transactions. Consent does not necessarily operate in the same way in different kinds of legal settings (e.g. it may be an empowering device, as in the notion of informed consent to medical treatment, or its imputation may be disempowering to women, as in rape cases).[6] But it does act as a powerful boundary marker, separating the public from the private and serving to deflect the exercise of state power. Consent turned out to play a prominent role in the civil proceedings that were the subject of the study reported here.

## REGIMES OF CONSENT

In the case of sexual harassment, complaints must be lodged with a state agency which is required, initially, to attempt to seek a resolution by conciliation (*Equal Opportunity Act* 1995 (Vic.), s. 112; *Sex Discrimination Act* (Cth), s. 52). The emphasis on conciliation provides the opportunity for private, confidential and low-cost settlement, but practical experience indicates that the conciliation process also provides the opportunity for long delays, for respondents to dig in and lie with impunity, and for complainants to give up and get on with their lives (Hunter & Leonard 1995). Only a very small proportion of sexual harassment cases is referred for adjudication. For example, in 1995/96, 234 sexual harassment complaints were lodged under the Victorian *Equal Opportunity Act* (Equal Opportunity Commission Victoria 1996, p. 39), but in the same period only two sexual harassment cases were scheduled for final hearing by the Victorian Anti-Discrimination Tribunal, and one of these settled at the door of the court.[7] Those that do not reach a hearing may have settled before that point, but some will have lapsed or been withdrawn.

Once a case is referred for hearing, the tribunal too will make every effort through the preliminary stages to encourage a settlement,[8] often successfully. The fact that settlements are almost invariably confidential means that there is no way of knowing their terms or assessing their adequacy. And the fact that few cases run (not all of which are successful) means that there is little opportunity for the tribunal to publicly identify harassing behaviour and state that it is unacceptable.

In the Family Court, settlements between the parties as a result of counselling, mediation or negotiations between legal representatives are also the norm, with litigation again very much the exception, although the overall caseload of the Family Court is much higher. Again, in those cases that are listed for hearing, every effort is made by the parties' lawyers, up to the door of the court and even during the hearing, to reach a settlement on which the parties can agree and to formulate consent orders for the court's approval. Moreover, the shortage of judicial time and court space available, and listing practices which mean that having a court date is no guarantee of a case proceeding, send a clear message to family litigants: judicial resolution of their dispute may be a long time coming, so they would be better off resolving it themselves. There is a particular emphasis, enshrined in the *Family Law Act*,[9] on the parties reaching agreement where children are concerned, on the basis that such co-operation is more conducive to the success of future parenting arrangements. Judges are always willing to give lawyers and parties extra time for discussions if a settlement seems possible. Since the whole institution of marriage is founded upon consent (O'Donovan 1997, p. 55) married (or formerly married) couples tend to be seen as prime subjects of consent. Yet in relationships that have involved violence, the capacity of the abused party to 'consent' must be highly compromised.[10] The Family Court itself recognises this by screening couples with a history of violence out of its mediation program.[11] But the same degree of concern is not extended to the 'private' settlement process. Even cases involving the most egregious violence inevitably include some consent orders on the file. These may often have been negotiated by lawyers rather than directly by the parties, but that is no guarantee that the existence of violence was accepted and taken into account. It may well have been put to one side in order to reach a settlement. (Elaborate contact handover arrangements may be the only sign of a woman's concern for her own safety.) Or the negotiation process may have involved further bullying of the woman by her (ex-)partner and/or by her lawyers. Further, the fact that interim custody and access arrangements were made by consent can be used at a later hearing to suggest that the violence alleged by the wife did not occur, was not as serious as she suggested, or had no significant impact on her capacity to negotiate with the husband.[12]

In relation to intervention orders, a whole new consent regime has developed. In Victoria, intervention orders may be sought either by an 'aggrieved family member' or by a member of the police force. In practice, however, police rarely exercise their powers under the legislation, leaving women who have been targets of violence to act on their own behalf. Women may apply *ex parte* for an interim order, which lasts for a limited period (usually one to four weeks). The applicant can then seek to have the order made final at a hearing at which the defendant is given an opportunity to contest the order.

Defendants may simply decide not to turn up for the hearing. This was the response in 41 per cent of the cases observed for this study where the defendant was notified of the hearing.[13] Not turning up constitutes an implicit (if somewhat defiant) form of consent to the order, which will almost invariably be made in minimum time, with minimum input from the applicant. Typically, she will be asked to enter the witness box, sworn, asked if she agrees with her previous statement (yes), if she fears for her future safety (yes), and the order will be granted.[14] Occasionally, the Magistrate might express some concern about the consequences for the defendant, especially if granting the application would involve excluding the defendant from the family home. In such cases the applicant may still obtain the order, but perhaps for a limited period, and after a grilling about whether it's fair and what alternative accommodation the defendant has available, even though the defendant, having been given notice of the hearing, has decided not to come to court to make these arguments for himself.[15]

If a defendant does arrive at court on the appointed day, the clerk will tell him that he has two (or sometimes three) options. He may contest the order, in which case the Magistrate will hear the case and he will be required to give sworn evidence and produce witnesses; or he can simply consent to the order; or he can consent to having an order made against him without admitting the applicant's allegations. It is the second option that is often omitted: consent without admissions is seen to provide a greater incentive. If the clerk has failed to persuade the defendant to consent, the Magistrate will sometimes repeat the options in court, with strong encouragement for the defendant to consent without admitting the allegations. Consenting saves considerable time for the defendant and for the court, and it also spares the Magistrate from having to listen to all the details of the alleged violence. In most courts, contested matters are scheduled after all the consents have been dealt with, so defendants who consent can avoid a long wait. In one branch court, final applications for intervention orders are heard one morning a week, with contested cases being adjourned to another court, a significant distance away, either for that afternoon or another day: a further powerful incentive for defendants to consent. Out of the 63 applications for final orders observed, only nine were contested.

If police were to play a more active role in applying for intervention orders, defendants might equally have an incentive to consent to orders being made against them, but the existence of police support for the complainant's allegations would render consent without admitting those allegations much less of an option.

In intervention order proceedings where women's consent is material, such as in applications for mutual orders or to revoke an order, there is rarely any interrogation of the freedom or fairness of her consent. If a defendant comes to court with a lawyer—and especially if the applicant is unrepresented—the defendant may agree to consent to an order only if she also consents to a tit-for-tat order against her.[16] There may be little or no behaviour on her part to justify such an order, and what behaviour exists is usually quite trivial compared to the behaviour she is complaining about. Yet again, since consent orders speed up the court process, there will be no stopping to question the appropriateness of her consent in these circumstances,[17] or to query whether obtaining a mutual order is just another instance of the defendant exercising power and control over her.[18] In relation to applications for the revocation of intervention orders, some Magistrates appear to hold highly romantic beliefs about the virtues of reconciliation and to exercise almost a wilful blindness to the possibility of coercion.[19] The clearest example of such a case that I have seen went like this:

> Young woman and young man are called into court. They enter together and stand side-by-side at the front.
> *Magistrate* (to woman): You want to revoke the order?
> *Woman*: Yes.
> *Magistrate* (to man): What do you think of that?
> *Man*: I want it, it was my idea.
> *Magistrate*: OK, the order is revoked.[20]

The following case (MC17), which also took one minute, went:

> *Magistrate* (to applicant): What's your relationship with the defendant?
> *Applicant*: He's my husband.
> *Magistrate*: Have you had a reconciliation or something?
> *Applicant*: I want to give him a chance.
> *Magistrate*: OK, fine, the order is removed. That's it.

## PROS AND CONS

It must be acknowledged that disposing of legal proceedings by consent has several advantages for women. It can bring the matter to a much quicker and less costly conclusion.[21] For sexual harassment complainants, reaching a settlement may be a great relief after the traumas of the harassment itself and the complaint process.[22] Arriving at consent orders also gives a Family Court litigant some control over the outcome of her case rather than leaving it in the hands of an unpredictable judicial decision-maker[23] (or a predictably hostile one). Unlike the parties to business transactions, parties to family law disputes have no option to walk away: they must either reach agreement or have one imposed upon them (Neave 1997, p. 114). Thus, a consent order may represent the best deal that can be made at the time,[24] in a context where there is no guarantee of a better decision.

In relation to intervention orders, encouraging defendants to consent may have many benefits for applicants. Pragmatically, the applicant gets her protective order, which is no less effective than one arrived at via a contest.[25] A breach of a consent order is equally culpable. A consent order also saves applicants the trauma of describing the details of their abuse to a courtroom full of strangers, or of facing their abuser in court, often in situations where the defendant is unrepresented and therefore may cross-examine the applicant directly. Conversely, if a woman does go into the witness box, there is a risk that her credibility will be undermined and the order refused.[26] A consent outcome may also prevent the defendant from becoming more aggressive towards the applicant, and therefore be more conducive to her safety.[27]

Lawyers involved in intervention order court support programs report that some women are quite happy with consent orders.[28] Women who are just in the process of separating from their partners might not need their say in court at that stage, or might not wish to speak if they are there without legal representation, so the consent option gives them an order quickly and with less stress than a contest.[29] However, no-one actually seeks the woman's consent in these situations. No-one asks her if she'd prefer to tell her story and prove her case; no-one asks her if she's happy to obtain an order while the defendant is allowed to deny his violent behaviour. While some women are happy with consent orders, others are frustrated or outraged by the choice given to the defendant to deny his behaviour.[30] How *could* he deny it? Or how *could* he be allowed to demand mutual orders?[31]

Furthermore, as Marcia Neave (1994, pp. 112–113) points out, all the evidence from both family and employment contexts points to the conclusion that women do poorly out of regimes of private ordering. Contrary to the assertions of liberal theory, women do enter into agreements they perceive as unfair—that is, they are the best they can achieve in the circumstances but they don't make them better off (Neave 1994, p. 114). And quite apart from the outcomes, consenting behaviour has some serious procedural consequences.

First, there is a lack of institutional affirmation of women's stories of abuse. There are few judicial findings that these stories are *true*. And the lack of such affirmation tends to reinforce the notion that women make up stories of abuse and use the legal process for collateral purposes—for example, as part of the manoeuvres in a property dispute, or to deny fathers access to their children (views expressed to the author by both defendants' solicitors and Magistrates in conversation). Second, there is a lack of public, legal condemnation of abusive behaviour. What happened is not clearly labelled as unlawful. And while public education campaigns can draw attention to the social unacceptability of and availability of redress for violence and harassment, publicity from successful cases does operate to empower other women—particularly in the case of sexual harassment—whereas private settlements have no flow-on effects. Third, men are not forced to take responsibility for their actions. This is especially so where mutual orders are obtained, which have the effect of putting the woman's self-defence or retaliation on the same plane as her partner's aggression. Fourth, the existence of violence against women, and the scale of that violence, fails to enter the realm of public knowledge. Men's denial and minimisation of violence is echoed by the state. Consent makes the 'problem' of violence disappear from view.

## CONCLUSION

I would argue that we need less consent and more talk about violence in court, not because telling their stories would be therapeutic for women, but because hearing women's stories would be educative for judicial officers, journalists, and society in general. Hearing might then start to translate into believing. Myths about violence can only be dispelled when more of the reality of violence circulates in public discourse.

Further, the fact that violence against women is unacceptable behaviour needs to be authoritatively stated again and again.[32] The consent regime in civil proceedings has helped to maintain the silence about abuse and violence. Consent continues to be invoked as the hallmark of the autonomous (non-gendered) legal subject (O'Donovan 1997, p. 47), and this, too, can only be challenged if the experiences of women are heard and understood in their systemic context.

I am not advocating the abolition of settlement options, or mandatory adjudication in proceedings concerning violence. But I would like to see consent problematised in relationships involving power and control. And I would like to see women given the opportunity, if they wish, to speak about their experiences of violence, to express their refusal to tolerate abuse, and to have the truth and the outrage of their stories affirmed.

# 5 | The case of the too hard basket: investigating the connections between 'ethnicity', 'culture' and 'access' to sexual assault services

*Mailin Suchting*

CRITICAL ENGAGEMENT WITH 'race',[1] 'ethnicity' and 'culture' in relation to sexual assault raises many issues. Even the most enthusiastic workers speak of moments when it feels too hard. It can seem easier for us to choose not to engage. But to do so is highly contentious because those who experience marginalisation based on 'race', 'ethnicity' or 'culture' in every aspect of their lives speak of not having such a choice. For it is the ability to choose that marks a position of privilege—creating an 'us' and 'them' debate, which I am calling 'the case of the too hard basket'.

The central questions in this chapter revolve around the concepts of 'race', 'ethnicity' and 'culture' and how these intersect with sexual assault work in New South Wales. This chapter seeks to provide insight into why 'improving access' to sexual assault services for people from non English speaking backgrounds might seem so hard, and for whom. This is a search for clues about the ways in which cultural, 'ethnic' and racialised difference are addressed in the provision of sexual assault services in New South Wales. But, first, let me be clear about what I mean by these terms.

Sneja Gunew makes the point that the terms 'race', 'ethnicity' and 'culture' carry highly charged meanings with contemporary significance to us all. She compares the distinctions between 'race' and 'ethnicity' with those that have been made historically between sex and gender—sex as a biological fact and gender as socially constituted:

> In comparable ways in the past, race was invoked as a science for differentiating in . . . essentialist ways among the various groups of people . . . Race was one of the irreducible differences and conveyed certain reassurance, as all irrefutable distinctions do. (Gunew 1993, p. 9)

Genetic and biological differences underpinning the notion of 'race' have consistently been shown to be trivial, and no case has ever been made to justify ascribing psychological, intellectual or moral characteristics to individuals or groups to justify arbitrary differential treatment. Paradoxically, racism remains recognisable and widespread, embodying the category 'race'. Where 'race' has been identified as a social construction it performs more usefully as an 'unstable and "decentred" complex of social meanings constantly being transformed by political struggle' (Omi & Winant 1986, p. 6). Ethnicity as distinguished from 'race' was seen as culturally and socially produced rather than biologically derived (Outlaw, quoted in Gunew 1993, p. 9). Gunew also notes that ethnicity has the quality of being self-chosen 'and in this aspect remains a central way of distinguishing it from "race": for example, ethnic communities and ethnic identity are self identified' (1993, p. 9). This is the meaning attributed to this term throughout this chapter.

So what of 'culture', which is perhaps the most contested of terms? Commonly trivialised to refer to lifestyle, food, dance and national dress, and privatised to refer to what people do in their domestic lives, culture is often paradoxically presented as a fixed characteristic of individuals or community, yet also constantly changing. This paradox is a common feature of multicultural discourse[2] where reference to 'other cultures' or, more recently, a 'diversity of cultures' or 'cultural diversity' is common. Revisiting the idea of culture from another perspective, Donald and Rattansi suggest that culture is:

> . . . no longer understood as [that which] . . . expresses the identity of a community. Rather it refers to the processes, categories and knowledge through which communities are defined as such: that is how they are rendered specific and differentiated. (1992, p. 4)

Such definitions serve as a reminder of the ways in which reality can be constituted through language and the way meaning can be constrained. Those involved in the examination of gendered discourses in critical work around sexual violence will find this type of analysis familiar.

## ACCESS

So, do we provide 'access' to sexual assault services to people from around the world who are now living in Australia? During the past two decades feminists working in a variety of settings have fought to provide a situation where services for women and children who have been sexually assaulted are available and appropriately resourced. Whilst this achievement of over 50 services in New South Wales is comprehensive and significant, there remain groups within the community for whom these services do not adequately provide. Migrant and refugee communities from non English speaking backgrounds[3] feature significantly as one of these groups[4] and provide the focus for this chapter. This situation is often described as one of *access* or rather a lack of *access*—a situation where part of the community is not getting what is available to the rest.

It is fair to say that lobby groups, funded services within the health and welfare sector and government have made attempts to improve 'access' to culturally and linguistically diverse communities guided by shifting policies of multiculturalism. These attempts have tended to be sporadic, short-term funded and generally geared towards maintenance of existing service structures. Hence, when Pamela Garrett (1992, p. 196) wrote that 'the provision of sexual assault services which provide equitable access to people of non English speaking background is fraught with structural and conceptual problems', she opened a case that remains quite familiar today. In a context where it is well recognised that rape and child sexual assault occur in all countries and communities (United Nations 1995), where over 80 per cent of Sydney's refugee community has experienced some form of sexual torture and where women are still being raped in every modern conflict (Amnesty International 1997), this issue is of great concern.

This chapter asks what it is about the context of sexual assault service provision that might limit access to migrants and refugees from non English speaking backgrounds. This revisits the often asked question of why so few migrants and refugees from non English speaking backgrounds 'access' sexual assault services (NSW Health 1995) more broadly, locating the problem politically rather than with individual migrants and refugees. It is, after all, over a decade since migrant women in New South Wales were first heard[5] to raise their marginalisation from the prevailing debates about incest and rape (Albie & Mowbray-d'Arbela 1987). In 1984 the NSW Women Against Incest phone-in survey (Waldby 1985) first documented a failure to reach non English speaking migrant women on the issue of sexual assault. In July 1986 a group of migrant women formed the Migrant Women's Network Against Incest in response to concerns about poor access to sexual assault services for women from non English speaking backgrounds.

This group provided community education about sexual assault to multicultural community groups and identified a vicious cycle of contemporary relevance. They noticed a classic Catch-22 situation: sexual assault services without workers speaking languages other than English—this lack of workers leading to little community awareness—no demand for sexual assault services from migrant and refugee communities because of a lack of awareness—leading back to no workers from non English speaking background being employed in sexual assault services because of no demand on services.

In 1987 the NSW Sexual Assault Committee coordinated a State-wide multilingual campaign on sexual assault. This involved the translation of the Women and Rape pamphlet into 11 languages and a radio, newspaper and poster campaign in 20 languages. Concurrently, the then Sexual Assault Education Unit within the Health Department developed training for migrant health workers, interpreters and sexual assault workers and produced a video about working with interpreters.

Although the relative effectiveness of these strategies has never been properly assessed, this remains the period of greatest focused activity around 'culture', 'ethnicity' and sexual assault in the history of the sector in New South Wales until 1996. From this time a number of projects began to emphasise local planning within services, relationship building with groups advocating on behalf of migrants and refugees, improving links between sexual assault services and migrant health services within Area Health Services and cross-cultural training. Despite this considerable body of work, sexual assault services continue to struggle conceptually with the meaning of improved 'access' and who the terms 'non English speaking background' and 'cultural diversity' represent. At a structural level, imperatives to increase the representation of non English speaking migrants and refugees in the client populations of services (NSW Health 1995), and increase the 'cultural sensitivity' and 'competence' of service providers continue and the statistics of actual service provision remain low.

Given this context it is my intention here to inspire a politics of difference. By this I mean first to '. . . recognis[e] "ethnic" and class differences between women as a starting point rather than as an embarrassing afterthought' (Jolly 1991, p. 53) in relation to sexual assault service provision, and second, to examine 'how our very notions of identity and difference are grounded in historical, political and moral relations' (Jolly 1996, p. 169). Extending this, I am also arguing that there will continue to be an 'issue' in the health system about 'access' for those marked as 'different' (read different from an imagined norm) whilst a notion of 'us' and 'them' persists. Until we are able to acknowledge that 'we are all "culturally different" rather than "we are normal" and "they are different" . . . and . . . "we are here to establish a dialogue between our differences" rather than "we are here to learn about cultural difference"' (Durie & Taylor 1997, p. 5) we will not have reached equity, the outcome of access. For aren't we all culturally and linguistically diverse?

Three propositions make it possible to interrogate the power relationships implicit here and challenge the workplace to consider changes in practice. The first of these suggests that the way in which sexual assault services have developed in New South Wales has created *structural constraints* to 'access' that require serious consideration. One example is the privileging of therapeutic models of intervention over the past ten years which has narrowed the potential client population to those familiar with counselling as a means of responding to trauma and grief. Such assumptions have been little challenged to date. The second proposition extends this analysis to a critique of the term 'culture'. Challenge is made to the idea that a group of people share a 'culture' that is fixed, able to be categorised and thereby 'accessed' with *the* right strategy. Links are made between the ways in which individual *'cultural' positioning* impacts on the pursuit of 'access' and how ideas about culture function within multicultural discourse.

Finally, this chapter offers some reflection on the *feminisms* that have guided the provision of sexual assault services in New South Wales and the ways in which issues of 'race' and ethnicity have been marginalised. The assumption that feminism speaks for all women in the same way has been well critiqued yet remains a prevailing idea in the sector. For true access to be achieved the sector must examine feminism in the light of a politics of difference.

## STRUCTURAL CONSTRAINTS

Many structural reasons have been identified over the past 20 years that seek to explain the lack of representation of people from diverse cultures in sexual assault services. These were perhaps most eloquently expressed by the report *Quarter Way to Equal* produced by the Women's Legal Resources Centre (1992). Summarised, the list reads as a failure of the system to provide people from 'non English speaking backgrounds' with appropriate information about legal rights, availability of services, referral and type of service; as a failure of services to plan effectively for all communities in regard to location, provision of outreach, employment of bilingual staff with relevant community languages, and links with appropriate services in the community; a failure of government to develop campaigns that provide information that people from many backgrounds can use; an inadequacy of training for key service providers in cross-cultural issues and for ethno-specific workers in sexual assault; and competing demands for resources.

Despite this type of rhetoric which appears in many reports, there continues to be a serious gap between the intentions of government agencies and the needs of people from non English speaking communities around the issue of sexual assault. Research like *Quarter Way to Equal* identifies interesting problems in the 'access' conundrum yet seldom offers a crucial piece of evidence to explain why 'they' don't use 'our' services. What if we were asking the wrong question? What if it were more important to ask what it is about 'us', rather than why 'they' don't come? Introducing 'us' into the picture (whoever 'we' are) starts a process of looking at the ways in which power is enacted through everyday practice. After all, the exercise of power can shape which claim is heard at a particular moment and given weight.

If 'we' stopped searching for how 'they' are different from 'us' and recognised that we are all 'culturally different' and that how our differences look depends on where we stand, we would open up the possibility of a dialogue between our differences (Durie &

Taylor 1997). The issue of 'access' could no longer be focused individually—it would have to include a broader political context. Such a shift would make it possible to look critically at the impact of some of the assumptions that guide some current work practice in the area of sexual assault and the way in which power is enacted through these. Some of these assumptions maintain:

- that 'Western' models of 'resolving trauma' and grief through counselling have universal application
- that 'state' based structures can offer services of value to those who may find it hard to trust the state
- that because issues around sexual assault have been so hard fought for in many arenas, they have been fought for on behalf of all 'others'
- that without 'our' help, 'they' will not be OK
- that 'their' differences are able to be determined and mark 'fixed' cultural identities that are 'accessible'.

For any worker these inspire thoughtful consideration about what it would mean to challenge such assumptions. This is where post-structuralist[6] perspectives have helped me most for they invite questions that relate to power and knowledge and provide a progressive framework for understanding the relationship between people and their social worlds. To understand the relationship between language, social institutions, subjectivity and power (Weedon 1987), post-structural feminism not only challenges the idea of the individual or 'culture' as a social construction resulting in a 'fixed' entity, but also recognises the way in which there are multiple and competing perspectives which claim to represent the truth of reality. For example, saying that *one* way to respond to grief around trauma is counselling, as opposed to 'the' way to respond to grief is counselling.

A service that accepts a multiplicity of ways of resolving trauma and therefore accepts the cultural specificity of current 'therapeutic responses' may begin to investigate 'access' differently. A worker who thinks about the multidimensional nature of power, who knows about the ways in which power is not just located in particular sites or institutions but also in everyday practice, and recognises how a service may be read by those to be 'accessed' may develop some insights into inaccessibility. My 'whiteness' may say a great deal more about power to one person than my gender may say about empowerment. This has to be taken into consideration when thinking of just what 'access' might mean.

Practically, it is important to recognise that adequate and appropriate funding is a prerequisite for 'accessible services'. This said, it is necessary to stop generating lists of structural constraints to 'access' as if the structures are faceless. It is important to examine the ways in which each worker enacts and critiques policy and to accept that it is time to move beyond the universalisms of 'us' and 'them' to acknowledge *our* part, be it wittingly or unwittingly, in colluding with structures that work against 'access'.

## CULTURAL POSITIONING

Take a card. Write a date on that card that marks your family's first contact with Australia. You may have a number of dates that you could choose but for the purposes of this exercise choose just one. Maybe you identify with one part of your family more than another. Perhaps you know more about one than another. If you are unaware of another date use your date of birth.

Mingle with each other and seat yourselves around the group in chronological order starting at around 60 000 years ago and ending at 1998. As we work through a number of recorded historical moments and policy shifts, call out when we reach the date you chose and tell us the story that connects you to this history of Australia.

This is an exercise that I have developed as part of my work that invites reflection about where each of us position ourselves, where we are positioned by others and where others are positioned by us in terms of 'race', ethnicity, 'culture' and history. In this exercise 'we' become markers of and players in Australia's 'racialised' history. The question of who 'we' are is important.

Recently, when I ran this exercise, many people expressed surprise when a young male worker identified himself with his 'white' father's birth rather than his mother's Aboriginality. Some members of the group acknowledged that they had already positioned him as Aboriginal and therefore expected him to identify with 40 000 years plus. In another group, a woman cried after telling the story of arriving here with her parents from Germany. Like many migrants at the time, her family anglicised their name under the pressure of assimilation policies in the 1950s. Although her family had spoken only German at home since they arrived, her work colleagues heard her identify as German for the first time in this group. They had positioned her as 'Anglo' within the Australian context.

The idea of positioning is located firmly in post-structuralist theorising around gender and 'culture'. Bronwyn Davies (1989, p. xi) explores the ways in which children are enculturated into ideas about gender in society:

> [I]ndividuals, through learning the discursive practices of a society, are able to position themselves within these practices in multiple ways, and to develop subjectivities both in concert with and in opposition to the ways in which others chose to position them.

Similarly, and more recently, Durie and Taylor (1997, p. 5) outlined a cogent explanation of the way positioning functions to assist us to make sense of our various 'cultural' positionings:

> We pointed out that we belong to more than one cultural grouping. [At the least] . . . we all have gender, sexual preferences, age, socio-economic background and ethnicity. We are likely to draw on our contradictory framings to make sense of our various cultural experiences. As our investments in particular positions often shift according to our contexts we are not necessarily consistent. Even without realising it we can move quite strategically between positions as we negotiate the 'real' world and our place in it. We must therefore place strong emphasis on our movements within and around cultural differences—our 'positionality'.

Over the past five years I have used the exercise described above many times with many different groups to explain the idea of positioning and the relevance of context. How 'we' identify culturally is not fixed and this has implications for working with difference. Stuart Hall (1990, p. 392) proposes that:

> identity [is] a 'production' that is never complete, always in process, always constituted within representation.

He notes that:

> we all write and speak from a particular place and time, from a history and a culture that is specific. What we say is always 'in context', positioned . . . [yet] . . . who speaks and the subject who is spoken of, are never identical, never exactly in the same place.

Understanding who 'we' are in this process of providing services to 'them' is another pivotal point for a discussion of 'access' as a political process. Yet it can be hard to know where to position ourselves. 'We' don't want to appear racist (and until recently politically incorrect) nor do 'we' want to be accused of cultural relativism. It can feel very difficult to act—easier not to hear, not to act, not to speak. Rather than relegating the idea of positioning to 'the too hard basket' I propose to model a strategy that goes some way towards explaining the ways in which each of us can understand ourselves differently and, in doing so, better engage with the complexities of 'culture'. I'd like to call this strategy a critical autobiography.

At the risk of falling into the trap that bell hooks (1990) describes of being a white woman/scholar investigating 'the other' from a standpoint of difference because it is fashionable, I am interested in examining my role in perpetuating a discourse that I believe actively marginalises immigrant women of non English speaking backgrounds from sexual assault services in particular. In doing so I am taking up the challenge of interrogating the role my 'whiteness' has played in my use of the discourses of multiculturalism, and of examining the power relationships that this exposes. This also forms the springboard for my analysis of the position of non English speaking background women within multicultural discourses and the ways in which this positioning impacts on 'access' to sexual assault services.

Although autobiographical material can sometimes activate a sense of personal experience as authority, I would like to follow the lead of Ien Ang (1994) and suggest that it is more important to ask why I want to be autobiographical. What relevance does it have to the question of why so few immigrant and refugee women present at sexual assault services? My answer is that the autobiographical comments I am about to make illustrate not only Hall's points but also the contradictions implicit in the term 'non English speaking background'. They politicise my relationship to the issue and seek to challenge the continuing attempts to fix categories around 'race' and 'ethnicity', as well as 'class', 'gender' and 'geography', in the discourse of multiculturalism.

There are two reasons why I want to position myself in this chapter. One relates to my constant confrontation with women through my work who are misrepresented by the term 'non English speaking background' when it is intended to identify who they are. Rather than acknowledge diversity, as the principles of multiculturalism have echoed over the past decade, the language works to limit what is knowable for any of us about each other. I am currently caught in a practice struggle that I think may be shared by some readers. The all pervasive language used to identify the people to whom the discourse of multiculturalism refers, those migrants or refugees from 'non English speaking background' (or NESB), has a universalising and numbing effect. Its overuse has dulled its purpose to the extent that there is little meaning left in the term. Every use of this form prompts my questioning of who 'we' are talking 'about'. I would like to suggest that every time workers in a sexual assault service focus on the issue of 'access' some of the first questions that are likely to be asked are 'which NESB?' 'who are we targeting?' 'how do we make a decision about "which" group?'

My second reason relates to my own location. As the daughter of a postwar German migrant to Australia and a third generation Australian of Scottish and Danish background, a feminist and a 'middle class' educated 'English speaker', I also experience shifting locations in relation to the term 'non English speaking background woman'.

The impact on my family of the assimilation policies of the 1950s and 1960s, and postwar sentiment about Germans, is one reason why I did not learn my mother's first language. Although, according to the Ethnic Communities Council definition of 'non English speaking background', I am statistically a 'non English speaking background' woman, my English skill and 'whiteness' locate me firmly with that mythical 'dominant Australia'. As a migrant on Aboriginal land, who is a lesbian and a parent with a Chinese first name and a family name from the shifting borders of Germany and Denmark (a name whose syllables resonate a Chinese tone), the limitations of any fixed category become more complex. Many people, when they first hear my name, expect me to be Chinese.

Why might this have any relevance to a discussion about access for 'non English speaking' migrants and refugees to sexual assault services in New South Wales? The following quote from bell hooks answers this well:

> Participants in contemporary discussions of culture highlighting difference and otherness who have not interrogated their perspectives, the location from which they . . . [work] . . . in a culture of domination, can easily make of this . . . [a situation] . . . where old practices are simultaneously critiqued, re-enacted and sustained. (hooks 1990, p. 125)

Improving 'access' has tended to require that staff develop 'cultural sensitivity' to 'different' groups through the practice of 'cross-cultural' training. This type of work is recommended by many documents and reports addressing 'access' issues for non English speaking people (Women's Legal Resources Centre 1994; Fairfield Multicultural Family Planning 1996). The perspectives informing cross-cultural training have hovered around defining 'culture', examining communication skills, understanding migration and refugee resettlement and, more recently, developing cultural competencies (Fitzgerald et al. 1996). Such training has seen a shift in focus from what workers need to know about 'others' in order to do their jobs, to skills that address 'cultural diversity'.

Cross-cultural training thus structured is one step removed from the 'checklist' approaches of previous years where lists of characteristics of particular 'cultures' were regarded as fixed and identifiable. In the context of 'cultural diversity' the rhetoric has changed to acknowledge 'culture as fluid and adaptive' rather than 'fixed and determined' (Durie & Taylor 1997, p. 5). Yet these two notions still co-exist in a number of ways. For example, the use of language like 'in Arabic culture' (a sense that there is one fixed, identifiable Arabic culture) sits paradoxically with comments like 'cultures are constantly changing and diverse'. I venture to suggest that we have been doing what hooks cautions us against, simultaneously critiquing, re-enacting and sustaining ways of working with these 'problem others'.

The current rhetoric which implores workers to develop 'cultural sensitivity' and 'competence' in order to work with 'non English speaking clients' lacks an analysis of power. There is an assumption that workers need to achieve a certain level of skill and they will be qualified to work with people who are culturally and linguistically different from them. There is no assumption that we are all different from each other—a subtle shift in identifying the 'problem', which implicates 'us' in an important power relationship. It is impossible to achieve 'cultural sensitivity and competence' without examining who 'we' are and who 'we' are being sensitive to.

For, as I have discussed, not only are 'we' different from each other but how 'we' are different changes depending upon who 'we' are with, what we expect from each other in different contexts, how 'we' present or position ourselves in relation to each other and what 'we' may share in common. Any worker must know who they are 'culturally' in different situations, how they may be 'read' and how their positioning might change in order to engage adequately with the way in which 'access' shifts.

## FEMINISMS

Sexual assault services in New South Wales, informed by radical feminism and brought into the State by liberal feminism, generated a comprehensive analysis of gender and power which has formed a very important foundation for the understanding of sexual assault. This analysis has, however, continued to marginalise issues of 'race/culture/ethnicity' and power. We know this by the ways in which issues for immigrant, refugee and Aboriginal women have seldom featured, or featured last, on conference programs, training programs, in literature, research and in client populations. This is ethnicity as the 'embarrassing afterthought' that Margaret Jolly's earlier quote is a warning against, and is a common critique of second-wave feminism.

More particularly, critiques of radical feminism hold that the reduction of the feminist struggle to one primary gendered struggle (the fight against male domination) alienated 'non-white' feminists who gave equal weight to the struggle against 'race'-based relations of domination. Radical feminism could not explain the interlocking ways in which class, race, sexuality and ethnicity differently shape the experience of gender (Rossiter 1997). In different ways, liberal feminism, in upholding the individual as a starting point, emphasised the need for state structures to protect individual women from discrimination.

Liberal feminists envisaged a society where laws and institutions reflect the interests of all and where differences like gender and ethnicity do not matter in terms of life chances. Such a society would aspire to full citizenship for women and anti-discrimination policy would pave the way. Critiques of this perspective maintain that, whilst laws and structures are developed to protect individuals, only some individuals can 'access' protection because the ability to use the system for protection requires knowledge and power to communicate with the system. In this way, an analysis addressing only the gender/power nexus is too limited.

Interestingly, Marxist/socialist feminisms have had little impact on the development of sexual assault services but have been the arena of second-wave feminism most concerned about intersections of gender, class and later 'race'. Whereas Marxists have historically seen class as the fundamental division in society, Marxist feminists were interested in expanding Marxism to explain how women are oppressed. Socialist feminists argued that Marxism is an inadequate theory to explain the oppression of women and that it was necessary to combine a theoretical analysis of class, capitalism and feminism. In the 1980s, following 'criticisms by Black women, "race" was added as a third category to be integrated' (Rossiter 1997). There was a great emphasis on connecting up the struggles of women, of 'ethnic' minorities and of oppressed indigenous groups around the world with those of the struggling working class.

I have spoken about these feminisms in the past tense not because they no longer exist but to mark the cultural moments from which they developed, historically. In contrast to these perspectives, difference has emerged as a central premise of feminism in the 1990s. Recognition of differences across 'race', 'class' and 'ethnicity' has challenged second-wave feminisms to acknowledge that not all women's experiences are the same. Feminism can no longer be said to represent all women's interests (Gunew & Yeatman 1993). These ideas of difference have emerged within post-structuralist thought and are often criticised for a lack of practical application. The argument goes something like 'It's all very well to see difference everywhere but what do we do about it?'

So what does difference mean for the feminism informing the work of sexual assault services and the feminists working there? Feminism must now cope with greater contradictions than ever before, and this is an uneasy and somewhat slippery position to be in. If we continue to think that gender is the only issue relating to power in relation to sexual assault then we will never address any differences enough to provide 'access'. The 'tack-on' approach will continue. We will continue to see 'NESB access projects' and 'disability access projects' with little real change.

The exoticisation of 'others' in a celebration of 'difference' and paying lip service to difference have long been critiqued as the legacies of colonialism. Mohanty draws to our attention the way in which difference expressed as benign diversity (as in the rhetoric of cultural diversity) '. . . bypasses power . . .' and suggests '. . . harmonious empty pluralism'. In contrast, difference could look like conflict, disruption and dissension '. . . situated within hierarchies of domination and resistance' (1989, p. 181). At least here power dynamics become transparent and, whilst this may feel uncomfortable, it is also likely to mean change.

It is of concern that the term 'feminism' is often used as if it were one unifying theoretical perspective. Locating ourselves in relation to which feminism informs our practice, and recognising the blindspots of the particular theoretical perspective we uphold can make it possible to investigate other ways of thinking. Feminisms are only some of the theoretical perspectives informing sexual assault work. Once each of us is clearer about which perspectives matter to us we can begin to engage with the complexities thrown up by theory, policy and practice. One thing is for sure: 'the ability to deal with difference is at the centre of feminism's survival as a movement for social change' (Gunew & Yeatman 1992, p. xxiv) and of crucial importance in this process is weighing and considering different perspectives alongside each other, listening and engaging and not 'turning our gaze away from those painful moments at which communication seems unavoidably to fail' (Ang 1995, p. 60).

Ang continues inspirationally to suggest that there is a problem with the assumption that common ground exists between us all and we just have to find it to communicate. She suggests we should perhaps start from a place assuming no common ground exists and that 'any communicative event would be nothing more than a speaking past one another'. Rather than regret this she suggests it could be the starting point for a

> more modest feminism, one which is predicated on the fundamental limits to the very idea of sisterhood (and thus the category 'woman') and on the necessary partiality of the project of feminism as such. (Ang 1995, p. 60)

In counselling and advocacy work around sexual assault, great investment is placed in successful communication informed by feminist approaches. To acknowledge the *partiality* of feminism here would require a worker to think about how differently they may see the world from the woman they are working with and the impact these differences could have on any communication. Practically, issues for refugee women in the Australian context come to mind. Many refugee women experience rape in situations of war, in flight and in refugee camps (STARTTS 1992). Understanding the context of the experience of many refugees and how much effort it takes to settle in a new country is important. The often contradictory feelings of relief about being (relatively) safe yet feeling disoriented, without support, anxious and guilty about those left behind and without the choice to return contribute to a particular understanding of what it means to be in Australia. Many of these so-called 'settlement issues' are the primary issues of concern for newly arrived refugees.

If I were to assume that my feminism would adequately guide my work with refugee women because of the 'sisterhood' principle (we are all women therefore share more in common than not) I may tend to see sexual assault as the primary issue at a time when it is not. Engaging with these debates is complex but to relegate them to the 'too hard basket' is to show blinkered interest in the impact of different feminisms on sexual assault work. Surely these are issues that must be debated in a sector proud of a feminist history.

## CONCLUSION

Multicultural health policy directions over the past ten years have moved towards mainstreaming and this is reflected in such documents as the NSW Government's Ethnic Affairs Action Plan 2000. This works to:

> ensure that resources are fairly distributed, that ethnic [sic] communities are consulted about decisions related to government program delivery, that the rights and responsibilities of all people are recognised, and that services are effectively targeted to meet the needs of ethnic [sic] communities.

Such a call for equity and access would be satisfied in the context of sexual assault service provision only when the demography of a local area is fully represented in the service client population, the assumption being that all aspects of the community are equally comparable because sexual assault occurs in all communities.

In this chapter I have argued the limitations of such perspectives, the need to think about 'access' differently . . . to think about what it means to involve feminist (sexual assault) practice in a politics of difference. The central question for discussion has been what is it about the context of sexual assault service provision that might limit 'access' to sexual assault services for people from around the word living in Australia? This has meant traversing the powerful and slippery terrain of language, structural constraints, different feminisms and cultural positioning in personal and theoretical modes.

Those of us within the health system in general, and sexual assault services in particular, have a responsibility to continue to engage with these debates thoughtfully and critically to develop a situation whereby we all acknowledge how different we are and act on the need for change in ourselves and our services. As the issue of 'race' continues to dominate our political agenda, the central issues of reconciliation between Aboriginal and non-Aboriginal Australia and who can, and should, be able to migrate to Australia will continue to feature significantly on the public agenda. The currency of the issues canvassed in this chapter provides a constant reminder of the danger of the 'too hard basket'. These issues will not just go away. They require and deserve the considered action of those prepared to speak to and past each other for as long as it takes.

# 6 | Systems that silence: lifting the lid on psychiatric institutional sexual abuse

## Jane Davidson and Lorna McNamara

> Despite the contribution of a feminist analysis of sexual violence, few of those who experience abuse today tell anyone. Silence reigns as the typical response of those who are sexually assaulted. Women, children, and men who encounter sexual abuse remain steadfastly quiet, despite all the publicity and changes in legal statutes and professional practice over these past 20 years. (Stanko 1997, p. 76)

IT IS A disturbing reality that, despite increased understanding in the community concerning sexual assault, the sexual abuse of women in mental health facilities continues to go unrecognised or is denied by health providers. Very often this has devastating outcomes for the victims. To understand how sexual abuse in institutions is possible, we need to examine the issue of silence and the use of silencing practices. These practices operate at a number of different levels: societal, systemic and institutional, and at the individual level—including the imposition of self-silencing strategies as a form of protection.

This chapter examines the findings in the research report *Every Boundary Broken* (Davidson 1997)[1] from the perspective of silencing practices. The study uncovered the sexual abuse of women in psychiatric facilities and made evident the failure of the system to respond to that abuse. Lack of awareness of the reality of sexual abuse within institutions was only one of the restraints identified within the system. Active resistance to the actuality of sexual abuse occurred at many levels within the hierarchy of psychiatric services, functioning to stifle and suppress the accounts of victims and any knowledgeable discussion about the subject of sexual abuse.

An analysis is also given, offering some reasons for this resistance by considering the historical and contextual basis from which the psychiatric system views the issues of sexual abuse, mental illness, power and gender, thus enabling it to remain insulated against the progress that has been made in society's understanding of sexual victimisation.

## THE RESEARCH

The community organisation Women and Mental Health (WAMH)[2] decided in 1995 to attempt to break the public silence around the topic of the sexual abuse of women patients during admissions to psychiatric hospitals and units. The Burdekin report (Burdekin et al. 1993) had brought into the Australian public arena the information that women were being sexually abused during psychiatric institutionalisation. Behind closed doors, in private communications and in individual public revelations, the topic continued to be raised both by women who had been abused, and by staff members. The members of WAMH decided that research was needed because, in this field, and particularly in the Australian context, there remains a marked paucity of published research. It was felt that qualitative research was the best means to achieve the recovery of the 'unspeakable', because it allows full voice to be given to these experiences, honouring the first-person accounts of those whose experience it was, whilst simultaneously meeting the demands of scientific rigour.

The study that resulted in the report *Every Boundary Broken* was designed in two separate modules: one involved in-depth interviews with ex-patients—'consumer participants'[3] who identified that they had been sexually abused when they were an in-patient during the last 15 years at a psychiatric facility. The consumer participants had to be over 18 years of age, not currently hospitalised, and mentally stable at the time of participation in the research. The other module involved in-depth interviews with staff or recent ex-staff of psychiatric facilities who identified that they had either witnessed or had disclosed to them incidents of sexual abuse of women patients during hospitalisation, and who had been involved in the care of the patient after the abuse. Staff and consumers resident anywhere within the Australian State of New South Wales were eligible to participate.

## Participation

Having heard anecdotally from so many consumers and staff about their personal experiences of the prevalence of sexual abuse in in-patient facilities, the research team[4] did not anticipate the difficulty the study would have in finding people willing to participate in the research process. In some cases this was attributable to timing: women who had wished to participate experienced episodes of unwellness and so decided not to participate.

Some service providers who were contacted to advertise the research through their services were extremely cautious and reluctant. They feared that their clients might be destabilised by participation, or that other clients might be influenced into having perceived delusional beliefs concerning sexual assault reinforced simply by knowing that the project existed (and therefore that someone thought that the *problem* existed). One professional warned his client, who had intended to participate and who had then begun to have flashbacks, that she should not participate because it would put her mental health at risk. Thus, maintaining the silence was seen by some professionals as vital to the individual's mental health. It seemed at times that some of these professionals had not considered that there may be a link between the incident of sexual assault and mental ill-health, and that it may be therapeutic to be able to talk about the experience. In fact, the *talking* about the abuse, rather than the abuse itself, became the identified trigger for unwellness.

This is not to trivialise a very real issue. Some consumer participants did initially have great concerns about the possibility of increased stress due to their participation. They feared this in case it might lead to a deterioration in their mental health, possibly resulting in a readmission—a prospect, considering their experiences, that was terrifying. However, the structure of the research included many strategies designed to ensure continuing support and safety for the consumer participants, both during interview and in the months following. The consumer participants unanimously reported that their involvement in the research had been a positive and empowering experience.

Those consumer participants who did eventually participate went through a long decision-making process first, fighting against fear and anxiety, and in some cases struggling with issues about loyalty and protecting the perpetrator. Many also had serious concerns that they not be identifiable, for fear of persecution during subsequent admissions, or during their use of other mental health services. Some staff members too talked about fear of being identified, with a subsequent impact on their careers; they also mentioned the pain of revisiting experiences where they had felt that there had been a failure in duty of care, either in responding to the sexual abuse, or in the fact that the abuse had occurred in the first place.

Twenty participants in all, from a variety of geographical locations, were interviewed for the research: nine consumer participants and 11 staff participants (comprising psychiatric nurses, psychiatrists and mental health social workers). The researcher, who was an experienced sexual assault counsellor, conducted all the interviews between May 1996 and January 1997. The participants described in detail a total of 34 separate incidents of sexual abuse, with numerous other incidents referred to in passing.

Consumers and staff spoke passionately and compellingly about the experience of silencing practices within institutional facilities. The currency of the findings of the research becomes obvious from the data when considering the date of occurrence of the sexual abuse: of the 25 individual incidents of abuse described in detail, two occurred in the early 1980s, and the rest took place in the 1990s, the majority between 1993 and 1996. The most recent had been some two months before interview. Of the nine incidents of ongoing sexual abuse described in detail, all but three concluded in the 1990s. The longest period of abuse described was 14 years.

Sexual abuse, as defined by the participants, and discussed in the research, included a continuum ranging from sexualised touching, exposure, masturbation and sexual remarks, through to sexual assault and sexual intercourse couched in terms of a 'relationship' (the latter almost exclusively perpetrated by staff). Some of the victims had been abused on one occasion; some had been abused more than once by different perpetrators; some had been re-abused by the same perpetrator on different admissions; and some had been abused by the same perpetrator on multiple occasions, sometimes spanning multiple admissions and many years. All of the latter type were perpetrated by staff members.

In the 34 incidents described in detail by the participants, the perpetrators were other patients, psychiatric nursing staff, and psychiatrists. All but two of these were male. Additionally, other perpetrator groups identified in the incidents mentioned in brief were visitors to the facility, and allied health staff (psychologists and social workers).

One of the notable findings of this study is that the patients abused by staff were the most silenced, particularly where the abuse was ongoing. Of the three incidents that were never disclosed or known to psychiatric staff, all were perpetrated by staff members. Of the remaining incidents of abuse by staff, in some cases the silence was maintained for years before disclosure. There was a variety of reasons for this. Sometimes the victim simply did not know it was abuse when it first began. This may have been because, through inexperience or lack of knowledge, and trying to make sense of what was happening, she thought it was part and parcel of being hospitalised and thus had to accept it, or because it was initially framed as being about 'love' and 'relationship'. Sometimes the victim was pulled into a web of indebtedness and secrecy because the perpetrator obtained special privileges for her; sometimes there were threats or punitive changes in medication in an attempt to keep the situation secret. Most frequently, when the silence was broken, the victim was met with inaction or further victimisation and, in some cases, threats of retribution.

## The perpetrators

In a parallel of the dynamics of child sexual assault, some victims maintained their silence out of a desire to protect the perpetrator from getting into trouble:

> I didn't want him to be hurt and think that I didn't appreciate the friendship, because I liked the friendship, I felt special and I think people need to feel special when they're in hospital—not for someone's own ends, but feeling special was important . . . That's why I didn't want to say anything, I didn't want him to be fired . . . So that is really an emotional conflict, because what he did was wrong. (Davidson 1997, p. 63)

Some participants talked about perpetrators, both patient and staff, deliberately targeting those most likely to keep the secret or maintain the silence. This was a description of abuse by a staff perpetrator: 'At that stage I was very quiet, I was very withdrawn . . . I was the perfect one to pick because I wouldn't have said anything at the time' (Davidson 1997, p. 37). And in describing an incident of abuse by a patient perpetrator, a participant said:

> . . . at the time she'd had large doses of [medication] . . . she'd also had sleeping tablets, so whether she would be able to even get herself out of bed would have been a moot point so really she wouldn't have been able to defend herself or say 'no' or do anything. She was very tiny. (Davidson 1997, p. 37)

Staff participants also discussed perpetrators, both staff and patient, who used the system to access vulnerable women sexually. The following descriptions refer to male patients:

> I guess they're predators. They go from hospital to hospital around the State, they would have fairly thick files and they are never really that unwell when they come in . . . I think they come into hospital . . . when they're without a relationship, without a partner . . . and there's always a vulnerable female that they can target when they come in . . . (Davidson 1997, p. 45)

> [When he's admitted] he has all of these wonderful little women of all ages, he doesn't discriminate about age, they're females, so he's touching them up all the time, because you can't do that at home, you can't do that in the street, I mean they'll get the police. But what do they do in the ward? They don't get the police. (Davidson 1997, pp. 45–46)

It was noted that predatory perpetrators, staff and patient, were conscious that they needed to move on, out of the ward or out of the hospital, if it looked possible that their repeated sexually abusive behaviour might be challenged or reported. However, it was clear from participants' accounts that such intervention was rare and often unsuccessful, and that predatory perpetrators often went on sexually abusing with impunity, sometimes for years. The dereliction of duty of care on the part of psychiatric facilities thus extended far beyond the victims described in this study.

## Legal issues

Of all the incidents described in detail, only five were reported to police, and criminal charges were laid in only one case. It was well known by both staff and perpetrators that police are unlikely to lay sexual assault charges in cases where both the victim and the perpetrator have a mental illness, because the victim is unlikely to present as a 'good' witness, and the perpetrator is likely to be acquitted on grounds of diminished responsibility. Thus, once again, women with a mental illness who have been sexually abused are denied a public hearing, this time the silencing originating from a system outside that of mental health.

In cases of sexual abuse by staff, where the abuse was framed as a 'relationship' between the staff member and the woman patient, the victims were also denied legal redress when they realised that they had been abused, as they were seen to have consented to the 'relationship'. Unanimously, participants in this study did not regard such a situation as simply 'poor boundaries', but as sexual abuse. The combination of the enormous power differential between the staff member and the patient, the patient's mental illness, and the fact that she was institutionalised and under the care of the staff member, ruled out any possibility of regarding this as an informed consenting relationship. However, under Australian law such sexually abusive exploitation of patients' vulnerability is not a criminal offence, because of the issue of consent. It is regarded as a breach of ethics in some professions and, as such, action may be taken on a professional level against the perpetrator; the sanctions, however, are quite different from a criminal charge of sexual assault. In addition, the victim has no recourse to, for example, the NSW victims compensation scheme.[5]

Having been denied a voice in the criminal justice system, both where perpetrators were patients and where they were staff, some of the victims in this study had sought, or were seeking at the time of interview, redress or protection through civil and other systems, to varying degrees of success, and at great personal cost.

**Disclosure and action taken**

Before referral to the police is possible, however, there must be a disclosure, and then action must be taken by the staff member to whom the disclosure was made. It is in this area that the wall of silence, which typically descended when a woman patient disclosed that she had been sexually abused, was most visible. It became clear from the responses of both consumer and staff participants that the question of belief was a key issue.

A central finding of the inquiry into responses to disclosure or witnessed events was that staff members on duty (apart from those who participated in the research) typically did not believe that the woman had been sexually abused. It was reported that among staff there was a continuum of responses: a small number who believed the disclosure (or witnessed incident) and believed that it was sexual abuse; those who believed the disclosure (or witnessed incident) but did not believe that it was sexual abuse, but consensual sexual contact; and those who did not believe that anything had happened at all—most frequently via a decision that the victim was delusional.

Woven among these responses were some from those who trivialised the incident to the victim: '[The victim] told one of the nurses, who thought it was a bit of a joke. She didn't doubt whether it happened, but she didn't think it was serious' (Davidson 1997, p. 67); from those who blamed the victim: 'Their first priority was to either keep me quiet or get me out of the way and . . . make it as if it was my fault, as if I was the nut case, and exonerating the [perpetrator] of any responsibility . . .' (Davidson 1997, p. 67); and from those who simply did not respond at all, leaving the victim to interpret their silence for herself.

> One of the effects reported by consumer participants of these negative responses to disclosures, was that it silenced them further: 'I suppose after that [disclosure] I just learnt to keep it to myself because of their negative response to me on that occasion, as though . . . I was doing something wrong rather than him.' (Davidson 1997, p. 68)

Victims were also very aware of the system within which they were placed. One victim was told she was delusional, and threatened with return to the seclusion room where she had been sexually assaulted by staff members. Another was aware that her disclosure had prompted staff to decide that her mental health had deteriorated, putting at risk her imminent discharge from the hospital where she had just been abused. In both these cases the victim made a conscious decision to pursue the matter no longer, one by making a retraction, and the other by going silent: 'I was shocked, I was angry, I was afraid, I was terrified that it might happen again. So I thought, well, the best thing is to just do what I'm told to do and shut up and get out as quick as I can' (Davidson 1997, p. 68). The truth has no bearing in a context where the only way to survive is to silence oneself.

Refusing to see or hear about the reality of sexual abuse on their ward, most staff took little effective action, with the exception of those few who believed that an incident of sexual abuse had taken place. So sure were the former that they did not seek any objective medical corroboration to their version of events: in fact, one patient who had requested a forensic examination to prove that she had been sexually assaulted (while unconscious from a forced injection of medication) was refused. The narrow paradigm of the medical model, through which the staff viewed patients, enabled them to ignore the manifest effects of the sexual abuse and interpret them as further symptoms of the psychiatric illness that simultaneously guided their treatment response (usually medication changes), and justified their conclusion that the patient was deteriorating and delusional, attention seeking or simply lying. Often the treatment of choice further silenced the victims:

> More [ECT] and more drugs, that's how they responded. If I would try and rage I'd be injected with something to calm me down. If I was grieving, then . . . they'd change the medication or they'd up the dose . . . That's all I got, was a different medication . . . The physical rape, that was bad, but the ECT and all that stuff was worse because I felt like that raped my mind. (Davidson 1997, p. 73)

## Workplace cultures

Staff, of course, do not work in a vacuum. They bring their own attitudes, prejudices, knowledge, training and experiences to the job. Too often it seemed that what was in fact a criminal matter became a matter of opinion, influenced both by those personal variables and the culture of the particular workplace. Frequent direct attempts were made to silence and punish staff who attempted to take action about an incident of sexual abuse. They were cast as troublemakers; they were accused of inciting patients to make up stories; they were ridiculed, reprimanded, discredited, 'let go'; their expertise was called into question; they were threatened: with loss of promotion, with transfer, with loss of favourable work hours; they were assigned the worst rosters and were refused leave at the times they wished to take it; they were given 'the silent treatment' and sarcastic remarks. Some of them began to feel fearful in the workplace.

Sympathetic staff were often silenced by many of the same systemic factors that silenced victims: the mental health culture of expertness, where the voices of those perceived as less powerful or less knowledgeable (by virtue of their profession, their place in the workplace hierarchy, or their gender)[6] were neither listened to nor believed; a treatment philosophy that was immersed in a model that focuses on individual pathology, interprets the person's distress as a symptom of that pathology and ignores the external realities of the individual's daily life; and a lack (often gender-based) of power to intervene effectively.

> I felt angry that the women [patients] weren't believed, but I felt angrier that I wasn't believed. I was a professional, I had given a professional judgment about something that had occurred on that unit, and I wasn't believed . . . I guess as a woman working in that system it was very hard for me to have a voice. It's impossible for patients to have a voice. (Davidson 1997, p. 92)

Many of the workplace cultures described by staff participants in this research were termed 'male-dominated' or 'boys' clubs', where managers and more powerful members of staff were either ignorant of, or had negative attitudes towards, the last two decades' accumulated knowledge and understanding about sexual abuse (and towards anyone who might refer to them) and where derogatory attitudes towards women, whether patients or staff, were the norm. A staff participant described an example of this:

> . . . one of our clients was sexually assaulted by [a] male client and the male boss at the time actually started laughing and said— 'well, you couldn't really expect much else because she was like a bitch on heat'. (Davidson 1997, p. 40)

It should be remembered that some of these cultures also had staff members working within them who were sexually abusing their patients. It would, of course, be in their interests to cultivate and perpetuate workplace cultures of derision and scepticism about the existence of sexual abuse, derogatory and sexualised notions about women, and environments permeated by sexual innuendo and comment. Another effect was seen to occur when staff members were abusing and getting away with it, which further affected the culture of the workplace. A staff participant said: 'The other male staff used to quite often ask [the patient whom the staff member was sexually abusing] for sexual favours, because if you're actually the bike then you might as well be the total bike' (Davidson 1997, p. 47).

Systemic factors, organisational cultures and individual staff members' attitudes combined with a patient population already made vulnerable by their illness and their institutionalisation provides a difficult context. As noted by Crossmaker (1991, p. 205): 'The people on the lowest rung of the institutional ladder—the residents—are reinforced for compliant behaviour, economically, physically and psychologically dependent, isolated and lacking in credibility; all factors increasing vulnerability to sexual abuse'—to create a psychiatric version of the 'rape supportive environments' described by Koss and Cleveland (1997).

## ECHOES FROM OUTSIDE

As a research team outside the system, it was interesting to find that we were not exempt from experiencing on a first-hand basis some of the barriers faced by those who had participated in the study. A particular difficulty that occurred at the beginning of the research best illustrates the power of the forces aimed at keeping the lid on the issue of the sexual abuse of women in mental health services. This constituted an attempt at another level to silence, by preventing the research.

Part of the process of conducting this research was the submission of the research protocol to Area Health Service ethics committees across New South Wales. During this process, one of the committees revoked approval one month after giving permission to proceed. The revocation was enacted following written advice from a peak psychiatric advisory group in that Area Health Service who recommended that the study not be approved. These communications were forwarded to the research team. Their intent seemed to be to stop the research from proceeding in that Area, since they offered no advice as to how the research design might be changed, and no avenue for negotiation.

In brief, the letters were damning of the methodology and scientific value of the research, questioned the ability of the research team, accused the research of providing opportunities for 'stimulation of false memory syndrome' (undefined), said it would build on patients' delusions, and that it could lead to 'self-fulfilling prophecies'—that is, that participating in the research could actually *cause* women patients to be sexually abused: after reading the invitation to participate in the research, women patients might then place themselves in a position of risk whereby they are sexually abused, therefore fulfilling the prophecy of sexual abuse in psychiatric hospitals. This particular concept manages to blame both the victim and the research team. Further, if we critically examine this, one could never recruit for research about sexual abuse because the questioning around it would actually produce the result.

The research team was completely unprepared for the approval to be revoked and for the comments from the psychiatric advisory group. We were left in a state of shock and disbelief; furious at the disparaging and patronising tone of the letters, but also fearful of the actual power that the group had to stop the study. While we were angry, our confidence had also been severely undermined: we felt that our professionalism and expertise had been denigrated, which we internalised in part, causing us to feel deskilled; we all experienced self-doubt, and began to secretly question our own abilities at some level. We had deep down a concern, as a group and as individuals, that we were not seen to command sufficient authority to influence the members of the advisory group. We feared our arguments could not carry the necessary weight because of who we were or, more pointedly, because of who we were not.

The only feelings that we initially shared with each other were the disbelief that it could happen and the anger that it had happened. What we did not share with each other at first was our fear that perhaps we were not good enough, our shame at being regarded as incompetent, our insecurity and our self-doubt. It was not until much later that we talked with each other about these issues. After the disclosure of our innermost fears and anxieties, we were then able to offer each other support and return to a realistic evaluation of the situation: that we were in fact competent, skilled and professional, and that the protocol was ethically and scientifically sound and thorough.

What the research team experienced as a result of the scathing criticisms of the psychiatric advisory group in no way matched the intensity, the depth or the seriousness of the impact on the participants of the sexual abuse and the subsequent silencing that they experienced. There were also some important differences in our situation: unlike the consumer and staff participants, we had a strong support group, both within the research team and via the steering committee for the project. And while the psychiatric advisory group could stop the research, it had no real power over us personally. It could not directly harm us: its members could not give us medication or fire us. However, it did have a marked effect on the research team, which can be seen as an echo of the experiences of both the consumer and the staff participants. It demonstrated how easily a powerful system can, through intimidation and 'expertness', gag discussion and engagement about sexual abuse issues, and diminish the sense of competence and self-worth of individuals.

The research team then decided to meet with the psychiatric advisory group in an attempt to reach a resolution. The psychiatric advisory group was comprised of professors in mental health fields, psychiatrists, neuropsychiatrists and clinical psychologists. Having first established the research team's expertise in qualitative research, the meeting moved on to the topic of sexual abuse of patients. We immediately noticed a marked lack of knowledge about sexual assault and the interface between sexual abuse and mental illness. We were concerned that women with mental illnesses seemed to be categorised by them into one class: as people who could not be telling the truth about sexual abuse, and who were assumed to be delusional or at best suggestible. There was no understanding that there could be times when these same women would be very coherent and very able to distinguish reality from non-reality.

The philosophical basis of their practice seemed to be that one does not believe what one's patients say, ever. The crucial issue, as the advisory group saw it, was that we could not know without doubt that our (consumer) participants were telling the truth. Again, to critique this argument, much sexual abuse research—indeed many types of research, whether qualitative or quantitative—would never be undertaken if proof of the veracity of participants was a requirement. In fact, this project had specifically put in place two safeguards in this regard: the employment of an interviewer who was experienced and skilled in assessment, and the availability of specific mental health professionals for consultation by the interviewer should there be any concerns about a participant's mental state.

The initial correspondence and the subsequent meeting revealed that members of the psychiatric advisory group held a number of assumptions: that they were the experts not only on mental illness, but also on research methodology and the sexual abuse of patients, and that the members of the research team lacked expertise in any of those fields; that all people living with a mental illness are chronically unwell and unable to distinguish reality from delusion; and that allegations of sexual abuse by such people should be regarded with scepticism, as the sources of the allegations are mentally unwell, probably delusional and definitely suggestible.

The meeting proved to be a turning point. We made some minor changes to the protocol, conceding that we had made a mistake in phrasing in one area, which had led to misinterpretation, and resubmitted the 'revised' protocol. Approval was given by the psychiatric advisory group, which stated that the protocol was 'greatly improved'. The Area Ethics Committee then re-approved the protocol, thus allowing the study to commence in that Area. Three months had elapsed from the time of receipt of the advisory group's letter, to re-approval. This delay was frustrating for the research team and stressful for the consumers in the Area who wished to be interviewed.

The meeting with the psychiatric advisory group had made obvious that there was not only a fundamental lack of knowledge about sexual abuse, but also a resistance to acquiring that knowledge and engaging with it. Mental health as a system has not grappled with the issue of sexual abuse, either as a reality in a consumer's everyday experience, or as a factor in their past history.

## THE CONTEXT

Given the findings of *Every Boundary Broken* and the experiences of the research team, a number of questions still beg examination. How can skilled and competent mental health professionals hold blatantly stereotypical views of women with mental illnesses, and how can they be so disbelieving of sexual abuse, given the volume of information on the subject?

To gain some understanding, perhaps we need to look to psychiatry's past, when psychiatric institutions were referred to as 'looney bins' or 'bins'. The term 'bin' was commonly used by staff to describe the complex system of psychiatric facilities in use during this century. It still holds currency in many places today. The word 'bin' conjures up strong images of somewhere dark and damp, and of waste and decay. It also conveys a sense of peering into the unknown and that when looking into a 'bin' we are looking in at something alien and unknowable. The unknowable in this context does not raise curiosity, rather it arouses fear. Fear that to rummage around inside might mean getting dirty or, worse, contaminated.

The word has powerful meanings for those who have been relegated to 'the bin'. It exemplifies the stigma and discrimination attached to mental illness. As Phyllis Chesler noted in *Women & Madness*: 'Madness is shut away from sight, shamed, brutalized, denied and feared' (1989, p. 26). Mental illness personifies the idea of other, of difference and of disempowerment. Indeed, those within the mental health system often perceive that it is the general community that stigmatises people experiencing a mental illness.

*Every Boundary Broken* challenges that assumption through its revelations about the attitudes held by some mental health staff towards their clientele. The process of defining someone with a mental illness as *other* can begin as early as their first contact with the mental health system. On arrival at a mental health facility, either through choice or force, and experiencing various states of distress and need, a consumer might find that their needs are pathologised, that the pathology is judged and diagnosed, and that the diagnosis, because of the mental health system's adherence to the medical model, becomes the *whole story*. The diagnosis often determines how a consumer will be treated. Because psychiatry positions itself as the expert in the understanding and explanation of that diagnosis, consumers are compelled to depend upon the system to help shape, explain, and through this process, define their lives.

For women, the issue of madness is complex and fraught. Phyllis Chesler (1989, p. 115) argues that:

> Since clinicians and researchers, as well as their patients and subjects, adhere to a masculine standard of mental health, women, by definition, are viewed as psychiatrically impaired—whether they accept or reject the female role—simply because they are women.

Psychoanalysis and modern psychiatry originated in the late 1800s and early 1900s. Much of the theory that was later to influence the evolution of cognitive, moral and personality development theory had its genesis at this time. The emphasis was on 'maleness' as the norm and 'femaleness' as an aberration of adulthood (Gilligan et al. 1988). Maleness as the exemplar of adult mental health was demonstrated in a study by Broverman et al. (1970) and replicated by Fabricant in 1974 (cited in Astbury 1996, pp. 15–16). Jill Astbury discusses the latter study, which found that male and female therapists both rated a substantial majority of descriptors of male characteristics as positive attributes of adult mental health, while the same therapists rated the vast majority of female descriptive terms as negative:

> This finding points up the difficulty women face in being able to resist or contest the highly negative view of the qualities seen to be intrinsic to their identity . . . For women, any attempt to be heard will first have to overcome the view that what they are saying is *prima facie* likely to lack reason, objectivity, impartiality and power. (Astbury 1996, p. 16)

Fabricant's study might be dismissed as being of historical interest only. However, the pervasiveness of the negative attitudes held by staff about women, particularly women experiencing mental illness, that were described in *Every Boundary Broken* demand that we question the impact and ongoing influence of theoretical paradigms that have at their foundation women as inferior and irrational.

Alongside the construction of women as mad was the equally powerful view that women were not to be believed. The connection between mental illness (specifically hysteria) and child sexual assault made by Freud in *The Aetiology of Hysteria* (1896) is comprehensively detailed in Chapter 1 of this collection. The pertinent point for this chapter, however, is that Freud, among others, ensured that women's allegations of sexual abuse did not have to be believed. Society could once again sleep peacefully, assured that the reality of sexual abuse was no more than a bad dream. Freud had provided a theoretical explanation, albeit quasi scientific, that succeeded in silencing not only the voices of children but also the voices of women for the next 100 years. Freud as the founder of psychoanalysis continues to have immeasurable influence upon the theoretical constructs of psychiatry. The two most powerful paradigms within the psychiatric sector—namely, the medical model and psychoanalysis—have at their foundation constructs that are impervious to the voices of sexually abused victims.

The construction of women as mad, unreliable and unbelievable, coupled with the belief that the mad are disposable and of little value, has created a cultural environment where the reality of sexual abuse in psychiatric facilities can and does go unrecognised, silenced or disbelieved. The sexual abuse of women in psychiatric facilities not only goes unnoticed by the general public but, perhaps more importantly, is disregarded by many of those whose job it is to care for women experiencing a mental illness.

The mental health system is lagging far behind in its understanding of and response to the trauma of sexual abuse. For there to be systemic change that is sympathetic, responsible and responsive to sexually abused patients, there needs to be a move away from active resistance at all levels of the hierarchy. What is called for is a genuine curiosity about and engagement with new knowledges about sexual abuse. Different theoretical models need to be incorporated which focus on more than individual pathology:

including, for example, a social analysis of trauma that encompasses domestic violence and sexual abuse. The system would only benefit from opening itself to the expertise and contributions of others, both those from within and those from outside—including, for example, consumers, mental health staff who have undertaken training in sexual abuse issues, and specialist sexual abuse agencies. If a safe environment for users of the mental health system is to be a goal, then individual and organisational attitudinal change must take place, including attitudes about gender, power and mental illness. Only when this systemic change has been undertaken will the mental health system be able to fulfil its promise of asylum.

# 7 | Recovered memories of child sexual abuse: the science and the ideology

*Anne Cossins*

IN RECENT YEARS, widespread media attention has been given to the alleged 'false memory syndrome' (FMS), a term coined by the False Memory Syndrome Foundation (FMSF) in America. The idea that a person could suddenly recall memories of being sexually abused as a child has been presented as incredible and as either evidence of the suggestibility of women to other people's ideas, bad therapy or even a deliberate conspiracy between therapists and daughters to destroy previously happy families.[1] Given the media coverage that has been devoted to the alleged false memory syndrome and the continuing attempts in the media to discredit adult survivors of child sexual abuse (e.g. Guilliat 1996a, 1996b, p. 17), there is likely to be a climate of disbelief which has influenced professionals and laypeople to believe that it is impossible to recover memories of sexual abuse experienced during childhood.

In light of the degree of uncritical acceptance of the claims of FMS proponents within both the scientific and non-scientific communities, the purpose of this chapter is twofold: first, to examine the empirical basis for the existence of the alleged false memory syndrome and, second, to examine the extensive body of scientific evidence on the phenomenon of delayed recall of memories of child sexual abuse (also known as traumatic amnesia). This chapter summarises the scientific data that show that delayed recall of traumatic events has been widely documented for almost 100 years, is an accepted scientific phenomenon which only became controversial when associated with memories of child sexual abuse as opposed to memories of war or accidents, and that delayed recall of child sexual abuse has been verified by documented medical histories of that abuse. The chapter then addresses the implications of this scientific evidence for the criminal justice system and the prosecution of child sex offenders.

## THE NATURE OF TRAUMATIC MEMORIES

At the outset, it is important to examine recovered memories of child sexual abuse in the broader context of the way memory functions in response to a wide range of traumatic events. As a scientific phenomenon, traumatic memories that are recovered or recalled at some time after a traumatic event are difficult to study (van der Kolk & Fisler 1995, p. 505). One of the reasons for this is that it does not appear to be possible to simulate, in the laboratory setting, the emotional responses that people experience after a traumatic event. As van der Kolk and Fisler (1995, p. 506) observe, '[c]learly, there is little similarity between viewing a simulated car accident on a TV screen, and being the responsible driver in a car crash in which one's own children are killed'.

If trauma is defined as 'the experience of an inescapable stressful event that overwhelms one's existing coping mechanisms', it is, therefore, questionable as to whether studies 'of memory distortions in normal subjects exposed to videotaped stresses in the laboratory can serve as meaningful guides to understanding traumatic memories' (van der Kolk & Fisler 1995, p. 506).[2] It is even more questionable whether everyday, 'commonsense' notions or understandings of the way memory works can also serve as meaningful guidance for understanding traumatic memories, although such notions have frequently been used in the media and in sexual assault trials to question a complainant's credibility (e.g. Guilliatt 1994, 1995a, p. 13, 1995b, p. 4). In fact, Williams (1995, p. 653) has observed that:

> the [scientific] literature on so-called 'false memories' . . . relies primarily on descriptions of anecdotal accounts from legal cases, the reports of adults recently accused by their adult children, and

laboratory studies on *general* issues of memory and suggestibility. [emphasis added][3]

What this literature has not made explicit is that there are recognised and documented differences between non-traumatic and traumatic memories. Indeed, the reasoning in this body of literature has been summarised by Whitfield as follows:

> since all memory is the same, and since one can 'implant' a 'forgotten' but false ordinary memory into up to one in five ordinary people like college students for an unknown amount of time, then that must also apply to all who remember past traumatic experiences after they have forgotten them for a long time. This reasoning is similar to: since apples and oranges are both fruits, then all apples must look and taste like oranges. (1995, p. 39)

The starting point for examining the nature of traumatic memories is to ask what scientists know about memory in general and traumatic memories in particular. First, memory is categorised according to type. Squire and Zola-Morgan (1991) classified memory into two different types according to function— that is, the explicit and implicit memory systems—both of which are distinguished from a third type called traumatic memory (van der Kolk & Fisler 1995, pp. 507–508).[4]

Second, there are several features of traumatic memory which distinguish traumatic memory recall from ordinary explicit memory recall and implicit memory recall. Explicit memory recall involves our conscious memory system in which we store a verbal account of facts or events that have happened to us, whereas implicit memory recall involves 'memories of skills and habits, emotional responses, reflexive actions and classically conditioned responses' (van der Kolk & Fisler 1995, p. 507).[5] The implicit memory system 'works automatically without our awareness' and 'processes conditioned emotions such as fear, and sensory information including smells, visual images, and sounds' (Kristiansen 1996, p. 4).

Traumatic memory is associated with trauma that causes a person to experience 'extremes of retention and forgetting: terrifying experiences may be remembered with extreme vividness or totally resist integration' (van der Kolk & Fisler 1995, p. 508), so that a traumatic experience can affect various memory functions and consequently the ability to recall the experience at all or only in part. Where such memories are retained they become 'fixed in the mind, unaltered by the passage of time or by the intervention of subsequent experience' compared with memories of ordinary events which have been shown to 'disintegrate in clarity over time' (van der Kolk & Fisler 1995, p. 508).

Third, because of these features of traumatic memory, it is hypothesised that 'traumatic memories may be encoded *differently* than memories for ordinary events' [emphasis added] due to the interference that extreme emotional arousal as the result of a terrifying experience may have on normal memory encoding (van der Kolk & Fisler 1995, p. 509). Thus, it can be said that, in order to understand traumatic memory in general and recovered memories of child sexual abuse in particular, it is the memory of trauma survivors that must be studied, not the alteration of memory in studies of 'college students looking at photos', an example of a typical type of study used by FMS advocates to challenge the veracity of recovered memories of child sexual abuse (Whitfield 1995, p. 13).

Fourth, since the late nineteenth century 'the loss or absence of recollections for traumatic experiences [has been] well documented' (van der Kolk & Fisler 1995, p. 509).[6] For example, amnesia with subsequent recovery or recall of the memory, in whole or in part, has been documented throughout this century in relation to natural disasters and accidents (Wilkinson 1983, pp. 1134–1139; Madakasira & O'Brian 1987, pp. 286–290; van der Kolk & Kadish 1987, pp. 173–190), combat soldiers during war (Southard 1919; Kardiner 1941; Sargeant & Slater 1941, pp. 757–764; Grinker & Spiegel 1945; Sonnenberg et al. 1985), victims of kidnapping and torture, and concentration camp survivors (Neiderland 1968, pp. 313–315; Goldfield et al. 1988, pp. 2725–2729; Kinzie 1993, pp. 311–319) and victims of physical and sexual abuse (Janet 1893, pp. 167–179; Briere & Conte 1993, pp. 21–31; Loftus et al. 1994, pp. 67–84; Williams 1994, pp. 1167–1176).[7]

Fifth, one of the significant features of traumatic amnesia is that it appears to be 'age and dose related' so that the younger a person is at the time of the traumatic event, or the more prolonged the traumatic event, the more likely it will be that the person will experience significant amnesia (van der Kolk & Fisler 1995, p. 509; Williams 1995). In addition, there is emerging evidence which suggests that traumatic amnesia for child sexual abuse is more likely to occur if a child's relationship with the abuser is one on which the child is dependent for survival (Freyd 1996, pp. 9–10).

These three factors are important for understanding the phenomenon of traumatic amnesia in the context of child sexual abuse and later recall, as are the facts that '[a]mnesia for traumatic events may last for hours, weeks or years . . . [and] recall is triggered by exposure to sensory or affective stimuli that match sensory or affective elements associated with the trauma' (van der Kolk & Fisler 1995, p. 509).[8] Thus, it can be said that, if recall does occur, it will be the result of a *chance* event which activates the retrieval of the traumatic memory. This point is crucial to understanding the phenomenon of delayed recall in the context of child sexual abuse, since it will not be within a victim's ability to *consciously* will a memory into existence (van der Kolk & Fisler 1995, p. 520), so that questions such as 'why has she suddenly remembered now?'[9] are irrelevant for ascertaining the veracity of a victim's testimony and clearly indicate the lack of understanding of the phenomenon of traumatic amnesia and later recall.

Whilst it is possible for fabricated memories of child sexual abuse or fabricated allegations of other crimes to exist, the popular media as well as the legal system rely on claims of fabricated memories and evidence which shows that memory can be distorted to invalidate all recovered memories that are reported (Freyd 1996, p. 30). This is equivalent to saying that because some insurance claims are false (in the case of planned car 'accidents'), then all insurance claims for car accidents are false. But what is the relevance of a study of *false* insurance claims to the frequency, type and reasons for valid insurance claims? The answer is probably very little *unless* a person adheres to the belief that all insurance claims are false, something few of us would believe because we all know that car accidents do happen. The same holds true for recovered memories of child sexual abuse: the only way that evidence of memory distortion or of fabricated memories of child sexual abuse (to the extent that they can be proved as opposed to being merely *claimed* to exist) could be relevant to a study of the frequency, type and triggering events of recovered memories of child sexual abuse is if it is believed that all recovered memories of child sexual abuse are false. Yet we know from empirical studies and other sources that child sexual abuse can and does happen.[10]

In light of the overwhelming evidence of the prevalence and incidence of child sexual abuse in Australia and other Western countries, and the nature of traumatic memory, the criminal justice system does need to find answers to such questions, as:

• How common is it for a child to experience traumatic amnesia after being sexually abused and then, at some time in the future, recall the abuse?

- How is that process of forgetting and remembering a traumatic event such as child sexual abuse explained?
- What factors (such as age, relationship with perpetrator, severity of the abuse, lack of maternal support) are predictive of traumatic amnesia for child sexual abuse?
- How accurate are memories that are recalled after traumatic amnesia?
- Do genuine recovered memories have features that could distinguish them from fabricated memories?
- Is it possible for perpetrators to falsely deny their activities?
- Are recovered memories of traumatic events only controversial at a scientific and cultural level if the traumatic event is child sexual abuse? If so, why is this the case?

## THE SCIENTIFIC EVIDENCE FOR DELAYED RECALL OF CHILD SEXUAL ABUSE

Recent studies do not support the prevailing belief in the media and of FMS proponents that recovered memories of child sexual abuse 'are fabricated by disturbed or vindictive adults or fostered by overzealous therapists' (Williams 1995, p. 650) or that adults with recovered memories 'are predominantly highly educated females who have received psychotherapy as adults and who come from well-educated, affluent families' (Wakefield & Underwager, cited in Elliott & Briere 1995, p. 645) who are highly suggestible to bad therapy or the influence of popular culture.

Studies of clinical samples (i.e. samples of adults undergoing psychological/psychiatric treatment) have reported varying figures for traumatic amnesia and later recall of child sexual abuse suggesting that it is likely to be a common occurrence. For example, Briere and Conte (1993) reported that 59 per cent of 450 men and women who were undergoing treatment for child sexual abuse had, at some time, forgotten the abuse experienced during childhood. Briere and Conte found that delayed recall of sexual abuse was more likely if: (i) the abuse occurred at a young age; (ii) the child feared death if they were to reveal the abuse to others; (iii) the abuse was associated with physical injury; (iv) there was more than one abuser; and (v) the subjects currently displayed more psychological symptoms associated with child sexual abuse than average. Other clinical studies have reported rates of between 40 per cent and 78 per cent for people reporting child sexual abuse who experienced a period of not being able to recall the abuse (Herman & Schatzow 1987; Cameron 1994; Gold et al. 1994; Loftus et al. 1994; Roe et al., cited in Whitfield 1995, p. 73).[11] However, clinical samples do not necessarily provide *representative* figures on the prevalence of traumatic amnesia and later recall of child sexual abuse within the general population. A clinical population can be expected to be biased (mathematically speaking) and unrepresentative of the general population, since '[t]hose with prior periods of forgetting may be more troubled by the experience and thus may be more likely to seek therapy' (Williams 1995, p. 650).

The most definitive study on delayed recall of child sexual abuse has been a prospective study by Williams which involved a non-clinical sample of adult survivors of child sexual abuse whose histories of sexual abuse were documented at the time of the abuse. Between 1973 and 1975, Williams studied 206 girls (aged from ten months to 12 years) who had been examined in a hospital emergency room as a result of reports of sexual abuse. In a follow-up study, Williams (1994) reported that, of the 129 of the original 206 subjects (i.e. those who, 17 years later, were able to be located and were willing to be interviewed), 38 per cent did not report any memory of child sexual abuse when interviewed. This figure suggested to Williams (1995, p. 650) that traumatic amnesia of child sexual abuse 'may be a fairly common event' within the general population,[12] although Williams recognised that failure to report an incident of child sexual abuse is not necessarily evidence of having no memory of being abused, since there can be other reasons why a person would not reveal such information.[13]

In 1995, Williams reported further results of her study of this group of 129 women, describing her results as the first 'to provide evidence that some adults who claim to have recovered memories of child sexual abuse *recall actual events* which occurred in child-hood'. Interestingly, and contrary to the claims of FMS proponents, her results also provide *no evidence* that the recovery of memories of child sexual abuse 'was fostered by therapy or therapists' (Williams 1995, p. 670) [emphases added]. These results pertain to a further study of the 80 out of 129 women who recalled the abuse documented in hospital records. Of those 80 women, 16 per cent[14] stated that there was a time when they did not remember the abuse. Williams (1995, pp. 656–662) reports that these women who recovered memories as adults:

- 'were on average three years younger at the time of the abuse than the women who reported that they had always remembered';
- were more likely to have been closely associated with the perpetrator (such as a close family member);
- 'were *less* likely to have been subjected to other physical force during the molestation';
- 'had received weak support from their mothers';
- 'were somewhat *less* likely to have received any counseling . . . [which] suggests, as do the women's accounts, that recovery of memories for these women was . . . unrelated to therapy';[15]
- were mostly African–American (86 per cent) and were not from white, affluent, middle-class backgrounds;[16]
- '[i]n general, had no more inconsistencies in their accounts than did the women who always remembered'. In fact, Williams observed that 'when one considers the basic elements of the abuse, their retrospective reports were remarkably consistent with what had been reported in the 1970s'.[17]

On the basis of her findings, Williams (1995, p. 667) concluded that:

> young age at time of abuse and having no or weak support from one's mother following the abuse increased the likelihood that the abuse would be forgotten and later remembered. These findings suggest that the cognitive, developmental features of the victim and the responses of others to the abuse may be critical in predicting the appearance of recovered memories.

Nonetheless, Williams considered that the women in her study were unusual, in the sense that their abuse was reported in childhood. This is contrary to evidence from studies that have reported the prevalence of child sexual abuse in general population samples (most of which is not reported to the authorities)[18] so that '[c]hildren who have never reported may have a different pattern of remembering and forgetting the abuse' (Williams 1995, p. 669). In addition, she considered that accurate recovered memories may have been more likely in the sample of women she studied because, when their memories were recalled, 'these women may have found it easier to retrieve an accurate account of the incident because they may have been able to recall conversations that they had had with others about the abuse' (Williams 1995, p. 669).[19]

One of the other interesting aspects of Williams' findings is that, although some of the women with recovered memories of child sexual abuse were reporting *actual* documented childhood events, they, *themselves*, 'were often very unsure about their memories and said things like "What I remember is mostly from a dream" or, "I'm really not too sure about this"' (Williams 1995, p. 670). As Williams recognises, these are the very types of statements that arouse the scepticism of judges, lawyers, journalists, therapists and laypeople. However, her study highlights the fact that 'such skepticism should be tempered' and caution must be exercised by the criminal justice system when dismissing a woman's account of recovered memories as false (1995, p. 670). When it comes to it, who would not feel some caution or uncertainty (if not despair and horror) about having to deal with a recovered memory of a traumatic childhood event like child sexual abuse? In fact, clinicians have reported that survivors of child sexual abuse commonly display chronic doubts about the reliability of their memories, whether recovered or not:

> [c]hronic doubts about what did and did not happen, along with a persistent inability to trust one's perceptions of reality, are perhaps the most permanent and ultimately damaging long-term effects of childhood sexual abuse. (Davies & Frawley 1994, p. 109)

However, in relation to the conduct of a sexual assault trial in which the complainant's account of child sexual abuse is derived solely or partly from recovered memories, Williams' findings compel judges and lawyers to rethink any biases they may have in relation to the idea of recovered memories and to question the scientific validity of their biases. As Williams states:

> [w]hile these findings cannot be used to assert the validity of *all* recovered memories of child abuse, this study does suggest that recovered memories of child sexual abuse reported by adults can be quite consistent with contemporaneous documentation of the abuse and should not be summarily dismissed by therapists, lawyers, family members, judges or the women themselves. (1995, p. 670)

Furthermore, 'there is no evidence that people who do recover memories . . . are less likely to be telling the truth' (Freyd 1996, p. 46) and there is, in fact, evidence which supports the converse: for example, Feldman-Summers and Pope (1994) have reported that 'the rates of corroboration for abuse memories are unrelated to whether there had ever been a period of forgetting. Similarly, Herman and Schatzow (1987) report high levels of corroboration for previously amnesic patients who had recovered memories of sexual abuse' (Freyd 1996, pp. 46–47). Both of these findings are consistent with Williams' findings that 16 per cent of women with documented histories of child sexual abuse had experienced amnesia in relation to their abuse and had later recovered memories of abuse that were consistent with what had been documented.

More recently, in 1996, Whitfield and Stock surveyed 100 people in a retrospective study who had 'identified themselves as having been abused before the age of 18'.[20] Thirty-two per cent of those surveyed reported that they had experienced total amnesia in relation to being sexually abused as children, whilst 36 per cent reported partial amnesia. In line with other studies discussed in this article, Whitfield and Stock (1997, p. 2) report that '[t]he younger the age at onset of the abuse was associated with more . . . amnesia' and '[t]he older age that the child was when abused was associated with more memory for the abuse'. Whitfield and Stock also report that only 3 per cent reported that a recovered memory occurred in therapy and that 63 per cent had external corroboration of the abuse, such as scars, eyewitnesses, earwitnesses, medical records, police records, diaries, notes or letters, report of the abuse to another person, confession by a perpetrator, knowledge of other victims or photo evidence.

Nonetheless, they found:

> no difference regarding the presence or absence of amnesia among the 59 analyzed subjects who found external corroboration. When analyzed and differentiated, these broke down to 22 with total amnesia for the CSA who had external corroboration, 22 with partial amnesia, and 15 who always remembered most. There was no significant difference among these verified groups regarding the external corroboration . . . Those who had always remembered had no increased corroboration than the amnestic group.
> (1997, p. 4)

In fact, Whitfield and Stock (1997, p. 8) have analysed a total of 31 studies from a current literature search[21] (including their own) which have studied the prevalence of traumatic amnesia among those who have either reported child sexual or physical abuse (25 retrospective studies) or, as children, had documented histories of child sexual abuse (six prospective studies). Although not all 25 of the retrospective studies investigated the issue of whether the subjects' accounts of child sexual abuse could be externally corroborated, of those that did (14 out of 31), Whitfield and Stock report that 85 per cent of subjects had their abuse experiences externally corroborated.

In the face of the scientific evidence which supports the existence of the phenomenon of recovered memories of child sexual abuse, it is possible to make the following conclusions:

- The phenomenon of recovery of traumatic memories has been known to science for more than a century and has been well documented.
- Studies on non-traumatic memory and commonsense assumptions of the way memory works are not valid methods for understanding the way traumatic memory is encoded in the brain.
- Recovered memories of child sexual abuse have been shown to accurately match actual events that have been medically documented.
- Traumatic memories cannot be consciously willed into existence and appear to occur in response to chance emotional triggers which resemble or evoke the stress of the original traumatic event.
- There is no empirical evidence to show that an adult's recovered memories of child sexual abuse are implanted or fostered by therapists.
- Recovered memories of child sexual abuse are independent of demographic factors such as sex, race and class.
- A person's uncertainty about their memory cannot, of itself, be used to conclude that the memory is false or unreliable.
- At the time of writing, 31 studies exist to verify the fact that recovered memories of child sexual abuse are a fairly common occurrence, with general population studies suggesting that between 16 and 51 per cent of those abused will suffer traumatic amnesia.

Thus, it can now be said that '[t]he questions "Does traumatic amnesia exist among CSA survivors?" and if so, "How common is it?" are now affirmatively answered' (Whitfield & Stock 1997, p. 8). However, one of the major questions that researchers should be investigating in light of the evidence that affirmatively proves the existence of traumatic amnesia for child sexual abuse, is '[h]ow common are traumatic . . . amnesia and false denial among child molesters?' (Whitfield & Stock 1997, p. 8). Since there is documentation of rapists who have reported memory loss of the rape (Schacter 1986; Clark et al. 1987; Brown 1995; Tayloe 1995), this raises the intriguing issue of whether it is a victim whose reports of recovered memories are really false or whether the perpetrator, himself, has suffered amnesia[22] or is in a state of denial (Salter 1995, pp. 6–7; Freyd 1997, p. 30).

## HOW DOES SCIENCE EXPLAIN THE PHENOMENON OF TRAUMATIC AMNESIA?

There are several hypotheses to explain why an adult will not remember an experience of child sexual abuse. First, if a child is very young at the time of the abuse, empirical research suggests that the ability to recall may be due to 'infantile amnesia', since memory appears to be impaired generally for events that occur before the age of three or four (Williams 1995, p. 651). It is believed that the part of the brain involving the explicit memory system (the hippocampus)[23] does not start to develop in children until 2–3 years of age so that, for children under the age of three, their memory is considered to be governed by the implicit memory system which involves the more primitive parts of the brain that do *not* store conceptual, factual and verbal material. This means that children under about the age of three, neurologically, may not be able to store an explicit memory of child sexual abuse involving full verbal memories but can have implicit memory of such events in the form of emotional reactions or the ability to draw representations of the event (Kristiansen 1996, p. 6). Thus, caution must be exercised not to dismiss abuse that is claimed to have happened at these young ages because the complainant 'fails' to produce a verbal form of memory which we, as adults, might be accustomed to thinking is the only valid form of memory.

For example, Terr (1988) studied 20 children who had been sexually assaulted before the age of five. All cases of sexual abuse had external corroboration and Terr compared the children's behavioural memories with the corroborating evidence, finding that the children's 'behavioral memories of trauma remain[ed] quite accurate and true to the events' that had caused them (Terr 1988, p. 96). Some of the behaviours described by Terr involved one girl pointing to her abdomen in response to questions as to whether she had ever been scared: Terr later saw pornographic photos of the child showing an erect penis 'jabbing at the very spot she touched in my office'. Another girl, aged almost three, was observed to undress a doll and poke it 'suddenly and violently in the vagina'. Again, pornographic photos showed that this child, as a baby, had been poked in the vagina by an erect penis (Terr 1988, pp. 98–101).

In addition, Whitfield (1995, p. 25) has surveyed numerous studies which have shown that 'people can and do remember traces, fragments or even the majority of experiences' under the age of five years in the form of memories associated with the implicit memory system. In one study of 34 children who had been sexually abused under the age of five in a day-care centre, all 34 of the children displayed somatic memories of the abuse, 82 per cent displayed behavioural memories and 59 per cent had visual memories which manifested in drawings (Burgess et al., cited in Whitfield 1995, pp. 25–26).

A second explanation for the existence of traumatic amnesia is that a child's inexperience with sex and sexual abuse 'results in [him] or her not having categories by which they may be encoded, which can influence how events are encoded or later retrieved' (Rogers 1995, p. 702). This, coupled with a child's fewer mental capacities, means that it can be difficult for them to construct 'a coherent narrative out of traumatic events' (van der Kolk & Fisler 1995, p. 510). Other researchers have suggested that longstanding or repeated episodes of abuse are more likely to result in amnesia (Terr 1991), or that traumatic amnesia is associated with more violent episodes of abuse coupled with young age (Herman & Schatzow 1987; Briere & Conte 1993).[24]

A third but more all-encompassing theory that is finding increasing acceptance in the literature is that 'it is the psychophysiological process of "dissociation", rather than repression or normal forgetting, that is primarily responsible for the nature of adults' memories of traumatic child abuse' (Kristiansen 1996, p. 3).[25] As van der Kolk and Fisler have reported, dissociation (which is a passive process and appears to rely on the brain's implicit memory resources)[26] affects not only the way experiences are encoded into memory but also the ability to retrieve that memory, the mechanism by which dissociated memories return and the fragmentary nature of them. There is evidence which supports the existence of the state of dissociation, its relationship with the brain's two separate memory systems (the explicit and implicit memory systems) and how they operate in parallel (Kristiansen 1996, pp. 4–9) and the strong relationship between the experience of trauma, dissociation and subsequent amnesia (Freyd 1996, p. 87).

For example, studies on the effects of stress on the brain support the proposition that mechanisms other than forgetting are involved in traumatic amnesia of child sexual abuse (Bremner et al. 1995, p. 545). In particular, 'neurological research shows that the brain structures of the conscious explicit memory systems are overwhelmed by the arousing impact of trauma' such that this system can actually be bypassed or impeded by trauma (Kristiansen 1996, p. 9). Where the explicit memory system is overwhelmed by trauma, the traumatic event will result in 'fragmented, emotional and sensory memories without the person being aware of the events originally responsible for the memories' (Kristiansen 1996, p. 9), so that there will be no verbal component to the memory (van der Kolk & Fisler 1995, p. 512).

Kristiansen (1996, pp. 8–10) documents studies that show that trauma causes neurochemical changes which are considered to interfere with the functioning of those brain structures responsible for processing information in the explicit memory system.[27] It is these neurochemical changes that are thought to be responsible for the lack of a verbal or narrative memory being encoded at the time of the trauma. In fact, the evidence suggesting that the explicit memory system is bypassed as a result of trauma is supported by those studies that report that the memory loss of child abuse victims 'varies systematically with the degree of trauma associated with their abuse' (Kristiansen 1996, p. 9)[28] or even the threat of violence at the time of abuse and level of distress experienced (Elliott & Briere 1995).

In other words, because increased release of neurochemicals during stress is believed to modulate memory function and affect the encoding of a traumatic event, it can be expected that the more traumatic the experience of child sexual abuse, the more likely the brain will be impeded from recording the experience (Bremner et al. 1995). In addition, the more times a child is sexually abused, the more likely it will be that the brain is impeded from encoding the experience due to the fact that 'repeated exposure to a stressor results in amplification' of the release of neurochemicals which impede the functioning of the explicit memory system (Bremner et al. 1995, p. 541). In fact, it appears that a person experiences the mental state of dissociation when the hippocampus has been impeded by the excessive release of neurochemicals, resulting in impaired encoding within the explicit memory system (Bremner et al. 1995, p. 543).[29]

Recently, Freyd has built on the research describing the link between dissociation and trauma and has posited that:

> the degree to which a trauma involves betrayal by another person significantly influences the traumatized individual's cognitive encoding of the experience of trauma. (Freyd 1996, pp. 9–10)

Freyd's betrayal trauma theory suggests that the closer the relationship between child and abuser, the greater the experience of trauma as a result of betrayal of trust and the more likely that encoding in the explicit memory system will be impaired (1996, p. 129). In fact, Freyd considers that abuse by an adult on whom a child depends or whom a child trusts (such as a parent) 'is a primary risk factor for amnesia' (1996, p. 44), since rates of traumatic amnesia have been found to be 'higher for incest survivors than for other sexual abuse survivors' (1996, p. 48). Freyd (1996, pp. 137–141) has listed seven factors which, according to betrayal trauma theory, predict that traumatic amnesia will occur:

1. abuse by a caregiver;
2. explicit threats demanding a child's silence (such as, 'I'll kill you if you tell');
3. a child is abused in a context different from a child's normal family life or environment (e.g. abuse in the middle of the night);
4. social isolation of the child during the abuse, giving rise to a lack of social validation of the child's experience;
5. young age at onset of abuse;
6. alternative reality-defining statements by caregivers (such as, 'this didn't happen'); and
7. lack of shared, explicit discussion of the abuse.

Freyd tested the validity of these factors by examining a number of studies that report on the prevalence of traumatic amnesia for child sexual abuse. For example, in an analysis of data from the Feldman-Summers and Pope (1994) study of 79 psychologists who had indicated that they had experienced either physical or sexual abuse as a child, Freyd found that 53 per cent of those who had been sexually abused by a relative had a period of amnesia in relation to the abuse compared with 30 per cent of all other abuse victims, a difference found to be statistically significant (1996, p. 143). Freyd observed that this difference between incest victims and those who suffered physical abuse may be due to the fact that 'sexual abuse is more likely to occur in isolation and with demands of silence', two factors which, according to betrayal trauma theory, are predictive of traumatic amnesia.

Freyd (1996, p. 149) also analysed the data in Williams' prospective study of 129 adult women (discussed above) and found that those women who had experienced incestuous abuse were more likely to have experienced amnesia in relation to the abuse, a result which Freyd (1996, p. 150) considers is 'highly congruent with betrayal trauma theory' and with Williams' own observations that the women in her study with recovered memories were younger at the time of abuse, were less likely to have received support from their mothers and had closer family relationships to the perpetrator (Williams 1995, pp. 649, 658).

Similarly, in an analysis of data from a study by Cameron (1994) of 45 women undergoing therapy for child sexual abuse, Freyd found a statistically significant correlation between those who had experienced amnesia for abuse and being abused by a parent. This finding again supports betrayal trauma theory, since 'sexual abuse by a trusted caregiver is the most likely sort of abuse to lead to amnesia' (Freyd 1996, p. 153). In fact, Freyd (1996, p. 156) has not found any studies reporting rates of traumatic amnesia in adult child sexual abuse survivors that showed that 'incest [was] negatively predictive of amnesia'.[30] Nonetheless, Freyd (1996, p. 157) has recognised that, whilst her analysis 'on the relationship between incest and amnesia tends to support predictions made by betrayal trauma theory', further work is required to show a correlation between each of the seven factors suggested by the theory and the experience.

## WHAT ARE THE CHARACTERISTICS OF RECOVERED MEMORIES?

The way that traumatic events are encoded within the implicit memory system is considered to be determinative of the way that traumatic memories are recalled. For example, van der Kolk and Fisler (1995) examined the way memory was processed by war veterans, victims of torture, child abuse survivors and people involved in traumatic accidents and reported that none of them said their memory returned as a complete narrative with a structured beginning, middle and end. In fact, regardless of the age at which the trauma occurred, all subjects initially recalled their trauma as flashback experiences (i.e. involuntary re-experiences) involving visual, tactile, olfactory, auditory or emotional experiences of the trauma (van der Kolk & Fisler 1995, p. 519)[31]—that is, sensations that are characteristic of the implicit memory system. In particular, like victims of other trauma such as war and concentration camps, 'when child abuse survivors' memories come back, they come back exactly the way they went in. That is, as raw, unintegrated relivings of the sensory, emotional and behavioural aspects of their traumatic experiences' (Bremner et al. 1995, p. 543; Kristiansen 1996, p. 14).

For example, van der Kolk and Fisler (1995, p. 513) document that, in their experience of treating traumatised patients over a 20-year period, 'patients consistently claim that their perceptions are exact representations of sensations at the time of the trauma'. Indeed, these clinical observations are supported by Williams' analysis of the 13 women in her study who had experienced delayed recall of documented sexual abuse, since Williams (1995, pp. 656–662) found that women with recovered memories had memories that were 'remarkably consistent' with what had been documented at the time of the abuse.[32] In fact, there is evidence to show that recovered memories of child sexual abuse have an accuracy rate of about 96 per cent which, according to American data, is an accuracy rate similar to that associated with crimes such as robbery or assault (Kristiansen 1996, p. 22).

One of the difficulties for a complainant in a sexual assault trial is that, if she is not able to supply a complete narrative of the abuse—that is, a full verbal account with start, middle and end (including explicit dates, place of abuse and details of who did what), then she is less likely to be believed and more likely to find her memories labelled as false. But in the face of scientific evidence that recovered memories of child sexual abuse *do not* have the same characteristics of memory that is stored in the explicit memory system, and the fact that memory is not 'solely a verbal system' (Whitfield 1995, p. 26), the question arises: How should the criminal justice system deal with the distinctive nature of recovered memories, other than to accuse complainants of making false allegations? This question is fundamental given the incidence of child sexual abuse in Western society, the intensely secret nature of the crime, the high degree of under-reporting of child sexual abuse, the fact that it is the crime *least* likely to be corroborated by independent witnesses and physical evidence,[33] and the demonstrated inability of the criminal justice system to prosecute the vast majority of offenders.[34]

Can traumatic memories be distinguished in any way from ordinary memory? Kristiansen (1996, p. 14) considers that '[t]raumatic memories are much more intense and more strongly characterized by decontextualized sensory re-experiences', indicating that they are distinguishable from non-traumatic memories and fantasised events and that people would be 'unlikely to mistake their explicit imaginings for implicit recovered memories of trauma'. Van der Kolk (1994, p. 258) has noted that '[c]linicians and researchers dealing with traumatized patients have repeatedly observed that the sensory experiences and visual images related to the trauma seem not to fade over time and appear to be less subject to distortion than ordinary experiences'. In addition, '[t]hey come out of the blue, they do not make much sense and, of course, their content is typically horrific' so they are likely to be accompanied by psychological symptomatology known as post-traumatic stress disorder (Kristiansen 1996, p. 14), with people typically experiencing flashbacks of the events and panic. In fact, Elliott and Briere (1995, p. 640) have reported that the men and women in their general population study who reported recovering memories of child sexual abuse within the two years prior to data collection displayed more psychological symptoms than other subjects who reported memories of child sexual abuse outside that two-year period.[35]

Is there any evidence from the foregoing studies to suggest that therapists have implanted memories of abuse? In posing this question, it must be borne in mind that, even if a person experiences delayed recall of child sexual abuse within a therapy situation, the conclusion that the therapist must therefore have implanted the memories does not necessarily hold. In addition, the claim that bad therapists implant false memories can be said to be nothing more than an unfounded diversion, since (i) it was first proposed by parents who had been accused of child sexual abuse, hardly a credible scientific source (Whitfield 1995, p. 68), (ii) there is *no* empirical evidence showing a positive correlation between a person's recovered memory and implantation of false memories by a therapist and (iii) there is sufficient empirical evidence that points the other way—that delayed recall of recovered memories occurs independently of therapy.

For example, 84 per cent of child sexual abuse survivors who reported recovered memories in the study by Kristiansen et al.

(1996, pp. 18, 20) 'said their therapist had never even asked if they had an abuse history' and 40 per cent of those women recovered their memories independently of therapy. These findings complement those of Williams (1995) that *none* of the 13 women who reported recovered memories of actual documented events in her study recovered those memories in association with therapy, and those of Elliott and Briere (1995, p. 637) that only 8 per cent of subjects in their study who had reported recovered memories had undergone therapy. Further, Whitfield and Stock (1997, p. 7) found that only 3 per cent of the 59 subjects who had reported delayed recall of child sexual abuse had experienced that delayed recall in a therapy situation.

In the face of the empirical evidence explaining the nature of traumatic memory and the neurological response to trauma, it is possible to make the following conclusions:

- Neurological evidence suggests that, during acute stress or trauma, an increased level of neurochemicals impedes the brain's ability to encode and store information in the explicit memory system.
- A state of dissociation is induced when the explicit memory system is impeded by the excessive release of neurochemicals.
- During this state of dissociation, memory of the trauma is encoded within the implicit memory system and the memory will be characterised by sensory components but will have no verbal component to it. In other words, memories stored in the implicit memory system do not have the same characteristics as those stored in the explicit memory system which stores a verbal narrative of events with a structured beginning, middle and end.
- Research on trauma victims shows that the recall of a traumatic memory is re-experienced, involuntarily, as a sensory experience with these sensations matching the original experience of trauma.
- Research on a wide variety of trauma victims shows that the experience of delayed recall of child sexual abuse is highly similar to delayed recall of other traumatic events.
- Delayed recalls of traumatic events are, to experts who work with trauma victims, distinguishable from non-traumatic or ordinary memories in that they are typically accompanied by psychological symptoms associated with experiences of trauma

and have the same emotional and/or sensory intensity for the victim as the original experience of the trauma.

- From an evolutionary point of view, there is 'a logic to amnesia for childhood abuse' since, as an adaptive response, 'amnesia may allow a dependent child to remain attached to—and thus elicit at least some degree of life-sustaining nurturing and protection from—his or her abusive caregiver' (Freyd 1996, p. 180).

- There is no empirical evidence to support the claim that recovered memories of child sexual abuse are false or that such memories are implanted by bad therapists.

## EMPIRICAL EVIDENCE VERSUS IDEOLOGICAL EVIDENCE

If a scientist claims to have discovered a new animal, virus, medical condition, atomic particle, planet or, indeed, a new psychiatric syndrome, empirical evidence is required to substantiate the claim. The scientific literature is replete with explanations and descriptions of experiments conducted including the methodology used, tabulated results and analysis of those results. In other words, the accepted scientific way is for scientists to expose their evidence to the scientific community to allow others to scrutinise and critique it and to enable replication of their experiments by other scientists.

However, Pope (1996, p. 957) has raised the issue that:

[c]omplex factors may shape the process by which announced discoveries and conclusions encounter or elude careful scrutiny. Such factors include prevailing scientific paradigms, historical contexts, and the bandwagon effect. They can influence the degree to which people are inclined, willing and free to question certain claims.

If an alleged scientific discovery is announced but is not accompanied by appropriate empirical evidence (i.e. a description of the methodology used and results verifying its existence), the critical question is: Should such an alleged discovery be accepted uncritically and is a scientist's emphatic belief in its existence sufficient to justify its existence? Or is 'independent examination of the primary data and methodology [that is] used to establish the validity and reliability' of a new scientific phenomenon, such as a new psychiatric diagnosis, 'an essential scientific responsibility' prior to applying the diagnosis to thousands of people? (Pope 1996, p. 962).

In the context of recovered memories for child sexual abuse, the puzzling question is how an alleged new psychiatric syndrome, the false memory syndrome, became so widely accepted within the scientific community, popular culture and the criminal justice system in the absence of empirical evidence to support its existence. What has made it a real and actual syndrome in the minds of those who believe in its existence, apparently afflicting at least 10 000 women in America, when there is no empirical evidence that verifies its existence? In other words, do people who believe it to be true make it true merely because they believe in it? If so, on what basis do these people believe it to be true?

These questions can only be answered by closely examining the various claims of those who believe in the existence of false memory syndrome. First, FMS proponents assert that 'many therapists—for reasons as diverse as well-meaning naivete, greed, incompetence, and zealotry—suggest a history of childhood sexual abuse to clients who have no actual abuse history' (Pope 1996, p. 957). As a result of such interference, 'clients who uncritically accept these suggestions and come to believe illusory memories of abuse with great conviction, suffer from an iatrogenic disorder termed *false memory syndrome*' (Pope 1996, p. 957).

Second, the syndrome is alleged to have reached epidemic proportions, since 'sufficient cases have been *diagnosed* to constitute an epidemic' (Pope 1996, p. 957) [emphasis added]. In fact, Pope (1996, p. 961) quotes one FMS Foundation information sheet as asserting that 'False Memory Syndrome [is] a devastating phenomenon that has affected tens of thousands of individuals and families worldwide'.[36] But has diagnosis been possible because sufficient cases have been studied and documented to enable a psychological profile of those who suffer from false memory syndrome to be constructed? Those allegedly suffering from false memory syndrome are said to display:

> a condition in which a person's identity and interpersonal relationships are centered around a memory of traumatic experience which is objectively false but in which the person strongly believes. Note that the memory is not characterized by false memories as such. We all have memories that are inaccurate. Rather, the syndrome may be diagnosed when the memory is so deeply engrained that it orients the individual's entire personality and lifestyle, in turn disrupting all sorts of other adaptive behaviors. The analogy to personality disorder is intentional. False Memory

Syndrome is especially destructive because the person assiduously avoids confrontation with any evidence that might challenge the memory. Thus it takes on a life of its own, encapsulated, and resistant to correction. The person may become so focused on the memory that he or she may be effectively distracted from coping with the real problems in his or her life. (FMS Foundation brochure, cited in Pope 1996, p. 959)

Pope has noted that the 'peer-reviewed scientific literature still lacks adequate information about [the] methodology' that has allegedly been used to assess those who are suspected of suffering from the syndrome and to state that, *in each case*, their memory was found to be 'objectively false' (1996, p. 959).[37] In other words, have FMS proponents surveyed *every* person who is alleged to be part of the (worldwide) false memory syndrome epidemic to determine that their memories are in fact false? If they have, by what methods was the survey carried out and where are the results? In posing such questions, Pope's response (1996, p. 962) is that:

It appears possible, on the basis of a reading of materials gener-ated by the FMSF, that some might not consider interviewing or clinically assessing the people supposedly afflicted by false memory syndrome to be an essential component of a study of the validity and occurrence of the syndrome. If, for this reason, the informed consent of or even direct contact with people diagnosed with false memory syndrome has been considered unnecessary in docu-menting specific cases or the extent of the phenomenon, it would be useful for FMSF and its Scientific and Professional Advisory Board to report any available scientific data about the ability to diagnose false memory syndrome without meeting the person alleged to have the disorder. *If the person reporting the so-called memory does not participate in the research, how do researchers conclude that the memory is objectively false (rather than simply subjectively judged to be false by those who have been accused)?* How do re-searchers determine that the center of a person's identity and interpersonal relationships is a particular false memory *without even meeting the person?* How do they examine all aspects of personality without interviewing, evaluating, or even knowing the person? [emphases added]

In light of the absence of empirical evidence to support the claim of a worldwide epidemic of false memory syndrome, has this alleged epidemic come into being merely because FMS proponents *say* it exists? For example, Pope (1996, p. 959) raises the issue that '[i]t remains unclear whether the protocol of any research purporting to validate the false memory syndrome diagnosis in large numbers of persons used any criterion other than the decision rule that all recovered memories of abuse are inherently false'. In addition, Pope (1996, pp. 959–960) has questioned:

> If there are validation studies for false memory syndrome and the epidemic that do not reflexively judge all reports of recovered memories of abuse to be objectively false, what was the research methodology for determining whether the reports were objectively true or false? Does the methodology yield an acceptable rate of false positives and false negatives? Assuming more than one person made each judgment, what was the interrater reliability? How was the methodology itself validated?

In the absence of empirical evidence to support the claims of FMS proponents, Pope has documented the type of evidence that has been advanced to support the epidemic nature of the syndrome. Such 'evidence' includes the apparently large family membership of the FMS Foundation; the failure to find corroborating evidence on the part of those claiming they were abused; an unspecified number of people who have allegedly 'retracted their claims of having experienced abuse'; evidence that prior to therapy a person had no memories of child sexual abuse; the lack of evidence that an accused person had a history of pedophiliac tendencies or sexual interest in children; and that the members of the FMS Foundation are, according to its Executive Director, 'a good looking bunch of people: graying hair, well-dressed, healthy, smiling . . . Just about every person who has attended is someone you would likely find interesting and want to count as a friend' (Freyd 1992, cited in Pope 1996, p. 960).

In addition, Pope (1996, p. 961) has suggested that '[i]t is possible that the impressive names, prestige, offices, and affiliations of the Scientific and Professional Advisory Board may have, however unintentionally, led fellow scientists, the courts, the popular media, and others to accept without customary skepticism, [and] care' the claims of FMS proponents as scientifically validated.

Nonetheless, the subjective nature of the 'evidence' should be obvious. But if such 'evidence' has been sufficient to convince the Scientific and Professional Advisory Board of the FMS Foundation, what subjective beliefs, prejudices and biases are held by those who find such evidence convincing? Consider the following argument by Pope (1996, p. 960): 'if self-reports of abuse memories are to be doubted in the absence of external "proof", why are self-reports about retracted memories presented as presumed valid in the absence of external verification? What scientific evidence supports claims that such factors as good looks, dress, health, and smiling *serve as valid and reliable indicants of whether or not an individual has engaged in child abuse?*' [emphasis added] Is the opposite, therefore, true—that all pedophiles are not good-looking, not grey-haired, badly dressed, unhealthy and do not smile? If factors such as good looks, dress, health, grey hair and smiling faces are persuasive as evidence of the non-pedophilic nature of the members of the FMS Foundation, are they persuasive because such features fit with a person's belief in the comforting stereotype of respectable middle-aged parents?

Further, why is a man's self-report of no history of sexual interest in or involvement with children a valid criterion of the truth, but a woman's self-report of being sexually abused as a child is not? Further, why are the claims of thousands of families (the number claimed to be members of the FMS Foundation) that there was no sexual abuse in their respective families held to be objectively true, whilst the claims of thousands of children are held to be objectively false? Are the denials of those accused of child sexual abuse likely to be a reliable scientific source?

Further, Pope questions why it is that '[c]laims that such factors as clothing, attractive appearance, smiling behavior, and chatting provide a reliable basis for concluding that a person has never engaged in child abuse' but that, according to some FMS proponents, 'it is not permissible to infer, or frankly even to suspect, a history of abuse in people who present symptoms of abuse' (Kihlstrom, cited in Pope 1996, p. 967). In other words, FMS proponents illogically but conveniently consider that symptoms of abuse can never be used to justify suspicions that a person has been sexually abused but that 'presenting factors such as clothing and appearance can reliably demonstrate that a person was not involved in child abuse' (Pope 1996, p. 967).

Third, FMS proponents claim that any memory of child sexual abuse recovered in therapy is thereby false, which has been observed to be 'a form of the logical fallacy *post hoc, ergo propter hoc* ("after this, therefore on account of this")' (Pope 1996, p. 966). Because such a claim denies the possibility that there has been no therapeutic interference, it therefore assumes that the therapeutic session must have induced the false memory. This is akin to saying that flashes of light in the night sky cause car accidents, therefore if you have a car accident at night it was caused by a flash of light. In other words, this type of reasoning *excludes* all other possible causative factors, such as poor brakes, poor concentration, consumption of alcohol, speed or tiredness and, in the case of recovered memories of child sexual abuse, excludes neurological factors associated with the storage of memory, as well as age at time of abuse, severity of the abuse or relationship with a perpetrator. This type of reasoning also fails to explain car accidents that do not happen at night and memories that are recovered independently of therapy. Therefore, the use of this type of reasoning, to the exclusion of all other reasons, is only believable if a person adheres to such beliefs, as that women are suggestible to ideas of being sexually abused, or that they or the therapist have a particular vindictive motive.

Further, even if a therapist can be shown to have engaged in unethical methods during therapy, that fact does not prove that (i) a memory has been implanted in the mind of a particular client or (ii) that the client believed the memory even if there was actual evidence of the therapist attempting to implant a memory. Furthermore, FMS proponents have expanded their claims by suggesting that women can acquire false memories by associating with other child sexual abuse survivors or by reading books about recovery from child sexual abuse. Presumably, if a person does not want to believe that it is possible to recover memories of child sexual abuse, it is easy to grab at straws and assert that, if it was not due to bad therapy, those with the recovered memory were suggestible to something they read, people they talked to or a movie they saw. In other words, there is an infinite number of ways to assert that a memory of child sexual abuse is false but these assertions cannot take the place of accepted methodology which involves interviewing each person claimed to be suffering from FMS and sound empirical data that shows that a recovered memory is objectively false.

Fourth, FMS proponents allege that it is impossible to forget or repress a traumatic childhood incident such as child sexual abuse. However, Pope argues that the 'evidence' for this assertion appears to be the assertion itself. Such assertions include 'people who undergo severe trauma remember it' (Wakefield & Underwager 1992b, cited in Pope 1996, p. 959) and 'memories of such atrocities cannot be repressed. Horrible incidents of childhood are remembered' (FMS Foundation, cited in Pope 1996, p. 959). When assertions like this are made without accompanying empirical evidence, it is akin to saying that there is life on Mars and the evidence I present for my assertion is the assertion itself. Therefore, there is life on Mars. Further, in making such assertions, FMS proponents need to explain 100 years of documented evidence showing that a wide variety of victims of trauma (war, concentration camps, accidents) experience traumatic amnesia. Even if they were to accept the validity of such evidence, they would then need to explain why child sexual abuse, as a traumatic event, is different in nature from other documented traumas for which traumatic amnesia has been reported.

Fifth, FMS proponents claim that the people who suffer from false memory syndrome are 'predominantly highly educated females who have received psychotherapy as adults and who come from well-educated, affluent families' (Wakefield & Underwager 1992a) 'not just anybody. They are women who already have problems, such as personality disorder, and they're likely to be unusually suggestible' (Sifford 1992, quoting Ralph Underwager, cited in Pope 1996, p. 961) or 'very angry, hostile, and sometimes paranoid . . . [and that] all will have demonstrated some type of psychopathology in earlier parts of their lives' (Wakefield & Underwager, cited in Pope 1996, p. 961).

Given that no study has shown that recovered memories of child sexual abuse are a function of either gender or psychopathology, it is clear that these assertions are merely representations of two particular cultural stereotypes of women: the mentally unstable female stereotype and the angry and vindictive female stereotype. Both stereotypes have significant cultural currency (NSW Department for Women 1996; Cossins & Pilkinton 1996, pp. 245–248, 258–261) and are easily used to dismiss the validity of claims of both adult sexual assault and child sexual abuse.

Another stereotype that has been used by FMS proponents is the Fascist stereotype which also has resonances with the vindictive female stereotype. Pope has documented that '[t]hose who disagree with FMSF have . . . been compared to Fascists' (Pope 1996, p. 970) and that FMS proponents have often resorted to 'Holocaust imagery' to undermine their opponents. For example, Pope reports the view of Wassil-Grimm that 'Hitler had the Jews; McCarthy had the communists; radical feminists have perpetrators', that Elizabeth Loftus, a member of the FMS Foundation Scientific and Professional Advisory Board, has compared the Foundation's work 'to those who risked their lives to save Jews from the Nazis' and that the Executive Director of the Foundation, Pamela Freyd, has described her daughter, Jennifer Freyd, as behaving in a 'Gestapolike' fashion (Pope 1996, p. 970). The cultural impact of these stereotypes is likely to be profound, reflecting as they do on anyone who disagrees with FMS proponents and on people, particularly women, who make claim to what has been shown above to be a legitimate psychological phenomenon accompanied by sound empirical evidence.

In conclusion, the claims of FMS proponents can be said to have little to do with objective scientific analysis. FMS proponents appear to have particular ideological objectives and use tactics such as picketing, misinformation and harassment (AAT&D 1996, pp. 25–29; Pope 1996, p. 968) to make claims that masquerade as science. The implications for the conduct of trials within the criminal justice system are profound if unfounded assertions in the guise of science are used to question the validity of a complainant's evidence of recovered memories, given the risk of prejudice to a complainant's evidence through the use of untested assertions and claims that have no empirical basis to them. But there is a logical fallacy associated with admitting into evidence so-called expert testimony relating to the alleged false memory syndrome. Because there is no evidence for the 'alleged clinical entity referred to as "False Memory Syndrome"', debating the characteristics of 'FMS' in the courts is about as logical as 'calling in experts to debate the characteristics of the man in the moon in the absence of any evidence that such a man exists' (Kristiansen 1996, p. 21).

Further, Midson (1995, p. 11) argues that false memory syndrome, as a scientific theory, does not meet the 'common-law rule requiring "general acceptance" for a scientific theory or technique before it may form the basis of an expert's opinion'[38] and should not do so until such time as adequate empirical evidence is found in the peer-reviewed scientific literature to substantiate the claim that the false memory syndrome is a real psychiatric diagnosis.

## THE IDEOLOGICAL BASIS OF THE CLAIM THAT RECOVERED MEMORIES OF CHILD SEXUAL ABUSE ARE FALSE

Given that (i) there is no empirical evidence for the alleged syndrome called the false memory syndrome and (ii) there is sufficient empirical evidence to confirm the existence of the delayed recall of child sexual abuse (suggesting that a recovered memory is more likely to be true than false), 'one has to ask why there is such intense social and professional concern about the validity of recovered memories of child abuse' (Kristiansen 1996, p. 22). In other words, if there is no scientific evidence for a syndrome that false memory proponents claim is a widespread epidemic, then it must be concluded that the recovered memory debate is more an ideological debate with specific ideological objectives than a legitimate scientific enterprise.

In order to test this hypothesis, Kristiansen (1996, pp. 24–25) conducted studies of two different population samples (university students and users of a laundromat in Ottawa) which showed that people with 'more negative attitudes towards women's equality were more likely to believe in FMS, required more stringent legal evidence and had more erroneous incest beliefs' and 'assigned more importance to the traditional values "family security" and "law and order" '. In fact, Kristiansen (1996, p. 26) found that 'the more people believed in FMS the more they endorsed [certain] derogatory ideas about women' which suggests that there is a correlation between those who believe women make false allegations or are suggestible to bad therapy and sexist beliefs about women in general. More specifically, and given the social context in which the term 'false memory syndrome' first surfaced, Kristiansen's results support the proposition that a woman's claim of incest by her father directly challenges the authority of the father and the sanctity of the family. Whilst it is true that men have reported memories of child sexual abuse, the *focus* of the false memory debate has been on women who have accused their fathers of abusing them as children. In fact, 'the demographics of the membership of the [American] FMS Foundation' indicates that 'sexual abuse perpetrated specifically by a parent is at the core of the delayed memory controversy' (Freyd 1996, pp. 140–141).

A fact that has not been publicised, to my knowledge, in the media is that the term 'false memory syndrome' (a term that 'convey[s] scientific and scholarly authority'—Freyd 1996, p. 56) was first coined by two parents who had no mental health training or qualifications. These parents, Peter and Pamela Freyd, set up the FMS Foundation in 1992 after their daughter, Jennifer, accused Peter Freyd of sexually abusing her as a child after she had recovered memories of the abuse (Whitfield 1995, p. 6). Jennifer Freyd is a Professor of Psychology at the University of Oregon and has an international reputation as a researcher in the field of memory. The irony is probably not lost on Professor Freyd that her parents' assertions that her memories were false have been considered more credible by many professionals (despite the fact that her parents have no professional qualifications in the field of psychology or psychiatry) than her claims of child sexual abuse. In 1993, she presented a paper at a psychology conference in which she publicly addressed these issues for the first time:

> At times I am flabbergasted that my memory is considered 'false' and my alcoholic father's memory is considered rational and sane. I wonder why people believe they can decide the truth of our family, and more, why they then decide that my father's memory is more reliable than is my memory. Is it academic success? No, I think by just about any measure I am as successful or more successful than either of my parents. Is it because I remember impossible or crazy things? No, I remember incest in my father's house. Is my father more credible than me because I have a history of lying or not having a firm grasp on reality? No, I am a scientist whose empirical work has been replicated in laboratories around this country and Europe, and until the last few years of parental invasion I enjoyed an excellent professional reputation without any scandal attached to my name. Is it because I have a questionable therapist or my memories emerged in some way indicating suggestibility? No, my first memories came when I was at home a few hours after my second session with my therapist, a licensed clinical psychologist working within an established group in [a] large and respected medical clinic. . . . Am I not believed because I am a woman? A 'female in her thirties' as some of the newspaper articles seem to emphasize? Am I therefore, a hopeless hysteric by definition? Is it because the issue is father–daughter incest and as my father's property, I should be silent? *If Peter Freyd were a man who lived in my neighbourhood during my childhood instead of my father, would he and his wife be so believable? If not, what is it about his status as my father that makes him more credible?* Indeed, why is my parents' denial at all credible? In the end, is it precisely because I was abused that I am to [be] discredited despite my personal and professional success? (Freyd 1993, pp. 3–4) [emphasis added]

The debate about false memories has been made in a context which has failed to recognise that the majority of the members of FMS groups are parents who have been accused of abusing their children (Dean 1996, p. 15), a group that can hardly be expected to be 'a source of objective information on the veracity of memories of sexual molestation' (Quirk 1994, quoted in Whitfield 1995, p. 2). The FMS Foundation in America also includes 'memory researchers who have not studied trauma, and who have a hard time understanding that memories of having been raped are qualitatively different from remembering nonsense words in a laboratory' (van der Kolk, cited in Dean 1996, p. 15).

The debate has also been made in a context which has failed to recognise that child sexual abuse allegations have a longstanding political history and that female child sexual abuse survivors have historically been treated as liars and/or hysterics (Russell 1986, pp. 3–9; de Mause 1994, pp. 77–91). The present debate as it has been presented in the media has a clear ideological objective, based as it is not on scientific evidence but on promoting inaccurate claims that recovered memories of child sexual abuse are the products of hysteria or witch-hunts (Guilliatt 1995a, 1996b; Freyd 1996, pp. 58–59). Such representations (which themselves appear to resemble the hysteria more than that they claim to describe) do not recognise that women have had very little to gain from claims of sexual abuse, be it rape or child sexual abuse, in terms of the documented ways they have been treated by psychiatrists, police, judges and defence barristers (e.g. Cossins & Pilkinton 1996), whilst men have much to protect from denial. Western society has a long history of denial of child sexual abuse and appears to have a significant investment in the myth of dishonest, suggestible or hysterical women who report child sexual abuse, and in the stereotype of the vindictive feminist seeking to destroy men and the family. In fact, the phenomenon of delayed recall of traumatic memories is a very old issue in psychiatry and only became controversial when studies on delayed recall of sexual abuse, as opposed to delayed recall of natural traumatic events and wartime incidents, began to be reported.[39]

In America and Britain, claims that an adult survivor's memories of sexual abuse are false are used indiscriminately by defence barristers.[40] Anecdotal evidence suggests the same is occurring in Australia. Yet we know that conservative estimates of the prevalence of child sexual abuse is approximately one in four to one in three for female children and one in ten for male children *and* that the vast majority of incidents of child sexual abuse are unreported at the time of abuse for many legitimate reasons. In other words, child sexual abuse is a reality for a significant minority of children whose only opportunity for seeking redress may not occur until adulthood. The criminal justice system needs to adjust to deal with the extent of child sexual abuse and with the reality of the phenomenon of recovered memories of child sexual abuse.[41] However, if the debate about false memories of child sexual abuse is a debate about ideology not science, the obvious question is whether it is appropriate for the criminal justice system to become a vehicle for perpetuating the ideological objectives of 'false memory' proponents.

The extent to which the false memory syndrome has become accepted as scientific 'fact' is exemplified by the Royal Commission into the New South Wales Police Service's warning that, in relation to cases of recovered memories of child sexual abuse, law enforcement bodies should determine:

- the time at which there was a first recovery of memory, and the circumstances in which it occurred;
- the extent to which that memory expanded or changed;
- whether there has been any intervention by a therapist or counsellor, and if so: the date/s and extent of that intervention; its nature; the modality of any treatment provided; the existence of any suggestive influence during the intervention; whether the therapist claims personally to be a 'survivor' and to have disclosed that fact to the complainant; and the personality type, mental status, and vulnerability to suggestion of the complainant;
- whether the complainant has had any exposure to outside influences which may have been suggestive of him or her having been a victim of abuse; that is, through incest or survivor groups, attendance at relevant conferences, the reading of books or newsletters, or through the viewing of films or TV programs dealing with the topic; and
- whether there is any corroboration available. (Government of the State of NSW 1997, p. 665)

In my view, if we are searching for the truth in a criminal trial, then the discrediting of a complainant's recovered memory evidence on the basis of myth and bias (rather than scientific evidence) can only bring disrepute on the criminal justice system, and, unwittingly perhaps, will allow it to operate to protect a significant proportion of child sexual abusers.

# PART II

## PRACTICES THAT CHALLENGE SECRECY AND DENIAL

# 8 | A different balance altogether? Incest offenders in treatment

*Lesley Laing*

THE RESEARCH THAT informs this chapter explored the impact on offenders, mothers and victims of, participating in the NSW Pre-Trial Diversion Treatment Program (Laing 1996). The establishment of the program, the first of its kind in Australia, was one of the most controversial recommendations of the 1985 Child Sexual Assault Task Force. The program has a legislative base and involves a coordinated response by the criminal justice system and the NSW Department of Health. Incest offenders who plead guilty and are assessed as eligible by the treatment program are diverted from the criminal justice process to a two-year treatment program, but can be returned to the legal system if they breach the stringent conditions of program attendance.[1]

The research addressed the following questions:

- Does participating in the treatment program increase offenders' acceptance of responsibility and empathy for the harm caused?
- Do changes in the offender's stance regarding responsibility and empathy assist the victim and mother (and their relationship) to recover from the impact of the sexual assault?
- Is there a shift in the power relationships in the family?
- Are the victim's needs and safety given priority?

This chapter is confined largely to a discussion of the research question regarding the program's goal of changing the power balance in the family.

## A TRADITION OF MOTHER BLAME

Prior to the advent of modern feminism, incest was held to be a rare problem, attributed initially to the seductive behaviour of the child. Later, influenced by the developing family psychiatry movement, incest was increasingly attributed to 'family dysfunction', the key to which was maternal deficiency and culpability. The theme of maternal responsibility for incest was the dominant one in the psychiatric and family therapy literature that informed the helping professions in the 1960s and 1970s. For example:

> Despite the overt culpability of the fathers, we were impressed with their psychological passivity in the transactions leading to incest. The mother appeared the cornerstone in the pathological family system. (Lustig et al. 1966, p. 39)

The women are described in this literature in pejorative terms such as 'frigid', 'distant' and 'hostile and unloving', these deficits rendering them failures in both the maternal and wifely roles. The notion of the wife 'abandoning' her husband as a precipitant to incest is a strong theme, whether this abandonment involves failure sexually, gaining employment outside the home, being hospitalised for the birth of a child, being ill, or attempting to leave a violent partner. The abandoned father is seen, quite naturally, to turn to his daughter to meet his unfulfilled sexual and emotional needs.

When incest was 'rediscovered' as a common problem in the late 1970s, this body of literature was vigorously critiqued by feminist writers (e.g. Wattenburg 1985) who exposed its underlying sexist assumptions and its failure to hold the offender accountable for his criminal behaviour. The contribution of feminism was to allow the voices of victims and mothers to be heard, without being filtered through the lens of theories that distorted their experience in the search for either victim or maternal culpability (e.g. Ward 1984; Hooper 1992). For the first time, the offender was held totally accountable for sexual assault and for other abuses of power within the family.

Despite the role of feminism in bringing the extent of incest to light, the child protection and treatment literature that subsequently emerged (e.g. Giaretto 1982; Furniss 1991) continued to reflect the themes of the earlier 'family dysfunction' literature, albeit stated in slightly less pejorative terms. A central theme was the responsibility of the mother who was now described as 'psychologically absent' or 'failing to protect' (Sgroi 1982). A rhetoric of offender responsibility now entered the literature, but at best this was responsibility shared with his partner. Men who sexually assaulted their children were constructed in this therapeutic discourse as different from other sexual offenders against children: the role of sexual motivation in the offending was minimised (Conte 1985) and they were seen as less dangerous, more amenable to treatment, and less likely to reoffend than extra-familial offenders who were viewed as dangerous predators. Incest offenders were viewed as troubled men in dysfunctional families, the incest a symptom of this dysfunction for which their wives shared equal responsibility. Reconstitution of the family was the goal of intervention, as reflected in the name of the best known and most influential of these treatment programs, the 'Parents United' program developed by the Giarettos in California.

The confusion arising from the notion of shared parental responsibility for incest is nowhere more clearly highlighted than in the treatment concept of 'apology' sessions, which are presented in family treatment as a key method of addressing the issue of responsibility. Trepper and Barrett (1989, p. 47) describe the apology session at the completion of the initial stage of family therapy in this way:

> . . . the abusing father apologizes publicly to the entire family for the facts of the abuse, and verbally takes responsibility for it. The nonabusing mother apologizes for her part in the abuse; for example, *she might apologize for not encouraging the type of relationship with her daughter that would have allowed the girl to tell her* when the abuse was actually occurring. [emphasis added]

This approach completely fails to address the tactics by which sex offenders, whether intra-familial or extra-familial, target potential child victims, engage the child in sexual activity, and use psychological and/or physical coercion to ensure that the victim keeps the sexual abuse secret. There is now an extensive body of research that explores the 'modus operandi' of sexual offenders against children (e.g. Lang & Frenzel 1988; Conte et al. 1989; Rogers & Renshaw 1993). This research indicates that sex offenders target a potential victim and carefully plan the abuse. A common approach to initiating abuse is one in which the offender gains the child's trust and sensitises the child to non-sexual touching before almost imperceptibly initiating sexual touching, often with the first sexual touch presented as 'accidental'. Thus the child, through consent to non-sexual touching, has become a 'participant' even before it is clear that abuse is occurring. After initiating the abuse, offenders use a variety of tactics, including threats and force, to continue the abuse and to prevent the child disclosing.

This body of research about the tactics of sex offenders has not commonly been incorporated into incest treatment programs because of an emphasis on family dynamics and the construction of the incest offender as different from other sexual offenders against children. Although presented in much of the family therapy literature as less dangerous than extra-familial offenders, incest offenders in fact have access to many opportunities in their role of caregiver to subtly set the scene for initiating abuse. In addition, their intimate knowledge of the child's particular situation and vulnerabilities assists them in finetuning their tactics: parental power to grant privileges and punishments is a powerful weapon which can be turned to the secret purpose of ongoing manipulation and entrapment of their victim.

While abuse of power is central to a feminist analysis of sexual assault, incest treatment programs have typically paid scant attention to the offender's other abuses of power within the family, despite numerous studies finding that a considerable proportion of incest offenders are also physically violent to their partners and children. For example, Stermac et al. (1995) found evidence of both spouse and physical child abuse in 52.7 per cent of incest cases, and Goddard and Hiller (1993) identified domestic violence in the families of 40 per cent of cases of child sexual assault presenting to a Children's Hospital.

There is also a paucity of studies of the effectiveness of such treatment programs. In particular, outcomes for victims after reunification have been the subject of minimal study, with little evidence of positive benefit to the victims found in the few small available studies. For example, Matthews et al. (1991) followed up five families that had reunited after completing family treatment. In four of five cases, the parents perceived the victims as happier and better adjusted than the victims perceived themselves. In only two cases did the victims feel that their wishes regarding reunification had been considered and two victims felt that their negative views about reunification would have been ignored if they had voiced them.

## THE NSW PRE-TRIAL DIVERSION TREATMENT PROGRAM

The NSW program differs in several significant respects from other programs in its stated goals and underlying premises. For example, the program is based on the explicit premise that women are not responsible for their partners' abusive behaviour, and family reunification is rejected as the goal of the program (NSW Pre-Trial Diversion of Offenders Program n.d., p. 8). Rather, it is a child protection program that aims to prevent further sexual abuse. One stated goal is to change the power balance in the family. In these respects, the program could be held to reflect a feminist analysis of incest, in which abuse of power is a key element, as exemplified by Herman:

> As long as mothers and children are subordinate to the rule of fathers, such abuses will continue . . . When men no longer rule their families, they may learn for the first time what it means to belong to one. (1981, p. 218)

In the NSW program, the offender is required to 'face up' (Jenkins 1990) to family members about the behaviours ('tactics') by which he entrapped, abused and silenced the victim and deceived other family members. In this, the treatment program draws on current developments in sex offender treatment, rather than focusing on the hypothesised family dynamics in cases of incest.

## THE STUDY

The research sample comprised two years of presenting clients who were accepted into the program and who were prepared to participate in the research. This was in fact the majority of clients, with 14 of the 15 offenders who were assessed as eligible to enter the treatment program agreeing to participate in the research, together with 13 of their women partners. All but one couple were committed to continuing their relationship.[2] Quantitative and qualitative data were collected from offenders and mothers at three stages of the two-year program: intake, mid-treatment and treatment completion, the data collected at program intake providing a comparative baseline.

There were 15 victims in the study, 14 female and one male.[3] Average age of the children at the time the sexual abuse commenced was 10 years, with a range of 5 to 14 years. In three cases, the sexual assault occurred on one occasion only, and was disclosed immediately. In the remaining 12 cases, the duration of the sexual assaults ranged from six months to eight years, the average being three years. Using the severity of abuse classification system developed by Russell (1986) based on whether or not force was used and the degree of sexual violation involved, the majority (11) of the victims in the study experienced sexual abuse at the 'very severe' level; three at the 'severe' level; and one at the 'least severe' level. Two of the victims referred in their police statement to their knowledge of the offender's capacity for violence, and one had been subjected to serious physical abuse in addition to sexual assault. The majority (ten) of offenders were stepfathers, four were biological fathers and one an adoptive father.

Summarising very briefly some of the broader findings, the results demonstrated the difficulty and complexity of assessing whether treatment goals such as increasing offender responsibility and empathy have been achieved, and the need to use multiple measures and multiple sources of data. In particular, the victim's view of the extent of offender change is particularly important, as exemplified by one young woman whose stepfather completed the program, but whom she described as failing to develop genuine empathy for the harm he had caused:

> He knows how it's hurt people, but he doesn't know the feeling of hurt, like he's cried and everything to my mum and I, but it doesn't mean anything, it doesn't change anything.

She also described his sense of entitlement about rejoining the family, and was able to take a stand against family reunification as her therapy proceeded:

> . . . [we] were giving him a really big chance and I don't think he accepts it, he accepts it but he doesn't feel really grateful, like he thinks 'Oh, they should have done it anyway.'

Fifty per cent of the offenders successfully completed the treatment program, and 50 per cent were returned to the criminal justice system. The most common reasons for exclusion from the program were breaches of the treatment conditions relating to unauthorised contact with the victim or other children in the family, or unsatisfactory progress in treatment. This result is open to a number of different interpretations. On the one hand, it may appear that the program was not very successful, since only half of the men who passed a rigorous assessment of treatment suitability completed treatment. On the other hand, it can be argued that these results indicate that achieving genuine change in incest offenders may be more difficult than has been reported in the literature. The NSW treatment program is extremely rigorous in excluding from treatment men who do not demonstrate evidence of accepting responsibility. Compliance with treatment conditions regarding contact with children in the family is actively checked by surveillance staff. This level of monitoring of treatment compliance is unique in sex offender treatment and proved extremely effective in a number of cases in obtaining evidence of breaches of treatment conditions and returning the offender to the court.

## A DIFFICULT START TO CHALLENGING THE OFFENDERS' POWER

While power is central to a feminist analysis of incest, less has been written about ways in which the power imbalance may be redressed through treatment. Fish (1991, p. 240) suggests that, in order to do this, it is essential for the therapist to form an alliance with the mother:

> The willingness of the perpetrator to habitually abuse power is a prerequisite for the occurrence of incest. This habit of abuse of power does not disappear when the perpetrator enters treatment, but continues unabated. The therapist must assess and counter the perpetrator's misuse of power from the beginning for treatment to proceed. To do so, the therapist must form a coalition with the perpetrator's family, based on the therapist's empowerment and support of the mother.

However, at the start of treatment, the program faced considerable barriers to establishing such an alliance. One of these barriers was the power the treatment program had to affect the women's lives by returning their partners to the courts for sentencing. The women feared losing their homes and income should their partner be imprisoned. This is not a context that is readily conducive to the women sharing their concerns and difficulties, but rather one in which the program can easily be framed as 'the enemy' against which the man and his partner must unite to preserve the family.

Further barriers were associated with delays between disclosure of the abuse and referral to the program. Only two families entered the program during the 6–8 weeks acute crisis period following disclosure. Apart from one couple, the crisis precipitated by the disclosure had been resolved with a decision to continue the marital relationship, based on the man's version of the abuse and his reassurance that he would not reoffend. As a consequence, most couples entered treatment believing that the issues arising from the abuse had been largely resolved. Such a situation clearly served the interests of the offenders who had managed to convince their partners that they were reformed and honest, without revealing either the full details of the sexual abuse, or the tactics used to perpetrate it. However, when the treatment program challenged this reorganisation—for example, by requiring the man to tell his partner the full details of the sexual abuse—the program, rather than the offender, was in many cases held accountable for the distress and disruption that resulted. This was a context in which the offender was in a powerful position to offer his partner support and to encourage her to ally herself with him rather than with the treatment program.

Paradoxically, one of the program's approaches to reducing the offender's power over family members provided the men with a vehicle with which to encourage their partners to take sides against the program. Removing the offender rather than the victim from the home is a widely recommended intervention that is compatible with the treatment program's therapeutic goals of the offender assuming responsibility for the abuse, and shifting the power balance within the family:

> . . . removing the father rather than the daughter assigns responsibility for the incest in a very powerful way . . . Removing the father actually begins to change the structure of the family. It redefines the victim as a child and as someone with an inherent entitlement . . . to receive some measure of caretaking. (Gelinas 1988, p. 59)

However, in almost half the cases, the offender had been permitted by the police and child protection services to remain living in the home after disclosure, while the victim lived elsewhere. Even in the cases where the offender had been required to leave the home, he had been permitted to have contact with the siblings of the victim. Thus the treatment program's requirements that the offender leave the home and have no contact of any kind with other children in the family were more stringent than those imposed by the other agencies. These requirements were then understandably seen as unreasonable by many of the women. Their distress about enforced separation proved a further barrier to engaging the women in treatment: the program was forcing them to live as sole parents and, as their partners were quick to assure them, all would be resolved if only the program were not impeding their return home. Such a situation of conflict between the mothers and the treatment staff enabled the offenders to avoid being held accountable by their partners for the family disruption resulting from the sexual abuse.

## SHAPING THE MOTHER'S VIEW OF THE ABUSE

The data from the (separate) initial interviews with offenders and their partners attest to the challenge involved in addressing offender's ongoing abuse and manipulation of power, particularly their attempts to shape their partner's view of the abuse. In their initial interviews, the men were eager to assert their total responsibility for the sexual abuse, unsurprisingly as this was a condition of entry to the treatment program. They were prepared to comply with program requirements, despite believing that treatment was unnecessary as they would not reoffend. In contrast, many of their partners were in active conflict with the treatment program, portraying its requirements that their partners fully disclose the extent and nature of their offending, and that the offender move out of the home and have no contact with any children in the family, as unfair and oppressive. Allied with their partner against the program and, in 50 per cent of cases, estranged from and angry with their victim children, it would be understandable to view them as 'collusive' mothers who were prepared to sacrifice their children for their relationship with the offender.

However, the offenders' apparent acceptance of responsibility was soon revealed to be quite superficial. Through their discussions about the sexual abuse and its impact, the men revealed that they were involved in a process of actively attributing responsibility for the abuse to other people—most commonly the victim and at times their partner—and to other factors such as alcohol or stress. Blaming the victim for encouraging, initiating or enjoying the sexual contact was a theme in the explanations for the abuse of over half the offenders. In fact, agreeing to plead guilty and claiming to accept responsibility for the abuse did not mean that the offenders were acknowledging the entirety of their victims' allegations. In half the cases there were discrepancies between the victims' accounts of what had occurred, and the accounts of the offenders in their interviews at program intake. They actively disputed their victims' accounts of the duration of the abuse, the extent of the sexual behaviours involved, and of their use of threats and force (despite both physical and psychological coercion being reported clearly in the victims' police statements). However, because of program entry requirements, some men explained that they were not disagreeing with the victim's account in their interviews with treatment staff. For example:

> I can't remember the details of what I did but I couldn't have got her pregnant, though I'll agree with anything that she says.
>
> [She] says a couple of times I came into her bedroom and pulled her out of bed. I don't remember, but it must have happened . . . I can't recall, but I won't argue.

Some offenders indicated that they admitted only as much as they had to, particularly where their partner was concerned. It appears that some men admitted aspects of the abuse to the police or the treatment staff but avoided revealing this to their partner until she would have discovered it anyway. For example:

> At disclosure [my wife] didn't know the full extent of it . . . it was only months later that I admitted it totally.

During that period of months, his partner had decided to reunite and as a consequence was estranged from her daughter. Another man explained that he was saying one thing to the treatment program, and another to his wife:

> I have to plead guilty to get into the program, but I don't agree with all that [victim] says. I told my wife it's not all true.

Thus, while claiming to be honest and reformed, the men were in fact carefully controlling the information they shared with their partners about the abuse, including the extent of the sexual behaviours involved, and in particular omitting the tactics by which they had perpetrated the abuse and deceived their partners. The vulnerability of the mothers to the offenders' accounts had several bases. They reported that their lives had been shattered by the disclosure of incest, and sought to make sense of how this could have happened. Often isolated by shame from friends and family, the women reported that their main (often sole) support was their partner, who was remorseful, supportive, ready to help her understand what had happened and committed to rebuilding their relationship. This placed the offender in a very powerful position to shape his partner's perceptions about the abuse, including the victim's role in it.

Notable also was the report by the women that there was minimal mother–victim discussion about the abuse (even in cases where the mother and victim were not separated or estranged). The silence between mothers and victims left the stage free for the offender to shape the mother's perception of events, and this was reflected in the way the women's explanations for the incest tended to mirror the explanations given by their partners. As the initial interviews revealed, many of the men were painting a picture of the victim as a willing participant in the sexual contact. Such assertions can be expected to have a devastating impact on the mother–victim relationship.

## MAKING TACTICS TRANSPARENT

The treatment approach of requiring the offender to 'face up' about the tactics of abuse is an important way in which the program attempts to counter the offender's power within the family. At intake, the men were shown to be actively resisting participating in this process but, by mid-treatment, the men who continued in the program now described in detail the extensive array of tactics by which they had planned and implemented the sexual abuse and attempted to avoid detection. These tactics included dividing mother and victim, creating opportunities to be alone with the child, making the child feel complicit, giving money and presents, reminding the child of the consequences of disclosure, being hard on the child to avert suspicion or, alternatively, showing favour-itism to the child, actively interrupting attempted disclosures and exploiting the child's curiosity about sex.

The most common tactic acknowledged by the men was that of dividing mother and victim. The power of this tactic lies in the isolation of the victim from her most likely ally, thus lessening the possibility that the child will disclose, or, if disclosure does occur, making it less likely that the child will be believed by her mother (Laing & Kamsler 1990). Offenders gave some examples of how they had gone about this:

> By manipulating my wife's thoughts towards [victim], that she was the problem, trying to drive a very big wedge between my

wife and daughter, so that my wife's feelings for her [victim] were negligible, and if she [victim] had said anything anyway she wouldn't be believed and she wouldn't take any notice of her feelings, so she [victim] wouldn't turn to her mother anyway.

[Victim's] trust was totally broken, she believed her mother knew what was going on. I was very clever in the way that I used to get my wife to tell [victim] to give me cuddles and all that sort of thing, so I manipulated my wife to break that bond.

Making the child feel complicit was another effective way of ensuring the victim's silence, because it promoted the victim's sense of responsibility and guilt about the abuse:

And you'd draw her into it with saying: 'If I ever try to do it again, just say no' and this sort of thing, so you're making her part of it, it's her responsibility now, it's not for me to stop it, it's for her to stop me.

It'd be the things I'd say to her to make her feel that she was part of the abuse, like 'we shouldn't have done it', to make her feel more part of it. 'We' being the word, rather than I shouldn't do this to you, making her feel as if she was taking as great a part as I was.

When offenders disclosed the tactics by which they had implemented and covered up the abuse, their partners reported experiencing a second crisis, perhaps more devastating than the one precipitated by disclosure, as they had to face the fact that their partners, despite their claims to honesty, had continued to deceive them for many months after disclosure, continuing into treatment. However, they reported that from this painful process they came to understand better, or in some cases for the first time, the suffering and entrapment of their victimised children. Importantly, once the offender made transparent to his partner the particular tactics by which he perpetrated the abuse, entrapped the victim, deceived her and contrived to keep the abuse secret, his power to divide mother and victim was diminished.

Three of the women reported that, from understanding the offender's tactics, they began to wonder whether their daughters had thought they knew about the abuse. When they asked their daughters and found that this was so, they were able to resolve this divisive issue with them, and begin to rebuild their relationship:

He had said all along, 'I always made sure you were in the house' . . . and then sort of I think, gee, [daughter] must have been under a funny impression if I was always there, and then I checked with her and said 'did you think I knew because I was always there?' and she said 'yes'.

Another impact of understanding the tactics used to abuse their children was the lifting of the women's feelings of guilt and responsibility for the abuse:

But in the beginning you do blame yourself. You feel guilty, but you know as it goes on that there's no way you could have known, because of the way it was done.

Once fully in the picture about the way in which the offender had set up and concealed the abuse, several women were able to acknowledge that, until that point, they had harboured fears about the victim's complicity. However, in a number of cases, the offender's tardiness in fully facing up to his partner about the tactics of abuse meant that any opportunity for mother and daughter to 'debrief' about the impact of the abuse and accompanying tactics on their relationship was lost—for example, where the daughter had left home and refused to have any contact with her mother.

One finding from the mid-treatment offender interviews was that in many cases the division of mother and victim had continued beyond disclosure and well into treatment. An example of this continuing division was provided by two of the men who described how they had used their victim's difficult behaviour after disclosure to continue separating mother and child. While they were solicitous about their wives' difficulties in managing adolescents in rebellion, they took many months to admit to their partners that the girls were in fact reacting to the particular tactics they had employed to divide mother and daughter. In one case the offender had told the victim, during each episode of abuse, that the abuse was the mother's fault. When he faced up to his partner about this, she understood why her daughter was so angry with her, and was able to begin to rebuild a relationship with her.

The data from the mid-treatment interviews further suggest that, in addition to continuing to divide mother and victim after disclosure, some offenders employed similar tactics of division (in which they are highly skilled) between the program and their partners. The benefit for the man of fostering such division is that he appears to be cooperating with treatment and avoids return to the criminal justice system, while avoiding fully facing up to his partner and risking losing her commitment to the relationship.

Dividing partner and program took a number of forms. One was for the offender to admit more to the treatment program than to his partner, a process described by several of the men. Another involved encouraging their partner's disaffection with the program, and discouraging their participation. When a cooperative working relationship is not established between the program and the mother, the offender can play a 'double game' and avoid fully facing up. The dividing of partner and treatment program also has implications for the victim, since the mother is less likely to encourage the victim's participation in therapy if her view of the program is negative. This provides the offender with another layer of protection against discovery of any remaining 'gaps' in his facing up, since the victim is the only other person who can testify to what occurred.

## SOME EVIDENCE OF A SHIFT IN POWER

The importance of countering the father's orchestration of power within the family is reflected in the end-of-treatment interviews with four of the young women who had been victimised, and their mothers. Looking back, the young women described their relationship with their mothers at the beginning of the program in terms of feeling blamed, and thinking that their mother must have known of the abuse:

> She just couldn't understand what had gone on and whose fault it really was and things like that . . . She didn't blame me directly, she didn't blame me, but she sort of implied that I had something to do with it you know, 'cause I hadn't told earlier.

> Like I just thought she wasn't a caring mother, she could have seen what he was doing, and therefore I couldn't talk to her, I couldn't face her with it.

In contrast, at the completion of the program, these mothers and victims described lives free of guilt and blame and closer mother–daughter relationships once the offenders' tactics had been made transparent and could no longer divide them.

> *Daughter:* When I went to the program I realised how he was hiding it and how he was being so awful to her that she couldn't

see anything, she could only see him because he was the main figure in the household, and everyone else just had to do things for him.

*Mother:* I still don't forgive [offender] for that [harm to the mother–daughter relationship]. That hurt me more than the actual abuse, I just don't know how he could have done it. That hurts, that still hurts me, what he did to our relationship, how he manipulated both of us. Once I realised how he went about it, how it was his fault that he did it and how he did do it, and the things he's put [victim] through as well, my God! Once I'd realised, that was my main aim, for my daughter and I [to] get our relationship back again.

The women and their daughters also reported other changes at the end of treatment which reflected a shift in the power relationships in the family. In contrast to the situation at the start of treatment when none of the women believed that she could cope while living apart from her husband, at the end of treatment they reported increased independence, and a reassessment of their power within the marriage. For example:

To put it bluntly, I was like a doormat to him.

Each of the four young women who participated in interviews at the end of treatment agreed that their mother was stronger, and had greater power in the relationship with the offender. For example:

She's much more her own person now whereas when dad was home she sort of did whatever dad said, she's like, got her own personality now.

## CONCLUSION

In cases where the offender completed the treatment program, some evidence was found in the interviews with mothers and victims of a reduction of the offender's power within the family. The nature of this power shift was powerfully summed-up by one of the women in her final interview:

See he knows he is no longer the ruler of the roost . . . he just knows that things aren't the way they were before, it's a different balance altogether.

However, the frequency with which the offenders were found to flout the most overt and concrete limitation to their power—the requirement that they move out of the home and the limitation on their contact with children in the family—suggests that their more covert abuses of power may be more extensive than have yet been identified. What does emerge clearly from this study is that the use of a treatment framework that focuses on the offender's accountability for the abuse, the accompanying tactics and his ongoing abuse of power provides an alternative view of the 'unsupportive' mother of the incest victim—as someone who is a victim of the offender's continuing use of the tactics of power and control. When the offender's abuse of power is challenged, and his tactics of abuse, silencing and division, are made transparent, new possibilities open up for rebuilding the relationship between victims and their mothers.

# 9 | Truth or fiction: men as victims of domestic violence?

## Kerrie James

ARE MEN HIDDEN victims of domestic violence? Over the past few years, a number of men have claimed to be victims of physical abuse perpetrated by their wives. The head of the Lone Fathers' Association was recently quoted as expressing relief that men are speaking out against being abused by their wives and from being excluded from receiving domestic violence services (Matheson 1996). Other claims have been made that the Australian Bureau of Statistics and the Office for the Status of Women have falsified and suppressed statistics that would otherwise have shown the 'true' extent of women's violence towards their male partners (Coochey 1995).

Government programs and health professionals, however, primarily view domestic violence as male violence perpetrated on a female partner and supportive services have been established for female victims of husband abuse. Male perpetrators, on the other hand, have experienced more organised and consistent intervention from the criminal justice system and therapeutic services aimed at decreasing their violence (see Chapter 16). Family therapists have also become more attuned to male violence against women. In many agencies, clear protocols for responding to domestic violence have been developed so that issues of women's safety and empowerment are addressed. No similar protocols and services exist for men who are victims of women's violence. It is no surprise, then, that when men claim to be victims of their wives' violence therapists are often suspicious, confused and unsure how to proceed. In particular, it is difficult for therapists to know whether or not such claims are legitimate; whether women's violence is the same as men's; and whether theories and interventions developed for male perpetrators are appropriate when applied to female perpetrators.

## ARE MEN'S CLAIMS OF FEMALE VIOLENCE LEGITIMATE?

How common is women's violence towards men? More common than most therapists believe. Surveys conducted in the United States during the 1970s and 1980s that examined the incidence of physical aggression in heterosexual relationships showed that men and women perpetrated violence at roughly the same rate. A study of 199 military couples found that, in 83 per cent of the couples, both husband and wife were physically assaultive (Langhinrichsen-Rohling et al. 1995). In a sample of engaged couples, 41 per cent of the women and 34 per cent of the men reported engaging in physical aggression against their partners in the year prior to the research (O'Leary et al. 1989). In reviewing 30 studies concerning the incidence of violence, Strauss concluded that the rate of assault by women on male partners is about the same as the rate of assault of men on female partners (Strauss 1993).

Strauss and Gelles developed the measure most used to ascertain rates of violence: the Conflict Tactics Scale (Strauss et al. 1980). In the most-quoted study, Strauss et al. used the scale to ascertain a range of physically violent acts. In samples of over 2000 couples in 1975 and over 6000 couples in 1985, they found that, in half, the abuse was mutual. They concluded that 'the resulting overall rate for assaults by wives is 124 per 1000 couples, compared with 122 per 1000 for assaults by husbands as reported by wives' (Strauss 1993, pp. 68–69). Severe violence was classified as kicking, hitting with an object, and assaults with a knife or gun. Strauss concluded that, in 1980, 3.8 men per 1000 couples were severely violent, and that 4.6 women per 1000 couples were severely violent (Flynn 1990; Campbell 1993).

While men's violence in the home towards women appears to occur at the same rate as men's violence outside the home (e.g. robbery, street gangs, organised crime, rape), women's violence is relatively non-existent in the wider community. As

Campbell (1993, p. 103) has stated: 'of all the forms of criminal violence, it is only those committed in the privacy of the home that do not show the usual marked gender differences.'

## IS WOMEN'S VIOLENCE EQUIVALENT TO MEN'S?

When researchers measure only physically violent acts and do not examine contextual factors, it is assumed that husbands and wives are engaging in comparable behaviours. What is often not taken into consideration is the use of other forms of violence (marital rape, verbal abuse, financial deprivation, threats and intimidation); the degree of severity of violence; the effect of violence on the victim; and the different motivations of men and women in perpetrating violence (Flynn 1990; McGregor 1990a).

When more closely examined, it becomes apparent that women's violence is not equivalent to men's violence in the following ways:

- Men's violence is more severe.
- Women's violence is often a response to frustration and stress, whereas men's violence is most often an attempt to dominate and control.
- Women's violence is more likely to occur in self-defence.
- Women's violence is often a reflection of dependence, whereas men's violence is a reflection of dominance.

### Comparing severity of violence

While it is true that earlier studies found men and women to be equally violent in terms of the acts perpetrated, the outcome or the effects of these specific violent acts were never examined. As Gelles himself has said: 'although men's and women's violence was recorded as equal, one would expect that if a 280lb 6ft 5in husband pushes his 5ft 4in, 120lb wife, he would do more damage than she' (Gelles 1979, p. 139).

When Strauss (1993) reanalysed data from the National Violence Survey of 1985, he found that, although men and women had been equally violent, men were six times more likely to inflict severe injury. Other studies have shown that male aggression towards females is more coercive and controlling than female aggression towards males, even when the severity of violence is the same (Cascardi & Vivian 1995).

At first glance it is hard to imagine that men's violence could be any more serious than the woman's violence described in the following excerpt. In Scutt's study of 125 couples, women were:

> more likely than men to throw things or use weapons. They were likely to hit men in the chest, punch, push, shove or kick a man in the shins. The husbands were slapped with an open hand or hit with hands; beaten with fists; kicked, scratched and beaten; had their hair pulled, hit with objects, including a fry pan, saucepan, skillet, brooms, mugs, an ashtray and a squeeze mop. Three were threatened with a kitchen knife, two had crockery thrown at them; one was poked with a peeling knife. One was pushed downstairs and one had a pannikin of hot, soapy water from the washing machine thrown over him. (Scutt 1983, p. 104)

It is salutary, then, to read Scutt's account of what women *did not do* (but which constituted tactics frequently employed by the violent men):

> . . . no woman punched her husband about the head and shoulders, or in the stomach. Punches were aimed at the chest. No husband was attacked in the groin. No wife directed punches so injuries would not show; nor did wives say this is what they would do . . . No husband was threatened with a gun, or chased with guns, knives, axes, broken bottles or by a car. Husbands were not kicked or stamped on with steel capped boots or heavy work boots; no husband was 'driven furiously' in the family car, nor was any tossed out at traffic lights. None was pushed against a wall or flung across a room; they were not held down in threatening positions, or against the wall unable to move. Strangling and choking were not used. No wife attempted suffocation with a pillow. Husbands were not locked out, confined to particular areas of the house, or isolated from friends, nor were any given ultimatums about time spent away from home shopping . . . No husband had arms twisted and fingers bent, none was frog marched out to the garden to hose, dig or mow the lawn. None was ordered to weed the garden whilst being kicked from the rear. Nor was any husband dragged out of bed at midnight to change the washer on the kitchen tap. (Scutt 1983, p. 105)

What is apparent from Scutt's description is that, whilst women may be capable of serious violence, men's violence is more humiliating, controlling and coercive. A woman's violence emanates from, and may be a refusal to accept, her less powerful position.

A man's violence, on the other hand, emanates from, and may be a way of asserting, his position of dominance.

## Women's violence as a response to frustration and stress

Unlike men's violence, women's violence is frequently a response to frustration and stress, resulting from pressure and isolation inherent in women's role in the family. Qualitative research has shown that women use aggression to let off steam and do so at the point of greatest stress or frustration (Campbell 1993). Women perceive their own anger and aggression as loss of control and as an expression of powerlessness in being able to effect change in their partner. In other words, women's aggression is expressive rather than instrumental or purposive.

It is because men's violence is generally instrumental that they frequently misinterpret their wives' expressive aggression as an attempt to control them (Campbell 1993). Men who are violent in relationships have usually learned to use aggression as a way of asserting dominance and control in their peer culture. A man's intention in using violence is most often to control the external source of his internal stress—that is, his partner. By generating a high degree of fear in his partner, he can then maintain dominance through the use of verbal abuse and intimidation.

> The point of men's instrumental aggression is not to signal emotional upset or to let off steam but to control the behaviour of another person, and this can be done effectively when anger does not get in the way. Men's strategic use of aggression as a means of instilling fear and gaining power finds its most sinister expressions in the exclusively male crime of rape and the predominantly male crime of robbery, both of which nearly always demand an aggressor who feels no anger toward the target of his violence. (Campbell 1993, p. 72)

In fact, it has been found that the most violent of men decrease their metabolic rate and calm themselves down during arguments with their spouses (Jacobson et al. 1994).

Even though men and women used violence equally in relationships, where women are not stressed their level of violence is 50 per cent that of their husbands. When women *are* stressed, their level of violence is 150 per cent that of men (Campbell 1993). Because women are socialised not to express anger, women are more likely to hold in anger until they are overwhelmed with rage. Then, their violence is explosive, hurting anyone in sight, and frequently involves throwing things, hitting and shoving.

Despite its explosive nature, men are often not afraid of women's violence and may mock and laugh at their wives' aggression (Campbell 1993; Jacobson et al. 1994). Women, however, do fear male violence. Apparently, it is clear to many men that they are ultimately in control, even when their wives are violent (Jacobson et al. 1994). While violent women experience themselves as out of control, violent men experience themselves as asserting ultimate control over their partners.

## Women's violence is in self-defence

Women's violence is more likely than men's to occur in self-defence within relationships where the partner is also violent (Saunders 1988). In comparing how often women used violence against abusive versus non-abusive husbands, Walker (1984, in Saunders 1988) found that, with abusive husbands, 23 per cent of women used physical force, while only 4 per cent of women used physical force with non-abusive husbands.

A study of women who killed their husbands revealed that there was a history of marital violence in 70 per cent of the cases, and that over half of husband killings occurred in response to an immediate threat or attack by the men (Ho & Venus 1995). Although a history of marital violence may lead to the killing of either spouse, men's and women's motivations differ. Marital separation and sexual jealousy are significant precipitants for men who kill their female partners. These factors are not precipitants for women, however, who are more likely to kill their husbands to obtain release from a lifelong prison of violence (Ho & Venus 1995).

Jacobson et al. (1994) studied couples where husbands were severely violent and found that a majority of women used violence in response to their husband's violence towards them. Frequently, women fought back or used what Saunders (1988, p. 107) has called a 'pre-emptive strike' in an effort to ward off another attack. The women's violence, however, continued only so long as their partners continued to be violent. On the other hand, the men continued their violence regardless of their partner's response, be it withdrawing, placating or violence. In other words, no matter what the women did, they were powerless in influencing their partners to stop the violence once it had begun (Jacobson et al. 1994).[1]

These same violent men and their partners were also observed during a non-violent interaction when they discussed a highly stressful or difficult issue in their relationship. In this situation, both the men and the women were angry and they equally showed belligerence and contempt. The women, however, also showed fear and sadness whereas the men did not. According to both partners, the women were not belligerent or contemptuous during actual violent incidences, but only during the non-violent interaction. This study sheds light on claims that some women provoke violence by being verbally abusive. It appears that women who perceive their partners behaving in a threatening or belligerent manner are more likely to withdraw or placate than to attack verbally.

One can conclude that, when their male partners are violent, a small minority of women will also resort to violence in order to retaliate or in an effort to defend themselves or their children.

## Male dominance and female dependence

Women's violence occurs in a society in which men hold the major positions of power. When women earn less money than men and are financially dependent on male partners, they are often trapped in abusive relationships because of emotional and material ties. Few men are so materially dependent that they cannot leave an abusive spouse. While they may choose not to do so, they are more likely to experience having the option to leave.

In contrast to women's socialisation, which discourages their expression of aggression, boys and young men are socialised to accept aggression as a way of maintaining dominance and control within peer groups (Campbell 1993). Families, schools and peer cultures inculcate in boys fear and discomfort about showing vulnerability and teach them to react with anger to feelings of hurt or humiliation. Aggressive women are seen as 'unfeminine'; aggressive men are seen as 'manly'. Men's violence, therefore, is buttressed by a culture which has traditionally sanctioned male dominance in both public and private spheres. Women's violence, however, is more akin to the risky violence of the oppressed as they make a claim for self-determination.

In conclusion, in comparing men's and women's violence, men's violence induces more fear in its victims and is capable of causing more extensive injury. Women's violence is expressive, a response to frustration and stress, particularly in situations where male partners are not violent. When men are also violent, women's violence is frequently in self-defence, and will, in most instances, result in increased violence from husbands. Finally, women's violence must be understood in the context of their subordinate status relative to men (i.e. their position as wives and mothers) and their lesser income and career opportunities. Men's violence, on the other hand, occurs in the context of their dominant position in society, which requires them to be stoical, in control, head of the family and not afraid to use aggression.

## IMPLICATIONS FOR PRACTICE

Given that women's violence is not the same as men's violence, how applicable to women are the policies and practices that therapists have developed in response to men's violence? In relation to women's violence, therapists must first distinguish between two possibilities:

1. that a woman's violence occurs in self-defence or retaliation and that she lives in fear of her partner's violence;
2. that a woman is violent towards a partner who is not dangerous and whom she does not fear. Instead, she may be belittling and contemptuous towards him.

In the former case, a woman's violence towards her violent partner puts her at an ever-increasing risk. Studies have shown that the man's violence increases in intensity and severity when the woman uses violence in self-defence or to fight back (Saunders 1988; Strauss 1993; Jacobson et al. 1994). Goldner (1994) emphasises the importance of assisting women to take responsibility for their own safety. This may involve encouraging women who are responding in self-defence to desist from violent behaviour, with the aim of decreasing the risk of their partner's retaliatory and increasingly severe abuse. It is also important to explore other ways of promoting a woman's safety: by encouraging her to obtain and invoke a Protection Order; to leave the relationship and/or their joint residence; if she is committed to staying in the relationship and her partner is trying to change, to help her accept her partner's need for 'time out' as a strategy he needs to use in learning to take responsibility for his violence (Goldner 1994). In this way, therapists can assist women to put safety before protest, and to achieve empowerment through more effective options. In assisting women not to respond violently, therapists need to be alert to the ambivalence that some women will experience when, by ceasing violent behaviours, they lose their only form of protest and retribution.

In the latter case of women who are violent towards their non-violent husbands, it is important that therapists take a position against violence just as they would with a violent man. A woman's violence may victimise and oppress her partner, even if in other respects he is in a more advantageous position. While some men minimise their wives' violence, those who seek counselling are usually distressed and want the violence to stop. In therapy, women's violence should not be condoned, regardless of how 'understandable' it is. Therapists should fully explore and acknowledge the man's experience, encourage him to use legal sanctions to protect himself and his children and help him leave the relationship and/or residence, if necessary.

In confronting a woman's violence, her level of stress, frustration and distress needs to be explored and acknowledged. It is important that her violence not be minimised. To do so would not only be a disservice to her partner and children, but a disservice to the woman herself, whose depth of rage goes unrecognised and unacknowledged. Therapy needs to address the perceived inequities in roles and responsibilities that often underlie a woman's anger and sense of injustice. Addressing her violence in this way does not become a substitute for her taking responsibility for her behaviour and for handling distress differently. Making reparation to those she has hurt is an important part of healing, both for herself and significant others. In working with women's violence, therapists must be able to contain within themselves the tension between exploring and understanding violence, while not condoning it.

In conclusion, whilst it is true that women can be violent and that women's violence can constitute a problem for their male partners, it is a fiction that their violence is equivalent to men's in intent, frequency, severity or outcome. Women's violence is a reality that needs to be acknowledged. This acknowledgment, however, should not be used to obscure another reality: that *more* women are victims of men's severe and repetitive violence, and are therefore at greater risk. As Strauss puts it:

Although women may assault their partners at approximately the same rate as men assault theirs, because of the greater physical, financial and emotional injuries suffered, women are the predominant victims. Consequently, the first priority in services for victims and prevention and control must continue to be directed towards assault by husbands. (Strauss 1983, p. 80)

The significant differences between men's and women's violence give us much greater cause to be more concerned about men's violence towards women than women's violence towards men, and legitimises current social policy direction and priority.

# 10 A forgotten group: working with adolescent survivors of sexual assault

*Jane Hutton*

EXPERIENCES OF ABUSE recruit young women into feelings of self-blame, self-hatred, mistrust and fear and into practices of self-abuse, isolation and secrecy. Dominant cultural discourses can act to reinforce these negative stories. This chapter describes some ways of working which have proved useful in my practice with this client group, drawing on the narrative approach to therapy. Issues in engaging adolescent clients, common themes that arise in therapy and approaches to addressing these within a narrative therapy framework are described. Brief reference is also made to work involving non-offending family members.

The first young woman who disclosed her story of abuse to me amazed me with her ability to share her experience and at the same time keep alive her sense of vitality and humour despite the effects of the abuse on her life. I felt overwhelmed with a sense of responsibility to connect with this young woman in a respectful way, a way that challenged her understandable doubt and mistrust of adults' motives. It was a struggle to be helpful, to challenge the beliefs about the abuse that stood in the way of her escaping its effects and to ensure that she experienced feeling heard, believed, and not blamed for what had happened. I felt I needed to stick by her through all her struggles, to support her in the painful process of working through the issues, and to create a sense of safety that would allow her to experience trust and undo some of the damage done by the abuse. I found myself feeling guilty and worried when I took leave and, when positive change occurred in her life, I always noticed it first. I remember the disbelief she expressed when I noticed positive developments in her life and the anger and sense of abandonment she experienced when I suggested making appointments less frequent as a result of these changes.

Around this time I became interested in the ideas of narrative therapy and started to wonder if my beliefs about therapy and abuse were restraints to change. I began to question the assumptions that child sexual abuse results in permanent damage and that my role was to find a solution and provide endless supplies of trust and nurturance. I began to make sense of my feelings of exhaustion and over-responsibility and my client's disconnection from her strengths within this restraining context of beliefs. I looked for ways to refocus the direction of my conversations with young women in this situation, towards inviting them to make new preferred meanings of their experience of self, instead of trying to convince them of mine. This focus invited information about how they had kept their hope and optimism alive, how they had rebelled against being recruited into self-blame, and what their survival told them about their strengths and resources.

Whilst it was a struggle to stick to this new way of thinking and interviewing and there were many temptations to give in to over-responsibility, I felt a sense of relief that I was not required to persuade these young women of anything, merely to invite them with questions to review their stories and assess whether these stories suited them or not. I was able to show my interest, support and caring without feeling responsible for the decisions and actions of these young women.

## THE NARRATIVE PERSPECTIVE

Gerald Monk (1997, p. 3) uses the analogy of archaeology to describe the task of the narrative therapist, suggesting that the therapist requires all the persistence and deliberation of the archaeologist to uncover and reconstruct a story located within a culture, albeit a living breathing one.

> With meticulous care and precision, the archaeologist brushes ever so gently over the landscape . . . With careful movements, she exposes a remnant, and with further exploration, others soon

appear. Disconnected fragments are identified and pieced together as the search continues. With a careful eye for the partially visible, the archaeologist begins to reassemble the pieces. An account of events in the life of the remains is constructed, and meaning emerges from what was otherwise a mere undulation in the landscape.

Whilst the narrative therapist is engaged in a process of investigating preferred stories, this is an act of collaboration with the client who is invited to participate actively in the identification of strengths and resources and whose knowledge and preferences are considered paramount. In the context of working with young women who have experienced childhood sexual abuse, these ideas provide a useful framework for understanding and challenging the oppressive beliefs and ways of being that are problematic for them, and for exploring the ways in which they have been recruited into these ideas and practices. It invites us to take an approach that is respectful and empowering of the young woman and challenging of the problem.

## DOMINANT DISCOURSES ABOUT ADOLESCENTS, WOMEN AND SURVIVORS OF ABUSE

When working with young women and exploring the dominant stories they have about themselves, their sexuality and their experience of abuse, it is important to have an awareness of our culture's dominant discourses or stories about adolescents, women and abuse.

### Adolescents

When I ask groups of therapists in training to brainstorm our society's dominant stories about adolescents, the story that emerges is overwhelmingly negative. The perception is that adolescents are difficult, disrespectful, rebellious, unsure, not knowing their own minds, threatening, sceptical of adults, irresponsible, untrustworthy, and sexually promiscuous. Adolescents are seen to be under the influence of peers and incapable of knowing what is best for them, unwilling to listen to or respect adults' knowledge or authority. At the same time there is another discourse running alongside this one that says this is the best time of one's life—that to be young, beautiful, carefree and idealistic is the only way to be. Adolescence is seen as a transitional time, with the negotiation of this transition being crucial to the success of the rest of one's life. Not achieving success in education and career choices at this time is seen to be setting the young person on a course of failure.

This discourse invites a negative or an idealised view of adolescents and can have the effect of putting distance and misunderstanding between young people and adults. It also puts pressure on adolescents and parents to 'get it right' or regret it, which can invite escalation of conflicts and polarisation. We need to be aware of the impact of this discourse on the young people we work with and the extent to which it has been internalised by us or them. The discourse limits the options that are available to young people and can have the effect of disconnecting them from their own voice and preferences.

## Women

The dominant discourse of women in our culture has described women as gentle nurturers and sex goddesses who exist to meet the needs of men and children, responsible for keeping them on track, or, conversely, responsible for tempting men with the evils of sex. Either way they hold a burden of emotional and moral responsibility for others. There is a pressure to be silent, to avoid expressing opinions and to maintain loyalty to family. Requirements are to be overtly sexy without expressing or acknowledging their sexual feelings and desires. Women are seen to be experts around the area of food, the provision of it to others on the home front, while at the same time thinner is better.

## Survivors of sexual abuse

A number of discourses about survivors of abuse exist in our culture. One is that they are damaged for life, unable to function, have relationships, or ever get over the assaults. Another is that they either made up the abuse, or perhaps even asked for it, or liked it. Yet another paints them as attention seekers who should get over it and get on with life, that surely it couldn't be as bad as they make out. These discourses describe them as dependent women, who are frightening and overwhelming in their needs. Another discourse invites doubt about their trustworthiness—people who are abused go on to abuse.

Many of the young women with whom we work following abuse will have internalised at least some of these discourses. In addition to the dominant cultural story, there is also the story promoted by the abuser about the young woman and the reasons for the abuse. These stories are characterised by the need for secrecy; the idea that the young woman is at fault and deserving of the abuse, either through wanting the abuse or being bad; and the idea that no-one would believe her if she did tell. Sometimes abusers promote the story that the abuse is in fact a special secret, a special game, and it is a sign of love and affection for the young person. Recruitment into this story can involve bribes, rewards, and special treatment as well as threats and intimidation. Whilst adolescents are still vulnerable to this kind of trickery, it is often at this time that they begin to challenge the idea that what is happening is special or indeed normal. Many young women report that it is the abuser's threats that coerce them into maintaining secrecy, whilst for others the power of the abuser's story is enough.

Amanda Kamsler (1990) discusses the influence of these oppressive stories, authored by the perpetrator, on the self-perception of women who were abused as children, describing the ways in which these women are recruited into strong gender stereotypical behaviour, not only in their relationship with the perpetrator, but also with others. These stories are reflected in the themes that commonly arise in therapy, and contribute to the particular challenges involved in engaging in the counselling process young women who have experienced abuse.

## GETTING STARTED

Sometimes sexual abuse is the presenting issue with young people, while at other times it emerges through the process of counselling for other issues, such as practices of self-abuse. Either way the process of engaging the young person in a therapeutic relationship can be difficult. Abuse recruits people into mistrust of others, a fear of not being believed and of being blamed and it is necessary to challenge these beliefs and invite the possibility of an alternative story before therapy can progress. We can only start where the young person is ready to start.

Notification can be an issue at this stage or later in therapy and I prefer to be transparent about my responsibilities in this area. Differences in legislation between States affect the responsibilities of practitioners and the likelihood of intervention by statutory child protection services with young people between 16 and 18 years of age. With young women under the age of 16,

I explain that all current abuse will be notified to the relevant authorities and that I will involve them in this process and allow them to maintain as much control as is possible. Over the age of 16, there may be the dilemma of not being able to notify and facing the idea that if a young person chooses not to proceed legally against their abuser we may be working with them in the knowledge that the abuse continues. Whilst this is difficult and anxiety-provoking for the counsellor, in my experience a respectful choice is to support the young person, continually increase their knowledge and understanding of their rights and options for action and challenge the restraints against that action through the process of therapy.

Trust is vital for therapy to progress. I communicate my assumption that lack of trust can be one effect of abuse and invite the young person to be cautious and to make their own judgements about my trustworthiness through the performance of trust tests. Exploring recruitment into lack of trust and unique outcomes around trust can be useful. Sharing the ideas and experiences of other young people with the invitation to compare if that matches, rather than making assumptions that we know how this person will feel, communicates respect and the belief that it is the young person who is the expert rather than the therapist.

Listening is important for engaging and establishing trust. It is also important to raise possible thoughts and feelings that the young person may be restrained by fear from saying aloud; to allow space for the young person to tell their story; and to ask them to reflect on how much they feel comfortable in sharing. Listening with an externalising ear is useful at this time, reflecting back the dominant problem story in an externalised way. For example:

| | |
|---|---|
| *Therapist:* | What have been some of the effects of the abuse on your life? |
| *Client:* | I feel really bad about myself, like there must be something wrong with me, I feel like the abuse was my fault, I should have stopped it. |
| *Therapist:* | So the self-blame really pushes you around and gives you a hard time? |
| *Client:* | Oh yes. |
| *Therapist:* | What other sorts of things does self-blame get you thinking or feeling? |

If the young person does not feel that you have heard how the problem has made them feel, they may find it difficult to move on to develop alternative, more positive stories about themselves.

Acknowledging and working with intense feelings is an important part of therapy. Many young people who have experienced abuse have concerns that their feelings are overwhelming for them and for others and it is important to communicate both an ability to accept and handle intense feelings and to offer a way of making them more manageable for the client. Sometimes just being prepared to stay with the feelings is important. Some feelings can be externalised and their significance explored by questions such as the following:

- To what extent has anger been a friend to you; to what extent has it got you into trouble?
- Has anger helped you to stand up to secrecy?
- Has getting in touch with your anger been a positive or negative development for you?

Other feelings may be addressed in the context of the relative influence of the problem on their life and their impact on the problem. For example:

- So self-blame has been pushing you around and gets you feeling suicidal, is that what you are saying?
- Are there times when you have been able to resist the self-blame and decide against dying?

Challenging the dominant story is an important part of the engagement process. Letting the young person know that you understand how abuse recruits people into negative ways of seeing themselves while being open that you haven't been recruited into the same views is important. Young people need to know that you believe them and don't blame them, even if they say they don't believe you. I often pre-empt my statement of belief in them and disbelief of the dominant story with a warning that the dominant story won't like what I'm going to say and that it will probably encourage them to doubt me. Inquiry about the tricks and strategies used by self-blame to discount your belief in the client can undermine the power of self-blame. This issue can emerge many times throughout therapy.

Goal-setting is part of getting started and getting clear about the priorities to work on. It can be useful to name the problem or problem story at this stage, using externalising language. By keeping goals small and specific, a situation is established where success is achievable. For example, even if long-term goals are stated in terms of 'being happy, leaving the abuse behind, feeling good about myself', break these big goals down into small pieces. Asking what is the smallest change they would consider significant is a useful way to set small steps. It is helpful to frame goals in positive terms, such as what will be happening in their life, what they will be doing and feeling, rather than what they won't be doing. Goals are framed in terms of steps away from the dominant story and towards a preferred story. For example:

- So you are saying that if you could choose you would get self-blame out of your life and start to give the abuser responsibility for the abuse you received?
- You have said that the abuse has had the effect of getting you to hate yourself. If you could have things as you want them, would self-hatred continue to bully you or would you be telling it where to go?
- What would be the first sign that you were getting the better of self-blame?

## ADDRESSING THE THEMES OF THE DOMINANT STORY AND INVITING THE DEVELOPMENT OF ALTERNATIVE, PREFERRED THEMES

Themes that emerge in therapy are considered within the context of the dominant story/alternative story framework. Questions are asked to explore the development and influence of each story, with an increasing focus on unique outcomes and the preferred direction. Earlier in therapy, questions are more likely to focus on understanding and challenging the dominant story, while later sessions work to build on unique outcomes and strengthen preferred stories. Therapy doesn't follow an orderly progression, however, and steps back and forth between the dominant and alternative stories and between different themes. There can be enormous change in an adolescent's life from week to week, both positive and negative, and it can help to weave these life events into the themes, exploring whether these experiences represent more the oppressive story or the preferred story.

The themes that come up most frequently when I am working with young women are now described, with examples of questions that might be asked to explore them.

## Self-blame vs freedom from self-blame

Stories of self-blame have the effect of silencing and isolating young women and inviting them to fear blame and derision from others. Self-blame may encourage practices of self-abuse and self-hatred. It goes hand in hand with the ideas that the young woman should have been able to stop the abuse or must have wanted it to happen. This story is often central to the dominant story and invites feelings of depression and hopelessness. It can act as a strong restraint to recognising strengths and positive qualities and to breaking secrecy.

- How does self-blame get you feeling?
- What are some of the other effects of self-blame?
- How does self-blame get you listening to it?
- Are there times when you don't listen, even if it's only for a minute?
- Who are the friends of self-blame, who are its enemies?
- How have you been able to start giving self-blame the slip and get free from it?
- How were you coached in self-blame?
- Who would be your best coach in freedom from self-blame, or would there be a team?
- As you continue to challenge self-blame, what other thoughts or feelings might you have?
- What else might you find yourself doing?

## Listening to the voice of others vs listening to one's own voice

Experiences of abuse can recruit young women into the belief that their voice has no worth, and this encourages practices of discounting their own opinions, thoughts and feelings. Reconnecting with their own knowledge and preferences can be an important part of the journey towards freedom from the effects of abuse. Possible questions to explore this theme include:

- What sorts of experiences do you think you have had that have invited you to discount the value of your own voice and defer to the voice of others?
- To what extent do you think you have been won over by the idea that you should listen more to the voice of others?
- Have there been times when you have felt angry at that idea?
- Can you tell me about a time when you have found yourself listening to yourself?
- How did you do that?

## Being for self vs being for others

Abuse offers strong training in the idea that the needs of others take precedence over those of the young person receiving the abuse. 'Being for others' can become a way of life that is supported by ideas such as 'thinking of yourself is selfish'. Many young people express a preference during therapy to challenge this story and work towards finding ways of being more for themselves.

- Do you think that the experience of abuse trained you more in being for yourself or more in being for others?
- What kinds of messages do women get in our society about this? Do you think that there are ways in which we are expected to be more for others than ourselves?
- How are these ideas put about?
- Do you think that these ideas make girls more or less vulnerable to further abuse?
- Are there times when you have rebelled against these ideas and thought of yourself?
- How does the being for others habit try and trick you into siding with it instead of siding with yourself?

## Self-hatred vs self-liking

Young women I have worked with often describe feelings of self-hatred and rejection, and express the desire to feel good about themselves instead. These stories can be associated with self-blame, or they may have been fed by other ideas or experiences.

- How did self-hatred come into your life?
- Who or what opened the door for it?
- In what ways did the abuse feed self-hatred?
- Have there been times when you have found yourself ignoring self-hatred and finding something you liked about yourself despite it?
- If you continued to follow the path that led to self-love or self-liking, how do you imagine things would be different for you?

## Self-depreciation vs self-appreciation

Habits of self-depreciation may accompany feelings of self-hatred and it can be useful to explore these and their possible alternative stories such as self-appreciation.

- Self-depreciation likes to see you putting yourself down—how does it work on you to get you doing that?
- What has made you vulnerable to self-depreciation?
- What sorts of things might you be likely to appreciate about yourself first if you were to escape the habit of self-depreciation and move towards self-appreciation?
- Who would be most supportive of self-appreciation?
- Have there been times when you have rebelled against self-depreciation and allowed yourself to appreciate one of your qualities?

## Secrecy vs openness

Secrecy is often central to the dominant problem story and can continue to influence therapy, even after initial disclosure. Secrecy may not allow a young person to disclose their experiences entirely and may continue to influence many of their relationships. Breaking secrecy may involve the young person making serious sacrifices in terms of family connections and this can act as a restraint to developing openness.

- How did the perpetrator coach you in secrecy?
- Were there other factors that supported secrecy instead of supporting you?
- How did the secrecy affect your relationships with others—your mother, your friends, your sisters and brothers?
- How did you manage to stand up to secrecy and tell someone what happened?
- What effects has this openness had on your life?
- Do you think secrecy makes children more vulnerable to abuse? How?
- What sorts of things make it hard to keep being open? What sorts of things make it easier?

## Isolation vs connectedness

Stories of self-blame, secrecy, and self-hatred can encourage practices of isolation and fear of making connections and putting trust in people. This can have negative effects on peer relationships which are important to young people.

- Has secrecy led you more in the direction of isolation or connectedness?

- Is this a positive or a negative?
- What would be the effects of more connectedness in your life? Of more isolation?
- Did anything else about the abuse lead you towards isolation?
- What sorts of things have you needed to do to make connections in the way you have?

## Self-neglect vs self-protection

Self-protection is an idea that needs to be considered carefully, and in such a way that it is clearly separated from self-blame or responsibility for the abuse. Young women in this situation describe feeling that they somehow deserved to be abused and have no right to safety or protection. Abuse also invites a sense of powerlessness which contributes to habits of self-neglect. Challenging these and other restraints opens up more options for self-protection where possible.

- Has the abuse left you more with the idea that you are deserving of neglect or more of protection? How?
- What would you say is more in charge at the moment, self-neglect or self-protection?
- What sorts of things does self-neglect get you doing or not doing?
- What steps have you taken towards self-protection, despite the influence of self-neglect?

## Self-abuse vs self-care

Self-abuse is frightening to face for both therapist and young person and it raises issues of responsibility and safety that can be difficult to resolve. Sharon Nosworthy and Kerry Lane (1996) have been doing some pioneering work on co-researching this area with young people. They found that exploring the influence of self-mutilation within a group context with the goal of understanding more about it, rather than engaging any of the young women in the goal of overcoming self-mutilation, had empowering effects for both the workers and young women involved in the project. This project not only shows the value of co-research in this area, but also offers something to individual and group therapy, and invites us to consider the value of exploring rather than working to convince and persuade.

- When is self-abuse most likely to be around?
- What forms can it take?
- Does self-abuse present itself to you as a friend or an enemy?
- What kind of friendship does self-abuse offer?
- Are there times when you could have given in to self-abuse but chose self-care instead? How did you do that?
- What are some other ways you have chosen to care for yourself?
- How does self-abuse get you listening to it instead of self-care?
- Is there anything that supports the voice of self-care?

### Sex as abuse vs sex for loving and pleasure

Adolescence is a time when many young people are discovering and exploring their sexuality with peers and experiences of abuse have a big impact on their view of sex. It may be that imminent sexual relationships with peers are what prompt disclosure or put added stress on the young person's ability to cope with feelings about the abuse. I have found that it is often not until later in therapy, when self-blame and self-hatred have been challenged, that it is possible to start to challenge the dominant story about sex as only bad, abusive and to meet others' needs.

- What effect has your experience of abuse had on the way you see sexual relationships?
- How has this got you being in your relationships?
- Have there been times when you have allowed yourself to recognise your own sexual feelings? How has that been for you?
- Has seeing sex and abuse as the same thing made it difficult for you to consider the possibility that a sexual relationship could give you love and pleasure?
- What would need to be different in order for that to happen?
- If you found yourself enjoying sexual intimacy with someone you chose to be with, what sorts of things do you think you would have already worked through?

Whilst these ideas have been discussed in the context of individual work, they can also be applied in group work which takes advantage of young women's affinity with peers (Wilson & Hutton 1992).

## FAMILY WORK

The dominant cultural discourse about adolescence as a time of individuation and independence means that, for many teenage women who are exploring the significance of abuse in therapy for the first time, it may be difficult for them to allow their non-offending parent/parents to join them in this journey. Sometimes, the effects of practices of isolation and secrecy have widened the gap between young people and their families to the extent that the young person does not feel safe or willing to take the chance to reconnect, even when their family is reaching out. One of the dilemmas of working with teenagers is that we must respect their choices about who is included in therapy.

Lesley Laing and Amanda Kamsler have written about the importance of working with mothers and children together to undermine the oppression of secrecy and isolation fostered by the perpetrator (1990, p. 172). I agree with them that, when a woman believes her daughter's disclosure of abuse, joint sessions are valuable opportunities for re-storying their relationship and their view of each other. In the absence of permission to include family members, it can be useful to explore the effects of the abuse on family relationships and the influence the young woman is able to have in determining those relationships. When a daughter is not believed by her mother, it is important to determine whether the mother has also been a perpetrator of abuse, and the ways in which she has been recruited into disbelief or blaming. Deconstructing the oppressive stories which the abuser has promoted about both mother and daughter is one way of keeping alive the possibility that a different relationship between them is possible.

In some work with older teenage women, parents may not even know that therapy is occurring. Without permission to contact families, it can be difficult to know to what extent family are supportive or not. The effects of secrecy and isolation can have young women doubting that anyone will support or believe them and these fears can act as restraints to seeking support from their mother or other family members. I try to invite young women to think about the ways in which the problem story coaches them in secrecy, isolation and expecting to be blamed and disbelieved, and to consider ways of being that support re-connection and trust.

## CASE STORY

This case example illustrates some of the points discussed in this chapter. Details have been changed to protect anonymity. Sophie (17) came to see me at the suggestion of members of a community group she attended and brought with her an adult friend from this group for support. It became apparent at the first session that this was one of several attempts by Sophie to find a counsellor with whom she felt comfortable. She had experienced not being listened to, and not feeling able to talk to counsellors in the past. She was seeking counselling for the effects of past childhood abuse by an uncle and also the effects of a more recent date rape.

In engaging with Sophie I wanted to have an understanding of what she was looking for, and how I could avoid making 'an idiot' of myself as she described other counsellors having done. I gave a description of the kinds of questions I might ask, and some of the ways I have worked in the past, and tried to acknowledge some of the fears and doubts I expected she could have. I invited her questions and comments about the ways in which she hoped counselling might help, and invited her to take some time to assess, after this first session, whether she thought something good could come out of working together. Whilst reticent at first to talk, Sophie relaxed a little and described what she hadn't liked about past counselling, and said that she wasn't sure what I could do to help.

I asked her permission to ask some general questions about the experiences that had brought her to counselling. She told me about being raped by a friend and being abused by her uncle throughout her childhood. I was interested to understand what the effects of these events had been on her life. She said the effects were quite separate but that the recent rape had also brought back the effects of earlier abuse more strongly. Some of the effects she described were isolation, trouble at school, loneliness, self-hatred, self-doubt, fear that she was mad or bad, and a feeling that it was all her fault. She said that it had made her depressed. She described the lack of support she had experienced from friends and family around the rape, her friends saying that what happened was normal, that she shouldn't have spoken out, and her mother not believing her. Charges were laid and Sophie described her treatment by police and medical staff as like being abused all over again. We had some discussion around dominant discourses about teenage sex, women and those who disclose rape or abuse. Sophie identified the disqualifying effects of these and stated her disagreement with what she saw as unfair ideas.

Whilst it had not been entirely Sophie's choice to make a statement to the police about the rape, she had followed this through to the court process, and took the stand as a witness. I was curious about how Sophie had found the strength to stick to her guns, when she hadn't felt supported. Her answers to questions about this were the start of an alternative story about her strength and courage and ability to challenge secrecy. Further inquiries about other occasions when she had resisted secrecy resulted in Sophie describing her disclosure about the abuse by her uncle to her extended family. Questions about areas of her life that Sophie had kept free from the effects of the abuse brought forth information about the responsible, full-time job she had held since leaving school. My curiosity about how she had managed not only to hold down a job, but to receive commendation and promotion, with everything else she was facing, was met with surprise and pleasure.

Answers to my questions were sometimes followed by long pauses and Sophie's friend would help fill in the gaps. When asked if it was painful to talk about these things, Sophie nodded. I continued to check with her if it was all right to go on, and stopped when she indicated that she wanted to stop. I speculated about the ways in which secrecy and self-blame might be working on Sophie to get her to be fearful of speaking about the abuse and this was met with a smile and a nod. I encouraged her to tell me only what she felt comfortable with and to listen to her own judgement—I warned her that secrecy could try to stop her coming back.

Therapy over the next six sessions focused on the themes of self-blame vs freedom from self-blame, self-hatred vs self-acceptance, and secrecy and isolation vs openness and connection. Sophie often laughed at my portrayal of self-blame, self-hatred and secrecy as vile villains, who were conspiring her demise. Each week there were unique outcomes around the new story and whilst at first it was difficult for Sophie to experience herself as strong, brave, free from blame and able to connect with others, she began to actively resist the old, oppressive story and to see herself in these new ways.

We explored the tricks and tactics of self-blame, self-hatred and isolation, and exposed their aspirations for her life. She was clear in her preference for moving away from their influence. At the same time, as trust developed and Sophie started to view herself more positively, she found the courage to make further disclosures about abuse and about self-abusive behaviours. This was obviously difficult and painful for her, and at times self-blame and hopelessness got her feeling suicidal. At one point it was necessary to make a 'no-suicide' contract, something I present in terms of an act of mutual trust and obligation.

Thus therapy was multidimensional, with these different issues all being woven into the dominant and preferred stories we were working with. Sophie preferred not to include her family in therapy for the time she saw me, and we talked about her assumptions about their beliefs and the family rules about who gets protected. She was clear that, at this time, it was more important to make connections outside the family and build up her strength and support network before addressing her relationship with her parents.

Six months after Sophie started seeing me she disclosed that abuse had resumed and that she was not safe. After clarifying with police and the relevant department that no action could or would be taken on Sophie's behalf without her agreement, I set about exploring what would need to happen to create safety for her. The first step was to increase the network of adults Sophie could turn to for support. This included police, a female general practitioner, and a number of accommodation services that could provide safe, supported accommodation. At the same time Sophie was challenging self-blame and starting to access her anger in a way that prompted action. Some acts of resistance against the abuse were putting up anti-abuse posters in her room, telling her abuser that what he was doing was a crime and finally moving into safe accommodation. Sophie chose not to lay charges but made it clear to her abuser that future abuse would result in her going to the police.

## CONCLUSION

Working with adolescents presents unique challenges and dilemmas and demands tenacity and the ability to situate oneself clearly beside the young person. It requires patience, respect and an ability to stand back and assess one's own participation with the problem story. It is vital to communicate optimism and equally important not to allow over-enthusiasm to inadvertently recruit the young person into siding with the problem. The narrative approach assists this process by reminding us to defer constantly to our client's preferences, and by externalising the problem so that we can be united with them against it. It also invites us to include the political as well as the personal and to be aware of the discourses that affect our practice.

# 11 | The courage to hear: working with people experiencing dissociative identity disorder

*Ann-Marie Hayes and Jane Tiggeman*

OVER THE PAST two decades or so, the recognition of, and understanding about, childhood sexual abuse/trauma and its effects have become more widespread. Not surprisingly, during this time many articles, books and ideas have been made available for therapists working with these issues. Some researchers (such as Herman 1992, pp. 28–32 and Summit 1992, pp. 16–18) have identified this period as a '. . . window of opportunity . . .' where the combination of a range of factors has resulted in a greater willingness to hear and acknowledge children's and adults' experiences of abuse, pain and betrayal.

While much has been written about the general effects of childhood abuse/trauma and strategies for working with survivors, one area that has recently gained specific attention is the issue of 'dissociation'. It is now widely acknowledged that dissociation is a response to trauma that is utilised both at the time of the traumatic incident and after, when recalling or relating childhood trauma/abuse experiences. Dissociative experiences can be seen on a continuum ranging from driving to a destination and not remembering the route you have just taken, to people experiencing themselves as multiple personalities within the same body.

Dissociation at the extreme end of the continuum can be described as 'an abnormal state, set apart from ordinary consciousness . . . where normal connections of memory, knowledge and emotion are severed . . .' (Herman 1992, p. 33). Block (1991) concluded that in extreme cases of dissociation there is a kind of fragmentation of self as well as an altered state of consciousness. Fragmentation of the self, or multiple selves, is well defined in the *Diagnostic and Statistical Manual* (DSM IV) under the category of Dissociative Identity Disorder (DID) as a

> failure to integrate various aspects of identity, memory and consciousness. Each personality state may be experienced as if it has a distinct personal history, self-image and identity, including a separate name . . . DID is often seen in combination with Post Traumatic Stress Disorder. (*Diagnostic and Statistical Manual*, 4th edn, 1994, pp. 484–485)

The emergence of traumatic memory phenomena as part of a post-traumatic stress reaction/disorder has been recognised as a significant problem for combat veterans from the Vietnam War and has been relatively well accepted by health and welfare professionals. However, as soon as this phenomenon was linked to the issues of child sexual abuse, rape and sexual assault, as in the latest *Diagnostic and Statistical Manual* (4th edn), the validity of traumatic amnesia or, more precisely, the remembering of these events within the context of therapy was questioned. The ideological aspect of this scepticism is well documented in other chapters of this collection and so is not dealt with in this discussion.

Rather, this chapter examines dissociative identity disorder and ways of working with people who experience dissociation as a result of childhood experiences of sexual abuse. Of central importance is an exploration of the therapist's courage in hearing the story of trauma while respecting the client and keeping pace with what aspects of their story they decide they need, or do not need, to tell. Throughout this chapter we use examples from our individual clinical practices, although information about individuals has been significantly changed to avoid identification.[1]

## THE INFLUENCE OF FEMINIST AND NARRATIVE THEORETICAL ORIENTATIONS

In our joint experience working with women and some men who have suffered childhood abuse and trauma, there are huge variations in how dissociation affects someone's life. In our therapeutic discussions, we have noted a continuum of dissociative responses.

This is not surprising—whilst many of the effects of abuse are similar, each person's experiences are compounded or affected by a variety of other factors unique to each individual, such as the age at which abuse began, its duration and its severity. We believe the quality of the therapeutic relationship is the primary therapeutic issue when working with people experiencing problems with dissociation. However, we would like to outline the theoretical orientation we have chosen to use, which we believe is effective in providing a comprehensive approach to the issue.

With survivors of trauma who use dissociation we work in such a way as to be open to their experience and how they name it. We have developed our own therapeutic style, drawing on feminist and narrative theoretical orientations. One of the main questions that guides us is 'What is the meaning of this event, behaviour or belief to this client?' We believe that every client story is unique and we see the task of the therapist as providing a safe context for clients to feel free from further damage in order to tell their story, in their own time and in their individual way.

Both feminist and narrative therapy frameworks enable and encourage the deconstruction of ideas. They support the therapist in assisting the person to separate the label from the self. In fact, ideas are challenged in a way that makes room for differing or alternative views of the client, thus encouraging their own sense of power. These approaches also support and encourage clients' ability to make sense and meaning out of their lives. Both theoretical frameworks take a position of interest; they are conscious of power relationships and the fact that the role of the therapist is to listen, support and assist, not define or give advice. This approach is very different from the ways in which many psychological and psychiatric professionals position themselves in relation to their clients.

Our primary focus is talking with the women we are working with and naming the dissociation in the way that they find most helpful. While we have found it very useful to know and understand the psychological and psychiatric terms associated with dissociation, we are conscious of the experience of being labelled and the enormous impact this has on one's perception of self. We were always concerned that a woman was not defined as 'a multiple', hence our deliberate use of the term 'someone who experiences herself as having multiple identities'.

We have found that at times the medical and psychological professions are associated with practices that can create a pathological context—for example, concentrating on diagnosis and symptomatology, rather than understanding meaning and possible ways forward from the client's point of view. In a few instances clients talked to us about their dissociation and what they rated on DES and DID scores, tests frequently used by psychologists when testing for dissociative identity disorder. Others talked about experiences of various medical professionals, who had told them that they had ten years of work ahead of them or that this was a 'problem' they would have for life. This was often perceived as unhelpful; it pathologised women so that they felt the inevitability and burden of a lifetime problem.

In exploring ways of working with clients with 'habits' of dissociation, in addition to our theoretical orientation of a feminist/narrative framework we allowed ourselves a level of openness to other approaches and ideas.[2] The women themselves often undertook huge amounts of exploration and study in the area of dissociation and shared valuable sources of literature. However, their life stories provided the best information. We heard from women the ways they had survived trauma and how dissociation was a part of their survival strategies. They sought to protect and keep in touch with what some women called their essence, soul, spirit or inner self. Women who had been traumatised as children described how dissociative skills had helped them to bear the unbearable—usually the betrayal by adult caretakers who were supposed to nurture them, not torture and abuse them.

From listening to the women we became aware of how children who use dissociation are able to fragment their sense of self so that they can 'wall off' very painful, unbearable experiences from their conscious mind. So, as an adult, the sense of self that presents to the therapist may not be aware of the other parts of the self that also have a story to tell and problems to overcome. Often women come for counselling when this previously helpful strategy is unravelling under other stresses, such as sexual and other intimate relationships, having children, the pressures of memories and the realisation of the effect of the abuse on their life. Some women talked about 'spacing out' or 'splitting off' as something they no longer wanted to do, or they wanted the dissociation to be modified so that they had more control of when and if it happened in their life.

In responding to such requests we ask clients their view of the value of the habit of dissociation. How has it helped them? Is it something they wish to keep? Does it hinder them in any way in their daily life?

Working with clients who experience themselves as more than one person has a range of aspects that is initially overwhelming. This includes changes in voice, tone and language, sudden variations in mood and tangential conversation. At times there is a sense of having 'lost track' of the person who walked into the session. It was important to understand the meaning of the various roles and protective strategies that the women found useful and had developed over time. Understanding these and working at the client's pace were crucial in setting up and maintaining what Neswald[3] calls 'a safe container'. Assisting clients to create some sense of order so they may begin to understand and make sense of the stories of abuse—when what they are saying sometimes seems like a third-person narrative—is part of the process of therapy with people experiencing dissociation. We believe there are three crucial issues that must be dealt with in the therapeutic relationship—power, developing trust and boundaries—for effective work to occur. This chapter now discusses these three issues.

## The issue of power

Central to the theoretical frameworks we use is an analysis and an understanding of power. Both feminist and narrative frameworks are built on understanding the impact of power, particularly as enacted in relationships and society generally. A feminist analysis clearly articulates issues of power in relation to gender. It identifies women's inequality within society and identifies the structures and processes that seek to maintain this. Our understanding of a feminist approach to therapy is that it positions the client within a socioeconomic and political context, which facilitates an understanding of the broad range of factors that impinge on an individual. It seeks to understand the effects of oppression and the ways women have been socialised into acting and interacting.

Within narrative and feminist frameworks the notion of the therapist as 'expert' is challenged. Instead, within these theoretical orientations, we see the woman as the expert in relation to her own life experiences. We, as therapists/counsellors, have expertise, knowledge and resources to support and assist a client, but we do not take the position of the expert on a person's life. We believe that the therapist does not know more than the client about that client's experience, rather the client is the expert on themselves.

The therapist is there to help clients to voice their own story safely in a way that will provide healing. This in turn creates an opportunity for them to move on with their lives so that the trauma story from the past is no longer intruding on the present in a damaging way.

As therapists we are given power by clients in order to combine our skills, techniques and personhood to assist them with the healing process. It is not something we necessarily seek and, even as we move to reduce power imbalances within the therapeutic setting, there remains a great deal of power in the position of therapist. Giving back power to the client is an ongoing issue that we are conscious of at all times. In relation to the client, we recognise that we have power not only as a therapist, but also in other ways by virtue of our education and economic position. An acknowledgment of these factors is important within a therapeutic relationship. We seek to be clear about the power in the relationship and take steps to redress the imbalance by working alongside the client.

Generally, making decisions about working in a way that is negotiated, or 'being alongside' rather than taking an expert role, provides many challenges. When working with people who have experienced trauma and dissociation this stance raises a number of issues. We have found at times that establishing and maintaining a balance is an ongoing struggle, especially when at times the urge or invitation to jump in and take over has been strong. We have talked about the importance of handing back power to a client rather than inadvertently maintaining or even building on the power of a counsellor. With this in mind, some of the things we have found helpful in our practice include defining and clarifying the different roles we have in the therapeutic relationship and being prepared to negotiate and discuss these roles. It is also necessary not to make assumptions, but always to check things out to make sure there is a shared understanding of an issue.

As we discuss later, the whole issue of setting limits and clear boundaries is a central feature of work with clients who dissociate. This is an adjunct to setting up a relationship that is safe, consistent and has clear parameters, and where the therapist is overt and transparent about ways of working and able to discuss this accordingly with the client.

Another way in which we pursued the notion of our clients as experts in their own life was to set up a 'study' group. The group comprised three women who experienced themselves as multiple, and us. We met on a 4–6 weekly basis to discuss ideas and critique papers and books on the subject of dissociation. This was a great opportunity to discuss at a theoretical level the issues related to dissociation that the women felt were relevant. We explored issues such as 'What would integration look like?' and discussed what limit setting offers to clients and therapists.

We both realise the privilege that meeting with this group entailed. This group provided an opportunity to discuss freely the implications of particular therapeutic strategies and unpick the orientations of various authors. We also benefited from the sharing of knowledge and ideas. Most importantly, we heard about things that had been helpful for them, either strategies they had developed themselves, or ways of working they had found helpful in therapy. These meetings informed and assisted our practice in a very meaningful way that also honoured the women and their lives.

Awareness of power issues and the ways these are reflected within the therapeutic relationship is a critical component of our work. However, inequities of power and the potential for clients to be re-traumatised can occur in interactions with wider systems outside the therapeutic relationship. Particular challenges around power issues arise when working with clients who are involved, through emergencies/crises or hospital stays, with the mental health system. Issues in relation to abuse and dissociation are still not widely understood or acknowledged within this sector. We have found many people who are allies, within the system or working as community mental health professionals. But the structures and ways of operating within hospitals do not fully support the notion that it is possible for 'patients' to have an active or central role in their own recovery.

Therapists in the medical model often assume that they know more about the patient, or that they know what is best for the patient, without involving the patient in the process. Most often the patient experiences this as a de-powering process. In the approach we have chosen, being open to understanding the meaning of problems from the client's perspective can be very challenging but it is a crucial aspect of allowing clients to be the expert about their own story. For example, a client disclosed to me that she had been raped and had undergone a medical examination. The ensuing diagnosis was that the wounds were probably self-inflicted. I was invited to see this client as manipulative. Rather than join with that view, I attempted to keep an open mind and try to understand what this could mean. As time went on I came to understand that the client may have been reliving traumatic memory and had re-enacted part of it by self-inflicting these wounds. It was her way of telling the trauma story rather than her being difficult or manipulative.

The trauma story can be told in other unusual ways. Basil van der Kolk (1991, 1994) has highlighted his findings of how the body, as opposed to the mind, can store memory. This was evidenced when a client talked about having continual vaginal bleeding but the doctor could find no medical reason. When it was suggested to the client that she consider whether her body was trying to tell her something, the client had a chance to reflect and became aware that it was a body memory of a traumatic abuse event that was coming up and being relived. This provided her with an opportunity to make a non-verbal memory of her earlier experience verbal, to tell the story of that aspect of her abuse.

So for us, when working with clients becomes difficult, due to crises in that person's life or when we are in contact with other systems, finding support for our alternative, non-pathologising way of working with clients is important in order to sustain ourselves. It also assists us to continue 'walking alongside' the person, rather than being invited by the expert model to jump in front and take over from the client. Maintaining our position in practice demonstrates our belief in people's strength, and their capacity to recover. This can at times be hard but it demonstrates our trust in the person in a concrete way—which is the second crucial issue that needs to be addressed in the therapeutic relationship.

## Developing trust in the therapeutic relationship

Being transparent about power dynamics and clear about the processes of therapy are important in building a trusting relationship. For most therapists who work with people who have experienced child abuse, rape or sexual assault, the issue of trust is paramount. Many clients have experienced abandonment, betrayal and hurt from people who are close. We have found that there is an understandable anger at being let down by people who should have protected them as children. There is also the generalising effect: 'if someone in this position can do this to me, who is trustworthy?'

For those who experience significant levels of dissociation, trust is an ongoing issue. Very often, clients alternate between being very trusting and very wary and utilising behaviours associated with their anger to keep the counsellor at a distance. The desire to trust the therapist is often apparent, although this may be mitigated by the desire to protect themselves, due to earlier and sometimes recent experiences of abandonment and pain.

An example of this tension occurred during a recent session with a client. There was a sense of sharing the sadness and pain over what had happened and the client expressed her relief at having a 'safe' person to talk to about these feelings. The tenor of the session changed dramatically as another aspect of this woman became angry and she declared, 'You don't care . . . this is just your job'. She then went on to give examples of how badly I was doing as a therapist generally. This left me feeling pretty battered although I understood the need for this woman to be close, but also to have space and to re-set the distance between us. At times we discussed this together and it seemed that, while it was about keeping me at a safe distance, it was also an opportunity to be angry, knowing that this would be OK and that she would not be responded to with abuse or anger.

In working with a survivor of trauma the therapist has to be worthy of trust and clients often have the need to test and retest our trustworthiness. When working with clients to build a trusting, safe relationship, it is important to be aware of the many variables that may have some effect on the therapeutic relationship. Early on we found it useful to think and respond to the women we worked with as if we were talking to 'everyone'. For women who experience themselves as multiple persons, difficulties arise from misunderstandings or assumptions made by the therapist. For example, it is easy to assume that there are only two or three important 'people' to know, or that the client's inner world is so compartmentalised that information is not shared. Over time we have found that what we are told is sometimes limited, for good reason, as the woman is testing to see our response—How are you going to manage this? We also discovered in conversations with women in a group setting that, while some information can be kept separate, it eventually filters through and around the internal 'system'.

Expectations of each other within the therapeutic relationship are also important and are interlinked with the concepts of power and trust. It was important to talk through this openly and on many occasions we talked about our beliefs about therapy/counselling, what we saw as our role, debunking the myth of expert and what that meant. While this was helpful at times, we both experienced clients perceiving us as 'bad' therapists who didn't know enough because we were not the 'experts' or because we didn't follow specific techniques they had read, or heard about. Consequently, it was crucial that we kept up with current therapeutic thinking (and the techniques women were talking about) and were prepared for a discussion highlighting the many ways that we could be helpful to them, but also explaining our own limits in terms of expertise and comfort. This type of discussion clarified our role as therapists, and the differences between this role and the role of friends or support people in their life.

People who experience themselves as multiple persons are highly sensitive to even subtle nuances or changes in the therapist's response. Any reaction, however slight, may be perceived by the client as the therapist having a negative response to them. It is often important to stop and explain what is going on—for example, a loss of concentration because the therapist is tired or has had a difficult day, and this intruded momentarily. Explaining openly and honestly within the session has been one way of overcoming a loss of trust. It is also a way for the client to realise that the therapist is human, which can assist in the client developing more realistic expectations of others. For the therapist it is a lesson in the power of honesty and talking through the issues with clients. It is an opportunity for us to explore the issue of past negative, traumatic experiences intruding on the present.

Some very practical strategies have been helpful around this issue, one being the timing of sessions. If possible, we found it desirable to see clients earlier in the day and even in the week, when we are fresher and more able to concentrate. It was also important to talk with the women about the length of sessions and ways of semi-structuring them, to ensure that issues are covered and that there is adequate time for the client to become grounded and leave the session safely. One woman devised a structure that ensured time limits for those 'parts' of her that were dominant, allowing time for others who wanted to check out the therapist or say something differently. This client was clear about the role the therapist played in ensuring this happened, which included intervening to remind the client of time limits, and taking responsibility for the implementation of agreed procedures for safety. These strategies were reviewed on an ongoing basis, and modified as required. For ourselves, reviewing the work we were doing with another therapist was extremely beneficial, as was participating in other forums around this issue such as the Network of Therapists

Working with Sexual Assault Survivors (NETTSAS). The use of reflecting teams, case conferences and peer review also provided opportunities for discussion with other counsellors/therapists.

Very obviously, trust is a vital element within any therapeutic relationship. One important way of establishing and nurturing trust is by developing and maintaining clear and consistent boundaries within the therapeutic relationship. This is the last of the three issues to be discussed in this chapter.

## Boundary issues

Maintaining clear and consistent boundaries is based on developing trust and maintaining appropriate levels of power within the therapeutic relationship. The concepts of power, trust and boundaries are inextricably interwoven. Over the time we have worked with people around issues related to trauma and dissociation, we have found that their expectations are often extremely high and at times unrealistic. Consequently, we are extremely mindful of safety issues in the therapeutic relationship, such as limit setting and boundaries, especially when working with someone who experiences themselves as more than one person.

The question that continually arises is how much the therapist should offer to the client versus what it is reasonable for the client to expect. Should the therapist be available outside office hours, taking phone calls from suicidal clients at 11 pm or 3 am? Should the therapist see the client for unscheduled emergency sessions? How long should sessions be—one hour, two hours or three hours? Should the therapist be able to take annual leave without clients becoming extremely distressed months in advance of the designated leave date? Many times survivors of trauma say things like 'You don't really care about me', when the context is that the therapist, after being so available, is now tired or sick, and needs a temporary break of a few days or weeks.

Of course, the therapeutic task is for the client to learn to trust that the therapist will return to the therapeutic relationship. However, for clients who have been abandoned so many times this is a difficult struggle. It is equally difficult for the therapist to see a client struggling when it can seem as if the therapist has somehow brought about the situation, by going on holiday or having private non-work time at the weekend.

There are many invitations for therapists to become over-responsible and inadvertently stretch their boundaries. With non-traumatised clients, sometimes giving that little bit more—such as an extra session or extended time—can often help the client to move that bit further, more quickly, towards overcoming their problem. With clients who are survivors of trauma, however, giving that little bit more tends to be unhelpful, as the client will often keep pushing or asking for more, trying to find the therapist's limit. Clients who are survivors of trauma would appear to need firmer and clearer boundaries than other clients. Perhaps this is because their boundaries have become so confused and they need to learn and practise in the relationship with the therapist what are reasonable boundaries.

The question 'Is this fair?' is worth considering. The expectations of a therapist can be measured in terms of what would be seen as fair or reasonable in the ordinary world. We believe being fair includes a preparedness to discuss issues with the client and to be clear about the limits, both personal and organisational. In addition, discussing the way you will work together and negotiating around this is an important part of the therapeutic process. As a therapist/counsellor, it is important for us to step back and consider such issues as: What can I sustain, in terms of time, over the long term? What am I prepared to do outside sessions? These questions can be helpful when developing some agreement about your role. If you decide to be available for telephone calls outside sessions, you may set limits about this occurring only between 9 am and 5 pm, but then discuss with the client their plan for crisis or support out of hours. We think part of the role of therapist/counsellor is to assist the client to utilise other networks, friends, support groups and crisis lines as an adjunct to the work we are doing.

We have found that clients who experience themselves as multiple persons often have unrealistically high expectations of the therapist. We have gone through the experience of meeting these expectations, only to find that they are impossible to maintain over time. This has meant we have had to stop and discuss issues about timing of sessions or availability after hours in a reactive way rather than in a planned, proactive way. While we acknowledge that adjustments to boundaries occur throughout the process of working with someone, to stop and reflect about these issues and set fair, reasonable limits at the outset of therapy is much more helpful to both client and therapist. Appropriate boundaries negotiated between therapist and client will help the therapist to be able to hear the story of trauma in an ongoing way. It also enables the therapist to develop relationships with multiple 'people' without succumbing to fatigue.

## DISSOCIATIVE IDENTITY DISORDER—ISSUES FOR THE THERAPIST

Working with people who experience themselves as 'multiple' is very different from working with other clients. Working with survivors of child sexual abuse involves a high level of skill and understanding and an exposure to trauma that can be distressing, but with experience over time we learn to manage our response and debrief reasonably effectively. In our therapeutic practice we have found that survivors of prolonged severe abuse, where disso-ciation was used extensively, have often been subjected to extreme sadism by both men and women, sometimes in a group context. The effects of this level of abuse reach a new order of magnitude.

Working with women who experience themselves as multiple persons is challenging work. The process of therapy is often painstakingly slow to ensure that talking about the inner world of the client does not destabilise her, or create overwhelming anxiety. For many women this is a painful process with the need to test and re-test the therapist to ensure that talking about their experi-ence of dissociation will be heard, understood and respected. It is for many women a time of extreme vulnerability, which adds to the usual complexities of the therapeutic relationship.

As the story of trauma slowly unfolds, associated extreme emotions such as panic, despair and physiological reactions emerge. Some clients report experiencing nausea, adrenaline rushes, disso-ciation or a sense of not being in the room, as well as describing situations and acting in age-inappropriate ways. Others would seem to be lost to the therapist for many minutes in a state of almost frozen affect. It is also not uncommon for clients to convey an extreme sense of urgency and immediacy, almost as if their life depends on the therapist. The message that something has to be done *right now* may pervade the therapy session. The powerful image of 'The Scream', by artist Edward Munch, comes to mind when meeting a client who has experienced prolonged and severe trauma for the first time and has used dissociation extensively. Not surprisingly, therapists may be invited into over-responsibility for the client both in and outside the therapeutic relationship.

Therapists may experience a feeling of bombardment as they

deal with the client's apparently extreme response. This can occur despite having worked with abuse for many years. Summit suggests that to accept dissociation exists can be a difficult thing for workers because:

> We are forced to understand that unremembered terror can happen, that it affects a person's identity, world view, emotional balance and emotional health . . . (1992, p. 22)

Even if only in a partial sense, the trauma can be re-enacted in front of the therapist very early on in therapy. Inevitably the unseasoned (experienced in every other problem but this) therapist is thrown into shock and confusion. This occurs not only in relation to the story of abuse that is unfolding, but also in response to the level of dissociation that may be experienced by the client during the therapy session, at times making communication very difficult. During the early days of working with clients around trauma and dissociation, we both experienced what is often described in the literature as a process of feeling deskilled, not knowing what to do and often feeling professionally inadequate. We believe it is important for therapists to recognise the possibility of this occurring for them in similar circumstances and to deal with it appropriately in consultation or peer review.

### The relationship between therapist and client

In working with people who experience themselves as dissociative and/or having multiple parts, we have found it to be very important and useful to focus on the nature of the relationship between ourselves and the people with whom we are working. Whilst we see some theoretical ideas and techniques as being helpful, we believe the strength of the relationship between client and therapist is the key to utilising creative ideas and practices successfully.

One of the most difficult parts of the therapy is the intensity of the client's connection with the therapist. This is possibly the case because clients may hope that the therapist can give them what they did not get as children, including appropriate nurturing and support. As a therapist there are many invitations to care for and reassure the abused child parts of the client. Facing the story of abuse with the client is often deeply disturbing to one's soul. However, in this process therapists have to realise that they cannot, even with the best will in the world, take away the fact that abuse occurred.

The grief for the client in coming to terms with the fact that nothing can change the reality of the abuse is enormous. No-one wants to feel the intensity of this grief and dissociation provides a way of hiding it—even from themselves. It may mean that a client never feels whole or properly connected. However, many clients decide that they want to become more integrated and connected in their sense of self and so choose to deal with varying levels of this grief. As therapists we try with the client to gain a better understanding of the meaning of their experiences by teasing out qualities of character, such as courage and creativity, that arise from the abuse. This process can be a way of fighting the effects of abuse and dealing with it. It seems that deriving some meaning in terms of the preferred qualities of character emerging from the abuse experience enables clients to gain a sense of re-empowering parts of themselves to be further freed of the traumatic experiences.

It is our view that no-one wants to have to face the fact that sadistic atrocities continue to happen to defenceless children. While many people do not know about the issues of abuse and their effects on people, many others choose not to know, which allows them to continue to believe in the safety of their world and maintain a distance from others' pain and suffering. Ironically, the survival technique of dissociation reflects this problem of 'knowing, yet not knowing'. When survivors of abuse choose to unravel their dissociated memories, we see them as heroically beginning to confront the abuse that society frequently prefers to deny. Survivors show immense courage and we believe that, by facing parts of their trauma experience, they are challenging themselves and others in the task of stopping abuse.

Likewise, when we as therapists choose to speak of these issues the responses we receive from others, including professionals, can appear to reflect those of the women we work with, including disbelief, isolation and a sense of being discounted. We have found that the way forward for us has been, and will continue to be, socio-political action to dispel myths that can be perpetuated about the issue of abuse and, more recently, about those who experience dissociation as an effect of abuse. Political action to stop child abuse is perhaps the ultimate way of debriefing and we believe that, until the personal incidents of child abuse that lead to dissociation become political issues, these problems will not be solved.

## CONCLUSION

Having the courage to hear and listen to clients telling their story of the nature of the abuse, and of how they fought the abuse, involves the therapist in the process of being a witness, in being able to stand with them against the experience of oppression and their oppressor. Being a witness to healing is an important component of the therapy. Tied in with being a witness to healing is supporting the client's choice of overcoming habits of dissociation, to acknowledge the *'not yet said'*, so that parts of the fragmented self can give voice to their story, which is frequently a story of heroism and survival. Once the parts of the self have been given the freedom to speak their alternative story of struggle against the oppression of abuse, the memory of the abuse is no longer dissociated. Instead, the experience of abuse can be integrated within the client's sense of who they are as a whole person. Only then can the client's sense of self become a rich tapestry of stories of heroism in contrast to the often dominant story of victimisation and powerlessness in the face of abuse.

# 12 Giving children a voice: the challenge of disability

*Frank Astill, Joan Bratel and Christine Johnston*

IF CHILDREN ARE to be protected from abuse, it is essential that they be given the opportunity to relate their experiences and that adults prepared to listen and understand. This applies in many contexts, including the criminal justice system. Listening to children requires understanding of the ways in which children's cognitive abilities differ from those of adults, particularly in court proceedings. This challenge has still to be fully met for children who are developing typically. How much more difficult, then, is it for children or adults with a disability to be heard since their credibility may be adversely affected by ill-informed community perceptions of decreased capabilities. This is particularly so for those who cannot speak for themselves—those who have no functional, spoken language. For them the difficulties are exacerbated both by their inability to relate their concerns easily and by the limited number of people who have the skills to understand them when they do attempt to do so. Children whose cerebral palsy affects speech production are very clearly in this situation.

Children, and adults, with moderate to severe levels of cerebral palsy, a condition that affects movement and posture due to damage to or lack of development in one or more parts of the brain, are particularly vulnerable to abuse because of a range of factors associated with the restrictions their physical disability places on them. They are likely to be dependent upon others for personal care and assistance. As a consequence, they are daily in situations with carers that might be described as intimate. Second, limited social skills and experience make it more difficult for them to assess other people's behaviour and intentions and to respond appropriately. Third, children with disabilities often lack information and knowledge about sexuality and sexual behaviour. This may be due both to a lack of formal education by parents and schools on issues related to personal development and to their having few opportunities to interact with a wide range of peers. Fourth, limited mobility makes it difficult, if not impossible, for them to remove themselves from a situation that has become untenable. Finally, and most importantly for the present discussion, the very difficulties they experience in communicating make them even more vulnerable as the child with no speech may be perceived as unlikely to be able to make their concerns and their abuser known.

The challenge confronting those in child protection is, therefore, twofold: to provide education about sexuality and appropriate sexual behaviour to children with disabilities and to explore the ways in which the voice of children who have no functional speech can be heard by those in the community and, importantly, in the judiciary. Both an educational and a legal perspective are therefore needed. Working with a small group of children with cerebral palsy who attended a school for children with special needs, our aim was to analyse the specific issues that related to children's ability to give evidence and to examine the impact a disability such as cerebral palsy may have in determining a child's credibility in the judicial system.

## THE DEVELOPMENTAL CONTEXT

There is now a sensitivity to and a significant research focus on children's ability to recall events and to be convincing witnesses (e.g. Goldman 1992; Steward et al. 1993). Building on this, we have focused on the implications of these findings for children with disabilities and particularly on the factors that should be addressed when conducting research about the ability of children with little or no functional speech to recount a narrative in a way that would be admissible in the giving of evidence.

What seems clear from our understanding of cognitive development is that, in order to relate instances of abuse, the child needs only to be operating at the concrete operational stage. Indeed, as

Goldman (1992, p. 83) has pointed out, some of what the child is required to do includes the identification and naming of particular objects or body parts. These are skills that might properly be seen as falling within the province of a lower stage of cognitive development, that of pre-operational thinking. This being so, there can be little reason for supposing that children with disabilities are not capable of such recounting unless they have a severe level of intellectual disability. In most circumstances, the concept development and skills required are well within their capabilities.

Recognition of developmental factors is essential in interviewing children, regardless of whether or not they have a disability. For example, children are likely to give different emphasis to events than adults; their life experience and ways of seeing the world are markedly different. To elicit the degree of detail that may be required it may well be necessary to ask very direct questions, particularly since it is likely that the child will be uncomfortable in describing what has happened. Goldman (1992), Steward et al. (1993) and Bussey (1990) all point to the embarrassment that children often feel in using sexual terms or talking about sexual behaviour. This is apparent from as early as seven years of age. This may well prevent their recounting the incident fully unless they are asked direct and explicit questions. The difficulty is, of course, that such questions are not acceptable in court settings.

These findings have direct implications for children with cerebral palsy. As discussed, they are likely to have had a narrowed range of experience and to have poorer social skills, making the task of talking to a stranger about an abusive situation even more problematic. Furthermore, if children do not have spoken language and are dependent upon augmentative communication systems, it becomes not just desirable that questions are short and clear and take account of the child's level of development but imperative since the slowness of the child's response will work against their credibility if long, complex questions put an additional and unnecessary burden upon memory.

Fear of reprisal and of being perceived as naughty will also serve to intimidate the child, particularly when the accused is present and the child is in the unfamiliar and alien environment of the court (Bussey 1990). It is for reasons such as these that there has been extensive discussion of the appropriateness of presenting children's evidence by means of either videotape or closed-circuit television in order to distance the child from the courtroom. The benefits of a supportive setting for interviewing apply equally whether the child has a disability or not. Children also need to have the vocabulary to describe what has occurred. The main difficulty is that sexuality is an area where a 'valid living language may be interpreted as offensive, or may be forbidden' (Sargeant, quoted in Goldman 1992, p. 89). As a consequence, children's sexual language is frequently a combination of pseudonyms and words peculiar to the family. Few clinical or anatomical words are used by children (Goldman 1990). Without an understanding of the sexual vocabulary available to the child, information proffered by the child is compromised. This problem is exacerbated where children have no spoken language. Whilst they may have the receptive vocabulary to understand sexual terms and what is being asked of them, unless they have been given specific ways of expressing those concepts or ideas by use of an augmentative communication system or have the ability to spell adequately, both the child and those working with them are greatly disadvantaged.

It is in the use of augmentative systems of communication that the greatest controversy has arisen. For children whose speech is restricted due to a disability such as cerebral palsy, an alternative means of communication such as signing, the use of a symbol board or an electronic communication device is necessary. A symbol board consists of a number of symbols or pictures and permits functional communication for individuals to express a variety of needs, relate information about past and future events and to partici-pate in successful interaction with others. Whilst a wide range of concepts and ideas can be generated using augmentative systems, including the construction of syntactically and grammatically cor-rect sentences, the vocabulary and concepts included in the child's communication system will affect what they can discuss with ease.

To date the use of such systems as a means of providing reliable, accurate information has been largely rejected by the legal profes-sions and the courts due to the risk of contamination of evidence. Such a view, however, ignores the clear distinction that can be made between facilitation that allows children to create their own message independently and where the role of an interpreter is simply to read that message, and facilitation that involves physically assisting children to select their messages, by, for example, sup-porting their arm. Research has been consistent in finding that the latter form of facilitated communication has limited validity (Moore et al. 1993; Jones 1994; Siegel 1995). Indeed, in almost every instance, the data suggest that it is the facilitator who is commu-nicating and not the person with a disability.

A number of studies describing the use of facilitated communication techniques with people with autism have also added to the confusion about the value of augmentative communication (Jones 1994; Richer 1994; Siegel 1995). Whilst it might be argued that those with autism would like to communicate, their lack of language is fundamental to the nature of the disability itself. Generally, they find it difficult, if not impossible, to interact with others on both verbal and physical levels. Their inability to communicate has not only a physical but also a psychological component. On the other hand, the inability of people with cerebral palsy to speak is a direct physical consequence of their disability: they want to communicate but are unable to do so. The need for those with cerebral palsy is not, therefore, to encourage them to speak but simply to find a method that will allow them to do this.

Parents, teachers and other professionals regularly use symbol boards to teach and communicate with people who have cerebral palsy and no functional speech. Establishing the efficacy of this technique in the context of criteria used for the reception of evidence has implications not only for courtroom procedures but for the wider community. This, then, provided the impetus for the current study.

## THE CONTEXT OF THE COURT

Our litigation system is adversarial: it operates on the assumption that the best results are achieved when opposing arguments are presented and tested as forcefully as possible. It is also based on a tradition of direct oral testimony. Courtrooms echo the values of fluent, decisive adult constructions of reality. The environment is not compatible with children, especially those with functional disabilities. There is a deep attachment to cross-examination as the acid test of the truth-value of evidence. It is the cultural touchstone of adversarial law. In the area of children's evidence, the procedural intensity, inflexibility and incompatibility with patterns of child narrative of the adversarial system are being questioned (ALRC 1997, Recommendation 30, 7.22–7.29). In this study, emphasis is put on the coherence of the narrative rather than the strategic techniques of cross-examination.

In criminal prosecutions, such as sexual assault hearings, there are strict procedures governing what evidence will be heard in court. The first two major control devices operating on the reception of evidence are the threshold issues of whether the witness is competent to give evidence, and whether the evidence is relevant. The second is whether the evidence is admissible. The third has to do with the probative value of what is said: the significance the court is prepared to attribute to the evidence in determining the matter being tried. Then there is the stringent standard of proof required in criminal matters. Proof beyond reasonable doubt means in effect that no other reasonable explanation is feasible. Any doubt that can be raised will be of great and usually conclusive benefit to the accused person.

Over the past decade children's evidence has attracted much legislative and research attention. Legislative reform has, in sum, made the satisfaction of criteria of competence easier, and given the judge or magistrate more discretionary power in dealing with the evidence. The Commonwealth and State *Evidence Acts* assume competence, putting the burden on others to show, on the balance of probabilities, incompetence (*Evidence Act* 1995 (Cth), ss 12, 13(5), 141(1)). A court will not receive a child's evidence if it is satisfied that 'the child is not able to respond rationally to questions' (*Oaths Act* 1900 (NSW), s. 33(3)(b)). The ability to differentiate between truth and falsehood is the key criterion as to whether a child is competent to give evidence, but unless the contrary is established, truth telling and ability to respond rationally will be presumed (*Oaths Act*, s. 33(4)). Under this section of the *Oaths Act* a child is a person under the age of 12 years (s. 33(4)).

There has also been legislative recognition of the difficulties the geography of the courtroom may pose for children. The NSW *Crimes Act* 1900 provides for closed-circuit television to be used in the reception of a child victim's evidence (s. 405D—for the purpose of this section a child is a person under the age of 16 years when giving evidence: s. 405D(5)). Further flexibility is provided for in allowing variations of seating arrangements in the giving of evidence, including taking into account the child's line of vision, the use of screens, and adjournment of the proceedings or any part of the proceedings to other premises (s. 405F(2)(a)(b)(c)).

These sympathetic structural changes do not, however, address the major impediments to the reception of evidence from a child with cerebral palsy. The need for assistance in communication and lack of motor coordination are the major obstacles to the giving of admissible or reliable evidence. Since communication is assisted, it faces the related challenges of being characterised as hearsay, or as evidence that is tainted by suggestive questioning and interviewing. The status of hearsay evidence varies according to circumstances, but it is suspect for the literal reason that it represents what has been talked about rather than observed. There are fundamentally two aspects to be dealt with: the time before trial and the possibility that the child has been led to believe certain events happened which may or may not have been within the child's direct experience; and during the trial when from the court's perception it is dealing with an interpreter who may be representing her own construction of what the child is intending to say.

In addressing both aspects, the common need is to devise an environment both inside and out of the courtroom where the reception of information from the child is demonstrably unaffected in its content by any form of facilitation. To this end a protocol devised in the light of the 'leading question' objection to evidence-in-chief was needed which could then be used to explore the ability of children who use augmentative communication systems to recount an event they have witnessed.

To summarise, four main issues emerged from the analysis of the developmental and legal perspectives as requiring exploration if the testimony of children using augmentative communication systems is to be accepted. These are the need for:

- children who have no functional speech to have the vocabulary necessary in symbolic or pictorial form to make it possible for them to communicate relevant information about situations of abuse and potential abuse;
- personal development programs to ensure that children develop concepts related to sexuality, personal safety and abuse and the opportunity to practise using the vocabulary;
- a demonstration that children with cerebral palsy can accurately relate a sequence of events that has occurred, using augmentative systems of communication; and
- a protocol to assist in adducing admissible evidence in situations such as alleged cases of abuse.

## THE RESEARCH STUDY

A five-stage study was carried out to consider these factors and had as its aim the exploration of two research questions:

1. Can children who have little or no functional speech and impaired language development, due to a disability such as cerebral palsy, accurately describe and recount a sequence of events including one related to abuse?
2. Can the use of an augmentative communication system such as a symbol board provide objective, reliable evidence admissible in a court of law?

Three short videos were used to provide the material to be recounted by the children. Each of these videos depicted a situation where the central character was at risk in some way. They were considered to address the issue of abuse in a realistic way and in contexts that would be meaningful for the child without being too confronting:

- *Truth and Dare* depicted the physical and verbal abuse of a young teenage boy by a group of older boys.
- *For Whose Sake?* (NSW Child Protection Council) showed a situation of neglect in which children in a classroom setting complain about a child being smelly and dirty.
- *The Secret* (South Australian Film Corporation) depicted a sexual abuse scene in which an adult male is minding a young girl and asks her for a goodnight kiss and attempts to fondle her while she is in bed.

The research was conducted as an adjunct to the already planned Personal Development unit that the children were to study during the school year, with appropriate parental consent and protocols should a child become upset by the content of the videos or the questions. The children were tested twice, the second time after an interval of six months.

Nine students participated in the study, six girls and three boys; the relatively small sample size was due to the low incidence of cerebral palsy and the availability of subjects able and willing to participate. Their ages ranged from 11 years to 15.8 years with a mean age of 13.3 years. All the children had a moderate to severe physical disability due to cerebral palsy, required an electric wheelchair for mobility and had limited functional use of their hands. All had been formally assessed as functioning within the normal range of intellectual ability and attended the same class in a school for children with cerebral palsy.

Only one male student had a degree of functional speech. However, the clarity of his speech deteriorated with the length of his sentences and the level of effort required to maintain breath control for producing speech, compromising his ability to communicate easily with strangers. The other eight students all used communication boards based on the compic symbol system. Of these, seven used finger pointing to indicate their responses with the eighth student using a light pointer mounted on a band worn on his head. All nine included in the study were literate and used an alphabet set out as part of their communication boards to spell out some of their answers. Every student was regularly seen by a speech pathologist, as part of normal service delivery, to enhance and develop speech and language concepts and to review and update their communication system as required.

## Stage 1: Devising the interviewing protocol

This involved the development of an interviewing protocol which, whilst taking account of the issues raised by the children's developmental status, would meet the 'leading question' objection to evidence-in-chief. A leading question is one that contains a prompt that can be interpreted as suggesting a particular answer. Allegations of problems in this area have dogged high-profile investigations in recent times.

Prior to the pilot of this project, scenarios were devised to illustrate the need for non-directive questioning, and discussed with the interviewer who conducted the pilot. They were constructed on a similar format to the project scenarios, but dealt with more neutral subject matter and had clearer true–false conclusions. Essentially, they were sensitisation exercises for the interviewer and indicators to the level of complexity of scenario that could be attempted in the time available. A scenario such as the episode described in the box on the following page was taped, and the descriptions compared with what happened. The mechanics of questioning, such as the role of the expert interpreter, were examined.

The protocol was constructed on the premise that non-suggestive questioning is possible once an interviewer is briefed on its basic principles. Those principles are that the interviewee is encouraged to relate a narrative through non-specific prompts, which can then become more specific by using information already provided. Four levels of questioning building on these principles are identified and outlined in the description of the protocol.

W is in a room with other children. She is facing the door. Three children are near the door. An adult, Bruce, walks up as the children begin a mild scuffle. One of the children slams the door, catching the adult's hand. Bruce exclaims (mildly). The adult has not seen who slammed the door, but says, 'Why did you do that, David?' David replies, 'It was not me, it was Alice.' Alice had run from the room by then, and nothing more is said.

In fact it was Peter who pushed the door, but it is clear he had no intention of hurting the adult, or even knew anyone was going to be hurt. He did it out of frustration. In the scene the scuffle is over who owns a particular ball, and there is some attempted snatching, which ends up with Peter in anger pushing the door as he lunges for the ball.

The Questioner (Q) wishes to know what happened. The witness (W) is interviewed immediately after the incident happens, and again, in almost identical fashion, two months later. In this sequence, however, it is two months later. The incident happened on October 18.

Q. Can you remember what happened on October 18?
W. No.
Q. Would you have been in your classroom?
W. Yes.
Q. Do you remember anything about that day?
W. Yes.
Q. What do you remember?
W. There was a fight.

The next group of questions will try to bring out a description of the scene without putting words and concepts into the witness's mind.

- What was it about?
- Who was it between?
- What happened?
- Did you see who slammed the door?
- What did Bruce say?
- What did David say?
- Who was correct?
- How do you know?

*Interviewing protocol*
The aim is for the interviewee to give an account of the episode that an independent observer would say is accurate and unaffected by the involvement of others, particularly the interviewer.

*Introduction*
> *Hello, my name is Louise. How are you today?*
> *We are going to watch a short video. When it has finished, I would like you to tell me all about what happened in it.*

[Show video]

*Level 1 questions: general narrative*
Aim at an accurate, visual, comprehensive, objective description. Courts prefer that witnesses tell what they actually perceived. Any evidence that is removed from the direct experience of a witness is suspect. So is a subjective opinion. You must avoid suggesting or implying a particular answer. So the first question is:

> *Now that we have seen the video, can you tell me what happened?*

It is best to proceed chronologically through the episode. If the interviewee reports a conversation in indirect speech, or that someone said something happened, ask the interviewee to say what was actually said, or what the interviewee actually saw. Hearsay is to be avoided. So, if the interviewee says, 'He said not to touch her', you should ask, 'What did he actually say?' or 'What were the words he used?' and persevere until you get an answer in direct speech.

If you merely wish to proceed, the next question is:

> *And what happened next?*

If you want to go back towards the beginning, you might say:

> *Did anything happen before that?*

If you are seeking elaboration:

> *Did anything else happen?*

*Level 2 questions: reflected prompts*
Once the interviewee has provided some information, it can be used to elicit further information. For example:

> *You said a man was in the room—*
> *What was he doing?*
> *Where was he?*
> *Was anyone else in the room?*

[Don't say, 'There was a man in the room, wasn't there?' or 'The man could have been on the bed, couldn't he?' If you cannot get the answer without resorting to this type of suggestion, let it go.]

*Level 3 questions: clarifying descriptions*
Every description must be as complete and objectively descriptive as possible. Don't leave undefined concepts undefined.
    If the interviewee says, 'He touched her', you need to ask:
    *Can you tell me exactly what he did?*

*Level 4 questions: clarifying interpretations*
The interviewee might say, 'She looked tense.' You then need a description of what that looks like, because as it stands it is subjective, a value judgement. This is a difficult area, because you cannot put words into the interviewee's mouth, but you need something further, like:
    *What makes you say she looks tense?*

*Conclusion*
You might ask:
    *Is there anything else you can tell me about what we have just seen?*
    If the answer is no, thank the interviewee, and say, *'Now we'll have a look at the next episode'*, or conclude.

## Stage 2: Establishing the subjects' ability to relate a sequence of events—pre-test

Each subject was shown *The Secret* and one of the other two videos. Both the other video shown and the order of presentation were randomly chosen. On the completion of each video, the child was immediately asked to recount the events shown. The interviewer used the interviewing protocol already described, addressing her questions directly to the child. The child then responded using the symbol boards (and sometimes spoken language).
    A teacher who was experienced in using augmentative communication systems such as the compic symbol board acted as interpreter. Her role was to read the response given by the child and relay it to the interviewer. The interpreter was encouraged not to anticipate responses from the child but to ensure that enough time was given to answer fully.
    Present during the viewing of the videos and the ensuing interviews were the child, the teacher who taught the class (and who acted as translator), the interviewer (unknown to the children

prior to the study), the three researchers and the camera operator. Although every effort was made to make the children feel comfortable, the situation had some elements which might give the impression that the child was being tested and, therefore, cause some measure of anxiety. In this it partly mirrored the courtroom situation where the child is questioned by strangers with a mix of people familiar and unfamiliar to the child in attendance.

Two cameras were used to tape the interviews. One was trained on the symbol boards that the child used so that the accuracy of pointing and the validity of the translation given by the teacher could be checked. The other filmed the child. In this way, when the tapes were combined, using split-screen techniques, both facial expression and body language could be matched with the responses given through the symbol boards. Transcripts of the interviews with notations about the child's reactions and the impact of the translator on the message given were made from the tapes. They were then analysed by each of the three researchers according to a scoring protocol which is described in the results section below.

## Stage 3: Development of a symbol board covering vocabulary related to sexuality and personal development

All students in the study used a communication system based on the international standards set down for the use of compic symbols. Additional boards were developed to ensure that the children had the vocabulary and means to discuss issues related to sexuality and personal development. These boards were devised in consultation with the speech pathologists who regularly worked with the children and were skilled in compic, the school principal and the teacher designated to teach the personal development course as part of the students' academic curriculum. The criteria used to determine the number of symbols required were based on a consideration of the complexity and size of the communication boards already being utilised by the students. The meaning represented by the symbols, as much as possible, was concrete and not open to interpretation. In addition to the symbols related to personal development, each student was given a board depicting line drawings of body parts. The specialised boards are set out in Figure 12.1.

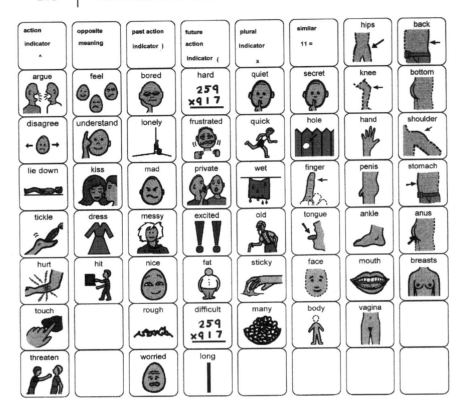

**Figure 12.1**  Symbol boards

A training program is required to familiarise students with new symbols and their location on the board and to give them sufficient practice to make their use meaningful and effective. Students were introduced to the boards over a six-month period and were encouraged to use them regularly within the personal development program.

## Stage 4: The personal development program

The students in the study all undertook the personal development course over two terms as part of their regular school studies. The curriculum was set down by the education authorities and covered a range of issues related to sexuality, sexual behaviour, personal safety and abuse.

## Stage 5: Establishing the subjects' ability to relate a sequence of events—post-test

The children were tested again after a period of six months. The same procedure was followed as in Stage 2 with the child being shown two videos again: *The Secret*, which had been seen in the pre-test, and the video not seen on the previous occasion. Once again, the order of presentation was random. The same interviewing protocol was used and the child was asked to recount the events immediately after watching each video sequence.

## RESULTS

The strength of the accounts given by the children was assessed on the criteria of accuracy, comprehensiveness and relevance to the proof of a possible offence. Fluency of communication and the role of the interpreter were also considered. In analysing the results, differences became apparent in how the children's performance should be judged according to whether a developmental or a legal perspective was taken. Thus, what might be deemed acceptable from an educational point of view might not be proof of a possible offence. Since the thrust of the study was to consider the children's ability to give evidence, the legal perspective was seen as primary.

Although most of the subjects relied on the interpreter to communicate their responses to the interviewer, the study shows that they are expressing their own ideas. It is clear that with the unknown interviewer the protocol worked to ensure that the story was the child's own. Clearly, the strongest approach is to see the purpose of the interview as the telling of a factual story, and prior discussion with the child that all that is wanted is what was actually seen might be desirable. Any intentional or unintentional leading could be eliminated with relative ease, particularly if the interpreter is unknown to the child.

The transcripts reveal the ability of several of the children to provide a narrative that carries sufficient independent meaning to be taken into account in building up a picture of what happened, and also factors that work against the cogency of the story. The most prominent of the latter is the lack of discrimination between certain words and concepts, which may come about through the necessarily restricted vocabulary available through the medium of communication. Another problem is the tendency of some children to infer situations which did not match the detail presented in the videos. It is then open to argument that the later filling in of detail follows the inference. Again, the reliance on inference is possibly a function of trying to communicate a 'rich' concept with restricted means.

Some examples that illustrate potential dangers to the reception of evidence in this fashion are the potential ambiguities arising from interpreter misinterpretation of meaning. *Behind*, for example, has a clear connotation in a sexually charged episode, but it is likely that in the context it meant either *before* or *after*. Two problems of meaning arise. One is determining which word was actually meant. The other is that it is often the case that words belonging to the same meaning cluster can have virtually opposite meanings—the meaning is usually clear from the context but here the paucity of context accentuates their possible ambiguity. One example, taken from Latin, is that *altus* means both high and deep. Other examples are scattered through the transcripts, such as *penis* being attributed to the speaker after only the first three letters, *pen*, had been indicated; drugs being seen as synonymous with cigarettes by one child; *always* perhaps being confused in translation with *alone*.

As problems with speech production are common to all the subjects in the study, difficulty with communication has always been a part of their lives. As a consequence they often have to work hard to be understood and are used to finding alternative strategies to get across their meaning. Despite or perhaps because of this, it was noticed that the children did, at times, become frustrated with the interpreter's ability to understand what they were trying to say. This was mostly apparent when the children were attempting to spell a word. Their poor spelling (very often phonetic) caused them and the interpreter great difficulty. When this happened they would sometimes curtail their account and simply move on to the next question. This frustration and the effort required is thus likely to limit the amount of detail given. Patience and great skill is needed by the interviewer, the interpreter and the interviewee.

The subjects made some use of the specialised communication boards (see Figure 12.1) which had been introduced to them before the second presentation of the videos. This enabled them to express intimate details more readily. Thus it was found that two of the nine children had a better understanding of the innuendo associated with the events portrayed in *The Secret*. The remaining subjects' recounting of the sequence remained unchanged although they were able to use a few more appropriate words to express themselves. It is to be expected that the before and after versions of the video should be basically unchanged as the subjects had been asked to recount, not to interpret, what they had viewed. A video sequence with more detail and where the recounting depends more upon the vocabulary learned by students in the personal development program might prove instructive. The ethics in doing this however, are, questionable, given the age of the children and the sensitive nature of the topic.

The ability to recount the events depicted in the videos is influenced by factors such as the child's understanding of the content, the quality of memory and the ability to express oneself. These are factors which affect the population at large, not just children with cerebral palsy.

Our perceptions of rationality and reality are heavily influenced by linguistic fluency. In the early stages of the study it was evident that the interpreter, who knew the children and was familiar with their idiosyncrasies, was inclined to finish sentences and make assumptions. Each of these traits might be sufficient for evidence to be seen as contaminated. The use of an interviewer who had no prior contact with the children curtailed, but did not eliminate, this type of interaction. The introduction of a skilled, independent interpreter would solve this difficulty.

The interviewer and the interpreter made the point that their viewing of the scenario before conducting the interview may have had some effect on their interpretation of the children's responses. This needs to be addressed in future studies.

## CONCLUSION

The results obtained show that there is now nothing to stop the giving of evidence by children with cerebral palsy, save preconceptions of incompetence. The High Court has warned against 'misconceptions often involving an underestimation of a person's ability' *(Secretary, Department of Health and Community Services v JWB and SMB* (1992) 175 CLR 218 at 239 per Mason CJ, Dawson, Toohey and Gaudron JJ).

The interviewing protocol developed for this purpose is simple and provides a framework for the accurate and reliable transmission of evidence. The interviewer was able to accommodate readily to the protocol, developing a routine of asking '*what happened next*' and '*you said . . . can you tell me . . .*' Integral to this framework is the mechanism of communication, which is the board, its enhancement, and the interpreter.

The amount of heightened imaginative overlay evident in the recounted episodes by some children suggests a need for caution and precludes a blanket confirmation of accuracy in terms of the narrative. That being so, we believe that four recommendations can be derived from the findings. These are that:

1. Use be made of expert evidence in determining whether the individual is capable of giving an independent response.
2. Court-appointed panels of professionals adept in the use of compic and other methods of augmentative communication be set up so that independent, expert interpreters can be called upon.
3. Judicial education be instituted to ensure that the issues involved in the giving of evidence by people with no functional spoken language be fully understood.
4. Due emphasis be given to the need for people with no functional language to be given the vocabulary and education needed for them to communicate and understand issues related to sexuality and personal safety.

We believe that the results obtained in this study provide confirmation that children can give a clear narrative using an augmentative communication system. As such, the protocol developed offers a platform for further exploration and application.

# 13 Melva's story: an Aboriginal approach to preventing child sexual assault

*Melva Kennedy*

ONE WOULD THINK anyone wanting to work in the area of child protection would have some sort of special motivation or ambition—for example, they may have had personal reasons, or have had contact with someone who had been abused. Or maybe they just wanted to help victims of violence. Strangely enough I began working in this area because I didn't want to work with a particular dentist. At that time I was working at the Aboriginal Medical Service in Redfern as a dental assistant. One of the dentists who was employed there at that time was not an easy person to get along with so I spoke to my employer and told her I did not want to work with him. It was about this time there was a position available for someone to train as a sexual assault counsellor. My employer then asked me if I wanted to work in child protection, to learn to work with children who had been abused. At first I was reluctant but when she explained I would have quite a lot of training in that area I told her I would give it a try on condition that I could go back to the dental clinic if I didn't find the other position suitable. She agreed, and the next time I went back to the dental clinic, it was as a patient . . .

I began attending workshops and courses on child sexual assault, counselling skills and whatever other kind of education I thought would help me to help my clients. I found it very difficult at first for many different reasons. I didn't like hearing about the horrible things that happened to children. It brought up some very deep feelings for me, such as sadness, anger, frustration and disgust. On the positive side I had good feelings about being able to help and support the families that came to see me. Some of them had been to other services but came to me because they said they felt better about seeing an Aboriginal worker. They felt I had a better understanding of their problems because of my Aboriginality. I actually started to become very enthusiastic about my work.

I knew when I started this position and began the learning, I was going to need all the support I could get. I spoke to my family, told them about the work I would be doing and explained that I would probably, at some time, need a shoulder to lean on and some TLC (tender loving care). I am very lucky to have such a caring family who have given me all the support I've needed. I am especially grateful for the extra support that comes from my two daughters and my youngest sister. They are always there for me when I need someone.

The hardest thing about the education I was receiving was becoming aware, not only of the incidence of child sexual assault, but the fact that it was happening in Aboriginal communities. Worse still was finding that Aboriginal men and some women were abusing our children. It was always easy to believe that this abuse would not happen to our children or in our community, especially when there was the history of caring and sharing in Aboriginal culture.

In addressing the needs of Aboriginal child protection I must mention a little about Aboriginal history. For anyone to begin to understand the needs of an Aboriginal person or their community there must be some awareness of the issues that began more than 200 years ago. The unfavourable treatment that Aboriginal people received after colonisation left them with feelings of great fear and a distrust of government bureaucracies that is still felt today. These feelings make it difficult, if not impossible for some Aboriginal people to seek help. It can be very intimidating for these people to ask for the assistance of government services such as police, hospitals, doctors, school teachers/counsellors, sexual assault services and, of course, 'the Welfare' (in New South Wales, the Department of Community Services).

These opinions of government bureaucracy can stand in the way of Aboriginal people being safe and healthy. They don't present to hospitals unless it is absolutely necessary. They don't want to seek counselling for any reason—they would rather battle on as best they can. They don't want to report offenders to police, not only because of the fear and distrust that was instilled in them, but for many other reasons—for example, backlash from their community and racist attitudes from some police officers and other service providers.

In 1988 I was invited to a Link-Up meeting. Link-Up is an Aboriginal organisation set up to find and reunite the Aboriginal children who, under government policy, were taken from their families. At this meeting I was asked by the organisers to speak to the group about child sexual assault. I agreed and was given a half-hour time slot. An enormous amount of interest was generated. This brought up lots of questions and long discussions, which finished about an hour and a half later. This was the first time I had spoken to a group of people about the issues of child sexual assault. I was surprised at the amount of interest shown, and the willingness of some people to talk about these issues.

After leaving the Aboriginal Medical Service, I worked independently as a consultant/educator. I presented workshops on child sexual assault for my people in communities throughout New South Wales. During that time I made a number of contacts in non-Aboriginal child sexual assault agencies, women's organisations and the Department of Community Services. Some of these contacts did not have a great deal of awareness of Aboriginal culture and were at a loss as to what to do for their Aboriginal clients. I had requests for advice on Aboriginal issues to help them understand better and assist their clients. This made me aware of the lack of knowledge and understanding some non-Aboriginals had regarding child sexual assault in the Aboriginal communities. It also made me aware that we needed our own system for addressing the issue of child sexual assault in the Aboriginal community.

To work with Aboriginal people and to make services accessible to them, service providers must be aware of the history of colonisation and the effects this has had on Aboriginal people today. They must also be aware of the 'cultural differences', not only between Aboriginal and non-Aboriginal but in the diversity of Aboriginal people and their communities. It is often assumed that all Aboriginal people are the same and have the same needs and beliefs.

To go into an Aboriginal community as a non-Aboriginal worker requires very careful preparation and demands a unique type of individual. Although I am an Aboriginal woman it would be disrespectful of me to plan something in an Aboriginal community without their permission. It is more appropriate to make contact with a person from the community I wish to visit, and to ask them if they would mind introducing me to other people in their community. If I require a venue for a workshop or meeting I explain to them what is needed and ask for help to choose a place that is suitable for everyone. It may appear to some people that I am referring to traditionally oriented communities, and I would like to explain that there is an 'Aboriginal way of being' or 'Aboriginal commonality' found among all Aboriginals whether traditional or city dweller (Dulwich Centre 1995). Therefore, many Aboriginal communities will relate, to some degree, to traditional cultural characteristics.

Until recently child sexual assault was not openly spoken about in our communities. In the past our people denied that it happened. Some Aboriginal people today still deny that child sexual assault happens in Aboriginal society. I believe the hesitation of Aboriginal people to discuss child sexual assault openly and acknowledge that it happens in Aboriginal communities as well as in others is due to the negative approach the government has used towards them in the past. The history of the Aborigines Protection Board 'stealing children' has caused great feelings of fear and distrust. In more recent times, the issue of black deaths in custody can make people more reluctant to notify—they don't want to feel responsible for the perpetrator possibly becoming another statistic.

Most Aboriginal people live in small communities, so they don't want to be labelled as a 'dobber' or 'police pimp'. They could also fear repercussions from families of the perpetrators and in some cases the victim's family. The victim's family may not want the abuse brought to anyone's attention, for many different reasons. Shame is one of the main reasons they may want to keep knowledge of the abuse to themselves. Most non-Aboriginal people have some difficulty understanding the concept of shame for an Aboriginal person, even though they recognise that it impacts powerfully upon their lives (Dulwich Centre 1995). An Aboriginal person who is experiencing shame will suffer a whole range of emotions, such as embarrassment, disgrace, dishonour and humiliation. This shame can have a huge influence on decisions they may have to make, and it could have a negative effect on their health and well-being.

The nature of child sexual assault makes it a very difficult and often painful subject for anyone to talk about. I feel the only way to make it easier to talk about is through education. Education is a powerful tool that can break down a lot of barriers.

Through colonisation, a large number of Aboriginal people have lost or had taken away from them their traditional culture and values, so most of my education and training came from non-Aboriginal people. During my childhood school years I suffered racism in the education system—which didn't do much for my self-esteem at the time or my ability to learn. I still experience racist attitudes today, which can be more hurtful, harmful and humiliating now than it ever was when I was a child. At least when I was a child I had some level of naivety—I thought people looked down on me because I was poor, or had daggy clothes, or maybe I wasn't pretty—but now I know it was all about the colour of my skin and where I came from and who I am. Racism still hurts and can generate a lot of damage: it can cause a 'big shame' leading to loss of self-esteem so that victims have no pride in themselves or their lifestyle; it causes a lot of anger which can motivate violence either towards the perpetrator or most commonly the victim or their families; and it causes psychological damage. All these effects of racism can actually lead to physical illnesses.

When, as an adult, I began attending workshops and courses, I found it extremely uncomfortable and intimidating to be the only Aboriginal person in a large crowd in a strange place, listening to all these strange, big words (jargon). Because I was in an unfamiliar place the learning process was much harder and took me much longer than normal. I had to write down the jargon and look in a dictionary to find out what it meant, but sometimes I didn't understand what was said and 'lost the plot'. Then I would have to find out in my own way, by looking for resources or talking to other people about what I needed to know. I eventually gained as much knowledge as anyone in the groups I was a part of, but I did it the hard way.

I decided I needed to share that knowledge with my people but in an easier way. I adapted most of the information and presented it in easy 'jargon free' workshops. These workshops consisted of clarified language in handouts, lectures, role plays and showing videos. Wherever possible the venue was chosen to suit the participants, usually in their own communities. I quickly realised that this was what my people wanted—workshops presented by Aboriginal people for Aboriginal people, gathering easy-to-understand but important information in a familiar place, and sometimes from a familiar Aboriginal face.

When planning workshops or meetings I must be aware of the different factions that usually exist in these communities and make sure I don't say or do anything that is traditionally or politically inappropriate. I visit these communities before each workshop to meet the people and talk with them about the workshop I will be presenting or the meeting I want to organise. I let them know who will be coming with me and basically what the workshop will consist of or what the meeting is about. I try to visit all Aboriginal organisations and to arrange visits to coincide with community gatherings, such as meetings or functions, in that particular area.

The Education Centre Against Violence and the NSW Child Protection Council have been instrumental in giving me the opportunity to share my knowledge with my people in their own communities in this more relaxed and less threatening manner. I have been able to present workshops in many Aboriginal communities throughout New South Wales, Canberra and the Northern Territory. Together, the Centre, the Council and I have developed suitable resources and have also achieved the accreditation of six Aboriginal trainers to present further workshops in child sexual assault, which I think is a very important first step towards preventing child abuse in Aboriginal communities.

These workshops have proved very popular with every community visited including communities in Canberra and the Northern Territory. There have been excellent responses from Aboriginal workers and community members. We have had up to 32 participants in some workshops. There have been some non-Aboriginal participants as well: these people are usually working with and accepted by the Aboriginal community. All the workshops generate fantastic feedback and I usually conduct follow-up activities with some members of each community. These follow-ups may include giving out more detailed information on certain issues or presenting smaller workshops for specific groups. Non-Aboriginal workers request workshops on Aboriginal issues to help them work with Aboriginal clients in a culturally sensitive manner.

Although there has been an enormous amount of time, energy and of course money spent on presenting workshops to Aboriginal communities on child protection, participants have continually raised the issue of the lack of specific, culturally appropriate videos and resources. I am currently involved in the production of two educational videos which hopefully will remedy this gap in resources. One video will address child sexual assault and the other, physical abuse and neglect, including domestic violence as a child protection issue.

## CONCLUSION

These workshops alone won't stop our children from being abused: there needs to be more community involvement, and there has to be huge awareness campaigns in the Aboriginal communities on children's safety. All services involved in the safety of children should come together to work out what role they can play in helping to enhance the safety of Aboriginal children. There also needs to be an 'Aboriginal Friendly' protective behaviours program designed especially for and made readily available to Aboriginal adults and children. There must be bigger and better advertising of 'Operation Paradox' in the Aboriginal community. This may help to alleviate some of the problems of reporting an offender. We also need to look at the possibility of having Aboriginal community controlled crisis and education centres against violence to children. There is a need for safe houses for these children and non-offending family members to access if the need arises.

There has to be a strong commitment to continue this work. There is much more to be done, more services and safety programs needed for our children, more communities to be reached, more Aboriginal trainers to be encouraged and supported, more children's lives to be protected and nurtured. These children are our future, this country's heritage. They are precious and the way they are treated today will influence their attitudes and behaviour in years to come.

# 14 Child protection: does community matter?

## Eileen Baldry and Tony Vinson

THE ANSWER TO the question posed in the title of this chapter is resoundingly affirmative if one has in mind the many studies here and abroad that have shown major variations in child abuse rates between neighbourhoods, defined operationally in terms of census collection boundaries.[1] The question takes on a more complex hue when we ask what lies behind these patterns of association, and in what sense the determinative influences are aptly described as communal.

The study described in this chapter focuses on the neighbourhood or local community as a potential source of support for families living in two socioeconomically depressed localities in Western Sydney, New South Wales. One area has a relatively high level of reported child abuse, the other does not. The study attempts to find out why this difference exists and relies for this purpose on the contrasting pictures of the sociopsychological environments of the two neighbourhoods, as indicated by the aggregate of individual characteristics (Unger & Wandersman 1982).

It is information about conditions of the community, as community, rather than its component parts, that needs to be kept in focus when pondering the issue posed by the title of this chapter. The details of individual families known to have maltreated children play no part in this study. The design emphasises the character of the neighbourhoods as social entities. The underlying assumption, consistent with the ecological approach, is that the characteristics of a neighbourhood as a whole may have an influence on social relations that is distinct from the influence of those characteristics on an individual level (Unger & Wandersman 1982). When this approach is maintained and random samples of the respective populations used to generate the sociopsychological data, a clear finding emerges: the two neighbourhoods are virtually indistinguishable in terms of all aspects of social climate and local organisation but one—the *structure* (not overall size) of their social support networks.

If 'community matters', a second major challenge is to determine how neighbourhood conditions actually infringe on the well-being of children. In the past, sociologists offered different explanations of the aetiology of child maltreatment. Gradually, with the maturing of the field of study, it has been recognised (Belsky 1980) that (i) child maltreatment is determined by forces at work in the individual, the family and in the community and culture in which the individual and the family are embedded, (ii) that these multiple determinants are ecologically nested within one another, and (iii) that much of the theoretical conflict that has characterised the study of child maltreatment is more apparent than real. Recent writers, notably Garbarino and associates and Belsky have adapted the ecological approach to human development conceived by Bronfenbrenner (1977) as an integrated framework capable of illuminating both the understanding of the aetiology of child maltreatment and ways in which we can attempt to prevent its occurrence.

Within this framework, the effects and interactions of factors as varied as parents' experience of abuse (*ontogenetic development*), children's abuse-eliciting behaviour, patterns of family interaction, spouse relations (the *microsystem*), neighbourhood resources and levels of social support (the *ecosystem*) and tolerance of violence, definitions of parenthood and methods of disciplining children (the *macrosystem*) can be studied (Powell 1979; Belsky 1980). It probably lies beyond the scope of any single project to straddle more than two or three of the conceptual levels outlined above.

Details of the current study are presented following an outline of the evolution of the theoretical framework within which it has been conducted.

## ECOLOGICAL APPROACH

Implied in an ecological approach to family functioning and child rearing is a view of the family as an open system, responsive to and dependent upon its environment. Families are constantly in exchange with social groups and neighbourhoods, which are major aspects of the family's immediate social environment. 'They are layers of the social environment which are in direct contact with the family system and serve as mediating structures which stand between the family and the larger society' (Powell 1979, p. 6). While this may be generally true, one of the best-documented characteristics of abusive and neglectful parents is their social isolation (Polansky et al. 1979; Belsky 1980; Salzinger, Kaplan & Artesnyeff 1983; Howze & Kotch 1984; Corse, Schmid & Trickett 1990). Conversely, the availability of social support has been shown in a Sydney study to be associated with parental and family behaviour likely to minimise child maltreatment (Homel, Burns & Goodnow 1987). Corse et al. (1990) have summarised other research evidence showing the benefits of parents having good social support.

The isolation of abusive and neglectful parents could have many causes: Polansky et al. (1981) believe, on the basis of a study of neglectful mothers, that social non-participation may long pre-date parenting problems. The same investigators, however, consider that the same evidence shows that the isolation of some neglectful mothers is due to rejection by people who disapprove of their methods of parenting and their lifestyle. Gaudin and Polansky (1986) have studied the relative social distancing of different groups from a hypothetical family which displays 'unacceptable' child-care practices. They have found that distancing oneself from families considered neglectful is greater among men than women, and greater among men and women of lower socioeconomic status (SES) than those of higher SES. Notwithstanding these differences, *most* of the respondents said they were inclined to distance neglectful families and that their communities would be even more rejecting.

Garbarino (1977) argues that the *sufficient* conditions for child abuse are in abundant supply in modern industrial societies. What is less apparent are the conditions that 'cause' this vulnerability to be translated into maltreatment. He argues that there are two *necessary* conditions for child abuse. One is the availability within families of a cultural justification for the use of force against children. As an Australian observer of the Swedish legal prohibition of corporal punishment (Ziegert 1983, p. 918) has stated, 'The "normality" of the use of force in punishment is not comprehensible without the silent or even expressly approbatory support of societal norms and values, including those of the legislator . . .'. The second necessary condition, of crucial importance to the present study, according to Garbarino, is isolation from potent support systems, especially those that exist at the neighbourhood and community levels. He quotes Caplan (1974, pp. 4–5) to make the point that support systems 'provide individuals with opportunities for feedback about themselves and for validations for their expectations about others . . .'.

The principal vehicles through which support system functions are achieved are social networks. They have been referred to as 'social circles'—an indirect chain of interaction based on common interest (Kadushin 1967)—and as 'natural social relationships' (Attneave 1976). Networks vary with respect to their (a) size and diversity of membership, (b) the interconnectedness among members, (c) the content of activities engaged in, and (d) the degree to which contacts are reciprocal. Social isolation need not be due entirely to external factors. It is necessary to distinguish between a lack of social supports and failure to use available supports. According to Garbarino, the failure to use social supports is common among abusive and neglectful families. In any event, the consequences are the same. Child abuse 'feeds' on privacy. It is more likely to occur only when feedback and support are inadequately available to caregivers, either because of an absence of social networks or through the presence of norms of parent–child relations which tolerate or even approve of abuse.

Understanding of the social support and cultural/educative functions of networks, and the connections between the two, has been further refined by Salzinger, Kaplan and Artesnyeff's (1983) study of mothers' personal social networks and child maltreatment. The study was based on the hypothesis that deficient social connections fail to provide parents with appropriate feedback on their behaviour towards their children or alternative models of parental behaviour, or the positive reinforcement required to change their behaviour. The authors conceived of the social network as mediating an individual's contact with the community and with society at large. It functions as a vehicle for the transmission of information, attitudes and values. So, although it is now part of conventional professional wisdom that social networks offer emotional support and protection against the effects of stress, 'they need not always function as a support system but may, in fact, be a source of stress as well' (Salzinger et al. 1983, p. 68; see also Cochran & Brassard 1979; Powell 1979; Corse, Schmid & Tricket 1990).

Some abusive families do not experience this latter type of stress because their particular form of insularity is a relative lack of connection between more immediate (usually familial) and more distant (usually peers) parts of the network (Corse et al. 1990). To test these contentions, Salzinger et al. (1983) compared the social networks of a sample of mothers in families being treated for disclosed cases of child abuse and neglect (the *clinic* group) and a matched sample of mothers whose children were not believed to be subject to maltreatment (the *control* group). The investigators found that the clinic mothers were more isolated than the control mothers in that they had smaller networks, especially peer networks, and spent less time with their networks. The clinic mothers were also more insulated in that their subnetworks were less connected to each other. It was speculated that, because the limited social contact the abusive mothers had was confined primarily to their immediate families who shared many of the same values, their patterns of behaviour were probably resistant to change and lacked the more varied discrepant input afforded by more distant parts of their network.

## 'HIGH-RISK' NEIGHBOURHOODS

Can we identify neighbourhoods that contain a disproportionate number of families that are vulnerable to child abuse and neglect? There are two senses in which families can be at high risk of maltreating their children (Garbarino & Kostelny 1991). The first stems from the well-documented link between low income and child abuse. For example, in a study of Omaha, Nebraska, socioeconomic status accounted for about 40 per cent of the variation across neighbourhoods in repeated cases of child maltreatment (Garbarino & Crouter 1978). A study of 246 Texas counties by Spearly and Lauderdale (1983) provided general confirmation of the foregoing results.

A number of Australian studies have shown a similar marked association between reported child abuse and low socioeconomic status (Nixon et al. 1981; Vinson & McArthur 1988; Vinson, Berreen & McArthur 1989; Skurray & Ham 1990). The disinclination of residents of low status areas to 'rat on' their neighbours and family, even while institutional sources (hospitals, schools, welfare agencies, and the like) may be more inclined to over-report in low income areas, has led Garbarino and Crouter to the conclusion that reported child abuse figures reflect a genuine inverse relationship between affluence and child maltreatment. This conclusion is supported by statistical analyses of the concentration of abuse in the lowest strata within the most disadvantaged sections of society (Pelton 1978).

The second meaning of high risk is that an area has a higher rate of child maltreatment than would be predicted knowing its socioeconomic character. This possibility was illustrated by Garbarino and Sherman (1980). They examined a pair of neighbourhoods, one high risk and the other low risk for child maltreatment, even though the areas were matched on socioeconomic characteristics. The two neighbourhoods presented contrasting environments for child rearing. The high risk neighbourhood was believed to represent a socially impoverished human ecology. Varied data was cited in support of this hypothesis. Mothers in the low risk area rated their neighbourhood as a better place to raise children and they rated their children themselves as easier to raise. In each of eight aspects of neighbourhood (e.g. public image, 'quality of life' and informal supports), the preponderance of the views of knowledgeable locals painted a negative picture of the high risk area. Support for the contention that child abuse is not predicted solely by socioeconomic deprivation has also been provided by a study of an inner-London Borough (Cotterill 1988). A later study by Garbarino and Kostelny (1991) of Chicago neighbourhoods basically replicated the findings of the Omaha project but with the added insight that the social service agencies in a community with an impoverished human ecology mirror the problems facing that community.

## CONCEPT DEVELOPMENT

One shortcoming of research into social networks is the lack of consensus regarding the conceptualisation of them. There is increasing agreement that the construct of support networks is a meta-construct with several dimensions, including structure, satisfaction and perceived support (Jennings, Stagg & Pollay 1988). However, even the central concept of 'social support' is not without its complications. In a timely review of the evidence supporting the parental isolation/child maltreatment thesis, Seagull (1987) was led to ask the basic question: 'What is the definition of social support?' Some of the grounds for Seagull's query (e.g. the non-supportive and/or non-social nature of some network experiences and the off-putting behaviour of some at-risk parents) have been dealt with by other writers and are discussed in the present chapter. What is more arresting is her citing of evidence (Henderson, Byrne & Duncan-Jones 1981), derived in part from community psychiatry studies, that an individual's *perception* of the adequacy of intimacy can be more important in buffering stress than embeddedness in large social networks. Clearly, the distinction between factors like perceived and received support, and measures which enable them to be examined separately, need to be employed in studies of child maltreatment and social support (Richey, Lovell & Reid 1991).

Not that progress is likely to be made via refinements to one term in the child abuse equation. As so often happens when a field of research is undergoing scholarly refinement, theoretical concepts at each level of the ecological framework, previously treated in an undifferentiated way, are now being more carefully defined and subdivided in the light of research findings. The work of Cummins (1988) is a case in point. It shows the added light thrown on the interactions between 'stress'/'social support'/'individual' where the first variable is assessed in terms of chronic stress ('hassles'), the second in terms of 'perceived' and 'received' support, and the third in terms of the 'internal'/'external' locus of control orientation of the individual. Then a number of differential effects can be seen. For example, individuals who perceived themselves as being in control (internals) achieve a positive buffering effect from received social support but a *negative* buffering effect from 'reassurance' of worth support. The latter seems to sensitise these individuals to stressful elements in the environment. Further conceptual refinements of this kind are to be expected and, provided the resultant schemes do not become too unwieldy, they will inform and sharpen the management of child abuse prevention programs.

It also seems probable that support for parenting is 'gendered' rather than undifferentiated (Breines & Gordon 1983; Parton 1990). In America, the descriptive data available on alleged perpetrators indicate some significant differences by gender. Females are more likely to be Hispanic, unmarried, young and poor. Males are more likely to be Anglo or Black, married, older and middle class. The personal resources of one group—females—are limited due to inequalities of gender, race, ethnicity and class. Awareness of this pattern led Young and Gately (1988) to hypothesise that the availability of neighbourhood resources would be of more importance in mediating maltreatment (and explaining variations in rates of maltreatment) by females than by males. In terms of the ecological approach expounded by Garbarino, they expected that 'drains' on neighbourhood social support would be more important in predicting female rates of abuse than in predicting male rates. Hence 'percentages of females in the labour force' was preferred over the previously used index 'percentage of females in the labour force with children under age six'. The investigators found that neighbourhood rates of maltreatment by females were lower when substantial numbers of women with access to material resources were available for support. Female rates were higher when there were relatively large numbers of newly arrived residents in a neighbourhood, presumed to have the effect of disrupting social networks.

These results are, in themselves, interesting but, in terms of the conceptual development of the field, the Young and Gately analysis is a major contribution on at least two counts: (i) it attempts to refine the broad concept of social support to take account of the stress experienced by women and the support available to them; (ii) it conceptualises the notions of neighbourhood environment more rigorously than is characteristic of the literature generally and operationalises measures so as to capture community level conditions rather than the situations of particular individuals. The study described below attempted a similar approach although it relies on survey rather than time series data.

## THE STUDY

A suburb of some 10 000 people and 3500 households in Western Sydney was nominated by the New South Wales State Department of Community Services as a locality with a relatively high rate of confirmed child abuse (22.5 per 1000 children under 16 years of age) over a three-year period. Each household in the suburb was assigned a number and a sample of households was drawn using a table of random numbers. Because of interest in the spatial distribution of reported abuse within larger social aggregates such as suburbs, the initial samples in two contrasting census units (known as Collectors' Districts) were augmented by additional random samplings. The number of households in the total sample was 633, of which 76 per cent granted an interview. Of these, 205 households had children and were eligible for inclusion in this study.

One of the census units, in the southern area of the nominated suburb, had the relatively high rate of confirmed abuse of 53.0 per 1000 children under 16 compared with a relatively low rate of 8.1 per 1000 in the comparison (northern) Collectors' District. The units were of virtually identical population size (approximately 880) and age distribution and had scores on an Australia-wide 'Social Disadvantage' index indicating low relative standing, slightly more so in the case of the southern unit which was two standard deviations below the Australian average. In the southern unit, the forms of reported maltreatment were evenly spread across the physical, sexual, neglect and emotional categories but for a slightly greater concentration in the last-mentioned category. In the comparison area, with the low rate of confirmed abuse, the problems were largely categorised as 'emotional abuse'. The present study is based on a comparison of survey responses of 51 adults in the southern (high risk) neighbourhood and 46 in the northern comparison neighbourhood, all of whom had the main or shared the main responsibility for looking after the children in the selected households.

In addition to demographic data, respondents were asked to indicate their degree of agreement with 18 statements in relation to their neighbourhoods. The items covered identification with and liking for the neighbourhood, patterns of friendships and association, sources of help and the presence of mutual support. Several questions canvassed the reasons for moving to the neighbourhood and the establishment of membership of it. Simple Likert-type scales assessed the locality as a place to raise children and each carer's particular experience of the neighbourhood, in that regard. The ease or otherwise of getting around the locality and maintaining contact with relatives and friends, directly and by telephone, was assessed by means of a number of forced choice and open questions.

The largest component of the questionnaire assessed the membership of nine subnetworks of each carer's support network. The nine subnetworks were: home, close family, distant family, close friendship, work, school/studies, neighbour, organisational and acquaintance. The individual members of the subnetworks were identified and the frequency of the carer's contact with each one ascertained. Once each carer's overall network had been compiled, the carer was asked to indicate whether each member knew each other member. In this way, a matrix of across-subnetwork acquaintanceship was developed. Following the helpful assistance of Dr S. Salzinger, the network data were analysed according to a method she devised.

Carers were also asked to indicate whom they would talk to about five kinds of problems (personal, money, child rearing, household and work/educational). The questionnaire was pre-tested and interviewers received in-house and field training. Each selected household was visited and, if a carer of a child or children was resident and willing to respond, an interview was conducted. If no-one was home that household received up to three calls at varying times before being abandoned. Quality control follow-up interviews were conducted in 5 per cent of cases. Interpreter services were used where language problems existed.

## SAMPLE

Before the residents of selected households were included in the study, it had first to be established that they had the main responsibility, or shared the main responsibility, for looking after resident child/children under 16 years. On that basis, 37 of the 51 respondents (72.5 per cent) in the southern statistical unit and 38 of the 46 respondents (82.6 per cent) in the northern unit were women. The majority of those interviewed were between 30 and 44 years (south, 62.7 per cent; north, 76.1 per cent). A further 27.5 per cent in the south and 21.7 per cent in the north were under 30.

The two samples appear to be generally representative of the populations of the two Collectors' Districts. The demographic and background data collected during the interviews permitted six direct comparisons to be made with the census data.[2] Four of the six comparisons show marked similarities with respect to employment and occupational status and professional/educational attainments. Indeed, ten of the 12 comparisons between census and survey findings revealed only minor differences. The relatively large number of 'overseas born' included in the southern area sample differed significantly from the census expectation. This difference could be a sampling error or reflect a change in the population since the last census. The same comment applies to the income comparison which indicates that the present sample of southern area residents included people of higher than to be expected income levels.

Whatever the explanations for these two findings for the southern statistical unit, their consequence was to make the two sample profiles very similar, with no statistically significant differences between them on the six points of comparison.

## KEY RESULTS

### The neighbourhoods as places to raise children

A majority of both northern and southern area parents took a somewhat pessimistic view of the child-rearing potential of their respective neighbourhoods. The same proportion in each area (39 per cent) described the child-rearing prospects as either 'excellent' or 'good'. The remaining parents divided more or less equally between those who considered the prospects 'so so' and those who thought they were 'poor' or 'very poor'. A variety of reasons were provided to justify these views: one in six of the southern parents considered their neighbourhood had a 'peaceful environment' but an equal number complained of the unacceptable 'lifestyles' of some families. One in five of the northern parents claimed that local children and youths were 'unsupervised'. The overall attitudes of the parents did not alter significantly when they were asked about their *personal* experience of their neighbourhood as a place to raise children.

### The neighbourhoods as places to live

If questioning about the child-rearing potential of their locality failed to reveal major differences of attitude between the southern and northern parents, essentially the same was true of their attitudes towards their neighbourhoods as places to live. An instrument comprising 18 statements covering feelings of identification with the neighbourhood, friendships and patterns of interaction and mutual support was administered. Interviewees indicated the strength of their agreement or disagreement with each statement. In terms of the numbers expressing agreement, the results for the two localities were either identical or virtually so (differences of less than 5 per cent) for half of the items. On the other nine items, the southern area parents consistently expressed the more 'positive' attitudes but the difference was only significant in one instance: *I think I agree with most people in my neighbourhood about what is important in life* (south, 54.9 per cent; north, 34.8 per cent).

## Social networks

The analysis of the social networks of parents in the two comparison neighbourhoods provided the most substantial differences uncovered by the study. Judged in terms of their size, there was little difference in the overall profile of the social networks of the two areas. The one obvious difference was that 11 in 52, or one in five of the southern area parents had networks of eight or fewer members. Only two in 46 of the northern parents had such small networks. The direction of the difference between the two samples remained consistent when the threshold was set at 12 or fewer network members (south 59.6 per cent; north 39.1 per cent). However, the number of southern residents with networks exceeding 15 members (28.8 per cent) was slightly greater than was the case among the northern residents (26.1 per cent). The net result was a slight (statistically insignificant) difference between the average network size of 13.85 in the north and 12.69 in the south.

Closer scrutiny of the structure of the networks in each locality reveals some pronounced differences. First, the relative sizes of the components of the networks. Northern residents had significantly larger average 'acquaintance' and 'neighbour' networks. On the other hand, the southern parents had a larger average 'home' network with the difference approaching statistical significance.

The second structural feature examined was the extent to which people in one component of a network interacted with individuals in other components of the same network. It has been hypothesised that such interconnectedness is important in exposing those with child-rearing responsibilities—essentially members of the 'home' network—to wider community values and practices which counteract tendencies to abuse children. Families whose social networks are characterised by this type of connectedness may fare better in the face of life pressures, such as socioeconomic deprivation, than families in comparable socioeconomic circumstances whose home networks are cut off from moderating cultural influences.

The findings of the present study lend support to the foregoing hypothesis. When examining the average number of interacting individuals for each of the 55 combinations of subnetworks within the southern and northern statistical units, in four instances the south/north differences are statistically significant. In all four cases it is the northern unit (the one with the relatively low abuse rate) that has the higher level of across-network interaction. The two instances involving home networks—home/acquaintances and home/neighbours—are particularly important in the light of the 'cultural monitoring' hypothesis.

The 'close family' network was second only in average size to the home network in both localities and its members may exert influence in the upbringing of related children. The greater connection between members of the 'close family' and 'acquaintances' networks in the northern area may indicate that stronger opportunities exist there for families to receive indirect exposure to alternative child-rearing ideas and practices. Similarly, the greater interaction between members of the 'close friends' and 'acquaintances' networks in the north may afford additional indirect and broadening influences on child-rearing practices.

### Social interactions generally

Questions regarding the scale and interconnectedness of networks were supplemented by others on different aspects of the neighbourhoods and wider social interactions. One point on which almost everyone in the northern and southern statistical units agreed was that the local railway was the dividing line between their respective neighbourhoods. Asked to outline their neighbourhood on a map, 88.8 per cent of the southern unit sample and 93.5 per cent of those in the northern unit drew the boundary at the railway line.

Sometimes the importance of making a social contact stems from the fact that one of the parties is faced by a worrying problem. To whom do the parents we have studied turn at such a time? In the vast majority of cases there is at least someone to whom they can turn, the choice to some extent being affected by the nature of the problem. However, the nominated source of help was either a relative or a friend for approximately seven out of ten parents, across the range of problems considered. The preference for seeking the help of relatives was general, but was more pronounced in the case of the southern area parents. A higher proportion of these parents nominated relatives as potential sources of help for each of the illustrative problems. Generally, with the exception of 'personal' problems, friends were less often contemplated as sources of help, and northern parents were more likely to have that preference.

While remembering that there may be a difference between people's general social interactions and those concerned specifically with obtaining help, the preceding findings are consistent with the results of the network analysis. The networks of residents of the northern area had relatively larger 'neighbour' and 'acquaintance' components, whilst the largest component of the southern area networks, in comparative as well as absolute terms, was that centred on 'home'. Less obviously linked to the earlier findings, given the slightly larger average size of the northern area networks, was the greater tendency for residents of that area to be unable to think of anyone to turn to for help with money problems (south, 5.9 per cent; north, 19.6 per cent). A similar, but statistically insignificant difference existed with respect to household problems (south, 7.8 per cent; north, 17.4 per cent). There may be some issues that, notwithstanding the availability of social contacts, residents of the northern area are less willing to discuss with others.

## IMPLICATIONS

Our study has uncovered one outstanding difference between the two localities, namely, the structure of the networks of the two samples of residents. Our findings in this regard are consistent with the findings of Salzinger et al. (1983), Corse et al. (1990) and those researchers whose work has focused on the relative lack of connection between more immediate (usually familial) and more distant (usually peers) parts of the social networks of abusing families. A difference in our study has been the finding that this network characteristic helps to differentiate relatively high and low risk *localities* and not just clinical and non-clinical populations. Our random sample of carers in the comparison (low risk) area had significantly higher levels of interaction between members of their 'home' and 'acquaintance' and 'neighbour' networks. Within the same group, there were significantly greater interactions between members of the 'acquaintance' networks and (respectively) the 'friend' and 'close family' networks. The picture is decidedly one of the insularity of parents in the higher risk area who, in the words of Salzinger et al., 'lack the more varied discrepant input afforded by more distant parts of networks'.

In the light of our findings, what community and network strategies are available for preventing child maltreatment? One of the best reasons for emphasising the prevention of child abuse is the considerable body of research testifying to the fact that treating individuals or families who perpetrate neglect or abuse does not reduce the subsequent incidence of child maltreatment (Cohn & Daro 1987; Caldwell, Bogat & Davidson 1988). This finding has led many in the field to the conclusion that the best strategy for reducing or eliminating child abuse and neglect is to prevent it. Unfortunately, to date, few demonstrably preventive programs have been documented.

Polansky et al. (1985) conceive of the treatment challenge as involving the forging of links between the parents who cause concern and their more supported and potentially supportive neighbours. They suggest a range of ways of effecting the suggested linkages, including the introduction of parent enrichment, education and mutual support groups that include both neglectful and non-neglectful families, cooperative child care (supervised by competent staff), and the identification and involvement of recognised 'natural neighbours'—persons in the community to whom others turn for help, advice or favours (Peterman 1981). Services intended to reduce the risk of child maltreatment may need to 'go with the grain' of existing social networks if they are to be taken up and used. Studies by Birkel and Reppucci (1983) show that the frequency of kin contact and the structure of a client's social network are important variables influencing participation in parent education. They infer from their findings that the group that made limited use of the parent education services may have needed a neighbourhood level of intervention; this might include the expansion of child-care services or the identification and use of neighbourhood opinion leaders in matters of child rearing.

One way of attempting to prevent child maltreatment is to devise programs that simulate some of the helpful child-rearing functions attributed to naturally occurring networks. These *devised social networks* are distinguishable from natural social networks by virtue of their being organised according to related functional roles rather than related social roles based on a history of established social exchange. Regardless of the type of network involved, it is advantageous for someone, often a professional worker, to coordinate the network at the community level (Turkat 1980). In many cases, the client, coordinator, service providers and the support system are brought together in a planning-linking conference (a social network assembly). A Child and Family Neighbourhood Program (CFNP), described by Powell (1987), overlaps the idea of devised networks. The concept of support afforded by the CFNP parallels the typical functions of parents' social networks. The program is designed to provide (i) child-rearing information and advice, (ii) emotional support, (iii) role models, and (iv) information about and referral to community resources. Essentially, the Child and Family Neighbourhood Program represents a strategic choice to graft temporary, new reference communities onto existing networks rather than relying on the mobilising of existing prosocial sources of support.

It is not possible nor desirable in this brief review to describe the content of more than a sample of the community and network-based prevention programs which have been developed. Others with different points of departure have not been included (see, e.g., Rosenberg & Reppucci 1985; Barth 1991). In a majority of instances the content needs to be determined in consultation with client groups.

The foregoing commentary has attempted to highlight some of the strategic issues involved if community is, indeed, to matter in the promotion of the well-being of children and the prevention of child maltreatment.

# 15 | A comprehensive approach: the family safety model with domestic violence

## Elisabeth Shaw, Akivra Bouris and Sheena Pye

SINCE ITS INCEPTION in 1948,[1] Relationships Australia (NSW) has been working with individuals and couples who present with, or are discovered to be experiencing, domestic violence. Over time it was recognised that an integrated and comprehensive strategy was required to address domestic violence, and that a specialist, rather than a generalist framework was required to address issues of safety and best practice. This chapter describes the development and operation of the Family Safety Program which aims to prevent violence occurring in family relationships and to resolve the effects of such violence. It is based on the premises that violence is the responsibility of the perpetrator, that all family members will be affected to some extent by the violence, and that members may have individual needs as well as needs in common as a result of the abuse.

The goals of the Family Safety Program are to:

- promote the safety of all family members including children, parents and grandparents and thus interrupt the intergenerational aspects of the transmission of violence;
- help family members cease violent, controlling, intimidating and belittling behaviour and to change attitudes associated with such behaviour;

- integrate the organisation's response to violence in all programs;
- diversify the range of services offered to clients involved in violence;
- promote staff well-being by providing a firm structure within which to work with violence;
- contribute to knowledge development about violence in families and effective interventions by undertaking research.

While the Family Safety Program targets all areas of family violence, this chapter focuses on the services that address men's violence towards women and children, those being intervention with: women, using groups and individual therapy; male perpetrators of violence; couples; and children.

## INTERVENTION WITH WOMEN

Our initial approach to intervening with women in violent situations was individual or couple counselling. However, concerns arose that couple counselling was often counterproductive, putting the women at greater risk of reprisals outside the session and silencing them about the abuse. These concerns led to counsellors recommending that each person be seen individually until safety was assured and couple counselling could proceed. Inevitably, the male perpetrator stopped coming to sessions and the counsellor worked individually with the woman, which was usually long-term work. It was recognised that individual work with women also held risks such as that of reinforcing the position of the woman. Women have been seen to be highly disadvantaged in the private sphere of the counselling room, imbedded as it is in a social and cultural context of secrecy in relationships and families (McIntyre 1984; Troup 1995). Feminist-influenced theory and models of counselling (e.g. James & McIntyre 1985) were adopted in an effort to be rigorous about our work and the process of change. In the mid-1980s group work was introduced as a service option, initially modelled on the Mutual Help Group program (Condonis et al. 1990), in order to service this client group more effectively.

### Principles and an approach to working with women survivors of violence

Different therapeutic approaches have been developed over time to address the needs of women but the overall aim of service provision has remained the same: the safety of the woman and any children she may have. The most effective service at this time is considered to include a combination of individual counselling and attendance at a support group. Services are made as accessible as possible in terms of time, location and cost. Confidentiality in attending counselling appointments is assured, and the support groups are held at secret locations—a fact that reinforces for all of us how unsafe these women are in the community. A woman may be attending counselling and the support group at the same time, or move from one to the other as her needs change.

In the current group work program, survivors of violence are able to share their experiences with other women; this process helps them to let go of feelings of responsibility for not having tried hard enough or for not having been a 'good wife'. A common aspect of domestic violence is the attempts of the male perpetrator to isolate the woman. The group offers what is often the first opportunity to build up a social support system outside the home; it is thus in an open format in order to be responsive to the needs of women who may not be able to attend every week. In all of our services to women the focus is on empowering them to work towards a decision about the future of the relationship. In particular, the following issues are addressed in the group work:

1. *Provision of information.* Whilst information about violence is given and safety emphasised, women must be enabled to make their own decisions without pressure for any one outcome to occur. This involves raising awareness of the importance of taking out an Apprehended Violence Order (AVO), and taking precautions to ensure she can escape the scene should it become necessary (e.g. an extra set of car keys placed in an accessible, secret place; knowing how to contact a refuge and the police; and having organised help from one family member or friend).

2. *The women are not responsible for the violence.* The effects of years of abuse and brainwashing need to be gradually unpacked and women helped to realise that they are not responsible for the violence and that violence is a criminal act. These women tend to be highly anxious, to have low self-esteem and to exhibit stress responses which include fear, depression, anxiety, difficulty in problem-solving and coping (Trimpey 1989; Perry et al. 1991). Counselling and group work provide a forum to heal, recover and develop strategies for change. Concurrent

with this, women get tremendous relief from telling their story and having it and them believed and validated.

3. *Unpacking the emotional bond/attachment.* In assisting women to leave violent relationships the therapist acknowledges and explores both the positive aspects of the relationship and their emotional attachment to their partner, as well as the negative aspects (Goldner 1994).

4. *Working through the effects of abuse.* During the course of counselling or group attendance women become aware of the extent of the abuse they have suffered. Many parts of the relationship that they had accepted as normal are now seen to be oppressive. This may include isolation, verbal and sexual assault and financial control. The women are encouraged to speak openly about the abuse they have experienced in the interests of reducing their feelings of shame. A theme in this work is that the abuse is the responsibility of the perpetrator and that by minimising the abuse women are inadvertently colluding in the oppression: abuse flourishes in private.

5. *Exploring the possibility of a temporary or permanent separation.* This can be an extremely difficult option for women to consider. Staying in the relationship often feels like the only way to get basic needs met, such as a roof over their heads, food to eat, and sufficient money to clothe and educate the family. The other choice could be to move periodically from refuge to refuge until there is sufficient strength mentally and financially to set up on their own. Group leaders do not put pressure on women to separate and care is taken to ensure that group members also refrain from pressuring others to separate. Nevertheless, women are encouraged to use separation as leverage to bring about change. In our experience, leaving and taking out an AVO have proved to be the most powerful leverage to bring about change. If they can effect a separation, it often results in the man seeking counselling and sometimes in his entering the perpetrators' program.

In this work the therapist faces many emotive issues and must be able to manage the transference and countertransference skilfully and responsibly (Hansen & Harway 1993). Sometimes women who have successfully left a relationship and established themselves appear suddenly to doubt their decision and return to the relationship. In such situations, counsellors often experience feelings of inadequacy as the woman returns to a violent situation. It is important that therapists and group leaders allow women time to make decisions and to understand the effect of the abuse on the choices they make. Stress and anxiety do not disappear in the short term and will prevent changes from being sustained. It is common for abused women to leave and return several times before making the final break. Counselling can assist women at this point to explore further the residual emotional attachment to her partner. Individual counselling offers an opportunity to explore issues deriving from family of origin and a history of past abuse in more depth than is possible in a group setting.

### Attending to requests to save the relationship

Whilst it is commonly thought that women who are with violent partners should be working towards separation and utilising legal sanctions, some women prefer to remain in their relationship but have the violence cease. Whether this is due to the difficulties of establishing herself independently or because she experiences herself as in love with her partner, the request for help is related to making the relationship work. A woman may report that her partner 'needs help' or that 'he has no-one but me'. She may minimise the violence, partly from fear or shame and partly because she hopes the relationship is salvageable. The woman herself can want to focus on the positive aspects. Usually, these women do experience aspects of their relationship as fulfilling, and are often emotionally invested and dependent on their partner. Consequently, many women request that their partner be included in therapy, either in individual or couple counselling. We consider such service requests in terms of their meaning for the woman. Any rejection of him can be a rejection of her too; that is, the service may be seen to be unsympathetic and inaccessible, and the woman will return to her private (unsafe) world of home and the relationship.

As the woman will experience her partner as 'needing help', suggestions about separation or legal sanctions seem incongruous and discrepant to her (although they must be made anyway). Such suggestions sound more like he's going to be 'in trouble' and she doesn't want the responsibility or the consequences of that stance. This is understandable—legal options such as the application for an Apprehended Violence Order require her to bear the burden of reporting on, and to some extent policing, her partner's behaviour, a position that can be unsafe, unfair and emotionally difficult. The availability of perpetrator programs enables the therapist to respond positively and convey that it is the male's responsibility to organise and be responsible for the change process himself. As women are desperate for something to succeed, they are often relieved when men take steps towards dealing with their violence.

Women's willingness to pressure partners into treatment provides significant leverage for some men who then take the first step towards change. In providing services to perpetrators, we believe that if some men can be assisted to cease or reduce violence, women and children will benefit in the end. It is essential, however, that therapists inform women that, while some men change, many do not. His involvement in a program should not be a reason to return to the relationship, relax vigilance around safety or not take out an AVO.

## INTERVENTION WITH MALE PERPETRATORS OF VIOLENCE

The idea of intervening in non-legal ways with violent men has resulted in much controversy since the early 1990s:

> Because men control power, property, jobs, and money in this society it is not surprising that wife assault, which is a male crime, should be so resistant to reform. Nor is it surprising that the crime is misinterpreted, misnamed as a problem rather than a crime, and that therapeutic help is offered to perpetrators rather than the appropriate legal response with its accompanying shame, humiliation and disruption to men's lives. (NSW Domestic Violence Committee 1991, p. 2)

In addition, there has been a low level of success recorded in outcome research of intervention strategies with men. Counselling and therapy are not seen in themselves to bring about significant change: men may leave therapy with new ideas, but live and work in contexts which do not support or reinforce these views. Consequently, they are slowly eroded and lost. It is also contended by some that counselling and therapy, when used as an alternative to the law, undermine the intention of the law (McGregor 1990).

Conventional criminal justice responses to other crimes of violence sometimes involve rehabilitation programs, including therapy, but only as a post-sentencing option. They are used as an adjunct to the criminal law, not as an alternative. This would also be the favoured option with the crime of domestic violence. However, as the legal sanctions currently available are limited and seem to have little effect on behavioural change for many men, and community demand for a response to the problem is great, some community organisations have taken it upon themselves to explore other options, ideally as an adjunct to the legal processes. Relationships Australia (NSW) was one of the first organisations to pilot specialist services to perpetrators of domestic violence.

### Service evolution

In providing services to perpetrators, the following concerns needed to be addressed:

1. The appropriateness of the service being provided separate from the legal system. Does this detract from violence as a criminal act?
2. The cost of the service. Does funding this service option involve any lessening of services to women?
3. The effect on the process of lobbying for increased legal sanctions. Does providing men's programs detract from these important changes?
4. The choice of a service model. Is there an appropriate model given serious concerns about a number of programs already in the community—for example, anger management, cognitive behaviour, couple and individual therapy?
5. Do such programs encourage women to stay and be hopeful rather than consider other options?

These issues were addressed in the context of a high service demand from couples and individuals requesting treatment, with one in four requests for counselling at Relationships Australia being related to men's violence. Perpetrators often present for assistance, angry and shamed from being rejected by public services. Consequently, they have attempted to manage their behaviour themselves. Women are also affected by the refusal of services to address the needs of these men. As previously stated, many women request that the relationship be salvaged but the violence stopped. A strong part of the couple's emotional bond is the sense that he needs 'help', and that she knows his 'softer side'. As services turn him away, or try to dissuade them from couple therapy, she is more likely to feel pushed towards him, to stand by him in the face of social rejection. Thus, simply denying service seemed to be cementing the relationship further, and disadvantaging women in the process. However, in relation to the available service delivery options, individual counselling does not engage most of these men beyond an average of four sessions. In deciding to offer a group program for male perpetrators, the following guidelines were developed:

- An educational program for men targeting violent and abusive behaviour was the treatment of choice.
- Where possible, and when the woman is willing, both man and woman are interviewed separately to ascertain the full extent of the violence, the safety of the woman and the man's motivation to change.
- The safety of women and children is given priority in each case.
- To discourage use of the program as a personal or social strategy for reconciliation with partners, a decision was made not to write reports or references, even in relation to court matters. Attendance at the program is voluntary.
- Program intervention is developed within the current legal and social framework in addressing violence. Legal sanctions are strongly emphasised and encouraged as an important step in establishing safety and change.
- Women and other victims are the essential reference point of change, and contact with them (if possible/appropriate) is maintained and encouraged.
- Services to perpetrators focus on behavioural and attitudinal change and assume that significant change can only occur with long-term intervention (i.e. six months or more).
- Other services (e.g. medical, drug and alcohol) are utilised to ensure adequate service provision occurs.
- Services are provided on a user-pays basis, and any 'surplus' monies are to be directed towards services for women.

The model chosen for intervention—'Power & Control: Tactics of Men Who Batter', commonly referred to as the 'Duluth' model (Paymar & Pence 1985)—was consistent with these principles. The Duluth model is a community intervention approach which relies on a commitment to enforce assault laws and civil protection orders, a consistent and uniform response to violence, a network of professional support, direct service intervention with male perpetrators as a post-sentencing alternative to jail, and community education. Devised by a team in Duluth, Minnesota, it operates in a context of high community education and awareness about domestic violence and its effects, a high arrest rate, and mandated referrals to the program. There has been five-year follow-up research that suggests a 40–50 per cent success rate.

Our program, based on this model, involves a two-week orientation followed by 24 weeks, two and one-half hours per week of input. Eight topics are covered with three weeks per topic: non-violence, non-threatening behaviour, respect, support and trust, accountability and honesty, sexual respect, partnership, negotiation and fairness. It is an educational program that focuses totally on attitudinal and behavioural change. It is not a therapy model, although the outcomes are partially therapeutic in nature and the program can lead to participants being more therapeutically engaged.

Whilst we do not operate our program in a context of formal community and legal support, the program itself does give a very strong message about the unacceptability of violence. In addition, by attending voluntarily, men have had to decide to make such changes and to commit to a six-month program. Ultimately, the motivation to attend rests with each participant (in fact, we ask them to convince us we should accept them). In this way, leaders can start from a position which assumes that men have taken some responsibility and do not have to spend time diffusing and processing the anger and resistance that more usually occurs with compulsory attendance.

Not all applicants are accepted into the program and exclusion criteria have been developed in the interests of effective service and client and staff safety. The exclusion criteria include: mandated clients and those referred from the criminal justice system (decided on a case-by-case basis);[2] when it is assessed that staff safety or the safety of family members could be jeopardised by our servicing the perpetrator; where serious mental illness is a factor in the perpetrator's abuse; there is a client history of sociopathic behaviour; or where a client has alcohol and/or drug addiction. Such men are referred to other services such as mental health or drug and alcohol, as appropriate.

### The effectiveness of perpetrator programs

The first question about these programs is: Do men stop being violent? This is a very hard question to answer for a number of reasons. First, longitudinal research is often hampered by a lack of resources in the community sector and the level of mobility and fragmentation of families experiencing violence. Second, it is difficult to define violence cessation. On the one hand, a goal to achieve cessation of all forms of violence, including verbal abuse, is laudatory. On the other hand, intervention that is limited to a few hours a week for six months will not necessarily achieve a complete reversal of attitudes and behaviour. Yet if we do not set absolute criteria for success, critics may accuse us of finding some level of abuse acceptable.

Our criterion for success is that significant change is reported by the men, their partners, the program leaders and counsellors involved at the end of the program and at 12 months follow-up. Ultimately, if the woman decides to continue the relationship, she must determine if the level of change is sufficient for her. Given variances in life experience, self-development, personal resilience and commitment to the relationship, this will vary from person to person.

In our follow-up studies of program 'graduates' (1992, 1993, 1994) we utilised separate, directed focus groups for the women and men or phone interviews if attendance was difficult. Women were invited to attend whether their partners completed the program or not, and whether they had separated or not. Approximately 50 per cent of program graduates and their partners were available for participation in the evaluation per year. In addition, other sources of information via the 1995 and 1996 programs (e.g. the ongoing contact with some participants and their partners in individual or couple therapy) have assisted us in evaluating the program.

Women reported that they had remembered our statements about the low success rate of the program in the initial interview with them. Despite this, they were hopeful when their partner was accepted into the program. It was interesting to note that coupled with the hope was the thought that 'This is his last chance'. This attitude arose from the woman's awareness that there were few remaining alternatives other than separation and jail. For most of the women we spoke to, if the man was violent after the program finished, they were more prepared to take out an AVO or separate than they were prior to the program. The women reported thinking 'He's had the treatment so if he is still violent, he doesn't deserve my support'. This was an unexpected but very important finding.

A majority of women reported that physical violence had stopped completely[3] and in the two instances where there had been an assault the men had been arrested and separation had occurred.

This outcome was due to women being more likely to use legal sanctions at that point. Verbal and emotional abuse was said to have decreased to a level that was seen to be 'acceptable' or more 'normal' for those women who were pursuing the relationship.

For the men who dropped out of the program early (usually around week five), most partners who were still together reported changes. These women reported that the men had become significantly less violent, although the change was not as great as for men who completed the program. A few men had left the program at the same time as leaving their partners. These men were unable to be contacted and their partners could not report any changes except the fact that the men had left the relationship.

Additionally, a number of women chose to separate or not reconcile about week 14 or 15 of the program. It seems that, after a period of feeling safer, some women had enough space to realise, or to feel comfortable to state, that the relationship was over. In all cases where this occurred, the men persisted with the program and the women were able to make their decision largely uncontested. Given that the separation time is a period of greatest risk, this could be a very important outcome for perpetrator programs. By the program's conclusion, about half of the men were still in relationships. Although the research is not conclusive, we believe that these findings are sufficiently convincing to claim that the program has some success in reducing violence and in assisting with separation in a large percentage of cases.

## PRINCIPLES OF A COUPLE APPROACH TO DOMESTIC VIOLENCE

Whether domestic violence may be treated via therapy and, in particular, whether it is good practice to apply a conjoint treatment model are issues that have attracted a great deal of debate in recent years (Dell 1989; Willbach 1989; James & McIntyre 1990; McGregor 1990; Lipchick 1991; Bograd 1992; Erickson 1992; Kaufman 1992; Meth 1992; Myers Avis 1992). Arguments against the use of couple counselling are that it may serve to reinforce patriarchal notions of women's roles and subjugation of the self, ultimately keeping the relationship fundamentally the same rather than promoting change on a structural and social level. Some models of counselling have also been considered as inadequate and unhelpful, such as the early systemic approach which has been identified as neglecting issues of power, control and gender (McIntyre 1984; Hatty 1985; Kaufman 1992).

Couple counselling also tends to seduce therapists into dealing with relationship issues and not focusing sufficiently on the man's violence (McGregor 1990). One critical concern is whether violence by men against their female partners is properly the concern of police and the courts or whether therapists might have a role to play (the 'social control versus therapy' dilemma). Within this debate, serious concern has been expressed as to whether conjoint therapy is safe for women, their consent to such notwithstanding.

The everyday reality for therapists, however, is that the potential to avoid working with domestic violence never quite exists. Myers Avis (1992) estimates that 50 per cent of the cases at the Marriage and Family Therapy Center at the University of Guelph had a past or current history of physical or sexual abuse and that this figure jumps to 80 per cent if other forms of coercion and control, such as verbal and emotional abuse, are included. Although comparable local statistics are not available, we would imagine, on the basis of anecdotal evidence, that these figures would come close to representing the Australian experience in generalist couple and family therapy practice settings. Certainly, one in four of the cases that present at Relationships Australia (NSW) involve a level of domestic violence. The real problem is not so much whether to choose to work with violence in a therapeutic way but to recognise and to name it (Kaufman 1992; Aldarondo & Straus 1994).

Further on the question of the social control versus therapy dilemma, we agree with Bograd (1992, p. 247) when she writes:

> To resolve this dilemma, people often either reject therapeutic practice and frameworks to uphold feminist or political beliefs or deny the contributions of a political perspective in order to maintain the purity of the therapeutic vision. But both positions have their truths, and neither can stand alone. Instead we must explore how understanding of gendered patterns of violence and control can be enriched by clinical insights and how therapeutic practices can be deepened by political and social wisdom.

The conjoint approach that we have adopted is very strongly influenced by the work of Virginia Goldner, Gillian Walker, Peggy Penn and Marcia Steinberg.[4] Their approach (1990) is 'multi-lens', combining principally feminist, systemic and psychoanalytic perspectives. The 'multi-lens' approach is their attempt to contain the contradictions that working with domestic violence evokes as, they argue, no one lens can adequately deal with the problem. The feminist lens allows the therapist to consider the socially prescribed power differential and abuse of power in the relationship, while the systemic lens facilitates an understanding of the interactional aspects of the relationship and can begin to deal with the question of why women remain in abusive situations. The psychoanalytic lens provides a theory of the individual and how males and females are 'gendered'. Goldner (1994) argues that the fourth lens, a narrative/social constructionist lens, allows for an understanding of how culture is internalised, of how culture 'enters minds'.

Mindful of the feminist objection to conjoint therapy as somehow implying a mutual responsibility for the violence, we carefully frame the offer of conjoint therapy to these couples. The 'therapy' is defined as a series of assessments/consultations, of preliminary steps that must be taken before 'therapy' can begin. The focus is on violence and not relationship issues. The men who have attended the perpetrators' program are told that conjoint therapy is not to be seen in their case as a right but rather as a possibility entirely dependent on their success (as defined by their female partners) in controlling their violence. The men from the general waiting list who have requested couple therapy are also quickly introduced to this idea at the beginning of their first conjoint session. The focus of our initial concern, indeed the only concern that we can legitimately have, is on the cessation of the violence and the safety of the woman and children. The assessment phase is framed as a testing ground and is deemed as necessary for the therapist to proceed. The therapist also expresses their own fears concerning their inability to monitor the couple outside the safety of the therapy room. The therapist needs to feel that the woman is safe before therapy can be allowed to proceed. This intervention is seen to act as a paradoxical injunction: 'therapy' won't proceed until the violence stops. However, the long assessment of the violence becomes in effect the 'grist to the mill' of therapy.

In a sense the merging of the social control imperative (the feminist concern) and the therapeutic response is a contradiction that is never resolved—it exists as an incongruent mix, a 'contrapuntal' mix (Goldner 1994). The dilemma is somehow reflective of the couple's own dilemmas. Particularly when individual sessions have not been held with clients, part of the therapeutic plan involves meeting with both partners individually (and, strategically, seeing the man first). The purpose of this is to elicit from the woman how safe she feels within the conjoint format. Once this is established, the central focus of therapy concerns itself with the dual tasks of the 'de-construction of the violent moment', particularly from the point of view of the man and the 'de-construction of the bond', particularly from the point of view of the woman (Goldner 1994).

The steps in this assessment phase are:

1. Individual sessions to assess the suitability of a couple for a conjoint approach. This assessment includes assessing the woman's desire to be seen with her partner; the safety of the woman if she were to be seen conjointly with her partner; the likelihood of the woman wanting to separate; and the ability of the man to accept challenge, and be accountable for his violence.
2. Conjoint sessions which focus on the violence as distinct from relationship issues. This includes a focus on the effects of the violence.
3. The therapist re-defines the presenting problem as the man's violence, rather than any relationship problem.
4. The therapist conveys that responsibility for the violence is with the perpetrator and confronts denial and minimisation.
5. The woman is encouraged to take responsibility for her safety.
6. The therapist utilises all possible sources of leverage in the absence of genuine motivation on the part of the man to work on his violence. This might include desire on the part of the man for a couple focus, to be rid of an AVO, to prevent separation or to reunite with his partner.
7. The therapist assesses the violence fully, including frequency, severity, effect (injuries plus other effects) and the most severe incident.
8. De-construction of the violence. The therapist works to understand the most recent violent incident, using a number of clinical and feminist lenses. In de-constructing the violent moment from the man's point of view, the therapist works to understand the internal dialogue and its historical roots and, using the language of choice, challenges the man to act differently.

This can best be illustrated in the following case example. For Geoff, as for many men we see, the trigger for violence is his internal somatic response (e.g. a sick feeling in the stomach) whenever he experiences his wife Sharon as differing and distancing from him in some way. This may be when she is speaking too long on the phone to her sister, momentarily preoccupied with a child, wearing certain clothes or her hair in a certain way, failing to give him a full picture of her everyday whereabouts, or refusing to comply with his preferred sexual activities. Internally he connects her 'difference' to him as 'against him', as a betrayal, as abandonment. He also experiences her sometimes bemused or sometimes assertive response to his complaints as further evidence of her not understanding him, of not caring—that is, as a further abandonment. When invited to consider where else he experienced himself feeling these feelings, Geoff is eventually able to talk about being 'ignored' as a child. As the middle of nine children, and born with a (rather insignificant) facial disfigurement which his father took as evidence that Geoff could not be his child, Geoff speaks about being invisible in the family. His father, Geoff remembers, singled him out among the boys for physical violence (although he sexually abused the girls) and his mother did not protect him. The idea that Geoff has substituted an 'acting like father' out of the painful failure to experience a close relationship with his father seemed to fit in this case.

Geoff's violence to Sharon is a learned response to a threat that he perceives as coming from her, but that is in reality a drama being played out in his own head. As a learned response Geoff has control and choice about whether to be violent, even if he feels he doesn't have any other strategies. Despite the knowledge that his chosen behaviour is damaging his relationship, he continues to use violence, initially physical and later verbal abuse, because it 'works' in the short term. Unpacking the violent moment, the therapist discovers that violence gives Geoff a momentary feeling of release from the internal anxiety that arises out of the fear of abandonment, because when he is violent Sharon stops her difference-making behaviour and attends to him. The momentary sense of control that Geoff experiences is very compelling and hence recurs.

9. De-construction of bond/attachment. The therapist works to 'unpack' each partner's bond or attachment to the other, so as to free up decision-making about a future relationship or separation. In the above example, Sharon's attachment to Geoff was based on the following: a loyalty to the 'nice' side of Geoff and sympathy about his tough childhood; a commitment to this relationship that, having begun as an affair, she wanted to

have succeed given she'd sacrificed her first (non-violent) marriage for it; and finally a sense of feeling 'at home' in a violent relationship that mirrored her parents' relationship where her father was violent to her mother. There was a part of Sharon that felt she didn't deserve her non-violent first husband, that she wasn't good enough for him. The elicitation and exploration of the attachment to Geoff helped Sharon to answer for herself the question that had so perplexed her and rendered her immobile—why indeed was it that she loved Geoff? It was only at that point that Sharon began to feel she had a real choice about whether to stay in this relationship or not.

10. Evidence of change. The therapist ascertains evidence as to the man's ability to be challenged and to be 'tested' in terms of managing himself differently.

Only when these aspects have been thoroughly investigated and safety assured would couple therapy be offered.

## ADDRESSING THE NEEDS OF CHILDREN

It is only in the last decade that research has started to focus on the effects of domestic violence on children. We now know that the majority of women being assaulted have dependent children, and that in 90 per cent of these cases the children who live in these families will be in the same room or in the next room when the violence occurs (Hughes 1992). Between 50 and 80 per cent of these children will be directly abused in addition to witnessing violence (Allbrook Cattilini Research 1992; Hughes 1992); they may be witnesses, co-victims or confidantes of their abused mother. Children are in fact profoundly affected by violence, and the effect on them 'has been equated with living in a war zone or being involved in natural disasters such as fire, earthquakes or cyclones' (Blanchard 1993, p. 31). Knowledge of the profound effects on children in both the short and long term has highlighted the need for appropriate, specialist resources for children.

Although Relationships Australia (NSW) has always provided family therapy services, within the Family Safety Program we initially focused on adult relationships. More recently we felt able to develop a focus on the needs of children specifically. For reasons of efficacy and service fit with the organisation, we chose to focus on family therapy and group therapy. In practical terms this has meant utilising a team approach to family assessment and developing a group intervention strategy for children where their fathers are in the men's program. The goals of intervention with children and their families are to:

- provide competent and thorough assessment of the actual violence and its effects on individual family members;
- heighten the parents' capacity to perceive and to respond to their children's needs separately from their own;
- emphasise that the focus of responsibility for the violence does not rest with the child;
- help parents make more child-focused decisions;
- protect children from conflict and ensure safety;
- break down the intergenerational transmission of violence;
- focus on more egalitarian relationships;
- heal and change family relationships.

The groups for children utilise age-appropriate activities to provide support, focus on identifying feelings including ambivalence about relationships with parents, identify strengths (to combat negative self-image) and teach protective behaviours and conflict resolution skills, emphasising the non-acceptability of violence. The goal is to promote change and healing for the child. The child's therapy involves the mother or primary caregiver. Fathers may also be involved if an ongoing relationship is likely, if they have completed the men's program, have demonstrated a capacity to focus on reparation and on developing a changed relationship with the child.

## CONCLUSION

The Family Safety Program has developed in response to the demands of our clients, with careful consideration of the social and political context. Services of this kind require organisations to attend to issues of accountability, staff and client safety, specialist staff training, and a preparedness to participate in the broader community debate. The Program offers an integrated, comprehensive service to families, which has the capacity to respond to the needs of individuals and subgroups without necessarily having to refer to other agencies and risk client 'fall out'. It also enables us to monitor the change process and identify any ongoing abuse by having access to the victim's feedback. The Family Safety Program is not seen to be complete at this stage. By its very nature it is constantly evolving to respond to the needs of our clients.

# 16 | Redressing the balance: child protection intervention in the context of domestic violence

*Chris Burke*

THIS CHAPTER OUTLINES a number of practice issues and pitfalls involved in child protection intervention with families in which domestic violence is also a concern. The intervention framework presented reflects my experience as Director of Jannawi Family Centre, a specialist child protection program located in the inner south-west of Sydney. In our work over the last eight years, domestic violence has consistently emerged as a contributing factor to the child protection concerns in 70–90 per cent of referred families.

## THE INTERFACE BETWEEN DOMESTIC VIOLENCE AND CHILD ABUSE AND NEGLECT

Over the last 20 to 30 years, professionals working with children and families have largely addressed the issues of domestic violence and child abuse as separate social problems requiring different policy and service interventions. This has changed in more recent years as: 'A growing body of research . . . suggests that spouse abuse and child abuse are clearly linked within families, with each being a strong predictor of the other' (McKernan McKay 1994, p. 29). For example, almost two-thirds of abused children are being parented by battered women, and women experiencing domestic violence are at least twice as likely to abuse their children (Stark & Flitcraft 1988); between 30 and 50 per cent of men who abuse women also abuse their children (Smith et al. 1996); and 70 per cent of children living in domestic violence situations are victims themselves (Cahn 1991).

Recognition of the devastating effects of domestic violence on children has resulted in child protection policy-makers in New South Wales including domestic violence as an identified form of child abuse. Also, when attending incidents of domestic violence in which children are present, police are now mandated to notify concerns to the statutory child protection agency, the Department of Community Services. This increased awareness, however, raises new dilemmas and difficulties for workers in developing effective child protection intervention with families in which men are violent and abusive towards their female partners. These include: how to intervene to protect children without reinforcing the woman's sense of guilt, self-blame and failure as a mother; how workers can avoid placing even more responsibility for protecting children onto women who are often powerless to act because of their own victimisation; and how workers can invite perpetrators to take responsibility for their violence and to be accountable for the impact of their actions on mothers and children (Burke 1994).

Challenges and dilemmas also arise for domestic violence workers assisting women to separate from violence. McKernan McKay (1994, p. 33) says that: 'Intervention with battered women takes the form of empowering mothers to seek new ways to protect themselves and their children' and suggests that workers in this role:

- help women to recognise how their children might have been affected by the violence in the home;
- make explicit the link between domestic violence and child abuse;
- help the woman to place responsibility for the violence with the abuser, or accept the necessity of altering her own parenting if she was abusive with the children.

## UNDERSTANDING THE IMBALANCE OF POWER AND RESPONSIBILITY

Traditionally, men have held socially constructed positions of power within families which allows those who choose to misuse their power to dominate and control other members of the family. They may use such tactics as verbal abuse, social control, physical violence, economic control, threats and intimidation, and sexual violence. Effective child protection intervention must understand perpetrators' real intentions as well as the real effects of their violence on women and children's lives and relationships.

The ideal context for raising children would be one in which there is an equilibrium in the distribution of power and responsibility between men and women. Men use violence in order to have power and control over their partners. This effectively upsets the balance, with men having greater power and women being disempowered. At the same time, perpetrators use their position of greater power to shift responsibility onto others through the use of blame and accusations which convince women and children to blame themselves or each other for upsetting or provoking the perpetrator. The perpetrator can then take a position of being 'under-responsible' for his actions as other less powerful members of the family are made to be 'over-responsible'.

This is demonstrated by Billy (eight years old): 'But he can't help it . . . he just loses it sometimes, but only when I'm naughty or when mum nags him' and by Lena (ten years old): 'I don't like it when dad yells and throws things at my mum. But dad said . . . she should know what upsets him by now!' (Burke & Moses 1996).

Women's and children's beliefs and behaviours are greatly influenced by the domestic violence context, especially their understanding of power and responsibility and gender roles. Because they are encouraged into self-blame, they do not attribute responsibility to their partner, father or male carer. This impacts on the relationships between mothers and their children. Children may be encouraged to blame or disrespect their mother, to see her as weak and ineffectual and needing protection, or as hopeless and uncaring, and the one who has failed to protect them. Mothers raising children who exhibit the effects of living with violence and abuse are presented with particular parenting challenges. If women do not understand the link between their children's behaviours and beliefs and the domestic violence context, they may be inappropriately punitive or rejecting of their children. They may see the children as 'just as bad as their father', or as misbehaving only to make life difficult for them as a mother.

When perpetrators attack and undermine women's role as mothers, they effectively diminish the mothers' confidence in raising children, and therefore limit their choices to leave the relationship and parent alone. This, coupled with the social and economic constraints of being a single parent, places pressure on women to keep the family together, and to maintain the children's relationship with their father. To achieve this family unity and harmony, women may believe that they need to try harder to be a better partner and mother. They may adapt their parenting to compensate for the partner's violence and abuse by becoming overly permissive, or overly vigilant and punitive in an attempt to avoid situations or behaviours that provoke or antagonise their partner (Smith et al. 1996). Unfortunately, in some cases the adapted parenting practices may be seen by child protection workers as inappropriate, inconsistent or ineffective parenting.

## PITFALLS IN PRACTICE

Workers in the fields of domestic violence and child protection intervention, like other professional groups, are strongly influenced by the evolving therapies and practices of their time. The following discussion illustrates the impact on men, women and children of particular theories and practices.

### Gender-biased interventions

Child protection has focused primarily on women as mothers, whose socially constructed role is the care and nurturance of children. Traditionally, women have also been seen to be responsible for the emotional welfare of their partners and their families. This is reflected in risk assessment tools, case plan goals and program strategies. The term 'parents' often camouflages the fact that it is mothers who are the subjects of assessments, the focus of intervention and the participants in programs.

Stereotypical ideas about female gender roles are reflected in practice interventions which refer women to services to make changes and improve their abilities in their primary caretaker role. Even when domestic violence concerns exist:

> The mother is all too often labelled a poor parent and becomes the sole focus of the intervention. Mandating her attendance at parenting skills groups or counselling reinforces the notion that she is to blame for the violence in the family and that her partner bears no responsibility. (Bograd 1990, p. 132)

It has been common practice for child protection workers not to speak to the male carer or partner because he may be at work, not at home when the worker called or not as cooperative as the woman. For example, Susan Heward-Belle's (1996) study of child protection workers' responses to domestic violence found that, in 51 per cent of the cases, workers spoke only to the woman. They asked her to give assurances that the children would not be exposed to further incidents of domestic violence. Notions about fatherhood and traditional male gender roles can result in workers not expecting or inviting men to reflect on the effects of their behaviour on their children or partner. The impact of men's misuse of power may be ignored or they may not be asked to make changes to ensure the future safety and welfare of the family. Instead, workers place the mother in both the 'super-responsible' and 'the messenger' role rather than speak to him directly. This practice perpetuates a great injustice and results in the woman being caught between two powerful forces—her partner and the statutory child protection agency. She is being asked to take responsibility for her partner's violence and abuse, this time by child protection workers.

### The 'invisible man' syndrome

Some people may remember *The Invisible Man*, a television drama program from the 1960s in which, due to an error in a laboratory experiment, a man was made invisible and could only be seen when wearing bandages from head to toe. When he removed his bandages he was able to move around and do things to others without anyone knowing he was there. The 'victims' appeared to be strange or weird because they would suddenly throw themselves against the wall or to the floor for no apparent reason; bystanders would look at them in a puzzled and confused way.

As child protection professionals working with the domestic violence context, we have often experienced 'the case of the invisible man, that is, we see the impact of his actions but we never see him' (Burke 1994, p. 19). We work to address the effects of the violence and abuse but ignore the very context and practices that have created the problems. An analogy for this is a punching doll, a child's toy that is weighted in the base so that it bounces back up after being knocked over. Services may focus interventions to assist the woman to 'bounce back', but fail to address the very practices that are 'knocking her down'. To be effective in child protection intervention, we need to address the real issues that are impacting on the safety and welfare of children and make visible the real effects of domestic violence on women, children and their relationships.

This emerging awareness about the link between domestic violence and child protection issues now places us in a position to 're-dress' the 'invisible man'. One way to do this is by posing questions to clients which reflect this context, such as:

> Are you a bad mother, or are the circumstances of your life making it hard for you to be the mother you would like to be?

> If you were not living with abuse and put-downs on a regular basis, how might life be different for you and your children?

> Would you see the actions of your partner as encouraging and helping you in your parenting role, or as working to undermine your confidence?

An example of the impact of the 'invisible man' syndrome is a female client who was living with her abusive partner who had stopped attending Jannawi's program. Throughout our contact she would swing from a stance of cooperation and active participation to one of aggression, distrust and blame of the worker and the child welfare department for causing problems in her family. When asked who else held these opinions, she named her partner and said that he was 'giving her a hard time' and telling her not to attend the program. She was swinging between doing what she thought was best for herself and her children, and following the 'advice' of her partner. This pendulum effect is an indicator of the perpetrator's continued power and influence and his ongoing attempts to isolate her from a program that was assisting her empowerment and safety.

If our modes of therapy and our theoretical knowledge do not include a socio-political analysis and an interactional focus to understanding the effects of domestic violence on people's beliefs and behaviours, we may inadvertently contribute to the 'invisible man' phenomenon. Individualising therapies within sexist notions of male and female roles and responsibilities can result in practices which allow the 'invisible man' to be even more invisible. For example, women may be diagnosed as suffering from depression or anxiety and be offered treatment without understanding how domestic violence may be a major contributing cause; and symptoms such as aggressive behaviour in children may be misdiagnosed, or the children labelled as having attention deficit disorder if there is no awareness of a domestic violence context.

## PRACTICE ISSUES TO REDRESS THE BALANCE

Child-focused family work with families in which there are both domestic violence and child protection concerns prioritises the safety and protection of children. At the same time, intervention aims to empower and ensure the safety of mothers by placing accountability and responsibility for the violence and its effects with the male perpetrator. The imbalance in power and responsibility between men and women must be addressed at all stages of child protection intervention: referral, intake, assessment, intervention and evaluation of client changes and progress. The following discussion describes aspects of such an approach.

### The 'zoom lens' approach

When undertaking risk assessment, workers can now draw on research knowledge which says that the existence of child abuse is a strong predictor that domestic violence may also be a concern. Therefore, workers should avoid an individual focus that 'zooms in' on the child or the mother only. Instead, by 'zooming out' they can take in 'the landscape' and incorporate a picture of the domestic violence context in which the family lives. As a result, workers gain greater understanding of the wider issues impacting on or contributing to the child protection concerns. Protective workers can then raise questions as to who is responsible, to whom and for what. They can then invite the relevant people to be accountable for their actions and the impact of their actions on others, and invite them to play a role in overcoming the effects of their actions on others and ensuring a safe future for the children.

### Men's role and responsibility

Jannawi Family Centre does not offer a domestic violence perpetrator program but, in aiming to be an effective child protection service, has had to look at ways to address the impact of men's violence on women and children. When accepting referrals, in collaboration with the statutory child protection worker, we first assess whether it is possible to work with the man. The following points have helped to guide this assessment:

- He believes that he needs to make changes, not just his partner or children.
- He wants the relationship with his partner, not just his role as a father to his child or children.
- He is prepared to make a commitment to not using violence in the future.
- He agrees to attend the therapeutic program and to cooperate with what is asked of him or his partner by statutory child protection workers.

If he agrees to the above, then the role of workers is an educative one, explaining how domestic violence and child abuse are linked and focusing on developing a responsibility plan for the perpetrator to demonstrate his intentions and actions to prevent further violence and abuse. Men's response to the 'assessment' can provide helpful information for workers and also for the men's partners who are needing to make informed decisions about the future. As a child protection service, if we did not address the perpetrator or invite his participation, then we would be inadvertently reinforcing the notion that the woman alone is responsible for the future safety of her children.

Workers can still be effective in addressing the power and responsibility imbalances if the man is not an active participant in the program. In our work with women and children we make conscious decisions about what we focus on, what we ask about and how we construct our questions. Naming the violence as central to the child protection concerns conveys a strong message of understanding and support for women. The way we construct our questions can also make visible the perpetrator's tactics and intended impact of violence and abuse. We could ask questions about the mother's budgeting skills, parenting difficulties or the children's difficult behaviours. Instead, consider the different impact when we construct our questions as follows:

- How has living with your partner's abuse and violence impacted on your thoughts and feelings as a mother?
- What is the effect of your partner's control of the money on decisions made to provide for the children's needs?
- What has living with violence and disrespect encouraged in your child's behaviours and interactions with you and others?

## Clear client priorities

It is crucial that workers have clear and consistent client priorities which serve to invert and counter the structural power of men over women and adults over children. The identified priorities at Jannawi are:

1. Safety and protection of children.
2. Empowerment and safety of women.
3. Responsibility and accountability of perpetrators of violence.

When dilemmas or potential conflicts of interest arise, it is helpful to refer back to and be guided by these predetermined client priorities. For example, if a woman is unable to, or chooses not to, act to protect the children, then someone else must ensure the safety of the children in the short term; if a man is not doing what the statutory child protection worker has asked of him by attending the program, we may choose to continue to work with the woman and refer the man to another service, such as services providing programs for men who are violent.

## Ensuring safety

It is essential to work in partnership with the wider system to ensure the safety of women and children. Jannawi first asks the perpetrator to make a commitment to a non-violent future and works from the assumption that the violence has stopped. If there are further incidents of violence, the precondition for ongoing involvement and support is that the woman takes out an apprehended violence order (AVO) for herself and her children, and that the man agrees to abide by this direction and attend the court.

The focus and goals of our early work with parents are to determine whether they wish to stay together or separate. Separate assessment meetings and counselling sessions are used to help develop safety plans for the women and responsibility plans for the men. It is through this process that numerous couples have decided to separate, either permanently or for a temporary period, to ensure the emotional and physical safety of the woman and the children.

If there is a breach once an AVO is in place, intervention focuses on ensuring appropriate action is taken by the police. If the woman is reluctant to act on the breach, we have encouraged the statutory child protection agency to invoke the use of separate undertakings (discussed below) to ensure effective protective action for the children in the family. These outline clearly what each parent is expected to do and have been used effectively as a pre-court option. This takes the decision for notifying future breaches out of the woman's hands and is intended to reduce the man's power and control over the woman and her decisions.

## Separate undertakings as a strategy

The use of voluntary undertakings is a common tool in statutory intervention. Initially, women were asked to sign undertakings and give assurances that their children would not be exposed to domestic violence. As awareness of domestic violence as a child protection issue grew, the practice of joint undertakings became common—both parents signed the same document which asked them not to fight in front of the children. However, this practice assumed equality in power and responsibility for the violence and abuse in the family.

Jannawi works with the Department of Community Services (DCS) to encourage the use of separate undertakings in which men and women are asked to sign different documents. This enables workers to directly address abuses of power and to counter imbalances in the responsibility taken by men and women throughout child protection interventions. For example, men may be asked to give undertakings that include accepting supervision by the District Officer; refraining from assaulting, harassing, intimidating or threatening their partner; not physically or emotionally abusing or neglecting the children; informing the child protection department if he returns to live at the family home; participating in relevant programs to address his violence and abuse; not undermining or discouraging his partner's attendance at support programs or her cooperation with DCS; leaving the home of his partner on her request; agreeing to the terms and conditions of an AVO; and not pressuring his partner to withdraw from legal processes or from an AVO.

Women's undertakings may include, for example: accepting supervision by the District Officer; attending support programs; not physically or emotionally abusing or neglecting the children; being willing to initiate an AVO to protect herself and her children; notifying DCS if the partner returns to the family home; notifying DCS or police if her partner uses or threatens violence towards her or her children; and notifying the police of breaches of any conditions of the AVO.

The use of separate undertakings can help to amplify a situation when the woman is doing everything that is asked of her and within her power to accomplish, but the man is not cooperating with what is asked of him and is well within his power—such as attending counselling, not perpetrating further violence, and supporting his partner. These are crucial realisations, not only for workers but more importantly for women. A woman may see that she is making changes but that her partner is not. For example:

> I realised that I was trying and trying, but that I couldn't change him, and he wasn't going to change. I could only change myself and I needed to get on and do that for my kids' sake.

Workers come to notice and appreciate women's cooperation and actions that clearly prioritise their children's needs. More importantly, women feel that their efforts are recognised by the workers and this contrasts with the non-efforts of their partners.

### Maintaining the focus on responsibility and power imbalances

The imbalance of power and responsibility is a constant theme which informs and shapes child protection intervention in the context of domestic violence. It is a helpful framework to apply to risk assessment, case management decisions, therapeutic intervention and evaluation of changes and developments in the family relationships and dynamics. The following case example demonstrates how workers can use this framework to reflect critically on how their case management decisions and intervention strategies may be reinforcing or working to counter the power and responsibility imbalances set up by domestic violence.

The investigation of physical and emotional abuse and neglect of two young children involved questioning a woman, hearing about her experiences of domestic violence by her partner, but not talking with the perpetrator because he was at work. Instead, the mother was referred for counselling and support, asked to sign undertakings and agree to act to protect herself and her children. This intervention placed a lot of pressure and responsibility on the woman without addressing the real issues of violence that were impacting on her and her children's welfare and safety. Thus, the imbalance in power and responsibility between the parents was reinforced.

Workers can use the framework of power and responsibility imbalances to review and assess progress and changes in individual clients, couples and family dynamics. For example, throughout counselling and therapeutic interventions, clients can be asked to reflect on how the distribution of power and responsibility has occurred or changed in their relationships. Some questions to ask women to elicit this new understanding may include:

- What has your partner/ex-partner been invited to take responsibility for as a result of the child protection intervention?
- How has this freed you from your previous super-responsibility role?
- In what ways do you feel you have more power, or what areas of your life do you have more control over?
- How has this come about? What have been the consequences for your partner's previous role of domination and control of you and the children?
- How might your children perceive family dynamics differently from how they did before the intervention?
- How have the changes you've made influenced how your children perceive you today?

This framework can also assist clients to assess their experiences of the intervention strategies and reflect on whether case management decisions reinforce the notion that men and women need to experience shared power and more equality in responsibilities for child rearing and family welfare.

## CONCLUSION

This chapter has invited workers to reflect on how case work decisions informed by individualising therapies and sexist notions of gender roles and responsibilities have made invisible the impact of men's violence and abuse on women and children. Effective child protection intervention in the context of domestic violence must recognise how the perpetrators of violence shape the beliefs and behaviours of family members. Intervention informed by a socio-political analysis of gender, power and responsibility redresses the balance and ensures safety, protection and justice for women and children.

# Notes

## CHAPTER 1

1   The choice of the term 'victim' in this context may initially be viewed as controversial, and should not be taken to imply that women and children in particular are victims generally, or that they lack agency over their lives as a whole. Most importantly, there is no intention to suggest that either adults or children passively accept violence, and therefore do not speak out against its imposition. Within the context of this chapter, the term 'victim' has been deliberately chosen to indicate, at the outset, that those adults and children who have experienced sexual and domestic violence were not, and are still not, responsible for its perpetration. Instead, they have been, and are, the objects of such violence.

2   For the purpose of this chapter a profession is defined as a knowledge system (and/or skills) that is characterised by a prestigious and exclusive organisational structure.

3   The use of Foucault in a chapter investigating sexual and domestic violence may appear dubious given Foucault's own opinions about incest and pedophilia and his total silence surrounding sexual and domestic violence whilst concentrating on violence against the body in works such as *Discipline and Punish*. For example, Foucault describes sexual relationships with children as 'these inconsequential bucolic pleasures', a phrase that characterises the tenor of his discussion of incest in *The History of Sexuality, Vol. 1* (1981, p. 31).

Similarly, his later submission to the Penal Code in France calling for the removal of the laws that forbid the incitement of minors to debauchery, and criminalise sexual relations between minors and adults is anathema to the views expressed in this work.

4   An example is the Henry Parkes' Select Committee on the Conditions of the Working Classes of the Metropolis 1859–60.

5   This paper was based on clinical studies of 18 patients (including two men) who suffered from hysteria. Objective verification of abuse was available in two of those cases and indeed in the well-known case of Dora. After recanting his earlier work, Freud insisted that Dora had fantasised her sexual trauma. Dora was infuriated with this assertion and left therapy. Dora was able, however, to obtain a signed confession from her attacker, which somewhat validated her stand with Freud (Masson 1988, p. 114).

6   Freud is unable to explain within this framework, however, accusations of sexual assault by more removed family members or family friends, nor perhaps the growing number of disclosures made by boys and adult men.

7   For example, Miller (1984) and Yeatman (1988).

8   For example, Gordon (1988); Kelly (1988); and Breckenridge (1994, 1995).

9   To talk of a women's movement as being representative of all women is fraught with problems, given the diversity of interests, beliefs, values and opportunities of women as a group and as individuals. This issue is comprehensively discussed in other works such as Breckenridge (1996) and Mueller (1994). Whilst it is beyond the scope of this chapter to address this difficulty to any great extent, one point may be helpful. That is, that the notion of a women's movement refers to a public fiction of unity and identity in relation to specific issues in order to achieve political goals.

## CHAPTER 2

1   Fundamentally this chapter concentrates on issues for mothers. This is not to deny that women may on occasion sexually abuse children. Rather, that the overwhelming pattern of both allegations and convictions in the area of child sexual abuse continues to show men as the prime sexual abusers of children (see Chapter 9 in this collection). In the context of divorce proceedings, Hume (1996) found one allegation in her sample of 50 in which the mother was suspected of sexual abuse.

## CHAPTER 3

1 Since the *Heroines* research, the rule relating to recent complaint has effectively been abolished in New South Wales through the introduction of the *Evidence Act* 1995 (NSW). Section 66 of that Act provides that previous statements are admissible where the statement was made whilst the matter to which it relates was fresh in the memory of the maker of the statement. The memory of whether one was sexually assaulted is likely to remain fresh for long periods and thus many more complaints are likely to be considered admissible in evidence. In a number of States in Australia, however, the old law of recent complaint is still applied. Anecdotal evidence suggests that in New South Wales the assumptions underlying the old common law rule continue to inform and influence legal decisions and directions on complaint.

2 This section was not abolished with the introduction of the *Evidence Act* 1995 (NSW) but remains in the *Crimes Act* 1900 (NSW).

3 Disturbingly, since the *Heroines* research the High Court decision of *Crofts v R* ([1996] ALR 455) has confirmed that, except in exceptional circumstances, a common law warning that the complainant can be discredited for her delay in complaint should be given alongside legislative provisions such as s. 405B to 'avoid a perceptible risk of a miscarriage of justice arising from the circumstances of the case'.

## CHAPTER 4

1 In Victoria, the relevant legislation is the *Crimes (Family Violence) Act* 1987.

2 The legislation applying in Victoria is the *Equal Opportunity Act* 1995 (Vic), ss. 85–95, and the *Sex Discrimination Act* 1984 (Cth), ss. 28A–28L. Another form of civil remedy for violence, crimes compensation, is not discussed here because of its different operation from the other proceedings discussed, and the fact that in Victoria the crimes compensation regime has recently been effectively dismantled (disallowing awards for pain and suffering).

3 *Family Law Act* 1975 (Cth), ss. 68F(2)(g)(i)(j), 68J, 68K. (The kinds of parenting orders the court can make regarding residence, contact, child maintenance and specific issues are set out in s. 64B.)

4 The notion that a party's violence during the marriage may constitute a negative contribution to marital property has only recently been recognised. See *Doherty and Doherty* (1996) FLC 92–652; Behrens (1993, p. 9).

5 *Jurisdiction of Courts (Cross Vesting) Acts* 1987 (States and Cth). See *In*

the *Marriage of Marsh* (1994) FLC 92–443, 17 Fam LR 289; *Re Q* (1995) FLC 92–565, 18 Fam LR 442.

6   See O'Donovan (1997, pp. 53–54). This observation draws upon the Derridean concept of 'iterability', which refers to the way in which the same term may appear with different meanings in different contexts. The law also makes it impossible to consent to some activities, though the infliction of harm in a heterosexual encounter has never been included on the list. This issue was discussed at a symposium on 'Narratives of Consent', Criminology Department, The University of Melbourne, 15 July 1997; particularly in the papers by Kerry Carrington (on the Leigh Leigh rape/murder case) and Les Moran (on the House of Lords decision in *R v Brown* [1994] 2 AC 212, dealing with homosexual sado-masochism).

7   In the year 1996/97, four cases were scheduled for final hearing, of which one was settled prior to hearing. Applications to strike out sexual harassment complaints were made in a further three cases, one of which was successful.

8   Tony Jacobs, Registrar, Victorian Anti-Discrimination Tribunal, private communication, 17 June 1996.

9   *Family Law Act* 1975 (Cth), s. 60B(2): setting out the principle that, unless it would be contrary to the child's best interests, parents should agree about future parenting of their children.

10   This argument is well developed in the literature on mediation. See, for example, Lerman (1984, p. 57); Astor (1990, p. 143); Astor and Chinkin (1992, pp. 257–260); Bryan (1992, p. 441). The issue has received less attention in relation to other forms of settlement.

11   Family Law Rules, Order 25A, rule 5 (listing factors, including power imbalance between the parties and family violence, that must be taken into account in deciding whether a dispute may be mediated).

12   Observation sample case FC1, June 1996.

13   Note that 26 out of 63 are actual or presumed family violence cases. (Some cases—especially where the defendant did not appear—were dealt with so summarily that the relationship between applicant and defendant was never specified. I have assumed that these were family violence rather than stalking cases, unless there was some clear indication to the contrary.) In a further six cases the defendant had not been served with the complaint and interim order by the return date, making it impossible for the application for a final order to proceed that day. In these cases, the interim order was extended for a period to enable further attempts at service.

14   A slightly longer version would include queries about any Family Court orders and whether the defendant has a firearm.

15   Observation sample case MC42, October 1996.

16   Hana Assafiri, Co-ordinator, Immigrant Women's Domestic Violence Service, Melbourne, interviewed 24 June 1997. In the observation

sample, however, applications for mutual orders were made in only six out of the 63 final order cases, and two of these applications were ultimately withdrawn. In addition, however, solicitors for defendants in four cases obtained undertakings from, rather than formal orders against, the applicant, apparently as a condition of the defendant's consent to having an order made against him.

17  Flora Culpen, Community Legal Education Worker, Broadmeadows Community Legal Centre, interviewed 17 March 1997.

18  Leanne Abela, Solicitor, Pearsons, Airport West, interviewed 16 January 1997.

19  Only a small number of revocation applications (six) were observed. Two of these were applications by the defendant without reference to the woman protected by the order. The other four were applications by the woman protected. In only one of these was the woman's freedom in making the application quizzed (by a female Magistrate): observation sample case MC86, June 1997. One other Magistrate in conversation described a practice of trying to satisfy himself that women's applications for revocation were made freely (especially when the defendant was present) and of making it clear they could apply for an order again at any time and would not be prejudiced by the previous revocation.

20  Observation sample case MC16, June 1996. The disposition of this case took one minute.

21  Assafiri, interview; Sally Hewitson, Solicitor, Gill Kane & Brophy, Melbourne, interviewed 14 January 1997.

22  Hewitson, interview.

23  Abela, interview.

24  Judith Peirce, Solicitor, Brimbank Community Legal Centre, interviewed 21 August 1997.

25  Assafiri, Culpen, Peirce, interviews.

26  Peirce, interview.

27  Culpen, interview.

28  For example, Peirce, interview.

29  Abela, interview.

30  Culpen, Peirce, interviews.

31  Culpen, interview.

32  Cf., for example, Cain (1983) arguing that, in debt recovery actions, Magistrates' Courts do not so much resolve disputes as constantly restate approved property relations.

# CHAPTER 5

1  Throughout this chapter terms such as 'ethnicity', 'culture', 'race', 'ethnic', 'different' and 'access' will feature in inverted commas. This

is done to acknowledge that these terms are highly contested and makes it possible for me to make transparent my need to use these terms critically whilst also using them in text in the ways they commonly occur.

2   Discourse here refers to the Foucauldian meaning of 'relatively well bounded areas of social knowledge' (McHoul & Grace 1993, p. 31).

3   I use the term 'non English speaking background' throughout this chapter in two different ways. The first is as the term continues to appear in multicultural discourses (in conjunction with the terms 'cultural diversity' and 'culturally and linguistically diverse') and as defined by the NSW Ethnic Communities Council:

> Someone whose first language is not English or whose cultural background is derived from a non English speaking tradition. In statistical terms, a person is of non English speaking background if they or one of their parents was born in a country where English is not the first language. Non English speaking background is therefore a cultural/linguistic term and may include English speakers or non English speakers, overseas born and Australian born. (Johnson 1994, p. 121)

> The second acknowledges that the term is highly contested and problematic in the way it fixes vastly different individuals and communities into the same category, assuming common needs on the basis of what they are not—not English speaking, and thereby marking 'them' as 'outside' the mainstream of 'dominant' Australia. This situation is further compounded by the narrowing of the term to the acronym NESB which I have resisted using despite its continuing popularity.

4   See Chapter 13 in this collection for a discussion of Aboriginal issues.

5   This is not to say that this is the first time immigrant and Aboriginal women began to speak [about sexual violence] but rather it is the first time that 'English speaking' Australian-born women (of which I consider myself one) began to indicate their intention to listen (Murdolo 1996, p. 72).

6   It is important to note at the outset that there is no single post-structuralism but that post-structural theorists do share a common philosophical base. For an introduction to post-structuralism and feminism, see Weedon (1987).

## CHAPTER 6

1   This report presented the findings of a research study into the sexual abuse of women patients during admission in a psychiatric facility. The study was the initiative of Women and Mental Health Inc.

2   A non-government organisation comprising consumers, carers,

advocates and service providers, Women and Mental Health (WAMH) was formed in 1993 to raise issues specific to women experiencing mental illness. Its aims include the promotion of research and community education on the needs of women with a mental illness; providing input to government; networking; and the provision of an annual conference. Currently, it is developing a training package to educate consumers regarding sexual assault and complaints mechanisms.

3     The term 'consumer' is of fairly recent origin and refers to a person who uses mental health services of any kind (e.g. in-patient facilities, rehabilitation services, accommodation services). It is the term of choice for users of mental health services themselves. For the purposes of the report, the term 'patient' was used to describe persons during an in-patient admission, and 'consumer' was used to denote an ex-patient (i.e. post admission).

4     Comprising Jane Davidson, the researcher; Lorna McNamara, the project supervisor; Elizabeth Watson (academic and qualitative research specialist) and Christine Wilson (consultant on research methods and ethics).

5     Under which victims of crime, including sexual assault, can apply for compensation up to $50 000 for emotional and physical injuries and loss.

6     For example, (female) nurses reported their frustration with (male) psychiatrists who overruled the steps they took with victims of sexual abuse; and a social worker participant described how both psychiatric nurses and psychiatrists regarded her input with suspicion because she was part of allied health, and therefore seen to be less knowledgeable about mental health, as well as being young and female.

## CHAPTER 7

1     Arguments made in FMS Foundation Newsletter, 1 October 1995; 1 November 1995; 1 January 1996. See also Hallam (1997).

2     These are the types of studies quoted as evidence that recovered memories of child sexual abuse are subject to distortion or are based on events that have not occurred, since one of the main claims of false memory proponents is that recovered memories of abuse are implanted by therapists (e.g. Loftus et al. 1994, pp. 1177–1181). In fact, such studies are meaningless for explaining situations where a person has recovered memories of abuse on their own with no likelihood of alteration by other people's suggestions. For a critique of such studies: Whitfield (1995).

3     See Wakefield and Underwager (1992); Loftus (1993); Lindsay and Read (1994) as examples of the literature on 'false memories'.

4    These terms 'refer to a distinction between ways in which memories are accessed' (Freyd 1996, p. 96).

5    That is, explicit memory is a cognitive form of memory in that it involves the encoding, storage and recall of verbal or visual material— ('the "facts" as opposed to the "feelings" ')—whilst implicit memory is an emotional form of memory that can only be evoked by stimuli 'which trigger recall for the original emotional state' (Bremner et al. 1995, p. 530).

6    Reports of traumatic amnesia began with those by Janet (1889).

7    For examples of case studies of different types of traumatic amnesia, see Bremner et al. (1995, pp. 533–534).

8    For example, Williams (1995, pp. 668–669) reports from her study of women who reported delayed recall of child sexual abuse that recall was often 'prompted by triggers (such as, seeing the perpetrator or someone who looked like him . . . )' or by a subsequent traumatic event (such as, a sexual assault); Bremner et al. (1995, p. 532) have found that '[t]raumatic recall often occurs in dissociated states which are reminiscent of the state in which the event originally was experienced. It may be that during states of arousal, release of neuromodulators such as norepinephrine . . . leads to pathological recall of traumatic memories for which the patient may have been previously amnestic.'

9    This type of questioning is commonly used by FMS proponents who claim that memories are 'implanted' by bad therapy or by women being involved in support groups (Toon et al. 1996, p. 75).

10   American figures for the prevalence of child sexual abuse in national random samples of women and men vary from 15–60 per cent for females and 9–16 per cent for males (Gilmartin 1994, pp. 41–43). In Australia, Fleming (1997, pp. 65–68) reported that 33 per cent of women from a national community sample had experienced at least one incident of contact or non-contact sexual abuse before age 16.

11   Variation in these rates may be dependent on the sample studied or methodology used (e.g. questionnaires versus face-to-face interviews). These studies are also retrospective (adults surveyed about past occur- rences of child sexual abuse), rather than prospective (followed up after being abused).

12   More recently Kristiansen et al. (cited in Kristiansen 1996, p. 9) found that 51 per cent of 113 community-based women who were survivors of child sexual abuse reported at least some amnesia for the abuse; a lower rate of 28.5 per cent was reported by Roesler and Wind (1994) who surveyed a random sample of 228 women who reported a history of CSA before age 16.

13   Williams (1994, p. 1170) tested the hypothesis that the 38 per cent of women who did not report being sexually abused as children did not do so because of a reluctance to talk about personal matters. She

found this group of 49 women were just as willing as other subjects in the study who did report such abuse to communicate confidential or potentially embarrassing information about their sexual histories.

14 This 16 per cent (13 women) constituted 10 per cent of the 129 women studied. If this group of 13 women is added to the group of women who did not report being sexually abused as a child (38 per cent), then a total of 48 per cent or 62 (out of 129) women in Williams' study can be said to have suffered traumatic amnesia at some time in relation to their documented histories of child sexual abuse. This conclusion is, of course, dependent on an acceptance that the 38 per cent who did not report such abuse were suffering from traumatic amnesia, rather than merely not informing the interviewers of abuse of which they were nonetheless aware. Nonetheless, this rate of 48 per cent is very similar to the rate of 51 per cent found by Kristiansen et al. (see n. 12) and the rate of 42 per cent reported by Elliott and Briere (1995, p. 640).

15 Elliott and Briere (1995, p. 640) also studied the prevalence of delayed recall in a general population sample and their findings support Williams' findings that there was no therapist influence on memory recovery, since only 8 per cent of their total sample were undergoing some form of psychological treatment and, of that sample, only 22 per cent reported being sexually abused as children. Of the group that reported such abuse, 42 per cent reported some level of amnesia for the abuse, with 20 per cent 'describing a period of time when they were completely amnesic for the abuse'.

16 Elliott and Briere (1995, p. 645) reported that, in their study of a general population sample, 'males, females, Blacks, Whites, affluent and relatively impoverished subjects all had an equivalent likelihood of reporting delayed memories of sexual abuse'.

17 The inconsistencies reported by Williams were categorised as inconsistencies due to minimisation of the abuse (small numbers of women with both recovered memories and continuous recall reported that the abuse had not been as serious as what had been documented) and inconsistencies due to elaboration of the abuse (small numbers of women with both recovered memories and continuous recall reported extra events that were not originally documented).

18 For example, Anderson et al. (1993) found almost one in three New Zealand women had experienced sexual abuse before age 16: only 7 per cent had reported the abuse. See also Fleming (1997).

19 This view is consistent with the shareability theory proposed by Freyd (1996, p. 108) which posits that 'through the process of information sharing we recode internal material to be discrete—stable across time and space—and hence more easily communicable': Further, '[s]hareability theory suggests that memory for never-discussed events

is likely to be qualitatively different from memory for events that have been discussed' (1996, p. 111).

20 Whitfield, C.L. and Stock, W.E. (1997) 'Traumatic Memory Among 100 Survivors of Childhood Sexual Abuse', paper in progress quoted with permission of the authors, p. 1.

21 Including: Herman and Schatzow (1987); Bagley (1990); Briere and Conte (1993); Gold et al. (1994); Loftus Polonsky et al. (1994); Roesler and Wind (1994); Williams (1994); Elliott and Briere (1995); Kluft (1995); van der Kolk and Fisler (1995); Burgess and Hartman (1996); Cameron (1996); Carlson (1996); Chu et al. (1996); Dorado (1996); Elliott (1996); Feldman-Summers et al. (1996); Grassian and Holtzon (1996); Herman and Harvey (1996); Williams and Banyard (1996).

22 It is considered that memory loss by a perpetrator is more likely to occur where the sexual assault has been violent (Kristiansen 1996, pp. 9–10) or where perpetrators experience their acts as out of control and unpredictable (Foa et al. 1989, p. 20).

23 See Bremner et al. (1995, pp. 534–536), for a summary of studies which have shown that the hippocampus plays a role in explicit memory encoding and recall.

24 Compare Loftus et al. (1994) and Williams (1995).

25 See van der Kolk and Kadish (1987); van der Kolk and van der Hart (1989, 1991); van der Kolk (1994); Bremner et al. (1995); van der Kolk and Fisler (1995); van der Kolk, van der Hart and Marmar (1996).

26 All people experience mild states of dissociation—for example, a person driving somewhere, seemingly on 'automatic pilot', who cannot consciously remember the act of driving (Kristiansen 1996, p. 3); Freyd (1996, p. 68) describes dissociation as 'a form of divided mental control . . . [that is] a lack of integration between mental activity and conscious awareness'.

27 In fact, both war veterans and survivors of child sexual abuse show the same neurochemical and neurostructural changes as chronically stressed animals (Bremner et al. 1995, pp. 538–539; Kristiansen 1996, p. 10). According to Bremner et al. (p. 539), these studies support the possibility that enhanced neurochemical release in the hippocampus as a result of stress similar to the original trauma may explain the subsequent recall of a traumatic memory.

28 Such findings have been documented by Herman and Schatzow (1987); Briere and Conte (1993); van der Kolk and Fisler (1995); Kristiansen et al. (1996).

29 This means that, neurologically, there is a lack of integration between the brain structures that encode and store the explicit memory system (the hippocampus) and those of the implicit memory system (the amygdala).

30  The Whitfield and Stock study (n. 20) also appears to support Freyd's betrayal trauma theory, since they reported that younger age at the time of abuse was associated with more amnesia, and the majority of subjects (72 per cent) had been victims of incestuous abuse. However, they did not investigate whether there was a statistically significant relationship between those who had experienced either complete or partial amnesia and their relationship with their abuser.

31  These findings complement the findings of Kristiansen et al. (1996, p. 12) who reported that women in their study with recovered memories 'said that their memories often came back as body memories and flashbacks' or intense emotions and images, and returned 'in fragments, gradually over time rather than explicitly, as complete narratives'. It is also recognised that '[t]rauma survivors may have intrusive recall of the sounds of an event while simultaneously being unable to recall the sights or vice versa. Or the feelings may be inescapably remembered over and over, without complete memory of the events that led to those feelings' (Freyd 1996, p. 22). Curiously, Elizabeth Loftus, one of the scientists who has been a key proponent of the alleged false memory syndrome (on the grounds that a person cannot forget traumatic events), has described her own (recovered?) memories of being abused by a baby-sitter at age six: 'The memory flew out at me, out of the blackness of the past, hitting me full force.' She has also described the lack of awareness of a substantial part of the events surrounding the abuse after struggling free of the baby-sitter whilst being sexually molested by him: 'After that, there is only blackness in my memory, full and total darkness with not a pinhole of light. Howard [the baby-sitter] is simply gone, vanished, sucked away. My memory took him and destroyed him' (Loftus & Ketcham, quoted in Freyd 1996, pp. 28–29). Freyd (1996, p. 29) has observed: 'Elizabeth Loftus's description illustrates the paradox of traumatic memory: how the survivor can have a memory of the event that is "indelible" yet so blocked that it causes the perpetrator to "vanish", a memory that was forgotten yet flies "out of the blackness of the past".'

32  Further, a study of children's ability to recall more accurately a genital exam (than a routine physical checkup) 'suggests that the types of events which form the basis of childhood abuse may not be as subject to distortions, insertions and deletions as more "mundane" memories' (Bremner et al. 1995, p. 545).

33  Many forms of abuse (e.g. fondling) do not result in physical evidence. In addition, unless medical documentation is made at the time, as in the Williams study, adult complainants have few opportunities of finding corroborating evidence irrespective of whether they have recovered or continuous memories of the abuse.

34  In NSW in 1994–95 there were 2955 substantiated cases of child

sexual abuse (Angus & Hall 1995, p. 25). For the period January–December 1994, 244 males were prosecuted in NSW Local Courts in relation to 316 sexual offences against children (35 per cent found guilty) and 419 people were prosecuted in the NSW District and Supreme Courts in relation to 863 offences (50 per cent found guilty) (NSW BCSR 1994, pp. 8, 62). Although the data on conviction rates in any given year does not necessarily represent a sub-set of the substantiated cases dealt with by the Department of Community Services, there is no evidence of a backlog in the courts such that it can be said that all DCS substantiated cases will eventually be prosecuted.

35 Briere and Conte (1993) also reported a relationship between recent recall of child sexual abuse and current symptomatology.

36 Hallam (1997) searched leading databases to find newspaper and magazine articles containing membership figures for the FMS Foundation and reviewed journal articles, transcripts from TV interviews and all FMSF newsletters. She discovered that the figure of 10 000 families, who were said to have merely contacted the Foundation, had been transformed into *documented* cases of FMS, even though 4000 of such contacts merely reported they had an unspecified family problem, whilst 7000 had called or written to the Foundation with questions and concerns. In fact, Hallam reports that 'the FMSF has no "documented" cases of false memory in its records. Pamela Freyd acknowledges that the FMSF does not investigate the story of the person on the other end of the phone, and admits that her Foundation has no idea whether the accusation is true or false.'

37 Pope (1996, p. 962) has noted that '[r]esearch involving human participants usually involves the informed consent of the participants' and comments that 'it would be useful if the procedures for obtaining consent—if consent was obtained—from people who were diagnosed as suffering from false memory syndrome were disclosed'.

38 Recently this test has been modified by American courts: *Shahzade v Gregory*, unreported, United States District Court, District of Massachusetts, Harrington, DJ, 8 May 1996, and *Daubert v Merrell Dow Pharmaceuticals, Inc.* (1993) 113 S. Ct. 2786.

39 Evidence given by Professor van der Kolk in *Shahzade v Gregory*, see n. 38, p. 4.

40 *Accuracy About Abuse Newsletter*, 14 February 1997.

41 For example, the District Court of Massachusetts recently held that so-called 'repressed memories' were admissible as evidence on the basis of expert evidence presented by Professor Bessel van der Kolk, Harvard Medical School. The Court was satisfied that the reliability of the phenomenon of repressed memories had been established on the basis that repressed memory evidence came within the definition of scientific knowledge—that is, it was grounded in the methods and

procedures of science and satisfied the following four criteria: (1) the theory has been tested; (2) the theory has been subjected to peer review and publication; (3) the theory's known or potential rate of error; and (4) the theory has attained general acceptance within the relevant scientific community (*Shahzade v Gregory*, see n. 38, p. 3).

## CHAPTER 8

1   These conditions include the offender moving out of the residence where his victim and family reside, having no contact of any kind with the victim and other children in the family without the permission of the Program Director, and making satisfactory progress in treatment.
2   As a condition of program entry is willingness of the offender's partner to be involved in the program, it is not surprising that this program is attractive to women who wish to reunite with their partner, despite the program's rejection of this as a treatment goal.
3   It was not considered appropriate to interview the young people until they had completed treatment.

## CHAPTER 9

1   The self-defence explanation for women's violence has been disputed. According to Strauss, in approximately 25 per cent of physical attacks, women were the aggressors when their husbands were not physically violent during a previous 12-month period. Another study found that, in approximately half of the attacks, women initiated the violence (Strauss 1993). Strauss urges caution, however, in interpreting these statistics. Women respondents may have been confused whether the interview question referred to: 'Who initiated the argument?' or, alternatively, 'Who initiated the violence?' He argues that women could have initiated an argument and then reported themselves as initiating violence. In addition, Strauss points out that there may have been an escalation of assaults throughout the relationship, with the original attacks by the man. The fact that the most recent incident happened to be initiated by the female partner ignores the history and the context producing that act, which may be one of utter terror (Strauss 1993).

## CHAPTER 11

1   In our work contexts of a Women's Health Centre and a private practice, we work primarily with women, so we refer mostly to

women's experience in this article. However, we acknowledge that men and male children who have been abused also employ dissociative strategies for the same reasons that women do, as a form of self-protection.

2    For example, Herman (1992) and van der Kolk (1995).

3    David Neswald presented these ideas in a workshop in Melbourne in 1994.

## CHAPTER 14

1    One problem, which will not be discussed in detail here, is that the definition of census collection boundaries is largely a matter of administrative convenience. While the boundaries may encompass elements of local social organisation, these features usually take second place in the studies to aggregate measures which are described as communal but, in fact, more often sum the attributes of *individuals* living in the localities in question. It will be seen later in this chapter that, when use is made of locality relevant statistics, like those that describe female participation in the labour force, the issue of whether one is dealing with an aspect of community often turns on the way the latter is conceptualised.

2    For a comprehensive presentation of the statistical results of the study, see T. Vinson, E. Baldry and J. Hargreaves, 1996, 'Neighbourhoods, Networks and Child Abuse', *British Journal of Social Work*, No. 26, pp. 523–543.

## CHAPTER 15

1    As the Marriage Guidance Council of NSW.

2    The reasons for this are the problematic effect of a mixed group of voluntary and mandated clients, and the effect of accepting mandated clients when the debate about the implications of a program as an alternative to jail has not occurred.

3    In our experience, where men continue to be violent they tend to drop out of the program or are asked to leave. One quarter of all participants do not complete the program for various reasons.

4    Since 1986 this group has worked with domestic violence cases under a project known as the Gender and Violence Project at the Ackerman Institute in New York.

# Bibliography

Adler, Z. 1987, *Reality of Rape Trials*, Routledge & Kegan Paul, London.

Albie, M. & Mowbray-d'Arbela, M. 1987, Paper presented by Migrant Women Against Incest for the Child Sexual Assault Services Program Conference, Dympna House, Sydney.

Aldarondo, E. & Straus, M.A. 1994, 'Screening for physical violence in couple therapy: methodological, practical & ethical considerations', *Family Process*, vol. 33, no. 4, pp. 425–439.

Allbrook Cattilini Research 1992, *Break the Cycle: The Extent and Effects on Young People of Witnessing Domestic Violence*. A report to the Youth Affairs Council of Western Australia.

Allen, J. 1982, 'The intervention of the pathological family: a historical study of family violence in NSW', in C. O'Donnell & J. Craney (eds), *Family Violence in Australia*, Longman Cheshire, Australia, pp. 1–27.

——1990, *Sex and Secrets—Crimes involving Australian Women since 1880*, Oxford University Press, Melbourne.

Anderson, J., Martin, J., Mullen, P., Romans, S. & Herbison, P. 1993, 'Prevalence of childhood sexual abuse experiences in a community sample of women', *Journal of the American Academy of Child and Adolescent Psychiatry*, vol. 32, no. 5, pp. 911–919.

American Psychiatric Association 1994, *Diagnostic and Statistical Manual of Mental Disorders*, 4th edn, Washington.

Amnesty International 1998, *Universal Declaration of Human Rights—50th Anniversary Campaign*. amnesty@www.universal/declaration/human/rights.com.au

**283**

Ang, I. 1994, 'On not speaking Chinese', *New Formations*, vol. 24 (winter), pp. 5–22.

——1995, 'I'm a feminist but . . . "Other" women and postnational feminism', in B. Caine & R. Pringle (eds), *Transitions: New Australian Feminisms*, Allen & Unwin, Sydney.

Angus, G. & Hall, G. 1995, *Child Abuse and Neglect Australia 1994–95*, Australian Institute of Health and Welfare, Child Welfare Series, No. 16, AGPS, Canberra.

Armstrong, L. 1996, *Rocking the Cradle of Sexual Politics—What Happened When Women Said Incest*, The Women's Press Ltd, London.

Aronson, M. & Hunter, J. 1995, *Litigation: Evidence and Procedure*, 5th edn, Butterworths, Sydney.

Astbury, J. 1996, *Crazy for You: The Making of Women's Madness*, Oxford University Press, Melbourne.

Astor, H. 1990, 'Domestic violence and mediation', *Australian Dispute Resolution Journal*, vol. 1, pp. 143–153.

Astor, H. & Chinkin, C.M. 1992, *Dispute Resolution in Australia*, Butterworths, Sydney.

Attneave, C. 1976, 'Social networks as the unit of intervention', in P. Guerin (ed.), *Family Therapy*, Gardner, New York.

Australian Association of Trauma and Dissociation 1996, *Newsletter*, November.

Australian Bureau of Statistics 1994a, *Crime and Safety, Australia, April 1993*, Cat. No. 4509.0, Australian Bureau of Statistics, Canberra.

——1994b, *Crime and Safety, New South Wales, April 1994*, Cat. No. 4509.1, Australian Bureau of Statistics, Sydney.

——1996, *Women's Safety Australia 1996*, Cat. No. 4128.0, Australian Bureau of Statistics, Canberra.

Australian Law Reform Commission 1997, *Report 84: Seen and Heard: Priority for Children in the Legal Process*, Sydney.

Bagley, A.C. 1990, 'Validity of a short measure of child sexual abuse', *Psychological Reports*, vol. 66, pp. 449–450.

Barth, R.P. 1991, 'An experimental evaluation of in-home child abuse prevention services', *Child Abuse and Neglect*, vol. 15, pp. 363–375.

Behrens, J. 1993, 'Domestic violence and property adjustment: a critique of "no fault" discourse', *Australian Journal of Family Law*, vol. 7, pp. 9–28.

Bell, V. 1993, *Interrogating Incest—Feminism, Foucault and the Law*, Routledge, London.

Belsky, J. 1980, 'Child maltreatment. An ecological integration', *American Psychologist*, vol. 35, no. 4, pp. 320–335.

Bender, L. & Blau, A. 1937, 'The reactions of children to relations with adults', *American Journal of Orthopsychiatry*, vol. 47, pp. 500–518.

Benedek, E. & Schetky, D. 1985, 'Allegations of sexual abuse in child custody and visitation disputes', in D. Schetky & E. Benedek (eds),

*Emerging Issues in Child Psychiatry and the Law*, Bruner/Mazel, New York.

Berliner, L. 1988, 'Deciding whether a child has been sexually abused', in E. Nicholson (ed.), *Sexual Abuse Allegations in Custody and Visitation Cases*, American Bar Association, Washington DC.

Birkel, R.C. & Reppucci, N.D. 1983, 'Social networks, information-seeking and the use of services', *American Journal of Community Psychology*, vol. 11, no. 2, pp. 185–205.

Blanchard, A. 1993, 'Violence in families: the effect on children', *Family Matters*, AIFS, vol. 34, pp. 31–36.

Block, J.P. 1991, *Assessment and Treatment of Multiple Personality and Dissociative Disorders*, Professional Resource Press, Florida.

Blush, G. & Ross, K. 1987, 'Sexual allegations in divorce: the SAID syndrome', *Conciliation Courts Review*, vol. 25, p. 1.

Bograd, M. 1990, 'Why we need gender to understand human violence', *Journal of Interpersonal Violence*, vol. 5, no. 1, pp. 132–135.

——1992, 'Values in conflict: challenges to family therapists' thinking', *Journal of Marital and Family Therapy*, vol. 18, no. 3, pp. 245–256.

Bordow, S. 1987, *A Survey of Sexual Child Abuse Cases*, Counselling Service, Family Court of Australia, Sydney.

Brandt, R. & Sink, F. 1984, *Dilemmas in Court-ordered Evaluation of Sexual Abuse Charges during Custody and Visitation Proceedings*, Paper presented at 31st Annual Meeting of American Academy of Child Psychiatry, Toronto.

Breckenridge, J. 1994, 'Intervention in child welfare: an inflicted evil or solicited response?', in M. Wearing & R. Berreen (eds), *Welfare and Social Policy in Australia*, Harcourt Brace, Sydney, pp. 137–154

——1995, 'The socio-legal relationship in child sexual assault', in P. Swain (ed.), *In the Shadow of the Law—The Legal Context of Social Work Practice*, Federation Press, Sydney, pp. 29–45.

——1996, *'Of Subjugation and Silences . . .'—The Ways in which the Women's Movement Influenced, Shaped and Changed Professional Discourses in Relation to Child Sexual Assault.* Unpublished doctoral thesis, University of New South Wales, Sydney.

Breines, W. & Gordon, L. 1983, 'The new scholarship on family violence', *Signs*, vol. 8, pp. 490–531.

Bremner, J.D., Davis, M., Southwick, S.M., Krystal, J.H. & Charney, D.S. 1993, 'The neurobiology of post-traumatic stress disorder', in J.M. Oldham, M.G. Riba & A. Tasman (eds), *Review of Psychiatry (Volume 12)*, American Psychiatric Press, Washington DC, pp. 182–204.

Bremner, J.D., Krystal, J.H., Southwick, S.M. & Charney, D.S. 1995, 'Functional neuroanatomical correlates of the effects of stress on memory', *Journal of Traumatic Stress*, vol. 8, no. 4, p. 527ff.

Bresee, P., Stearns, G., Bess, B. & Packer, L. 1986, 'Allegations of child sexual abuse in child custody disputes: a therapeutic assessment model', *American Journal of Orthopsychiatry*, vol. 56, pp. 560–569.

Briere, J. 1989, *Therapy for Adults Molested as Children: Beyond Survival*, Springer Publishing Co., New York.

Briere, J. & Conte, J. 1993, 'Self-reported amnesia for abuse in adults molested as children', *Journal of Traumatic Stress*, vol. 6, no. 1, pp. 21–31.

Brody, J.G. 1985, 'Informal social networks: possibilities and limitations for their usefulness in social policy', *Journal of Community Psychology*, vol. 13, pp. 338–349.

Bronfenbrenner, U. 1977, 'Toward an experimental ecology of human development', *American Psychologist*, vol. 32, pp. 513–531.

Broverman, I.K., Broverman, D.M., Clarkson, F.E., Rosenkrantz, P.S. & Vogel, S.R. 1970, 'Sex-role stereotypes and clinical judgments of mental health', *Journal of Consulting and Clinical Psychology*, vol. 34, no. 1, pp. 1–7.

Brown, D. 1995, 'Pseudomemories: the standard of science and the standard of care in trauma treatment', *American Journal of Clinical Hypnosis*, vol. 37, pp. 1–24.

Bryan, P.E. 1992, 'Killing us softly: divorce mediation and the politics of power', *Buffalo Law Review*, vol. 40, pp. 441–523.

Burdekin, B., Guilfoyle, M. & Hall, D. 1993, *Human Rights and Mental Illness: Report of the National Inquiry into the Human Rights of People with Mental Illness*, AGPS, Canberra.

Burgess, A.W. & Hartman, C.R. 1996, *Sadistic Child Abuse and Traumatic Memories*, paper at Trauma and Memory: An International Research Conference 26–28 July, University of New Hampshire, Durham.

Burke, C. 1994, *Being an Effective Advocate for the Child: Children who experience Domestic Violence*, NSW Child Protection Council, Sydney.

Burke, C. & Moses, S. 1996, *Change Could Come*, video script, Jannawi Family Centre, Sydney.

Bussey, K. 1990, *The Competence of Child Witnesses*, paper presented at the Australian Child Protection Conference, Sydney.

Byrne, K. 1991, 'Mental health professionals in child custody disputes: advocates or impartial examiners', *Australian Family Lawyer,* vol. 6, pp. 8–11.

Cahn, N. 1991, 'Civil images of battered women', *Vanderbilt Law Review*, October.

Cain, M.E. 1983, 'Where are the disputes? A study of a first instance court in the U.K.', in M.E. Cain & K. Kulscar (eds), *Disputes and the Law*, Akademai Kiado, Budapest.

Caldwell, R.A., Bogat, G.A., Davidson, W.S. 1988, 'The assessment of child abuse potential and the prevention of child abuse and neglect: a policy analysis', *American Journal of Community Psychology*, vol. 16, pp. 609–624.

Cameron, C. 1994, 'Women survivors confronting their abusers: Issues, decisions and outcomes', *Journal of Child Sexual Abuse*, vol. 3, pp. 7–35.

——1996, *Adult Memories of Child Sexual Abuse: A Longitudinal Report*, paper presented at Trauma and Memory: An International Research Conference 26–28 July, University of New Hampshire, Durham.

Campbell, A. 1993, *Out of Control: Men, Women & Aggression*, Pandora, London.

Campbell, M. 1991, 'Children at risk: how different are children on child abuse registers?' *British Journal of Social Work*, vol. 21, pp. 259–275.

Caplan, G. 1974, *Approaches to Community Mental Health*, Tavistock, London.

Caplan, P. 1989, *Don't Blame Mother*, Harper & Row, New York.

Carlson, E. 1996, *Sex Differences in Amnesia for Childhood Physical and Sexual Abuse in Inpatients*, paper presented at Trauma and Memory: An International Research Conference 26–28 July, University of New Hampshire, Durham.

Cascardi, M. & Vivian, D. 1995, 'Context for specific episodes of marital violence, gender and severity of violence difference', *Journal of Family Violence*, vol. 10, no. 3.

Cassens Moss, D. 1984, 'Abuse scale', *ABA Journal*, December, vol. 1, p. 26.

Chesler, P. 1986, *Mothers on Trial: The Battle for Children and Custody*, McGraw-Hill, New York.

——1989, *Women and Madness*, Harcourt, Brace Jovanovich, Florida.

Chu, J.A. et al. 1996, *Childhood Trauma and Dissociative Amnesia: Issues Concerning Correlation, Corroboration and Suggestion*, paper presented at Trauma and Memory: An International Research Conference 26–28 July, University of New Hampshire, Durham.

Clark, M.S., Milberg, S. & Erber, R. 1987, 'Arousal state dependent memory: evidence and some implications for understanding social judgments and social behavior', in K. Fiedler & J.P. Forgas (eds), *Affect, Cognition and Social Behavior*, Hogrefe, Toronto.

Cochran, M.M. & Brassard, J.A. 1979, 'Child development and personal social networks', *Child Development*, vol. 50, pp. 601–616.

Cohn, A.H. & Daro, D. 1987, 'Is treatment too late? What ten years of evaluative research tells us', *Child Abuse and Neglect*, vol. 1, pp. 433–442.

Coleman, L. 1986, 'False allegations of child sexual abuse: have the experts been caught with their pants down?' *Forum,* January/February, pp. 5–14.

Condonis, M., Paroissen, K. & Aldrich, B. 1990, *The mutual help group: A therapeutic program for women who have been abused*, 2nd edn, Redfern Legal Centre Publishing, Sydney.

Coney, S. 1988, *The Unfortunate Experiment*, Penguin, Auckland.

Conte, J.R. 1985, 'Clinical dimensions of adult sexual abuse of children', *Behavioural Sciences and the Law*, vol. 3, pp. 341–354.

——1995, 'Assessment of children who may have been abused: the real world context', in T. Ney (ed.), *True and False Allegations of Child Sexual Abuse*, Brunner/Mazel, New York.

Conte, J.R., Wolf, S. & Smith, T. 1989, 'What sex offenders tell us about prevention strategies', *Child Abuse and Neglect*, vol. 13, pp. 293–301.

Coochey, J. 1995, 'All men are bastards', *The Independent Monthly*, November, pp. 48–51.

Corse, S.J., Schmid, K. & Trickett, P.K. 1990, 'Social network characteristics of mothers in abusing and nonabusing families and their relationships to parenting beliefs', *Journal of Community Psychology*, vol. 18, pp. 44–58.

Corwin, D., Berliner, L., Goodman, G., Goodwin, J. & White, S. 1987, 'Custody disputes: no easy answers', *Journal of Interpersonal Violence*, vol. 2, pp. 91–105.

Cossins, A. & Pilkinton, R. 1996, 'Balancing the scales: the case for the inadmissibility of counselling records in sexual assault trials', *The University of New South Wales Law Journal*, vol. 19, p. 222.

Cotterill, A.M. 1988, 'The geographic distribution of child abuse in an inner city borough', *Child Abuse and Neglect*, vol. 12, pp. 461–467.

Crittenden, P.M. 1985, 'Social networks, quality of childrearing and child development', *Child Development*, vol. 56, pp. 1299–1313.

Crossmaker, M. 1991, 'Behind locked doors—institutional sexual abuse', *Sexuality and Disability*, vol. 9, no. 3, pp. 201–219.

Cummins, R.C. 1988, 'Perceptions of social support, receipt of supportive behaviors, and locus of control as moderators of the effects of chronic stress', *American Journal of Community Psychology*, vol. 16, no. 5, pp. 685–700.

Davidson, J. 1997, *Every Boundary Broken: Sexual Abuse of Women Patients in Psychiatric Institutions*, Women and Mental Health, Sydney.

Davies, B. 1989, *Frogs, Snails and Feminist Tales*, Allen & Unwin, Sydney.

Davies, J.M. & Frawley, M.G. 1994, *Treating the Adult Survivor of Childhood Sexual Abuse*, Basic Books, New York.

Davies, L. & Carlson, B. 1987, 'Observation of spouse abuse. What happens to the children?', *Journal of Interpersonal Violence*, vol. 2, no. 3, pp. 278–291.

Dell, P. 1989, 'Violence and the systemic view: the problem of power', *Family Process*, vol. 23, pp. 1–14.

de Mause, L. 1994, 'The history of child abuse', *Sexual Addiction and Compulsivity*, vol. 1, pp. 77–91.

de Young, M. 1981, 'Incest victims and offenders: myths and realities', *Journal of Psychosocial Nursing and Mental Health Services*, October, vol. 19, no. 10, pp. 37–39.

Dean, M.C. 1996, 'Interview with Professor van der Kolk', *Australian Association of Trauma & Dissociation Newsletter*, vol. 4, no. 4, November.

Donald, J. and Rattansi, A. 1992 (eds), *'Race', Culture and Difference*, Sage, London.

Dorado, J.S. 1996, *Remembering and Coming to Terms with Sexual Abuse for Incest Survivors*, paper presented at Trauma and Memory: An International Research Conference, 26–28 July, University of New Hampshire, Durham.

Ducote, R. & Harrison, D. 1988, 'Aggressive advocacy for parents protecting children in child sexual abuse cases', in E. Nicholson (ed.), *Sexual Abuse Allegations in Custody and Visitation Cases*, The American Bar Association, Washington DC.

Dulwich Centre 1995, 'Reclaiming our stories, reclaiming our lives', *Dulwich Centre Newsletter*, no. 1.

Durie, J. & Taylor, A. 1997, *Teaching through Difference*, paper presented at Australian Association for Research in Education (AARE) Conference 30.11.97 to 4.12.97, Brisbane, Queensland.

Elliott, D. 1996, *Traumatic Events: Prevalence and Delayed Recall in the General Population*, paper presented at Trauma and Memory: An International Research Conference 26–28 July, University of New Hampshire, Durham.

Elliott, D.M. & Briere, J. 1995, 'Post-traumatic stress associated with delayed recall of sexual abuse: a general population study', *Journal of Traumatic Stress*, vol. 8, no. 4.

Elterman, M. & Ehrenberg, M. 1991, 'Sexual abuse allegations in child custody disputes', *International Journal of Law and Psychiatry*, vol. 14, pp. 269–86.

——1995, 'Evaluating allegations of sexual abuse in the context of divorce, child custody and access disputes', in T. Ney (ed.), *True and False Allegations of Child Sexual Abuse*, Brunner/Mazel, New York.

Epston, D. & White, M. 1989, *Literate Means to Therapeutic Ends*, Dulwich Centre Publications, Adelaide.

Erickson, B.M. 1992, 'Feminist fundamentalism: reactions to Avis, Kaufman and Bograd', *Journal of Marital and Family Therapy*, vol. 18, no. 3, pp. 263–267.

Estrich, S. 1986, 'Rape', *The Yale Law Journal*, vol. 95, May, pp. 1087–1184.

Everson, M. & Boat, B. 1989, 'False allegations of sexual abuse by children and adolescents', *Journal of the American Academy of Child and Adolescent Psychiatry*, vol. 28, pp. 230–235.

Fairfield Multicultural Family Planning 1996, *Many Voices, Different Stories—Speaking Out about Cultural Diversity and Sexual Assault*, Fairfield: FMFP.

Faller, K. 1988, 'Criteria for judging the credibility of children's statements about their sexual abuse', *Child Welfare*, vol. 67, pp. 389–401.

——1991, 'Possible explanations for child sexual abuse allegations in divorce', *American Journal of Orthopsychiatry*, vol. 61, pp. 86–91.

Faludi, S. 1991, *BACKLASH—The Undeclared War against American Women*, Crown Publishers, New York.

Feldman-Summers, S. & Pope, K.S. 1994, 'The experience of "forgetting" childhood abuse: a national survey of psychologists', *Journal of Consulting and Clinical Psychology*, vol. 62, pp. 636–639.

Feldman-Summers, S., Pope, K.S. & van der Kolk, B. 1996, *The Nature of Traumatic Memories following Adult and Childhood Trauma*, paper presented at Trauma and Memory: An International Research Conference 26–28 July, University of New Hampshire, Durham.

Finch, L. 1993, *The Classing Gaze—Sexuality, Class and Surveillance*, Allen & Unwin, Sydney.

Finkelhor, D. 1984, *Child Sexual Abuse: New Theory and Research*, Free Press, New York.

Fish, V. 1991, 'Abuses of power by father-daughter incest perpetrators in treatment: the necessity of the coalition', in M. Bograd (ed.), *Feminist Approaches to Men in Family Therapy*, Harrington Park Press, NY, pp. 227–242.

Fitzgerald, M., Mullavey-O'Byrne, C., Clemson, L. & Williamson, P. 1996, *Enhancing Cultural Competency*, video and manual training package, Transcultural Mental Health Centre, NSW.

Fleming, J.M. 1997, 'Prevalence of childhood sexual abuse in a community sample of Australian women', *Medical Journal of Australia*, vol. 166, pp. 65–68.

Flynn, C. 1990, 'Relationship violence by women: issues and implications', *Family Relations*, vol. 39, pp. 194–198.

Foa, E.B., Steketee, G. & Rothbaum, B.O. 1989, 'Behavioral/cognitive conceptualisation of post-traumatic stress disorder', *Behavior Therapy*, vol. 20, pp. 155–176.

Foucault, M. 1980, *Power/Knowledge: Selected Interviews and Other Writings 1972–1977* (ed. C. Gordon; trans. by C. Gordon, L. Marshall, J. Meplam & K. Soper), Harvester Press, London.

——1981, *The History of Sexuality, Volume One: An Introduction* (trans. R. Hurley), Allen Lane, London [first published in French in 1976].

Franklin, B. 1989, 'Wimps and bullies', in P. Carter, T. Jeffs & M. Smith (eds), *Social Work and Social Welfare Year Book 1*, Open University Press, Milton Keynes.

Franzway, S., Court, D. & Connell, R.W. 1989, *Staking a Claim—Feminism, Bureaucracy and the State*, Allen & Unwin, Sydney.

Freedman, J. & Combs, G. 1996, *Narrative Therapy: The Social Construction of Preferred Realities*, Norton, New York.

Freud, S. 1984, 'The Aetiology of Hysteria', in J. Masson (ed.), *The Assault on Truth—Freud's Suppression of the Seduction Theory*, Penguin Books, London, pp. 259–290 [first published 1896].

Freud, S. & Breuer, J. 1986, *Studies on Hysteria*, Penguin Books, London.

Freyd, J. 1993, *Theoretical and Personal Perspectives on the Delayed Memory Debate*, paper presented at the Center for Mental Health at Foote Hospital's Continuing Education Conference: *Controversies around Recovered Memories of Incest and Ritualistic Abuse*, 7 August, Ann Arbor, Michigan.

——1996, *Betrayal Trauma: The Logic of Forgetting Child Abuse*, Harvard University Press, Cambridge MA.

——1997, 'Violations of power, adaptive blindness, and betrayal trauma theory', *Feminism and Psychology*, vol. 7, p. 22.

Freyd, P. 1992, 'How do we know we are not representing pedophiles?' *False Memory Syndrome Foundation Newsletter*, 29 February.

Furniss, T. 1991, *The Multi-professional Handbook of Child Sexual Abuse: Integrated Management, Therapy and Legal Interventions*, Routledge, London.

Galanter, M. 1974, 'Why the "haves" come out ahead: speculations on the limits of legal change', *Law and Society Review*, vol. 9, pp. 95–160.

Game, A. 1985, 'Child sexual assault: the liberal state's response', *Legal Services Bulletin*, vol. 10, no. 4, pp. 107–110.

Garbarino, J. 1977, 'The human ecology of child maltreatment: a conceptual model for research', *Journal of Marriage and the Family*, vol. 39, pp. 721–736.

Garbarino, J. & Crouter, A. 1978, 'Defining the community context of parent–child relations', *Child Development*, vol. 49, pp. 604–616.

Garbarino, J. & Kostelny, K. 1991, 'Child maltreatment as a community problem', personal communication.

Garbarino, J. & Sherman, D. 1980, 'High-risk neighbourhoods and high-risk families: the human ecology of child maltreatment', *Child Development*, vol. 51, pp. 188–198.

Gardener, R. 1987, *Sex Abuse Legitimacy Scale*, Creative Therapeutics, New Jersey.

Garrett, P. 1992, 'Monocultural to multicultural—issues of services equity for immigrants', in J. Breckenridge & M. Carmody (eds), *Crimes of Violence: Australian Responses to Rape and Child Sexual Assault*, Allen & Unwin, Sydney.

Gaudin, J.M. & Polansky, N.A. 1986, 'Social distancing of the neglectful family', *Children and Youth Services Review*, vol. 8, no. 1, pp. 1–12.

Gaudin, J.M. & Pollane, L. 1983, 'Social networks, stress and child abuse', *Children and Youth Services Review*, vol. 5, pp. 91–102.

Gelinas, D.J. 1988, 'Family therapy: critical early structuring', in S.M. Sgroi (ed.), *Vulnerable Populations Volume 1: Evaluation and Treatment of Sexually Abused Children and Adult Survivors*, Lexington Books, New York, pp. 51–76.

Gelles, R. 1979, *Family Violence*, Sage, California.

Giaretto, Henry 1982, *Integrated Treatment of Child Sexual Abuse*, Science and Behaviour Books, Palo Alto.

Gilligan, C., Rogers, A. & Tolman, D. 1991, *Women, Girls and Psychotherapy: Reframing Resistance*, Harrington Park Press.

Gilligan, C., Ward, J.V. & Taylor, J.M. (eds) 1988, *Mapping the Moral Domain: A Contribution of Women's Thinking to Psychological Theory and Education*, Harvard University Press, Boston.

Gilmartin, P. 1994, *Rape, Incest and Child Sexual Abuse: Consequences and Recovery*, Garland Publishing, New York.

Goddard, C. & Hiller, P. 1993, 'Child sexual assault in a violent context', *Australian Journal of Social Issues*, vol. 28, pp. 20–33.

Gold, S.N., Hughes, D. & Hohnecker, L. 1994, 'Degree of repression of sexual abuse memory', *American Psychologist*, vol. 49, pp. 441–442.

Goldfield, A.E., Mollica, R.F., Pesavento, B.H. & Faraone, S.V. 1988, 'The physical and psychological sequelae of torture: symptomology and diagnosis', *Journal of the American Medical Association*, vol. 259, pp. 2725–2729.

Goldman, J. 1990, 'The importance of an adequate sexual vocabulary for children', *Australian Journal of Marriage and Family*, vol. 11, no. 3, pp. 136–149.

Goldman, J.D.G. 1992, 'Children's sexual cognition and its implications for children's court testimony in child sexual abuse cases', *Australian Journal of Marriage and Family*, vol. 13, no. 2, pp. 78–96.

Goldner, V. 1994, 'Gender and Violence: A Couple Therapy Approach', workshop, Sydney.

Goldner, V., Penn, P., Sheinberg, M. & Walker, G. 1990, 'Love and violence: gender paradoxes in volatile attachments', *Family Process*, vol. 29, no. 4, pp. 343–364.

Goldthorpe, J.E. 1987, *Family Life in Western Societies*, Cambridge University Press, Sydney.

Gordon, L. 1988, 'The politics of child sexual abuse: notes from American history', *Feminist Review* (28), pp. 56–64.

Gottman, J., Jacobson, N., Rushe, R., Wu Shortt, J., Babcock, J., La Taillade, J. & Waltz, J. 1995, 'The relationship between heart rate reactivity, emotionally aggressive behaviour, and general violence in batterers', *The Journal of Family Psychology*, vol. 9, no. 3, pp. 227–248.

Grassian, S. & Holtzon, D. 1996, *Memory of Sexual Abuse by a Parish Priest*, paper presented at Trauma and Memory: An International Research Conference 26–28 July, University of New Hampshire, Durham.

Graycar, R. 1995, 'The gender of judgments: an introduction', in M. Thornton (ed.), *Public and Private: Feminist Legal Debates*, OUP, Melbourne.

Graycar, R. & Morgan, J. 1990, *The Hidden Gender of Law*, Federation Press, Sydney.

Green, A. 1986, 'True and false allegations of sexual abuse in child custody disputes', *Journal of the American Academy of Child Psychiatry*, vol. 25, pp. 449–456.

Grinker, R.R. & Spiegel, J.P. 1945, *Men Under Stress*, Blakiston, Philadephia.

Guilliatt, R 1994, 'Abused memories', *The Sydney Morning Herald*, 5 November (Spectrum).

——1995a, 'Demons from the past', *The Sydney Morning Herald*, 1 February.

——1995b, 'Family sex abuse claims "untrue"', *The Sydney Morning Herald*, 21 November.

——1996a, 'Abuse and justice', *The Sydney Morning Herald*, 29 June.

——1996b, 'Hosing down the hysteria', *The Sydney Morning Herald*, 1 November.

——1996c, *Talk of the Devil: Repressed Memory & the Ritual Abuse Witch-Hunt*, The Text Publishing Company, Melbourne.

Gunew, S. 1993, 'Feminism and the politics of irreducible differences', in S. Gunew & A. Yeatman (eds), *Feminism and the Politics of Difference*, Allen & Unwin, Sydney.

Gunew, S. & Yeatman, A. (eds) 1992, *Feminism and the Politics of Difference*, Allen & Unwin, Sydney.

Halberg, W. & Rigne, B. 1994, 'Child sexual abuse—a study of controversy and construction', *Acta Sociologica*, vol. 37, pp. 141–163.

Hall, S. 1990, 'Cultural Identity and Diaspora', in J. Rutherford (ed.), *Identity: Community, Culture, Difference*, Lawrence & Wishhart, London.

Hallam, S.J. 1997, 'Is there a false memory epidemic?', *Treating Abuse Today*, vol. 7, pp. 29–38.

Hansen, M. & Harway, M. (eds) 1993, *Battering and Family Therapy: A Feminist Perspective*, Sage, California.

Hatty, S. 1985, 'On the reproduction of misogyny: the therapeutic management of violence against women', *Conference Proceedings, National Conference on Domestic Violence*, Australian Institute of Criminology, Australia.

——1991, 'Of nightmares and sexual monsters: struggles around child abuse in Australia', *International Journal of Law and Psychiatry*, vol. 14, pp. 255–267.

Henderson, S., Byrne, D.G. & Duncan-Jones, P. 1981, *Neurosis and the Social Environment*, Academic Press, Sydney.

Herman, J.L. 1981, *Father–Daughter Incest*, Harvard University Press, Cambridge, Massachusetts.

——1992, *Trauma and Recovery: The Aftermath of Violence—from Domestic Abuse to Political Terror*, Basic Books, USA.

Herman, J.L. & Harvey, M. 1996, *Adult Memories of Childhood Trauma: A Chart Review Investigation*, paper presented at Trauma and Memory:

An International Research Conference 26–28 July, University of New Hampshire, Durham.

Herman, J.L. & Shatzow, E. 1987, 'Recovery and verification of memories of childhood sexual trauma', *Psychoanalytic Psychotherapy*, vol. 4, pp. 1–14.

Hersko, M., Halleck, S., Rosenberg, M. & Pacht, A. 1961, 'Incest: a three-way process', *Journal of Social Therapy*, vol. 7, pp. 22–31.

Hester, M. & Radford, L. 1996, *Domestic Violence and Child Contact Arrangements in England and Denmark*, Policy Press, Bristol.

Heward-Belle, S. 1996, *All Care and No Responsibility? A study of the responses of child protection workers to domestic violence in families*, unpublished masters thesis, University of Sydney.

Hlady, L. & Gunter, E. 1990, 'Alleged child abuse in custody access disputes', *Child Abuse and Neglect*, vol. 14, pp. 591–593.

Ho, R. & Venus, M. 1995, 'Domestic violence and spousal homicide: the admissibility of expert witness testimony in trials of battered women who kill their abusive spouses', *Journal of Family Studies*, vol. 1, no. 1, pp. 24–32.

Hollingsworth, J. 1986, *Unspeakable Acts*, Congdon & Weed, New York.

Homel, R., Burns, A. & Goodnow, J. 1987, 'Parental social networks and child development', *Journal of Social and Parental Relationships*, vol. 4, pp. 159–177.

hooks, b. 1990, *Yearning: Race, Gender and Cultural Politics*, South End Press, Boston, MA.

Hooper, C-A. 1992, *Mothers Surviving Child Sexual Abuse*, Routledge, London.

——1994, 'Do families need fathers? The impact of divorce on children', in A. Mullender & R. Morley (eds), *Children Living with Domestic Violence*, Whiting & Birch, London.

Horowitz, J., Salt, P., Gomes-Schwartz, B. & Sauzier, M. 1984, 'Unconfirmed cases of sexual abuse', Office of Juvenile Justice and Delinquency Prevention, *Sexually Exploited Children: Service and Research Project (Final Report)*, Washington DC.

Howze, D.C. & Kotch, J.B. 1984, 'Disentangling life events, stress and social support: implications for the primary prevention of child abuse and neglect', *Child Abuse and Neglect*, vol. 8, pp. 401–409.

Hughes, H.M. 1992, 'Impact of spouse abuse on children of battered women', *Violence Update*, August, pp. 9–11.

Hume, M. 1996, 'Study of child sexual abuse allegations within the Family Law Court of Australia', Family Court of Australia, Second National Conference Papers, Sydney.

Humphreys, C. 1990, *Disclosure of Child Sexual Assault: Mothers in Crisis*, unpublished doctoral thesis, University of New South Wales, Sydney.

——1993, *The Referral of Families Associated with Child Sexual Assault*, Department of Community Services, Sydney.

Hunter, R. & Leonard, A. 1995, *The Outcomes of Conciliation in Sex Discrimination Cases*, Centre for Employment and Labour Relations Law, University of Melbourne, Working Paper No. 8, August.

Jacobson, N., Gottman, J., Waltz, J., Rushe, R., Babcock, J. & Holtzworth-Munroe, A. 1994, 'Affect, verbal content, psychophysiology in the argument of couples with a violent husband', *Journal of Consulting and Clinical Psychology*, vol. 62, no. 5, pp. 982–988.

James, K. & McIntyre, D. 1985, *Therapeutic approaches to domestic violence*, Conference Proceedings, National Conference on Domestic Violence 11–15 November, S. Hatty (ed.), Australian Institute of Criminology.

——1990, 'Is psychology a crime too? Further reflections on violence, relationships, and therapeutic responses', *ANZ Journal of Family Therapy*, vol. 11, no. 2, pp. 71–72.

Janet, P. 1889, *L'automatisme Psychologique*, Alcan, Paris.

——1893, 'L'amnesie continue', *Revue Generale des Sciences,* vol. 4, pp. 167–179.

Jenkins, A. 1990, *Invitations to Responsibility*, Dulwich Centre Publications, Adelaide.

Jennings, K.D., Stagg, N. & Pollay, A. 1988, 'Assessing support networks: stability and evidence for convergent and divergent validity', *American Journal of Community Psychology*, vol. 16, no. 6, pp. 793–809.

Johnson, P. 1994, *Pathways to Ethnic Communities: Communicating with People of Non English Speaking Backgrounds—a Guide*, Ethnic Communities Council, Waterloo.

Jolly, M. 1991, 'The politics of difference: feminism, colonialism and decolonisation in Vanuatu', in G. Bottomley, M. de Lepervanche & J. Martin (eds), *Intersexions: Gender/Class/Culture/Ethnicity*, Allen & Unwin, Sydney.

——1996, 'Woman Ikat Raet Long Human Raet Ono? Women's rights, human rights and domestic violence in Vanuatu', *Feminist Review*, no. 52.

Jones, D.P.H. 1994, 'Autism, facilitated communication and allegations of child abuse and neglect', *Child Abuse and Neglect*, vol. 18, no. 6, pp. 491–493.

Jones, D. & McGraw, J. 1987, 'Reliable and fictitious accounts of sexual abuse to children', *Journal of Interpersonal Violence*, vol. 2, pp. 274–275.

Jones, D. & Sieg, A. 1988, 'Child sexual abuse allegations in custody or visitation cases: a report of 20 cases', in E. Nicholson (ed.), *Sexual Abuse Allegations in Custody and Visitation Cases*, American Bar Association, Washington.

Justice, B. & Justice, R. 1979, *The Broken Taboo*, Human Sciences Press, New York.

Kadushkin, C. 1967, *Why People go to Psychiatrists*, Atherton, New York.

Kamsler, A. 1990, 'Her-story in the making', in M. Durrant & C. White (eds), *Ideas for Therapy with Sexual Abuse*, Dulwich Centre Publications, Adelaide.

Kaplan, S. & Kaplan, S. 1981, 'The child's accusation of sexual abuse during a divorce and custody struggle', *Hillside Journal of Clinical Psychiatry*, vol. 3, pp. 81–95.

Kardiner, A. 1941, *The Traumatic Neuroses of War*, Hoeber, New York.

Kaufman, G. 1992, 'The mysterious disappearance of battered women in family therapists' offices: male privilege colluding with male violence', *Journal of Marital and Family Therapy*, vol. 18, no. 3, pp. 233–243.

Kelly, L. 1988, *Surviving Sexual Violence*, Polity Press, London.

Kessler, W. & Fein, G. 1979, 'Variations in home-based infant education: language, play and social development', cited in D.R. Powell, 'Family—environment relations and early childrearing: the role of social networks and neighbourhoods', *Journal of Research and Development in Education*, vol. 13, no. 1, pp. 1–11.

Kinzie, J.D. 1993, 'Post-traumatic effects and their treatment among southeast Asian refugees', in J.P. Wilson & B. Raphael (eds), *International Handbook of Traumatic Stress Syndromes*, Plenum Press, New York, pp. 311–319.

Kluft, R.P. 1995, 'The confirmation and disconfirmation of memories of DID patients: a naturalistic clinical study', *Dissociation*, vol. 8, no. 4, pp. 253–258.

Koss, M.P. & Cleveland, H.H. 1997, 'Stepping on Toes', in M.D. Schwartz (ed.), *Researching Sexual Violence against Women*, Sage, California.

Kristiansen, C.M. 1996, *Recovered Memory Research and the Influence of Social Attitudes*, paper at conference Beyond the Controversy: Recovering Memories of Early Life Trauma, Peterborough, Ontario, 23–24 May.

Laing, L. 1996, *Unravelling Responsibility: Incest Offenders, Mothers and Victims in Treatment*, unpublished doctoral thesis, University of New South Wales, Sydney.

Laing, L. & Kamsler, A. 1990, 'Putting an end to secrecy: therapy with mothers and children following disclosure of child sexual assault', in M. Durrant & C. White (eds), *Ideas for Therapy with Sexual Abuse*, Dulwich Centre Publications, Adelaide.

Lang, R.A. & Frenzel, R.R. 1988, 'How sex offenders lure children', *Annals of Sex Research*, vol. 1, pp. 303–317.

Langhinrichsen-Rohling, J., Neudig, P. & Thorn, G. 1995, 'Violent marriages: gender differences in levels of current violence and past abuse', *Journal of Family Violence*, vol. 10, no. 2.

Larson, M. 1990, 'In the matter of experts and professionals, or how impossible it is to leave nothing unsaid', in R. Torstendahl & M. Burrage (eds), *From the Formation of the Professions—Knowledge, State and Strategy*, Sage, London.

Law Reform Commission of Western Australia 1991, *Report on Evidence of Children and other Vulnerable Witnesses* (Project No. 87), Perth.

Lerman, L.G. 1984, 'Mediation of wife abuse cases: the adverse impact of informal dispute resolution on women', *Harvard Women's Law Journal*, vol. 7, pp. 57–113.

Lindsay, D.S. & Read, J.D. 1994, 'Incest resolution psychotherapy and memories of childhood sexual abuse: a cognitive perspective', *Applied Cognitive Psychology*, vol. 8, pp. 281–338.

Lipchick, E. 1991, 'Spouse abuse: challenging the party line', *Family Therapy Networker*, vol. 15, pp. 59–63.

Loftus, E.F. 1993, 'The reality of repressed memories', *American Psychologist*, vol. 48, no. 5, pp. 518–537.

Loftus, E.F., Garry, M. & Feldman, J. 1994, 'Forgetting sexual trauma: what does it mean when 38% forget?', *Journal of Consulting and Clinical Psychology*, vol. 62, pp. 1177–1181.

Loftus, E.F., Polonsky, S. & Fullilove, M.T. 1994, 'Memories of childhood sexual abuse: remembering and repressing', *Psychology of Women Quarterly*, vol. 18, pp. 67–84.

Lucas, B. 1995, 'The problem with "battered husbands"', *Deviant Behaviour: An Interdisciplinary Journal*, pp. 95–112.

Lustig, N., Dresser, J.W., Spellman, S.W. & Murray, T.B. 1966, 'Incest: a family group survival pattern', *Archives of General Psychiatry*, vol. 14, pp. 31–40.

MacKinnon, C. 1987, *Feminism Unmodified*, Harvard University Press, Cambridge MA.

Madakasira, S. & O'Brian, K. 1987, 'Acute post-traumatic stress disorder in victims of a natural disaster', *Journal of Nervous and Mental Disease*, vol. 175, pp. 286–290.

Masson, J. 1984, *The Assault on Truth—Freud's Suppression of the Seduction Theory*, Penguin Books, London.

——1988, *Against Therapy*, Fontana/Collins, London.

Matheson, A. 1996, 'Battered husbands: fact or fiction?', *The Sydney Morning Herald*, Tuesday, 23 April, Agenda, p. 13.

Matka, E. 1991, 'Domestic violence in New South Wales', *Crime and Justice Bulletin No. 2*, NSW Bureau of Crime, Statistics and Research, Sydney.

Matthews, J.K., Maker, J.R. & Speltz, K. 1991, 'Effects of family reunification on sexually abusive families', in M.Q. Patton (ed.), *Family Sexual Abuse: Frontline Research and Evaluation*, Sage, Newbury Park, pp. 147–161.

McDonald, T. & Marks, J. 1991, 'A review of risk factors assessed in child protective services', *Social Service Review*, March, pp. 112–132.

McGregor, H. 1990a, 'Conceptualising male violence against female partners: political implications of therapeutic responses', *ANZ Journal of Family Therapy*, vol. 11, no. 2, pp. 65–70.

——1990b, 'Yes, psychology is a crime (metaphorically speaking)', *ANZ Journal of Family Therapy*, vol. 11, no. 3, pp. 73–74.

McHoul, A. & Grace, W. 1993, *A Foucault Primer: Discourse, Power and the Subject*, Melbourne University Press, Victoria.

McIntyre, D. 1984, 'Domestic violence: a case of the disappearing victim?', *Australian Journal of Family Therapy*, vol. 5, no. 4, pp. 249–258.

McKernan McKay, M. 1994, 'The link between domestic violence and child abuse: assessment and treatment considerations', *Child Welfare*, vol. LXXIII, no. 1, Jan/Feb.

Meth, R.L. 1992, 'Marriage and family therapists working with family violence: strained bedfellows or compatible partners? A commentary on Avis, Kaufman and Bograd', *Journal of Marital and Family Therapy*, vol. 18, no. 3, pp. 257–261.

Midson, B. 1995, *The Law and Recovered Memories*, paper at Australian Association of Trauma and Dissociation Fourth Annual Conference, *Trauma, Memory and Dissociation*, Melbourne.

Miller, A. 1984, *Thou Shalt Not Be Aware: Society's Betrayal of the Child*, Farrar-Strauss-Giroux, New York.

Mills, T. 1984, 'Victimisation and self-esteem: on equating husband abuse and wife abuse', *Victimology: An International Journal*, vol. 9, no. 2.

Minow, M. 1990, 'Words and the door to the land of change: law, language and family violence', *Vanderbilt Law Review*, vol. 43, pp. 1665–1700.

Mohanty, C. 1989, 'On race and voice—challenges for liberal education in the 1990s', *Cultural Critique*, no. 14, pp. 179–208.

Monk, G., Winslade, J., Crocket, K. & Epston, D. 1997, *Narrative Therapy, The Archeology of Hope*, Jossey Bass, San Francisco.

Moore, S., Donovan, B., Hudson, A., Dykstra, J. & Lawrence, J. 1993, 'Brief report: evaluation of eight case studies of facilitated communication', *Journal of Autism and Developmental Disorders*, vol. 23, no. 3, pp. 531–539.

Mueller, C. 1994, 'Conflict networks and the origins of women's liberation', in E. Larana, H. Johnston & J. Gusfield (eds), *New Social Movements—From Ideology to Identity*, Temple Press, Philadelphia, pp. 100–130.

Mullender, A. & Morley, R. 1994, *Children Living with Domestic Violence*, Whiting & Birch, London.

Murdolo, A. 1996, 'Warmth and unity with all women. Historicising racism in the Australian women's movement', *Feminist Review*, no. 52.

Myers Avis, J. 1992, 'Where are all the family therapists? Abuse and violence within families and family therapy's response', *Journal of Marital and Family Therapy*, vol. 18, no. 3, pp. 225–232.

Neave, M. 1994, 'Resolving the dilemma of difference: a critique of "the role of private ordering in family law"', *University of Toronto Law Journal*, vol. 44, pp. 97–131.

Neiderland, W.G. 1968, 'Clinical observations on the "survivor syndrome"', *International Journal of Psychoanalysis*, vol. 49, pp. 313–315.

NSW Bureau of Crime Statistics and Research 1995, *New South Wales Criminal Courts Statistics 1994*, Attorney-General's Department, Sydney.

NSW Child Sexual Assault Legislative Reform—*Hansard Report Legislative Assembly and Legislative Council*, 12 November 1985, GPS, Sydney.

NSW Department for Women 1996, *Heroines of Fortitude: The Experiences of Women in Court as Victims of Sexual Assault*, Sydney.

NSW Domestic Violence Committee 1991, *NSW Domestic Violence Strategic Plan*, Women's Coordination Unit, Sydney.

NSW Health 1995, *Victims of Sexual Assault 1992/93–1993/94 Initial Contact at NSW Sexual Assault Services*, Sydney.

NSW Pre-Trial Diversion of Offenders Program (undated), 'Pre-Trial Diversion of Offenders Program', unpublished, Westmead.

NSW Service for the Treatment and Rehabilitation of Torture and Trauma Survivors, *STARTTS News*, April 1992, vol. 1, no. 2.

NSW Sexual Assault Committee 1993, *Sexual Assault Phone-in Report*, Sydney.

Nixon, J., Pearn, J., Wilkey, I. & Petrie, G. 1981, 'Social class and violent child death: an analysis of fatal nonaccidental injury, murder, and fatal child neglect', *Child Abuse and Neglect*, vol. 5, pp. 111–116.

Nosworthy, S. & Lane, K. 1996, 'How we learnt that scratching can really be self-abuse: co-research with young people', *Dulwich Centre Newsletter No. 4*, pp. 25–31.

O'Donnell, C. & Craney, J. (eds) 1982, *Family Violence in Australia*, Longman Cheshire, Melbourne.

O'Donovan, K. 1997, 'With sense, consent, or just a con?', in N. Naffine & R.J. Owens (eds), *Sexing the Subject of Law*, The Law Book Co., Sydney, pp. 47–64.

Office of the Status of Women 1995, *Community Attitudes to Violence: Detailed Report*, Department of the Prime Minister and Cabinet, ACT.

O'Gorman, T. 1991, 'Defence strategies in child sexual abuse accusation cases', *Queensland Law Society Journal,* June, pp. 195–204.

Okin, S.M. 1989, *Justice, Gender and the Family*, Basic Books, New York.

O'Leary, K., Barling, J., Aries, I., Rosenbaum, A., Malone, J. & Tgree, A. 1989, 'Prevalence and stability of physical aggression between spouses', *Journal of Consulting Clinical Psychology*, vol. 57, pp. 263–286.

Omi, M. & Winant, H. 1986, *Racial Formation in the United States*, Routledge & Kegan Paul, London.

Packman, J. with Randall, J. & Jacques, N. 1986, *Who Needs Care?*, Basil Blackwell, Oxford.

Parke, R. & Collmer, C.W. 1975, 'Child abuse: an interdisciplinary analysis', in E.M. Heatherington (ed.), *Review of Child Development Research Vol. 5*, University of Chicago Press, Chicago.

Parkinson, P. 1995, 'Custody, access and domestic violence', *Australian Journal of Family Law*, vol. 9, pp. 41–57.

Parton, N. 1990, 'Taking child abuse seriously', in *Taking Child Abuse Seriously: Contemporary Issues in Child Protection Theory and Practice*, The Violence Against Children Study Group (ed.), Unwin Hyman, London.

Paymar, M. & Pence, E. 1985, *Power and Control: Tactics of Men who Batter—An Educational Curriculum*, Duluth, Minnesota.

Pelton, L.H. 1978, 'Child abuse and neglect: the myth of classlessness', *American Journal of Orthopsychiatry*, vol. 48, no. 4, pp. 608–617.

Perry, B.D., Conroy, L. & Ravitz, A. 1991, 'Persisting psycho-physiological effects of traumatic stress: the memory states', *Violence Update*, vol. 1, no. 8, pp. 6–11.

Peterman, P.J. 1981, 'Parenting and environmental considerations', *American Journal of Orthopsychiatry*, vol. 51, no. 2, pp. 351–355.

Pilisuk, M. 1982, 'Delivery of social support: the social inoculation', *American Journal of Orthopsychiatry*, vol. 52, no. 1, pp. 20–31.

Polansky, N.A., Chalmers, M.A., Buttenwieser, E. & Williams, D.P. 1979, 'Isolation of the neglectful family', *American Journal of Orthopsychiatry*, vol. 49, no. 1, pp. 149–152.

——1981, *Damaged Parents*, University of Chicago Press, Chicago.

Polansky, N.A., Gaudin, J.M., Ammons, P.W. & Davis, K.B. 1985, 'The psychological ecology of the neglectful mother', *Child Abuse and Neglect*, vol. 9, pp. 265–275.

Pope, K.S. 1996, 'Memory, abuse and science: questioning claims about the false memory syndrome epidemic', *American Psychologist*, vol. 51, pp. 957–974.

Powell, D.R. 1979, 'Family–environment relations and early childrearing: the role of social networks and neighbourhoods', *Journal of Research and Development in Education*, vol. 13, no. 1, pp. 1–11.

——1987, 'A neighbourhood approach to parent support groups', *Journal of Community Psychology*, vol. 15, pp. 51–62.

Radford, J., Kelly, L. & Hester, M. (eds) 1996, 'Introduction' *Women, Violence and Male Power*, Open University Press, Buckingham, pp. 1–17

Richer, J. 1994, 'Facilitated communication: a response by child protection', *Child Abuse and Neglect*, vol. 18, no. 6, pp. 531–537.

Richey, C.A., Lovell, M.L. & Reid, K. 1991, 'Interpersonal skill training to enhance social support among women at risk for child maltreatment', *Children and Youth Services Review*, vol. 13, pp. 41–59.

Rodwell, M.K. & Chambers, D.E. 1992, 'Primary prevention of child abuse: is it really possible?', *Journal of Sociology and Social Welfare*, vol. 19, no. 3, pp. 159–176.

Roesler, T.A. & Wind, T.W. 1994, 'Telling the secret: adult women describe their disclosures of incest', *Journal of Interpersonal Violence*, vol. 9, no. 3, pp. 327–338.

Rogers, G. & Renshaw, K. 1993, 'Covert communication between sex offenders and their child victims', *Annals of Sex Research*, vol. 6, pp. 185–196.

Rogers, M.L. 1995, 'Factors influencing recall of childhood sexual abuse', *Journal of Traumatic Stress*, vol. 8, no. 4, p. 691.

Rosenberg, M.S. & Reppucci, N.D. 1985, 'Primary prevention of child abuse', *Journal of Consulting and Clinical Psychology*, vol. 53, no. 5, pp. 576–585.

Rossiter, P. 1997, *Feminisms: Issues in Theory and Practice 1970s–1990s*, notes from presentation for Education Centre Against Violence, 12 February 1997, Parramatta, NSW.

Royal Commission into the NSW Police Service, *Final Report Volume V: The Paedophile Inquiry*, August 1997, ISBN 07313 09162.

Russell, D. 1984, *Sexual Exploitation—Rape, Child Sexual Abuse and Workplace Harassment*, Sage, California.

——1986, *The Secret Trauma: Incest in the Lives of Women and Girls*, Basic Books, New York.

Salmelainen, P. & Coumarelos, C. 1993, 'Adult sexual assault in New South Wales', *Contemporary Issues in Crime and Justice Series No. 20*, NSW Bureau of Crime, Statistics and Research, Sydney.

Salter, A.C. 1995, *Transforming Trauma: A Guide to Understanding and Treating Adult Survivors of Child Sexual Abuse*, Sage, California.

Salzinger, S., Kaplan, S. & Artesnyeff, C. 1983, 'Mothers' personal social networks and child maltreatment', *Journal of Abnormal Psychology*, vol. 92, no. 1, pp. 68–76.

Sappington, J., Reedy, S., Welch, R. & Hamilton, J. 1989, 'Validity of messages from quadriplegic persons with cerebral palsy', *American Journal on Mental Retardation*, vol. 94, no. 1, pp. 49–52.

Sargeant, W. & Slater, E. 1941, 'Amnesic syndromes in war', *Proceedings of the Royal Society of Medicine*, vol. 34, pp. 757–764.

Saunders, D. 1988, 'Wife abuse, husband abuse, or mutual combat? A feminist perspective on the empirical findings', in K. Yllo & M. Bograd (eds), *Feminist Perspectives on Wife Abuse*, Sage, California.

Sawer, M. 1990, *Sisters in Suits—Women in Public Policy*, Allen & Unwin, Sydney.

Schacter, D.L. 1986, 'Amnesia and crime: how much do we really know?', *American Psychologist*, vol. 41, pp. 286–295.

Schaefer, M. & Guyer, M. 1988, *Allegations of Sexual Abuse in Custody and Visitation Disputes: A Legal and Clinical Challenge*, paper at 96th Annual Convention of the American Psychological Association, Atlanta, GA.

Scheppele, K.L. 1989, 'Foreword: telling stories', *Michigan Law Review*, vol. 87, pp. 2073–2098.

——1994, 'Manners of imagining the real', *Law and Social Inquiry*, vol. 19, pp. 995–1022.

Schudson, C. 1995, 'Antagonistic parents in family courts: false allegations or false assumptions about true allegations of child sexual abuse?', *Journal of Child Sexual Abuse*, vol. 1, pp. 111–114.

Schuman, D. 1986, 'False allegations of physical and sexual abuse', *Bulletin of the American Academy of Psychiatry and the Law*, vol. 14, pp. 5–21.

Scutt, J. 1983, *Even in the Best of Homes*, Penguin, Victoria.

——1990a, *Women and the Law*, The Law Book Co., Sydney.

——1990b, 'Confronting precedent and prejudice: child sexual abuse in the courts', in K. Oates (ed.), *Understanding and Managing Child Sexual Abuse*, Harcourt Brace Jovanovich, Sydney.

Seagull, E.A.W. 1987, 'Social support and child maltreatment: a review of the evidence', *Child Abuse and Neglect*, vol. 11, pp. 41–52.

Sgroi, S.M. 1982, *Handbook of Clinical Intervention in Child Sexual Abuse*, Lexington Books, Massachusetts.

Sharland, E., Seal, H., Croucher, M., Aldgate, J. & Jones, D. 1995, *Professional Intervention in Child Sexual Abuse*, HMSO, London.

Siegel, B. 1995, 'Brief report: assessing allegations of sexual molestation made through facilitated communication', *Journal of Autism and Developmental Disorders*, vol. 25, no. 3, pp. 319–326.

Sirles, E. & Franke, P. 1989, 'Factors influencing mothers' reactions to intrafamily sexual abuse', *Child Abuse and Neglect*, vol. 13, pp. 165–170.

Skurray, G. & Ham, R. 1990, 'Family poverty and child abuse in Sydney', *Australian Journal of Marriage and Family*, vol. 11, no. 2, pp. 94–96.

Smart, C. 1989, *Feminism and the Power of Law*, Routledge, London.

Smith, J., O'Connor, I. & Bethelsen, D. 1996, 'The effects of witnessing domestic violence on young children's psycho-social adjustment', *Australian Social Work*, vol. 49, pp. 3–10.

Sonnenberg, S.M., Blank, A.S. & Talbott, J.A. 1985, *The Trauma of War: Stress and Recovery in Vietnam Veterans*, American Psychiatric Press, Washington DC.

Southard, E.E. 1919, *Shell-Shock and Other Neuropsychiatric Problems*, W.W. Leonard, Boston.

Spearly, J.L. & Lauderdale, M. 1983, 'Community characteristics and ethnicity in the prediction of child maltreatment rates', *Child Abuse and Neglect*, vol. 7, pp. 91–105.

Squire, L.R. & Zola-Morgan, S. 1991, 'The medial temporal lobe memory system', *Science*, vol. 253, pp. 1380–1386.

Stanchi, K. 1996, 'The paradox of the fresh complaint rule', *Boston College of Law Review*, vol. 37, pp. 151–184.

Stanko, E. 1997, 'I second that emotion: reflections on feminism, emotionality, and research on sexual violence', in M.D. Schwartz (ed.), *Researching Sexual Violence Against Women*, Sage, California.

Stark, E. & Flitcraft, A. 1988, 'Women and children at risk: a feminist perspective on child abuse', *International Journal of Health Services*, vol. 18, no. 1, pp. 97–118.

STARTTS (NSW Service for Treatment and Rehabilitation of Torture and Trauma Survivors), *STARTTS News*, April 1992, vol. 1, no. 2.

Stermac, L., Davidson, A. & Sheridan, P.M. 1995, 'Incidence of non sexual violence in incest offenders', *International Journal of Offender Therapy and Comparative Criminology*, vol. 39, pp. 167–178.

Steward, M.S., Bussey, K., Goodman, G.S. & Saywitz, K.J. 1993, 'Implications of developmental research for interviewing children', *Child Abuse and Neglect*, vol. 17, pp. 25–37.

Strauss, M. 1993, 'Physical assault by wives', in R. Gelles & D. Loseke (eds), *Current Controversies on Family Violence*, Sage, California.

Strauss, M., Gelles, R. & Steenmetz, S. 1980, *Behind Closed Doors: Violence in the American Family*, Anchor/Doubleday, New York.

Stuart, D. 1993, 'No real harm done: sexual assault and the criminal justice system', in P. Easteal, *Without Consent: Confronting Adult Sexual Violence Conference Proceedings*, Australian Institute of Criminology, no. 20.

Summit, R. 1992, 'Opinion: Misplaced Attention to Delayed Memory', *The Advisor*, vol. 5, no. 3, Summer.

*Sydney Morning Herald*, 'Privacy issue as rape therapist jailed', *The Sydney Morning Herald*, 15 December 1995, p. 1.

Tayloe, D.R. 1995, 'The validity of repressed memories and the accuracy of the recall through hypnosis: a case from the courtroom', *American Journal of Clinical Hypnosis*, vol. 37, pp. 25–31.

Terr, L.C. 1988, 'What happens to early memories of trauma? A study of twenty children under age five at the time of documented traumatic events', *Journal of the American Academy of Child and Adolescent Psychiatry*, vol. 27, p. 96.

——1991, 'Child traumas: an outline and overview', *American Journal of Psychiatry*, vol. 148, no. 1, pp. 10–20.

Thoennes, N. & Tjaden, P. 1990, 'The extent, nature and validity of sexual abuse allegations in custody/visitation disputes', *Child Abuse and Neglect*, vol. 14, pp. 151–163.

Toon, K., Fraise, J., McFetridge, M. & Alwin, N. 1996, 'Memory or mirage? The FMS debate', *The Psychologist*, February.

Torrey, M. 1991, 'When will we be believed? Rape myths and the idea of a fair trial in rape prosecutions', *University of California: Davis Law Review*, vol. 24, pp. 1013–1071.

Trepper, T.S. & Barrett, M.J. 1989, *Systemic Treatment of Incest*, Brunner/Mazel, New York.

Trimpey, M.L. 1989, 'Self-esteem and anxiety: key issues in an abused women's support group', *Issues in Mental Health Nursing*, vol. 10, pp. 297–308.

Troup, M. 1995, 'The Family Law Reform Bill No. 2 and its ramifications for women and children', *The Australian Feminist Law Journal*, vol. 5.

Truesdale, D., McNeil, J. & Deschner, J. 1986, 'Incidence of wife abuse in incestuous families', *Social Work*, March–April, pp. 138–140.

Turkat, D. 1980, 'Social networks: theory and practice', *Journal of Community Psychology*, vol. 8, pp. 99–109.

Underwager, R. 1986, *False Allegations of Child Abuse*, Institute for Psychological Therapies, Minneapolis.

Unger, D. & Wandersman, A. 1982, 'Neighbouring in an urban environment', *American Journal of Community Psychology*, vol. 10, no. 5, pp. 493–509.

United Nations 1995, 'Power and Influence', *The World's Women: Trends and Statistics*, United Nations, New York.

van der Kolk, B.A. 1994, 'The body keeps the score: memory and the evolving psychobiology of post-traumatic stress', *Harvard Review of Psychiatry*, vol. 1, no. 5, pp. 253–265.

van der Kolk, B.A. & Fisler, R. 1995, 'Dissociation and the fragmentary nature of traumatic memories: overview and exploratory study', *Journal of Traumatic Stress*, vol. 8, no. 4, p. 505.

van der Kolk, B.A. & Kadish, W. 1987, 'Amnesia, dissociation, and the return of the repressed', in B.A. van der Kolk (ed.), *Psychological Trauma*, American Psychiatric Press, Washington DC, pp. 173–190.

van der Kolk, B.A. & van der Hart, O. 1989, 'Pierre Janet and the breakdown of adaptation in psychological trauma', *American Journal of Psychiatry*, vol. 146, pp. 1530–1540.

——1991, 'The intrusive past: the flexibility of memory and the engraving of trauma', *American Imago*, vol. 48, pp. 425–454.

van der Kolk, B.A., van der Hart, O. & Marmar, C.R. 1996, 'Dissociation and information processing in post-traumatic stress disorder', in B. A. van der Kolk, A.C. McFarlane & L. Weisaeth (eds), *Traumatic Stress: The Effects of Overwhelming Experience on Mind, Body and Society*, Guilford Press, New York, pp. 303–327.

Vinson, T. & McArthur, M. 1988, 'Why child abuse appears to have increased', *Modern Medicine*, September, pp. 62–73.

Vinson, T., Berreen, R. & McArthur, M. 1989, 'Class, surveillance and child abuse', *Impact*, April/May, pp. 19–21.

Wakefield, H. & Underwager, R. 1988, *Accusations of Child Sexual Abuse*, Charles C. Thomas, Illinois.

——1992, 'Sexual abuse allegations in divorce and custody disputes', *Behavioral Sciences and the Law*, vol. 9, pp. 451–468.

Walby, C. 1985, *Breaking the Silence: A Report based on the Findings of the Women Against Incest Phone-In Survey*, Dympna House, Sydney.

Ward, E. 1984, *Father–Daughter Rape*, Women's Press, London.

Wattenberg, E. 1985, 'In a different light: a feminist perspective on the role of mothers in father–daughter incest', *Child Welfare*, vol. 64, pp. 203–211.

Weedon, C. 1987, *Feminist Practice and Poststructuralist Theory*, Blackwell, Oxford.

Weinberg, K. 1955, *Incest Behaviour*, Citadel Press, USA.

White, M. 1991, 'Deconstruction and therapy', *Dulwich Centre Newsletter*, no. 3.

——1995, *Re-Authoring Lives: Interviews and Essays*, Dulwich Centre Publications, Adelaide.

Whitfield, C.L. 1995, *Memory and Abuse: Remembering and Healing the Effects of Trauma*, Health Communications Inc., Deerfield Beach, Florida.

Wigmore, J. 1961, *Wigmore on Evidence*, 3rd edn, Little Brown, Boston.

Wilkinson, C.B. 1983, 'Aftermath of a disaster: the collapse of the Hyatt Regency Hotel skywalks', *American Journal of Psychiatry*, vol. 140, pp. 1134–1139.

Willbach, D. 1989, 'Ethics and family therapy: The case management of family violence', *Journal of Marital and Family Therapy*, vol. 15, no. 1, pp. 43–52.

Williams, L.M. 1994, 'Recall of childhood trauma: a prospective study of women's memories of child sexual abuse', *Journal of Consulting and Clinical Psychology*, vol. 62, no. 6, pp. 1167–1176.

——1995, 'Recovered memories of abuse in women with documented child sexual victimization histories', *Journal of Traumatic Stress*, vol. 8, no. 4, p. 649.

Williams, L.M. & Banyard, V.L. 1996, *The Impact of Gender and Sexual Abuse Characteristics on Memories for an Incident of Child Sexual Abuse*, paper presented at Trauma and Memory: An International Research Conference 26–28 July, University of New Hampshire, Durham.

Wilson, A. & Hutton, J. 1992, 'Groups for incest survivors: a new context', *ANZ Journal of Family Therapy*, vol. 13, no. 3, pp. 129–134.

Women's Legal Resources Centre 1994, *Quarter Way to Equal: A Report on Barriers to Legal Services for Migrant Women*, Keys Young, funded by the Law Foundation of New South Wales.

Woods, G. 1981, *Sexual Assault Law Reform in New South Wales: A Commentary on the Crimes (Sexual Assault) Amendment Act and Cognate Act*, Department of Attorney General and Justice, Sydney.

Yeatman, A. 1993, 'Voice and representation in the politics of difference', in S. Gunew & A. Yeatman (eds), *Feminism and the Politics of Difference*, Allen & Unwin, Sydney, pp. 228–245.

Young, G. & Gately, T. 1988, 'Neighbourhood impoverishment and child maltreatment. An analysis of the ecological perspective', *Journal of Family Issues*, vol. 9, no. 2, pp. 240–254.

Young-Bruehl, E. 1990, *Freud on Women*, The Hogarth Press, London.

Yuille, J., Tymofievich, M. & Marxsen, D. 1995, 'The nature of allegations of child sexual abuse', in T. Ney (ed.), *True and False Allegations of Child Sexual Abuse*, Brunner/Mazel, New York.

Ziegert, K.A. 1983, 'The Swedish prohibition of corporal punishment: a preliminary report', *Journal of Marriage and the Family*, November, pp. 917–926.

Zuravin, S.J. & Taylor, R. 1987, 'The ecology of child maltreatment: identifying and characterising high risk neighbourhoods', *Child Welfare*, vol. LXVI, no. 6, pp. 497–506.

# Index

Page numbers followed by an 'n' indicate endnotes.